PRAISE FOR
NORTHERN WRATH

"Packs a punch worthy of the
Thunderer himself. It rocks!"
Joanne Harris,
author of *The Gospel of Loki*

"Ferocious, compelling, fiercely beautiful.
Fantasy at its very best."
Anna Smith Spark,
author of the *Empires of Dust* series

"This is fantasy as it should be written:
savage, liminal, full of wonder and magic."
Gavin Smith,
author of the *Bastard Legion* series

"The author joins a somewhat
exclusive club as having provided me
with one of my favorite stories."
Kris Larson

"When you're reading in the garden
on the hottest day of the year and can feel
the cold of the Viking North..."
Ebookwyrm's
Blog Cave

First published 2020 by Solaris
an imprint of Rebellion Publishing Ltd,
Riverside House, Osney Mead,
Oxford, OX2 0ES, UK

www.solarisbooks.com

ISBN: 978 1 78108 819 7

A CIP catalogue record for this book is available
from the British Library.

Designed & typeset by Rebellion Publishing

Printed in Denmark

NORTHERN WRATH

PART ONE OF THE HANGED GOD TRILOGY

THILDE KOLD HOLDT

SOLARIS

To all past, present and future Vikings.

EINER

Chapter One

BLOOD DRIPPED FROM Einer's fingertips onto the crisp snow.

The sound brought him back to his senses. His sleeves were bloody, his entire coat was, and his trousers too. The left side of his ribs stung. His coat was torn there. The wool flayed in long strips. Einer pressed a hand against his ribs. Fresh blood warmed his fingers.

He must have been attacked, although he did not remember it, or much at all; only that he had set out with the others before midday. He did not remember jumping down from his horse, or tearing off his gloves, or being wounded, or anything much. He did not even know what the last thing he remembered was.

His lips tasted of iron and salt. There was too much blood on his coat and hands for it to have come solely from his wound. Someone else was there, or had been. He must have fought.

A trail of Einer's own bloody steps disturbed the otherwise white snow. The steps led straight back a few paces, up the bare slope of the dale.

With one hand clenched around his chest not to upset his

ribs, Einer forced his legs through the heavy snow, following his own bloody footprints. He searched the forestless mountain for Sigismund and his friends. They would not have left him on his own. Unlike them, he did not know one dale from the other.

Ten strides up lay Einer's horse at an awkward angle. Its skull was crushed and its stomach exposed, as if a hunter had sliced it open and wrenched out its guts. To the right of the horse lay the hunter; a great white bear with an axe through its skull. The snow was tainted red around the beast. On its hind legs, it had to be twice Einer's height.

The trail of Einer's steps led straight to the white bear. The axe in its skull was his.

He tried to dry the blood off his hands onto his trousers, but they were equally smeared with red. Frantically, he washed his bare hands in the snow, and the arms of his coat and his trousers, but the blood had already stained itself into the fur, and wool, and dried into his skin.

He had thought he would not lose control again. The last time had been so long ago.

The sight of the bear, and the thought of it all, made him shake, or perhaps it was the cold, for his freezing hands barely bent to his will.

His eyes swelled with tears at the thought that it had happened *again*. If his father heard about it, Einer would be sent away again, and if his mother heard about it... He couldn't imagine what she would do, but he knew that it meant never returning home to Ash-hill. No one could know.

Even as he stared at his axe in the bear's skull, Einer could not make sense of it.

The berserker inside him was supposed to have been repressed, and yet there he stood, in snow to his knees with blood on his hands and his axe planted into the skull of a great white bear, shaking at the thought of what he must have done. He felt trapped inside his own body.

Einer took a few deep breaths, focused on calming his

emotions, and took in the landscape. He imagined that was what his mother would have done, had she been there. She would have calmed him down first, and then assessed what needed to be done.

The winter days were short this far north. Since the sun was still in the sky; he could not have been out for long. He needed to find a way back to the village before sunset. First, he needed warmth.

Einer limped towards his horse, searching for his gloves, or something else to warm his hands. The horse smelled of manure, and the smell was worse than the sight of its exposed intestines and stomach. Einer bent down by its open guts where the heat steamed out. He leant into the steam, let his face thaw, and shook the ice out of his hair and hat. The smell of iron poured out of the horse and filled his nostrils. He reached in past the horse's ribs to heat up his hands. The warmth seared into his flesh and tore at his bones. His fingers numbed, and when the pain returned, he tried to bend his fingers, again and again, until they listened.

For a moment, he kept his hands in the heat and watched the quiet dale to calm his racing heart and decide on his next move. When the snow fell this far north, it covered everything, not like back home, where there would be trees with patches of earth underneath them. There were not many landmarks to steer by here, and Einer did not recognise the shape of the hills, but the position of the sun told him which way was west, and they had ridden east out of the town in the morning.

The white bear twitched.

It wasn't dead, not yet.

Determined to finish the deed, Einer pulled his bloody hands out of the horse and approached the bear. The bear kicked out with its hind legs. Before Einer could reach it and retrieve his axe from its skull, the bear rose.

Einer backed away with his eyes locked on the bear. He crouched behind the dead horse to shield himself, fully aware that he would not be able to run with his wounded ribs. Not that running would have given him much of an advantage.

His weapon belt was empty.

The bear was enormous. Even on all fours, it was taller than Einer.

Einer searched around the horse for a weapon, for *something* to defend himself with, if it came to it. Don't turn around, don't turn around, he chanted in his head, hoping the bear would listen.

Before long, the bear would notice Einer. He needed a weapon before then, but moving in to reach his axe was too risky. A quiver was fastened to the back of the horse's saddle. Einer pulled out the arrows and lay them in the snow besides him. There were only three. His bow lay pressed underneath the horse. Einer dug the snow out to reach. His hands were freezing once again.

The white bear stumbled a few steps forward, and then its eyes caught the horse. Einer slid his hands out from underneath his dead ride. It was too late and he had no bow. He grabbed an arrow in each hand. The bear eyed him, and slowly, as if its large weight barely allowed the bear to move, it stepped towards Einer.

Einer tried not to breathe; perhaps the bear had not seen him yet.

He clenched his hands around the arrows. His hands were numb from the cold. His ribs stung, and still, the bear trod ahead, one heavy step after the other. Its cold eyes were locked on Einer. There was no doubt they had both seen each other.

Einer rose from his crouched position. His chest wound forced him to hunch in over himself. The closer it came, the larger the bear seemed to be.

He braced himself to fight. At the very least, he needed to die with valour, like a warrior, so Odin might choose him and allow him to pass on into Valhalla in the afterlife. Be brave, he told himself, but his limbs were shaking, and his ribs hurt as if he was being stabbed over and over, and he did not feel very brave at all. 'Be brave,' he whispered aloud. 'You've already survived one attack.' The thought did not make him feel brave, only more terrified, because he had never heard any stories about someone surviving a white bear attack *twice*.

The bear pushed itself up to its hind legs. It cast a long shadow across Einer. Before he could change his mind, Einer yelled and plunged forward with his arrows. He hopped up against the bear's fur, aimed for the heart, and pushed both arrowheads against its chest. The wood snapped. The arrow tips fell helplessly down into the snow. The bear bumped into Einer, so he fell onto his back. He fumbled for the last arrow, grabbed it with both hands, and wormed backwards. 'Go away,' he said, trying to sound threatening, but his voice shook from the cold and did not carry much strength.

The bear roared, tall on its hind legs. Its voice resonated around the dale.

'Go away!' Einer bellowed, finding all the courage he possessed. He slashed out at the white bear with the arrow in his hands. 'Leave me.' He felt silly for yelling. The bear looked down at him, tilted its head, and then it let itself fall forward. Einer held his breath, ready to be crushed under the bear's weight. The tip of his last arrow hit the bear's chest and splintered like the others.

With a thump, the white bear landed in the snow with a great paw on either side of Einer. Its breath smelled of rotten fish and the stench made Einer's eyes tear up. Or perhaps it was the fact that he could not remember anything. He did not know why the others had left him to ride off alone, or how the white bear had found him, or how he had planted his axe in its skull. He had nearly killed a white bear, and he did not even remember it.

The bear eyed him, and lifted its black lips in a snarl to reveal its sharp yellow teeth. Its face was smeared with blood, and its jaw so wide it could close down over Einer's head.

Einer felt himself shrink at the bear's blank stare. 'Forgive.

I... I... I don't remember,' he admitted. 'Forgive me. I wasn't myself.'

The bear leant closer to him, and Einer rummaged to pull away, but he was trapped between the bear's large paws. He tightened his grip around the splintered arrow. The white bear bent in close to his face, and just when Einer thought it would bare its teeth and crush his skull, its wet nose touched his. It nudged him, as a mother might nudge its cub. Its breath thawed his face and Einer's cheeks and ears prickled to life. He lay still, and sniffed to stop the melting snot from running down over his face. 'Forgive,' he muttered to the bear, staring into its black eyes.

The wind ruffled the bear's fur.

'You should leave,' Einer said. The beast moaned in response, swayed its heavy head from one side to the other, and as if it understood him, it rose to its hind legs, turned, and slumped down, away from Einer.

One gloomy step after the other, the white bear lumped away, past the dead horse, and up the slope of the dale.

Einer waited until he could no longer see it from where he lay. With the bear out of sight, he let go of the broken arrow in his grip and exhaled loudly. He rubbed his hands together and cupped them around his ears. His heart raced. He pushed himself up to sit, and brushed the snow off his coat.

The bear trampled out over the icy valley, moving fast on all fours. It almost seemed as if Einer had imagined their encounter, or dreamt it. It seemed impossible. The bear had been so much stronger than him.

Far to the right of the dale, where the wind blew in, a rider trotted across the white fields, headed for Einer. The bear must have smelled someone coming, and decided to leave.

'I'm here,' Einer yelled. He waved his hands over his head, and then slumped back down into the snow, waiting for the rider to reach him. Somehow, he needed to keep his berserker craze a secret.

Sigismund and the others would question what had happened, and when his father heard that his berserker craze had returned, Einer would be sent away, no longer fit to be the son of a chief.

The crunch of the horse's hooves in the snow became louder and louder. Einer pushed himself back up, ignoring how much his hands and ribs hurt.

The rider was Sigismund. It felt strangely discomfiiting to see Sigismund covered in fur and skin jackets when he usually wore colourful clothes full of embroidery. His fur hat hid his blonde curls and his neck-warmer reached up over his chin and hid the thin stubbles of the beard he tried to grow.

A few paces away from the bloody outline of the white bear in the snow, Sigismund slid off his horse and pushed his boots through the knee-high snow. He stared down at the white bear outline, and warily approached. The horse trod nervously at the smell of death.

Einer gulped and rubbed his hands. 'My hands are freezing,' he said in a rough voice.

'Found your gloves,' Sigismund mumbled. He seemed to have completely forgotten. He shifted his attention away from the patch in the snow, to Einer, and it made Einer feel as if he had interrupted something. Sigismund stumbled ahead, holding Einer's thick wool gloves.

With a thankful nod, Einer took them. They were stiff from having lain in the snow. He slapped the snow out of them, and when he put them on, clenched his fists to gain some warmth.

'Thought we'd lost you to the ice,' Sigismund said. 'Didn't think you were... chasing bears..?'

'It got my axe,' Einer said. 'Lucky you arrived and scared it off.'

'White bears don't flee...' Sigis mumbled. 'Where *is* your axe?'

'With the white bear,' Einer said. 'Stuck in its skull.'

Sigismund stilled at his answer, and Einer just knew he had said something wrong, again.

The wind seemed colder for the sudden silence and distance between them.

'It'll be dead soon, then.' Sigismund shook his head in disbelief. 'Fifteen summers old and already a white bear slayer. Three summers younger than any of us,' he mumbled as if he had just remembered it, again. No one ever quite let go of that fact. 'How did you do it?'

Einer did not know the answer. Thinking of it made him miss his mother. 'I'd like to go home,' he said instead. 'It's cold.'

Sigismund agreed with a nod. 'We need to patch you up,' he said.

In silence Sigismund bound Einer's wound. Einer started to feel dizzy from the cool air and the pain in his ribs. The whole day exhausted him, and he just wanted to get home, not only back to the village and warm himself, but to set sail and get home to Jutland and Ash-hill, and Hilda.

Sigismund helped Einer up on the horse and mounted at the front.

Clouds had blown in during the day, and the sun hung low in the sky. It had been dark when they had woken up and prepared to set out. Winter days were so short up north, and Einer missed the warmer weather from back home. After today's events, he missed it even more, and all he wanted was to sit by the fire while their skald told stories about great heroes.

It seemed like they had ridden for a long time, but when Einer glanced back over his shoulder he could still see the dot of his dead horse and he knew they could not have ridden for that long.

In silence, they set into tölt and left the dale. After the trot with which they had started, the steady tölt was almost soothing, and Einer's ribs hurt less than before.

Einer knew Sigismund had something to say from the way he rummaged on the horse, searching for the words. Finally, Sigis spoke: 'Did you really attack…?'

'I did,' Einer confirmed. He tried not to mind the way

Sigismund hesitated to talk about it as if they hardly knew each other, although they had been friends for half a dozen winters.

Einer starede at the back of his friend's head and became so acutely aware of how different from each other they were, and perhaps always had been.

The horse heaved and thumped out over the snowy landscape. The clouds tainted yellow.

'The gods steered your hand.' Sigismund had selected his words with care.

In silence they rode on for so long that the day turned dark and the lights of the village finally entered into view, in the far distance.

'The gods didn't steer me,' said Einer, having thought about it all this while. 'They let me go.'

HILDA

Chapter Two

Nine Winters Later

WHENEVER HILDA LEFT her father's side, she forgot how drained he looked. How old and wrinkled he had become. How close to death he was.

The sound of Midsummer song was loud outside.

The smoke-heavy house smelled of burnt oak and wet sheep. Smelled like winter, not summer. The fire had been lit for her father to stay warm. The light was dim and barely reached the richly-coloured heroes painted on the walls of their longhouse.

'Hilda,' her father muttered. His voice was frail and his hand stretched out towards her. Five silk pillows supported his back.

'Hei.' She took his hands and stroked his long hair. Pushed a greasy lock away from his face.

'I heard about the attack from south,' her father said, worried about the future, as always. Worried about her, but forgetting that she was twenty summers old and had always taken care of herself. Even in this state, he worried.

'It's just rumours,' Hilda said. 'You have nothing to worry about.' She wondered how he had heard. Who had told him about the rumours of southerners planning a raid on Jutland. She didn't want his last moments to be full of worry.

Hilda caressed his hand. At the Midsummer feast, the warriors had urged her to speak to him.

'You have to go with them, Father.' She said it softly to convince. She knew that he was tired and hurting, but this was important. The entire village was anxious at his decision to die in bed.

'I can't fight with a limp,' he said, and he raised his eyebrows a little as if it were the simplest thing in all the nine worlds to understand.

'Don't blame this on your leg.' She shook her head. 'You've always had that limp.' She tucked her father into his furs as she spoke. It wasn't fair of him to choose to die in bed like a farmer. To shame the entire village, when he could so easily join the raids and go to battle, or die in single combat against the chief. He would die anyways, might as well die with honour. 'You don't need to go to battle to win, you just need to leave us the right way.'

'Great warriors have ended up in Hel's realm before me,' her father said, and choked on his own spit. His hand squeezed hers, and it sounded as if his insides were being coughed out.

Hilda rubbed his back until it stopped.

'This is the destiny my actions have gifted me,' her father said with a strained voice, as if his throat still tickled. 'And no one, not even the gods, can escape their destiny.'

'Valhalla is your rightful place.'

'I won't go to Valhalla. I'll go to Hel.' He was as stubborn as her.

'We could sail together on Frey's day,' she insisted. 'Make this my first raid and your last.'

'Nej,' he snapped. His lips quivered in resolution. 'And stop saying you want to fight,' he added, annoyed with her like only a child or an old man could be. 'You won't join the warriors on the raids. The chief promised me.'

His words cooled her to the bone.

Never before had it been so clear to her that almost everything her father did was to keep her from becoming a warrior. Maybe his decision to die in bed was also to keep her away from the raids. To stain the family's warrior reputation. 'Why don't you want me to become a shieldmaiden?'

'I want to keep you safe,' he said, not giving it a thought. 'Like I should have done with Leif.'

Despite how her brother had passed on, Hilda wanted to fight. Her father refused to understand that this wasn't something he was meant to decide, that she needed to find her own path. The path the nornir had spun for her. She opened her mouth to tell him, but then she saw him there, old and worn, and he seemed so fragile.

She said nothing, just held his hand tight and looked into his eyes, blue like the ocean. She used to think her father would never grow old. Now he had three deep wrinkles on his forehead, a few in the gap between his eyebrows and two at the corners of his mouth. He was old, and soon he would pass on. There, in his bed, in the dark of their longhouse.

Regardless of how betrayed she felt, he was the only true family she had. A dying man. She searched for words that would help her father pass on with a peaceful mind.

'You don't have to worry about me. You leave me in good hands,' she assured him. 'The villagers will care for me. They always have.'

He forced a smile for her between more fits of coughing.

She rubbed his back. Stayed with him until his hacking stopped. Until the thrall arrived to care for him, and then Hilda stepped back out into the Midsummer night.

The wind scooped around her with its whispers. A couple of young lovers ran down the street past her. Drunk and giggling. The sun had set and the moon was out. It hung low over the ash tree in the inner circle. The night was warm with talk and song. Hilda almost wanted to pull off her yellow under-gown. To wear nothing but her strapped red dress and the two brooches that held it up.

Hilda walked up the hill to join the festivities. The Midsummer pyre blazed in the middle of the village near the great ash. The inner circle was filled with people. Around the fire, two dozen villagers held hands as they sang and stomped their feet in rhythm. Two steps to the left and one to the right. Their song was deep and powerful, as though a thousand people sang.

The shadows of dancing villagers swirled up against the edges of the inner circle. The laughter and conversations were loud. The smell of smoke lingered on everyone's tunics.

Hilda moved through the crowd towards the tables by the ash. Chanted the verse, longing to escape thoughts about her dying father.

As you take,
Don't take it all.
Leave fortune,
Good harvest and hope.

A broad man with long hair stood by one of the ale tubs twenty arm-lengths away, back facing the Midsummer fire. His hair was long and well combed, his strong arms covered with painted symbols and images. The back of his left hand was blood-red from the newest addition; the bindrune of fortune.

'Heill, Finn,' she said.

The warrior glanced at her and smiled. 'No moonlit flowering for you, Hilda?' he asked, and took a deep gulp of ale from his rune-carved horn. A cup was easier to manage, but a horn was better, and larger too.

From her belt, Hilda freed her own horn, dressed in silver.

'By Mimer's head!' he blurted when he saw it.

Her wealth usually impressed, but not always so much. She stretched over Finn, towards the tub of ale, but couldn't quite reach, and without making her ask, he took her horn and filled it for her. The ale flowed over the border and dripped from the silver tip when he gave it back.

'Takka,' she said.

'So, will you finally join us on the raids on Frey's day?' he grinned.

She watched him plunge his empty horn into the wooden bucket to refill it with ale.

'I'll fight,' she answered, though once again the chief had denied her requests to prove her worth. All because her dying father didn't want her to raid.

'To your first raid. May we raid together or meet in Valhalla.' Finn raised his drink. 'Skál!'

He emptied half the horn at a stroke and a burp escaped his throat as he raised his drink to her again. His breath stank of onions. Hilda lifted her own horn and drank and drank, so the ale flowed down her throat and filled her stomach. The drink wasn't as sweet as she liked it, but it was stronger than she had expected. The horn was nearly empty when her thirst was quenched. She dried her lips with the back of her hand and forced out a burp of her own.

'By Ymir's frosty balls,' Finn exclaimed. 'You drink more ale than me, shieldmaiden.'

Glad to be treated like a true warrior, Hilda giggled as she watched him down the remainder of his own drink. When he finished, he no longer looked at her.

Hilda turned to see what had taken his attention.

Einer was there, tall behind her. His straw-like hair had been brushed away from his face to reveal his green eyes. 'Hei, Hilda,' he said and smiled as he always did when he saw her.

'Hei,' she piped. Quickly, she combed her hair with her fingers and arranged the two brooches on top of her breasts so the beaded necklace between them hung nicely.

Einer caught Finn's glare then, and raised an eyebrow at him. Finn held the stare. For a while the two men glared at each other and Hilda felt as though they were having a silent conversation in which she wasn't allowed to participate. Finn broke the stare, submerged his horn into the wooden tub to refill it. He glanced at Hilda, regained a grin for a heartbeat, and turned away.

Einer's eyes fell back on Hilda.

She had waited for a chance away from the feast table to speak with him. 'Why haven't you talked to the chieftain?' she immediately asked. She had to lift her chin to be able to look him straight in the eyes. 'I talked to your father, and he refused to take me on the raids. Why didn't you try to convince him?'

He almost seemed embarrassed to look at her. 'He doesn't listen. Forgive,' he said. 'I've tried.'

Hilda didn't forgive so easily. All she had ever worked towards and trained for was to join the raids. Einer knew how much it meant to her. Better than anyone. He knew.

'Have you talked to your father?' Einer asked. He didn't look into her eyes as he had used to do when they were younger. Freed a plain cup from his belt and filled it with ale, instead. The cup was too modest for the son of a chief. It surprised her that he hadn't taken one of his horns, or at least a prettier cup. Not that Einer ever boasted about his family's wealth, or cared that he looked like a poor farmer.

'Have *you*?' she asked.

Einer nodded.

'And you forgive him?' She didn't want to ask, but she had to know.

'Hilda, he's like a father to me,' he answered without truly answering.

She had thought he would understand, but things had been different since Einer had started raiding. He was no longer as eager for fights and battles as her.

'You have to take him along on the raids and let him die with honour,' she insisted.

'We've all tried. He doesn't want to come.'

'He's just saying that so he won't be a burden for you.'

Einer nodded, but didn't respond. He took a quick sip of ale, and stared at her for three entire heartbeats. Hilda wanted to look away, no longer used to him staring straight at her. His gaze felt different. Since that night on the beach.

As if he knew it made her uncomfortable, Einer diverted his eyes. 'My father says it's because he misses her,' he said.

'Who?'

'Your mother.' He spun the drink in his hand and his lips trembled. 'Dying like this is the only way he can see her again.'

'His rightful place is in Valhalla, as was hers. Leif too.'

'I know.'

'Then why won't you take him on the raid?'

'When I went to see him this morning he said something he once told us as children: "Think fondly of the dead, whether death took them in bed or in battle".'

It was her father's voice that Hilda heard. Those words and the smell of smoke on her clothes brought her right back to that rainy afternoon in the longhouse. She remembered how he had said it as he gazed into the fire. Hilda and Einer had been mere children. Had asked about her mother's death. 'Think fondly of the dead, whether death took them in bed or in battle,' was all her father had told them; and never again had they talked about her.

Tears rolled over Hilda's cheeks before she knew what was happening. Her vision blurred and her face felt warm. She blinked to force the tears back and peered up at Einer. His cheeks were flushed, and she knew he hadn't expected her to cry. Not that she had expected it either.

'Forgive,' he muttered, drying her tears with the back of his hand.

Hilda brushed his hand away and dried the remaining tears with the sleeve of her dress, so no one else would see her. Swallowed her feelings up and hid them away. Warriors didn't cry.

Einer looked down at the drink in his hands. 'Are you going

to pluck flowers and dream of your future husband?' he asked, and she knew he wanted to make her think on other matters.

'Nej.' She sniffed to stop her nose from running and turned away from him, towards the wooden tub of ale to refill her horn. She refused his help although he offered. 'Had you spoken to your father, I wouldn't need to consider it. I would have sailed with you on Frey's day.'

She took a big slurp of ale, but didn't empty it like before.

'Shieldmaidens have husbands too,' Einer muttered, maybe more to himself than her, but she didn't fail to hear, and didn't allow him to have the last word.

'I have all I want.' She began to walk away.

'Hilda,' he said.

She lifted her eyes to the dark sky and faced him, again. Her leather shoes sunk into the mud.

Her childhood friend didn't speak, though he had called for her, and it seemed as if he had lost his words. Unlike him; Einer had always had a smooth tongue. 'Will you jump across the fire with me?'

She didn't answer. Didn't know why he asked.

'Not now. Later. After the flames have died down,' he continued. 'Like we did when we were younger.'

For a bit longer, she watched him and tried to find out what he was really doing. Why he asked. He couldn't honestly mean for them to declare their love.

She laughed, at him, at herself, at the situation, the absurdity, and glanced over the crowd to see if his friends were there somewhere and it was but a dare, but she couldn't find them.

'You're like a brother to me, Einer,' she said. 'Jumping the Midsummer fire isn't something brothers and sisters do.' With those words, she walked away, leaving Einer alone. And though she wanted to see his reaction, she didn't turn back to look, but for some reason she felt awful for having laughed and for leaving him like that, and the wind whisked around her with disapproving whispers.

'I'm not your brother,' she heard him say, and she knew he was right. Einer would never truly feel like a brother. Especially not since that night on the beach.

Hilda shook her head to forget about him and pushed her way in towards the fire. There were only embers, and through the hot air she saw Finn. He had bound his hair up with a red strip of linen. Their eyes caught each other, but when she blinked, he was gone.

Eager to get lost in the music, Hilda stomped her feet along to the song.

Right when the deep hum of the song was at its best, someone tugged at her braided hair.

She swung around and Finn let go of her blonde hair. Smiled to her, and it was as though she couldn't quite focus on him, though she tried. He caught her as she staggered and they laughed. Even when he no longer did, Hilda couldn't stop laughing. She held Finn's overtunic for balance. Glanced to the ash tree where Einer sat with his friends. He was looking at her. At once, her laugh was forgotten. Despite everything that had happened between then, she missed spending time with Einer, doing nothing and everything. They had used to always be together.

'He doesn't want you to go on the raids,' Finn said after a while. 'Einer.'

Hilda didn't let go of Einer's stare. Einer and her might have drifted apart over the last few summers, but apart from her father, Einer was the closest she had to a family. Soon her father wouldn't be around anymore. Einer was all she had. The only one who took her side no matter what, and always had. Despite what Finn said, Hilda had no doubt that Einer wanted the best for her.

'I could help you,' Finn said.

'How?' she asked, not out of interest, but in surprise.

She examined Finn's sly smile. The few times she and Finn had spoken, it had always been about Einer, and never in a good way. Einer had never mentioned Finn, and Hilda did not know how well they knew each other, or if she could trust Finn. He was an older man and a more seasoned warrior.

'We could go down to the tents and talk about it.'

Hilda scoffed. 'You want to go to the tents with me?' she mumbled. Her voice was smoothed with ale and though she knew perfectly well what men and women went there to do, she'd never expected to be asked to go there. No one dared ask a woman of Hilda's status to go down to the tents. She wasn't just anyone, she was the skald's daughter.

She shook her head. Not wanting to go to the tents, and least of all tonight.

'Come,' Finn whispered into her ear, and before she could say anything, he dragged her along, out of the circle, away from the crowd and though she didn't know why, Hilda turned her head to find Einer in the crowd. But they were going too fast and she couldn't see him.

Finn's grip was stronger than hers. She knew she wouldn't be able to push him away, but she was smaller and she could wriggle out of his grip.

'Stop,' she said, pulling Finn in the opposite direction, back up the hill.

'Come on.' Finn dragged her wrist so she stumbled a little further down the road.

Again, she shook her head. 'I won't go to the tents, Finn.' She was baffled that she had to say the words aloud. Finn was the same age as her aunt, and married too.

'Hilda,' a man called from behind, interrupting their conversation.

For a moment, her heart stopped beating and relief flushed over her: Einer had followed them down the road, he must have, but when she turned and saw that it wasn't him at all, her heart sank. The man who had called her name wore yellowed clothes that had once been white. A thrall, but not just any thrall; her father's loyal servant, and in his arms, he carried something big and heavy.

There were few lit torches along the road, but Hilda could see the rich red cloth of father's tunic. Ragnar Erikson was carried out in the arms of his thrall like a child who couldn't yet walk.

Hilda wrenched Finn's hand off her wrist and rushed up towards the thrall and her father.

'Where are the other servants?'

Her father didn't look at her, though she was standing right in front of him. His eyes were wide open and far away, and he stared out into the distant night.

'He has been sending them on errands,' answered the thrall

'You can't carry him like this.' She waved Finn over, but he didn't come. Shook his head and kept his distance. 'Finn,' she called to him. 'We need your help.'

Finn continued to scowl for a few moments, and glared at Hilda, but then the frown on his forehead softened and he took a step towards her. 'What do you need?' he asked.

'A chair for my father to sit in.'

Finn moved like he was on a mission. Banged on the door of the nearest longhouse and entered before anyone answered.

Hilda turned back to the thrall. 'What were you thinking?'

'He ordered me to carry him out.'

'You should at least have come to get me,' she argued.

A hand reached for the sleeve of her dress. 'Hilda,' her father whispered. 'Hilda.'

'Did you give him mead?' she asked the thrall, refusing to look at her father for a little longer as she tried to control the tears that swelled up in her eyes.

The thrall nodded without meeting her stare. 'And a few dream caps,' he said.

'Good.' She swallowed her spit. It took all her courage to look down at Ragnar and speak. 'I'm here, Father,' she said. 'Hilda's here.'

Before her father could respond, Finn arrived, hauling a heavy chair, and her father's concentration floated away from her. Images were carved into the wood, of Odin's lone travels in Midgard; a chair worthy of the village's storyteller. And Hilda was certain it was the biggest one Finn had been able to find. She gave him a thankful nod.

He put the chair down on the wooden belayed part of the road and helped the thrall move Ragnar towards it.

'I see Odin's runes,' Ragnar mumbled as they sat him down in the large chair. 'Odin's runes.' Then he forgot about the runes and murmured Hilda's name instead, over and over, though he didn't look at her, and she wasn't sure anymore if he knew she was there with him.

In her mind, she repeated what Einer had told her: "Think fondly of the dead, whether death took them in bed or in battle," and struggled to keep her posture. She couldn't cry. Finn was there, and shieldmaidens never showed weakness.

Her father was frail and tired, and so old. He had never looked old before, but a few stray hairs had become white over these past months and his skin was pale, almost grey. He looked dead already.

'I forgive you, father,' she said. 'I forgive you.'

She waited for him to speak and tell her that everything was in order, and that he didn't blame her for being angry with his decision to die at home, and that he was glad she forgave him. But when he spoke, those were not his words. 'I see Odin's runes,' he said. 'Everywhere, Hilda.'

She wasn't sure he had understood or heard her. 'I forgive you, Father,' she repeated. Tears rolled down her cheeks and though Finn was there and watching, it didn't matter. 'I forgive you.'

'Odin's runes speak to me,' was all Ragnar said.

She dried the tears under her chin while her father continued to mumble about the runes. The wind swirled around Hilda, and its loud whispers made it difficult to focus on her father.

'Your eyes.' He waved his left hand at the thrall. 'His are red, but yours—yours are golden. You have a golden future, Hilda.'

She swallowed the lump of spit in her throat and glanced to Finn. He didn't pay attention to Ragnar or her. Tapped his foot to the distant song from the circle. Maybe he just pretended not to see her cry, but the sight of him not noticing, relieved her.

'Where else do you see the runes?' she asked her father, and dried the last few tears.

'They're everywhere,' he whispered. 'There are more lights in the sky than there has ever been. And runes, everywhere.' His focus became faint. 'And Hilda,' he called and grabbed her wrist, as if he remembered something of importance. 'The runes on the house were cracked and faint. It will fall.' His grip tightened and it began to hurt. He stared at her, waited for her to respond and held her tighter.

She nodded and smiled. 'I understand, Father.'

Ragnar rambled on and on, about how everything in Midgard suddenly made sense and the runes shone to him. 'They shine, they shine, Hilda,' he kept saying. 'Odin's runes are true. They tell the truth.'

Hilda could do nothing but force a smile and try to accept that he would die like that. He should have died in battle, but instead he would leave a stain on the family's warrior reputation, like her mother had. She forgave him. How could she not? He was her father.

'The raven. It's here for me,' Ragnar mumbled. 'Like your mother's snow fox. Hurry I have no time. I need to speak to them, speak once more. You'll tell them what I said, ja, Hilda? You'll tell them?'

'I'll tell them,' she assured him. Though she didn't know who she should tell and what she should tell them. The old man had drunk too much mead, eaten too many dream caps, and the sound of death had to be ringing in his head. He no longer made sense.

Ragnar smacked his lips and grinned in satisfaction. 'The raven can take me now,' he mumbled. 'You can—Nej, I need to speak.' He clawed at the thrall's arms. 'Take me to the ash.'

Hilda nodded to confirm her father's words. If he wanted to tell the villagers one last story, she would make sure he did. She turned to Finn. Immediately, as though signalled, he rushed over and joined the thrall. Between them they lifted Ragnar's chair. But they advanced slowly, too slowly for her father. 'Faster!' he yelled and lifted his arm above his head to order them to hurry. 'Faster, thralls!'

Hilda noticed Finn glare up at Ragnar, but her father was old and dying, and to make it better Hilda laughed and laughed until Finn too would be able to see the fun in it all. 'Come, Father, come,' she told Ragnar, as she too rushed the two men further up the hilly road until they could see the crowd gathered in the circle.

The dim light from the Midsummer fire glistened against the planks on the road. The villagers' stomps could be heard throughout Ash-hill. The song was strong, like it had been at the beginning of the celebrations. Her father mumbled along and tried to stomp in the rhythm of the song, though his feet only tapped the air.

'Ragnar Erikson shall speak,' Hilda called to the hundreds of villagers still gathered around the inner circle. 'Our skald shall tell his last story!'

The ones who heard her repeated the shout, and it didn't take more than half a verse before the song ended and the villagers parted for Ragnar to be carried up close to the remains of the Midsummer fire.

Finn and the thrall put the chair down while the villagers gathered around the embers, ready to warm themselves on Ragnar Erikson's last tale.

To give him strength, Hilda sat down next to him.

Ragnar fiddled with the fabric of his own tunic, and gaped like a small child who couldn't speak and didn't know the world. The villagers watched him, and many chuckled at his ways. 'Too much mead,' a small girl giggled.

'The old ash, Ratatusk's home,' Ragnar muttered.

'We can't hear you. Speak up, Father,' Hilda whispered to him. His eyes lit up as she said it. At her reassuring smile, her father regained a little of his courage and focus.

A warm hand was placed on Hilda's shoulder. She looked up. Einer was there, and he smiled to her. She smiled back, glad to have him with her through this.

'Behold Yggdrasil's kinsman,' Ragnar yelled. The villagers turned to the great ash in the middle of the inner circle as her father talked about the beautiful tree. 'Ratatusk's home is how the gods communicate with us. It is written in the runes on the bark of the ash tree, and on its branches and leaves. We must take care of it, never let it become frail. We must always care for it, as if it were Yggdrasil itself. Every morning if it hasn't rained, water needs to be poured on Nidhogg's fodder so the roots can grow deep. And stories shall always be told, right here, under the great ash of Ash-hill.'

Ragnar had spoken about their ash-tree with much conviction, but then his focus simmered away once more. He stared at the air right in front of him, though there was nothing there to see. 'The raven. The raven is here for me,' he whispered ever so faintly, so only Hilda could hear. 'The snow fox watches us. Your mother is here.'

He opened his mouth to speak again, but instead he wheezed and coughed and seemed to no longer be able to breathe. Hilda knew she should hold him, but she couldn't make herself move. Just sat and watched as his eyes opened wide, though it didn't appear as if he could see.

'If Yggdrasil's kinsman falls,' he wheezed, his voice nothing but a whisper, though the silence was so complete that every being in Ash-hill could hear him. 'If the ash falls, we're doom—' His cheeks reddened, tears rolled down his face and Ragnar gagged. For four entire heartbeats, his eyes looked as though they were being pushed out of his skull, and then he dropped in over himself.

Hilda saw her hands reach out towards her father. She pushed his shoulders to make him sit up. She was not in control of her own body; she could only see it happen and feel the soft wool of his tunic under her fingers. His head hung as though his neck was broken and when she crouched down, she saw that his blue eyes were wide open though they weren't looking. There was no life behind them. She felt a knot in her throat, removed her hand from her father's shoulder. As soon as she let go, his upper body fell down again. Limp and lifeless.

Her heart felt as if it were being clenched tight in a fist. She had hoped she would never have to see him die like that. But there he was, in his rich red tunic instead of his armour, bending in over himself as though he were broken, or maybe listening to what the earth had to say.

Your journey will be long,
But do not fear, old friend.

The chanter's voice cut through the night. Her sharp song seemed to make the knot in Hilda's throat swell all the way down to her stomach. The villagers stomped their feet in rhythm. Einer's hand was warm on her shoulder.

This is your beginning,
We'll meet before the end.

Even the whispers in the wind were singing for her father.

Hilda heard the flap of wings. A raven sat on her father's back. Its long claws were buried into his skin. Its feathers were greasy, its eyes blue, like her father's, and on its black beak were runes; Odin's runes.

'The raven,' Hilda whispered. The one her father had mentioned.

The bird blinked at her softly, like her father had used to do when she had been younger. She had never seen a raven with eyes like that before.

Glory you leave behind,
To last and ever shine.

The raven didn't let go of her gaze and Hilda didn't blink, afraid the bird would disappear if she did, and along with the few hundred villagers, she sang.

Greet the gods, greet our kin,
Someday we'll meet again.

The raven cawed in answer before it took flight. And in front of Hilda's eyes, it faded into darkness.

EINER

Chapter Three

RAGNAR'S FUNERAL PYRE lifted high up into the air like no pyre Einer had ever seen before. It was almost as large as the Midsummer fire.

'There you are,' his mother's voice cut through the crowd. Her slender fingers touched Einer's arm to make him turn away from his friends, towards her.

As always, she looked almost too elegant for the occasion, even for a grand funeral like this. Her long golden hair was braided in the old style, and her dress looked as though it had been embroidered by the goddesses themselves, for it was almost too perfect to belong in Midgard.

Einer gave her the hug she asked for, and together they walked up the slope towards Ragnar's funeral pyre.

'Are you ready to sail off tomorrow?' his mother asked as they walked past a flowery field where a stallion galloped around. The black horse looked like night against the sunny day. Its mane whipped in the wind. It knew both tölt and flying pace, and was a beautiful horse with a fitting temperament.

'Ja. All packed,' Einer said. He attempted to find Hilda in the crowd.

At the middle of the stacked wood, lay Ragnar's corpse. Ragnar looked older than he had alive. Flies had settled on his wrinkled, grey face. His clothes were decorated with gold and around him lay the offerings: his sword, two daggers and a seax; golden cups filled with mead; food for Ragnar to enjoy on his journey; and rings, neck-rings, arm-rings and jewels. Nothing lacked.

The stallion stopped galloping.

Relentlessly Einer searched for Hilda's blonde hair and blue hairpiece.

'Einer.' His mother forced them to stop up. She looked at him with her unavoidable stare that meant she was about to say something very important. 'I had a visit from Ragnar.'

'Ragnar? Before he passed on?'

'Afterwards. In my dreams.'

Einer gulped and listened more carefully. His mother's dreams always came true, like the visions of a runemistress, and if she mentioned it, there and then, instead of waiting until tonight when they were alone, then it was important.

'He said it was time.'

'For what?'

She brought forward something she had hid in her palm. It was an old neck-ring with a bracteate attached, a big gold coin, onto which the image of the oldest tree in the nine worlds had been hammered. A clear image of the sacred ash, Yggdrasil.

'Wear it. Always,' his mother instructed, as she lifted the chain over Einer's head.

Although the bracteate was light, it felt like a heavy burden, and although Einer wanted to ask its significance, people were moving into position for the funeral, and there was no time.

A stone bowl as big as two palms stood on the grass five arm-lengths north of the pyre. Einer walked to it and took his position behind it, with his parents. He checked that his shield was safely strapped to his back and that he could reach it for the song.

The villagers moved into a large circle surrounding Ragnar's funeral pyre. Not a single freeman, woman or child had stayed home. Everyone had come to honour Ragnar Erikson. Ragnar had meant a great deal in northern Jutland.

The horse he had seen earlier neighed and then Einer noticed Hilda, at the stallion's side, leading it in a full circle around the pyre. In front of Einer and his father, she stopped up and struggled to make the horse stand still.

Foam dripped from the stallion's muzzle as it was brought before them. It was big, and its back was so tall that it reached Hilda's shoulders. She attempted to hold it still, but Einer could see that she was nervous by the way her eyes darted around; Hilda normally always had focus.

Their eyes found each other. She gestured to the horse. He nodded. Hilda rarely asked for help, and Einer gave it willingly. He walked to the horse's side and stroked its neck. The stallion's black hair-coat was drenched in sweat and white from foam. It did not turn its head to look at him, but its ears twisted back and forth, and its hooves marked the ground. It knew.

Einer positioned himself in front of the horse. It turned its head away from him, breathing heavily. He waited for it to settle. The stallion neighed and cast its head upwards, away from Einer. Its ears were flattened back.

With both his hands, Einer clasped around the bridle, brought the horse's head back down, and waited for the animal to steady. He held it still so the horse could no longer look away. The whites were showing in its eyes as it tried to battle free, and it stomped its hooves. Einer kept its head fastened between his hands, waited, and gave it time to realise that it was forced to settle and look at him. Its nostrils continued to flare, but not with the same intensity. Its ears moved around, quicker than he could follow. They settled in Einer's direction. The horse looked at him. Under his fingers, he could feel the blood race through its body.

Einer tried to ignore the hundreds of people watching, imagined that there was only him and this stallion, nervously stomping. It no longer resisted Einer, and did not look away. He let go of the bridle with one hand, closed it into a loose fist and held it out for the horse to see. Then he lowered it to his hips. He knelt and guided his hand further down towards the earth. The horse followed and knelt down with him, its front legs to begin with, and then the rest of its body until it lay down entirely on its side. Einer could not help but smile at the success. He had not trained horses since he was a boy shy of raids, but he had not forgotten the ways.

He grabbed the bridle again, careful not to startle.

'Blót,' Hilda called out.

The horse kicked and attempted to get up, startled, but Einer held its head so it could not move, and calmed it under the stare his mother had once taught him.

'Blót,' hundreds of villagers repeated in loud roars. Einer's father sounded the blowing horn.

The stallion kicked again. Its ears darted back and forth, but its eyes stayed on Einer. It would be all right. With his thumbs, he caressed the side of its head to calm it.

The warriors brought out their round shields. They began to tap them, more and more joining in, so the sound rang all around.

The stallion neighed, shook its head and its eyes showed the whites again. Einer clasped his hands tighter around the horse's head.

'Many summers will pass before we find another skald as great as Ragnar,' Einer mother announced to the crowd. Ragnar had been born to tell stories.

'Aesir and vanir hear us,' Einer's father called out to both kinds of gods, following the rhythm of the taps on shields. 'High Odin, in your honour we offer our strongest stallion, allow it to accompany our skald, Ragnar Erikson, son of Erik Ivarson, on his last journey. Allow him to ride to Hel so he will not have to walk.'

In death, Ragnar would have more greatness in front of him.

Einer's father crouched down, touched the stallion's stomach and guided his hand further up, to the neck. The horse flinched but quickly found Einer's gaze.

On the other side of the stallion, Hilda crouched down too, ready with the stone bowl. It looked as though it had been made for her; was the exact size of her two palms, and when she held it her fingers spread out prettily like flower petals.

Einer's father knelt in front of the horse, grabbed his dagger with both hands and lifted.

The stallion breathed rapidly. Its nostrils blew warm air on Einer's forearms. The rhythm hastened as the warriors tapped their shields faster and faster, with as much force as they could, until they were tapping out of pace.

Einer's father plunged the dagger down. He stabbed the stallion in the throat, just under its jaw. Blood splattered out and hit the back of Einer's right hand. His father carved through the flesh, pushing the dagger all the way through the horse's throat to finish it quickly.

The horse kicked and made a gagging noise that reminded Einer of Ragnar's dying moments.

He never looked away from the stallion's eyes, stayed with it until the end, when the last strength left the animal.

His father pushed his fingers to the horse's neck. His hand was dark with blood when he pulled it away, and he marked his own face with the colour, from the forehead down to the cheek. Then Einer's mother crouched down and marked her own face too.

Hilda held the bowl underneath the horse's neck to fill it up. When she was done and stood up with the stone-bowl full of blood, Einer placed the horse's head down on the blood-red grass.

He rose from its side, walked to Hilda's and glanced at her. She held the bowl of blood high above her head as the warriors continued to bang their shields, and for a while she silently communed with her father's dead body, laid out on top of the nine-wooded pyre in the middle of the wide circle of villagers.

Einer did not take his eyes off her. He knew the stone bowl was heavy, but Hilda showed no sign of struggle. She was strong.

Without warning, Hilda turned to him, arms outstretched, holding the bowl. Einer dipped his fingers in the blood and marked his face, as his parents had done. The smell of metal was overpowering. When he was finished, Hilda handed him the bowl, wet her own fingers and flicked blood onto her own face.

One of Einer's father's thralls advanced with the golden bowl of blessed mead. Hilda took it and gave Einer a nod.

Behind them the horse was carried away, out of the crowd; out of sight. Its meat would be prepared and cooked for tonight, its bones offered onto Ragnar's grave.

With the stallion's blood, Einer blessed everyone who stood close to the pyre; everyone who in life had been close to Ragnar. To all who had blood on their face Hilda served the sacred mead. She had to refill the bowl several times.

The stone bowl began to feel heavy in Einer's hands by the time he reached Finn's wife. He smeared the blood on her cheeks and moved along to her husband. Finn's smile stank of superiority. Recently Finn was everywhere; with the famed warriors, at Einer's father's side, and at Hilda's, with that cold stare that Einer doubted he would ever grow to understand.

It was a relief to move along to Hilda's uncle and aunt, and their daughter, Tyra, who was as good as a sister to both Einer and Hilda. Einer dipped his fingers in the blooded bowl one last time, smeared the dark colour onto Tyra's face and dried his hand on the back of his blue tunic. With his bloody fingers, he rearranged a flower in Tyra's hair, and smiled to her. Hilda took his place and offered Tyra a sip of the blessed mead.

Together Einer and Hilda walked to Ragnar. The warriors hammered their shields in rhythm.

The pyre was so tall that Ragnar lay a handspan above Hilda's head.

The skald's arms and fingers were covered with rings; he would not go to Hel bare. His fingernails had been cut short so Loki could not use them in the afterlife, and his hands rested on the hilt of his unsoiled sword that had never had a chance to taste blood. Ragnar had never been fit to go back into battle. His limp had kept him away for more than two dozen summers; a sad destiny.

It hurt to see Ragnar like this. The smell that surrounded the old man was heavy and foul, like that of a rotting animal left behind by a pack of wolves.

Einer coloured his fosterer's face with the stallion's blood. The pyre was so tall that even Einer could not reach to the middle of it. In turn, Hilda climbed up the side of the stacked wood and leant in to reach Ragnar and pour the sacred mead over his lips so it flowed over his cheeks and chin and dripped out over the silk pillows he lay on. More carefully and gracefully than Einer had known her capable of, she climbed down again.

Two thralls rid them of the heavy bowls. Einer's hands had been steady throughout the ceremony, but they began to tremble almost as soon as he let go of the blooded stone bowl.

The villagers stomped their feet. The air was tense and expectant as the sound resonated from the burial ground, out towards Ash-hill.

A thrall was guided up the slope towards them, in through the crowd and around the pyre like the stallion had been. It took two thralls to hold him up and make him walk. People turned to look as he passed. He was brought around once, outside the crowd, for all to see, before finally being guided towards Einer's father.

The admirable thrall was Carlman. Before Einer had begun raiding, he had often stayed in Ragnar's longhouse during the summers when both his parents were abroad, and during those times, it had been Carl who had taken care of him.

The thrall would serve Ragnar well. In honour of his choice, he had been given both mead and dream caps, more than he had ever been given before, and he was brought before the villagers free and unbound; an unusual but brave choice. He was a thrall, but had chosen to be there.

'Ragnar Erikson, son of Erik Ivarson,' Einer's father yelled loud for everyone to hear. 'May this thrall serve you always, with as much vigour and care as he served you in Midgard.'

The villagers took steps back and forth, commencing the dance. The two thralls who had brought Ragnar's servant to the burial ground let him stand on his own.

Einer's father turned to Carl. 'Speak, thrall!' he ordered.

The servant was dressed modestly. He swayed and Einer feared the dream caps and mead had made him forget his words.

'In life, I served my master,' Carl shouted, just when Einer was certain he was in no state to speak at all. 'In death I shall follow.'

They yelled and roared as loud as they could. Einer swung his heavy shield around from his back and tapped it with his fist, along with the hundreds of other warriors. When they stopped, and the burial ground quieted again, there was only the stomp of their feet left. The rhythm accompanied the thrall as he walked towards the pyre, arms raised in the air.

He slipped when he climbed up the wood.

It pained Einer to see Carl leave, but he was proud that the thrall had decided to sacrifice himself, and he was certain that in return Carlman would gain the knowledge he sought in the afterlife. Sacrifices were always rewarded.

For a short moment, Carlman stood on the top of the pyre, his hands raised in the air. The warriors banged their shields for him. Then Carl knelt down besides his master.

The two thralls who had helped him to the burial grounds climbed up to tie his wrists to his ankles with horsehair rope.

A torch was brought forward. Hilda took it and walked

towards the pyre. Carl gaped at her with fear in his eyes, but he did not move. Einer could almost hear the servant's blood pound, like the stallion's had.

Hilda stopped in front of her father and raised the torch high into the air. The warriors stamped while they tapped their shields. Einer's throat was tight. Carl cried as he watched Hilda. Carlman had served Hilda her entire life. It was befitting that she was the one to send him on his way. She held the burning torch in outstretched hands.

'Death,' the chanter sang from the other side of the pyre.

Everyone began to sing as Hilda lowered the torch in outstretched hands.

Hear our voices,
Hear our song,
Though your journey
Will be long.

Hilda sang as loud as them all, and on top of the stacked wood, the thrall muttered the words along with them. He had heard them many times before. They all had.

You will not be
All alone,
We will guide you
To Hel's home.

The burning torch touched the wood. Hilda let it drop and took a step back. Carl sang loudest of all. Einer began to tap his shield with more force, and when the song continued, they all did their best to sing so loud that the thrall's voice would be drowned by theirs.

Now take a step,
And take two.

We will help you,
To pass through.

The fire caught and the wood began to smoke as the flames rose. Carlman shook and coughed, though no one heard.

Walk all nine worlds,
Through them all.
The last will be
Helheim's hall.

Carl screamed so loud that the stomp of their feet and the taps on their shields could not drown his squeal. He coughed and spat and shook, but did not attempt to run and did not jump down from the pyre, knowing, as well as all, that he would be thrown on it again if he tried. It was better to die with pride.

Knock on the gate,
Call Hel's name.
Many others have
Done the same.

Carl wriggled like a worm. His instincts urged him to get away. The strongest of warriors too would have done the same. The smoke surrounded him. Flames began to lick Ragnar's feet.

With open arms,
Hel will hum:
"Welcome Ragnar
Erikson."

Barely visible through the smoke, Carl collapsed face down, halfway on top of his master.

Now your journey
Shall begin.
Greet the gods and
Greet our kin.

They swung their shields around to hang on their backs again. Einer looked longingly at Ragnar as he stamped in rhythm with the others.

'Goodbye Ragnar, skald of Ash-hill, son of Erik Ivarson,' he said. 'I hope you'll never have to go to Hel,' wishing from his entire being that Ragnar would be allowed into Valhalla, where he belonged, instead, and as he watched the pyre burn, Einer felt a deep sense of calm as if the gods had listened to him and his wish had been granted.

In death.
In death, we shall meet.

The fire felt as though it burned Einer's face and chest. His chest hurt.

In death.
In death, we shall see.

His flesh burned where the gold bracteate his mother had given him touched his skin. Einer clasped his teeth together, and tried to suppress the roar of pain. The song drowned his pained moan, like it had drowned Carl's squeals.

To death.
To death we shall leave.

Einer tore the gold ring from his neck.
The gold was cool, as though he had left the bracteate outside on a winter night.

Through closed teeth Einer breathed deeply. He looked at the flat gold coin that had burned him in disbelief. He did not understand how he could hold it in his hand. He knew how hot it had been.

His mother put a hand on his shoulder, knowing, as she always did, that something was amiss.

'Something is wrong with it,' he told her.

'You used it,' she answered in a distant tone.

Einer glanced up at her and saw that she was not looking him in the eyes, but instead she stared at his chest. He gazed down.

The flesh above the neck of his tunic smoked. His flesh was blood-red, marked with the image of his bracteate. The tree of life was burnt into his chest.

DARKNESS

DEATH, PAIN, AND fear.

Ragnar opened his heavy eye-lids to the afterlife with a longing smile on his lips. Complete darkness surrounded him. The distant echo of a song called him towards a tall light ahead; a veiled entrance to the afterlife.

Finally, he would see his wife again. Finally, he would see his son. His mind was clear from the influence of mead and dream caps from his life, his body felt healed from ills, and Ragnar was ready to start his long-awaited afterlife in Helheim.

He sat on a horse, scarcely outlined by the light from the veiled exit. He smiled at the sight. The villagers must have sacrificed the horse for him. Eager to pass on into the next life, Ragnar grabbed hold of the reins and made the horse move. His tunic felt expensive.

He wore his finest clothes, the yellow coat lined with gold that he wore for special ceremonies. His arms were heavy with rings, and his neck too. He could not remember what he had been wearing when he had passed on from Midgard, but this had not been it. He smiled. No freeman passed on and went to see the gods in drab clothes.

Someone walked at his side. 'Ragnar?' said the familiar voice of his thrall.

'Carlman,' he responded in a welcoming tone, and the honour of it all made him swell with pride. His thrall had chosen to serve him in the afterlife too.

The villagers had given him a worthy burial.

Ragnar kicked the horse to make it move towards the slit of light while the distant voices of those alive were singing and guiding the way for him to the afterlife.

Now your journey
Shall begin,

Their voices guided him forward. He heard his daughter sing for him, accompanied by the voices of villagers that he knew well. The sound of them made him miss his life, already, but in Helheim his wife and son would be waiting, and he missed them most of all.

Greet the gods and
Greet our kin.

The blessed afterlife of Helheim was finally within sight. The veiled opening was so near. Ragnar's heart sped up at the thought of seeing his wife again. The closer he came, the more clearly the light fell on him, and the horse, and his servant. Carlman was smiling as he walked at Ragnar's side, and the horse's ears flicked forward with interest. Ragnar kicked it into trot, eager to pass on into Helheim and see his family.

The slit of light disappeared.

With no warning, it vanished.

The voices faded and their last word echoed around the cold Darkness. *Kin, kin, kin...*

The song had not yet come to an end; there was one more verse, but their voices had stopped.

Ragnar glanced around to see if the slit of light had appeared elsewhere, but saw nothing. Everything was pitch black, and the silence was complete.

He blinked and concentrated to see something, but there was no light at all, and he heard nothing, and felt nothing.

The horse whickered.

'Where did it go?' Ragnar asked his thrall.

An axe hacked into Ragnar's shoulder. Blood splattered out over his arm and up his neck. The horse reared. Ragnar was cast off its back, too shocked and breathless to scream. His head bumped to the floor. His neck snapped.

Death, pain, and fear.

HILDA

Chapter Four

THESE DAYS, HILDA trained twice as hard. With her father in the afterlife, nothing and no one stood in the way of her becoming a warrior.

As on any good summer day, women were gathered around the ash in the inner circle. They had pulled out benches and tables to work. Together they would cook all day, or make soap, or clothes, or whatever else needed to be done before the raiders returned home. Hilda smiled. She had never joined them, and never would. Her path was that of warrior. Next summer, she would raid.

The chieftain's wife, Siv, sat on the longest bench, right next to the Ting stones, sewing a coat. Hilda glanced around and found Tyra on a nearby bench, enthralled by Siv's old tales.

With a smile, Hilda walked towards her. Tyra's long hair had been braided in the olden style, like that of the chief's wife, and with her dagger the girl carved a wooden figurine.

'Who is it?' Hilda asked.

Tyra bent over the figurine to hide it. 'Don't look.'

'Is it for me?'

'Maybe.' Tyra without a doubt tried to sound mysterious, but her broad smile gave her away.

'It is, then.' Hilda said.

Tyra nodded, no longer denying it. 'As thanks for teaching me how to fight.'

'I'll look forward to seeing it,' she said and gave Tyra a sharp pat on the back. 'Practice tonight?'

Tyra nodded enthusiastically. 'Did you dream about them last night again?' she asked. 'Odin's runes.'

'As if the gods want me to remember what my father said.'

Hilda winked to Tyra, smiled to the chieftain's wife, raised a short greeting to her aunt, and then she set out towards the boundaries of Ash-hill. Well aware that many of the women whispered about her behind her back.

She skipped down the wooden road and through the gate of the rising sun. Past grassing cows and sheep and the Christian church and out into the forest.

The wind whistled at the top of the trees. Sunshine glistened against the bark. The woods were loud with the twitter of birds. The trees' leaves were no longer bright green as they should have been, and a few had already begun to change colours. Summer was almost over.

Einer's bear cub roared. It stood in the clearing to her right, behind the gate of its little yard. It had grown considerably, almost reaching Hilda's shoulders now, but Einer had trained it well before the beginning of summer and it no longer snapped out after her when she came to feed it in the afternoons.

'I'll feed you when I'm back, Vigir,' she yelled to it and rushed off, further into the forest. She got a roar in response.

Before long, any sign of the village disappeared in the dark of the woods. The tight crown of trees let only occasional patches of sunlight through.

A few days ago, Hilda had seen the flicker of a white tail disappear between the trees out in these woods, and since, she had been at the search of the animal. It had been too small to be a wolf tail. She was convinced that it belonged to a snow fox, though she had never seen one. Had never even heard of a snow fox so far south.

A few dream caps rummaged in her pocket and reminded her of how her father had sounded in the end, after he had been fed some. The night he died. In his dying hour, he had claimed to see the Runes, the very ones Odin had discovered when he had hanged himself in Yggdrasil. The same Runes she heard in her dreams, like the whispers she had always heard in the wind, only clearer. He had mentioned a snow fox, too, her mother's snow fox, and now it was here, in the forest. Hilda had never given up on anything in her life. If the snow fox really was there, in the forest between Ash-hill and Horn-hill, she would find it.

As she walked further into the woods, she had a feeling that someone was watching her. The wind rustled the leaves, and whispered, as ever. Listening to the whisper of the wind was like trying to understand a language she had never heard. Words escaped before she could hold on to them, but the whispers continuously came to her in the wind that rustled at the treetops. They never stopped, and never halted long enough for her to catch their meaning.

A man's scream pierced through the forest.

Hilda stopped up.

The scream didn't repeat, but Hilda heard muttered voices nearby. A group of men were talking. Hilda snuck closer to hear what they said, but no matter how much she listened, she couldn't make out the words. Just like with the wind's whispers. She was certain of one thing; the voices weren't from Ash-hill and they weren't from Horn-hill either.

Careful not to make a sound, Hilda tiptoed towards the men. Tested the ground before stepping to make the least amount of noise. The slightest sound might give her away. The tree trunks shielded her. A couple of arm-lengths were enough to hear their words clearly, but they spoke a tongue she didn't understand.

Hilda reached for the battle-axe tied to her belt and held it in a tight grip with both hands. She snuck closer and peered ahead. There were four men clad in armour. Their clothes were a strange choice of brown and grey.

Silently, she moved. Kept her gaze fixed on the men to assure herself they didn't see her.

She needed to find out who they were, but she couldn't give her position away. Four warriors were too many for her, certainly without her shield and armour.

Hilda continued to observe the men. The men were facing away from her. Two of them wore helmets; the other two had dark short hair, like thralls, but thralls didn't walk around dressed for a fight. They were men from the south, she realised.

She tiptoed and tried to see more. All of them stared at something on the ground. At what, she couldn't see.

A branch cracked nearby. Hilda jerked around. A small fox stood two arm-lengths away. Not just any fox; the snow fox. The one her father had seen. The snow fox's fur was a mixture of grey and brown, but its tail was thick with white winter fur and a black tip. The colour of its eyes was blue, exactly like her own.

She felt an instant sense of kindship. She didn't know what to do. She hadn't exactly thought about what she would do if she actually found the fox.

It had a deep scar above each eye where its patched brown summer fur no longer grew. More scars covered its lean legs. Somehow it looked both vicious and gentle.

It glared at her, and then it called out with a high shrieked bark.

Hilda shielded herself behind the trunk of an old oak, so the men wouldn't see her, if they looked to the fox. The snow fox continued to call and wail with its eyes closed.

Suddenly, its wail stopped. It eyed Hilda; took a tentative step forward and barred its teeth at her. It jerked its attention towards the men. For a moment, Hilda watched the animal without moving, but it felt as if it wanted her to look as well. She peered out from behind the oak behind which she had hidden.

The southerners' backs were still turned to her, as though they hadn't heard the barks, or, at least, were not alarmed by them.

Of course. Hilda should have known the moment she had seen the snow fox and its blue eyes. This was no ordinary snow fox. It had to be her animal follower; her fylgja, come to warn her that the southerners would kill her if she walked out into their midst.

Her mother's fylgja must have been this snow fox. It must have been hers, and Hilda had inherited it at her mother's death. Passed down the bloodline, as fylgjur often were. That must have been why her father had mentioned the snow fox and said her mother was watching. He must have seen Hilda's fylgja when he was dying, like she had seen his.

Alert, Hilda shifted her attention back towards the snow fox, but it was gone. Its barking wail rang in her ears. It really was her fylgja then. This was the first time she had seen it. Hopefully, it would be the last.

Fylgjur warned of death. The snow fox had revealed itself to Hilda to warn her that death was close. To give her a chance to counter the destiny she was headed for. Its visit wouldn't be in vain, Hilda decided.

She clenched the axe tighter in her grip, ready to fight, and glanced back at the men. Like the fox, they too were gone.

A couple of heartbeats passed before Hilda ventured out of hiding. She was barely out of her hiding place when she spotted what the warriors had gathered around. A body sprawled on the mossy ground. The man's left hand clenched onto his wood-chopping axe. Any warrior could have told him that it would have been more powerful in his right hand, but in the end, she doubted it would have made any difference. A single farmer had no chance against four armoured warriors. The weapon that had pierced his body had half shattered his axe shaft on the way.

Hilda walked to the young man, crouched down beside him. She rolled his body over, but his face remained planted into the ground, body and head parted with a messy hack. Blood flowed out from both his stomach and torn throat.

It felt as if Hilda's mind had detached from her body. Her hands acted without her orders, as they had when her father had passed, and pushed the man's head around to face upwards like his body. The dead man's mouth was wide open and his eyeballs had rolled back so far it looked as though his eyes were white. His muddy face was stained with fear. His neck looked oddly like that of a butchered cow, or perhaps a pig.

She knew who he was. He lived in Horn-hill, a farmer like his parents. Sometimes he came to Ash-hill to worked on Tormod's farm. Bard was his name.

At least he had died an honourable death with an axe in his hands. Her father's face flashed before Hilda's eyes. Her father had passed on like a farmer, while this young man had fought to his death like a worthy warrior.

Hilda rose from his side. For a moment longer, she gazed at him and wished she could swipe away the fear on his face. 'Meet you in the afterlife,' she muttered, and then she turned away.

The earth of the forest cooled her feet through her slim soles. She no longer felt her toes, but she didn't care. Horn-hill wasn't far away anyways; in the next clearing, she would see it. But before she reached it, she saw the smoke, and smelled the death.

Horn-hill was burning. The closer she came, the more the forest rang with voices. There was laughter, and talk, all in the foreign tongue of the south, as if a thousand warriors were assembled nearby. Exactly as the summer rumours had warned.

Hilda turned back.

It wasn't just four southern warriors. This was the rumoured attack. The one they had been assured was nothing but unfounded rumours. The one their Christian had assured them would never happen.

Hilda stopped suddenly. She hadn't gone very far. Five arm-lengths to her left a man clothed in blooded white stood on the top of a gravemound; urinating, by the sound of it. A sword in a scabbard was slung across his back, ready to march far, not to fight. He hadn't seen her yet.

She clenched her axe, and snuck closer. Careful not to let the forest betray her presence and slowly, so as not to be spotted, she moved to a tree to her right.

She glanced around, searching for other southerners, but couldn't see any.

The snow fox she had gone searching for had been her fylgja. The snow fox had come to warn her of her death, and her search for the fox had led her to the southerners. What would she say back in the village? Her story would have more credibility if she wasn't alone.

The flicker of a thick white tail disrupted her thoughts. Then a crunch came from behind, and another. Crunch, crunch. Hilda swirled, looked, and there he was; the leather-clad southerner from the gravemound.

He seemed as startled as her. He took in a deep breath. He would yell out to the others, Hilda realised. Before she could think what to do, she had run the three steps to him as he fumbled to free his sword. He yelled. Hilda's closed fist punched him in the throat.

The man wheezed for breath. Hilda's axe hung loose in her right hand. She should kill him. He would be her first, but she should do it, and silence him properly. Only, he was worth more to her alive. She needed proof of what she had seen. Besides, she didn't want to let the southerners know that they had been discovered.

Quick as a fox, Hilda stepped aside, out of his grip, and kicked the man at the back of the knee. He tumbled forward, scrambled to get away and then he yelled words Hilda couldn't understand. Raising an alarm. Alerting his friends. Hilda kicked him to the ground. That stopped him.

Hilda let out a ragged breath. Her hands and feet had reacted faster than she could think. She had never before been tested in a real battle, but there was nothing wrong with her warrior reflexes.

The smell of death from Horn-hill spread across the forest. There was no time. More southerners were out there, and at any moment they could come running through the woods. She needed to warn Ash-hill of the southerners' presence in Jutland. Before it was too late.

There was no telling how many more southerners were travelling up through Jutland, but if they were at Horn-hill, they would come to Ash-hill too. They would be there in the morning, at the latest.

Hilda grabbed his greasy short hair, and lifted his head to see. He had passed out, though she hadn't hit him all that hard. It was nothing compared to the fights she sometimes got into with the young warriors. His face was bloody from the fall, though. His beard was as greasy as his short dark hair. She lifted her axe-hand to his nose. He still breathed.

Voices approached. Warriors yelled in search of the man.

Hilda darted to her feet. A large oak tree cast shadows over them. Its trunk was wide enough to hide behind. By the padded armour, she dragged the southerner to the trunk of the oak tree.

The southern voices neared. Eyes warily scouring through the forest, Hilda went back out. She kept low, and covered up their bloodied trail. She couldn't risk leaving a mark. She moved carefully, not to make a sound and not let panic grip her. Panic was a warrior's worst enemy.

Axe clenched in her hand, Hilda shielded herself behind the large oak tree. She stayed crouched down next to the southerner and listened. Stayed until she no longer saw any men and the sound and smell of them grew distant.

The snow fox didn't appear and warn her that she might die. Hilda waited for a moment longer, searching the woods for southerners, and for the fox. No one arrived. It was just him and her. At least for now. She needed to get the man she had struck away and fast, before he woke and yelled for reinforcements.

Hilda fastened her axe in her belt, and grabbed good hold of the man. She dragged him a hundred paces. Shielded him behind another tree-trunk and went back to cover the tracks.

The road home to Ash-hill was long and the southerner was heavy to drag, but Hilda neither wanted to risk coming home without proof of what she had seen, nor risk leaving a trail. She worked as fast as she could. After a while it began to feel like one of Einer's training exercise.

Eventually, she was far enough away that she stopped covering the tracks, and short after, she heard Einer's bear roar for food. The forest didn't go on much further. She heard a roar again, and saw the brown fur of Einer's bear. The cub shook two of the wooden poles of its fence.

The southerner grunted. He was waking up. Hilda left him and skipped to Vigir's cage. She untied the thick, long rope that closed the door to Vigir's cage. Her eyes never left the waking man. Her fingers worked fast, digging into the knot.

Vigir roared and rocked the wooden poles. The man blinked himself awake. The rope came free in Hilda's hands. She undid it from the cage opening. At once, Vigir burst forward. Pushed the wooden door open and darted. Hilda tried to grab its collar, but the bear was too fast.

Meanwhile, the southerner had lifted his sword from its scabbard and readied a swing. Vigir raced towards the southerner. Knocked the man to the ground with a swift swing of the right claw. The man squealed. Vigir stood above him, and growled as loud as a grown bear. Showed its deadly teeth.

The man fumbled to lift his sword. Hilda didn't take her eyes off Vigir and him. Again, the bear cub hit the man on the armour-covered chest. The southerner was knocked backwards.

Vigir fell down onto all four, and began to tear at the man's leg.

'Vigir,' Hilda called, to make the young bear turn its attention to her and stop trying to tear the man's leg from his body. 'Vigir, Vigir. Let the man live.'

Einer's bear cub didn't understand her, but it always liked when she spoke to it. She struggled to pull the bear cub away by the collar. Vigir moaned. She caressed the top of its head to thank it.

With the rope in her hands, Hilda grabbed the neck of the southerner's padded armour. He squealed as she dragged him to the nearest birch. The man sobbed. He had stopped fighting. With her foot, Hilda pushed his hand open, and the sword away.

'You'll have to catch your own food for a while, Vigir,' she told the bear and began to tie the southerner to the birch tree. 'There are more people like him out there.'

Vigir had left deep claw marks in the man's padded armour. Scratches that went all the way through to his flesh. Hilda winced at the sight of them, she could understand why he was sobbing.

She used all the knots she knew, until there was no more rope left to tie. Then, she took a few steps back until she was out of the man's reach, and him out of hers. His back was bound tight against the birch. He sobbed, terrified of what was to come. He was just a boy like any other, but his hair was short and dark, and he wore armour, and he was not the only southerner in northern Jutland.

Hilda stared down at the young man she had captured. She clenched her axe. She really should kill him, although he would be her first. She needed to learn what it was like to kill. She knew what came next. The southern warriors would march on Ash-hill and she didn't want to hesitate in battle.

He would be her first, and Hilda knew enough warriors to

know that her first would not be as easy as she wanted it to be. Killing someone was not easy. Not at first, at least. Warriors lost themselves sometimes. Especially after their first kill. Their first battle. They came home changed from summer raids. Hilda had always known that, but she wanted to be a raider all the same. Killing was the price. The horror of battle was the price.

But maybe, once he stopped crying, this man might be able to tell her how many others there were out in the forest, though, and what they had planned. Not that he spoke her tongue.

Had the raiders been home, they would have taken over and killed this southerner for her. Though Einer might have stopped them. He would have insisted that the kill belonged to her. He would have wanted her to do it on her own. Give her a quiet moment to accomplish her first kill, but Einer wasn't there and he couldn't help her. Couldn't help any of them.

Hilda turned away from the man.

Running came easy to her.

Vigir skipped ahead, contently snorting as it did whenever Hilda brought it a rich meal. It slowed when it reached the sunny road towards the village. With a happy roar, the bear strutted off the road, past the old stone tower, straight towards the beehives. Two thralls out on a field yelled after Hilda. She knew she ought to stop Vigir before it reached the beehives, but there was no time. If she didn't warn the villagers soon, the damage Einer's bear cub did would be the least of their trouble.

DARKNESS

DEATH, PAIN, AND fear.

Ragnar felt himself come alive again. Shaking from his many previous deaths, he opened his eyes to the same Darkness as before. His heart pumped heavily from the shock. His neck ached where it had been broken mere moments earlier. He had died. Again. He had felt the pain and jolt, and he had died, for certain. More than a dozen deaths he had suffered already.

Ragnar stood on his feet in the cold Darkness, trembling from fear. Around him was the same pitch dark as before. No song and no escape.

The horse was long gone. Carlman too. At least, he didn't hear anyone.

With the sleeve of his tunic, Ragnar dried the cold sweat on his forehead. His eyes found nothing to rest on, only cold Darkness. His throat felt tight, his chest heavy from his last death, and no matter how much he tried, Ragnar could not calm himself. His hands were clammy.

This was not how it was supposed to happen. This was not

what had been promised in the afterlife, and somehow, he knew he would suffer another brutal slaughter. Any moment now, something would kill him. His entire body shook with the knowledge. His legs shuddered from fear, but he needed to make them stop, so he could search for a way out of this place. He so desperately needed to leave, and find the way to Helheim.

It would hurt to die again, but waiting for it to happen was painful too. A quick end might give more relief, Ragnar thought to convince himself to stop shivering and take that first step.

'Is someone there?' He knew he was alone, asked only to break the complete silence. 'Carlman?'

He took a step forward. An axe gutted him. The second blow opened his chest. Ragnar cried out as the pain trickled down to his heels. His right hand clasped his wet stomach. The blood flowed out through his fingers, warm over his hands. His knees were weak.

Death, pain, and fear.

THE COLD DARKNESS wrapped around Ragnar, anew. Fear consumed him like a shadow, grabbing his chest. He felt as if he were being watched, and he did not dare to move, frightened of what might see him. Again, he had died.

The deaths were as real as the one back in Ash-hill that summer evening by the Midsummer when the blue-eyed raven had come for him. He had thought his first passing would be his last. Never would he have guessed that he would wake to this Darkness and so much pain.

Ragnar shut his eyes and tried to imagine himself away from the Darkness. His chest was tight and his head dizzy. He focused on his breathing, as the warriors had once taught him. Two short breaths in, and a long one out. He tried to imagine the green forests at home, and the yellow fields, but he could not recall how colours looked, and he no longer remembered the faces of the people he had loved when he had been alive. Already, he had begun to forget what it was like to live and it was impossible for him to remember how long he had been trapped in the dark. It could have been an entire summer or half a day. He did not know if it mattered.

There had to be a reason this was happening. A reason he was there, and a reason the Darkness killed him. A dozen deaths he had experienced. Or was it two dozen? His memory was clouded. He had spoken this time. The last time too. Perhaps it was his voice.

The silence was so complete that Ragnar could hear the many sounds his own body produced, as if he was made up of thousands of small creatures, puffing and moving and talking. The blood surged through him, reaching the back of his ears and the tip of his fingers at different times, accompanied by the sound of his own saliva accumulating in his mouth. He was so acutely aware of himself that he could even hear his hair ruffle and his stomach stir.

His breathing was wild again, and he focused on it. Two short breaths in, and a long one out.

His legs shook as if he had been running for days, although he had only been standing there, waiting to die. Ragnar fell to his knees and lay down flat. The ground hardened, as if the Darkness wanted him to stay awake.

Help. His lips formed the word without making a sound. His limbs were shaking at the thought of experiencing the pain of death again, and tears streamed from his eyes. Help.

He rolled onto his side. His head knocked against something.

In the dark, he fumbled for it. His left hand knocked against a bone-and-metal stave a little shorter than two arm-lengths. Holding his breath, Ragnar sat up and felt it with his hands. The bone at one end was twisted as though it had been wrung, and came to a point. He turned the rod in his hands. Not an ordinary bone, then: a tusk. A narwhal tusk. At the mid-point, polished iron twined around the bone, curling ever more tightly until Ragnar could no longer feel the tusk and the stave was entirely metal, then parting again, as if around an apple or pear, to meet in a smooth disc at the very top.

What he held in his hands was a distaff, Ragnar realised, but not the wooden sorts used for wool spinning. This was the long distaff worthy of a runemistress, perhaps even a goddess.

He had asked for help in his mind and the Darkness had given him a tool. Holding the rod in both hands so the hollow bulge was in front of his face, Ragnar rose to his feet. He tapped the rod on the floor, as he had often seen runemistresses do when they prepared to glean the past or the future. Once, twice. His hands and the distaff emerged from the dark, as if lit by a dusted light. The Darkness swallowed the sound of the taps.

An axe swung down on Ragnar's head. He screamed from pain, but all that came out was a gag. His hands froze, his insides felt cool, and the blood ran warm over his cheeks.

Death, pain, and fear.

PONTIUS

Chapter Five

'SOUTHERNERS!' A YOUNG girl shouted outside. 'Southerners.'

Pontius rushed out of his church and saw her blonde hair and green dress flap in the wind as she ran up the hill towards the town.

'Southerners,' she shouted again. It seemed as if a great weight was on her shoulders, for she did not run as young women her age did. She darted up the hill with the heavy stomps of a warrior.

Before he could decide what to do, Pontius was already running after her to catch up. He needed to stop her; no one could know that warriors from the south were on their way, no one but him. If they knew, they would ruin everything. They would fight, they would resist, and they would die.

The old landowner walked out, out of the farmhouse across the road from the church. 'Hilda, have you seen Bard?' Tormod shouted after the young woman.

Pontius hadn't recognised her.

Hilda glanced back at Tormod as she ran. 'Forgive,' she yelled and sped up. Pontius panted and knew he could not catch up with her, but he continued to try, as she shouted the same word over and over, every time a little further away: 'Southerners. Southerners. Southerners.'

'Father, what's happening?' Tormod called to him.

Pontius halted his run. 'I heard her yell,' he said and remembered how Tormod had been a raider before Pontius had settled in Ash-hill. Christianity had made Tormod see the truth and abandon his old ways, but he was a villager, and would always protect the townsfolk. Tonight, he would die for that.

'She used to do this all the time,' Tormod said. 'When she was younger. She used to come running through town and warn of all the dangers she could think up.'

That was good; the others might not believe her, then.

'Of bears, and armies, and winged serpents. There's no need to run after her.'

'Even so, I'll go and see,' Pontius said and resumed his run up towards the village, with a little more ease this time.

'Father,' Tormod shouted after him. 'Have *you* seen Bard?'

'Not since yesterday,' he yelled back and further behind him, he heard Tormod grumble something about the Horn-hill kid being a waste of food.

It would be fine, Pontius assured himself, but a small part of him was afraid. In the past, Hilda might have lied about dangers, but this was different. She spoke the truth this time, and Pontius knew. This was what the message had said.

He tried not to think of it.

He passed through the inner town gates, and heard Hilda yell up ahead. All Pontius could see of the inner circle was the tip of the ash tree. Taking a deep breath, he began to run as fast as he could in his long robe, while the heavy cross at his neck bumped against his chest.

'I saw them!' Hilda yelled.

Several women spoke at once and Pontius could not make out the individual voices, but he could see them now. They sat in small groups on a dozen benches around the ash. Mostly they sewed and weaved, but a few women stood by large tables and prepared dinner for them all. He spotted little Tyra on a bench closer to the ash. Wide eyed, she stared as Hilda spoke. The sweet little girl that these barbarians wanted to turn into a killer.

At the edge of the circle, Pontius dropped down to rest his hands above his knees and catch his breath. He did not want to interrupt, but he needed to be ready to jump in if the villagers showed any sign of believing Hilda.

She stood in front of the chieftain's wife. Siv had put away the winter jacket she was sewing and watched Hilda with honest consideration, unlike the other women who'd scoffed and returned to their work. Pontius scowled at her; he had never liked Siv, and after all these years in Ash-hill, he still did not understand how a mere woman could be trusted to make decisions for the town when her husband was away. That right should have been given to a capable man; someone like Tormod.

'They killed that boy, from Horn-hill,' Hilda muttered. 'Bard.'

'Bard? Isn't he working?' asked a woman Pontius could not make out in the crowd.

'I was out in the woods. By Horn-hill. They'd killed him.'

'The southerners killed him?' Siv enquired.

'Ja, the southerners. Killed everyone else, too.'

'How did you get away?' Those women always had to act as if they knew best, when only Hilda and Pontius knew who hid in the woods, waiting for the fall of night.

Heaving for breath, Pontius straightened his back and clenched his cross in his hand to muster his forces after his run.

'When I saw him and Horn-hill too... I came back here to warn you.' Hilda looked exhausted, as if she had run the entire afternoon. Her face was flushed red. 'They're all dead.'

'I understand, Hilda,' Siv said with a woman's care and

concern, not the stern decisiveness a chief needed. 'But we need proof.'

'I knew you would say that. I captured one of them.'

A short moment of silence followed as the women watched each other and then they burst into laughter. Had Pontius not known better, he too might have laughed. It seemed impossible.

Only Siv did not laugh, and that made Pontius bite his nails, an old nervous habit he had long forgotten.

'You captured someone?' Siv asked.

'I tied him to a tree at the edge of the forest.'

'Don't bother, Siv, she's trying to trick you again,' howled a large woman.

'I'm not,' Hilda said. 'You can come see for yourself.'

Siv looked as if she were about to respond but a few of the women laughed and before anyone could say anything more, Hilda abruptly snapped, 'I'd be concerned if I were you.' Then she turned back the way she had come, and that made the women laugh louder. All except Siv.

Pontius let out a relieved sigh. Partly he felt sorry that no one believed Hilda. He felt as if it were his fault, and in a way it was, but it would be better if the villagers were taken by surprise without time to mount a defence. It would be easier if they surrendered. The warriors were away, and Pontius was certain the army from the south would be made of capable warriors. The villagers did not stand a chance against the attack.

No, it was not an attack, he reminded himself, it was an act to *free the heathens from their false beliefs*, in the exact words of the message he had received. It ought to be a praiseworthy deed, but he knew God would not approve of this method.

It fell to Pontius to enforce God's will, to make certain no blood was spilled, and to save the Jutes so they would see the bliss of God and so he could help them onto the right path, but as he watched Hilda run down the road, it pained him deeply that he could not help her now. If the villagers knew about the attack, they would fight, and they would die. Their only hope of salvation was to submit, and Pontius would make sure they did.

He watched Hilda leave the circle, and then his eyes caught the beautiful cross on top of his wooden church. The church was carved with intertwined patterns; he recalled how the villagers had built it for him. He had not asked for help, but when they had seen him trying to flay the wood on his own, more and more of them had gathered. All Pontius had to do was point and say what he wanted where, and every day more villagers had come to help him finish his church. They had accepted him into their village, despite their many differences. He had never met such kindness from strangers before, even when he had studied in Colonia.

Pontius shook his head firmly; he was forgetting that the Jutes raided. As the message had stated. They had killed and plundered men of God. They needed to be stopped.

Yet he had so many memories there.

One late summer night the villagers had gathered in this circle for a feast in honour of the returning raiders and merchants. It had been Pontius' first summer feast. A farmer had approached him and asked what made Pontius so certain Christ had been sent from "this God he spoke of." The priest told him about how Jesus had cured the fatally ill, which the locals claimed any good runemistress capable of, and then about how Christ had walked on water.

The Jutes had laughed so loudly that Pontius had been tempted to run back to Cologne, had he not been forced to stay to make these barbarians see the truth of Christ. He had stood up and demanded they stop laughing at Christ; they should submit to someone with such holy abilities, but the villagers had not stopped. The laughter had gained in force the more Pontius spoke, the more he demanded, and asked—and, finally, pleaded—for them stop.

'All men can walk on water,' a bulky Norseman had claimed when the roars gave way for speech.

The young man Pontius had been had not known how to respond and his confused expression had been met with louder laughs than his truths about Christ.

'When winter comes, we'll show you, and maybe you too will walk on water then,' an old man at his side had said.

That winter he had learnt laughter. The second week of snowfall they had come to show the ignorant Christian how to walk on water. Farmers, children, women and raiders, no one had forgotten. They came to bring him out of town, down to the inlet, despite the biting wind. There, they sat in the snow by the frozen water and tied bones to the sole of their shoes, one on each foot.

The children were the first to run out onto the water, past the priest, in too much of a rush to be polite. They jumped onto the ice, glided on the bones under their soles and danced on the frozen inlet.

Pontius had understood then, what they meant by walking on water. He could have shouted this was not what he had meant when he had spoken of Christ, but it had not mattered; not there, and not then.

Instead, he had laughed himself warm, until he started crying and the tears froze on his cheeks, and then he had asked for a set of bones and let the children show him how to dance on the ice.

Since, he had never judged the Jutes for their ease with laughter. It had warmed him on the coldest of winter days, and he understood it was necessary to survive in the raw weather up north.

After that, Pontius had begun to accept their ways as he tried his best to enlighten the poor heathens who knew no better than to pray to the false gods they believed in. Even now, so many years later, he often had to remind himself not to judge them for their mistake; Romans, too, had once praised mortals as gods.

* * *

THE WOMEN IN the circle brought him out of his thoughts. Hilda was far down the road on the way out of town, but the chatter had not picked up again.

'If there really were southerners this far north in Jutland, someone would have seen them and told us,' a woman finally dismissed.

'Someone just did.' Siv's answer killed the laughter.

In sudden decision, Siv rose from her bench, left her coat behind, and walked out of the circle, down the road, after Hilda.

A few of the women shouted for her not to waste her time, but Siv did not stop.

Pontius bit his nails. They might ruin this, he thought, as he watched Siv chase after Hilda down the road. In their womanly stubbornness, they would bring on the destruction of Ash-hill.

SIV

Chapter Six

Siv's FEET BARELY touched the ground as she glided down the road after Hilda. Siv knew not to underestimate the warnings of the skald's daughter. Einer held Hilda in high esteem, so Siv took Hilda seriously, as her son would have.

'They attacked Horn-hill?' she asked.

Hilda smiled, seeing Siv following her. 'The whole northern part of Horn-hill's woods reeked of corpses and smoke,' she answered.

Side by side, Hilda and Siv walked past the Christian church, out towards the forest. There was chaos out on the fields. Thralls were running to shelter. Siv was about to set off, the carving knife from her belt already drawn, but Hilda stopped her. 'It's just Einer's bear,' she said.

Siv took a whiff of the southern air, and caught the scent of the bear's hunger and the honey on its paws. In her focus, she even heard the bear's grunts and the buzz of bees. There was something else out there; the scent of a long-lived, like her.

She had smelled the scent before. All summer a long-lived

70

had lurked at the edge of Ash-hill, but had never approached.

As they walked, Siv searched the fields beyond the beehives and the farmhouses and forest for southerners; sharpening her hearing to be sensitive to every snap of a branch, but there were too many fields to search and the forest was too vast for her to find any.

Hilda brought Siv into the edge of the forest. The solid fence Einer had built for his cub had splintered. The gate stood open, and there, nearby, was a southerner, tied to a birch tree, exactly as Hilda had said he would be.

He stared at them. His eye was swollen and his entire face was smeared with blood. He was crying too, sobbing even, at the sight of them.

Hilda took a proud stance at the southerner's side. 'I saw four more like him. All armoured. Heard more people out in the woods, hundreds of voices.'

Siv crouched down in front of the scared southerner, stroked a finger across his bloody cheek. Her touch made him tremble, and she sensed his fear, his anger, and a foreign something she could not place.

'How many more of you are there?' she asked the man, although she knew it would make no difference. He would not tell them anything, nor could he, when they did not speak the same tongue, but she did not ask to gain an answer, she asked only because Hilda expected her to ask.

Siv rubbed the southerner's blood between her fingers and asked again. 'How many southerners are coming?'

She closed her eyes and focused on the southerner's breathing and on his heartbeat. His blood was different from that of the Jutes, and her nose and ears sharpened at the close proximity of the unsteady pump of his heart.

Through these woods that she knew so well, she searched for more like him, with greater focus this time. Past the spirits in their gravemounds, past the animals of the forest, the squirrels, the birds, the deer and pigs, the roaming sheep and grassing goats, and there, beyond it all, beyond the water creek where frogs were bathing, and beyond the rye fields, Siv sensed foreigners. They had that same strange air as this man; minds that she could neither comprehend nor influence.

Hilda was right. There were more out there; many more. Now that Siv was outside of the town's barricade and away from the crowd, she could feel the southerners' presence. They were not far north of Horn-hill, but there were many of them; many loud thoughts and many heartbeats. Had Hilda not brought her attention to it, Siv might not have noticed it until it was too late.

'He won't tell us anything,' Siv said, and brought forth her little carving blade, quick to put it against the man's throat.

Hilda stopped her with a hand on the wrist. 'I'll do it.'

Siv stepped back and stuffed her small knife into her apron belt. The southerner was yelling for his life and screaming, but Siv stared at him, and reached for his weak mind to silence it. His screams and sobs halted and the southerner stared up at Siv, recognising, as no short-lived was supposed to do, that it was her silencing him.

Hilda prepared to deal the fatal blow. From the grassy ground, she picked up a southern sword with a bloody tip. She placed the sword at the man's neck, held it in both her hands and tested her swing. Again, she placed it at his neck and retraced the swing of the sword, until she stood with the blade raised, staring down at the man with a fierce anger in her eyes.

'He is your first,' Siv observed.

'My first,' Hilda repeated. 'But he won't be my last.' With those words, she swung the sword into the man's throat. His eyes popped open, and his tongue hung out of his mouth. His loud foreign thoughts stopped, and then, so did the pulse of his heart. Blood spilled out of his throat. His head snapped to one side, but Hilda was not yet done.

She grabbed some locks of his dark hair to hold up his head, and with the sword she chopped through his neck. The sword clonked against the bones in his neck, but Hilda persisted, lifted up his head a little further so she could see into the wound, and look for the best way to carve through it.

The first was never easy, and with the southerners' arrival, Siv suspected that many would make their first kills tonight. Women and men who had only ever slaughtered cattle would be forced into battle. Hilda was lucky to have had a calm moment to go through her first kill. Trained warriors too often struggled with their first.

It took Hilda five good chops to cut through the southerner's neck-bones. Her sword cut into the birch tree and the southerner's head rolled off.

They both stared down at the head and knew that this was something Hilda had needed to do before the battle to prove to herself that killing a person was no different from killing a pig.

With her bloody left hand, Hilda grabbed the dark greasy hair of the southerner and lifted the head. She was calm at the sight of it, and gave Siv a short nod for them to go back up to town.

'What now?' Hilda asked without looking up.

Siv took a moment to consider as they walked out of the forest. 'You said you saw four in armour. And heard voices of hundreds more,' she said, so Hilda would not question the nature of Siv's knowledge. There were many of them out there, more than Siv could count and distinguish, but there were things that Siv knew she could not share for fear of revealing her blood-line.

Hilda nodded and awaited Siv's instructions.

'We gather everyone,' Siv said. 'We tell them what happened and then we prepare for the attack: light the warning pyres, warn the nearby farmhouses, and gather the children to send them off to the winter campsite with food and furs and riches.' Siv listed the steps aloud, to ensure that she had not forgotten anything. 'We gather everyone, every farmer and thrall to fight. We close the gates. We keep watch. We hold Ash-hill's last feast, and then we wait.'

'What do you need me to do?' Hilda asked. As long as Hilda had trained to be in a battle, this was not the sort she had trained for. Like other hopeful raiders, she had hoped to fight abroad, not at home at the peril of losing everyone and everything she loved. As a warrior, she knew how to combat it, to face it straight on, by focusing on one small task and achievement at a time. She needed clear instructions to help her focus.

'Assign eight villagers to keep watch from the barricade, and enough riders to warn the outlying farmhouses. Then go get your armour, and ride up to the warning pyre,' Siv said. 'Set it ablaze, and call the guards home.'

Hilda nodded in answer.

They started up the wooden road towards Ash-hill, past Tormod's farmhouse and the Christian church. Hilda's sword scraped against the wooden road as they marched. The head dangled at her side, back and forth along with her arm movements, and the, dripping blood was thrown all around the street. Hilda's green dress was dark with blood stains, and with every step, her gaze hardened as she prepared for what was to come.

Laughter rang out from the inner circle where women and children were still gathered around the old ash, oblivious to the happenings in the forest. Siv smiled at the sight of the sunlight hitting the ash-tree's dark leaves. She would protect this place at any cost. Among the hundreds of places where she had lived in her long life, Ash-hill had been the warmest. A village worth protecting.

The women and children in the inner circle stopped their doings when they saw Hilda in the bloody dress with the head dangling at her side.

Hilda walked past them all, without glancing at them. She stopped inside the Ting ring. Then, she let go. The head dropped to the ground and splashed mud on the near-standing women. Blood and mud stained the man's face. The hair on the head was darker than the mud, and his dark brown eyes stared blankly at the villagers.

'Is it...?' someone muttered.

'The southerner,' Hilda completed. She turned and walked away, out of the Ting ring and out of the circle, on a mission to complete the tasks Siv had given her.

Siv walked past the southerner's head, stepped onto her husband's Ting stone and reached up into the ash-tree for the ox horn that hung from one of the low branches. Hundreds of eyes were on her, as she brought the horn to her mouth and blew it.

The sad ring echoed out over Ash-hill's fields and lands. Three times she blew it.

Villagers darted across the fields and up the streets and burst out of their homes to join everyone else in the inner circle by the ash where Old Ragnar had passed on at Midsummer. Hundreds of curious faces peered up at Siv. Most of them would no doubt die tonight.

'There are southerners out in the woods,' Siv announced when the villagers had gathered. 'They have attacked Horn-hill. If they wanted to attack us during the day, they would have been here already. They're waiting until night-fall.'

She sensed a small part of an army's presence in the animals stirring in the forest, and occasionally she could also smell them in the breeze. They were massing their forces. Together they would attack Ash-hill, as they must have attacked every larger town in Jutland to reach this far north. They had come not to conquer land, but to burn it. All of Jutland was already burning. Now that she searched for it, Siv could smell the smoke of fields and houses in the southerly breeze.

The crowd stirred and protested, but Siv spoke through it. 'We need to send the children off to the winter campsite. Gather enough food and furs for them to be warm and fed no matter what happens. Then I want you to go home, get into comfortable clothes, and take whatever armour and weapons you have at home that you won't use yourself and bring it up here. Shields are a priority. We also need to finish cooking so we can eat before tonight.'

'Are you telling us to stay and fight?' a young man finally asked. 'Shouldn't we pack up and leave while we can?'

'Our husbands and wives and children are off fighting abroad. They count on us to keep Ash-hill safe while they're away. A sacred promise pledged between them and us. We will honour it,' Siv answered. 'If the southerners think they can come here and scare us away from our home and lands, and everything we hold dear, they are wrong, and they will meet our wrath. We might not be warriors, but we protect our home, whatever the cost. We make the gods proud so we can stand tall when we meet them in the afterlife.'

'How do we even know there are southerners?' asked a sceptic old farmer.

Siv pointed to the evidence at her feet; the severed head of the southerner Hilda had captured and killed.

'How do we know there are more? How do we know they'll come here?'

'You're asking us to believe the impossible,' another villager chimed in. More scared farmers voiced their worries.

'I'm not asking you to *believe* anything,' Siv answered in a loud, clear voice that shut them all up. 'I'm *telling* you what to do. As the chief's wife, I'm in charge of Ash-hill, and I'm giving you very clear instructions. You will do what I ask of you.'

No one argued with her after that.

Siv continued to give commands. 'First, we need all the children to gather. And Aegil.' She found his bald head in the crowd. 'You need to leave with the children too. They're going to need a lawspeaker.'

'My daughter, Dagny, is fifteen winters old,' Aegil answered, and gestured to the young woman at his side. Dagny had long outgrown her father: she was almost as tall as Siv and easily glanced over the heads of the villagers. 'She knows the law better than me, even the clauses I sometimes forget.' No one

76

laughed at Aegil's attempt at a joke, although yesterday they might have. 'She will be their lawspeaker.'

With a nod, Siv accepted Aegil's sacrifice.

'The grown thralls shall be given a choice to stay or leave with the children,' Siv announced.

'If we stay...?' asked a brave thrall, his bare ears were red from the cool breeze.

'If you stay you will most probably die like the rest of us.' Hiding the brutal truth was of no need, even with the children listening. It was better they knew. 'But if you fight and kill an enemy, your courage will be rewarded with freedom, both yours and that of your children.'

The prospect of freeing their children made the thralls chatter among themselves, reconsidering their chances and discussing the choice.

'We need at least four of you to go with the children,' Siv added to reassure the servants that leaving Ash-hill with the young ones was not a cowardly deed. 'It's brave to choose to fight,' Siv said, as she had once told a young son, hundreds of summers ago. 'But it's just as brave to protect the young ones who can't protect themselves. Don't forget that.' Her words calmed the nervous herd.

Siv had expected protests from the crowd of freemen, but there were none.

'Before the fight, I suggest you take a drink for courage, but we need everyone at their best, so know your limit. As Odin warned: "One knows less the more one drinks."'

It was funny to think she was the only one who knew Odin's voice and could hear him say those words. No one else in the village had ever met the Alfather, although many of them soon would.

At her final signal, everyone dispersed with their respective tasks; the farmers went off to release their farm animals to find fodder for themselves, and the thralls Siv designated went off to gather food and furs for the children, while everyone else gathered every weapon and armour they owned. Arm-rings were exchanged and passed on, so the children would have wealth to survive on if the village fell. The young ones clenched onto the furs and food their parents prepared for them.

THE SUN WAS already half-way on its descend towards the hills when the villagers began to gather again. Some of the children had decided to stay with their parents' approval, and they walked around the ash-tree with their families and friends to find armour and weapons that fit their size. There were many choices of weapons, more shields and chopping axes than anything else, and Siv did not see much armour.

Women wore tunics and trousers and bound up their hair to look like men. Siv too had changed into Einer's old trousers and tunic, put on her own weapon belt and helmet, and she carried a chieftain's broad shield at her back.

The children readied to leave. Left in the village would be half a dozen children, two hundred farmers and a handful retired warriors. All of them had been armed, although even with weapons, most were not warriors. They would all fight, and they would all die with pride.

The voice of a young girl caught Siv's ears. 'I won't go. Even Ingrid's staying,' Tyra said, and when Siv turned her head towards the north road she saw Jarn's chestnut hair bump up and down and then the rest of his family emerged too; Gunna and all four of their girls.

'Tyra, you have to leave,' Gunna said as the family entered the far edge of the inner circle.

'I'm not a child anymore,' said Tyra. 'I've made my choice. I'm staying.'

Siv glided through the crowd towards Jarn's family, listening to their talk as she approached.

'You didn't choose to learn fighting to die a week later,' Gunna said.

'Nej, but I didn't choose blindly either, I knew what it meant when I picked the seax, and I haven't changed my mind,' Tyra insisted. 'I'm staying.'

'But—'

'I won't let you all leave for Valhalla without me.' Tyra's words shut up her parents. With determined steps the girl shuffled through the crowd, straight past Siv. Her hair was braided away from her face, her tunic looked large and big on her, and in her arms she hugged five axes. Behind her, Siv saw Tyra's parents and sisters exchange concerned looks before they moved after Tyra.

'Jarn,' Siv called as she reached them. 'I need a moment.'

'Walk with me,' Jarn said. In his arms he carried two pieces of heavy chainmail armour. On a different day, they would have sold for a fortune.

The crowd was thick, but still parted for them.

'I want you to lead the defence,' Siv told him.

She could see him hesitate, and knew he would ask why she would not do it herself, when she too had fought in battles. 'I've never played a tactical part,' she said before he asked. 'Not like you.'

Besides, she did not trust herself to keep her lineage hidden throughout the battle. If she led the defence, those who survived would shun her as a result. 'This is not a time to be modest, Jarn,' she said. 'You're the most qualified person we have and we need you.'

He mused on her words. 'Do we know how many are out there?'

Siv attempted to feel it with her mind, but she had trouble to distinguish the southerners from each other. She shook her head. 'Nej, but we must assume there are more than us.'

'And they're better trained too,' Jarn said. He pushed through the last of the crowd. Siv helped him put the chainmail down by the roots of the ash tree. Almost as soon as she let go, the amour was taken from her hands by farmers without proper armour of their own.

'The southerners are not so different from us,' Jarn said, and stared straight ahead.

They stood in the shadows of the great ash looking out over the thick crowd of villagers busily shouting to each other and rushing up and down the streets with armour and weapons and food.

'If we can take down their leader, we can probably split them up,' he reasoned.

'You think they'll make it through the gates?' she had not thought that far ahead.

'They will. It's only a question of how soon,' Jarn said and rolled up his sleeves as he talked. He was ready to lead them into battle. 'If they're in Horn-hill, they will probably attack from the south. I want you in charge of the villagers furthest west. Gunna and I will take the centre, and Tormod will lead the eastern wing.'

Siv nodded. She was ready to give her long life, if it meant saving these short-lived. Despite her lineage, she belonged in Ash-hill, and always would.

'I have a favour to ask of you,' Jarn said after they had stood blankly staring at the crowd for a while. 'Your reputation assures me you're as good a warrior as Gunna and me.' He gulped and looked up to the sky. 'I know my daughters. They'll insist on joining Gunna and me on the front lines.' He bit his upper lip and his voice was nothing more than a whisper. 'They all stayed home this summer because of Tyra's choice.' He took a slight pause and Siv could see him strain to surmount the calm to say any more. 'I don't want Tyra to see us all disappear to our deaths.' The tip of his nose became red as he said it, his eyes glistened with tears that he held back, and Siv could feel his blood boil in a mixture of mourning and anger. She attempted to soothe his feelings with her mind, but Jarn was a determined man and it did not work as successfully as she would have liked. His lips quivered, ever so slightly. Had it not been for Siv's blood, she might not have noticed, but she did.

'It would be an honour to fight alongside Tyra,' Siv said, knowing what he would ask. 'I'll do everything in my power to keep her safe.' They were big words, but she intended to keep them. It was the least she could do for the sacrifice Jarn and his family would give to protect Ash-hill.

A slim smile crossed Jarn's lips, and then it broadened. 'At the very least, teach her some good insults to yell after those bloody southerners.' He looked at her then, his eyes lightly tainted red. 'I'll take care of our defence.' With his usual broad smile, he disappeared into the busy crowd.

Siv allowed the magnitude of her promise to dwell on her. Tyra was her responsibility now. The young girl did not stand a chance in battle; Tyra was inexperienced and too young, but a promise as the one Siv had given to Jarn could not lightly be broken. Even if she had to reveal her true lineage, she would keep her word and make certain Tyra survived.

TYRA

Chapter Seven

'ARE WE REALLY going to die?' Tyra asked.

'One more mouthful, Tyra,' her sister Yrsa said instead of answering. Tyra had already eaten too much and she felt as if she was going to be sick, like Ingrid who had already been sick three times.

Her father saved Tyra from Yrsa's insistence. The villagers went quiet as he rose from his seat. Not that they had been loud before. He stepped up on his bench so everyone could both see and hear him.

'Our seasoned warriors are out guarding the gates,' her father said. 'They have placed bows and arrows along the outer barricade, and as we speak they are lighting the fires between the posts.' There was complete silence. Everyone swallowed her father's words as if he was Odin himself, speaking to his warriors. 'Wherever you stand, you will work in pairs.'

The farmer boy Tyra had been paired with found her eyes in the crowd and nodded reassuringly to her from afar.

'We don't know how many southerners are hiding out in

the forest, but there will be more than us.' Gravely, her father looked around at them as he spoke. 'But we're Jutes from Ash-hill, and Jutes don't back down!'

The crowd timidly cheered.

'Use your shields as often as your weapons, and don't foolishly charge into the crowd alone. Any questions?'

The villagers looked around at each other. No one had any questions. Tyra's father gave a short nod and stepped down from his bench. 'Now eat plenty. We'll need our full strength.'

Silently, Tyra finished her portion. She had never sat at such a quiet long-table. It felt all wrong.

When the meal was over, Astrid and Yrsa helped Tyra into her armour, and her mother tightened her bright helmet for her.

Together they headed out to the barricade as the sun set behind the hills. Her parents and sisters bathed Tyra in kisses and made sure she knew which bow was hers and where she should stand. Her place was easy to find since Tyra's bow was her own training bow, shorter and less powerful than the others. Astrid waited with Tyra for Hilda and Siv to join the lines, and only when the darkness of the night settled around them, and the barricade was thick with armoured villagers, and Tyra insisted that it was time for Astrid to find her own place, did her sister leave.

Tyra didn't want Astrid to leave, she didn't want any of her sisters to leave, and certainly not her parents, but they were leading the defence and were demanded elsewhere, and Tyra knew she had to accept that.

All around her adults fiddled with their weapons. The shields rested against their legs so they didn't need to hold them while they waited.

Siv and Hilda—and Aegil's wife, and the two farmer boys who had been paired with Hilda and Tyra—tried to make Tyra laugh and smile. Hilda told a funny story about how she fought better in dresses because trousers itched, but Tyra was too scared to really laugh.

The sorrowful blow of a horn pierced the silence.

Southerners were coming.

The smoke from their torches in the night was visible over Hollow Hill. They came through the slim forest between Ashhill and the outer farms. Their torches blinked in the dark. Tyra's hand tightened around her bow.

'How many do you think there are?' Hilda asked. She had that frown on her forehead the warriors sometimes got when they recalled their first fight.

'More than I can count,' Siv answered.

Tyra stared down at the timber flooring of the barricade and tried to hold in her tears, using every trick she knew to keep from crying.

They stood at the top of the timber wall and stared at the lights, shining through the night in the far distance. When the lit torches reached the edge of the forest, flames rose up. A long row of flames burned up towards them. The southerners were burning the fields.

Smoke blew up towards them and made Tyra's eyes tear up.

'What does it feel like?' Tyra asked, breaking the silence. 'To kill someone?' She was crying and she didn't know if it was from the smoke or from fear.

'You've killed game before,' Siv said.

Tyra nodded but the thought didn't reassure her. People were coughing all around her.

'It's like that,' Hilda completed. 'It's like killing pigs.'

Down to their left some women were laughing. Their giggles spread down the rows.

'Cowards,' a woman shouted loud enough for the southerners to hear her.

'We'll slay you like pigs,' another chimed.

'You hear?' Hilda howled to Tyra. 'Just like killing pigs.'

They began to chuckle, all the way down the rows, as more and more insults were flung at the southerners.

'You're so ugly even trolls would be scared,' Siv yelled.

They laughed and laughed so tears rolled, and their stomachs hurt, and they coughed from the smoke. Tyra cried and coughed so much that she lost her balance, but the farmer boy behind caught her. Still, she could not stop, and crouched down, terrified of what was to come.

'What if the gods won't take me to Valhalla and I'm forced to go to Helheim?'

'The valkyries will take you to Valhalla,' Siv responded.

Tyra looked up at Siv, and tried to smile. She didn't think she succeeded.

'But not tonight,' Hilda said. 'Tonight, you'll show the southerners what your parents and your sisters taught you. Tomorrow the valkyries will come.' Her hair was hidden by her helmet and her eyes were barely visible from the shadows the fire cast on her face. She looked like a warrior. She *was* a warrior. A true one.

Tyra nodded in resolution and told herself to be strong. She dusted her knees and stood up again, holding her bow in a firm grip, as she imagined a real warrior would. The fields burned quickly. The smoke was too thick to see the southerners.

'Are you ready to fight?' her father shouted from top of the southern gate to their left.

The villagers roared and yelled in response.

'Are you ready to meet Odin in Valhalla?'

The rumble of their voices gained force.

'Are you ready to kick these southern cowards in their asses so they fly all the way to their Helved?'

All tapped their shields with their weapons, shouted like there was nothing else in Midgard. Tyra howled. They made all the noise they could to scare the southerners who ran up the hill from Muddy Lake.

'Archers,' her father thundered.

Tyra reached for her first arrow.

'Ready!'

They took their stance as one.

'They're going to kill us all,' Hilda concluded. Tyra had never heard her speak like that before. 'Aren't they?'

'They're going to try,' Siv gravely responded.

Tyra took a few deep breaths to steady herself and blinked the last tears out of her eyes. 'Let them come,' she whispered under her breath.

Her hands were steady as she lifted the bow. Without their torches, the enemy couldn't be distinguished in the dark. But she could hear them run up the hill. She narrowed her eyes to find a target.

'Arrows,' her father yelled.

Her arrow carved up with a hundred others. Together the arrows hurled ahead, as though all loosed from one enormous bow.

Tyra fumbled for the next one. The four remaining arrows had been wrapped in cloth just below the iron tip. She secured her grip around the arrow and readied for her father's signal.

'Fire,' he yelled.

She dipped the arrow tip into the fire between her and Hilda until the cloth caught the flames. Breathing deeply to calm herself, she resumed her stance and nocked the burning arrow as she had been taught, careful not to burn her hand.

'Arrows!'

She tensed the bow and let her fire arrow fly. The fire-tipped arrows carved through the air and lit up the enemy line. Hundreds of southerners were out there, beyond the barricade. They had armour and horsed men. There were so many of them! And then the lights of their arrows were put out. The fields no longer burned and their vision was hindered again.

'Roof,' her father shouted.

The farmer behind Tyra pulled the shield over her. Arrows hammered down above them like hail on the wooden road a stormy night. They bounced off the shield-roof. And finally stopped. The farmer retreated with the shield. But Tyra felt reluctant to go out uncovered. Quickly, so she wouldn't stand unshielded for long, she grabbed the next arrow.

Tyra lit up her arrow and fitted it to the bowstring. Her heart raced and her hands were shaking. Her breaths were short and broken and she tried to concentrate on steadying her breathing like Hilda had taught her. And holding the bow correctly, so she wouldn't burn her hand.

Next to her, Hilda sent off a burning arrow. Tyra followed her lead. Their arrows were joined by the deep ring of a song.

Cattle die,
Kinsmen die,
We must die likewise.

The chanter sang loudly, and almost as soon as she had begun the song, many voices joined hers. Siv and Hilda smiled, and Tyra tried to find the same strength within herself. But all she really wanted to do was to cry because her parents had been right; she wasn't ready for this. But she also didn't want to be left in Midgard all by herself when they had decided to fight and pass on.

The farmer shielded her again. Arrows hammered down around them. Tyra stood completely still hoping that her feet were small enough to not be hit. The villagers around her groaned as the enemy's arrows fell.

The renown never dies,
The one who gains glory in life.

The villagers sang. The shield was lowered above her. Tyra reached out for her fourth arrow, lit it and took her aim.

She lost sight of her own arrow as soon as it was released. It joined a flame row high in the air and hurled down towards the enemy. Some arrows fell short and she saw another enemy wave coming towards them. The shield wasn't above her. She swirled around to face the farmer and rush to safety. He was sprawled out behind her. Two arrows had pierced through his stomach, his hand was tight around one of them, and he groaned and squirmed.

An arrow flayed both clothes and skin from Tyra's left forearm. She felt a poke against the leather armour on her back and the sting of something sharp like a needle. A falling arrow bounced off the wooden floor and hit her leather shoe.

The law-speaker's wife thrust her shield above Tyra and sheltered her from the attack.

The arrows rained down over the farmer as he lay without protection, his left arm too wounded to lift his shield. Arrows bounced off his chainmail, pierced through his arms. All the while, Tyra watched with wide eyes as he clenched his teeth to keep from screaming.

All around, the villagers repeated the chanter's song. Their voices rang in the deadly night. Under the safety of their shield, Aegil's wife sang softly. And Tyra felt as though the villagers were singing for her. To make her realise that this was how it would end.

Cattle die,
Kinsmen die,
We must die likewise.

Her eyes swelled up with tears. The dying farmer she had been paired with gave one last grunt and ceased to move.

'Arrows,' her father yelled.

I know one thing that never dies,
The repute each gains in life.

Tyra blinked the tears out of her eyes, sniffed and turned to reach for her last arrow. She lit it before her father could give the order, and with steady hands, she fitted it to the bowstring and took aim. She loosened at the same time as the others. Their fire arrows lit up the enemy lines, one last time. The southerners were lined up by the gates.

'Spears,' Tyra's father shouted. 'Grab your shields!'

Tyra cast her bow up against the barricade, out of everyone's way, and reached for her own shield. She didn't have a spear to throw or the strength to throw one, so she moved closer to the barricade and held up her shield to protect those further back.

Next to her, Hilda and Siv both readied themselves to throw their spears. The southerners were closing in. Through the slim gaps of the barricade Tyra could see the moonlight flashing on their armour as they ran up the hill.

'Cast!'

Hilda and Siv flung their spears at the enemy. Now that she stood pressed up against the barricade, Tyra could hear the southerners scream as the spears hit their targets.

Arrows fell on Ash-hill from the skies.

'Roof,' her father shouted.

Their shields moved up over them to take the blows of the arrows. Tyra rushed to the right so her shield would cover Hilda. She struggled to hold it still as arrows smacked into the wood.

The villagers shouted insults as they had before the battle. but Tyra couldn't fully hear them over the noise of the arrows beating her round shield. Her helmet was heavy on her head. Her armour felt tight. Her shield-arm bled from where the arrow had torn the skin. The wound was warm, as if she had been burned.

The pounding stopped, and Tyra moved away with her shield so Hilda could cast another spear.

'Die, dicks,' Siv yelled to Tyra's left and hurled a spear at the southerners.

Tyra gazed through one of the slim gaps in the barricade and followed the weapon with her eyes as it darted towards a man on a horse. He saw the spear come at him, but couldn't get down from the horse. He was still trying to rein it in when the tip of the blade pierced through his face.

Another set of arrows hailed down. Again, Tyra leapt towards Hilda with two other farmers, and when she was there, and the arrows began beating on their shields, she noticed that Siv stood without cover. Aegil's wife was dead, as well as the three young farmers behind her, heir tunics and flesh pierced with arrows. The villagers further back them stumbled over the corpses, holding their shields above themselves.

Siv huddled close against the barricade. The arrows flayed her clothes and skin as they hit. Like many of the villagers, she wore no chainmail or leather armour, only a helmet. Arrow after arrow hit the back of her helmet. One pierced Siv's shoulder, and another closer to her heart, and one more through her right arm. Terrified, Tyra watched, wishing she could stop the southerners from sending more arrows. They were killing Siv, just like they had killed the others.

Just then, the rain of arrows abated.

Siv rushed out and grabbed her last spear. Thick blood flowed from her shoulder and stained her tunic. The arrows were still stuck in her shoulder and arm, but she reached for a spear and flung it out over the barricade with unrivalled force. The arrow close to her heart had gone straight through her. Tyra saw the tip poking out at the front. The blood continued to flow, and villagers and southerners screamed all around them, but Siv didn't even seem to know that she had been hit. She glanced at Tyra. Only then, did she look down at her shoulder and see the arrows there. With her free hand, she reached for the one in her upper arm, broke off the feathered end and pulled it out with a grimace. Even over the battle-cries and screams, Tyra heard the wet noise as it came out.

Siv threw the blood-soaked arrow down and reached for the one close to her heart. She broke off the feathers and slid the wood through her chest. Tyra cringed, almost feeling the pain.

'Roof,' someone shouted and Tyra darted ahead to shield Siv

from the incoming attack. The arrows made her shield splinter at the edge.

'You need to help me push it through,' Siv said.

'What?' Tyra gulped as she stared at the thick blood staining Siv's tunic. The last arrowhead was stuck somewhere inside her shoulder.

'Push the arrow through,' Siv repeated.

Holding her shield one-handed above both of them with a strength she did not know she had, Tyra reached for the arrow with her right hand. Her fingers clasped around the fletching. She took a deep breath. Siv's blood flowed out from the wound and stained Tyra's hand. With all the force she could muster, Tyra jerked the arrow further into Siv's shoulder, cringing as she felt Siv's flesh tear. Through and through she drove the shaft until the head poked out of Siv's skin under her breast, dark red with blood. She broke the feathers off, and Siv pulled the arrow back out. There was blood all over Tyra's fingers.

Siv didn't scream, didn't seem to feel any pain. And as soon as the arrow was out, she picked up her last spear and took her stance as if nothing had happened. 'You fight worse than old bitches,' she yelled and cast her spear.

Around them, the battle had turned bloodier. Hilda stood over the barricade, swinging her axe, and Tyra knew the southerners had already reached her. They would soon break through the gate.

'Grab your weapon,' Siv yelled to her.

Tyra was still clenching the bloody arrow she had pulled out of Siv's shoulder. The blood had dried, sticking the arrow to her hand, and she had to shake it off. She fumbled to pull out her seax from her weapon belt, raised her shield and took a deep breath. She crept closer to the barricade and peeked out through the gaps in the wood.

The invaders were already at the southern gate, pushing to get through. They filled the path all the way up. The corner to Muddy Lake couldn't be seen anymore. It wouldn't be long before they broke through, and then the longest and bloodiest part of the battle would start. Tyra was almost surprised she had survived this long, because when she looked back at the trampled corpses behind her, it was clear that many hadn't.

The surviving villagers leant in over the barricade, sheltered under their neighbours' shield-roofs, and knocked the enemy's heads with their spears and axes. Tyra didn't dare. And she was too short to reach.

'You stay close to me,' Siv told her and turned her attention to the southerners, axe in hand.

'Turn!' Tyra's father yelled.

Tyra's heart raced at the thought that the southerners had broken through the gate.

'Break into walls!' Siv yelled back. Tyra heard both her father and mother echo the call elsewhere.

It was all happening too quick. Far too quick.

Siv pulled her shield around from her back, and Tyra pushed her own up against Siv's so they overlapped. Behind her a tall villager joined his shield to hers, and all the villagers around them did the same. Their round shields formed a long, tall wall stretching up and out to either side. Tyra glanced to her left, looking for Hilda, but next to her was a woman she couldn't recognise beneath the heavy armour, and then another, and Hilda seemed to be nowhere. Tyra glanced back, under the arms of the tall villager behind her, and when she looked at the villagers' feet, she saw the hem of Hilda's blue dress. Hilda was pushing through the villagers, in towards the middle of the shield-wall. She would get herself killed.

'Hilda, come back,' Tyra shouted but Hilda didn't hear her. Tyra removed her shield from the wall to follow Hilda, but the tall farmer was pressed up so close behind her that she couldn't get away unless she left her shield behind.

A strong hand on her shoulder kept her from going anywhere. 'Stay here,' Siv hissed.

'But Hilda—'

'Stay,' Siv repeated and as she said the word, Tyra's will to find Hilda disappeared from her mind entirely, as if the gods had changed her mind, and she couldn't make her feet move away. She joined her shield to the others again, but it felt like someone else raised her arm for her.

'To the gate!' Siv shouted. Their long wall broke into smaller ones. Each wall was held up by a dozen farmers. They had to march slowly so they wouldn't break ranks as they moved. The tall man behind Tyra set her pace. He extended his spear through the gap between their shields.

The enemy forces could be heard storming through the southern gate.

The tall villager behind Tyra enrobed her in the smell of sweat, and she wrinkled her nose. He was so close to her, and Siv so close to her right, and someone else to her left, that the sweat dripped from her forehead and she had to heave for breath.

Tyra looked at the ground to find her way, but she had no idea where they were anymore, other than they were close to the barricade. On the blood-stained ground lay an unmoving farmer in padded armour. Tyra tried to leap over him without pulling her shield away from the others, but the man behind her pushed against her back so she stumbled over the body instead. Villager after villager trod on top of what that same morning had been a neighbour and friend. Another corpse came into view. Tyra gulped and tried to imagine it wasn't someone she knew when she stepped onto the bloody woman. The fresh corpse warmed her feet through the soles of her shoes.

She tried to shut out the cries and clatter of armour, but with every step, they moved nearer to the gates, nearer to close combat, nearer to death.

'Cattle die,' she whispered and attempted to imagine that everyone on the other side of their shield-wall were just cattle waiting to be slaughtered.

Someone in their formation yelled, and their wall drove

against the first southerners. Tyra felt a jolt in her shield and staggered, but she kept her stance strong and watched Siv push her axe under the shield-wall and cut straight through a man's trousers and flesh. The blood trickled down over his foot, then he fell. Another villager hit him in the face with an axe. Blood and spit splashed up Tyra's trousers.

To both her left and right, the villagers grunted as they slashed out and stabbed toes and feet to make the southerners fall on after another, and they pushed their shield-wall further ahead and marched over the enemy's warm, bleeding bodies.

Their wall joined with another, and Tyra glanced back to see where they were. Beneath the smelly armpit gaps of the tall man behind her, Tyra caught a glimpse of the road that led to the inner circle. They were right by the southern gate, at the furthest front of the battle. Southerners continued to bash against their shields.

A sword poked up under Tyra's shield, straight at her. Tyra tried to move back without breaking the shield-wall, but the tall man behind her stood too close, and she couldn't get out of the way. Siv's axe clashed against the sword and diverted its course. The blade cut Tyra's leg. The wound stung.

The southerner on the other side retrieved his sword, and Tyra pushed her seax back after it. She felt a jolt and heard his scream. She had successfully hit his leg.

Siv slashed out after him too and he fell almost immediately. His head banged against the ground at Tyra's feet. His eyelids were pressed closed as he squirmed and rolled from side to side.

'Get him,' said the deep voice of a farmer to Tyra's left. She didn't allow herself to hesitate, and thought back to her training. *The neck, right between the helmet and armour that's where you hit them,* she heard her father say, as he had yesterday morning out in the field by their honey bees.

'Finish it,' the deep voice shouted again. Tyra thrust her seax at the squirming southerner at her feet. She aimed for the neck. He squirmed too much. She missed and slashed again and again. Finally, she her seax cut into him. The weapon came back soaked in blood.

Tyra was pushed ahead by the man behind her and stumbled over the southerner she had killed. The tall villager behind her jabbed at southerners from above with his spear.

Tyra jarred when another southerner bumped against her shield. And she struggled to hold her part of the wall. The tall man behind her and the other villagers pushed and pushed, so she was pressed up against the side of the shield-wall and could hardly breathe.

'Get back,' Tyra wheezed, but she didn't have the strength to yell it. Her shoes were covered in slippery, sticky blood and she couldn't get a proper foothold to press against the thin wooden shield which was all that stood between the southerners and her. She was squeezed up against it, so much that she feared her shield would break and she would land on the enemy's sharp weapons. 'Move back!' she cried, and her face was wet from blood, sweat and tears.

'Stop pushing,' Siv yelled. At once the tall man behind Tyra moved back, just enough so she could breathe again and wasn't flattened up against her shield. Swords and axes came down upon them. The southerners attacked from above.

'Let them through when I say,' Siv shouted, changing strategy. Tyra got a tight grip around her seax, ready to slash. 'Open!' Siv yelled and moved her shield away, at the same time as the farmer behind her. A short southerner who had pushed against their shields fell into their midst. 'Close!' Siv yelled as soon as the man was through. She moved in with her shield again. Tyra poked her seax through the southerner's neck in the way her father had taught her. Siv followed, and with two blows he was dead.

The sound of galloping horses resonated up the road where they fought. Horsed men stormed through the gates. Between two shields, Tyra could see them riding straight towards them. The riders' spears and swords reached easily over the shield-wall. The tall man behind Tyra leant in close. His breath was on her neck. He shifted his shield against hers to form a roof above them, but many villagers had already died and the wall wasn't as tall further down as it was around Tyra. There were too many horses on the other side, and they were too far away from the wall to reach with anything but a spear—and most of the surviving villagers only had axes. To Tyra's left, the horsed warriors cut down her neighbours one after the other.

Somewhere in the crowd a horn was blown. Her father's. 'Yrsa, Astrid, Hilda, Aegil, Tormod! Swine array,' he yelled.

A swine array. Her father had abandoned all hope then. No one who went into a swine array survived. Not in a crowd like this. It was certain death. And her father had called her sisters and Hilda, but he hadn't called her mother, and Tyra didn't want to think about what that meant. But her eyes teared up regardless, and she just wished all of this would end.

Tyra poked her seax through the gaps of their shield-wall, both above and below, but it didn't feel as though she hit much. Clothes, shields and air. Not flesh, and nothing but flesh mattered.

It didn't feel real, and Tyra didn't feel like herself, but her arms continued to stab with her seax and she held up her shield with a strength she didn't know she possessed. She was so tired.

She heard the shouts to their right and knew a wedge—the swine array—had broken loose from the shield-wall and was pushing into the enemy lines like a wild boar.

Tyra's legs and shield-arm were warm from wounds, her helmet was heavy on her head, and sweat had drenched her tunic. She continued to slash after the southerners as their yells intensified and their horses brayed.

She tried to imagine the success of the swine array; the three-sided shield-wall cutting its way through the enemy in search of the leader. Horses, riders, and warriors equally scared and surprised.

Tyra looked up as a horse to her left neighed and reared

above them. The rider fell, landing on his own men, cut to pieces by friendly swords.

'Kill!' she heard her father shout at the snout of the swine array somewhere straight ahead in the enemy crowd.

Siv opened their wall again. This time she let two warriors in. Together they killed the southerners almost as soon as the wall closed behind them.

'Push ahead,' Siv ordered the shield-wall. Each of them put their weight into their shields and pushed hard against the warriors on the other side to make them stumble and fall, so they could walk over them, hacking the fallen southerners to pieces as they passed.

'Close formation!' Tyra's father shouted.

Someone in the swine array had died, Tyra understood. It was madness. They would all die out there. Hilda, her sisters, her parents, all of them. Tyra was the only one left.

'Cattle die. Kinsmen die,' Tyra whispered to herself. 'We must die likewise.' There was nothing to be afraid of—they would all pass on and fight elsewhere in the life beyond—but even though she knew that, her heart beat like never before. And tears mixed with the sweat on her face. And she heaved and heaved for air. And she never wanted to fight again.

Their shield-wall lost strength. The villagers were tired, they were done. And so was Tyra. They, like her, knew what the break of the swine array meant. Their best warriors would die. Her father and sisters were as good as dead.

'The renown never dies!' Siv yelled loud and clear at her side.

'The one who gains glory in life!' they shouted back, and for a moment the villagers gained strength, fought for themselves, for the children they had sent to safety, for the raiding warriors, and for the glory they would leave behind for all to see. Tyra felt herself gain strength as well, but it was too late and it was not enough.

DARKNESS

DEATH, PAIN, AND fear.

Ragnar's hands tightened around the distaff the Darkness had given him. The Darkness weighed him down like a winter coat. His feet were cold and his legs shivered from the shock of yet another death.

Again, he could see nothing, not even the distaff, or his own hands. He had seen for no more than a heartbeat before the axe killed him. This time he had not spoken, but he *had* made a sound. He could not risk tapping the distaff again, although that was what runemistresses did to look into the future.

An idea formed in his mind. *Tap, tap*, he said in his head, and pretended to hit the distaff on the ground, but without letting it touch.

Light lit both his hand and the distaff, like it had before, as if the distaff pushed away the heavy Darkness, but there was nothing else to see. There was no one but him.

Ragnar braced for the upcoming death. The muscles in his neck and shoulders tensed as he waited for an axe or a sword to slash and kill, but neither appeared. It was just like when he had asked for help. He had not said the words aloud so the Darkness could not hear him.

He relaxed his shoulders, and stood up tall. He wielded the distaff in his right hand, like a runemistress would.

Under the hollow pear shape, Odin's holy runes had been carved into the metal. They shone bright blue. A shining thread surged out from the hollow part of the staff, and with it came a sound like a hundred knives scraped against glass. The hair on the back of Ragnar's neck rose.

The thread from his distaff tore a hole in the Darkness. A bright, veiled hole into another world, extending further and further up, opening wider and wider from the shriek of knives against glass.

The veiled exit to Helheim.

Goosebumps rose up his body. Ragnar ran towards the veiled opening, and passed through.

The air was humid and heavy, the shriek gone.

Everything had changed.

Ragnar's heart raced, but his legs no longer trembled. With the runic distaff extended in front of him, he took a cautious step ahead. The ground was hard.

There was something to his right, at the edge of the Darkness: a rock, but more than just a rock. It was a whole wall hacked out of stone, blurry as if seen through a mist. With a glance, Ragnar followed it back, and although he knew the veiled opening had been there, now he could only see the wall stretching on behind him.

He was not in the Darkness any longer. This was a step in the right direction, or so he hoped. Maybe it was the outer gate to Helheim, although the roof did not appear to have been made of gold, as the stories told. It certainly was a cave of some sort.

Ahead was an echo of dripping water.

For a long time, Ragnar walked towards the sound before he heard anything but the drip. The wall at his side had long disappeared into the dark when a hushed song reached his ears. Someone else was there with him. Ragnar had spent his life learning all the songs in Midgard, but he did not know this melody; and he could not hear any words, just the hum.

Drip. The water was somewhere ahead.

The humidity made Ragnar sweat. His lips were salty and he struggled to breathe. He heaved loudly, realising what he was doing too late. A blade slit his throat. It came from behind, cold against his neck. He felt his knees buckle. The blood trickled down over his neck and chest.

Death, pain, and fear.

HE WAS BACK, on his feet, in the dark. For a moment, he calmed his breathing and prepared himself. Determined to continue on and escape the Darkness, he clutched the distaff and tapped it, making the sound in his head. The shrieks of daggers against glass made him wince as his distaff created an opening in the Darkness. Ragnar ran through the veil.

The cave came into view. He stood at the very place where he had died moments before. With cautious steps, he walked towards the hummed song and there, in the middle of this humid cave, his staff pushed away the dark to reveal a foot twice the size of his own, and then another. The ankles were tied with chains disappearing into a rock that rose from the floor, and the legs were similarly fastened. The man was naked, and his torso was bound so tight that his chest hardly moved as he breathed. He was huge; not just because he was taller than Ragnar, he was bigger than any man Ragnar had ever seen before. The man was a giant. A jotun.

Ragnar stepped closer to let the runic distaff push the Darkness away to reveal the man's face. The giant did not look at him; did not appear to realise that Ragnar was there. The song was still whispered through the giant's half-open mouth. His hair was dark and red locks grew at each temple, his beard a mixture of both black and red. His lips looked as if they had been scorched. His mane had been allowed to grow so long that it touched the stone floor.

The giant did not look at Ragnar, just stared up into the dark and whispered his song.

Ragnar leant in to listen, so close his ear nearly touched the man's charred lips, and, as he did, he realised that the giant was not singing, but talking to himself. 'The Alfather has abandoned you,' he muttered to himself. 'Blood-brother…'

The Alfather's blood-brother. Ragnar's eyes opened wide and he leant back until the giant's whisper turned back into a hummed song. The leader of gods' blood-brother. This was not just any giant. This was Loki. The very Loki Ragnar had told hundreds of stories about during his life in Midgard. The clever giant who lived with the gods; treacherous Loki all children loved to hear about.

Loki looked so dishevelled and wild, nothing like the well-groomed man Ragnar had always imagined him to be. He knew the story of Loki's punishment well, had told it hundreds of times. This was it, the very scene he had so often described. The treacherous giant, bound to a rock in the depths of a cave, destined to a slow death.

Ragnar became acutely aware that something was missing. Something that had been there before.

There was no dripping.

Ragnar gulped, already knowing what was there, above him, before he tilted his head back.

A snake hung from the ceiling, tied by the tail. The dripping sound had not come from any water, but from the beast's poison. That was why Loki's lips were charred. The snake's focus was no longer on Loki. It looked directly at Ragnar, hissed, and burst forward.

Ragnar screamed as the snake's fangs planted themselves into his eyes.

Death, pain, and fear.

HILDA

Chapter Eight

YRSA HAD FALLEN. They were as good as dead, everyone in the swine array. Hilda knew it, but refused to think about it. Pressed against Astrid's back, she tried to keep her side of the wedge.

She couldn't hold the wall, not alone. Jarn tried to compensate, but the formation had a gap. With Yrsa's death, they were a warrior short. No matter how they positioned themselves, they would still be a warrior short.

Hilda planted her axe into the neck of a southerner, wrenched it out again. Hacked out after the next one. Her swing was large, compared to theirs, axe-shaft long. She was taller too, and reached them easily. But there were too many, and she couldn't see their leader anymore. As soon as he had seen the swine array come for him, he had ridden out of the gates. A true coward.

Jarn too had noticed their peril. 'I love you,' he shouted to his daughters, and perhaps to all of the villagers and the entire town too, for all of them were doomed. All would die. Ash-hill would die.

'I love you too,' cried Astrid at Hilda's left flank.

Hilda did her best to hold the wall long enough for them to say their last goodbyes in this life.

A spear planted itself into Hilda's thigh, and just as quickly, it was torn out again. The pain didn't startle her. The wound didn't matter. In the afterlife, it would heal.

Hilda took in a deep breath. Saw the flicker of her snow fox's tail between the southerners' legs. The snow fox. Her death was near. She couldn't escape it this time. This was it. She was ready, and she would take a hundred warriors with her to the afterlife.

'Meet in Valhalla,' Jarn breathed, and then he gave the order. 'Break!'

They launched into the thick crowd of warriors. Each on their own, fighting their last battle.

Hilda smiled and cried at the thought of Valhalla. She swirled around and hacked out after the enemy. Moved in every direction and none at all. Moved in any way the southerners wouldn't expect. Cut down one man after the other. Anyone who approached her. Slammed them with her shield. Stepped on their toes.

They were more experienced than her—stronger men too—but they feared death and Hilda no longer did.

Her snow fox fylgja ran at her side and let out a sharp bark. At the fox's warning, Hilda turned to see a warrior sneaking up behind her. She punched him with her shield and sunk the sharp tip of her axe into his throat.

The snow fox barked again, demanding Hilda's focus. Further down the road, she spotted Ash-hill's Christian. Calm, as if this slaughter was like any other night, the priest stood and chatted with southern warriors. His casual posture made Hilda's insides turn. Anger flared up inside her. Only one word could describe him now. 'Murderer!' she roared after him.

The coward's eyes met hers. The priest diverted his gaze, pretended not to have noticed, but his face flushed and betrayed him. The priest knew that it was him she called. He knew, but he chose to ignore her. He might have lived in Ash-hill among them, but he was part of this betrayal. He had told them the rumours were false. He had tricked them.

The priest moved into the shades of the night, out of Hilda's sight. Deliberately, she knew; scared she might do something and ruin his show. And she would. He had called the southerners, summoned them over the summer. Now it was clear to her. It had been his doing and she would make him regret it.

Her fox barked and snarled at her side. Hilda no longer cared. She was nearly ready to allow the fox to take her to the afterlife. Like her father, in the end. She only had one task left. The priest.

She peered through the mob as she fought, with quick, darting glances. Annoyed by how much her helmet hindered her vision. Her blows became stronger as she cut her way towards Pontius the Murderer.

It didn't take her long to get close to him. She barely noticed the sword and spear wounds she suffered in her approach. They didn't matter. They would leave proud scars in the afterlife.

For a heartbeat, the wind's whispers reached Hilda and the crowd parted in front of her, so she could see the priest, straight ahead. Pontius held the reins of a tall horse, preparing to mount and ride away. Dastard.

She lunged forward, shouldered her shield, grabbed the dagger from her weapon belt and plunged it into Pontius' ankle as he swung onto the horse. He screamed. She pulled the dagger towards herself, the blade still in his ankle. Dragged him off the panicked horse. She hoped it hurt.

In a heartbeat her dagger was at his neck. The mount made its escape, but it didn't matter. Pontius was hers now. With the dagger to his neck, she made him stand tall in front of her.

Her shield and helmet covered her from the back, and Pontius from the front. She secured the battle axe in her belt. The southerners couldn't kill her with a single move now; they would need to strike twice, and before their second blow she would have plenty of time to finish off their dear priest.

She glanced at the warriors surrounding her and smiled. The snow fox wasn't there anymore. The southerners wouldn't kill her. If the fox wasn't there to warn her of her death, it wasn't her time yet. She was a shieldmaiden, and stronger than a hundred of them. She had survived the warnings of the fox with blue eyes. Had escaped her own death, more than once. They couldn't possibly kill her now. It was a good lie, and she needed to believe it.

An arrow scraped Hilda's left shoulder and plunged into the head of the warrior in front of her. Clenching onto Pontius, Hilda spun around, turning his body with her own. 'I'll kill him!' she shouted, and grinded her teeth to suppress the pain at her shoulder.

The priest wailed. Hilda tightened her grip on the dagger and held it close until she could feel his racing pulse.

The warriors didn't move away.

'Tell them!' she yelled, and pressed the blade until she felt a faint flow of blood drip down her arm.

'Don't kill me,' he sobbed. 'Hilda, you know me.' The drops were tears, Hilda realised, disgusted. Pressed the knife against the priest's neck so blood stained the blade, real this time. He shrieked at the warriors, and forced them to back away.

'Make them retreat,' Hilda snarled, leaning close to his ear as she pressed the blade closer yet. His hair stank as if he hadn't washed the entire summer and the stench threatened to make her pull away from him. She struggled to keep her breathing steady so she would have enough air for her next move, no matter when the opportunity came.

Through the dagger, she could feel the priest breathe, and when he spoke to the southerners her hand moved up and down with the lump in his throat.

'I'm not—' Pontius said in Norse when he was done, but Hilda kept him silenced. 'You don't understa—' he tried again, but to no avail. She pushed her dagger against his throat until blood trickled down her hand. Warm, at first, but quickly cooling in the air, and turning sticky.

'I want to save you,' he managed to yell. He dared to speak and dared to come up with such utter lies. A coward like him shouldn't be allowed to live. But she needed him, for now.

'I'm sure you do,' she answered, her teeth clenched. 'Anything to save yourself. So, make them clear the way for us.'

The priest didn't protest this time. In a shaky voice, he translated.

Hilda glanced over her shoulder to the shield-wall the remaining villagers held up. The defence was thin and breaking up. Few had survived this far into the fight, and those who had would all die. The southerners would never retreat at this point. The southerners too had suffered losses, but not as many, and there was so many more of them. They would kill every last villager. Nothing she could do would stop the slaughter now.

The cold northern wind came with its usual whispers. It pushed against her back as if to urge her to escape. She didn't want to leave. When so many had passed on and fought to death, it didn't feel right to leave, though with the priest as hostage, she had a chance to make it out, perhaps even alive. A raven flew over the crowd, and cawed above Hilda's head.

She didn't have time to see if it had runes on its beak like her father's raven, but she still felt as if her father was there, watching over her. He would have wanted her to leave.

'If anyone attacks, or follows us, you're dead,' Hilda whispered into the priest's ears and pushed him forward towards the outer gates.

The priest yelled and screamed to the bewildered southerners. Even so, they followed Hilda and the priest to the southern gate, and she knew they wouldn't let the priest out of their sight. At the first opportunity, they would strike Hilda to save Pontius the Murderer.

A roar rang around the village, and screams erupted. Southern warriors fled from the gates, terrified.

For a moment, they all seemed to forget about Hilda and the priest, and Hilda did not need more than a moment. She pushed the priest ahead of her, towards the chaos by the southern gate, ignoring his protests and his clawing at her arms.

Another roar shook fear into the crowd; the last few still pointing their weapons at Hilda faltered. Hilda smiled as the crowd parted. By the southern gate, Einer's bear cub had risen to its hind legs and roared.

Vigir hadn't fled from the sound of the fight. It must have sensed the danger and wanted to protect its home. It clawed out after those who tried to keep it away with their arrows, axes and long spears. A southerner managed to poke Vigir's arm, and the bear launched at the culprit. The southerners screamed and backed away, afraid of the wild beast.

Hilda made her way towards the bear. A few southern warriors yelled after her—urged others to do something, and to stop her—but Hilda was too quick and they were too worried about the bear, and themselves.

The priest was crying under her arm. Still. His tears fell all over Hilda's hands. His entire body was shaking from fear. Hilda pushed him closer to the wild bear.

The warriors were bewildered, not knowing if they should level their weapons at Hilda or at the bear, and yelling at the thought of their holy man being eaten alive or clawed to death.

'Vigir,' Hilda called as she approached, so the bear would know that it was her and not an attacker. She hoped it wouldn't attack her. She knew she didn't look like herself in her full armour, hidden behind the Christian priest.

The bear halted its mad frenzy at her voice and tilted its large head in her direction.

'Vigir,' she called again.

It padded towards her, growling at anyone else who attempted to get closer.

'Good bear.' Hilda cornered away from the southerners, with the Christian priest as her shield and the bear as her weapon.

'Stay,' she told the bear as she backed out of the southern gate.

The bear waddled along with her.

'Stay,' she insisted, but the bear continued to pad after her. 'Stay!'

The wind and its whispers pushed the bear back up towards the village. The bear growled and roared for Hilda to change her mind. It was scared. Scared like the rest of them. Like the screaming villagers, and the frightened southerners.

Despite its protests, Vigir listened to her and to the wind. It stopped following.

Hilda continued out of the gates. 'Einer would be proud,' she yelled. The bear roared.

A few brave warriors tried to exit the town, past the bear. With a loud growl, Vigir turned away from Hilda and faced the Christians, lashed out after them.

Clear of the gates, Hilda made the priest spin around, and forced him into a run down the hill, past his stupid church and past Tormod's farmlands. Into the forest. The long shaft of her axe slapped against her knee, and the shield tapped loudly at the back of her helmet.

As soon as the shadows swallowed them, Hilda slowed. Hidden by the dark of the woods, she made them walk west out past the old stone tower, toward the stables, careful not to leave a trail. She watched the hill they had come down. Four southerners had escaped the bear's clutches and chased after her. The priest tried to yell out to them, but Hilda silenced him with the dagger. Moving with him was difficult, but she needed him alive until she was far enough away to make her final escape.

They moved further out west along the farmlands, hidden in the shadows of the forest. The further they went, the clearer it became that they weren't being followed. Unlike her, the southerners didn't know these lands in the dark of the night. Horses neighed. The stables were close and someone had forgotten to let the horses go.

Screams travelled across the farmlands from Ash-hill, and sent a chill down Hilda's spine.

She stopped walking, glanced around to ensure that no southerners were at her back. She allowed herself time to watch Ash-hill from afar. The bloody remainders of home.

The inner circle was thick with people. The villagers had retreated up to the ash tree. They were still fighting. No longer for their life, or for the village, but for their legacy. Hilda wished that she was up there and not safe, as her father would have wanted her to be.

Another squeal wrenched at Hilda's heart and made tears prickle in her eyes. This was the last time she would see her home, and she was well aware of it.

The priest tried to scream for help, but at the first small yelp, Hilda made blood trickle from his neck, careful not to slice deep enough to kill.

'Why?' she asked and forced him around to face Ash-hill. The night was lit by the torches on the barricade. Fresh blood glistened against the outer wood. Corpses leaned over the barricade. 'Why would you do this?'

'It's the same,' the priest cried and tried to turn his head away from the scene, to avoid to look at what he had caused. He was trembling from fear.

She grabbed his chin and made him look. 'The same as what?' she demanded to know.

'Your raids.'

His words made her shake with anger. 'This is nothing like a raid,' she hissed into his ear. 'That up there is a slaughter.' She let her tears, supressed throughout the battle, fall down her cheeks as she watched her old home and heard the cries of her dying friends and neighbours. Children were screaming—mere children, not yet old enough to make their choice or know the world. Children who should have been sleeping this far into the night. 'Don't you hear them? A slaughter. Devoid of honour.'

She knew Christians did not abide by the same code of

honour as Jutes or other northerners, if they abided by any at all. They didn't take pride in fighting, even the few who made it their trade, and every last one of them feared to meet their god. Hilda could never understand how someone could fear the long-awaited meeting with their own god; to finally be in the presence of one so powerful, the greatest privilege in the nine worlds.

'This isn't for honour,' the priest said in a distant voice, as if he had said the words a thousand times. 'It's for God. To save God's good men from the horrors of your raids.'

Hilda knew there was no point in arguing with a Christian, and yet she did. 'No one up there raids. You know that.'

Squeals Hilda feared she might never forget cut through the night and wrenched at her heart. Her knuckles were white, so tightly did she clench the dagger against his throat.

The priest had known his Christian warriors wouldn't stand a chance against the raiders, so he had decided to attack during summer, when all the capable warriors were away. At summer, when there were only farmers and children at home.

A long time ago the chief had allowed the priest to stay in Ash-hill. Had it been Hilda's decision, he never should have been allowed into the village. Would have been killed on sight, same as any Christian who came after him. Others had accepted him into the village as one of their own, but Pontius was nothing but a southerner. Never had been anything else. A true little shit.

'If you hadn't built your church in Ash-hill, they wouldn't be dead. They wouldn't be dying,' she told him. 'Jarn, Gunna, Yrsa, Astrid, Ingrid.' Her heart tightened at the thought of Ingrid who had never wanted to fight. 'Ingrid. You knew her. She defended you. And you killed her. And Tyra.' Hilda swallowed her tears at the thought of Tyra being killed like this. It made her tremble with despair. She grinded her teeth and focused on what she could see. Replaced her mourning with a warrior's pure anger. 'You killed your own neighbours,' she snarled. 'You killed friends. You killed children. Go meet your god. Explain *that* to him.'

She brought the dagger away from the priest's throat and down to his stomach. Sliced and pushed in so far that had the blade been any longer she would have stabbed herself too. She carved up through his guts. The blade halted when it reached the priest's ribs and she had to put in an additional effort to finish the task and reach his heart. The blood was all over her dagger and hand and arm. Two breaths and it was done.

TYRA

Chapter Nine

TYRA'S FATHER NO longer shouted. He had been yelling commands throughout the battle. Now, he had been silent for far too long. As long as he could fight he would have yelled, she knew he would. Her mother too.

Her parents hadn't made it. Her parents who had raided for two dozen summers hadn't made it. Tyra had no chance of survival and all she wanted now was to join her parents and not be left when they would all be feasting in Valhalla's halls tomorrow morning.

She couldn't see her sisters either. There weren't many villagers left. The tall farmer behind Tyra, pushed, and Tyra struggled to hold up her shield. Her legs and arms were weak from effort. Sweaty and weak.

Their shield-wall was falling apart.

There were too many warriors on the other side. In the end, there were too few villagers. And they weren't warriors, and they weren't prepared.

'Back up!' Siv shouted at her side. They had already retreated into the circle at the top of the town. Southerners arrived up every street. There was nowhere to retreat.

Still, at Siv's command, Tyra took three steps further back. Her left heel knocked against one of the Ting stones. Tyra put her full weight into her shield. Her arm was sore from holding it for so long, and she wanted to switch hands, but she couldn't put her weapon away.

Ravens cried above her. Tyra flinched and lifted her eyes. Two ravens sat in the ash-tree and their dark eyes were staring down at her. Recognising her. They cawed, and Tyra almost thought she heard them croak her name, but she was pushed up against her shield again, and lost her concentration, and then the birds were gone.

The southerners were in full formation. Only Siv had the brute force to fight back, but then even Siv stopped attacking. All of them were tired.

This was the end.

The few dozen surviving villagers were forced to retreat. Closer and closer together. Nearer the ash, until there was no room, and Tyra was pressed against Siv's hip. Still the southerners advanced. Tyra couldn't turn to see who else had survived, but they weren't many. And in the end, none of them would make it through. They would be killed one by one. She just knew they would, and she would have no chance to fight back, and she would never make it to Valhalla and she would never see her family again, and she would be all alone for the rest of eternity.

Siv removed her shield from the wall.

'You follow me,' she said and Tyra looked up too see the chieftain's wife staring at her. At Tyra. And she could do nothing but let the tall farmer behind her step in to replace her in the shield-wall, and follow Siv.

Siv shuffled back to the last Ting stone, up close to the trunk of the ash-tree. 'Set down your shield,' she ordered.

Tyra did as she was told.

Siv leant down close, like Einer always did when he spoke to Tyra. 'You need to crawl up into the ash tree,' Siv said.

Tyra glanced up to where the ravens had been. People were screaming all around them, and fighting, and dying. And Tyra didn't understand what was happening or why Siv was telling her to crawl up in the tree.

'There will be a hole up there,' Siv continued. Her intense stare demanded Tyra's full attention. 'Crawl inside the hole, and—now, this is very important—don't make a sound.'

Tyra didn't quite know why, but listening to Siv's instructions made her cry. The tears ran down her cheeks and the thought of the fight, and of her parents and sisters, of everyone around them, made her cry all the more. Siv set down her own shield, and put a hand on Tyra's shoulder. Immediately, Tyra's mind calmed. She found the resolution to do exactly as Siv had asked of her.

Siv lifted Tyra up by the hips and helped her to climb onto the lowest branch on the tree. 'Don't make a sound,' Siv warned again. 'I will come get you.' And then she took out her axe, picked her shield back up, and darted back to fight.

The slim shield-wall was breaking apart. Siv pushed through the crowd with her shield, and warriors fell before her. They were four, five, seven southerners trying to kill her, and none of them were a match for Siv. She was taller than them, stronger. She overmanned every big warrior as if they were nothing more than puppies. The biggest of them only reached Siv's shoulder, and she pushed everyone and everything out of the way with a brute force Tyra had never seen before, not even when the warriors fought sometimes at the tavern by Knifed-hill.

The battle raged on, but hidden in the leaves of the ash-tree, Tyra didn't feel as if she were part of it any longer.

She sniffled. The tears still flowed down her cheeks, but she pushed her lips together fiercely, and turned her attention to the tree. She fumbled for a branch to hold onto and climbed to the trunk.

Branches clanged against her helmet, and her head was

sweaty, but her ears cooled with the northern wind that shook the tree's leaves.

In the dark, Tyra felt around the tree trunk for the hole Siv had told her about. Tyra had never known there to be a hole in the ash tree, but then her left hand glided over a hole, and she groped for the edges of it. It was large. Large enough.

Tyra slid her feet into the hole. It went deep, and she couldn't feel where it stopped. It was wide enough for her to slip inside. She shuffled closer so her legs dangled into the hole and then slid into it entirely, as Siv had instructed her to do.

The loud clangs of battle disappeared, suddenly.

The hole was big and cold. Tyra could hear her own heart beat loud, and hear her breath, and the rustle of her hairs inside her helmet. And Siv's warning for her not to make a sound made her too afraid to move, or do anything.

For a long, long time, she stayed in the dark, waiting, and trying to listen for the fight going on outside the tree, but she couldn't hear it, and she didn't know what had happened, and the only thing that was worse than the actual fight was not knowing.

Siv ought to have come for her by now, if the villagers had won. Siv didn't lie, and she had said she would come for Tyra. But Tyra couldn't help but think that maybe even someone as strong and powerful as Siv hadn't made it through. There had been so many southerners.

Tyra stared up at the hole she had climbed through, but she couldn't see it for the Darkness was so complete. She reached up for it. She had an urge to know the wind on her face and to hear something, to *feel* something. Anything.

There was nothing above her, no wooden edge where she had passed through. It hadn't been much of a drop—she ought to be able to touch the wooden edge—and yet it wasn't there. Tyra stared up, but above her, where the hole was supposed to be, was only complete darkness. And then somewhere below her, further into the tree, far away in the distance, a man screamed.

DARKNESS

DEATH, PAIN, AND fear.

The Darkness wrapped around Ragnar. His scream before his last death resonated around the dark. He was unable to shake the image of the snake out of his mind and forget the pain of its fangs planted into his eyes.

It had not been the road to Helheim after all. It had not been the same slit of light that he had travelled towards with his stallion and with his thrall at his side. He had used the runic distaff to see the future, as runemistresses did. He had gleaned the far future in which Loki would be punished for his crimes against the gods and be tied up inside that cave, waiting for the final battle of Ragnarok, when the gods would die and the nine worlds would perish.

This was not the afterlife Ragnar had expected.

His heartbeat sped up on its own. It rested all the way up in his throat and he could hardly breathe for fear that something would jump out at him.

Tap, tap, he said in his head and pretended to knock the

distaff on the ground. His runic distaff pushed the Darkness away in rhythmic pulses, and from the hollow apple-shape, a thread surged out through the dark. With the sound of a hundred knives sharpening against glass, the thread cut a veiled opening out of the Darkness.

Ragnar ran towards it and straight through, escaping the horrid sounds.

It was dark beyond the veil; dark as night. Although Ragnar illuminated the surroundings with his distaff, he could not see far. At the edges of what he could see, the Darkness pulsated in the rhythm of his own heartbeat.

Ragnar started at a loud clang. His shoes slid over muddy grass.

A howl shook the ground. Ragnar flinched away, his feet slipping on the wet grass. He caught himself with a hand on the ground. His palm came back red. The grass was not wet from mud or rain; it was dark and slippery from blood. Black blood clots covered the ground. Ragnar gulped and dried the blood onto his trousers.

Clashes of steel echoed around him. Horrid screams and slurps, and roars, and horns blowing.

Ragnar's breaths were heavy. His heart raced. He turned around himself, worried that something would attack him. He wished that he could see what was going on around him.

Trying to calm himself, he shut his eyes tight and wished and wished that the Darkness would retreat and allow him to see further; and when he was calm enough to face the Darkness and the blooded grass and all the horrid sounds, Ragnar opened his eyes again. The Darkness had retreated, and with every pulse of his distaff it retreated further yet.

A warrior twice Ragnar's height burst out of the dark to attack a much smaller woman. Her chainmail was made of silver, and her hair was long and golden. The goddess Sif, Ragnar knew as soon as he laid eyes on her. Fiercely, she fought the giant. She thrust a spear into the giant's kneecap to make him fall, and with her axe, she went in for the final kill. Blood splattered out over her hands and face. Quick as lightning, she spun away from the giant corpse and rushed along the battlefield.

Ragnar gaped after her. A goddess, in this bloody battle, and a giant too. He swallowed nervously. This was the famous battle of Ragnarok, which had been foretold at the beginning of ages. On this battlefield, Ragnar's gods would die.

He could not allow it to happen.

Make me fearless, he begged of the gods. Then, determined like his daughter Hilda had always been, Ragnar darted across the battlefield after Sif, searching for her gold locks. He ducked under the legs of giants and raced past lesser known gods and beasts. He couldn't let her die; not any of the gods. They needed to survive so the nine worlds would survive, and so he could go to Helheim and be reunited with his wife and son.

The sky was dark and ashes rained down over the battlefield and swooped into the blonde hairs of fierce gods in expensive chainmail. Blood rained down over Ragnar as he ran through the crowd. In large clumps, it dripped onto his shoulders and soaked his tunic.

No one matched Ragnar's searching stare. No one noticed him. Almost as if he wasn't there, and perhaps he wasn't. An observer with a distaff. Just a runemistress, glancing into the future.

Giants and gods fought to the death. Their corpses piled like great hills and mountains, and Ragnar crawled over them. Through the crowd of fighting giants and gods.

A great howl shook fear into everyone on the nearby battlefield.

The length of three longhouses down the hill from Ragnar's mountain of corpses was a huge wolf. Ragnar saw it at the edge of the pulsing Darkness. Its teeth were longer and sharper than any he had ever seen before. They glistened and wrenched through three warriors at a time.

The warriors around the frenzied wolf parted for a fierce one-eyed man who fearlessly approached. His silver beard had been braided and partly coloured in blood. With his sharp spear, he pushed warriors and giants out of his way, all of whom looked small in his presence. His eye was set on the big wolf. Pieces of guts dangled from his jewelled chainmail; not his own guts, but that of giants and beasts he had slain.

Ragnar's heart caught in his throat at the sight of the great Alfather.

Then, the panic washed over him.

This was how Odin, the great Alfather and leader of gods, was destined to die; his bones broken by the wolf's sharp teeth. The future seers had foretold it, hundreds and hundreds of winters ago.

Ragnar stumbled down the mountain of corpses towards the Alfather. His fear of the Darkness was not enough to make him stop.

The yells of the fighting warriors, and the loud clashes of swords and axes, and the thunder above, were too loud for Ragnar to be heard. Odin would die at Fenrir's lack of mercy.

Run away, run away, Ragnar repeated loud in his mind, like he had thought about tapping the distaff and like he had thought about making the Darkness retreat. *Run away, run away*, he thought to his god, and all the way into his heart, he wished that the Alfather would listen to him and leave the battlefield, before the wolf could get him. Before he died.

Run away from the wolf, Ragnar thought, and as if all the powers in the nine worlds were bestowed upon Ragnar, his god listened.

EINER

Chapter Ten

THEY WERE SO close to home. Einer was not the only warrior who hoped they would sail soon again, now that they were so close to Ash-hill.

'We should pack tomorrow and sail before midday,' Einer urged his father as they walked through the tavern. Einer's father always dreaded having to get in and out of ports. For preference, he put as much time as possible between those two manoeuvres, but Hedeby was too expensive a harbour for them to stay in for more than a few nights.

'It'll rain tomorrow,' his father reminded Einer.

Einer nodded. He would have to push harder to convince his father. The summer had not been prosperous, neither in terms of riches nor fights. They had only gotten into two skirmishes, one of them in a tavern, and so far, the little they had won for themselves barely covered the warriors' minimum pay and ship maintenance. Raiding was no longer the glorious and profitable profession it had used to be. It was no wonder that many warriors had turned to trading in recent summers.

Sometimes, Einer wondered if Hilda understood the reality of it, and if that was partly why she was so ardent to join the raids, to ensure the future of a dying art. She had always been a protector.

A wealthy man waved Einer and his father over to his table where he sat with a group of warriors, whose eyes were wild as if they had eaten too many berserker caps. Einer did not know the man, but only a truly flamboyant leader would wear clothes coloured in expensive blue. It had to be the wealthiest chief of southern Jutland; Harald of Jelling, son of Gorm the Sleepy.

Einer and his father walked to Harald's table with smiles that matched their low expectations. For Harald wore a deep blue overtunic, and an equally blue woollen cloak, lined with gold. The shiny pin that held his cloak in place was bigger than Einer's palm. Chief Harald truly did have a greedy tooth for the expensive colour of blue; exactly as the tales told. It was no wonder he had gained the horrid calling name "Bluetan."

'Chief Harald,' said Einer's father. 'It's been a long time. Not since your father was chief.'

'I'm no longer a chieftain, old Vigmer,' said Harald. 'I'm the King of Danes.'

Einer and his father burst out laughing; a mouthful of mead splattered out of Vigmer's nose which made Einer laugh harder. He howled with laughter until he noticed that Harald and his berserkers watched in silence.

No matter if it was true or not, it was a laughable matter. Any good man unexpectedly turned king would have laughed at his own fortune. Yet Harald did not laugh, and although they had been called over, Einer and his father were not invited to sit. Perhaps it was because he lived close to the southern border, but Harald acted like a southerner, and he truly thought himself King of Danes.

'Soon I'll be the King of Jutes too,' Harald said through clenched teeth, still unable to laugh at his own sudden fortune.

'Who do you think we are?' Einer's father laughed. He seemed unaware of the seriousness in Harald's tone. 'You think we're Christians?' Einer's father continued. 'Why would anyone pay you for protection? We're raiders, that's what *we* get paid for. We can protect ourselves.' He laughed, alone, and finally, even he noticed the hardened expressions on the faces of Harald and his berserkers.

In recent winters, kings had begun to emerge throughout the Norse lands, and Einer had often wondered how long it would take before Ash-hill, too, would be confronted with someone claiming control over their lands and riches. That time was now.

'No one in the nine worlds would want you as their king.' Einer's father took another slurp of mead as he turned away from Harald's table. 'Who would want a king who can't laugh at himself?'

'Chief Torsten, Chief Ralf and Chief Ulf acknowledge me as their king,' Harald said and then he named all of the important chiefs in the Dane lands. Einer found it impossible to believe that so many allowed the fool to take their riches and rule over their lands from a distance, yet, Harald kept naming more chiefs.

Einer narrowed his eyes at the man in blue. Harald was no king, but they could not take the declaration lightly. Unlike chieftains, kings were not elected. They had no right to rule over land, and they knew it, which was why they ruled through fear and destruction, and turned away from the old gods who encouraged opportunity for personal advancement.

'There is no way Ulf would pay for a king to take his driftwood,' Einer's father insisted. He was still struck by those first three names Harald had listed. 'Torsten and Ralf might be rich and dumb enough to think it funny, but not Ulf.'

'Times are changing,' Harald said without responding to the provocation. 'Chiefs like Ulf acknowledge that.'

It sounded as if Harald had already taken over most of the

Dane lands. The lack of protests from the Dane warriors in the tavern was their proof. If he had not earned the title, he would not call himself King of Danes so openly in a large tavern such as this, but even if he truly was a king, he was not King of Jutland. Perhaps he had already gained the favour of larger trading towns like Alebu, but clearly Harald understood the importance of Ash-hill as the last true raiding town in northern Jutland. That was why he called them over.

The confrontation was a poor end to a disappointing summer.

'We need to be able to respond to threats,' Harald said. 'We need to show a united force.'

'A united force?' Einer's father repeated. 'We don't need a king for that. I've sailed in raiding parties with half a thousand warriors. I've raided with dozens of other ships.'

'And when was that, Vigmer? Back when my father was chief, and not too tired to raid, nej?'

The entire tavern had fallen silent. Warriors watched the exchange between the two chiefs, or rather, between the chief of Ash-Hill and the King of Danes.

Einer's father scoffed, but they all knew that Harald was right. It had been many summers ago since Norse chiefs had last sailed united. 'We could still show a united force, if we wanted. But why in all of Midgard would we? I remember how your father split the winnings that summer.'

'You truly think you could unite that big a raiding party in times like these?' Harald retorted. He was insistent, set on getting them to agree with him. Set on getting them to acknowledge him as a king. 'That many chieftains together? Who would decide?'

Einer's father sighed at Harald's insistence.

'Four ships sail under my command. I have no need of more raiders,' he dismissed and beckoned to Einer. They began to walk away.

'All a kingdom means is wealth in everyone's pockets,' Harald called after them, although considering how angry Einer's father was getting, he would have been wise to let them leave.

Vigmer grumbled and took a deep gulp of mead. Finally, he turned on his heels, back towards Harald. 'Nej. It means wealth in *your* pocket,' he hissed to Harald. 'We negotiate fine with our own swords and axes. We don't need a king to take our share.'

'A kingdom is something the southerners understand. We can win so much more if we unite,' Harald argued and Einer knew that he would keep at it. Ignoring Harald would only make the matter worse. They needed to show Harald that he would never be King of Jutland.

'The southerners seem to understand the hack of an axe just fine,' Einer said, but Harald spoke over him.

'If we show them that they can reason with us—'

'Reason with us?' Einer's father laughed. 'Then I suppose we should all become Christian and stop raiding too.'

'If that's what it takes.'

'You must have rubbed your head in troll shit,' Vigmer hissed and shook his head.

Harald's berserkers were shaking from the will to burst up and fight, but Harald kept them seated. Their eyes bulged and Einer thought their drinking horns might shatter in their grips. He put a hand on his father's shoulder. They could not risk a fight, certainly not in a tavern in Hedeby.

Harald too knew it. He could have chosen to speak to them anywhere. 'Are you declaring war on me?' Harald asked.

Vigmer was still shaking his head in disapproval. 'I'm telling you that I don't care what you call yourself, but Ash-hill will never agree to call you King, Chief Harald.'

'You'd be wise to join me, like Chief Ulf was. Soon when you sail abroad, the threat of your lone axe won't be enough. Soon your approach to negotiation won't work anymore, and that's a summer raid from which you won't be coming home.'

'My approach to negotiation won't work? I'll show you how well it works,' Einer's father retorted. 'Here is a proposal for you. You can shut up now, Harald, and sail back home to your Jelling in a few days, or you can keep talking and you can crawl instead.'

Complete silence surrounded them as the words settled. All the warriors in the tavern listened.

Both Vigmer and Harald were silent for many heartbeats.

Even if Harald decided to attack them right there, with his great berserkers and his great fleet nearby, there were still the farmers and villagers back in Ash-hill. Winning a single battle would not make the chieftaincy of their lands pass onto Harald.

A smile flicked across Harald's lips as he stared at Einer's father. 'There's no need for us to fight each other,' he said. 'Not when we have a common enemy we can fight against.'

Einer's father leant away from Harald's table and shook his head again. 'You're a shiny stink-fart, Harald, and Ash-hill won't be funding your blue dresses.'

With those words, they left Bluetan's table. Einer's father paid their tavern debts and they swiftly left with their crews.

'Gather the warriors and pack up,' he ordered Einer and the dozen warriors who followed them out. 'We sail at first light.' It was unlike him to sail out when the weather was rough and Einer knew he was eager to get Harald out of his sight. None of them protested; they all wanted to sail home.

Einer went from tavern to tavern and gathered their warriors, many of whom were too drunk to sail in the morning. He doubted that most of them could even find the ships. A few warriors were still missing after he had visited every open tavern, so Einer set out through the dark streets of Hedeby in search of them.

A scream caught his attention. Einer rushed down a narrow road until he found the source. Whimpers came from the backside of a closed tavern. A familiar voice laughed.

Finn stood above a crying Christian who had fallen to his knees, praying and mumbling and begging for help from his god. Finn twisted the tip of his sword into the Christian's left arm to make the man squeal and scream. His bloodlust was high from the many drinks he had bought in the night.

'Kill him with honour or let him go,' Einer urged and approached. He could not watch a fellow Jute ignore Ash-hill's code of honour. Especially not in a big harbour like Hedeby, and drunk too.

'He insulted me. Move on, Einer,' Finn hissed, and pushed his sword harder into the Christian's arm with a hungry glint in his cold eyes. Ale always made him act without thought for anyone but himself and his own satisfaction. Drunk minds revealed who people really were deep down, and the dark secrets they hid, and Finn was a cruel man who loved to make people suffer.

The Christian wailed and grabbed Finn's arm to try and wrench free of Finn's sword, but Finn knocked the hand away and stepped on the fingers so they broke with a loud crack.

'Kill him or let him go,' Einer repeated. 'Don't bring our reputation dishonour.' He put a hand on Finn's shoulder to urge the drunk warrior to listen.

'Roast your own cock,' Finn growled, and with the crazed eyes of a drunkard, Finn thrust his sword out of the Christian's arm, and turned to Einer.

The tip of Finn's sword slammed into Einer, wrenched through his tunic, skin, and into his gut. The blow made him grunt. The air was sucked out of his lungs. The jolt of Finn's blow rang through Einer's every limb. The blood spilled out over Finn's hands, onto the road.

Einer hunched in over himself. He kept himself up with the support of his hand that still rested on Finn's shoulder. The movement tore at the corners of his open wound.

Finn's face flushed with the realisation of what he had done. He retrieved his sword with a mumble. The cold pain stung as the blade slurped out of Einer's guts.

The Christian wailed at the sight of them, his voice scraping inside Einer's head, from one side of his skull to the other. Einer just wanted the noise to stop, and wanted Midgard to stop spinning. His chest began to heat up as if an unstoppable fire had been set deep within his heart.

Finn silenced the Christian with a sharp stab through the head. Einer was thankful.

Midgard waved before him. His mind was dizzy. His chest burned like a Midsummer fever.

The night howls and chants of drunk warriors were distant. Einer heard blood pump through him, and felt the pulsations on his forehead.

He pushed against Finn's shoulder and managed to stand up tall, but words failed him. It had to have been an accident; Finn was cruel in many ways, but he was not someone who would stab a kinsman, and the shock of his actions was profound to see on Finn's face.

As if he knew exactly what Einer was thinking, Finn controlled his expression, as much as the ale in his stomach would allow. His eyes dispelled their surprise and narrowed in their usual cold way, and he pressed his lips together. 'Shouldn't interfere in another freeman's fight,' Finn told him, but his voice did not carry its usual calm and provoking tone.

With no will to talk or fight, Einer pushed away. He supported himself with a hand against the back wall of the closed tavern, and stared down at the dead Christian Finn had tormented.

Einer's chest burned up like it had at Ragnar's funeral. The bracteate his mother had given him hammered against his chest with loud jolts as if it were Thor's hammer.

With a wound like the one through his stomach, he should not have been able to stand; should not have been able to move at all, but only his chest hurt, right where the bracteate burned.

He could not take the heat anymore. It made him dizzy and feverish and he wanted his mind to clear. His mother's words of warning never to take off the bracteate rang in his head, but Einer could hardly stand up straight from the heat anymore.

He wrenched off his gold neck-ring, hoping his chest would stop burning, then.

Straight away, he felt the change. Pain kicked the air out of his lungs. His body felt heavy as if he were carrying a rock in his chest. He collapsed from shock and pain.

This time, it was not his burning flesh that hurt. It was the wound Finn had inflicted upon him. A mortal wound.

SIV

Chapter Eleven

THE LAST JUTE fell at Siv's side, head hacked off by a sharp blow.

Siv was the lone survivor in her part of the shield-wall. There were more villagers out of her reach, fighting for glorious deaths, no longer for life. Everyone she knew and loved was dead, and their loss had mounted as a lump in her throat. They had been betrayed. All that was left was those cowardly Christians who thought they were brave because they had spent the summer killing farmers and children and old folk.

The town was in flames. Her home.

Hundreds and hundreds of southerners flocked around her. In front of her and at her back. They stumbled over the corpses of Ash-hill's farmers and children to get to her. They stepped on the corpses of her neighbours and her friends. For the mere chance to kill the last warrior in Ash-hill.

They had her cornered. Their eyes were eager, but they thought she was like the others, and they were wrong.

Siv threw down her shield. An old Christian smiled, thinking that she had surrendered. Others laughed at their success.

129

The anger flowed up within Siv. They had killed children and farmers and they had come in the night. They had ambushed the village and slaughtered all in sight.

She roared like a wild bear, roared so it shook them to the core. She called forth the ancient rage within her. Her forefathers had long rested idle inside her, and now they needed to be released. Once their rage took her, they would kill everyone.

The southerners started at her roar and stumbled a few feet backwards.

At the risk of losing herself to their rage for all eternity, Siv welcomed the ancient forces within her. She felt the forefathers' anger burn up her arm. She let it. She felt their anger flood her mind. She welcomed it.

Without her shield, she was faster. She unsheathed her axe. Her spear was in the other hand.

Siv shattered the shield of a southerner. Pierced him in the chest with her spear. Slashed a man in the eye with her axe. Hacked through the bridge of his nose to free her weapon, and stabbed a southerner coming up at her back.

Flames rose around her. Her home was burning.

The forefathers made her stronger and precise. She kept everyone away with the spear. Slashed through armours and necks with the axe. The forefathers made it so easy to kill, but there were too many southerners. They organised themselves in groups, and attacked as one. She would need to let the forefathers out further to survive. Allow them to take over entirely, and no jotun came back from that. If she did, she would lose herself and be a killing beast for the rest of eternity.

Besides, there was Tyra, hidden away inside the dark of the ash-tree.

Further down the road, southerners screamed. Not because of her, not because of the fire. Someone else roared. She was not the only beast to fight for Ash-hill.

Siv ran through the crowd liked a berserker. Down the road another long-lived raged, like she did. The same long-lived she had sensed these past days. He was a giant and twice the size of any of the southern warriors. Like Siv, he had let the forefathers out and raged uncontrollably through the town. Smacked southerners out of his way. The Christians ran from him, screaming for their god.

The forefathers killed around Siv while she watched him.

The southerners didn't see the giant, like Siv saw him. He wore a Midgard hood, which meant that all the screaming southerners saw was their friends die around them. Bloodied to the core, spines broken.

'Witchcraft!' Christians shouted in their cowardly tongues and fled like scared cattle. Down the road and out of the gates. Siv's forefathers made her chase them. Roaring and screaming, flailing her weapons.

She took a deep breath. The forefathers had not been out for long. She could still control them. Could still push them back and lock them away.

The giant roared. He was further gone in his berserker rage than her. The flames were tall around him. He did not have his forefathers under control. Not like Siv did. Unless she helped calm him, he would be lost to the forefathers forever. A berserker raging through the nine worlds for centuries to come, on a mission to kill. His gaze caught Siv. The only one who did not flee from him. He charged at her, entirely lost.

Siv stood her ground and took a deep breath. Just a young giant, she told herself. She had handled the rage of many young giants before, but the last time had been over two centuries ago.

With a loud growl, the giant charged. The forefathers made him target Siv. They knew that she was a long-lived, but they did not care. Their rage was too great for them to think clearly, if at all.

The rage within her was wild too, and as the giant approached, the rage got stronger. The urge to fight and kill made her taste blood.

Siv glanced up at the giant. There was only one way to stop him. She had to take on the forefathers' rage for him. All the rage he could not control. She matched his stare, and opened her fist to feel the forefathers. If she let more of them out, they would retreat from the giant. They would flood her instead for she was the stronger vessel. Willingly, she opened her fist, and let them.

The long-lived in front of her was too young to survive, but Siv could, if she were smart. She welcomed their rage. Revelled in their age-old anger. They took over.

THE SNAP OF fire brought Siv out of her berserker rage. She opened her eyes. She was standing outside Ash-hill, by the Christian church. She had thrown her spear away. Looking down, she realised she held the sundered arm of a Christian in her spear hand. She let it plop down to the ground.

She did not remember what had happened. The forefathers had taken over so completely that she had been pushed away from her own mind and was unable to remember anything. So completely that she had thought she might be lost to them forever.

Ash-hill burned. A black cloud of smoke hung over the town. There were southern corpses all the way up and down the streets. Killed by the forefathers in Siv's berserker rage.

The giant was nowhere to be seen. Siv closed her eyes and sniffed the air. She smelled him; he smelled of burnt rocks, and of moss too.

'I saved your life, at least reveal yourself,' Siv said, knowing that he was hiding from her, as he had been hiding from her all summer.

'You saved more than my life,' came the answer of a deep long-lived voice. Raw like fire, and familiar, although she knew that she had never heard the voice before.

The giant had let out his forefathers to come to her rescue on the battlefield, at the risk of losing himself, and no matter how Siv thought about it, she could find no reason for a long-lived to risk the centuries of life ahead of him for a slim chance to save another.

'I knew you would bring me back,' he answered to her unspoken question. He emerged from the flames of Ash-hill, comfortable as if that was where he belonged; in fire.

His arms and legs had cuts and bite marks that Siv knew had not been there when she had taken over his rage. They must have fought, the two of them, while the forefathers flooded her mind.

Despite his hood, his dark hair played in the soft breeze. He was young for a long-lived, perhaps no more than half a century old. And he was controlled. He had not let the forefathers go simply because he could not contain them within himself, as some young giants did.

'I've always wanted to meet you.' Again, he answered her unspoken question. If she had died in the battle, then he could not meet her. That was his reason for interfering. 'They never talk about you,' he said.

'Who are "they"?'

'Our parents.'

Siv had no brother, but she recognised his features. The green eyes, and heavy eyebrows were like her father's, and his pointy nose resembled her mother's. Siv had her mother's high eyebrows and golden hair, and her father's straight nose. This man had everything of their parents that Siv did not.

'Find me in the passage, when the time is right,' her brother said. 'When the Alfather isn't watching.' He turned away from her, and then he was gone.

RUNEMISTRESS

Chapter Twelve

THE CREAK OF the wooden floor gave the stranger away.

A young woman, less than half of Tress' age, stood in the doorway to the small hut. Her face was hidden in the shadows of her helmet, her tall, muscular body scarcely outlined by the moonshine, and her chainmail shone. Her hair was messy and bright, as Tress' own had once been, and in the young woman's hand was something bright and sharp. The blood on the axe did not drip off; it had dried and settled there. The kill had been made earlier in the night.

Wary and alert, Tress glanced around in search of her fylgja. Often it had come to her in the form of a hare to bring Tress warning. Her fylgja would show itself to her if this woman posed a threat. But Tress saw no hare. No other animal. Tonight was not a night she had to fear for her life.

'Are you the runemistress?' the woman asked and shifted to lean against the doorway. She was wounded.

'Perhaps,' was her answer. Tress had learnt the runes as a child. Her mother had borne the name before her and when her mother had died, Tress had been given it, her young name forgotten. But she was not *the* runemistress. Just Runemistress, or Tress. That was her name.

The woman did not speak, but stared at her fiercely. Judging, as if the woman could tell just by looking if Tress was the runemistress or not. A wind caressed the woman's blonde hair and pushed the door further open. Her expression softened.

'Perhaps?' the young thing repeated scornfully. 'Is it true or not?'

'Truth is but a word creatures like us gave meaning,' Tress answered.

'Spoken like a true runemistress,' the armed woman said, but she did not enter the hut, stayed by the threshold with her axe ready to slash if the words that came next did not please. 'Tell me my fortune,' she demanded.

'To receive you must give.' Tress rubbed the runes she had once painted into the skin on the back of her pale, wrinkled hand. 'Reveal your lineage so I can speak without fear.'

'I've killed,' the woman said in a husky and quiet voice. 'Not long ago.'

Threats did not give answers. Tress stayed calm and searched for her fylgja, but it did not show itself and that meant that this woman had no intention of harming Tress.

'I could kill you,' said the young woman.

'Kill me and gain no knowledge,' Tress snapped back.

The young woman hesitated in the doorway and then, she limped through, into the hut. Her steps heavy, yet careful, as though entering would trap her in a spider's web. 'I'm Hilda Ivardóttir, the smith's daughter,' the woman said and kept her distance.

'Well met, daughter of Ivar.' Tress' words brought a strange relief to Hilda.

Tress crouched down by the embers in her fireplace and covered them with three logs of wood. The smoke was thick at first, but soon enough the fire brightened her hut. She glanced at the runes. The ones the full moon night had made her carve into the wall. They were filled with shadows and appeared to be even deeper and darker with the light all about them.

She moved to the back of her hut, and sat down on the sleeping bench by the table on which her pouch rested, filled with carved runes. She gestured to the stool at the other side.

With hesitant steps, Hilda came further into the hut, past the fire, and collapsed onto the stool so her chainmail clinked. The blue dress she wore under her armour had a hole up the thigh, and the skin beneath had a wound; deep like Tress' runes. Yet the injury did not hinder Hilda's determination.

Hilda pulled off her helmet and shook her blonde hair free from their restraints. Her face was made of rough features, as if it had been carved. Her chin was angular like that of a warrior, and Tress had seen those sparkling blue eyes before.

'You're from Ash-hill,' Tress said, recognizing Hilda. It suddenly made sense to her. What she had seen in her visions last night. It had been the present, not the future as she had thought. 'You've come from the battle,' she said. 'You survived.'

'I didn't *survive*,' Hilda said scornfully. 'I cut my way out of there.'

'I saw,' Tress answered.

Tress and Hilda examined each other. Restlessness filled Hilda's eyes and something else too. Uncertainty. Hilda was hiding something, and Tress intended to find out what. 'Tell me what you seek, Hilda Ivardóttir.'

'My future—' Hilda glanced around the room before she continued, 'And I'd like to know about the whispers in the wind.'

'Whispers in the wind,' Tress repeated. A most unusual request. 'Can you pay?'

Hilda reached into her sleeve and forced a silver arm-ring off her wrist. She put it down on the table between them, eying it without letting go of it for a little while, as if she considered if it was worth to parting with it or not. Then she let go, but she still stared at the twisted arm-ring as if it meant something more to her than the cold piece of silver it was.

Tress reached in over the table and took. She pulled the ring over her wrist. A tight fit.

Hilda still clenched onto the bloody axe underneath the table.

Tress pulled her new silver arm-ring over her sleeve so its beauty would not be hidden. 'If you release your weapon, I'll speak with a thankful heart,' she said.

'I never leave my weapon. You've got your payment.'

'Then put the blade where both our eyes may look upon it.'

Hilda put the axe on the table. Her hand did not let go; tense and ready to pounce. So much mistrust was not good for the mind.

'Let's begin with your future,' Runemistress said, pushing her suspicions aside.

She reached for the leather pouch on the table. Inside were the runes she used for casting. Each one had been created with care, burnt into small pieces of wood, carved and coloured. She brought her hand into the pouch and caressed one of the flat, round coins with her thumb. Upon one side of each coin runes were carved. Her fingers knew each of them so well that she could tell which rune was on which wooden coin without looking.

This was her oldest set, the one she had created before her mother had passed, when she had borne a regular name.

This very set was the set she had used that once, when the one-eyed man had entered her hut. He had known all about the runes, even more than her. He had come in the night, as Tress' visitors usually did. She remembered how he had hidden his missing eye with his long grey hair and how his voice was deep, as if it came from the earth. His clothes had been made from blue linen, yet somehow it looked modest on him, like a rich man turned beggar.

From the moment his leather shoes had touched the floor of her hut, she had known who he was. Her heart had raced with the knowledge and she could hardly think, but he had made her sit and pull out her runes to read his future.

'I'm Bileyg,' he had said, but they both knew it was a lie. She had pulled out this very set of runes, caressed them as she did now, and read his future. He knew the runes better than her and he had taught her some, not much, but some, and although he had called himself Bileyg, she suspected, and mostly she knew, he had been Odin, the great god and Alfather; master of runes.

Tress glanced at Hilda and bent in over the table to brush it clean. The field for casting needed to be pure. 'I will pick out the first rune and cast it here.' She pointed to the centre of the table. 'Then you shall pick eight others, casting them in rows of three, like this.' Again, she pointed to the specific places. Three rows of three, nine runes in all. They would tell her everything she needed to know about Hilda.

As Tress reached down into the pouch and felt her way through, she kept her eyes on Hilda. A rune fell into her palm. She rubbed her fingers around the soft wood and pulled it out to cast it on the field at what would become the bottom right corner.

She passed the pouch to Hilda, who plunged a hand into it, refusing to let go of her axe with the other. Hilda cast the second rune onto the field, above the first. Thor's rune, the rune of chaos. The pieces found their way into Hilda's hands and soon the third emerged, Tyr's rune. Then Reid, put down in reverse, followed by Fe, the rune of wealth.

The young one had claimed to be the daughter of a smith; Hilda Ivardóttir. But the runes revealed a truth Hilda had not.

Hilda continued to cast runes, until nine of them lay in three rows on the field. Then she posed the pouch on the table and looked to Runemistress for interpretation.

'Fe, the rune of wealth,' Tress said and pointed to the fifth one, without touching it. 'It reveals your lies. Your true lineage carries wealthy blood.'

The blue-eyed woman did not answer.

'You asked me to be truthful, yet you were not.'

'Truth is but a word,' the woman who was not Ivar the smith's daughter repeated.

'A word with a meaning you asked of me, why should I help you when you bring weapons and lies?' Tress was more intrigued than previously. Why did the daughter of a blessed family lie and have so much mistrust? More so than before, she wanted to know the truth about the woman, but Tress did not appreciate being threatened. Hilda had wealthy blood, and powerful blood too, but even giants knew when to show respect.

'Because I paid you,' the woman snarled.

'I'll tell you because you have no other place to go.' And because she was curious. 'Remember that it's not the axe in your hand that gets you these answers.'

The young woman's grip on the handle tightened a bit. 'What do the runes say?'

'The runes in your wind, or the runes on my field?'

Involuntarily, Hilda's attention shifted to the wind, to listen to the whispers there.

'The whispers are getting louder, aren't they? Clearer?'

The way Hilda was barely able to sit still, and the way her concentration simmered away made it obvious that Tress was right.

'Tell me my future,' Hilda demanded. 'I paid you already.'

'Until you tell me your true lineage, my runes will remain devoid of meaning,' said Tress.

The woman rummaged and her tongue darted out to wet her dry lips.

Tress simply watched, and waited.

'I'm Hilda. Daughter of Ragnar Erikson, the late skald of the chief of Ash-hill.'

Tress had been right, wealth had meant rich blood and rich blood the woman had, although that was not all, but perhaps Hilda was not aware of the rest.

'Now I can see your destiny,' Tress said and moved her eyes to the cast runes.

She held her right hand above the significator, Pertho, the one she had picked herself, and eyed Hilda as she spoke. 'Although the thread of your destiny has already been spun by the nornir, you have a choice to change what has already been decided.' She moved her hand to the second rune, the first one Hilda had chosen; Thor's reversed rune of chaos. 'You can defeat death. And I believe you already have, at least once before, warned by your blue-eyed snow fox.'

Hilda did not move in the slightest, barely blinked, as if she did not want to let Tress know how accurate her reading was, but Tress knew that she was right.

Hilda had been destined to die, but she had survived; and now her destiny was not certain, although death was close behind, intending to catch up. Hilda knew what the snow fox meant, knew it came with death and doom. Although perhaps she was not truly aware of what the snow fox said of her ancient lineage.

Seeing the nature of someone was sometimes tricky and this particular reading was one Tress had never seen before, and maybe never would again, but in some ways, it reminded her of the one she had once given the one-eyed man who had called himself Bileyg. This was why Odin had done her the honour of a visit. This was the reading he had prepared Tress for.

Before he had left, their hands had touched, as he had given her the promised payment. His hand had been colder than the coins he had given her. A chill had travelled through her, and that fickle touch had changed everything. Suddenly she had known the runes better than ever before.

Tress moved her hand up the row, to Tyr's warrior rune at the top right corner of the field, and the traveller's reverse rune, next to it. 'A long time ago, you chose the path of the warrior, but you have been stalled from fights and missed your meeting with death.'

Her hand moved to the fifth rune. 'The rune of wealth is how I recognised your lies,' she said. 'It could not have been cast by the daughter of a smith.' Tress kept what else the rune told her to herself. It did not just speak of rich blood, but also of the old norn blood that flowed in Hilda's veins, though she doubted Hilda knew about that, and about how it provoked those whispers in the wind.

Tress moved her hand to the wooden rune closest to herself. It lay face down, not revealing its nature. She picked it up and turned it. Odin's messenger rune. She put the rune down as it had been cast. It was not commonly seen in relation to health, and this altogether was no ordinary reading.

'I see three admirers, and the time will come when you will have to choose who to trust,' Tress said, of the next two runes of necessity and wealth.

'The future.' She touched the very last rune with the tip of her finger. 'Isa.' She paused and glanced up at Hilda. Usually, the rune of ice represented a lack of movement, but in this case, it seemed to her as though Isa referred to Hilda's destiny: slippery and difficult. Ever changing.

'There is no future for you.'

Hilda narrowed her eyes as if to see the words and better understand them, but then she gave up, and asked instead. 'No future?'

You have escaped the holds of the nornir's plans, and even the gods no longer stand in your way, Tress thought, but answered otherwise. 'To begin with, the beginning had not begun,' she said, half incanting runes, not offering a challenge, but using the melody of flyting. 'Because change changes and does not change back. And, in the end, the ending will not come to an end.'

Hilda remained silent for a long moment. The wind blew through the open door and dimmed the fire. Tress noticed how much the young woman paid attention to the gust. How her head tilted towards the door, as though she listened to something outside.

The wind came and went and the flames shifted and then burned out, and still, Tress sat and waited. She doubted the young woman had understood the fortune that had been told. But some day, when the time was right, and when the events predicted came to pass, Hilda might remember what she had heard this very night, about the runes and her destiny, and then she would understand.

Hilda Ragnardóttir was no ordinary woman. *The runes speak to her*, Tress thought, *the nornir's blood flows through her. She hears their whispers, and perhaps someday she will control them.*

Tress fumbled with the wooden pendant that hung from her neck, caressed the engraved bindrune, and stared at the runes she had carved before Hilda had come.

Her runes had been deep enough to cut through the veil of the world, but already they were being undone. 'You're using my runes,' Tress muttered.

HILDA

Chapter Thirteen

THE WHISPERS IN the wind swirled around Hilda, louder than ever before. Almost as if the runemistress' hut gave them strength to speak. They were still muffled, but sometimes a word stood out. *Hang... Done... Corpse.*

Hilda stared across the table. Stared at the runemistress. She tried to keep her focus on the task at hand. Tried to ignore the whispers in the wind, like she had her whole life, but they were getting louder the longer she stayed. *Hanged... Done... Corpse... Rot.*

'You should listen to the nornir's whispers,' the runemistress said, and suddenly, the wild haired woman launched in over the table, and grabbed Hilda's hands. A cold sting went through Hilda, like Thor's lightning strike.

The voices in the wind picked up. They shouted where before they had been mutters. *The Hanged God will abandon you,* they howled.

Hilda cast her head around after the wind, to see where the whispers came from. Her eyes widened at their words. *In the river, your corpse will rot.*

Her sight snapped back to the runemistress. 'What did you do?' she hissed. She could barely hear her own voice over the loud snap of the wind's voices.

'I merely sharpened your hearing,' the woman replied.

The whispers were loud around her. The Runes, as the runemistress had called them. *The Hanged God will abandon you.* The same words over and over, like a loud warning call.

The great Alfather would not allow her into Valhalla should she die.

'You must follow them,' the runemistress urged. 'You must heed their warnings.'

Hilda put her helmet back on. It didn't do much to shield the loud voices of the Runes. At the runemistress' insistence, she limped out of the smoky hut. *In the river, your corpse will rot.*

Outside, her horse grassed in the moonlight. Hilda gathered its reins and mounted. Set its head north away from the runemistress' hut, up towards the hillside from where she could see the fiord to Ash-hill. From there she would be able to see the raiders' ships when they returned home.

The wind pushed against her. *North is for peril. In the river, your corpse will rot.*

The words made Hilda uneasy, and somehow, she couldn't help but wonder what the Runes knew that she didn't. Maybe the southerners were heading further north than Ash-hill, or maybe, they also waited for the warriors to return, like her.

She shook her head at herself. She wouldn't have doubted her decision if it hadn't been for the wind's whispers. If it hadn't been for the runemistress' warning.

She pressed her legs around the horse and forced it into trot.

North is for peril, the Runes whispered, louder than before. Their warning rang around her. *In the river, your corpse will rot.*

The snow fox appeared in her path. Hilda halted the horse, blinked, and then the fox was gone.

Warily, Hilda made the horse move forward again. Once more, the snow fox appeared. Exactly as it had, and then it barked at her. The snow fox was as convinced as the Runes that death waited for her further north.

Hilda turned the horse around. She rode south past the runemistress' hut, and up the steep hill on the other side. This time, the snow fox did not appear in her way. Not as she set into trot and rode on, but when she glanced back, over her shoulder, it was there. The snow fox ran after her, preventing her from going north. Preventing her from riding to her death.

DARKNESS

ODIN STOPPED IN his tracks. The Alfather turned away from the fight and ran, exactly as Ragnar had desperately wished.

At Ragnar's silent plea, the great Alfather fled the battlefield. Ragnar's thoughts had influenced Odin; there could be no other explanation, for the Alfather had been so certain of himself as he approached the huge wolf. Ragnar had made it happen.

His distaff pushed the Darkness far back. He scrambled down the mountainside of corpses and across the slippery blooded grass after his god, but he was not the only one to follow the Alfather. The great wolf Fenrir, too, had caught sight of Odin, and pursued him out of the crowd.

Never before had Ragnar run so fast, nor had he thought himself capable of it, but the urgency was too great not to run, for he ran not for his own life, but for the survival of the Alfather and all the nine worlds.

Odin was faster. Even Fenrir could not keep up. The Alfather disappeared into a hall. *Close the gates, close the gates,* Ragnar begged as he raced towards the hall. He barely made it inside before Odin closed the tall gates, listening to Ragnar's silent demands.

For a moment, the Alfather just stood there and stared at the great gate with his single eye. He seemed confused by the sight of it, by the knowledge that he had run. He rubbed his blooded beard, and clutched onto his famous, crooked spear like a walking stick that he leant on for support.

Ragnar let out a quiet sigh. The gates were locked. He had managed to save his god, even if Odin might not understand the reason behind his own actions. All that mattered was that the Alfather was safe from the wolf that was supposed to inflict his bane wound.

Odin clung onto his spear and moved away from the gates, down the hall. Guts from all sorts of beasts dangled from his jewelled chainmail and slapped down onto the floor, leaving a gory trail of pieces of ears, torn lungs, and flaps of skin.

Ragnar hurried after his god. His distaff pushed the Darkness back in pulses that matched his fast heartbeat. A fire ran down the middle of the hallway. The walls and the floor were made from smooth sand-coloured stones that reflected the light from the narrow fire, like mirrors. Ragnar's shoes were bloody, but unlike his god, his steps left no bloody traces. As if Ragnar wasn't there. Just a runemistress, watching the future with his distaff.

Something hammered against the gates from outside. Fenrir had reached them. Ragnar heard the wolf claw the wooden gate. At any moment, it would break through.

Barely had the thought formed in Ragnar's mind, before the gate broke. Wood splintered into the hallway. It clanked against the bright floor, and then the wolf's fangs wrenched an opening.

At Ragnar's side, Odin took his stance, unafraid, like before Ragnar had gotten involved. His spear was ready to welcome the wolf, sharp tip towards the target. Odin's single eye was focused, and his stance was solid like a trained warrior, but

Ragnar knew how this fight would end, and he saw only one solution.

Run, he urged his god. *Run from the wolf.* Incomprehension flashed across the Alfather's face, as he turned away from the wolf, away from the fight, and scrambled down the length of the hall.

The wolf burst inside. Its claws screeched across the floor.

As Ragnar had commanded, the Alfather continued to run, but even Ragnar could see that the wolf was too fast. Down the hallway it hunted Odin. Its teeth snapped out after his heels.

Fight it, Ragnar commanded, but there was no time for Odin to act out his wishes. The wolf clasped its sharp teeth down over Odin's arm, threw him to the side. Odin's helmet fell off. The beast snapped out and tore off the Alfather's scalp.

Odin's spear clanged against the stone floor, and the Alfather fell to the ground. The wolf growled and dug into Odin's guts, ripping them out, and fed on the Alfather's corpse. The corpse of a god.

Horrified, Ragnar watched. Tears fell down his cheeks at the sight he had so often told stories about. To witness it was something different, and he had never thought it would have been such an honourless death. Worse was the fear that filled Ragnar then, that it had only happened because he had commanded Odin to run. Perhaps the reason Odin was destined to be killed by Fenrir was not because he would have lost in a fight on Ragnarok's battlefield, but merely because Ragnar had urged him to run.

Odin had approached the wolf with confidence, so certain of his move, despite what the premonitions said. He must have known he could win in a fight, and then Ragnar had ruined it all.

The wolf was tearing the proud god apart, limb from limb, and gnawing on his bones. Odin's single eye was wide open. His brain hung out of his crushed skull.

Ragnar just wanted the wolf to stop and leave the Alfather,

and in that exact moment, right as Ragnar thought it, Fenrir turned around and peered back. It was not the loud fight outside that the wolf looked at; it was Ragnar himself who had caught the great wolf's eyes.

He gulped and spun around. He ran with all his might, down the hallway, away from the wolf and his dead god, and everything. He shook his head as he ran. Refused to believe that this was happening. Not the wolf, not the huge beast. He thought it as loudly as he could, in the hope that Fenrir would hear him and obey, like Odin had. But Fenrir was not a god, and the big monster did not listen to Ragnar.

High-pitched screeches echoed when the wolf's claws scratched against the stone floor. The deep snarl that threatened to make all nine worlds disappear came closer with every heartbeat.

Ragnar continued to run.

He could not die like this. He had not given himself away, had not said a single word.

But that did not matter, for the wolf was coming for him, close behind, and his god was already dead. The beast's snarls made the fear inside Ragnar mount, and he could no longer keep himself from screaming. He yelled and ran as fast as he could, but the beast was faster.

Fenrir snapped his sharp teeth and caught Ragnar's shoulder. It felt like a dozen daggers poked through his flesh, and through his bones and lung.

The wolf released him and snapped again, and this time Fenrir caught his legs. Ragnar's head smacked hard against the stone floor as his feet were lifted into the air. His body was thrown from side to side, his legs torn to pieces. He yelled, screamed, cried. He was stabbed by the beast's teeth, and his head hit the stone floor again, and again, as he was thrown about, until the last bite caught around his neck and he could smell death from deep down the beast's throat.

Death, pain, and fear.

TYRA

Chapter Fourteen

A VOICE CRIED and wailed through the Darkness, a scream that got more and more desperate and seemed to come from every direction and none at all. Then there was a loud crunch, like the sound of bone breaking, and the scream stopped.

Tyra was shaking from fear. Her heart raced, loud in her chest. Her eyes searched through the Darkness, but there was nothing to see. Nothing to hear anymore, either.

She closed her eyes and wished and wished that Siv would come and get her out of this dark tree. She couldn't climb out on her own. She couldn't even find the exit.

Tears raced down her cheeks and she didn't remember any calming thoughts. Her mother, and her father, and her sisters; none of them were going to come for her. Maybe Siv wouldn't come either. Maybe the southerners had killed her and she would never come for Tyra. Maybe Tyra would die in the dark. A slow and honourless death of starvation. She would never go to Valhalla.

Already, it felt as if she had stayed in this dark for an entire night, and three nights, and longer than that, as long as she could remember, and at the same time, it felt as if she had just arrived.

Another distant scream pierced the Darkness. Tyra jolted and closed her eyes really tight, trying to wish herself away.

'Tyra,' Siv's voice called out, and right as Tyra was about to yell out to it, Siv stopped her. 'Don't say anything. Reach up for my hand.'

Tyra looked above her, but there wasn't anything to see. She reached up, although she knew there was nothing there. She had tried to find the exit so many times before.

Her hand knocked against something cold.

'Grab my hand.'

Tyra found the cold hand and grabbed onto it, and with a jolt, she was pulled upwards and out of the Darkness into Siv's warm embrace.

The night was loud with the snaps of fire and the call of crows. The light of flames in the night was blinding after the Darkness. The smell of rot and puke surrounded them. Tyra blinked to look around the inner circle. She smelled a fire burning, and when her vision settled, she saw the smoke everywhere in town. Ash-hill was burning.

'Come, Tyra. We need to leave,' Siv urged and got them both to their feet.

The circle was filled with corpses. They lay thick around the ash-tree, where they had taken their last stand. They had been dead for at least a day, maybe two days, for Tyra thought she saw maggots move on the corpses' faces.

Siv dragged Tyra to her feet. 'We need to go, come on,' she urged, but Tyra still stared at the corpses and tried to make sense of it all, and then she glanced back to the ash-tree, but it wasn't there.

The tree had fallen and all that was left was a hacked, uneven stump. Their holy ground had been ruined. The ash lay on top of the ten Ting stones, and there was no hole in the tree. None at all.

Siv took Tyra's hand and forced her to move. Tyra's legs were shaking. Her head was fixed in the direction of the fallen tree. The orange leaves danced in the smoking night wind. The tree was rotting along with the many corpses.

The inner circle smelled of a funeral, only much worse. Flames rose from houses down the road. Tyra hunched over as they walked down the smoky road filled with corpses. They walked faster than Tyra liked, for it was dark, almost as dark as inside the tree, and there were corpses everywhere.

She stumbled over another corpse and looked down.

The helmet had rolled off her mother's head. Her blue-pale cheeks had been pierced by a spear, her eyes were wide open but far away, and her face looked like it had been painted on. Tyra felt her knees weaken at the sight, but Siv's resolution to keep going made it impossible for her to linger.

Siv pulled her ahead. Tyra stumbled over her mother's dead body. Tears and sweat dripped from her chin and dried in the heat of the fires and the wind in the night.

They passed the open southern gate. Halfway towards the Christian church, Siv let go of her hand and brought them both to a stop. Finally, Tyra could breathe.

'You were brave, Tyra,' Siv said. 'It's over now.' She leant down to give Tyra a warm hug, and the embrace, and the words of reassurance, made Tyra feel a hundred different emotions at once. She had been so afraid of the dark, and the fight, and death, and of the scream in the Darkness, and the southerners outside, and she had thought she would never ever get out, and now her home was burning and her mother was dead.

The tears burst out before she realised what was happening and she wailed into Siv's strong arms. 'Mother,' she cried and cried.

'It's over, Tyra.' Siv caressed her armoured back. 'The battle is finished. You're with me now.'

The words made Tyra cry all the more, because her parents weren't there and they never would be and her sisters wouldn't come either and it felt like there was no one in the nine worlds but her and Siv, because everyone else was dead.

Siv continued to hug her, and caress Tyra's back, and with every caress from Siv, Tyra calmed a little. Soon her wailing stopped and then the tears too and she sniffed to dry her runny nose. 'What happens now?' she asked.

'Now I take you to the winter campsite with the other children. And then, soon, the warriors will be home from their raids and they will keep you safe.'

'But—' Tyra didn't want to say it, but as she looked at the flaming town, all she could think was that she no longer had a home, and everyone who had used to belong there was gone. Ash-hill was gone.

'The town will have to be rebuilt,' Siv completed for her. 'The warriors will come home soon, and when they do, they will rebuild.' She said it so simply that it almost made Tyra feel like this was no more of a problem than an old fence that had to be redone, but then she noticed that Siv hadn't said that that *she* would come back.

'What about you?'

Siv didn't answer that question.

'Wherever you're going, I'll go.' Tyra's lips trembled and her nostrils flared. 'I don't want to come back here,' and she tried not to cry again, but she couldn't help herself.

The town snapped with fire at their backs.

'We will go together, then,' Siv gave in. She dried Tyra's tears with her cold hand and lifted Tyra up to her feet.

They began to walk out towards the forest. Siv's hair lit up because of the light from the flames from Ash-hill and her smile seemed to caress Tyra and tell her that all was well.

Tyra slipped her hand into Siv's. 'I'm yours, now,' she said. 'Don't leave me.'

With Siv she felt safe. Siv was such a strong, beautiful woman, she almost couldn't be human. But Siv wasn't prettier than most other women, but she had something no one else did: a kind of light that shone out from her, almost. Though it wasn't visible, just something that Tyra could feel sometimes when Siv smiled.

'What are you?' Tyra finally asked. The question had burned at the back of her throat since the beginning of the battle when she had first noticed the extent of Siv's power.

'Much the same as you.'

Tyra didn't question it, but she knew, like Siv, that it wasn't the truth. They were different, ever so different. Tyra couldn't pull arrows out of her own shoulder without so much as flinching. She couldn't make a dozen warriors fall with a simple push from a shield, and she couldn't make people do as she wanted simply by staring at them, or taking their hand.

She couldn't open secret hiding places either. 'Siv... What was that place in the tree?'

Siv didn't answer, so Tyra thought up another question. She had so many, she hardly knew where to start. How had Siv survived the battle? Being strong did not seem like enough to scare away thousands of southerners. How had Siv hidden Tyra away in that tree? Why hadn't Tyra been able to get out on her own? How had Siv pulled her out again when all that was left of the ash was a stump? There were so many questions to ask, but Tyra supposed that only one of them really mattered.

'What was sacrificed?' she asked. 'What was the price for saving my life?'

Being hidden away in the Darkness inside the tree had saved Tyra's life. Old Ragnar had always said that no gift was free, least of all the gift of life. It had to be expensive.

'No price,' Siv said. 'It was just a hiding place.'

They both knew that wasn't true. Tyra hadn't simply crawled up into a tree, she had disappeared *into* one. She had never heard of anyone capable of doing that. Only in the old sagas. The tales of future. Of the survival of human kind after the fall of gods and giants. At Ragnarok, a girl and boy would hide inside a tree, to survive the final battle. That was what the stories of future told. The price for their survival would be the death of everyone else.

The price for Tyra's survival would be steep too.

Siv seemed to know that her answer hadn't been convincing enough. 'The price is my burden, Tyra,' she eventually said. 'Not yours.'

Tyra wanted to argue, because she was the one who had crawled into the Darkness, so she knew that the price could not solely be Siv's to pay. She too would have to pay, someday. She tried to say so, but when she looked into Siv's eyes, her voice was sealed away by Siv's stare.

She couldn't force any words out, and she knew she ought to be scared of Siv and what she could do, but Tyra had no one else to trust in all of Midgard, so she simply buried her questions deep within and clenched Siv's hand.

Hand in hand, they stumbled down the road towards the forest.

Bodies were piled on top of each other by the Christian church. The southerners had tried to get through the door into their holy church, but they had been killed. They too had paid a price for their actions. They had attacked Ash-hill and killed Tyra's family and friends. The price paid was steep but fair. In the end, they had been abandoned by their god.

HILDA

Chapter Fifteen

THE HANGED GOD will abandon you, the northern wind reminded Hilda.

She had to appease the gods, or the Alfather wouldn't allow her into Valhalla in the afterlife.

Hilda rode along a lilac heath. Two days since the battle and her battle wounds had already begun to heal. The spear wound in her thigh too. She still limped, and worried that she always would, like her father had.

There had been nowhere to rest up. All of Jutland had been ravaged by southerners. The gods were angry and needed to be appeased. It was good she hadn't stayed in northern Jutland and waited for the warriors to return home. Someone needed to act, and Hilda was the only one there to do it.

Her chainmail clinked as she rode, and her helmet weighed her down. Even the axe in her weapon belt was heavy. The mare was tired too, but not like Hilda. The horse had rested while Hilda had been kept awake by the whispers in the wind.

Rain and thunder will mark the plunder, the Runes whispered through the wind.

Hilda watched the threatening sky. Rain and thunder. Her mare was growing uneasy at the approaching storm. They needed to find shelter, but on the heath, the best she could see was a jotun passage grave, and only the gods knew what kind of forces hid in old gravemounds. Gravemounds poked up from the old heather-covered field, but only one of them had a passage that might provide shelter. She had passed it already.

A blurry line of rain gathered on the horizon. Hilda threw away the rest of the bitter root she had been chewing and licked her teeth clean. She pressed her legs around the horse and trotted across the heath towards the woods far ahead. The broad, yellow leaves would at least provide some shelter.

The wind whipped against her face, and whispered. *The Hanged God will abandon you.*

The sky rumbled. The horse neighed and lifted its head. It stopped up. Its head settled in the direction of an ancient gravemound the length of a longhouse ahead. A lone tree grew on top.

'Come. Come. All is good,' Hilda told the horse and clapped it on the neck. The mare's body was tense and attentive. Something was amiss.

The whispers in the wind told her what the horse had sensed.

Rain and thunder will mark the plunder, the Runes repeated. This time Hilda listened, and understood what they wanted to say. Hilda wasn't alone at the far edge of the Oxen Road. She couldn't tell if the Runes wanted to warn her about a plunderer or if they wanted *her* to plunder. Either way, it didn't matter.

She kicked the horse into trot to reach the nearby gravemound on top of which a lone tree grew. Behind the gravemound she glided off the horse's back and hoped the small grave would keep them both out of sight. The lilac heather and wild grasses reached her knees.

Hilda removed her helmet to look less suspicious, bound it to the horse's saddle next to her shield so she wouldn't lose it. Her dress still showed bloodstains; she had tried to remove them but they had dried into the skirt.

A heavy drop fell on her forehead. Rain poured over the yellow and red thicket of a forest ahead, and then over the flowers around her. The drops hit hard, almost stung as they landed.

Hilda leant against the gravemound to peer ahead. The high, dark yellow grasses prickled the palms of her hands. She narrowed her eyes to keep out the rain that dripped from her eyebrows.

Through the dense rain she saw a wagon drawn by an ox, trundling from the forest path. It was too heavily loaded to move fast across such bumpy land.

A strange choice for anyone with a wagon to travel off the Oxen Road in rainy weather. Anyone in such a hurry, and who didn't travel the safest and fastest way, couldn't have honest motives. Mostly thieves or outlaws travelled like this, she knew. If he was an outlaw she was legally expected to kill him. He would be branded, but she wouldn't be able to tell until she came closer. The Runes seemed to want her to think that the figure ahead was a thief, but Hilda didn't want to presume anything. The wagon-rider could also be travelling off the Oxen Road because of the southerners, like her.

The heavy rain blurred the figure ahead. The rigid grass on the gravemound tickled Hilda's neck, and for a moment she thought she saw whoever had been buried there, hundreds and hundreds of winters ago. A draugar rose through the grass; a man, pale and bony, stared right at her, but his eyes had long been eaten by worms and left only dark holes. His hiss came, not in the wind like the Runes, but directly in her head. Her heartbeat caught in her throat. Hilda pushed away from the gravemound, and the draugar simmered back into the high grass.

She gulped and stared at the spot where she had seen the draugar. The ancient dead ought to never be disturbed. She hoped she hadn't woken him; she didn't need any more misfortune and death.

Hilda turned her eyes back to the wagon. It bumped over the uneven ground of the heath with difficulty and tipped, one of the wheels catching in mud. The ox struggled to pull it out and the man jumped off to push from behind.

Lightning struck in the distance, behind the man and his wagon.

'Rain and thunder mark the plunder,' Hilda whispered. No doubt remained as to what the Runes wanted her to do. The excitement of it all made her heart race. Listening to the Runes felt like the games of dare-or-die that she and Einer had used to play as children, only real.

Hilda took three short breaths and leapt out from behind the mound. She approached the muddled figure in the dense rain. Her dagger was in her belt behind her back, and her axe hung exposed at her hip. The downpour covered the sound of her steps, but her chainmail rustled.

She glanced back to the gravemound to make sure the mare waited where she had left it, but the rain was too heavy to see that far.

'Well met,' the ox-riding man shouted before she could turn back towards him and his wagon. 'I was going to ask for help, I thought you were a man. Forgive, the rain blurred my vision,' he said.

His brown hair stuck to his forehead and half-shielded a scar that covered the right side of his face. 'It's unusual for women to travel alone,' he said and glanced up and down at her.

He wore a green coat with a fur ridge at the top and dull brown clothes underneath. He didn't look like a merchant. From how he talked to her, he had to be a Christian—or someone who had grown up in the south, both were much the same. So, he didn't travel off the Oxen Road because of the southerners. Had to be an outlaw or a thief, then. A man dangerous and deadly to anyone who came too close, and Hilda already had.

'Going north?' she asked in return.

The man shook his head, carefully so his hair didn't part from his face and reveal the ugly scar he tried to hide. 'East. Sealand to trade.'

He didn't look like a trader. His clothes were too simple, out of fashion, and his posture was huddled, not proud, like the merchants Hilda knew.

'You look cold,' he said. 'Care to buy a fur?'

'You selling?' She walked closer to have a better look, pretending to be an interested buyer.

The man smiled slyly and reached for a large wooden chest on the wagon, dragged it to the edge and opened it a little so the lid still shielded the contents from the rain. Inside it were all kinds of furs. There was even an expensive white snow fox coat. 'I sell silks too,' he announced. 'But they might ruin in the rain.'

She nodded. Though the Runes had told her to steal, these weren't things she had any interest in. There had to be something else. Well, maybe she could use a fur to keep warm at night.

Lightning struck again right as Hilda noticed the full coin pouch hanging from the man's belt. The Runes' intentions were clear. She didn't have anything to trade for shelter or food.

Hilda fondled the furs, and glanced at the seller. He was a thief and murderer, she told herself. He had stolen the wagon and ox, and these furs too, and from the way he had glanced at her when he had first seen her, he wanted to steal from her too.

The rain poured over them. Hilda glanced around. If the snow fox was there, it would make itself known. It always did if she was in danger. But it was nowhere, and the Runes had no news for her. They had told Hilda what they wanted, and the runemistress had told Hilda to listen to them.

'How much is that fur, there?' she asked and pointed to the chest, to no particular fur at all.

'This one?' the man asked and lifted a sheepskin at the top of the chest ever so slightly, so it wouldn't get wet. With his right hand, he reached for something at the front of his wagon.

He stretched so the flesh at his neck became visible from under his coat. Hilda caught the flicker of something white. Her snow fox. Quick as the lightning above, Hilda reached for her dagger and sliced through the man's wet skin so quickly that he didn't have time for words. She caught him as he fell, held him up by his moist armpits.

His right hand was tight around the hilt of a seax, his knuckles were white from the death grip. He must have hidden the weapon on the wagon, and was reaching for it when she had asked about the fur. Had she hesitated, her throat would have been slit, not his.

'Never underestimate your prey,' she told him.

The rain washed the blood from the man's neck. His eyes were already distant like her father's had been, and his face contracted with a horror no one would see.

His soaked body and coat weighed her down. Her fingers, slick with blood, fiddled for the coin pouch and released it from the man's belt. She placed him with his back against the mud-locked wheel, opened the pouch—already stained with his blood, or maybe that of its previous owner—and took a look. A dozen silver coins filled it to the top.

It felt like stealing to take the bloody pouch, but the man at her feet was an outlaw and a thief, and such people had no possessions. If he didn't own anything, how could she steal from him?

She tied the pouch to her own belt, then washed her dagger in the rain, polished it on her skirt and slid it back into her leather belt. From the wagon, she grabbed a curly sheepskin but left the rest untouched. A woman with too much would be noticed. Especially this far south, it was best to go unnoticed. She clawed through the wagon and found some dried meat to chew on as well. Not much, but enough to sustain her for a day or two.

She released the dark brown ox, which still faithfully trying to pull the wagon out of the mud.

'Go find a new master,' she said and clapped the ox to move it along. The ox disappeared across the muddy heath. The rain had become so heavy that she could hardly see three arm-lengths ahead.

Hilda walked back in the direction of the gravemound where she had left her horse. She did her best to avoid the muddiest areas on the heath. A difficult task, and she promised herself to light a fire tonight so she could wash her clothes and warm herself. She needed it.

She reached the mound with the lone tree on top and looked for her horse. She circled the mound, twice, but the mare was gone. The rain was too thick. No chance of finding it in this weather. At once she regretted having released the ox.

Rain had already soaked her dress. Her long hair fell out of its braid and down the sides of her face. Her helmet and shield were still fastened to the horse's saddle. She should never have taken them off. Not even the nornir knew where her ride was now.

'Head-cleaving mare,' she grumbled. At least she hadn't taken off her chainmail.

The heath's high grasses produced a hiss that reminded Hilda of the old draugar she had seen. Immobile, she stared at the gravemound to her left, barely breathing so as not to be heard. Another wind hissed and a dark shadow approached in the rain at the foot of the grave. The draugar.

Hilda rushed away, in the direction of the woods, though she couldn't see them through the gloomy rain. She went fast so the grave corpse wouldn't be able to follow her.

The draugar must have spooked the horse. No wonder it had left without her.

'I've got your coins,' she told the wind as she ran. 'Where to now? How do I appease the gods?'

South forged will be an offering to please, the Runes whispered in response to her wishes.

'You want me to follow the southerners into their godless lands?' Hilda asked in disbelief. The mere thought of it made her flare with anger. 'After everything they did.' Yet she couldn't go north; the snow fox blocked her way and warned her of death whenever she turned around. There was only one way to go.

Hilda's stare hardened as she ran through the rain with new purpose. 'If I go south, I won't come back. I'll appease the gods in more ways than one.'

EINER

Chapter Sixteen

EINER COUGHED FOR air. His bracteate burned into his scarred chest and jerked him to life. He had thought he had died. His body felt so weak he could not find the strength to sit up, so he lay as still as he could, felt the warmth of his furs, and hoped the pain would subside.

'Osvif!' someone yelled above Einer. 'He's awake!'

Einer opened his eyes, and for a heartbeat or two, the bright light blinded him.

A warrior popped in and out of sight as he rowed. He flashed a yellow smile when he saw Einer's open eyes. 'Welcome back to this life,' he said.

Einer felt the rock of the ship. He wondered how long the warriors had been rowing. Last he remembered was a storm, but perhaps that had been nothing more than a fevered dream. The previous times he had woken, he had taken no more than a glimpse. He could not keep track of the days, and he had thought he would not need to keep track. He had thought he would die.

His hands tightened around the hilt of his sword. He felt his shield at his back. He was laid out on the deck of the ship like a dead warrior. No one had thought he would survive.

'He's alive?' a familiar voice shouted above Einer.

A warm hand graced against Einer's left cheek. Startled, he flinched away from it.

'You've come back, my friend,' said Osvif and felt Einer's forehead for a fever. His hands were burning like the bracteate at Einer's neck. 'I thought we had lost you to Valhalla.'

'I won't die so easily,' Einer said to dismiss the voice in his head that said he would die within the day. It hurt to speak. His voice was a wheeze and his lips were both itchy and bloody.

'How long have I been here?' he asked, to show his resolve to survive. A dying man would have no reason to ask such a question.

'It's Moon's day,' Osvif answered.

Three days since the night by the tavern, then.

'I told them you wouldn't die like this, I told them,' Osvif's voice broke.

Einer forced his eyes open. His eyelids were heavy and his body was difficult to control, as if he had forgotten how to make it obey his commands after laying down ready to die for so long.

Immediately, Einer noticed the unfamiliar rowing thwarts, and the unfamiliar feel of the planks under his feet. He was not on his own ship. This was the *Wave Crusher*.

The rower from before had given up his rowing place for Osvif. All the rowers were staring at him. They rowed on half oars which meant that there were twenty warriors, ten on each side, rowing in a slow rhythm. If this was as fast as they could row, they must have rowed for long already.

Osvif pressed his curly red hair away from his face and Einer knew well that Osvif only did that when he was worried. Finally, Osvif looked down at Einer for answers. 'What happened?'

'I don't remember,' Einer said, although he did.

'I was ready to tell everyone how you bravely killed a great winged snake while the rest of us were busy drinking, and how you had to allow it to claw you to get close enough to kill it. "And that is the story of Einer Vigmerson's bane," I'd say.'

'I won't die,' Einer insisted to reassure Osvif that he would not have to part with a friend this summer too. Last summer, their old friend Ralf had joined Valhalla's ranks and the one before it had been Osvif's father.

'Why am I on your ship?' Einer asked.

'You needed someone to look after you.' Osvif nodded towards a young warrior. 'Arne learnt from my father. The chief put Finn in command of the *Northern Wrath*.'

After what he had done, Finn dared to sail home in Einer's ship, and there was nothing Einer could do about it, not now, not in this state. At least someone would benefit from Einer's death.

'Can I borrow your mirror?' Einer asked his old friend.

Osvif coughed awkwardly. 'Lost mine on the way out.'

'No wonder you look like a troll,' Einer chuckled, but the resulting pain in his stomach made him stop quick. He knew that Osvif wanted to spare him the sight, but he needed to know how bad it was.

Einer pulled his sword from its scabbard and held it up, to see himself in the reflection of the smooth blade. His flesh was pale. It had never been so pale before. His eyes were distant as though life was leaving him. Black waves curled under his eyes and made him look like a corpse. His lips were badly chapped, and that explained why it hurt to speak. Einer glared at his reflection. It reminded him of how Ragnar had looked at the very end.

All of this because of Finn Rolfson. One drunk moment of blood rush.

His chest burned too much for him to move far, but Einer let the sword fall to his side and sat up against the side of the ship. His wound was bound, but fresh blood soaked through from his movements. Young Arne sprang forward and begun to remove the long piece of bloody cloth. The last sliver clung onto the wound and Einer clenched his teeth when Arne tore it off.

His whole belly seemed like it had taken blows. He was black and blue all about, and the skin around the gash was green where herbs had been used in an attempt to cure him. The wound was deeper than Einer remembered it to be, and it had not succeeded in scarring. The edges were blue and green, as if his skin was rotting. No wonder they all thought he would die.

Fresh blood flowed from the gash down over his lower stomach and onto his trousers. Arne said something about having to bind the wound again, and went to work.

He was going to die. Einer had never seen anyone recover from a wound like that; it was already a wonder he had survived for as long as he had. He would not make it back home.

'You dressed me for a funeral,' Einer said.

They had dressed him in his best tunic, placed his hands on his sword, and from his neck they had hung the gold bracteate his mother had given him.

'Ja, and then you woke up, as if you felt the jolt of the jewellery being hung from your neck.'

The gold neck-ring felt like it burned all the way to his heart. He could hardly breathe. His chest blazed with heat, but the more his chest burned, the more bearable the pain in his stomach became.

All Einer hoped was that he would not die there, but would survive long enough for their arrival home, and get one last glimpse of Ash-hill, to see Hilda smile to him one last time.

'Are you good, Einer?' asked his friend.

Einer did not answer for he did not yet know the answer.

With a force he knew himself capable of, but doubted the others did any longer, Einer grabbed his sword and rose to his feet. The sudden movement blurred his vision with white spots. Osvif offered his shoulder, so with Osvif's support, Einer walked aft out along the ship. The warriors gaped at him in bewilderment as Einer balanced on top of rowing thwarts, almost too easily, and made his way to the aft-ship with Osvif.

'How can you stand with a wound like this?'

Osvif was right to ask. The pain shot through Einer's body with every movement, yet, he somehow thought that if he did not acknowledge the cut, it would eventually cease to hurt. Besides, the burning skin under his bracteate hurt more, and not entirely in a foul way.

Cringing as if he too could feel the pain, Osvif helped Einer lean against the helmsman's bench at the very back of the ship where the two sides of it met and the tail curled upwards.

Ash-hill's three other ships sailed in front of the *Wave Crusher*. The ships rowed along the familiar shores of home. The flat land of Jutland stretched at either bank of the outer fiord.

'We'll be home soon,' Einer observed, determined to stay alive long enough to get home.

Soon they passed the pole blocks by Geese-swamp's fishing village. Hundreds of times before, Einer had sailed into their fiord from the Limsound, but through the eyes of his dying body everything seemed both familiar and new to him.

Einer leant out the side of the ship to look down at the sand-bed below. The waters were nice and shallow and the sand fine and yellow, not coarse as most of the beaches abroad. Einer smiled when he saw small fish swim away, shoved to the side by the waves the ship produced. Even they felt familiar, as if he knew every fish and each of them swam along the side of the longship to greet him. Geese took flight and flew right past them. Einer gazed at them until they were too far away to be seen. The birds, the fish, and the landscape, all seemed to welcome him home, for the last time.

He was glad he had survived so long; perhaps he would get it as he wanted it, and would be able to set eyes on Ash-hill. The village was most beautiful with the golden colours of early winter he supposed it would have now. Perhaps he would be able to see Hilda smile to him in his last moments. That would be decent. That would be good.

When the rowers brought in their oars, they chanted the homecoming song:

A ship is for swift journeys
And a shield for protection,
A sword for blows
And a maiden for kisses.

Einer muttered the words with them. No one could remember the rest of the song, at least not without the help of a chanter, so they repeated the same verse over and over and a few of the shieldmaidens on board insisted that it was "a man for kisses," and not a maiden at all, as the rest of them knew it was.

Einer's hand tightened around the hilt of his sword. His chest burned worse than ever before.

Arne approached with a washed and fresh cloth to bind Einer's stomach. The fabric of Einer's overtunic stuck to his wound and he winced when Arne ripped it off. The cut must have bled again. Arne moved closer to examine the wound, but the clean-shaven warrior did not wrap it.

'I don't under—' Arne began and looked up at Osvif for confirmation.

Osvif leant in close as well, and squinted as if he could barely see from all the sunlight. 'Einer, your wound…' was all he managed before his voice faded, as though he could not believe what he was about to say.

Einer glanced down at his stomach, expecting the rot to have spread. Instead, the black and blue colours, which had covered his stomach when he had woken up, were gone. The cut had scarred. The skin around the wound was pink, like a new-born's.

'I truly thought you would leave us for Valhalla,' Osvif laughed.

Nothing could explain it, except for Einer's mother's bracteate, hot against his chest.

He had taken it off before he had collapsed, although she had told him to always keep it on. Now he knew why, and embraced the burn more easily. The gold necklace kept him alive. For some reason, an ancient artefact had deemed him worthy of life. The work of gods.

Einer smiled with newfound hope as they carved into Ash-hill's inner fiord. His mind full of memories, he eyed the top of Rat Mountain where the two cow-tit gravemounds stood and remembered how Sigismund had been disappointed the first time they had sailed this way together with their parents as young kids. Proudly, Einer had pointed out what, to him, had been one of the tallest mountains he had ever seen. Sigismund had laughed and said: "That's not a mountain, it's a bump in the earth." Only when they had sailed to Frey's-fiord and Einer had seen the great mountains Sigismund called hills had he understood why his friend had laughed. After that, they had given the mountain at home a new name: Rat Mountain, and Einer had never looked at it in the same way.

He had many memories up there. As a young man, before his raids, he had often stood on top of Rat Mountain between the gravemounds and looked out over the waters, hoping to see Ash-hill's longships arrive. The guards by that warning pyre were the nicest. He had used to take a horse, so he could ride back to Ash-hill and welcome the warriors home with the rest of the villagers. Twice he had taken Hilda up there too, but she did not like to wait around.

Einer snickered, recalling once when she had lit the warning pyre because she had been too bored. The villagers had put up full defences and closed Ash-hill's gates, expecting an invasion, but instead Einer and Hilda had ridden home, after a hasty escape from the two angry guards on Rat Mountain. They had gotten into a lot of trouble for that.

Einer searched the tree-less hill. He supposed either Tormod or Torsten would be up by the pyre today, but he could see neither of them, and as they sailed closer, the homecoming horn was not blown. No one was up there to keep a watchful eye on the horizon and Einer knew what that meant.

'The warning pyres,' he muttered as he stared at the empty top of Rat Mountain. 'They've burned the warning pyres!' he yelled with more force.

Einer reached for Osvif's blowing horn, fastened at the warrior's hip. With all the strength he had in his stomach he gave it a proper blow. His burning bracteate hammered against his chest. The sound resonated across the waters. Thrice he blew it, so they would all notice, and know.

The crew muttered amongst themselves, and soon yells and shouts resonated, and many blew their horns to announce their arrival. They all hoped, together, that it was not as it seemed, but when there was no answer to the cries of their horns, they knew not to expect a welcome.

It did not take long before the yells and the sad echo of their horns died, and all they heard was their warships pushing through the inner fiord and the wind pulling at their clothes. No one sang anymore.

It seemed like an eternity passed before they reached the harbour. The fishing boats rocked in their places. All of the boats were there, on a nice day like this. The harbour lay abandoned.

They docked their longships by the port. Einer's father told the warriors to keep their calm but he also ordered them to bring carry their weapons and prepare for the worst.

Einer leapt off the *Wave Crusher* with the others. The harbour was lifeless. No guards stood on the hill by the small house and tents. Death had roared nearby, but not in the harbour; the battle had been fought elsewhere. In the air was a faint smell of smoke. They all thought it together, although no one said it: Ash-hill.

The warriors ran inland. Their steps were heavy and Einer could not hear anything around him; he did not know if it was because no one talked, or because his ears were ringing.

Einer too wanted to run inland to reach Ash-hill, but he did not have the strength, so instead, he stumbled through the crowd towards the river-boats. Each small boat had six oars and could take ten warriors, but most were too impatient to sit and row. Einer had already put two oars in the water, ready to row on his own, when Osvif and Hormod climbed in and forced the oars out of his hands.

'Don't strain yourself,' said Hormod. His long grey hair was hidden by his helmet. He was dressed for battle, had put on his chainmail and taken his shield. Most of the warriors were as fight-ready as Hormod, and Einer felt bare without his armour and shield, not that he had strength to carry either.

Osvif's expression was grim. His teeth were clenched together. Osvif had already lost hope for his family, Einer realised; his wife was from abroad, terrible at fighting, and his daughters were too young to learn. Had Osvif been anyone else, Einer would have assured him that his family would be fine, but Osvif was a clever man and Einer did not know any words to soothe his worried mind.

Osvif and Hormod began to row them upstream. Something white fell and settled in Osvif's red hair. A snowflake, and then one more, and when Einer peered up at the sky he saw grey snow fall. It settled in their hair, on their shoulders, and fell into the flowing stream. Ashes from Ash-hill.

The smoke inland was deadly and destructive, but there were darker things in the air than the smoke and ashes; crows circled above their town. There were corpses in Ash-hill.

Einer caught glimpses of the village through the heavy vegetation along the stream. Most of the houses were black and burnt and some, it seemed, were still in flames. Bodies were coming into view, slumped over the barricade, and Einer could hear the roars of warriors who had arrived, and discovered their loved ones.

Docking the river-boat required patience; all three of them wanted to jump out and run up the hill to the village that had once been, but this place was not home to them anymore.

On a sunny day like this, there would be cloths drying on the racks; wool and linen of every colour blowing in the soft and fresh breeze, but today the racks were empty. A lone, bright yellow cloth fluttered on the wooden fence where the town's shared animals were penned; the gate was open and the sheep were gone. The grass and farmland up the hill towards the village had been burned. This place was a blackened shadow of the glorious village that had once been.

Bees flew around his feet in search of the season's last flowers beneath the ashes.

There were corpses up the hill towards the town; Christian corpses with sword-crosses on their shields and clothes. Invaders from the south.

Einer wanted to see what lay beyond the gates and the barricade, but at the same time he did not. All of them felt the same. All of them dreaded to find their children, friends, and loved ones, and to see the despair which must have grabbed Ash-hill as it burned. In this moment, none of them were warriors, only fathers and mothers, sons and daughters, who had lost too much.

Einer walked up the northern slope of the hill to the outer barricade, through the piles of Christian corpses. His knees felt soft and his mind repeated the many times he had run up this hill to get home. The villagers usually filled the hill when raiders returned and those who were late would storm out of the gates to welcome them. And the drums would be struck and flutes were played and the horns blown and they would sing and dance and laugh.

Crows cawed as they circled above the burnt village.

The northern and western gates were closed from the inside. Arrows were fastened into the outer barricade. There were more and more as Osvif and Hormod and Einer walked around at the edge of the barricade towards the southern gate. Einer concentrated on the sound of them walking through the high, half-burnt grasses to keep himself from looking up at the corpses at the top of the barricade. He feared to find Hilda's face among them.

Instead he watched the outer village, where every field was empty, and where the crops were ruined and black. Rakes lay abandoned on the burnt fields. Warriors spat at the Christian church as they passed, the only building that had escaped the fire.

The southern gate was wide open, and Einer had not even reached it before he saw what lay inside the town. More stinking corpses, some burnt and unrecognisable. Many of the warriors were too afraid to go further. They faced away from the smoking embers and half-burnt corpses, as if they were scared to look. It was easier to shout for revenge than to look at what had been done. Only a few tiptoed into the village, cautious not to wake the spirits of their slaughtered kin.

The loud hum of thousands of flies overwhelmed Einer, swarming around the remains. Corpses of farmers, both men and women, there were, even a few children. Among them the Christians, clad for war and battles in expensive armour.

The stench was unbearable. Many of the warriors shielded their noses and mouths with the sleeves of their tunics. Einer did not bother.

The corpses were not yet swollen, but they were of a blue-green tint. Crows sat on faces and hacked at the flesh. Maggots crawled out from missing eyes where crows had already feasted. Faces and entire bodies were hidden in the mud. They had been stepped on, and over, so many times they had nearly disappeared into the earth. Guts had been torn out; the wolves had already been there. They must have left, sensing the arrival of the warriors.

Face down in the mud lay a young boy. His limbs were long, like most boys his age. Maggots crawled around the back of his chestnut-coloured head. Einer crouched down and pushed the cold body around. Flies covered the boy's eyes, and maggots wriggled around from the back of his head to his cheeks and nose and eyes. The hum of the flies was loud, and more and more of them settled on the boy's face.

An unusual calm rushed over Einer. He ignored the flies and cleaned the boy's mudded face to reveal the blue features underneath. With his bare hand, he caressed the boy's cold cheeks in hope of making the wriggling maggots fall off into the mud, but they had bitten themselves too far into the skin, and the flies rose for no more than half a breath. Long enough for him to recognise the corpse as Hormod's youngest son. A boy three summers away from the prospect of raiding. He would have done well.

Einer leant in and kissed the boy's forehead. His cheeks brushed the slimy maggots.

With a sob, Hormod fell to his knees. The mud splashed up his tunic. He brushed the stiff hairs on his son's head as the tears streamed down his rosy cheeks, into his beard.

Never had Einer thought he would see the old man cry.

He placed a warm hand on Hormod's shoulder and for a moment, they just knelt there, with Hormod caressing his boy, tears streaming down his face as he shook his head.

Einer left Hormod alone with his son and ventured further into the village. He leapt over the corpses, his eyes searching through the dead piled along the streets and at the edge of the barricade. Faces he knew stared up at him. Friends and neighbours he had never expected to see smeared with blood after having fallen in battle, and all so different from how they had looked alive. Einer recognised Ivar the smith, dead from a blow to the head that had knocked his helmet in, and Gertrud from the tavern by Knifed-hill whose guts had been wrenched out by wolves. He knew each one of the villagers, even if he could no longer recognise most of them.

More warriors had joined the chant for war and revenge but Einer just wanted them all to stop and look down at those who were dead, and acknowledge the sacrifice their loved ones had made.

Einer felt as if he were far away as he looked down at the faces and the backs of the dead villagers' mostly helmetless heads. This could not be true. It was a dream, like the fever dreams in which Hilda had laughed at him. Where was she? Where would he find her? On the barricade? Had she died in the first wave of arrows? It was possible. She was too good a warrior to die so early, but Einer knew that sometimes being a good fighter was not enough.

Einer acted as if he were drunk on death. He moved calmly, but his eyes were frantic as he turned a woman in the mud, and then another. Cleaned their dirty faces, so they were free of death, and kissed every maggot-covered forehead he recognised as a friend, and the cheeks of those he barely knew, or whose faces had been distorted in the battle and he could not recognise.

His eyes caught a woman with bright blonde hair beneath her helmet. Her chin was square, and few girls had a chin like that. Hilda had a chin like that. He crouched by the woman's side, and removed her helmet. Her head was stuck well inside, but when the helmet was off he noticed her strong eyebrows, and although her face was bloated and different from how it had been, he could not stop the tears from streaming down his face and blurring the vision of Ingrid lying there.

Like Tyra, Ingrid had been like a sister to him. He brushed her bright blue clothes clean; she had always had the most beautiful clothes, and as he arranged her tunic, he felt the bump of her stomach. He had not known she was with child, and he wondered if the rest of her family had; if Hilda had known, and if Tyra had. They would have been close to protect her. The entire family would have been.

The burning pain in his chest made him more desperate. Einer felt his way through the dead at Ingrid's side, turned over the rotting corpses, wrenched the maggots and flies away to see their familiar faces, desperately searching for Hilda.

HILDA

Chapter Seventeen

The Runes guided Hilda across fields of the south.

A passage deep rests in the hill, whispered the wind.

In the middle of a field to Hilda's right rose a hill that hadn't been used for harvest. The grasses were both high and wild, as if no one had touched them for a hundred winters.

Hilda stumbled through the soft earth to the hill and its wild grass, and up. *South forged will be an offering to please*, the Runes reminded her as she hiked up.

The cloudy night made it difficult to see far. On the top of the hill was another smaller hill: A grave with a dark, stone-lined hole leading inside.

Hilda walked towards the passage grave. Her feet scraped across the first stone, right outside the grave. She groped the edges of the passageway, and stopped by the grave opening. Being so close to an ancient grave reminded her of the draugar she had seen on the heath. Her palms were sweaty and her heart beat all the way up in her throat. She took a deep breath, her hands flat against the entrance, then ducked to enter and smelled the grave's moist rocks.

Hilda's eyes adjusted to the dark of the jotun passage grave. A large stone blocked the end of the passage. A dead end. 'Just a grave,' she hissed to the wind, but all the same, she stepped inside.

The Runes still hadn't told her where they were leading her. Maybe the smith from whom she was to buy the weapon to appease the gods was dead. Maybe he was a draugar, dead within this grave.

Hilda shivered at the thought. She crouched down to keep her head from knocking against the stone ceiling. The Runes were eager to talk. Even inside the passage grave, wind blew around her. *Passages open for noble blood,* the Runes whispered.

She touched the big stone at the end of the passage. It was smooth in the middle, as if it had been polished.

Passages open for noble blood.

Following the whispers in the wind, Hilda reached for her dagger and sliced into her little finger. Just a little. The blade came away bloody. She smeared her blood onto the rock, and it all—the dark, the smell of blood, the weapon in her hand, all of it—reminded her of the battle at Ash-hill. Yrsa trampled to death by the warriors, Ingrid left behind, Jarn and Astrid pushed out of the crowd, out of sight. The screams in the night.

The passage grave rumbled. Hilda kept her bleeding hand flat on the rock that blocked her way.

Keep your eyes clear of Muspel's furnace. A constant fire burns within, the Runes mysteriously warned. *Cover their sight as you leave.* Never before had they talked as much.

Rocks clattered around her, and for a moment the burrow seemed to be crumbling. Then, under her palm, the stone rolled aside. Hilda reached into the widening gap. The passageway continued inside. She walked through the opening. The first stone her feet reached was lower than where she stood; the next, lower again. The rocks were steps, leading down into the grave.

Keep your eyes clear of Muspel's furnace, the Runes instructed again. Their voices echoed down the steps. *Cover their sight as you leave.*

Hilda walked down three steps before the rock had finished rolling away from the end of the passage grave, and reached above her. Her fingers didn't reach the ceiling, so she rose to stand up with a straightened her back.

Keep your eyes clear of Muspel's constant fire. Cover their sight as you leave, the Runes repeated. *Cover their sight as you leave.*

'I'll close the furnace,' Hilda agreed, to end the Runes' constant plea. They never whispered so much; this had to be important.

The ground shook again, and the stone rolled back into place. Blocked out any light so there was only darkness. The wind stopped, and with it, the whisper of the Runes died. The rock sealed tightly behind her Hilda was trapped in the dark passage way.

No wind played with her dress or hair anymore. If the Runes hadn't spoken to her, Hilda might never have noticed the lack of wind, but now it was all she could think about. For the first time, she felt naked and alone. All her life the whispers in the wind had been with her, no matter how faint, but now, for the first time, she was alone. In the dark.

Her heart raced as she took a blind step down. Her steps rang out as she walked into the depths of the grave. It was deep. She trod carefully, afraid the draugar who lived inside this ancient grave would hear her and wake.

For a long time Hilda walked, until she no longer had the strength. Then she curled up on a step in the dark to sleep. As she sank into sleep, she whispered to the Runes, hoping they might hear her, but no response came. Whispering her questions, she fell asleep, and soon she woke and began to move down the steps again.

'The stupid man stays awake all night, and worries about

everything,' Hilda recited as she began to move again. 'Come the morning he's worn out, and everything is as bad as it was.'

The smallest of things reminded her of her father and what he had taught her. He had kept her away from the raids for so many summers. She had thought she wouldn't miss him much after he passed on, but she did.

An unexpected ache gripped her chest when she thought of him and how he had looked in the end. She had dreamed about him when she had slept, and the reality that he had passed on— that all the farmers in Ash-hill were dead—was hard to grasp. There was just the warriors and the children left. She hoped they were all still alive.

To keep the hunger away, she munched on a root. It had been long since she had eaten a proper meal. Her legs were sore from how she had been on the move since the battle in Ash-hill four nights ago. During these past days, she had walked so far that the leather at her soles had become thin like linen and blisters had begun to form on her feet.

Hilda stumbled on a step. Navigating down the bumpy stone steps in complete darkness took courage and patience, the latter of which Hilda had never possessed. She kept a hand on the left wall to keep her steady. The cold of the grave made her shiver as she continued to descend.

Her fingers felt frozen. She removed her hand from the wall, and wished she had more furs to wrap herself in. They said graves were cold and the dead were too, but she had never thought a grave would be *this* cold. She huffed in and out, to feel a bit of warmth on the top of her lips. Her nose was runny and she was certain it wouldn't be long before her snot turned to ice.

Hilda staggered, and caught herself with a hand on the wall to her right. Unexpectedly, the air became heavier, and warmer. Her head was dizzy and she was prickly all over, as if a thousand needles jabbed her skin. Her frosty nose heated up and ran freely again. The right wall was warm.

The left side of the passageway was cold like a winter night, but the right was hot like an oven.

Hilda continued down the stone steps, walking in the middle this time. It felt strange to be frozen on one side and hot on the other. Her right hand was wet with sweat and her left felt as though it had turned to ice. Her fingers were numb. Sweat dripped down from her right eyebrow, stung when it fell onto her eyelashes and dripped into her eye. Her head hurt from both heat and cold.

The sound of her footsteps rang down the never-ending stairway and her breathing was loud and exhausted. Twice she stopped for food, although she didn't have much. She couldn't tell for how long she had walked: two rests or an entire day? After every step, there was another.

Her left eyelashes felt like they were frozen onto her skin. She blinked the right one to avoid getting sweat into it and peered ahead. Then she noticed it: feeble light, glimmering through a few gaps at the edge of a large stone down the way. She had reached the end of the passage.

Had she seen the light sooner, she might have sped up, but the frost and warmth had slowed her, and she didn't have more strength left than what would barely get her there.

When Hilda was so close that she could see the smooth texture of the rock, she turned around to warm the frozen side of her face, and cool the other. Her head spun, as if she had eaten dream caps. She wanted nothing more than to lie down in a comfortable room, neither too warm nor too cold, but whatever lay on the other side of the passageway, she was certain that wasn't it.

'Before you advance through the door,' Hilda recited to herself. 'You must look about, and peer around, because you cannot know for sure where enemies will sit in the hall.' Her father had made sure she knew the great Alfather's sayings as well as a skald.

This was a grave, she reminded herself, and graves meant

draugar. Her hand was ready at her weapon belt. She reached for her dagger and sliced into her little finger and let her blood drip onto the rock, like she had done at the top of the steps.

The ground shook again, like before, and the rock rolled away.

After spending so long in the dark, the light was blinding. Hilda walked into the room beyond the dark steps. For several heartbeats, she blinked, before muddy shapes began to take form.

The room was a forge. Behind a sturdy wooden table with a single leg was a big closed furnace and a wide empty floor. Water surrounded the round forge, as if it were an island. Across from the entrance was a waterfall that created foam and bubbles in the water.

To the left, beyond the forge and the water that surrounded it, was ice. It sparkled in all shades of blue. Every shard of ice Hilda looked at shone a different shade. Shades she had never seen before, and colours she had never known. Closer to the forge, red light gleamed in the ice, reflected from the right side of the room, where glowing red embers flowed like water. Sometimes dark and almost black on the surface.

Fire-licked embers dripped from somewhere above too, and when Hilda looked up there was no change in the scenery. Frost to the left, fire to the right. As far up as her eyes could see, embers filled one side and icicles the other.

Hilda settled her eyes back on the furnace. The one the Runes had warned her about. Her hand was tight on her dagger. Her heart raced at the thought of seeing another draugar.

Something rummaged behind the one-legged table.

Someone was standing there, staring at her.

EINER

Chapter Eighteen

EINER'S BRIGHT YELLOW tunic stood in stark contrast to the grey village.

Einer's father rose to speak. His eyes lingered on the empty Ting stones, which had belonged to the land owners. Every last one of them had passed on in Ash-hill's battle, and their absence was deeply felt on the silence. Even with the children returned to Ash-hill from the campsite, the town was too quiet.

They had finished burning the bodies the previous night. There had been more than they had expected. Still, some bodies were missing. Einer had neither found Hilda nor his mother, and he refused to think that they were among the unidentified half-eaten corpses, although his father did.

'Before we open the Ting there's an important matter we need to settle,' the chief announced for all who had gathered. 'Has every child gained a new parent? A new father or mother? If there is anyone who still don't know where they belong, please step into the ring.'

The quiet that followed made it clear that every young child had gained new parents.

'Very well. I now summon our new lawspeaker, Dagny Aegildóttir,' he announced, much louder than needed; used to a larger crowd. In a single summer, so many had passed on. 'May she open her first Ting and over time prove as worthy a lawspeaker as her father did before her.'

With nervous steps, Dagny replaced the chief in the stone ring, found the worn earth in the middle where her father had used to stand. She pushed her soft red hair away from her face using the back of her hand, took a deep breath, and straightened her back before she addressed the freemen.

'Under the circumstances, this early winter Ting will also serve as a general assembly to allow us to change the decisions we took before summer,' she said in a loud, steady voice, and slowly spun around to face them all in turn as she spoke. 'As an early winter Ting, it shall last at least a day, but no longer than two nights. As at a general assembly, all freemen shall be present throughout.' Dagny stopped turning when she faced the tree-stump, and delicately raised her hands in the air as her father had done so many times before her. 'I now declare the Ting open.'

The warriors and children stomped their feet and clapped their hands. Einer put more effort into it than ever before and he could hear that he was not the only one to stomp and clap louder than usual. They all tried to fill the silence left behind by the many who had passed on.

'Our first matter is a plan for winter,' Dagny announced. 'May any warrior with a plan—man, woman, or child—come forth and speak.'

A big warrior, older than most, pushed his way through the crowd. 'We need to avenge our wives, husbands, friends, and children,' he stated, 'so they can rest and enjoy their afterlife. Do you want them to roam in loneliness because we fear we're too small in number?' The man stroked his grey beard and paused. Warriors and young children shouted their support and agreement and many stomped their feet, Einer too. 'I say we leave before the wind rises again.'

'You're crazy,' a bulky warrior from the *Mermaid Scream* broke in. 'You say it yourself,' he spat after the older warrior, as the man left the ring. Enjoying the many eyes on him, the bulky warrior took his time to say any more. 'The winds will rise again,' he finally said. 'How do you expect us to sail in the grim winter weather?'

Muttered agreements erupted through the ranks, but not as many as the warrior had expected, because he said his next words carefully. 'We can travel down over land instead, and join forces with Harald Gormsson. He can protect us.'

At once the warriors protested, and none took the time to move into the ring to speak.

'There's nothing left to protect!' one yelled.

'It would mean submitting to him,' another cried. 'We don't need a king to sit on our riches.'

Two dozen warriors had already left for Harald's Jelling. Warriors who had not known the patience to stay and plan for a proper revenge, and had not had the calm to care for the children and replenish themselves. They had left after the bodies of their loved ones had been burned and been safely sung into the next life.

'We need Harald. He has more ships than us,' said someone who stood behind Einer. 'He can protect us.'

'We don't need Harald's help,' Thora yelled over them all. 'We can go to Valhalla without him!' She stared down the warriors she could see, as if challenging them to a duel if they dared to disagree with her. 'Dagny, let's take the first vote,' she urged.

Their young lawspeaker took the stone ring. 'Let every freeman in favour of joining forces with Harald Gormsson raise a hand.'

Finn and Osvif's helmsmen were the only men of influence

to vote in favour, and in the circle around them only a small portion of the freemen raised their hands. The vote was clear; they would not join forces with Harald, and the discussion resumed.

Finn was quick to rise. 'I agree that action needs to be taken as soon as possible, but we're too close to winter. Next summer, when the weather is with us again.'

A few people in the crowd stomped their feet in support of Finn and his preposition, while others shouted insults, but Finn continued, unbothered by the rising voices. 'Over the winter, we can gather our full strength and come up with a plan that'll get us a proper revenge. A careful plan always beats a hasty action.'

Even Einer had to agree with that.

'Finn's right,' he shouted to make it known. 'It's too dangerous to sail out while the visibility is so poor, and once the visibility improves it'll be too icy. But... while we gather our forces, our enemies also gather theirs, and they outnumber us. We need a surprise attack that will take them aback. Then, perhaps, we'll have a chance. They won't expect us in the winter. But they might think we'll act on impulse, so we need to give them enough time to forget us, but not long enough for flowers to bloom.'

The freemen considered his argument and as Einer regained his seat, he noticed several nods.

The next warrior agreed with Einer's proposition and added that they ought to start rebuilding Ash-hill and attack once the children had houses to live in.

Dagny announced another vote. As one, Osvif and Einer raised their hands, and that was half the ship owners. Thora and Vigmer were still undecided, and several freemen too. They would need a stronger argument to win over the majority.

This time Osvif took the word. 'Many of you knew my uncle and cousins—they built most of your houses—and it's from my uncle that I know: building takes time, and we can't build proper houses in the wet winter. It'll be difficult to stay here.'

To give his words impact Osvif held out his arms and gave them a few heartbeats to look around the fallen houses. Lone pillars and half-burnt walls plotted the village like an old skeleton.

'Soon it'll be too cold to live in the tents, and there will be more rain,' Osvif continued. 'Our winter provisions burned with Ash-hill and the weather continues to cool. That leaves us two options: either we attack this winter, or we seek shelter elsewhere.'

The freemen did not need to discuss it further before Dagny demanded another vote, and this time, the vote was clear. Almost everyone trusted Osvif's judgement and agreed that staying in Ash-hill any longer was impossible.

When the vote had passed, Ingolf, the fastest rower on the *Northern Wrath*, pushed through to speak. 'I say we winter elsewhere. Our only option is to seek shelter with Harald.'

Roars of disapproval rose from the freemen. 'The vote was passed,' they shouted. And a few added that Bluetan was stupid, rash, cowardly, each word was worse than the last. Einer remained silent, fidgeted with his bracteate, and watched the others insult each other.

'I know, I know,' Ingolf said defensively as the yells intensified. 'We agreed not to join Harald, but where else do we have allies we can trust? Other raiders?'

'In Normandy,' Osvif roared. 'We have old ties in Normandy. They owe us! Or in Frey's-fiord!'

A small group of older warriors lifted their spears and axes high into the air in agreement, but the remaining freemen were not convinced, and again they were in disarray. They discussed and argued; half of them wanted to attack right away and the other half wanted to wait until the weather improved.

Several votes were taken but not once did a vote fall through. The clouds were heavy and drizzle fell over them. The ash tree had used to keep them dry when it rained during a Ting, but now there was just a blackened stump left. The endless discussion, and hearing the same arguments over and over from a hundred different mouths, drove Einer close to madness. The dark of evening fell around them; by now, everyone had aired their arguments, but still no decision could be made.

A small figure pushed through the crowd and entered the ring to speak. 'Am I allowed to voice my suggestion?' a girl asked, barely loud enough for people to hear. 'I'm just a thrall,' she explained, and normally she never would have been allowed near a Ting, none of the children would have, but these were not regular times.

The girl did not walk past Thora's Ting stone into the ring, for she knew that it was a place for freemen. 'My name is Unn, I'm the property of Hilda Ragnardóttir,' she announced.

At the face of such a young girl, Einer's father did not insist that Hilda was dead, torn apart by wolves, as he had yelled at Einer that morning. 'Did your parents die in the battle?' he asked instead, not sure whose daughter she was. Indeed, she had grown a lot over summer, her hair was significantly longer, and had become bright from sunshine. Her limbs were long too and her face had slimmed.

Unn shook her head. 'My mother died in childbirth, and my father accompanied Ragnar Erikson to Helheim.' She looked at the ground as she spoke.

'You're Carlman's daughter!' Vigmer exclaimed. 'A good thrall and dear family friend.' Many nodded their agreements. Einer smiled, remembering Carl's sacrifice on the pyre. Few thralls were as loyal to their master and as honourable as Carlman had been. 'Your new parents can speak for you.'

'I have none. I belong to Hilda,' Unn repeated.

It was understandable that a thrall girl was the only child who had not gained new parents. With the recent loss of houses and shelter, keeping a thrall who was entitled to adequate shelter and food was a commitment that few would be ready to take.

The chief watched the crowd to judge their expectations.

'This is no regular Ting,' he said. 'And we've all voiced our opinions. If you have something to add, then speak.'

The crowd fell silent as the skinny thrall gained the circle. The children who had spoken before her had been eager to join the fight despite being several winters too young, apart from a young boy who thought no one should quarrel anymore.

'Without a word, I've listened to all of you,' Unn said, and indeed every freeman had spoken his or her mind, most more than once. 'Some of you say we should go right away.'

The ones who were of that mind roared, and of all of them, Einer's voice was the loudest.

'Others say we should wait until summer.'

This time Finn cheered loudest. Einer knew that his father was of the same mind, but as chief he could not voice his approval quite as easily.

'I say: think of the many we lost when the southerners took Ash-hill.' Unn spoke slowly, like a well-trained skald, or more accurately, like a thrall who had learnt to only speak when she had something important to say. 'Do you not want to see your wives and friends happily feast in Odin's halls? Do you want them to keep their heads low in embarrassment? Do you not want them to lead their afterlife with pride because you've avenged their deaths?'

Throughout the crowd, more and more nodded in agreement.

'This cannot wait.'

Mumbles rose through the rows, arguments for and against, the same that had already been voiced, but Unn did not stop to listen.

'Some of you mutter words of disagreement now,' she said. 'Do you really believe you just forget what happened here?' With a harsh stare she must have learnt from Hilda, she turned around so everyone could see her, no matter where they stood.

'I'll always remember the panic in the eyes of those who stayed. Their hundreds of torches in the night. The yells that we could hear even out by the campsite. The screams throughout the night. We sat together, around the campfire, all of us, and listened to parents and friends die. Last night too, I cradled young Torstein and Aslak in my arms as they woke from nightmares. Saw their parents dying, again and again. And you want them to just forget that?'

Her knuckles were white where she clutched her grey dress.

'I won't forget,' she nearly whispered. 'Don't be fooled. It doesn't end here. Sure, we can rebuild. But those memories will never go away, and the southerners will always think they won. Unless we prove them wrong.'

Einer was thunderstruck that such a small girl could speak with such conviction.

'Silently I grew up listening to Ragnar the Brave teach battle strategies. The best skald in Midgard. So, it's not in ignorance I speak.' She took a longer pause for the warriors to acknowledge her worth. 'I say we send word out to all possible allies. Strike now.' And with those words, she left the inner ring.

A young man broke the near-silence Unn's speech had left. 'With Harald's influence in the south, we have no allies,' he said it quietly, as if afraid to be beaten for questioning the wise words of a thrall girl.

Thora rose from her Ting stone and repeated Unn's last phrase: 'All *possible* allies. We send word to Tyr's-lake, Odin's-gorge, up to our Norse friends in Frey's-fiord and further, all the way to the land of the Finns, and out west to the settlers on the islands.'

'They aren't our allies, they won't fight with us,' protested a shieldmaiden behind Einer.

'In this they will,' Thora insisted. Her voice, the voice of a ship commander, gave credibility to Unn's speech. 'If the southerners pose a threat to our lands, they pose a threat to theirs.'

Einer nodded his agreement, and he was not the only one.

'You are right to be bitter,' she continued, and her words took him aback. 'They won't send their ships and their best warriors. But freemen will rush to fight with us, and we'll have more warriors and be more fit to fight than we are now.'

The silence was like a buzz, as if every freeman's thoughts could be heard as they considered what decision to make, and what side to take.

'Say they send us warriors to fight,' said Einer's father. 'Do you suggest we just march south into the cowards' lands?'

'Nej,' Thora replied. 'We set sail and strike where it hurts. We shake their throne in the north.'

'Hedeby?' Finn questioned in a mocking a tone. 'That's what the warriors who left for Jelling wanted to do.'

'Hedeby isn't really theirs. Nej, I'm talking about Magadoborg, way up the Albis river.'

As soon as Magadoborg was mentioned the discussion erupted among the freemen again, and even Einer was shocked at her suggestion. But at the same time, he had an indescribable urge to agree with Thora and pass the vote.

As if nothing had happened, and as if her suggestion to attack the fortified city had been as casual as suggesting they move their camp further inland, Thora sat back down on her Ting stone.

The crowd was loud with discussion. People yelled back and forward, but Unn's brave words had left a deep impression on them all.

Dagny walked to the middle of the ring. Her back was straight, her eyes observed the crowd like a hawk watching a field. Despite her soft red hair and her big eyes, she looked so much like her father when he had been their lawspeaker. 'Let every freeman in favour of Thora's proposal raise a hand.'

Einer was the first to cast his vote; Thora and Osvif were quick to follow. One after the other, freemen raised their hands; Chief Vigmer too, voted in favour and when he showed his hand, many more did. All around the circle, people voted in favour of Thora's crazy suggestion. A suggestion that might get them all killed.

The freemen stirred and still discussed amongst themselves. Patiently, Dagny waited for them to quiet and be certain of their choice. Even Finn raised his hand.

'Good,' Dagny finally said, and they lowered their hands. 'We shall gather allies and attack Magadoborg.' Einer roared with approval for as long as he could, and freeman stomped their feet in rhythm and cheered for the result.

In the crowd, across from Einer, Unn beamed with joy.

'We still have some general decisions to make,' Dagny said. 'What shall we do with the young children and the thralls? We can't leave them here without shelter and food.'

With increased confidence from her last contribution, Thora rose to speak. 'I think we all agree that the children can't be left here. I propose that my crew and I take the children up to Kar in Frey's-fiord. I know he'll take care of them as if they were his own.'

No one else had anything to add, so Dagny had them vote. The decision was unanimous, and loud cheers were given when Dagny declared it done. Now that they had decided what action to take, the details were easily solved.

Einer volunteered his own ship to sail to Normandy in search of help. His father and Hormod who had once fought with the Norman chief both agreed to join Einer's crew.

The late hour of the day showed on the tired faces in the crowd. Yet, despite how night fell around them, no one sat down on the ground, and no one appeared to want to end the day's Ting.

Never before had Einer witnessed such a short, peaceful Ting. It almost felt wrong, as if their rituals had been broken and nothing was as it were supposed to be. There were no neighbour feuds. No endlessly rehashed discussion about whether Jarn had to move his beehives further out of town because Gudrun's son had been stung two summers ago and he had swelled to the size of the ale-barrow. Not a single protest at Einer raising a bear cub, although of course he no longer had a cub to raise; it had escaped before the battle like the farm animals, and had raided Jarn's beehives on the way.

Dagny declared the end of the Ting. 'It is decided! On the morrow, we shall send word to every ally whose favour we may hope to gain, and when our answers come, we shall sail up Albis River to strike Magadoborg!'

The freemen clamoured their approval.

HILDA

Chapter Nineteen

A MAN STARED at her, his smile fading; whoever he had expected, it had not been Hilda.

Hilda kept her grip on the dagger firm, and out of his sight. She had expected to see a draugar at the bottom of the grave, but this man wasn't a draugar. He didn't look anything like the one she had seen out on the moor, which had spooked her horse. He wasn't tall, like a draugar, and he was too simple, too plain. Too frightened. He was scared of her, she realised.

Neither of them spoke.

Hilda glanced around the room to be aware of any threats, as the Alfather advised. The furnace behind the short man was a large, round oven with a closed metal door. In front of the man was a wooden table that looked as if it had been grown there, in the middle of the island.

The ice and fire on either side of the water made Hilda uneasy. Like two of the nine worlds came together in this place: the fire world of Muspelheim and icy Niflheim, the first two worlds. As impossible as it seemed, she had left Midgard and was staring at the tale of creation. The place between ice and fire where life had formed.

She needed the Runes to tell her that this was just her imagination. But what she saw was more real than anything she had ever seen before, as if her life in Midgard had been a dream.

There was wind in the forge. It came from the waterfall, but carried no whispers, only the soft crackles of fire and ice. The Runes weren't there to help.

'It's not like you to stay quiet,' she whispered to the wind that caressed her skin. Waited for a response, though unconvinced she'd get one. The Runes had left her at the top of the steps, and Hilda couldn't stop wondering what they had wanted, and if they would ever be back.

The short man still hadn't moved. His slim eyes examined her.

Hilda took a step further into the forge. She didn't want to be the first to speak, in case she said something she shouldn't, but obviously neither did the man.

Maybe the Runes had led him there, as they had led her. Maybe the Runes had intended for her to meet this man, whoever he was, for he was not a draugar. Maybe they had told him something that they hadn't told her.

'Did you hear the whispers too?' she finally asked. Her voice echoed around the forge.

The man narrowed his eyes at her question. 'What whispers?'

He hadn't, then, or he would have known.

His voice was coarse, as if he hadn't used it in a long time. 'How do you know this place?' he asked in return.

Hilda remembered her father's advice. Lies always had to be told with calm to be believed. With all the time in the nine worlds, she approached the wooden table. 'Luck,' she answered, as she stared around at the ice and the fire that surrounded the forge. But the man didn't believe her, and she hadn't expected him to.

'No one could find this place by luck alone,' he said with certainty. 'Someone must have brought you here.'

Hilda's father had always said that someone who spoke without restraint was a liar, but someone who held back, spoke the truth. She didn't volunteer any more information, and for what seemed like hundreds of heartbeats, they stared at each other in absolute silence.

'No one took me here,' she finally said.

Her revelation prompted another question. 'What are you?' he asked. 'Aesir? Vanir?'

Hilda didn't dignify his question with a response. If he wanted to believe that she was a goddess, he was free to do so.

She searched around the forge for her snow fox, with its many scars up the legs and its long puffy tail, but it had been a while since it had shown itself, which meant that she was safe, at least for now. But, it didn't necessarily mean she could trust this man in front of her. He had to be a smith. This was a forge after all. Suddenly, Hilda knew exactly what to do.

'Who I am shouldn't concern you. Only why I'm here,' she said.

The man took a step back. One, two, and three steps, until he stood with the water directly at his back, as if he thought drowning would be better than talking to Hilda. 'Why are you here?'

'I need a weapon. An axe worthy of a goddess,' she said.

He hadn't expected that answer.

'You *are* the smith?' Maybe she had assumed too much.

'I can forge,' he answered, but he didn't say more.

To receive, you must give, Hilda thought. That was what the runemistress had told her. She plunged a hand into the bloody coin pouch she had stolen out on the moor. Grabbed a silver coin and flicked it across the table to the smith.

He caught it, by instinct, not because he had wanted to. Turned it in his hands and brought it up close to his plump face.

'Payment,' she said.

'Fake,' he answered. 'Tin.'

He flung the round piece of metal back at her. It hit her hidden chainmail, clanged against the table and rolled back towards the smith. Hilda took another coin from the pouch. Up close, she looked at the obscure portrait on the coin and the foreign letters in a circle around it.

A tin coin, not silver as she had thought. She couldn't understand why the Runes would have made her kill for six tin coins. They had definitely been silver when she had last looked at them.

For a moment, she questioned it all: the Runes' motives, her destiny, her presence there, even the will of the gods. Her questions were meaningless. She was there, and as with everything and all encounters, there had to be a reason.

'Look again,' she said.

The smith eyed her, and then he approached. He was skinny, and so short, compared to her, but he had the strong arms of a smith. Hilda still clutched onto her dagger. Discreetly, she touched her dress and felt the chainmail underneath it. Her axe hung from her hip.

The smith picked up the small coin he had flung back at her, glanced up at Hilda, then looked more closely at the coin. 'Is it—?' he asked with a raised eye-brow.

Hilda nodded, without knowing what he asked. She trusted the Runes. They wouldn't have betrayed her.

The corner of the smith's lips curled in a broad, wicked smile. 'How much more do you have?' he asked. He placed the shining coin on the table. His eyes were eager.

'Enough,' she answered.

'How much?'

She didn't think it wise to give him everything she had, but she didn't have any use for it, and the only way to truly gain this smith's trust was by trusting him first.

'Six coins,' she said. 'Enough.'

'Plenty.' He smiled to her.

'You can have all of them if you'll make a worthy axe for me. Do we have a trade?'

'We do.'

He got to work immediately. Brought his tools out from underneath the table, hammers and tongs and small bags of things. Finally, he pulled forth two melting pots.

'I only need one axe,' Hilda said.

'A weapon for you, a weapon for me,' he replied. 'The coins.' He stretched a hand out over the table, towards her.

Warily, not liking the idea of paying first but feeling like she had no other choice, Hilda dropped the bloody pouch onto the table.

The smith frowned at the blood on the pouch, but did not ask any questions. He dug the coins out and dropped three into each of the melting pots, as though he was going to melt the coins and use their metal to forge with, but they were so tiny and three would not be enough to make an axe. Hilda didn't find it wise to question him. She wasn't sure he would be as eager to make an axe for her if he realised she wasn't a goddess.

'What spirit bone?' the smith asked. He was crouched down by a bag, clawing through it. 'I have bear, white bear, eagle, elk, snow fox, and lynx.'

'Snow fox,' Hilda said. The choice was easily made.

Hilda watched him weigh out the bone piece. The smith knew his craft well. He worked like a skilled dwarf smith. Maybe he *was* a dwarf. He had the right height, and almost looked skilled enough too. It would explain why his forge looked like it melted together two of the nine worlds, and why the Runes had brought her there.

She walked around the edge of the island. Apart from the table and the broad furnace, the island was empty. Nine arm-lengths wide from every edge. The river from the waterfall parted in a perfect circle around the island. Hilda stretched her hands out above the stream of water towards the hot fires of Muspelheim. The heat wrapped around her fingertips like a glove.

The smith clasped onto the melting pots with a long pair of tongs, and faced the closed furnace.

'I'll open the furnace,' he said in a warning voice, and shut his eyes.

Hilda recalled the Runes' words of warning—*Keep your eyes clear of Muspel's furnace*—and quickly she shut her eyes, like the smith.

The metal door to the furnace clanged opened. Voices emerged. For half a heartbeat Hilda thought the Runes had returned to her. But the voices didn't come in the wind, and they weren't the Runes. They were deep, dark and crackling. She couldn't understand what they said, though she felt an intense will to stare into the furnace and see where they came from.

'Don't listen,' she whispered to herself. The desire to look was so strong that she had to repeat the phrase louder and louder inside her mind; *Don't listen, don't listen, don't listen.*

The crackle of the voices made them sound hot, as though they belonged to fire. Of course, they did, she realised. The forge was built on the border between Niflheim and Muspelheim. The furnace had to open into the heart of the world of fire: the Runes had spoken of Muspel's children. What she heard had to be the voices of demons of the fire world.

The voices gained in strength, and became so loud Hilda had trouble resisting the urge to open her eyes and search for them. They snaked around her, burning and humid. Tried to pull Hilda in and make her open her eyes to see the fire demons.

It took all of her concentration and resistance to keep her eyes shut and her head turned away.

Metal clanged and locked away the demons' voices; the smith had closed the furnace. The forge was almost silent after the clamour that had surrounded them moments earlier.

Hilda exhaled loudly and tried to forget the demons' dark

crackle. They left an ache in her heart like waking from a nightmare, still gripped by the memory and pain.

'They'll need to be in there for a while.' The smith's voice pulled Hilda away from her thoughts. He had put both melting pots inside.

'How long?'

'Long enough to eat and get some sleep.'

She nodded at that.

'Did you bring food?'

'Just roots,' she said, and she was tired of chewing them.

The smith crouched down by his food skin and handed Hilda a piece of dried meat no bigger than her hand. It wasn't much—she was hungry enough to eat at least ten times as much—but it was more than she had expected.

Hilda sat by Niflheim's cool side as she munched on the piece of meat. It tasted salty, slightly bitter too, and chewing it made her jaw hurt. It was nice to taste salt on her tongue again. The smith's meat was a lot better than what she had gotten from the wagon on the moor. In a cupped hand, she scooped up some water from the stream to drink.

Neither of them mentioned the voices of Muspel's children. The smith must have heard them often before, but Hilda had never imagined such alluring voices, and her thoughts kept circling back to them. She was exhausted from the long day, too—or the long *days*. She had no idea how long she had walked in the dark, or how long she had been in the forge. Without any daylight, it was difficult to judge, and she was impatient to get moving again. She didn't know how long ago the battle in Ash-hill had been. When she came out of the forge again, she could figure it all out. The battle had been one night before full moon.

When he had eaten, the smith lay down by the water close to Niflheim to sleep, and Hilda at the other side of the forge, by Muspelheim's heat and the furnace. She attempted to sleep, but after staying awake for so long, sleep wouldn't come and her eyes seemed to open on their own every time she tried to close them.

She often glanced to the smith, not knowing if she could trust him. Without the Runes, there was no one to warn her if he decided to attack her while she slept.

For what felt like an entire day she lay there, eying the flowing fires of Muspelheim, listening to the burning fires and creaking ice, and the smith's heavy breaths. Until she could take it no more and moved to the waterfall to bathe and unwrap her battle wounds.

The spear wound in her thigh had healed well considering how deep it had been. The wound had crusted, though her thigh was still blue from bruises. Most of her skin was blue from the fight, for that matter, but her wounds were crusted scars now, and only stung when she pressed on them.

Keeping her head above the surface by the waterfall she washed herself and peed in the water. She rubbed off her old skin, careful around her wounded thigh, and then she rinsed her hair in the waterfall. The ends of the long blond locks were ragged and she imagined that her eyebrows needed to be plucked too. Her nails were beginning to grow long as well, especially her toenails; when she wore her shoes, she could feel her nails against the leather.

After such a long time, it felt good to clean herself. Afterwards, she sat by the waterfall balancing her feet in the water until the smith woke and warned her that he was opening the furnace again.

Barely had he opened the furnace before the calls overwhelmed Hilda. The demons dried her wet hair and filled her ears with crackles so loud she wanted to scream. Anything to block them out. The voices tickled and wrapped warm around her. Hilda kept her eyes shut, repeating the Runes' words in her mind as loud as she could; *Keep your eyes clear of Muspel's furnace.*

The furnace door slammed shut. The clang of the metal door echoed around the forge. Relieved, Hilda opened her eyes.

The iron the smith had retrieved from the furnace shone like stars in the night-sky. Hilda was mesmerised by the heated metal's beauty as the smith hammered the melting pot off. It felt as if the metal called her like the demons' voices. The coins had melted and more than tripled in size, and still the metal grew. The smith began to pound.

At a distance, Hilda stood and watched, too tired to focus, and when her legs lost the little strength they had, she sat by the waterfall. Absentmindedly she watched as the smith hammered and hammered, and hacked away to form the eye of an axe.

Listening to the blow of his hammering, she fell asleep.

A HISS WOKE Hilda. She opened her eyes wide, and hated herself for having fallen asleep. The smith stood by the ice water at her feet. He didn't notice her wake. Clasped in each hand was a pair of tongs, which he had extended underwater, cooling the two weapons he had made.

Steam rose from each blade. The surface of the water began to boil. The shine of the blades lost intensity and faded. For a good ten heartbeats, the smith held them underwater.

Hilda sat up to stare down at the cooling blades. The surface cleared. The bubbles slowed. The smith pulled out the iron. Smoke wrapped around the blades, caressed them, as though it came, not from the steam and water, but from the blades themselves. He put the axe and sword down on the table. Through the steam Hilda stared at the axe. It was the old kind, with a long beard. A working axe, not a war axe like her own, which was pointy at the tip. But when she drew closer, she saw it was slight, meant for battle.

'Just need to polish them,' the smith told her. 'Sleep first.'

The smith lay down by Niflheim. Like the first time, Hilda couldn't sleep. Impatiently, she rummaged through the shelf under the one-legged table, searching for a polishing stone. There were hammers, tongs, flasks and other things. A chain rustled around in there too. Finally, she found a polishing stone, grabbed her axe and sat down by the waterfall to work. She knew how to care for weapons, and she didn't need someone to polish the axe for her.

When he woke, the smith tried to take over the polishing work on the axe, but Hilda was already so far into the work and it felt good to do something, so she told him to work on his sword instead.

Their meal portions were consistent, but as she polished her axe, Hilda's mouth watered for richer food. For fresh meat, hare maybe, and a rich stew. She craved the softness of cheese, the taste of a sour apple, a horn-full of milk, and sweet mead.

Her arms were sore from the repeated motion of sharpening the axe. Her reflection was clear on the blade. The iron inlay didn't show yet, but otherwise the axe was both smooth and sharp.

She brought the axe-head to the smith. He put aside the pommel he was working on for his sword and focused on her axe. He polished a little here and there, but then rummaged through his tools for a small flask.

He opened it and let a few drops of a clear oil onto the axe, made them roll out over the blade like butter on a pan. The iron inlay became visible.

He had branded the weapon intricately, and Hilda knew how difficult that was. As a child, when she had watched old Ivar brand his weapons, he had often told her: "Only the finest smiths dare to do this, Hilda. You'll never see a travelling armourer with inlaid weapons. You simply won't."

The beautiful image of a snow fox had been inlaid on the axe head. The animal's slim face and thick tail set it apart from a regular fox. It had been carved in the current style, marked by thin and precise lines. The snow fox's body was dotted, elongated and twisted into knots. The legs interlaced with each other. The tail swirled around, in between the legs, around the neck, and curled around the axe-eye to the back. Hilda was transported by its beauty, and as if she were a costumer at a market, she wanted to possess it, but it was not for her. It truly was a weapon worthy of gods.

The smith pulled Hilda's attention away from the axe-head and made her choose a handle for the axe. She weighed out the different shafts and settled for a tough ash with light images carved into it. As he sawed and polished the wood, and readied to hammer it on, Hilda walked around the table to look at his sword.

Although it missed pommel and handle, it had been fully polished, and like her axe, it bore a brand. An inlay of foreign symbols. Hilda recognised the image they produced. +ULFBERH+T.

'It's not an Ulfberht sword,' she blurted. 'You're not Ulfberht.'

The smith frowned at her. Slowly, he cornered the table to stand right in front of her. She was taller than him, but he had a presence that made her swallow to stand so close. 'Then what's my name?' he asked.

She didn't know the answer. She hadn't thought to ask for his lineage. All that had mattered was that the Runes had led her to him. That he could forge an axe worthy of gods.

Something moved behind the smith.

Its tail flowed in the wind and its teeth were barred as they often were. Its blue eyes reflected the light from the ice behind Hilda. Her snow fox, warning her of death.

The smith intended to kill her.

He had a hammer in his hand.

Staring at him as harshly as she could, Hilda grabbed her old axe from her weapon belt and unsheathed it with a slash that made blood trickle down his left arm. The smith grabbed her right wrist before she could strike again, tightened his grip. Squeezed until she had to let the axe fall. She tried to grab the axe with her left hand, but the blade cut her palm and clinked against the floor. The smith kicked it so it skidded over the edge of the forge and into the water.

'I could easily push you in as well,' he hissed. His grip was firm on her right wrist. Her skin was stained white where he held her. 'And with that mail you'd drown.'

For five heartbeats, they stared at each other, neither looked away, nor gave in.

'How did you know where to find this forge?' he finally asked. Somehow, he no longer believed her half-lies from the beginning. 'Did Lundir send you before he passed on? Did Bafir?'

'No one sent me,' Hilda maintained.

The smith closed his eyes and smelled the air. 'You don't belong to the aesir,' he said when he opened his eyes again. 'Nor vanir. Someone sent you.' His grip was tight on her wrist. She couldn't wriggle free.

Hilda gulped and spoke the truth. 'The whispers in the wind sent me.'

'Who sent you?' he bellowed.

He didn't believe her. The truth wouldn't solve this.

He was shorter than her, enough so that she couldn't easily headbutt him; but he was only holding onto one wrist. Hilda brought up her free hand, jabbed two fingers into his eyes. Quick, she retreated. Leaned in over the table to grab the new axe head. With it, she pushed his sword off the table so the smith couldn't reach it, and found foothold again, axe head in hand.

Meanwhile, the smith had recovered. His hands were ready to grab her and make her drop the axe-head like he had made her old axe fall. She wouldn't let him get close enough for it to happen this time, and took a step back. Felt the weight of the axe-head in her hand.

The fox circled the smith. It growled low in its throat. The smith took his stance, with his right foot in front of him, ready for a fight, a large hammer in his left hand. Before Hilda could do anything, he swung it at her belly. Her stomach tightened as the blow landed, the chainmail dug into her skin. Her ribs hurt, and the pain made her bend in over herself, and cough. Despite it all, Hilda regained control of her body. She stood up as tall as she could, the new axe-head ready. Had it not been for her chainmail, that swing would have crushed her.

Surprised at her quick recovery, he backed away from her, towards the furnace. The fox snarled at him. Hilda followed, one step forward. The axe head felt right in her hand. It wanted the kill as well, all three of them did, Hilda, the axe, and the blue-eyed snow fox.

He stood close to the furnace. Hilda took another step ahead. Kept her distance so she could move out of the way if he tried to attack first. Again, she felt the weight of the axe, to make sure she knew it well. This was a risky move.

His hand moved towards the furnace door. There was no time. Hilda took her aim, pulled her arm back, and cast the axe-head with all the force she had.

The smith opened the furnace door. The loud voices of demons nearly drowned Hilda. A demon reached out of the furnace with its long slender fire-enrobed fingers. It saw her, its eyes so dark and deep she was certain they could swallow her whole.

Her own eyes were still open. Still watching as her axe carved through the air towards the smith. A bump and a splash followed.

The heat bored into her eyes, and the demon snickered. Hilda screamed from the pain that melted through her. The fire, the horror, the pain. Deeper and deeper into her head the heat went, as she gaped and saw the demon crawl out the furnace.

Everything lost shape and turned white. The demons' loud voices resonated inside her head and made her want to stare again, but she couldn't.

Her eyes were open but saw nothing.

SIV

Chapter Twenty

MORNING FROST COVERED the grass. Siv smiled, welcoming the colours of winter. The cold reminded her of where she had grown up in the northern mountains of Jotunheim, where the snow never melted and Niflheim was only a passage grave away.

She strolled into the broad-leaved forest at the edge of the clearing where Tyra and her had raised the tent last night. Tyra was still sleeping.

The air was crisp. The trees were covered in white crystals, which would melt when the sun rose higher up in the sky. Dark red leaves almost ready to fall. The ground rose in hills, like waves, and a little further ahead was the old burrow. Two oak trees grew to mark the jotun passage grave, one on either side of the big rocks. The stones had been mounted thousands of winters ago.

Thinking of her old life, Siv walked towards the ancient grave. She had not used this passage since she had first arrived in Midgard. She preferred not to pass through it, but she needed to know if anything had changed in the other nine worlds, and if Midgard was safe. Her brother would know.

The thought of having a brother was still strange to her, especially since she had not known he existed until he had come to her rescue during the battle at Ash-hill.

Siv walked to the passage grave. Three stones had been raised like a doorway into the hill. The grave looked small to her now that she had seen so many others, but when she had first arrived, the barrow had seemed huge, compared to how tiny she had expected everything to be in Midgard.

Taking a deep breath, she pulled out her seax and made a slim cut on her finger, just enough so a single drop of her precious blood appeared. She secured the seax on her belt again and reached her arm into the grave so her bloody finger touched the stone at the end. The stone gave way, opening the passage, and Siv closed her eyes.

She focused on herself; on the length and thickness of her bones, the size of her entire body, trying to make everything shrink. For so many hundred winters, she had gone about her life in a body made as small as a child, although she was still tall compared to most short-lived. It had become almost as normal to her as her true height. But to compress herself to be even smaller seemed as hard as it had been when she had first changed her height.

From lack of practice she was unable to contain the force within herself. The earth began to shake and she called for the runes to help. The wind whipped around her, and when it stilled, Siv was one fourth of the size she had been.

Her clothes fell off her shoulders in a puddle around her, and her shoes and wet seal socks were big and heavy. But the passage grave was tall enough for her to walk inside without needing to bend her neck.

Siv removed both shoes and socks, and heaved her clothes into the passage grave to hide them, so no passing short-lived would think to poke around. She picked up the seax and brought the weapon with her. It was heavy and long like a fitted sword, although the hilt was thick and she had to hold it with both hands. Her body was naked and the cool wind blew around her, saying its goodbye.

Siv walked into the dark steps she had not taken for half a hundred winters. She took a deep breath, and walked through. The rock closed behind her, blocked out the fresh air, and left only the smell of the moist cliff that all passages were made from.

Without waiting for the dark to feel stuffy, she thought of the rune of fire, Kauna, and when it was all she could think about, the passage lit up. Flames hung underneath the rock above her head, all the way to the end of the passage, thousands of steps down.

Using the seax as a walking staff, Siv began to descend, feeling awkward and fragile in her small body.

In her reflection on the blade in her hands, she saw a blurry image of her naked self. In the firelight, the red shine in her hair more obvious. Even braided in the old style, her hair reached far down her back. The humidity made her sweat; she felt droplets trickling down her spine. For a long time, she walked down, alone with the echoes of her bare feet rubbing against the steps and the clang of her seax.

She was half a hundred steps away when the rock at the other end of the passage opened. A man, naked like her, walked through, his face barely lit by the fires above. For a moment, Siv thought it was her father, with his large shoulders, shining green eyes, and bushy eyebrows, but he was younger than her father would be now, and the way he moved was the exact image of her mother.

The rock closed behind Siv's brother. He walked up towards her. In his hands, he held a jotun dagger. Its blade was as long as Siv's seax, but thicker, with a larger hilt.

'I never thought you'd come.' It sounded as though he had waited a hundred summers for her to walk down this very passage. 'I'll walk back up with you,' he said enthusiastically when they reached each other on the steps.

Siv turned to walk back up with him at her side. It was strange to think she had a younger brother.

'We hear the cries of corpses in Niflheim,' he told her, knowing that she had come for news of the nine worlds. He smelled of moss, just like last time. He had been to Alfheim to see the alvar again.

'It's too early,' Siv said. She knew the prediction of Ragnarok as well as anyone. It was not yet time for the final battle between gods and giants, and this was not how it was supposed to begin.

'The runes are weakening,' her brother said, staring at her as they walked. Siv attempted to ignore him by glaring at the next step, and the next, and the next.

'The Runes too?' she questioned.

He nodded.

The Runes and the forefathers' old anger within her had felt weaker to her mind, she had thought it was because she had finally stayed in Midgard too long and begun to lose her grip on the other eight worlds. This was much worse.

'They're still powerful back home,' her brother said. 'But they won't continue to be. I suggested that you could help us,' he said with a secret smile. 'Surt sent me to you.'

Siv's heart caught in her throat. After all of these summers, Surt had finally caught up with her. The time had arrived to pay for what she had done. She had always known the day would come when either Odin or Surt would find her, but she had hoped it would be in some hundred winters or more. All of her other sons had died early, one after the other, but she would not allow Einer to pass. Even if Surt had found out what she had done, she would defend Einer until her last living breath, and in death too.

'What does Surt want?' she urged, breathless with the thought of what was to come.

Surt rarely left the fire demons of Muspelheim, and when he

did, no long-lived was safe. Back then, before Siv had arrived in Ash-hill and before she had struck a deal with the woman in the shadows, she had known that stealing from Surt could result in nothing but complete destruction. But the then-recent loss of yet another child and the shadowed woman's promises had made her do it, against all reason. All she had ever wanted was what the shadowed woman had promised her; to never witness the death of another of her children.

Stealing from Surt had been surprisingly easy, and she had been so certain that he had not woken, had not seen her, or known that she was there. Of course, she should not have kept the bracteate she had taken. If she had given it up, then perhaps Surt would never have searched for her, or known about her. But with the golden amulet of Yggdrasil in her hands, and the power she could feel within it, she had known, as soon as she had touched it, that her next child could outlive her if he had it.

How Surt had known who had stolen from him, and how he had found her in a mere thirty summers, was no mystery to her. The shadowed woman must have told him, out of spite that Siv had kept the gold bracteate.

'Surt needs your help,' her brother said. 'We all do.'

Siv could barely believe her brother's words. Surt had not searched for her to kill her and Einer? The almighty Surt, guardian of fire demons, needed her help. Siv swallowed her thieving guilt and focused on the task ahead.

'What does he need from me?' She was almost afraid to ask, for she knew it would be about the bracteate.

'Midgard is drifting apart. We don't know why. You need to find out, and stop it.'

It was not what she had expected.

'Why me?' she retorted. Somehow, she could not help but think that Surt was making fun of her: having this long-lived come to her and pretend to be her brother, to give her a mission. No one ever received a mission from Surt.

'You're my sister,' he answered, as if that explained everything.

'And apart from Odin and his kin, you're the only long-lived with some knowledge of Midgard.'

She knew it to be true, but it did not make it any easier. She was their last chance. Had she not been, Surt would have given the task to another. Anyone would have been better than someone banished for betraying her kinsmen.

'What exactly do you know?' she asked.

'It's as if the runes no longer have a stronghold in Midgard. As if the old faith is dying. We feel it in the other nine worlds. It got worse this summer.'

The attack on Jutland had not been significant enough to change so much. People died every day. It was something else. 'It got worse this summer, but started winters and summers ago, did it not?'

'Do you know what it is?' His question answered hers.

'For many winters now, chiefs in Midgard have fought to become kings. They abandon their faith to strengthen their claim.' This summer another chief must have done the same. Used the opportunity of a weakened Jutland to assert himself.

'Can you do something?' her brother asked.

'I'll do what I can,' she replied, and still she hardly dared to breathe. Surt knew of her, he had to know what she had done. She did not know what it meant that he entrusted this task to her, but she knew that she had no option other than completing it, by whatever means necessary.

Her brother and her walked on in silence, both caught in their own thoughts.

From the smell on him, there was no doubt he had visited the alvar recently, and if so, he knew more about the situation than he had said. Out of all beings in the nine worlds, the alvar always knew most. 'You've been to Alfheim,' she said, hoping it would make him speak.

'The alvar didn't tell me anything,' he said, and for a moment she thought that was all he would say, but then he continued. 'So I went to Svartalfheim.'

Siv took a deep breath and found the faint smell of parched soil of Svartalfheim, so subtle that she had not noticed it before. She shuddered. She had only been to see the svartalvar once, as a child when her parents had wanted to show her how gruesome the short-lived were, so she would no longer want to go to Midgard. In the end, she had left anyway, as soon as she had been of age to change her size, but never could she forget the horrors the svartalvar had made her see.

'They helped me,' her brother said. His voice was calmer than she would expect.

'What did they make you see?'

'They didn't give me sight,' he said and the discomfort that had settled around Siv's throat, without her even noticing, was undone. She walked with more ease and her thoughts felt light in her head.

'They made me listen.' Her brother stared emptily ahead as if to remember exactly what he had heard.

'They opened a door for me, a door down to the heart of Muspelheim's heat,' he said. 'In exchange, they wanted to know what I heard. Not many of them know the language demons speak.' Siv was impressed that her brother did; few creatures ever lived to learn the language of beasts and demons.

'So, I closed my eyes,' he continued, 'opened the door and listened and I heard the fire demons' crackle and laughter.'

'Muspelheim's demons are laughing?' She could not believe it. It could only mean one thing.

'They're stronger than ever. They're preparing to take over Midgard,' her brother said, confirming her worst fears.

Her feet felt heavy and she almost had to drag herself further up the steps. The knowledge rang in her tiny head. It was difficult to think in this little body.

Siv concentrated on the stone steps, struggling to calm herself. She had not expected to be so shaken, but this was the beginning of the end, and she had never thought it would come so soon.

'There's still time to postpone fate,' her brother said.

Despite what else she had heard, Siv's thoughts rested with Surt, and because of it, she noticed, perhaps for the first time, her brother's dusky skin. Next to him, her own looked like old milk. Over the winters, she had almost forgotten how the snow could colour someone. When she had been a small girl, her skin had been the same pretty tan as his was now, and it almost made her miss the days she had spent outside in the snow, far away from the house. It was all she would ever allow herself to miss from her homeland.

They were nearly at the top of the stairs. 'You haven't asked about them.' Her brother's voice was so quiet that Siv almost did not hear him.

'Who?'

'Our parents.'

With all her might, Siv tried to ignore him; she did not want to talk about them, or home, none of it. The hours spent in the snow, away from them, were the fondest memories of her childhood, but that was all she had. It was bad enough to have the existence of a younger brother to remind her of that past. She had left for a reason.

'You've never asked my name either,' he said.

She did not want to know, but when she saw that he was looking at her with eyes wide and deep, like those of a cat, she could not help but ask: 'What is it, then?'

'Buntrugg.' A rough-sounding name of typical jotnar roots, like the one Siv had been given at birth; Glumbruck. It had been a relief to discard it and pick something easier on the tongue.

Not knowing what else to do or what to say, she nodded.

They were ten steps away from the top of the passage.

'Good luck,' he said.

'Takka,' she answered, and because he did not turn around to walk back down, but waited for her to leave, she added something else, 'Tak, Trugg.'

He smiled.

Quickly, Siv turned away, so he would not expect her to say more. She made a cut on the tip of her little finger with the large seax and smeared the blood onto the stone at the end of the passage. It opened for her, and without a glance back at her brother, she left. There was too much to think about and her small, naked body could not hold it inside for much longer. Her chest visibly shook with her heartbeat, and her mouth was half open, heaving for air.

Overnight, she had become a tool for jotnar, vanir and aesir alike. A tool for all beings in the nine worlds, although most of them did not know she existed, and perhaps never would. Still, their fates rested in her hands. The future of the nine worlds rested in her hands.

HILDA

Chapter Twenty-One

HER EYES WERE open; they were. Hilda felt them with her fingers, poked her eyeballs. But she couldn't see. Could only feel the heat from the furnace on her skin, and hear the loud crackle of the fire demons, laughing at her.

Keep your eyes clear of Muspel's furnace. She knew the words—the Runes had warned her—but it would be alright. Her eyes only saw white because she had peered into something too bright to be looked at. Like those times when she stared directly at the sun and her eyes became prickled with colour. Though now everything was white. Just white. No prickle of colour.

Heat wound itself through her core. Hilda roared. It felt like her eyes were touching embers. Like the fire had burned into the back of her eyes; like her eyes were melting. She screamed and reached for her face; a thick fluid flowed down it, covering her cheeks, lips, and chin. She tasted salt. It burned, and kept burning.

Hilda closed her eyes. Maybe with some rest her vision would return. Through her eyelids, she felt the heat and light of the furnace. The demons snapped with laughter. She wanted them to stop, to leave her alone. More than anything, she wanted to get out of the jotun passage grave and back home before winter. *Keep your eyes clear of Muspel's furnace.* Maybe she'd never see the colours of early winter again. Or the white snow on a late winter night. The lush green of summer.

The fluid from her eyes stung. Hilda clenched her teeth to suppress the pain. Her eyes watered too, which only made everything hurt more. The heat bored itself into the darkest corners of her skull.

Keep your eyes clear of Muspel's furnace.

It had happened so fast. A glance, and that had been it. A simple glance. She hadn't meant to look, but the fire demon had been right there. Her entire face prickled with pain and her eyes felt swollen.

Hilda rubbed her eyes with the back of her hands, accidently smeared the stinging liquid all over her face. It burned like a hot iron. Frantically she lifted the skirt of her dress to wipe it off. She wiped and wiped to remove the fluid from her eyes and make the pain stop.

Tears ran down her face. No matter how much she dried them, her face stayed wet with tears, and that burning fluid. And everything hurt, as if needles poked through her face, and her hands too. Embers rested behind her eyes; burning, and boring into her skull.

She couldn't stay there. She had to move. She swallowed her tears and let the moist skirt of her dress fall down. Her blue dress. She knew it was blue.

Hilda opened her eyes.

Resting her eyes had helped. The heat made it difficult to look, but she could see the bright colours of fire, around her. Long arms of fire reached for her. The fire demons chuckled inside the furnace. And outside it, too. She saw them, their heat. She didn't need the Runes to tell her that they were dangerous. She needed to leave.

Her eyes hurt so much. They hurt more and more, and Hilda knew that was a bad sign.

Nej, she needed to keep hope.

She couldn't ask the gods for help. They were angry with her. They had allowed Ash-hill to be attacked, and the Runes had warned her that the Alfather would abandon her. She couldn't rely on the gods until she had delivered the axe to appease them, but she could rely on the Runes. When she went back through the passage and reached Midgard, the Runes would heal her. She knew they would. They could make the wind rise around her. They had led her into another world to forge a weapon for the gods; surely, they could heal the burn in her eyes too.

Her eyes itched, too. The wind swirled around her, but the Runes didn't whisper, and she missed their warnings. The Runes would help her. If only she could get up to them, if she could get away from this forge, then she'd be saved. The Runes would save her.

First, she had to find the axe-head. She had come here with a purpose, and she couldn't leave without having fulfilled it.

Shaking her head to dismiss the pain, Hilda stumbled ahead. Her feet were unsteady. Her foot kicked something. She heard it roll on the floor, and crouched down to grab whatever it was. Her hands fumbled over the stone floor until they knocked against an object, soft like a sponge. Her fingers stroked it. There were small bumps on the soft surface, and hair too.

His head. The smith's head.

Hilda spun the head until she found the stubble on the smith's chin and then his neck. Tight, she clenched her eyes to ignore the deep ache in her head. With her fingers, she searched through the sticky blood for the bone of his neck. The axe had been sharpened well. The cut of the bone was so smooth she didn't really trust that she had found it. Soft like her father's once clean-shaven head. Never before had she seen or felt a cut as smooth as this.

Wherever the axe was, she needed it. She twisted her head in search of it, though she wouldn't be able to see it. She could only see the long slender fingers of fire demons.

The cut was clean. The axe head had gone straight through. The smith had been standing by the furnace, his back dangerously close to it, and Hilda's aim was good.

She crawled towards the heat and the fiery fingers that reached for her. Her eyes felt like someone pinched them from the inside and the ache in her head made her dizzy. Her hands felt the bottom of the furnace. She closed her eyes to focus and to keep the vision of Muspelheim and its demons out, then rose to her feet and felt the furnace. Back and forth, up and down. Patiently she brought her hands around, hoping to find the axe head.

Nothing.

Hilda roared with frustration. Slower and with more care, she probed the surface of the furnace, until her fingernails clinked against something embedded in the surface. Hilda smiled; she had been right. It had been a clean cut. With a forceful jerk, she wrenched the axe head free.

The axe lacked a handle, but Hilda had already picked one. Smiling at her own idea, Hilda searched blindly through the air for the table she knew was at the middle of the forge. Her left palm knocked against the table edge. She groped the tabletop for the shaft she had picked out, and a hammer. She couldn't go out into the big wide world of Midgard without a proper weapon. Her own axe was long gone, but the axe for the gods was right there, and the smith had already prepared the shaft.

It required a lot of care, and guessing, to hammer the shaft into the eye of the axe, but focusing on something helped her ignore the pain in her eyes, like focusing on orders to ignore the pains and sorrow of battle.

Finished, Hilda put the new axe into her weapon belt, fumbled her fingers over the edge of the table and found the dwarf's tools. For a little while she sorted through sharp, heavy objects she couldn't name, and a few she could: iron ingots and files, some thin strips of leather and a few fine polishing stones. Her hands found a skin-bag and she pulled it out. Various tools clanged on the floor and hit her feet. There was something inside the skin, something that smelled salty. The meat the smith had shared with her.

Hilda cornered the table and swept the floor with her feet to find the Ulfberht sword, stomping carefully so she wouldn't cut herself. After a long search, she found the blade and placed it into the skin with the food, the sharp end upwards so it wouldn't poke a hole at the bottom of the bag. The tip poked out far at the top.

Hilda lifted the bag up and let it hang across her body from her right shoulder. Ready to leave.

A whimper from her right wrenched her out of her thoughts. It came from the waterfall. She knew the voice; her snow fox.

The smith was dead. There had been no one else in the forge. The snow fox was there to warn here of the fire demons. The whimper gave her an idea. She could use the company and warnings of the snow fox. If only it would stay with her and not disappear.

Her chainmail rustled as she crept towards the waterfall, and then she remembered: the chain. There had been a chain among the smith's tools. She had seen it when she was searching for a polishing stone. At once, she turned to the table and found the chain under a tong. She yanked it free and tested the strength of it. It felt light in her hands, but strong too.

Paws scrabbled on the stone floor a little further towards the waterfall.

Hilda searched through the fire demons' fiery fingers. There was a faint red heat of something small, standing on four legs. Hilda crawled towards it, careful not to startle the snow fox. It whimpered again. Maybe the fox was hurt like her. Maybe it had looked into the furnace as well. Nej, if its eyes hurt like her own, the fox would have howled in pain, anyone would have.

She jumped towards the fox. Her hands grabbed its furred body, squeezed to hang onto the fur. The fox's slim body slipped away under her touch, but Hilda jerked after it. Fire demons laughed and the fox barked at her.

Hilda clenched her fist shut around the fox's tail.

With all her strength, she pulled the tail closer. The fox cried out and she heard its sharp claws against the stone floor, struggling to free itself from her grasp.

It snarled at her, but her fist was closed around its puffy tail. With her other hand Hilda grabbed the skin at the fox's neck. 'I won't hurt you,' she muttered. 'You're safe with me.'

The fox yelped a bark and she felt it snap at the air a mere fingertip or two away from her skin, threatening to bite.

'I won't hurt you,' she whispered, holding the fox by the neck and tail. 'I need you.' The yelps lost conviction. 'I need your help.' The fox's muscles relaxed.

For a few heartbeats longer, Hilda held it, and then she let go of its tail. It tried to wriggle out of her grasp, but she kept it fastened with her grip at its neck. Hilda was as stubborn as the fox, and she didn't allow it to get away. Unafraid, she tied the chain around the wild animal's neck. She let go of the neck of the snow fox, and hung onto the chain.

As soon as she let go, the fox yanked on the chain, pulling with all its might, but then it stopped, suddenly, as though it had realised its struggle was of no use. Hilda didn't loosen her grip on the chain. Five heartbeats passed before the fox tried again; Hilda held it back and waited for the fox to realise that it was impossible to get away.

'I need you,' she repeated.

Her words provoked a threatening growl, and barely had Hilda opened her mouth to speak again before the fox let a bark escape.

'You're bound to me now.' She lifted the chain a little. 'I go where you go, and you go where I go. You need to be my eyes.'

The fox growled, but didn't snap this time.

There was so much light and heat in the forge. Everything hurt more and more the longer Hilda stayed there. She needed to escape. The burning shadow of her snow fox became clearer every time Hilda blinked. It was easier to find too, bound to her with the chain.

Hilda tied the end of the chain around her right hand three times so she wouldn't accidently let go of it, and then she rose to her feet. Her head was heavy from the scorching pain in her eyes. The fox blended in well with the heat of Muspelheim, a mere shadow, but Hilda saw it.

'Take me to the passage way,' she commanded. The fox straightened the chain and led Hilda away from the table. The roar of the waterfall was loud; the left side of her vision was blank white and the right full of fire and demons.

'I know that's not that way,' she snarled and yanked the fox towards her. She moved along the table. Full of mistrust, she stepped ahead. The fox tried to drag her in the opposite direction, but every time it did, Hilda tugged on the chain. Before every single step, she tested the ground with the tip of her toes, terrified of falling into the water, to her death.

It felt like half a day had passed before she reached the big rock at the edge of the forge. The one that led into the passageway and up to the daylight above, up to the Runes that would heal her.

The rock needed her blood.

She moved her hand down to her weapon belt. A deep cut of the godly axe opened the skin on her palm. Hilda touched her hand to the rock in front of her.

The forge didn't shake like the passage way had, but the rock underneath her palm did, and then it rolled to the left. Hilda rushed through, dragging the struggling fox in with her before the opening could close. She staggered up the first few hot steps. The fox tried to yank free and run away, but Hilda forced it to stay at her side. The rock closed behind them.

The sound of Hilda's steps echoed up the passageway.

'I *will* tame you,' she snarled to the fox and walked up the steps. She needed guidance and reassurance now that she could hardly see, and only the fox could provide either.

Her white Muspel sight showed her fox clearer, now that they were away from the overwhelming heat and amber light of Muspelheim. She saw herself too; the warmth of her body.

It was a relief to be on her way again, but it didn't take much more than half a rest for her enthusiasm to fade. Her eyes stung worse and worse. The fox ran too fast, or refused to walk at all, and Hilda had to haul it up most of the way.

'Come, come,' she called when the fox refused to go anywhere for the hundred-and-twentieth time. The journey seemed longer than the one down, and the only comfort Hilda had was the thought that the Runes would heal her when she stepped out of the jotun passage grave.

Heat had burned into her and given her a different form of sight, Muspel sight. The Runes would give her back her normal sight. Yet the doubt that they were even still up there, in the wind, waiting for her, rested at the back of her mind. Nothing was certain.

After a long walk Hilda sat down on a step to eat. The snow fox lay down on the step above her, its fur brushing her arm, and Hilda broke off a piece of the meat and held it out. The fox sniffed the food, poked it with its nose, curious, and turned its snout away.

'You don't eat?' she asked.

The fox ignored her. Hilda wanted to leave the meat next to the fox for it to take when its pride would allow, but there wasn't enough food to spare. There would be enough to get her out of the jotun passage grave, but that wasn't the end of her journey. She needed to head home to Ash-hill once she got out, so she could offer the axe to the gods and beg for their forgiveness.

Her eyes throbbed. They were in constant tears, and that made it worse. It felt as though they had been sewn shut. They hurt unlike anything had ever hurt before. Even more than the wound in her thigh from the battle in Ash-hill.

Hilda lay down flat on the steps. She tried to sleep, though she couldn't. Even so, it felt good to lie down and do nothing for a while. To just lie with her eyes closed and pretend that she was almost back home in the longhouse in Ash-hill, and that her father was alive, and that everyone else was too.

Something wet touched her bleeding hand. The fox sniffed, and then its nose poked her fingers, its tongue licked her hand, bloody from her entrance into the passage. The fox cared for her, after all. Though it was stubborn like her and didn't take orders. Her fylgja was just like her.

Its long fur rubbed against her arms as it walked up to her face. Again, she heard it sniff, and then it poked the side of her head and its tongue licked her eyes. The pain receded with her fylgja's care. The burning sensation receded, for a while. When it began to hurt again, Hilda got up, took her things and resumed her walk.

Four more times she stopped for food. Each time she offered the snow fox something to eat, though it ignored her. It didn't try to escape any longer either.

At last, she reached the top of the steps. Hilda sat down with her back against the closed exit and took out a small piece of dried meat. The fox whimpered, as though pleading with her to open the passage. Hilda munched on her meat, and stared down the hundreds and thousands of steps she had walked up, and couldn't see. Her eyes stung. The thick fluid the fox had licked away had formed anew. The pain sped up her heartbeat and made her short of breath.

Outside, the Runes waited for her in the wind. They'd be there, she thought, to convince herself, and they would heal her eyes and make her see normally again. She would go to Ash-hill, and then she would be with the warriors again, and with Einer, and together they would avenge Ash-hill.

Hilda leant her head back against the rock, took three short breaths, slit open the wound on her little finger, and rubbed the blood onto the rock behind her.

The passage grave shook. Hilda rose to let the rock roll away for her.

Hilda. Hilda. Hilda. The wind and its whispers overwhelmed her with their force, like the many voices of the fire demons in Muspelheim. She had expected the sound of them to soothe her, she had expected to be overcome with relief at their return, but she wasn't. Instead, she trembled with unknown fear. *Did you cover Muspel's furnace as you left?*

Hilda crawled out into the grave. She couldn't see anything apart from the snow fox and herself, burning with heat like fire demons. The passage loudly closed behind the fox and her.

Did you cover Muspel's furnace as you left? the Runes demanded to know.

The wind rose around her. Hilda sat down inside the grave, her head turned away from the opening. She couldn't bear the idea of going out when there was nothing for her to see. Nothing but white light. When her eyes hurt, and burned, and were useless.

You saw Muspel's children, the Runes realised, making the wind swirl fast around her.

'Heal me,' she ordered. She didn't dare to breathe as she waited for the Runes to comply. Furiously she blinked her eyes, each time convinced she'd see normally again. Convinced the burning sensation would recede, finally, as it had for a short moment in the passageway when the fox had licked her eyes. But the pain and the white light persisted.

It has passed through. We cannot heal you.

'Make me see again,' Hilda yelled, to make the Runes listen, and make them heal her. They *had* to heal her. They knew so much. They could make the wind rise. Always, they knew what she had to do. They could fix everything. As they always did.

Despite our warnings, you saw Muspel's children.

'Make me see!' Her eyes were filled with tears. She closed them.

The Runes could heal her, she knew they could, they had to. They were her only hope. If the Runes couldn't save her, then...

It has passed through. Nothing can free you.

DARKNESS

RAGNAR WANDERED THROUGH the Darkness, alone and with no idea of where he needed to go.

He struggled to shake the memory of the wolf tearing him apart, and of his god dying. He had brought on Odin's death, and he had watched as his god was torn apart and devoured.

The memory made him shiver.

No matter how long he waited and how many deaths he suffered, the big bright veil into Helheim would not open for him, as if even Helheim did not deem him worthy.

Walking through the chilly Darkness almost made him feel like a true farmer again. That was all he had ever been; a farmer, no more. He had never belonged in Ash-hill. He had lied about everything, and his lies had allowed him to stay there and become their skald. The villagers had believed his words; had regarded him as a hero. They had made him into the person he had been the last winters of his life in Midgard. Alone he was no one. He was not clever, not brave, not capable. He was just a farmer's boy.

He was unworthy of what he had owned back in Midgard, and he had lied his way to all of it. Right from the moment when he had first woken up in Ash-hill's campsite and they had asked who he was. Vigmer had found him floating on a raft that had survived from the burnt longship from which he had escaped. It had been before Vigmer had become chieftain, back when Bjorn was chief of Ash-hill, long before either Hilda or Leif had been born.

When they had asked Ragnar where he came from, he had realised, despite the dream caps and ale he had been given, that they knew little if anything about why he was there and who he was. So, he had lied. It had been so easy.

He had told them of the great battle he had fought, how he had been the lone survivor, had killed everyone else. How their ships had been burned, and how he had bravely navigated across the open sea on the remaining planks, and passed out from the effort.

But he was a farmer's boy, and had never been more. He had never killed a man, had never hunted, had never been brave, never wanted to raid and had only survived as a young man because he had run from the battle before it had begun.

Perhaps they had learnt the truth before they had finished burning his corpse, and decided not to give him the honour after all. Perhaps that was why he was here and not in Helheim.

His lies and dishonesty, his greed and his fears had brought him right into this Darkness that had no end and no light and no good at all. He had provoked his own misfortune.

The irony dwelled on him and he had to restrain himself from laughing. The madness swelled up inside him. He was a fool, a true fool, walking blind through the dark, wanting to laugh at himself and his situation, despite the fact that he knew it would get him killed. He was a coward who deserved this sentence the gods had given him.

He took a loud breath to calm his madness, gulped, realising what he had done. He had made himself heard.

EINER

Chapter Twenty-Two

EINER SHOOK THE rain out of his hair and pulled his oar back hard. When they rowed, they drew breath together, and moved in the same beat, but from lack of practice, Einer had needed a few moments of clumsy struggle. Being allowed to laugh at their commander's unusual clumsiness had relaxed the crew, and made Einer feel like a young sailor again.

His father commanded the *Northern Wrath* in Einer's stead.

All morning as they rowed, Hormod had told them stories of Normandy. Nearly two dozen summers ago, he had helped Richard of Normandy take back Rouen.

'Just a young boy, back when I knew him, but already fond of wars and women.' Hormod laughed. His husky voice made it sound like a cough. His stories helped to make them relax at the thought of arriving in Normandy. Much must have changed since Ash-hill's old warriors had been there, for despite the praise Hormod had for Richard, Normandy was Christian land. By going there to seek help, they risked everything. They risked their lives and the strike they had planned to honour their families and friends. All of it.

'He has a funny name,' one of the two youngest raiders piped; the unshaven and stinky one Einer had forced to bathe on the first day because the smell of him made them all sick.

'Ja, being Christian is his biggest flaw,' Hormod said. 'Like not washing is yours, Geir.'

They all howled with laughter, Einer probably louder than he should have; a commander should never act quite the same as the rest of his crew.

'Richard might be Christian, but that's because Rollo turned his faith,' Hormod continued. 'Richard keeps the religion his grandfather chose.' Some of them grumbled a little at that and none of them could imagine the shame it must induce to be kin of a man who had abandoned his gods.

'He was an honourable kid. He will be true to the promise he made after his father's death. He'll lend us his strength,' Hormod assured them.

To sit and row for so long felt strange; Einer had raided for no more than two summers before he had been given command of his own ship, and since then, he rarely rowed or held a rope. His body dripped with sweat, and every time he pulled, he shook his head, so the mixture of sweat and rain would not run down into his eyes. His arms were not sore, as he had thought they would be, but he could feel his sword-muscles heat up and remembered, for the first time in many summers, that rowing was good practice for fighting.

Einer was too focused on maintaining the rowing pace to give much attention to Hormod's words, but he acknowledged that it soothed the mind to have someone on board tell stories; a skald like Ragnar, although Ragnar had never been fit to come with them on the summer raids. Having a story to concentrate on made the crew work with more rigour and less complaints. Perhaps he himself should start to tell stories next time they had to row.

The call of a horn made them peer out to port side. The river was wide in comparison to the narrow fiords and inlets back home. Inland, a dozen riders galloped along the river. The rider at the front yelled something to Einer's father. The warriors were quiet and tried to listen, Einer was too far away to hear much over the rain, but he could see the riders over the side of the ship. Their bows were nocked. A bad sign.

The riders were from Rouen, a party sent out to meet them. Three of the riders turned back where they had come from, but the rest set into trot and, on land, they followed Ash-hill's ship up the river. Another bad sign.

A quiet chatter rose among the crew. Everyone was nervous. Einer too felt his heart beat in his chest, and not because he had been rowing; his heartbeat only rose like this in battle.

They risked sailing straight into an ambush, they risked death by rowing on the little way left to Rouen, but they would risk anything to avenge those who had passed on. If they died there, then so be it. They would feast in Valhalla. Yet, Einer had no intention of letting any of his warriors die. His mind raced, trying to figure out how he could get them through this safely, and he kept a watchful eye on the riders as they followed them up the river to Rouen.

When the *Northern Wrath* turned the next bend in the river, the edge of the city came into sight even for the rowers. Stone and wood buildings blended in with each other; some tall and built close to each other, but most of Rouen's houses were small, like two thrall homes put together.

The rain turned dusty and then so fine that it did not feel like rain at all. Bells rang, announcing their arrival. They had come on friendly terms, but it tasted like a raid. Bells always sang for them when they raided at high-day.

Perhaps it was merely due to the heavy clouds above them, but the city seemed grey and sad. Around the market by the harbour they steered for, there seemed to be no colours and no light, no laughter and no song, just long faces.

The sound of the bells grew louder as they approached.

Einer's father commanded the *Northern Wrath* into the first empty port. The warriors put away their oars and readied themselves to go ashore. They changed into dry clothes, put on their armour, but left their helmets and weapons behind to show that they came on friendly terms. Einer changed into his bright yellow tunic that matched his hair and put a few silver arm-rings on, to show his rank. The last arm-ring was the twisted one Ragnar had given him winters ago. Hilda had one too, exactly like his. He wondered if she was feasting in Valhalla.

Three dozen guards or more were scattered around the harbour. All of them were men, but not a single one was large enough to defend against Ash-hill's warriors, had they truly come to raid.

Einer gathered ten of his best sailors. In a hushed voice, so neither the guards nor his own father would be alarmed, he ordered them to stay on the ship with weapons close and to row out at the shallow end of the harbour once the warriors had left, away from the harbour but close enough so the warriors could waddle through the water to the ship. He ordered them to defend the *Northern Wrath* at any cost, and to stay on high alert until every last sailor had returned to the ship. His request uneased them, and their expressions hardened.

Locals gathered by the harbour to see the warship with half-hidden curiosity. They pointed at the newly-arrived strangers and whispered to each other. The guards, too, looked on with interest; some of them seemed frightened, but as warriors did, they hid their fear and unease.

'This is all very different now,' Hormod mumbled as he legged off the *Northern Wrath* behind Einer. 'Things change. Things change.'

Einer joined his father and Hormod at the front of the harbour. Einer's father had spoken to a guard but no one had come to greet them yet. The riders they had met on their way should have arrived in plenty of time for Richard to meet them by the harbour. It was not a good sign that he was not there yet to greet them like a friend and good host.

'I didn't think they would speak our language,' Einer said to think of something else. At the time of Rollo's rule, the Normans had been true northerners like them, but that was long ago.

'Back then, some of them did,' Hormod said. 'Richard learnt quickly.'

Einer smiled but could not help but think that if his mother had still been alive, they would not need to have this conversation. His mother had always had a gift for foreign tongues, she would have laughed at their concern and said: "It's the same tongue, just a different song."

'The guard understood,' Einer's father said, a little late as though he had to think about whether he was right or not. 'When I mentioned Richard, he ran off.'

'Perhaps you scared him,' Einer said and laughed.

Down from a muddy road to the right of the harbour arrived a man who stood out from the colourless setting. A man who could be no other than the Norman chief. He wore gold as a warrior would wear armour. Around his neck hung a flat gold chain inlaid with glass and jewels of all sizes and colours, which complemented the jewelled rings on his arms and fingers of both silver and gold, equally ornamented with jewels. Even his clothes were decorated with gold borders. Either Richard was very wealthy, or he wanted to make everyone believe that he was.

His outer coat was sharp blue with a round cut, not the usual square one from home. At his side walked a younger man, although Einer suspected that anyone would look young next to Richard.

The young man would have had more ease blending in with the Jutes than the Normans. His shoulders were covered with a fur and his hat, short and round in Norman style, had a silk trim.

The two men walked directly towards Einer's father. 'Welcome, old friends,' Richard said in a thick accent that curled the 'r'.

He stopped in front of them and smiled. Einer's father stared blankly at him, but did not respond. For someone who had been born in the south and had never lived in northern lands, Richard's Norse was good, but he had to repeat himself twice before Vigmer understood.

'I'm Vigmer Torstenson, the chief of Ash-hill,' he finally said and forced a grin.

'Vigmer,' the jewel-covered man responded. 'I'm Richard Williamson.'

'We've heard much about you from Hormod, who once fought with you.' Einer's father gestured towards Hormod.

'It's good to see you after so many summers, Richard. You've grown,' Hormod said, a little too fast, so he had to repeat himself with a nervous stutter before he received a reciprocal smile. Richard's welcome held no warmth, and Einer assumed that he either could not remember the old raider, or had never noticed him in the first place.

'You predict to stay long time?' Richard asked Vigmer, ignoring Hormod. He put an excessive stress on the word *predict*.

'If you'll allow it.'

'Ja, ja.' He nodded without as much as a smile. 'Our northern brothers are always welcome in Normandy.' Einer could not help but notice the cold tone of voice; perhaps he was imagining it.

'Takka,' his father said in an equally cool undertone. Einer had not been alone in sensing the hostility.

'What you bring here? And voyaging with women.'

'What we bring?' Einer's father asked, and it was a wonder that he had not reacted to Richard's dig at their shieldmaidens.

'Ja, why are you here, in Rouen?'

'Maybe we can discuss this after a meal. It's been a rough journey.'

Richard nodded. 'Ja, ja. You must be hungry and tired. Come. I will show you something on the way to the hall.'

Richard's smile unsettled Einer, and made him glance around the market to count the Norman guards. Thirty, that he could see. There had to be more elsewhere in town that he could not see. They were a full crew on the *Northern Wrath*, but even so, they were only forty warriors. With ten sailors on the ship, only thirty of them followed Richard into his town. Without their weapons, they would be vulnerable if it came to a fight.

They were guided up the roads of Rouen, past stone houses, big and small, while the sun hung low on the horizon and the clouds in the sky turned to bands of red and dark blue.

The fur-wearing man shadowed Richard, who pointed to the houses they passed, telling them which important Christian lived where. The Jutes responded with a few grunts from time to time and an occasional nod when a grunt was not enough.

The locals scowled at them and kept their distance, and although the locals were nearly as tall as the Jutes, they were weak shadows of northerners. Einer could not find a single man who looked like a warrior, although they made a game out of trying.

Throughout the walk, Einer and his warriors exchanged concerned glances. Rather than watch what Richard pointed out for them, they glanced down the dark streets, searching for figures in the shadows. It did not feel right to walk there, in the evening, as the sun was about to set.

'We've arrived,' Richard said, as they turned up a big street to the right. Ahead was a stone church. 'Rouen Cathedral,' he proudly announced. 'One time finished, it will be the most magnificent cathedral in Normandy.'

The building was as tall as three longhouses on top of each other; the slanted wooden roof was so far up in the air that it could almost touch the clouds.

'We still work on the outside, but inside it is nearly finished.' He stopped to eye the building in front of them, smiling, as though the sight of it was enough to make him happy.

Einer looked up and tried to see what Richard saw, but he could not. He did not understand why someone would need or want something like this. Such a big place would be difficult to keep warm, and take a lot of time and effort to build, and it seemed to have no real purpose other than to show off wealth, which could be done by throwing a few good feasts instead.

'Here, I think to put a statue of our Archbishop,' Richard explained. He added something else in Norman that made no sense to Einer, and on he went about what needed to be done and how it would look when it was finished.

No longer listening, Einer wondered why they had been brought to see this big stone church. Perhaps it was a threat, or perhaps Richard wanted them to change their faith in return for his hospitality and help. If so, he was not as clever as Hormod gave him credit for.

'Enter,' Richard showed them through a big wooden door.

Every part of Einer roared for him not to enter. It was not the same as going into the wooden church at home. This felt different, like a trap. Not just his mind, his entire body rebelled against entering the church. All the same, he forced himself through the wooden door after his father, along with the rest of the Jutes.

Inside was a single big room with thick pillars to support the roof, which was uncomfortably distant. The air was cold and damp inside, and candles had been lit around the big hall. Thin gaps in the high walls allowed a little evening light to enter as Richard led them further into the hall past several statues, some of them carved into the pillars.

'This is what I want to show you.' His voice echoed down the hall, or room, or whatever this was. 'This is where he rests.' Richard stopped up in front of an image hacked out of stone on the floor.

'Rollo?' Hormod asked. He was the first to recognise the face of the picture they stared at.

'My grandfather, Robert.'

A Christian name that dishonoured Rollo's legacy.

As he gazed down on the stone statue of the first Norman chief, Einer felt a knot in his stomach. Rollo was pictured praying like a true Christian, with no weapons in his hands, and nothing in the image to suggest the kind of man Rollo must have been. The kind of man the stories about him said he was: a fierce leader and conqueror who had tricked a king into giving him Normandy, but who in turn had been forced to abandon his faith. There was nothing fierce about him. Only a docile, praying Christian. That was all that was depicted. That was how he was remembered in Normandy.

Einer had never quite understood what could lead a man so fierce to abandon what he believed in, but as he peered down at the image of Rollo carved in the stone by their feet and glanced to Richard, walking around with his glittering jewels, it all made sense.

Rollo had become Christian for wealth.

He had abandoned his faith in favour of power.

'And this is my father, William.' Richard showed them another stone carving on the floor.

The others followed, to politely examine the grave, but Einer could not move away from the docile image of Rollo.

It had been a mistake to enter the church.

Einer wanted nothing more than to be free of the thick stonewalls that surrounded them, and to get away from the faces of the statues looking down on them, but Richard had positioned himself at the furthest end of the hall to address them all, and it was not the time to leave.

The sun had set and, in the dark of the hall, it was difficult to spot possible danger; but it was there, and Einer's thoughts wandered to the silent fur-wearing man who had still not been introduced to them. His body felt cramped, and the bracteate on his neck-ring hammered against his chest. Something was amiss.

'I've shown you around,' Richard said, standing in front of them all. 'So, tell me, Vigmer Torstenson, why have you come?'

The ringing silence filled the cool with a howl. Einer could almost hear his father think.

'Richard,' his father finally said. 'We come to ask you to fight with us, as you asked us to fight with you nearly two dozen winters ago. Ash-hill answered your call, and we hope you'll answer ours.'

'Because of the battle this summer?' Richard rubbed one of his many finger-rings, without as much as glancing up at Einer's father.

There was a long silence. No one had expected Richard to know. If he did know, then perhaps he had been one of the people behind the attack on Jutland.

The warriors' previously nervous stares hardened.

Einer's blood boiled, not with anger, but with something else. He needed to leave this place, before he suffocated. He needed to get back to his ship and sail far away.

'Ja, I have heard talk about the battle in your Dane lands.'

'Jute lands,' Einer's father corrected.

The Dane lands was what Harald had called his own lands. Even before Richard could speak again, it was clear how he had known about the battle.

'This man,' Richard turned to the young fur-wearing man who had not left his side all night. 'I've not introduced you. He is the envoy of Harald Gormsson.'

Whispers erupted between the men and women in the Christian hall.

Unaffected by the sudden chatter, Richard continued his speech. 'He told us that faithful Christians arrived in the north to make you see the truth of Jesus Christ.' Spoken like a true southerner and Christian.

No one said anything, but Einer knew he was not the only one to clench his fists in anger and keep his teeth shut so hard they might shatter. His chest was tight and his breathing heavy.

'They met a violent resistance and were forced to fight. Harald Gormsson fought them too, to Hedeby, and down to Danavirki.'

If Harald had taken over Danavirki, they would have known. He would have sent for all Jutes and Danes as soon as he had taken over Danavirki. He would have sent for everyone, to man the barricade and keep the southerners out. There was only one possible explanation.

'There he saw the truth of Christ and gave up his old faith.'

Harald Bluetan, the Rollo of southern Jutland. He would be the death of them all.

'The coward,' Einer's father exclaimed, and although they were all thinking the same word, the hall went quiet. They understood the impact of their chieftain's words. Those words would not be pardoned.

'All this I know. So, tell me, Vigmer Torstenson,' Richard spat the name. 'Why have you come?' Richard's steps echoed along the hall, and the silence stretched.

'To ask you to seek revenge with us.' The words escaped Einer's mouth before he could stop them. They could not give up. They had sailed so far.

'Revenge? You're not the ones who should seek revenge.' Richard did not settle his gaze on Einer, instead he looked out over the crowd of Jutes. 'But if you convert and acknowledge your wrongs, God will forgive your violent past.'

Einer knew his father was too taken aback and embarrassed to speak, so again, he spoke in his father's stead. 'Our friends, our kin—brothers, sisters, parents and children.' Einer looked the Norman chief directly in the eyes. 'They were slaughtered by these faithful Christians this man has told you about.'

'The Christian envoys met violent resistance,' Richard insisted.

'From farmers and children?'

'You can't know what happened,' Richard hissed. 'You arrived *after* the battle. You can't know how it started when you weren't there.'

'We helped you back when you were chased from your lands,' Einer's father said, ignoring their bickering. 'Will you help us now that we've been chased from ours?'

Richard peered at the men and women in the hall, licked his teeth, and even before he opened his mouth to speak, Einer knew his answer. 'Convert and God shall help you.'

Einer's father scoffed at the suggestion. 'You refuse to help us now that you no longer need help yourself.' His father was not asking, he was making an observation, and one that did not please.

'Convert and God shall help you,' Richard repeated.

'You *owe* us your help,' Hormod said through clenched teeth. He stood further down the hall, and when Einer turned around and saw the old man's hurt face, he felt his heart tighten. Hormod had expected Richard to help them; had spoken so fondly of him. And then, behind Hormod, Einer saw Norman guards standing outside the church, and at once he understood why his heart felt so tight and why the bracteate burned at his chest. They had been led into a trap. Convert or be killed as they exited the church, those were their options.

'We should never have come,' Einer's father muttered. He too had noticed the guards outside.

'At least now we know.' Einer was not proud to admit it, but it was the truth. 'Now we know exactly what awaits us back in Jutland.' He walked towards the exit. He had made his choice.

His steps echoed along the hall. They all watched him, but no one stopped him. He would clear the way for his warriors, and give them options. He would clear the street before anyone would manage a fatal blow. He would give them a path back to the ship.

His choice was easy. Hilda was no longer there. In the next life they might meet. In Valhalla, they would find each other. He rushed at the open door.

Guards outside braced themselves, and pointed their weapons at him, but Einer was taller and larger than them, and they could not have been in as many fights for one of them was shaking.

At the door, he stopped. His chest burned and his lungs were tight. He wanted nothing more than to leave the suffocating church, but he knew churches were sacred places to Christians, and of all places, they had planned an ambush on their own holy ground. He would make certain that they would suffer the consequences.

The guards watched him, reluctant to enter their holy church and force Einer outside. Their leader barked at his men, kept them in line outside; an older man with a stern look. A man used to Christian battles and strategies.

But Einer was no Christian.

One of them lunged forward, sword first, aiming for Einer's neck.

Einer clapped, as if the sword was no more than a fly, and caught the blade between his palms. He pulled the sword towards him, and the warrior stumbled a few steps to hold on. Others tried to pull him back into their midst, but Einer let go of the sword, didn't mind the cuts on his hands. He grabbed the corner of the man's shield and tore it out of the man's grip.

Einer stepped back into the church, wheeled the shield around and took his stance. He glanced back over his shoulder, hoping to see Jutes at the throats of Richard of Normandy and his fur-clad attendant, but the Norman chief was gone. So was Einer's father and a half a dozen others. There must be another way out of the church; they were in pursuit.

Outside, the guards retreated further from the door as Jutes joined Einer's flanks. Hormod was the first, raising a small chopping knife he had hidden in his clothes. Einer used his shield to cover the two of them. They stepped forward, selected their target.

Einer kicked the man's shin, and Hormod pulled him into the church. The man fell forward, face first. His chin smacked into the stone floor and Hormod sliced his neck from the back.

Blood spilled over the holy church floor. The guards outside were yelling.

The dead guard's armour and weapons were stripped from him, secure in the hands of Jutes. Another guard was pulled inside, killed on the stone floor. They bathed the church in Christian blood.

Outside, chaos erupted. Einer's father arrived from behind, an elbow into the back of the head of a Norman. Einer, Hormod, and the many at their backs took the opportunity to force their way out of the church. Einer slammed his shield into the head of a Norman, using it both for cover and to attack. Normans were fighting to keep their weapons, while Jutes attacked with nothing to lose.

Einer kicked his way forward. Hormod sliced off Norman's fingers with a blooded smile. One Jute fell at Einer's feet, and then another.

There were fifty guards and more, and thirty Jutes fighting for their life. At the first opportunity, they ran down the street, straight towards the river and their ship.

A spear pierced through the man running at Einer's left side. He collapsed, but there was no time to stop and haul him along. Einer kept running, with the swoosh of arrows at his back and the shouts of Norman guards.

The dark of the night made it difficult to recall the right way down to the harbour and market place. Einer ran after those in front, not knowing where he was or where they were going. Hormod and him were separated. There was no light but those that escaped the cold houses. The night was covered. Even the stars were hiding.

'The ship is gone,' someone yelled further ahead.

'Down the river,' Einer shouted. 'In the shallow waters!'

He heard splashes of water as the first Jutes jumped in.

Norman guards were chasing them down across the market place. Einer held his ground so his crew could get ahead and out to the ship. He stood with the shield high, searching through the fleeing Jutes for Norman guards.

His father rushed past him, Hormod too. Einer held his end, waiting in the dark. His senses were on high alert. His warriors splashed into the water at his back, and when he could no longer see anyone else heading down to the river, Einer too raced along the harbour to the shallow end and jumped in.

The cold water enrobed his feet. He waddled through until the waters reached his chest. There were screams everywhere. Einer tried to see where he was going. There was so much commotion. He heard yells behind him, and ahead besides, and pushed through the shallow waters towards them. A Jute floated dead in the water, an arrow in the back. Einer could not see who it was. He forced himself further ahead through the dark, towards the yells out on the water.

He rushed the last distance to the *Northern Wrath*. There were many warriors in the water, hanging onto the timbers; at least a dozen. Einer heard his father's voice, and a grunt that could belong to no one but Hormod.

They lay in the water, holding onto the *Northern Wrath*, waiting their turn to crawl onto the ship. Einer was shaking from the cold water. They all were, but they would row themselves warm.

From where he stayed and waited in the water, Einer counted less than two dozen warriors. So, few, and whoever was left was lucky to be there.

'Everyone has betrayed us,' his father said, voice shaking from the cold. 'We're on our own.'

HILDA

Chapter Twenty-Three

HILDA HADN'T MOVED. Sitting on the stone floor at the deep end of the jotun passage grave, she clenched the Ulfberht-made chain in her right hand.

She didn't know how long she had been sitting there, but her left hand no longer bled. Maybe half a day, maybe all day and night. There was no way to tell, and knowing wouldn't change the facts. Never before had she felt incapable of doing anything. Yet there she was, in the passage of an old grave, motionless and petrified with fear.

The thick fluid had settled around her eyes again and sealed her lids.

'Heal me,' she demanded of the wind, as she had too many times already. Her throat was dry and her voice sounded like the croak of a toad, not like her own at all. 'Help me.' A coarse whisper.

We cannot heal you.

Her eyes throbbed and she tried to concentrate on anything other than her eyes and the pain, but couldn't. Her entire head burned, and nothing could make it stop.

It has passed through. We cannot free you.

'I know that!' she yelled and she was crying now. Her tears melted through the thick fluid, ran down warm over her cheeks, gathered at her chin. Her entire face burned from it. 'I know.'

She would never see normally again. She would never become a shieldmaiden, would never be able to do anything on her own. She would always need someone at her side and a stick to walk with, like those old women who spent their lives weaving threads in the dark of a longhouse. She was too young for that. She hadn't done anything yet. Hadn't raided, hadn't proven her worth.

It was all the smith's fault.

Despite our warnings, you looked at Muspel's children. The Runes whispered as though they could hear her thoughts and knew that she was blaming her hardship on someone else. They were right; it was her own fault. She should have known—should have been careful and shut her eyes—but she hadn't. And now she was nothing, no one, and it was her own fault.

Rough fur caressed her leg. The snow fox leant against her leg for warmth and comfort.

Her face was wet and hot. Her nose ran, her lips tasted salty and her cheeks felt swollen. With the back of her left hand Hilda dried the tears at her chin and then her nose. She rubbed it from side to side and dried the snot. She couldn't sit there forever.

She had to go on.

She had set out from home and come all of this way. At least she needed to deliver the axe that would appease the gods, and return to Ash-hill, but she couldn't find the way on her own. Not like this.

The wind whispered something Hilda couldn't fully hear. A comforting whisper. The time in the forge had made her miss the Runes.

'You need to—' she sniffed sharply, and tried to ignore her unstable voice. 'You need to help me.' Everything was white, and strange. She had never known light to be feared. She had never known the world to be such a scary place.

It has passed through. We cannot free you.

'I know!' she yelled so and she felt so angry, as if a fire was being fed within her. 'I'm not talking about that!'

She didn't deserve this. She hadn't done anything to deserve it. The anger surged through her. All her life her father had prevented her from following the path she was destined for, and now this. As if she needed more hindrance. The nornir were cruel to wound her when there was so much more to achieve. They were all cruel; her father, the chief, the nornir; all of them.

She would show them.

She took a deep breath, she puffed out her cheeks and let the air escape a little at a time to calm herself and make the tears stop.

The Runes didn't talk, but she knew they were there. She felt the air caress her skin inside the passage grave. Her eyes itched and she wanted to scratch them, but she knew it would make the pain worse.

This wasn't the end. As the sole survivor of Ash-hill, she needed to get through this so she could accomplish something; so her life wouldn't be wasted.

The living man gets the cow, her father would have said.

The snow fox's thick fur felt warm against her legs and the wind was pleasant on her skin. She concentrated on that and took another deep breath. Her sight wasn't bare. She saw the snow fox, and herself. She saw heat sources. She wasn't alone, either; there were the Runes and the fox. If they helped her, she could get through this. Maybe, with rest, her sigh might improve.

Again, she dried the tears from her chin and cheeks, and her running nose, too.

'I need to find them,' she said when she felt certain that she wouldn't burst into tears. 'I need to find the others—you have to help me to get back to the warriors.'

The wind gave no answer, but it blew strong around Hilda, and the Runes muttered to themselves. Maybe they thought she was incompetent. Maybe they were deciding if she could be trusted. If that was the case, she needed to show herself capable and prove that even without her usual sight she would be useful to them.

Eyes shut, Hilda ensured that she had both the bag with the Ulfberht sword on her back and that the god-worthy axe was well fastened in its leather loop in her belt. Gathering all her courage, she took one last deep breath and turned to crawl out of the passage grave. But the chain she had tied around her right hand refused to budge; the snow fox didn't move with her.

Her muscles were tight and her body was sore from all the time she had spent sitting down, but she needed to move. Now. Before she could change her mind.

'Come on,' she called with a shaky voice, giving the chain a sharp jerk. 'Let's go.'

The iron loosened in her grip, as the snow fox rose to follow her. Its fur brushed against her right thigh, and then her arm, as her fylgja pushed past her out of the passage grave. To the best of her ability Hilda held it back. It moved too fast for her.

Patting the smooth stones on the ground, which had been placed there by giants thousands of winters ago, she found the wall and followed it out. She crawled so she wouldn't hit her head. When the wall stopped, she continued until moist grass brushed her fingers and tickled her knees. Only then did she rise to her feet.

The fox pulled on the chain, wanting to go further and fast, but Hilda held it back. The wind blew stray hairs in front of her face. Out of habit Hilda pushed them away, though it mattered little. Her new sight showed only her and the snow fox.

'Which way?' she asked the Runes and pretended that she didn't know she was crying.

Her mind was half focused on trying to stop her tears, half filled with anticipation of action. The wind whipped her hair around, but gave no answer. 'Tell me where to go.'

The wind pushed a little harder, as if telling her to find patience, but she had none to find. She had already wasted enough time feeling sorry for herself. It was time to *do* something. But she didn't dare to take a step forward without the help of the Runes. The way down from the gravemound was steep, she recalled.

The white light tricked her to believe it was day, but the air was cool, though maybe that was only because she had spent so long down in the protected grave. She couldn't hear any birds; maybe that meant it was night.

Above her was a ball of light, a small brilliant circle. The sun. She could see the sun above her. So, it was day, after all.

You didn't heed our words. The Runes' response wasn't what Hilda had expected.

'If you help me, you'll get what you want,' she said, not knowing what the Runes wanted. They had led her to the smith to get an axe made for the gods and now she had that very axe. She felt the weight of it on her belt. They had helped her so much. They had to want something in return.

The sharp wind made her shiver. *Despite our warnings, you looked at Muspel's children.*

She knew that. She hadn't done what they had told her to do, and she didn't need the Runes to remind her. She just needed them to show her where she had to go now. The warriors would be up in Ash-hill, by now. Maybe further north if they had gone elsewhere to seek shelter.

Only when the nornir have spun the thread in your favour do you listen to us. The nornir hadn't spun her destiny in her favour. Fate didn't go her way; it never did. The Runes had brought on this horrible fate for her. If they hadn't whispered to her, she wouldn't have searched for the forge, and she wouldn't have looked into the furnace.

You didn't heed our words. Your promises can't be trusted.

'I've learnt,' Hilda said, surprised at herself. 'Tell me what you want and I'll give it to you. Just— help me find the warriors. Help me get home.'

The snow fox sprinted suddenly ahead. The chain stiffened, and Hilda stumbled a few steps forward. She felt weak. The wind made the small hairs at the back of her neck tickle. The Runes needed convincing. 'I'll listen to you, I promise.'

You will lay an oath to heed our words?

Hilda nodded, impatient to move. Her stomach rumbled.

First: Did you cover Muspel's furnace as you left? She had forgot that the Runes had told her to cover the fire of the furnace. She had been so distracted by everything else. *Did you cover Muspel's furnace as you left?*

Her stomach felt as tight as her throat. How could she have forgotten? They had repeated their plea over and over before the passage had closed. She so wanted to tell them that she had covered the furnace, but she couldn't, because it would be a lie and though Hilda didn't always tell the truth, she didn't want to lie. Especially not to the Runes.

'What does it matter?' she dismissed and took a step forward, to the great excitement of the fox that strained on the chain. She walked a little way behind it, feeling the decline under her bare feet. No socks or shoes. She had taken them off when she had bathed and forgot them down in the forge too.

Muspel's sons will blaze through Midgard. So, tell us now, Hilda, did you cover Muspel's furnace as you left?

She walked after the fox, trying to go a little faster and ignore the Runes' insistent question. They would ask her to return to the forge and cover the furnace if she admitted the truth; and she couldn't go down there again. Couldn't. Her entire body rebelled at the mere thought of it, and her eyes stung in memory of the furnace.

Hilda, you did not cover Muspel's furnace.

'I did,' she yelled through the pain, and the guilt of the lie settled like a dark shadow firmly bound around her heart. 'I covered it.'

Then she opened her mouth again, and tried to say that it wasn't true, that she hadn't covered it, to admit the truth. But her voice was stuck, and she couldn't say it. The words halted deep down in her throat as though someone held them back.

The fox continued to pull her down the hill and Hilda stumbled over a knot of grass. She yanked the chain back, to force the fox to a halt.

Above her, the sky rumbled. A thunderstorm was coming.

You heeded our words, so your axe will join the battles of the south.

They weren't listening to her. 'Nej, nej, nej,' Hilda said. 'I need to find Ash-hill's warriors.' It would be so easy to go with the Runes and the snow fox, but Hilda had responsibilities. Even if they had returned, the warriors didn't know how Ash-hill had fallen or who had done it. She needed to tell them so they could avenge the dead, and Hilda was the only one who could tell them. 'I need to get home.'

Your axe will join the battles of the south.

'I need to find the warriors,' she insisted. 'If you won't tell me how to get home, then I'll have to do it on my own,' and although she feared falling down the hill, she bravely stepped forward. The fox put its full strength into dragging Hilda further.

'I need to find them,' she repeated. How could a half-blind woman hope to fight in battles of the south? The tears swelled up in her eyes at the thought. She would never raid. She would never fight again. An entire life of training lost and wasted.

The Runes were as reluctant to give in as her. *Your axe will join the battles in the south.* She needed to be more convincing.

'You desire something, like the dwarfs desired Freya, and like Freya desired the neck-ring Brisingamen.' The wind rose around her. Hilda knew that the Runes would listen to her this time. 'If you grant me my Brisingamen now—if you lead me to the warriors—I will grant you a wish too. I will do what you ask, if you do what I ask.' Alone she would never find Ash-hill. There were other worries too. Soon she would need to find shelter and food, and that, too, she would never manage on her own. She needed the Runes and she hoped they still needed her.

You'll heed our words, the Runes said in an acknowledging tone. She had succeeded. The Runes would grant her wish. *A soup to fill your stomach is being heated in a house further west. Your warriors will make camp south from there. Your axe will join their battles.*

The Runes had tricked her. All along they had known that the warriors were travelling south.

'And how can I find west like this?' she yelled at the Runes. An unfamiliar anger flared inside, reinforced by the pain that continued to burn at the back of her eyes, inside her head and all across her face. 'And I'm not hungry!' she screamed, though she was.

We have granted you your Brisingamen.

'But how am I supposed to find west?'

You'll know which way to go.

'I *don't* know,' she yelled, but the wind was different now. It didn't whisper to her or swirl around her and she knew the Runes were somewhere else. They had abandoned her, now that she needed them the most.

BUNTRUGG

Chapter Twenty-Four

THE MOUNTAIN TREMBLED with heat and anger from another world. Muspelheim's demons were fiercer and warmer than Buntrugg had ever witnessed them before.

The snow melted and trickled down the rocky slope like a river. The sweat ran along Buntrugg's arms and legs and gathered on his bushy eyebrows and eyelashes. He had begun his hike up the snowy foot of Muspel's mountain long before Surt had commanded his presence.

Buntrugg came to a stop. He released a dagger from his belt, and prickled his little finger with the dagger so a few drops of precious blood dropped onto the scorching rock.

Surt's passage cave opened for him. The mountain shook with the knowledge of his arrival, alerting the great Surt to his presence. Buntrugg hurried inside the dark cave, and the entrance shut behind him.

Usually, the cave was cool, but not today. The loud cackle of demons resonated inside the cave and burned Buntrugg's ears so it felt like he had a fever. The outside of the mountain was so hot that he had thought the passage to Muspelheim was open, but it was shut.

The scorching voices of the demons stopped suddenly.

Surt was coming.

Surt's steps alone made the cave in this world tremble and shake. Boldly, Buntrugg waited for the fire giant to appear.

The loud steps approached, and then they halted, on the other side of the sealed rock that separated Jotunheim from the world of fire. Buntrugg held his breath and looked down at his blackened shins, to avoid looking at Surt when he came through.

The rock at the end of the passage cave did not open, as he had expected.

'I thought I had given you a task, Buntrugg.' Surt's voice was as sharp as half a hundred blades, even through the rock that separated them. Since birth, Buntrugg had run errands for Surt, yet even now, the giant's voice sent shivers through him.

Buntrugg remained silent. He had thought he had completed his task to close and lock all openings to Muspelheim. He had sought out the Svartalvar and struck a deal with them. His task had been accomplished, and the nine worlds were safe from the unstoppable fire and wrath of the fire demons.

Or so he thought. 'A furnace is still open.' The words rang around the cave and scratched Buntrugg's ears as they echoed back to him, full of Surt's disappointment.

Buntrugg didn't understand. When he had been in Svartalfheim, dwarfs had hurried away to lock their furnaces. Each dwarf had been as worried as the next that they might take the blame for the escape of a fire demon. Buntrugg had reported to Surt that the matter was dealt with, and he had believed it. He still did. He had done what he had been sent out to do. He was certain.

'The dwarfs closed their furnaces,' he bravely retorted.

Surt did not respond, but through the rock, Buntrugg heard the demons in Muspelheim whisper about him. No one ever dared to contradict Surt, and despite how calm Buntrugg tried to sound, his left leg trembled.

'Buntrugg!' Surt roared. The fire giant's sharp voice scratched inside Buntrugg's head and made him wince from sheer pain. Yet, Buntrugg was thankful that Surt had not entered the passage cave to greet him. If not for the thick rock that separated this world from the next, the fury in Surt's voice alone might have killed him.

'I will find the furnace and I'll close it,' Buntrugg swore. 'Muspelheim *will* be silenced again.'

HILDA

Chapter Twenty-Five

THE FOX DRAGGED Hilda away from the passage grave, and down the steep slope of a hill. Despite her best efforts to keep up, she stumbled. Her companion kept running, pulling her with it, but her feet couldn't follow. She lost her foothold; her knees hit the ground and scraped against the grass, followed by her chest. The fox dragged her through high grasses. She sledged down the hill on her stomach.

Clenching her teeth, she yanked the chain back and the fox stopped. Hilda scrabbled against the ground until she came to a halt. The chain was limp for no more than three breaths before the snow fox nearly tore it from her hand, again.

She couldn't allow the fox to decide where they should go and how fast. She was the one in control. The fox pulled and pulled, but she held it back. It was like taming a dog, she told herself. Except the snow fox was surprisingly strong. Like a bear cub, maybe. But unlike Einer, she had never tried to tame a bear.

'Are you there?' she shouted to the wind, but received no response. For the first time in her life she truly needed help,

255

and for the first time, no one offered. Neither the Runes nor the fox.

She shook her head to shake the tears away. There was no time for this. She needed to find west. Only she didn't know how, and her eyes wouldn't stop stinging.

Taking a deep breath, she tried to find her bearings. From Ash-hill, she had walked south through Jutland. When the Runes had led her to the forge, it had been dark and Hilda had been following directions, not looking at the landscape. She had no idea which way they had gone. But the forge had been inside a passage grave, and those kinds of burrows belonged in the north. She didn't remember passing Danavirki. Maybe she was still in Jutland. Maybe not.

She bent her legs in to her chest.

The Runes had given her an impossible task. West. North. Now that she couldn't see even the simplest of things, like grass and trees, they were only empty words that she had used some time in the ancient past.

The sky rumbled, the same thunder she had heard earlier. It was drawing near. It wouldn't be long before the rain would fall. She could smell it in the humid air already.

She tried to rise to her feet. Her knees were hot; they must have been scraped open when she had been dragged down the hill by the fox. But even with her knees and her hand still bleeding, her eyes still hurt so much more. The pain was almost worse now than when she had first been blinded and her head was dizzy too.

It was only pain. It hurt though, as if someone poked her eyes from the inside with a hundred heated needles and the thick fluid that settled around her lids was her own melted eyeballs.

Hilda heard rain fall onto grass and felt a drop on her left foot. Then another on her forehead, one on her arm, and soon the drops were everywhere, falling from the sky as the thunder intensified. The rain fell on her, and the thick fluid that sealed her lids was smeared across her face, burning.

The fox whimpered at her side, and cuddled close.

'You took the pain away, on the steps,' Hilda remembered. The snow fox's licking had made the pain recede. Hilda groped the chain and followed it until her fingers touched the fur of the fox, moist from the run down the hill, through the wet grasses. She stroked the fox. It snarled in response.

Its fur had grown so much since the first time she'd seen it in the forest. Its winter coat was dense and hot like a thick woollen glove. It was muddy up the scared paws where its long hairs no longer grew. 'You licked my face on the steps.'

Maybe its drool had soothing effects. It was no regular fox after all. It was a fylgja. Hilda held her right hand by the snow fox's snout. The fox growled as loud as the thunder above, but then it sniffed her hand, poked it with its wet nose and gave it a lick. Immediately, Hilda smeared the snow fox's drool into her eyeballs. It hurt, as if she were rubbing sand into her eyes, and the pain didn't recede. No matter how many times she batted her eyelashes.

Maybe it wasn't the fox that had made her feel better. At least, it wasn't its drool.

'Are you there?' she shouted to the wind, but received no response.

The rain splashed over the field where she sat. If she continued to sit there she would catch a chill, and out there, without shelter for the night, a chill could kill.

'Come,' she told the fox, and stumbled to her feet.

They needed to find shelter. The passage grave wasn't an option: it was the driest place nearby and free from brisk rain and wind, but she couldn't go back. There had to be somewhere else.

The grasses were high and she knew the land was too flat to find good shelter. Finding west as the Runes had told her to do was her only hope. There had to be a way. The rain washed the stinging fluid from her eyes down her face and chest, burning all the way.

There had been trees between the fields, she recalled. She just needed to find the edge of a field.

'Come,' she said to the fox, and jerked on the chain to make it stand.

She rushed ahead, as fast as she dared, her feet cool on the ground, and tried to make herself light so her feet wouldn't get hurt. The skin on her knees was rigid. The fox sprinted along, dragging her with it. The sky thundered above. The storm gained intensity. Then she heard raindrops on branches. Could even smell it, that early winter smell of dying leaves.

With her hands stretched out in front of her, Hilda staggered ahead until the tip of her fingers hit the trunk of a tree. The trunk blocked the wind, so the gust only ruffled the hem of her dress and cooled her feet. Of course; that was how she could find her path. The coldest winds came from the sea, and now that the Runes weren't making the air rise around her, she could trust the direction of the wind. The trunk blocked the rush of air, so the ocean was ahead of her. That was it. It didn't tell her where west was, but it was a beginning.

Hilda searched her mind for a method to find her original course. She knew the stars best, and they were the most reliable to follow, but she couldn't see them.

There was something about trees, too. They never looked the same from every side; grew densely in the direction of south. Maybe she could still hear where the layers of branches and leaves were the thickest from how the rain fell. Where more leaves provided better shelter from the storm would be where the tree was densest, and hence the direction of south.

Hilda moved slowly around the tree, listening to the sound above her until she stood where the tree provided the best cover from the storm. She faced the trunk. Faced north.

The wind blew in from northwest, and the strongest storms came from the ocean. Likely northwest was also where the sea was. If she turned to her left now and walked so the wind came in a little to her right, for about one rest, like the Runes had said, she would find shelter. Proper shelter where she could rid herself of the chill that had already begun to sneak up on her. Maybe she could also find a pair of socks to warm her feet and some furs to sleep in, and have a warm meal.

'You need to help me now.' She looked down at the snow fox, her only companion in her white blindness. It looked up at her. 'We have to walk straight and keep going west.'

She turned left and began to walk. With almost every step she took, she flinched, thinking she might walk into something, or trip and fall. It took all her willpower to continue marching.

'The faster the better,' she muttered and sped up her pace, moving as fast as she dared. Her walk was bumpy from the uneven ground and she raised her knees high to avoid tripping over a patch of grass, a bush, or a big rock, or something else. She watched the snow fox to know what to expect, and she still stumbled, yet, she had no time to feel her way.

Her left hand was still bloody from having opened the passage grave. She could barely bend her fingers, and her eyes burned more and more from the rain that washed the thick fluid out over her face. With her left hand, Hilda rubbed both her eyes. They were hot on the inside, but, as she wiped them, the burning sensation withdrew and her eyes hardly stung anymore.

A warm yellow web appeared in Hilda's vision, and disappeared as suddenly as it had arrived. Thunder followed. She had seen lightning. Lightning, which was warm, like her own body. Only more so. Hot like the fire demons.

Again, lightning struck, as if Thor was riding across the sky, watching her and confirming her thoughts. The gods were on her side.

Hilda's eyes almost felt normal. The left hand she had rubbed them with was still bloody from before. Red Thor made the lightning strike and showed Hilda the truth. Down on the steps, the fox had licked her bloody hand first, and then her eyes. It was blood, not drool.

It didn't feel as though she had walked for long before her

eyes stung again. With the axe Hilda made a slim cut on her forearm; her left hand needed to heal so she would be able to grip onto a shield. She lifted her arm up to her face, rolled her head back, and let blood drip from her forearm into her eyes.

The pain retreated. It truly was blood.

Without rest, she walked on, concentrating on the path ahead, dripping blood into her eyes, every once in a while, when the pain returned. Half the time she had water up to her calves. Her forehead was hot and she was certain it was sweaty too, but it was difficult to tell—every part of her was wet from blood and rainwater.

The storm continued to worsen and the thunder seemed to never retreat. Thor was on his way to fight giants somewhere in Jotunheim.

In front of her, something appeared out of her white blindness. Something warm. A fire, she realised as she came closer, and people. Two of them, one large and one skinny. Hilda inhaled the air. Fire and roasting meat. It had to be the place of shelter the Runes had told her about.

She rubbed more blood into her eyes and as she did, the wind picked up and swirled around her. The Runes returned with their distant whisper: *You knew which way to go.*

'You could have told me how to find west,' she said. They had come back to find her, hadn't abandoned her. They had bent to her will, the fox ran obediently at her side and she had found her way, had done it all alone, without her usual sight.

Hilda slowed her run when she approached the warm figures and the fire. One figure was large and the other smaller. A man and a woman, she guessed.

The storm continued to rise and she was drenched from it.

Before Hilda could announce herself to the couple, she ran into something; her head banged against it before she could stop. A wall. She felt it with her hands.

The two weren't outside on the field, but in a house, yet still she could see them move about. Feeling her way with her hands, she followed the wall until she touched the wood of a door. She knocked. Kept a flat hand on the door to know when it opened. The warm outline of the bigger body came closer. Only the door was between them.

Hilda's throat was dry and her stomach empty. The cold had chilled her and the axe felt so heavy in her hand. She needed drink, needed food, and needed rest.

The voice of a man reached her. The door was still closed. She couldn't understand what he said, not because of the door between them muffled his voice, but because the language he spoke was one Hilda didn't know. This wasn't Jutland, she realised. Somehow, she had passed Danavirki and she was further south than she had imagined.

The man repeated himself and Hilda tried to listen, to find similar words and guess what he was saying, but it was more difficult than she would have thought.

She cleared her throat. 'Can I come in? I'm lost,' she said, putting on her sweetest, most girlish voice. 'I was hoping you might share some food, and a drink. Maybe somewhere dry to sleep.'

She heard quiet talk behind the door, quiet, but talk nonetheless. Then it opened with a creak, to leave a narrow gap. The large man leant closer, as if he was leaning in against the door to peer outside, at Hilda. The other figure, inside the house, backed away.

The rain continued to fall and Hilda shivered. 'Can I come in?' she asked.

The man grunted. He stalled for a moment and then he slammed the door shut.

'You lied to me,' Hilda said in a tired sigh, and she wasn't talking to the man.

Never did we say the door would be open.

She should have known. Nothing was ever simple with the Runes. She laughed at the absurdity.

She needed shelter or she would die, yet this man closed the door on her after seeing her standing there, a young half-blind girl soaked in the rain.

Hilda dripped more blood into her eyes to lift the veil of pain that had crept back into her mind. Already she had made five cuts up her left forearm. New wounds bled more than old ones, and she needed a lot of blood to soothe her eyes, but with every new slit she felt a little fainter. The loss of blood drained her. If this continued, it would kill her, she knew, but she couldn't think straight with the pain throbbing in her eyes.

'Open this door!' she demanded, knowing that the two people inside would hear her and understand what she wanted from the anger in her voice.

No response came, and she didn't wait for one. Instead, she undid the chain around her right hand and fastened it to her left, pulling the fox around to her other side.

She lifted the godly Ulfberht axe. She hated to have to use such an elegant battle-axe in this manner, but the man inside had given her no choice. She needed shelter.

Without any hesitation, she struck the oak door. The axe splintered the wood. She both heard and felt it. She had never known an axe with such power. A newfound rush of energy surged through her and she hacked again. She fumbled for the door. Still locked. The two people inside backed away. Her third strike cut a clear hole by the lock, and with all her force, Hilda kicked the door in.

The fat man who had closed the door on her lifted his left hand. He held a weapon no doubt, though it was his left hand. Every warrior knew to hold weapons in the right hand. This man had never been trained in battle. It was clear from his stance, which exposed his body, made him an easier target. Behind him, on the far side of the fireplace, stood the woman.

Standing in the threshold, Hilda heaved for air and at her side the snow fox yelped its vicious bark. She had never felt so much like a shieldmaiden before, and so strong. A flash of lightning struck in the distance. Hilda smiled; Thor was watching.

Squealing like a pig, the man launched at her with his left hand raised, with the weapon, whatever it was.

Hilda dodged out of his way and hit him in the right hip with her elbow. Skilfully she moved around him so she faced his back. He wasn't as fast as her. Before he could turn, she had hit him in the back of the head with the flat side of her axe.

The fat man dropped onto the floor. Like the man in the forest. Southerners truly went down fast. The woman screamed.

Without putting her axe away, Hilda grabbed the collapsed man by the ankles and towed him into the house, though the effort nearly made her collapse along with him. He was much heavier than he looked, like hauling a fully-clad warrior across the floor, shield, chainmail and all. It didn't feel like he wore armour, though. Just a tunic.

Hilda's body felt so weak, and the honeyed smell from the man's drink seemed to want to lull her to sleep. He had been drinking mead, not ale as she had expected. This wasn't a poor household.

When the man lay inside the house, and rain no longer poured over his legs, Hilda found the door and pushed it closed as far as she could.

'He'll be fine,' Hilda said and turned her full attention to the other person. The woman who had screamed. It looked like the woman's back was pressed against a wall. She held something in both hands. A weapon, maybe a knife.

Gently, so as not to startle her, Hilda shook her head. 'Put it down.' She lowered her axe, so it didn't look as threatening. 'Put it down,' she repeated.

The woman stepped forward, but not to charge. Her hands let go of what she held, which clanged onto a table. The woman backed away and showed the supposedly empty palms of her hands.

Hilda walked towards the place where the woman had dropped the knife, towards the table near the hot fire. With her eyes locked on the woman, she felt for the table top and searched until she found the knife. She secured her axe in her belt and sat down at the edge of the table.

'I won't hurt you like him, unless I need to,' she said to the woman and held out the knife in warning. Even with her blood coursing through her from the brief fight, she was beginning to feel sleepy.

She approached the fire and sniffed the air above it. A stew was brewing, like the Runes had promised. Hare and mushrooms, and spices she couldn't name.

The man lay face down on the floor. Hilda walked to him with an idea forming in her mind. She crouched down at his side, reached for his head, and felt around for a wound. A little blood trickled down over the man's forehead, from where he had knocked his head when he had fallen. She drove two fingers over the wound to gather as much blood as she could. She let the blood drip into her eyes, already stinging with pain anew.

The man's blood didn't mix into her eyes and soothe them. It dripped out as she blinked and made no difference. It didn't soothe like her own blood did.

With a sigh, Hilda rose and walked back to the fire, holding the knife loose in her hand. She found the table again, and a bench too, pulled it out and sat down. With the blade, she gestured towards the stew. The woman approached the pot hanging above the fire.

The snow fox hopped up on the bench to sit at Hilda's side. It growled in warning at the woman. Hilda smiled. Maybe the snow fox didn't quite listen to her, but it was definitely *her* fox.

She turned the knife in her hand, felt it with a finger. Such a simple blade, not even that sharp, not in comparison to her axe. With it, Hilda made another cut on her forearm, held her arm up, tilted her head back and dripped the blood into her eyes. A few red drops ran out over the edge of her eyes, down over her cheeks.

'You don't talk much,' Hilda said to the Runes, and the woman yelped, frightened. Hilda ignored her and listened to the wind. She knew the Runes were there, but no answer came.

TYRA

Chapter Twenty-Six

SIV RARELY SPOKE. Tyra didn't talk that much herself, at least she didn't think she did, but all her life she had lived in the skald's house where Ragnar, or her father, had told stories. Both of them had passed on, now.

It was just Siv and her left. Just the two of them.

Siv was already halfway down on the other side of the hill by the time Tyra reached the top, and she skipped down the hill, over the wet leaves. Descents were the best, because she could run in a rhythm that made it seem as if she were a horse. And her legs didn't feel tired because she wasn't a girl anymore; she was a horse. The noises were fun to make too. But Siv didn't want her to be loud, so she only made the sounds in her head.

Halfway down the hill was a hut, hidden between the trees.

Siv had already reached the hut. Tyra galloped towards it. The closer she came, the better she saw the hut. Runes were carved into the walls and on the roof, too. They were everywhere, on top of each other, some coloured with blood and some not.

A mutter came from the front of the hut, where Siv had

disappeared, and when Tyra turned the corner, she saw the runemistress who lived there, pressed up against the side of her hut, hands high above her, holding a dagger and carving a rune into the edge of the roof.

The woman didn't acknowledge them; didn't notice them at all. Her hair was messy, as if she didn't own a comb, and her clothes were edged with fur instead of silk. Tyra didn't understand why anyone would want to dress that way.

Her clothes looked as if they hadn't been washed in weeks, and so did she. Her skin was dirty and she smelled.

Siv put their things up against the outer wall. 'We'll sleep here,' she said and entered the hut, not even glancing at the woman, who was muttering the names of runes as she carved, as though in a trance.

Tyra had often seen runemistresses in Ash-hill, but she had never been this near one before. Since she had been marked by battle, she supposed it was all right to walk this close to someone who had learnt the runes, but she still tried not to stare too much. Her mother had told her how dangerous those who had learnt the runes could be.

This woman did look dangerous. Around her neck bindrunes were painted in black, the kind that were pushed into the skin with needles, like warriors got after they had killed for the first time. Tyra would be allowed one around her wrist, and on her shoulder as well. She had spilled her first blood and she had been in her first big battle too. Tyra shook her head to dismiss the thoughts of the battle before she could think about her parents.

She focused back on the strange woman in front of her.

The runemistress had black images everywhere on her skin. Her fingers had runes and her wrists had several too, though they were different from the ones the warriors had. All the markings were runes and bindrunes. Some of them were also crooked as though she had done them herself. And around her left wrist hung a twisted silver arm-ring. A small piece of it had been chopped off, similar to how Hilda had chopped a piece off her arm-ring last summer when they had been in Alebu, throwing axes.

Hoping the scary runemistress wouldn't notice her, Tyra hurried inside the tiny hut after Siv.

The home was as strange as the woman. Tyra had never seen the house of a seeress or runemistress before. It was a lot smaller than what she had imagined. Seeresses were always so certain of everything and so powerful, and Tyra had always assumed they lived in great halls surrounded by servants, or perhaps nowhere at all.

Inside were more runes. On the floorboards, the walls, the ceiling, the table, the benches. Runes everywhere; the old kinds, the new ones, and bindrunes too.

Fascinated, Tyra walked to the nearest wall and touched one of the carvings. The wood was smooth, as if worn down by winters and winters of rain and snow. She muttered the names of the runes she recognised: Tiwaz, Pertho, Isa. She only knew the new ones, hadn't learnt the old runes yet, and bindrunes were still a mystery to her. The light from the fire made the carvings look like living creatures. And right there, as she looked, a carving was undone. A blink and the rune was gone. And then again with the rune of Isa, and Pertho.

'Look! The runes are disappearing,' she said and pointed towards them.

Siv didn't look surprised. 'When they're all gone it'll be the end of the nine worlds as we know them,' she said to herself.

For the first time a proper answer, an explanation.

'Why?' Tyra asked, hoping to get answers to all of her questions. Her eyes were locked on the many carvings, and everywhere she looked, more were vanishing.

Siv crouched down by the fireplace where some wood had been stacked. The hut was nearly as cold as the air outside. Tyra watched as Siv brought a hand in over the firewood and it burst into flames. Siv only needed to stare at the wood with her harsh grey eyes to make fire. Even wood was scared of her.

'The runes belong to that which keeps the nine worlds together.' Siv walked around the table and sat down on the sleeping bench at the other side, staring at the runemistress through the open door. 'Come inside,' Siv ordered.

The runemistress came inside, her concentration on her runes forgotten. She looked almost startled and afraid, but her expression hardened when she saw the two of them inside her hut.

'Who makes you carve these runes?' Siv asked.

A sly smile crossed the runemistress' lips. She had no intention of telling Siv anything. It wouldn't do, Tyra knew; she would have to tell. She *would* tell, whether she wanted to or not. Siv would make her say it.

Tyra was right, she could see it on the runemistress' face. Her features became tight and it looked as though she was fighting with her own mind. But she would lose. Siv always won.

Sure enough, the runemistress began to speak. 'The great Alfather came here. Long ago.'

The runemistress clutched onto a wooden bindrune hanging from one of the twisted cords on her neck-ring. Tyra wondered what it protected her against. Whatever it was, it didn't protect her from Siv.

'He makes me carve runes for the norn girl. The skald's daughter.' Then, the woman pulled her hands up to her wild hair and pressed them against her ears, perhaps to keep Siv's unspoken commands out. '*For Hilda Ragnardóttir,*' the woman blurted with such force that her body rocked forward. It seemed like the words had been pulled out of her.

Hilda. So, Hilda was alive and not in Valhalla at all.

The runemistress cried and cried, and then stopped to heave for breath. She looked exhausted.

'Go back to your rune carving,' Siv commanded. 'We were never here.'

She didn't need to say more. The runemistress raised her dagger and into the nearest wall she began to carve the same bindrune as the one on her neck-ring. And as soon as she was done, she moved the knife to the left and carved the shape again. Her movements were quick but precise, and Tyra wondered if she could someday learn to carve runes that quickly and well.

'Are we here to look for Hilda?' Tyra asked. That had to be why Siv had refused to go back to Ash-hill with the children and thralls.

Siv shook her head. 'Hilda is on her own path,' she said. 'Sit, Tyra. Perhaps it's time for me to answer your questions.'

Slowly, so she had time to think up good questions, Tyra pulled her eyes away from the disappearing runes on the wall and sat down on the bench opposite Siv, her back to the open door and the scary runemistress.

Tyra was so taken aback by the fact that Siv wanted to answer her questions that she had long forgotten every question she had ever formed in her mind. She looked around the hut and the many carvings, for more questions. 'Why are the runes disappearing?'

'Because the nine worlds are drifting apart.'

'Why?'

'The end is coming.'

'Why?' she asked again.

Siv did not answer that time.

'You're trying to slow it all down,' Tyra said. 'The runes, and the end of the worlds. That's what you're doing with *her*.' She nodded towards the woman behind her who carved her runes over and over, like an empty being. As long as she created new runes to replace the ones that were being undone, they couldn't all disappear. 'What Odin is doing with her.'

Siv nodded to confirm, and Tyra smiled. Lately, she had been good at guessing. 'Do you work for Odin?'

'I don't,' Siv answered.

Tyra wasn't sure if that was reassuring or scary. 'Why not?'

Siv stared into the fire as if she remembered something from a long time ago. 'The Alfather and I don't want the same things.'

'What do you want?'

'I want you, and Einer, to grow up well.'

Tyra rolled her eyes and she knew Siv was holding back, but at the same time, the answer made her feel warm inside.

Siv looked at Tyra with a sweet smile. Whenever Tyra looked into Siv's grey eyes she forgot everything else. Siv's eyes looked like they were made up of fierce animals, curled around the black dots in the middle. Two wolves, maybe, who enchanted Tyra to forget what she wanted to ask, except she wouldn't allow Siv's fierce eyes to win this time. Tyra stared down at the carving-covered table and searched her head for the right questions to ask.

'So, you're here to stop the runes from disappearing,' Tyra said. It wasn't really a question, but saying it aloud helped to make sense of it.

'It's not just the runes,' Siv said. 'The runes are merely one form of that which keeps the worlds together.'

'What do you mean?'

Siv opened and closed her fist, watching it, as if she could feel something there.

Tyra narrowed her eyes, an idea forming in her mind. 'It's about that dark place inside the ash tree,' she realised. 'Isn't it?' Right before he had died, Ragnar had said that the ash tree was how the gods communicated with them, and that it shouldn't be cut. Like Siv said, the runes were part of what kept the worlds together.'

'You're very observant,' Siv praised.

It made Tyra feel very clever to be praised by Siv, who never said anything she didn't mean. 'Is that how you made the opening in the ash-tree? With runes? And fire, just now?'

'The runes are deep,' Siv said and stared down at the many deep runes the runemistress had carved on her table. 'So deep that they cut through to the void between the nine worlds. Those who know the runes well, can carve them with words.'

'But you didn't say anything,' Tyra said. Siv had just swept her hand over the firewood and it had burst into flames.

'Not all words need to be spoken aloud.'

'What does it have to do with what's inside the ash-tree? What is that place?'

'It's not a place,' Siv mysteriously answered, and that made no sense at all. Tyra had been inside it, though it hadn't been like anywhere else she had ever been.

'There is no time, no place,' Siv continued. 'It's the past. It's the present. It's the future. It's everything and nothing. It's the Ginnungagap. The void between the worlds.'

Tyra didn't know what to say to that. Ragnar had often told her of the of Ginnungagap and the creation of the nine worlds, but she had never thought she could actually have been inside that great void of everything and nothing. Ginnungagap had created everything, but Tyra had never thought that it still existed; she had thought all of it had been used up to create the nine worlds.

'If that is the Ginnungagap, then how is it inside our ash-tree?'

'Because the Alfather put it there,' Siv said. Again, her eyes were distant and she seemed to remember something, or someone. 'To contain it. To control it.'

'Is that why they cut it down?' Tyra asked. The southerners had felled the ash-tree as if they knew exactly how important it was, although until now even Tyra hadn't quite known.

'Maybe,' Siv answered. 'Maybe they could sense the Ginnungagap within. Maybe they cut down the ash because they were scared of the dark void. Those who don't know what it is, often are.'

Tyra nodded and tried to remember what else she wanted to ask. She traced one of the runes in the table with the tip of her fingers; Tiwaz. She had always thought it looked like an arrow shooting up into the air. Like her own arrow at the beginning of the battle in Ash-hill. Joined by hundreds of others, which fell down towards the enemy at Muddy Lake. Arrows had torn through flesh and helmet-less skulls around her. Hammered down on the shields above them. Three arrowheads had pierced Siv's shoulder. Blood, everywhere, and screams. A puncture through her mother's cheek.

A chill travelled through Tyra and she shook her head to make the memories go away. 'Why was Ash-hill attacked?'

'There are some questions even I don't have answers to, Tyra.'

'But there are many you *do* have answers to. Answers to questions I didn't even have before you took me with you.' Siv was unlike anyone else Tyra knew or had ever met. Special, and strong and powerful too. 'You're not from this world, are you?'

Siv smiled, and Tyra knew with pride she had been right. She smiled; she liked to be right about important things.

'I'm not. But you've known that for a long time.'

'Ja,' Tyra said with a nod. Since the battle in Ash-hill, she had known, perhaps even before then. She wondered if she should push it, ask more to find out which world Siv came from, now that she knew it wasn't Midgard. Would even tell her? Probably not.

Siv's gaze didn't leave hers. And the two fierce animals in her eyes seemed to swell in size as Tyra looked. They weren't wolves, she decided, wolves were too reckless for someone like Siv. She was more elegant. Cats suited her more, but they weren't nearly fierce enough. Lynxes, that's what Siv's eyes looked like; grey lynxes.

Tyra forced her gaze away from Siv to regain some clarity. 'Why do you answer my questions now? You never really did before.' Siv was able to silence Tyra with a mere stare. She didn't need to tell her anything.

Siv didn't answer. Something was wrong.

'Are you dying?' Tyra wouldn't let her. Never again would she be abandoned.

'We're all dying,' Siv said routinely, but with a certain sadness, which could only mean she didn't expect to live much longer.

Tyra's fingers still followed the carving of the rune Tiwaz. Over and over, tracing it, and then, under her very touch it began to fade. The wood filled in, until the rune was entirely undone and there was only a plain wooden surface left.

'When all the runes disappear, the nine worlds will drift apart,' Tyra said, repeating what she had learnt, wishing it would make more sense if she said it, instead of just listening. Her finger traced the arrow shape where the carving had been, though now there was no indication there had ever been anything. 'The nine worlds will drift apart... But then what about the people who pass on?' She jerked her head up to look at Siv.

This time she did not receive an answer, but somehow Tyra already knew what would happen to those who died. If the nine worlds drifted apart, how could the dead pass on into one of the other eight worlds? Tyra was not afraid to die, but if there was nowhere to pass onto, then death had an entirely different meaning. Then death would be the end of everything.

'Will we die? After all the runes have disappeared?' This was the very last question on her mind, and it seemed the most important. If the nine worlds were no longer together as one when they died, their existence would simply be undone, like the runes. And then Tyra would never go to Valhalla and she'd never meet her sisters and her parents again.

'Cattle die. Kinsmen die. We must die likewise,' Siv softly said.

Another rune was undone under Tyra's touch. On her own, she muttered the last lines of the song that was their battle cry: 'I know one thing that never dies. The repute each gains in life.'

FINN

Chapter Twenty-Seven

FINN'S TROUSERS WERE heavy with mud. He grumbled and left the campsite through the slim trail in the woods, heading for his shift on the East Road. His hair was tied back in a long braid and made his uncovered ears feel as cold as the tip of his crooked nose.

They were nearly done gathering food for the journey south, and so far, only five longships had joined them at the mouth of the Albis river. The *Northern Wrath* had returned from Normandy with half a crew. Thora's ship hadn't arrived. Finn no longer believed that she would come back. Any ship commander trying to sail on the open sea in winter had to be crazy.

Finn walked out onto the road. The forest was dark brown and yellow and the ground covered with fallen leaves. Two men stood hidden on either side of the East Road, which despite its name was nothing but a dirt path through the forest, wide enough for carts to pass without too much trouble.

One of the two men was an elder raider with long white

hair. The other wore his clothes sloppily, his belt was fastened underneath his tunic so the tunic hung free. Finn sighed when he recognised old Hormod and stinky Geir. He grumbled a little, already regretting his decision to take an evening shift.

'Finally. I thought everyone was trying to avoid this shift,' Hormod said with an enthusiasm, and Finn realised that he was about to be stuck with the stinky one who refused to bathe. 'I'll head back and get some rest.' The grey-haired warrior tapped his smelly companion on the back and hurried away, a little too quickly.

Warily, Finn approached, hoping the day's rain had washed Geir clean and taken away his usual smell of wet fur and unwashed hair. It had not.

'He's the third person to leave me like that,' Geir said. 'I've been here since morning.'

Finn took his position at the opposite side of the road, but the wind brought Geir's foul smell towards him and no matter which way he faced, he found no escape. All he could do was wrinkle his nose and open his mouth to breathe. 'Don't you ever wash?'

'Only when I have to. It takes too much time,' Geir answered as if it were the simplest reasoning in Midgard. 'Who're you in a tent with?'

Finn didn't answer, not wanting to encourage conversation. Most of the young men could talk endlessly for days and days. The older ones could too, but the chances of learning something from an old raider were significantly higher.

'They put me in a tent with four others,' Geir said, answering his own question, and shook his head. 'And we have a small tent. It's so cramped and humid in there. None of us can sleep.'

Finn could scarcely imagine being crowded in with someone this smelly.

'I guess that's how it is to be one of the young warriors,' Geir continued. 'How many summers did you raid before they no longer treated you like that?'

'It doesn't matter how many summers you raid,' Finn said. 'It depends on when a new set of faces join. We always need someone to torment. So, until someone worse comes along, it's going to be you.' Finn hoped that would be enough to shut Geir up. He just wanted to stand guard in silence.

The young man nodded pensively but then opened his mouth to speak again. Finn rolled his eyes.

'It's been strange throughout the day,' Geir said. 'We've had five people pass through already.'

That was unusual, not a lot of people travelled at the beginning of winter.

'From Hedeby?' Finn asked.

'From further south.'

'Think they were scouts sent out to find us?' Richard of Normandy would have had plenty of time to send messengers to his allies and warn of the attack they had planned.

'Nej, don't think so.'

Finn eyed the empty road ahead, unsure that he trusted Geir's opinion. The wind rustled at the treetops and fallen leaves scurried over the earth.

'Hormod didn't think so either,' Geir said after a while, as if he'd heard Finn's thoughts. 'They talked about this woman who appeared last night in the next village east. They say she's an undead.'

'A draugar?'

Geir nodded eagerly. 'All five of them said they were travelling west to get away from her.'

From experience, Finn had learnt that body language was something every man and woman could understand, no matter if they were Jutes or southerners, but he could not think of a single way in which five southerners could have successfully communicated so much to a dimwit like Geir.

'And they all described the same person. A girl with white skin, who cries bloody tears. They say she smells of corpses and kills anyone who stands in her way.'

A shiver travelled through Finn's body. A draugar was the only kind of creature that could make the hairs at the back of his neck stand up from fear.

He dried his sweaty palms on his over-tunic and blankly stared at the empty road. He breathed through his nose, already tired of waiting for someone to come and replace either Geir or him.

'Go back,' Finn hissed to Geir between closed teeth when he could no longer stand the smell. 'Take a good long bath and get some sleep.'

'But we're supposed to always be two out here.'

'Then send someone else.'

He did not have to say any more for the inexperienced warrior to wave a quick goodbye and rush down to the hidden path to camp.

As soon as Geir was gone, Finn took a deep breath of fresh air, filled with the wonderful smells of moist bark and wet earth. The air was different from back home; not as good. It felt colder, yet heavier, and then there was the muddy camp. Finn did not want to spend another day there. All he wanted was to leave this place and set sail up the Albis river, so they could reach Magadoborg and begin the battle they had left Ash-hill to fight.

For a long time, he stood guard. He wrapped up in the fur he had taken with him, keeping his right hand on the hilt of his sword. The air began to cool. The sun was setting. The wind rose and crispy leaves scurried down the passage in the woods, and there, far ahead, someone rode straight towards Finn. The wind rose around the shadow, sending leaves flying as it galloped ahead.

Finn walked out to the middle of the road to make the rider and horse slow down and stop. Crows cawed nearby and the wind rose as they approached. The saddle-less rider was a young woman. Her blonde hair hung free and the skirt of her blue dress beat in the wind. Red leaves whisked around her.

And then Finn saw it: crimson tears streamed from her

bloodshot eyes and dripped onto her chainmail. Her skin was pale.

It looked as if the wind blew straight from her. She came closer and closer.

Finn's mouth was dry and he could feel his heart pounding rapidly in his chest. This was the draugar Geir had talked about.

It seemed as if all of Midgard slowed for her as she arrived. The horse's hair-coat was sombre, almost black, but its mane was bright, like the rider's hair. In her left hand, the woman held onto a chain, which ended in a loop above the ground, which hung in the air as though wrapped around something unseen.

Finn debated with himself whether he should get out of the way or stand his ground as the rider continued to approach. Nervous spit filled his mouth accumulated in a thick ball. The horse galloped closer.

A mere three feet in front of Finn, the horse stopped. The shock made Finn choke on his spit. His hand tensed around the hilt of his sword and he was ready to draw it, should the rider make a threatening move.

He coughed, cold sweat drying on his forehead, and peered up at the draugar. The leaves flew in the wind between them. Slim cuts covered her left arm and a fresh one at the top of her forearm bled so much that the blood trickled down her arm and dripped onto the horse's mane from the tip of her fingers. Her skin was so white it almost looked transparent and her eyes were hot like embers; like fire itself. Red tears coloured her cheeks and lips.

The whirl of leaves flicked around her. Her face felt familiar. Her skin peeled off like a summer sunburn, though it was winter and it had not been a sunny one. The woman had a strong jaw, an angular chin and harsh eyebrows that could not easily be forgotten. He even knew her cold glare.

'Long time,' she said in a husky voice, her lips forming a smile, and then he knew.

'Hilda?'

Her smile broadened. 'Finn?'

Finn could hardly believe it. She was nothing like the young woman he remembered from Ash-hill. Her pale skin, her bloody eyes and arm, made her into something else. A frightening figure that no one, not even he, would dare to contradict.

Still, this was Hilda. Just little Hilda from Ash-hill who dreamt of becoming tough like a shieldmaiden, to raid and pillage and fight until death. Just little Hilda, who was not so little anymore.

'Wha— how—?' He could not form his question; did not know what he wanted to ask. It *was* her, but he thought she had died up in Ash-hill, with the others. They had all died, everyone who had fought. They had burned all the corpses.

It could still be a draugar; it could be Hilda's draugar.

'I need to see the chief,' she said and kicked the horse with her bare feet until it began to trot. Finn had to leap out of the way to avoid getting trampled.

Unable to take his eyes off her, he followed behind. If she really was an undead and as dangerous as she looked, he could not allow her to pass through on her own. Besides, she wouldn't know how to find the camp without his help. Together they followed the road, she on the horse and he walking by her side, the rustling chain hanging in the air between them.

'How did you find us?'

She did not answer, but there was no way she could have known they would set camp there, and no way she could have found them by herself. Unless, she truly was a draugar.

They approached the hidden path to the camp, and Finn was about to point it out, but Hilda pulled the reins to make the horse walk up the slim track through the woods before he could speak.

'How'd you know?' His heart beat fast again. Perhaps she really was a draugar; she certainly looked like one.

'There was a trail,' she answered. She rubbed her eyes with her forearm, smearing blood all over her face. They had passed three other trails before this one, hardly visible in the dark. Even if she had seen them, she could not have known which one to take.

The wind had calmed a little, but Finn's thickly braided hair still beat at his back.

Hilda did not speak, so neither did Finn, though he had so many questions.

The fires from the camp came into view through the last trees at the edge of the forest, and then the river of mud and once-white tents. Warriors sat under the wooden roofs and talked by the fires.

Hilda steered the horse straight through camp, as though she knew exactly where they were going. She smiled to the warriors and shieldmaidens as she passed. Everyone stared, but nobody stopped them.

Suddenly, she made the horse stop and hopped down. She waved over a nearby shieldmaiden, who was almost as young as Hilda, but otherwise her exact opposite: brown hair and eyes, heavily built where Hilda was slim and tall. The shieldmaiden wore a clean yellow over-tunic like a man, again contrasting Hilda's bloody, blue dress.

When the woman reached her, Hilda handed her the reins and waved her away. The shieldmaiden's mouth dropped open and her stance stiffened, but Hilda did not waver and did not seem to notice the other's discomfort, so the woman took the reins and led the horse away without protest. Finn grinned. It took a real shieldmaiden to deal with another.

They had stopped in the middle of camp. The wind only brushed Finn's skin, but beside him, the skirts of Hilda's dress flapped like a sail. She tugged on the chain in her left hand, and then it moved ahead, rustling as if alive. Finn could hardly believe his eyes, and he was not the only one; men and women gathered at a safe distance from them to glare and whisper.

Hilda stopped in front of a tent and turned to Finn. 'Can you bring the chief out for me?'

Finn glanced to the white tent. She had known how to find them, but apparently not that the chief had put his tent up further into camp.

'The chief's in there,' Hilda said, as if she knew what he was thinking. Like a seasoned warrior, she went straight to the point. 'Will you get him for me?'

Unconvinced that the chieftain would be in the tent, and not wanting be ordered about like a simple animal, Finn was about to tell her she could go inside herself, but when he turned to her, Hilda had an axe out. It shone brighter than any weapon he had ever seen and had been engraved with the image of a slim animal a dog or fox. The weapon was an old kind but it looked new and strong enough to carve through mountains as easily as skulls.

Hilda didn't point the axe at Finn or threaten to kill him. Instead she sliced open the skin under her left elbow, next to the many other fresh cuts. She pressed the skin around the new cut so it began to bleed and then she held her arm up, tilted her head back, and dripped the blood into her eyes; directly into them. When she blinked, her ember-like eyes had dimmed a little, and blood ran down over her cheeks, covering older streaks that had already dried and cracked.

For a moment, unknown fear swelled up inside Finn; fear that this monster would hack him down without a fight, denying him Valhalla, if he did not do as she asked. He walked around her to the tent and took a deep breath before he pushed the fabric open and stepped inside.

On a sleeping bench lay a naked woman half covered in her furs. At her side, the chieftain, snoring like a pig, almost louder than Stein back in Finn's own tent. A used fish-bladder had been tossed on the grass at the foot of the sleeping bench next to a small jar of expensive rue; in such times as this, the prospect of a bastard child could compel even a brute like Vigmer into discretion.

One of the chieftain's hairy legs was pressed against the side of the tent. Finn leant in to shake it. The naked shieldmaiden woke and peered up at Finn. He did not so much as acknowledge her, instead tapped the chief's calf again. The chief grumbled and opened one eye, then rolled the shieldmaiden over and kissed her. From where Finn stood it looked as if his beard swallowed her whole.

'Hilda's here,' Finn said, without waiting for Vigmer to realise that Finn was standing there in the tent with them.

The chief pushed himself up. 'Finn?'

'Hilda's right outside,' he said and turned away. 'And she isn't very patient,' he added before he pushed the fabric aside and walked back out into the mud.

Hilda stood before the tent, in the middle of the path through camp. A group had gathered in a wide circle, keeping as far away as possible from the bloody-eyed monster. The camp had begun to stir with her presence. Geir and Hormod had clearly talked about what they had heard on the East Road, and the gossip travelled from ear to ear.

Unbothered, Hilda looked down at the chain she held. Her right hand moved oddly back and forth in the air by the floating loop. She petted the air and whispered something as the wind whipped around her.

Cold sweat dripped from Finn's forehead, and more because he felt he had to than because he wanted, he walked to stand at Hilda's side.

HILDA

Chapter Twenty-Eight

THE PAIN NEVER left Hilda's eyes. Something strange moved in her Muspel sight. Around her were the hot shapes of warriors, but there was something else too. Animals everywhere; dogs and stags and birds flying above.

Her snow fox looked at the animals. It saw them, like her. They belonged to the warriors, like the snow fox belonged to her. Just like she saw her fox, Hilda also saw everyone else's fylgjur, like she had seen her father's when he had died. Like she had always heard the whispers in the wind, until the runemistress had touched her and made them clear. Her Muspel sight just made the fylgjur easier to spot.

The people Hilda had encountered on her way to the camp hadn't had any animal companions, but they had been Christians. Maybe that was why. A hawk had been flying over Finn, and had followed them to camp; she had thought it was a wild bird, but she understood now that it was his fylgja.

The longer she watched them, the clearer the fylgjur became, and in the distance, she saw a great bear approach, far too big to be a brown bear. A white bear. Hilda wondered to whom it belonged. A great warrior no doubt. It couldn't be the chief's though, because the Runes had told her he was one of the two warm bodies inside that tent, slowly getting out of their warm furs, and dressed.

A tall body joined the thick crowd that had formed around Hilda. Einer. Even with her Muspel sight, she recognised him immediately for he was much taller than any other warrior. His walk was not slow and careful like everyone else's. He pushed out of the crowd and embraced her.

'You're not dead.' His voice broke. His arms were warm around her, and for the first time since Midsummer, Hilda felt safe again. 'You're alive,' he said and then he let go.

He seemed to look straight into her eyes, though she couldn't quite tell. She stared up at a face that she couldn't see. His head was a large shining mass. The white bear stood at his back. It was a huge fylgja, and it was definitely his.

'Who did this to you?' Einer asked.

'The gods,' she answered.

'What happened?' he asked, and again, 'Who did this to you?' Always that concern for her well-being, before everything else. Always that mundane concern and care.

'The gods have abandoned us,' she told Einer. It felt good to say it aloud and to someone she trusted. Someone who would believe her.

Einer stared at her for a long moment without saying anything and she wished she could see what his eyes were trying to tell her. His eyes spoke his inner thoughts so clearly, but she could no longer see them.

'I have something for you,' Hilda said. She removed her furs and reached for the skin-bag she had carried since the forge. She was careful with it because the Ulfberht blade poked out at the top.

The smith had made the sword with white bear bone, the same kind as Einer's fylgja. It seemed obvious to her that it was destined for him. Maybe the Runes had known that too, and simply not told her. They seemed to know everything.

Flat on her hands, Hilda offered the sword to Einer so all the gathered warriors could see the glorious inscription.

'An Ulfberht,' someone whispered in the crowd.

Yet, Einer did not take it from her. He seemed to stare at it though. Again, she wished that she could see his face and see what he was thinking. Instead, she waited for him to speak.

'It's beautiful, Hilda,' he whispered so only she could hear. It sounded like he smiled too, but she couldn't know for certain. 'A gift worthy of gods,' he whispered. That was exactly what she had set out to find, but the gods would be satisfied with the axe that hung from her belt. The sword belonged to Einer. She wanted him to have it.

Yet, still, he didn't reach for it.

'Hilda,' he whispered. 'I can't accept it. A gift like this should go to the chief.'

Hilda stared up at Einer. Again, he gave way for his father, as he always did and always had. She knew that he was right, but the sword was destined for Einer. She didn't want to give it to another, though she supposed that if the chieftain got it, Einer would eventually gain it as part of his inheritance, and then the Ulfberht sword would find its rightful owner.

She nodded to him and lowered the sword.

At Einer's back, the chief finally crawled out of his tent. Hilda walked around Einer to see the chief who looked down at himself, fumbling with something. His belt, perhaps. Finally, he looked up. 'Hil-Hilda?' he stammered, keeping his distance. His boar fylgja took a step back.

'Ash-hill was attacked by southerners,' she said for all to hear. 'They came in the night, thousands of them. I'm the sole survivor.'

'We know,' the chieftain said in simple shock.

So, the warriors had been home and they had seen what the southerners had done.

'The gods are angry,' Hilda said, hand on the axe she needed to deliver to calm the gods' anger. 'But I know how to calm their anger.'

'Ja, that is why we're here,' the chief said. He was pacing and seemed eager to get on with other matters. Any other matter. He wasn't listening to her.

It felt like all those times she had asked him to join the raids and been refused without being given a chance to prove her worth. The chief was as dismissive now as he had been to her then, summer after summer.

Hilda scoffed and shook her head in disbelief.

They had to listen to her, but she knew that she could not talk about the Runes. If she explained that the whispers in the wind told her the will of the gods and had guided her there, none of them would believe her. Even Einer might not believe her, then. She glanced to him over her shoulder.

He stood tall at her back and watched. He would fight for her. She knew he would, against his own father, too, if it came to it. She couldn't let him do that. For the last few summers, Hilda and her own father had been fighting and then he passed on. In times like these, there was no telling how long any of them would live. She could not allow Einer to oppose his father. She would not allow them to fight over her.

The chief was about to go back into his tent. His boar of a fylgja had already turned away from Hilda and the commotion. Yet, the circle of warriors around Hilda had thickened with warriors and fylgjur. She needed to convince the chief, but she also needed to convince all of them.

The chief had always liked flattery.

'I have a gift for you,' Hilda said, and lifted the Ulfberht blade for the chief to see. She offered it to him with less formality than she had offered it to Einer. It didn't feel as special to give the sword to the chieftain.

'An Ulfberht blade,' Einer's father muttered, striding straight to Hilda. 'A precious gift,' he said and took it. 'Takka.'

'The gods demand a worthy offering,' Hilda said and tapped the axe from her belt to make them all look at the godly offering she had gained. She couldn't quite tell if the chief was watching, but she had to assume that he was.

'You said you were here to appease the gods,' Hilda said. She assumed that the warriors had assembled this far south with the intention of striking a southern town in retaliation. She had expected them to strike but not so soon. 'I'm ready to fight,' she said.

The Runes had faithfully guided her there. The snow fox warned her of mortal danger. Despite her Muspel sight, she felt confident that she could fight. Her glare was hard, unmoving. Blood tickled down her cheeks.

The chief appeared taken by the Ulfberht blade she had offered to him. He did not look at her when he spoke. 'You should ride home,' he said. 'I promised your father not to take you on raids.'

Each summer the chieftain had brushed off her request to join the raids without as much as giving her a fair chance, because of her father, but this was different.

'This is no ordinary raid,' Hilda hissed to the chief. She shook her head in disbelief that he had refuted her claim to raid, after everything that had happened. She scowled at him, and his boar, and without waiting for him to say anything more, she grabbed her furs and bag; lifted them from the mud and walked back to her horse.

She rode the horse through the thick crowd of people and away.

Nothing more waited for her there if she couldn't be treated as an equal warrior. No fights and no glory. She had the Ulfberht axe for the gods, and no doubt the Runes knew how to deliver it. A much greater destiny than staying there. A much greater honour than any the chief could give her.

Einer called her name. The sound of his rapid steps was catching up with her. He had convinced her to stay before. She couldn't let him convince her again.

Hilda didn't stop.

Her head was dizzy from pain, but she kicked the horse into a trot, pushed through the crowd and lost Einer in the early night.

Her arms and legs were shaking. She felt faint, and brought a hand to her hot forehead. Blood loss would kill her, if she kept it up, and Hilda didn't want to die. In battle, someday, but not yet, and not on the road like this.

Her blood gave her relief, but nothing more. Her Muspel sight was a part of her, and she had to accept that.

She wouldn't be the first warrior to be half-blind. Even the god Höd was blind, though he was no warrior, and misguided by Loki's whispers, he had killed his brother Baldur. Unlike Höd, Hilda had good guidance. She could trust the snow fox, and she could trust the Runes.

EINER

Chapter Twenty-Nine

EINER RAN OUT after Hilda, mud splashing up his trousers The forest wrapped around him and shut out the little light from camp.

'Hilda!' If only she would let him catch up. She was fast, and the tight forest made it impossible to see anything. The sun had already set.

'Hilda! Where are you?'

The cold wind was blowing through the forest and the hoot of an owl answered his call, but Hilda did not. He ran faster, hoping at the very least to catch another glimpse of her so he knew he was on the right path. The forest was too dark; he would not see her unless she stood right in front of him.

Convinced that his attempt to catch up was futile, Einer stopped running. Perhaps if he stayed quiet he might hear her horse. Sounds of running water and the creak of rope tightening around wood; he was nearby the river where their ships were docked. He heard a horse mark its place. Leaves scurried at the bottom of the forest, rising around his feet.

Einer turned around, and there she was.

'Don't follow me. I'm done here.' Hilda had unmounted from the horse and her skin was so pale it almost shone in the dark.

Her eyes weren't blue as they were supposed to be. They shone like embers.

'Where are you going?' His heart was gripped with fear. She had only just arrived.

'That doesn't concern you.'

His heart caught in his throat. 'Are you really leaving?'

She didn't hesitate. 'Ja.'

Some warriors laughed in the distance and the wind increased in force, swallowing their voices, and Einer could not think of a single thing to say to convince her to stay, and not leave him.

'I'll talk to my father again. I'll make him agree to let you come,' he said, trying to keep his cool, although his hands shook from the thought that she might leave. 'It wasn't right.'

The wind calmed. The sounds of laughter returned, and Hilda stared out towards the warriors, refusing to look at Einer. 'I don't want to be *allowed* to come,' she said.

Einer did not know what to do. 'Then, what do you want, Hilda?'

She took a deep breath, and they were both so quiet, and the warriors in the distance too, that although two arm-lengths separated them, Einer felt as if her words were whispered into his ear. 'I want to find my place,' she said. 'To earn it.'

'You will. I'll talk to my father again. I'll convince him. Whatever it takes.' He meant it. Even if it meant single combat, he would demand that Hilda was allowed to fill her rightful place as a raider. 'No matter what.'

He couldn't let her leave like this, bloodied and hurt. The wind rose around them both. Blood from Hilda's eyes dripped onto the chainmail.

'Don't go. You're hurt.'

Hilda released a deep breath. 'You won't make your father change his mind.' Then she gazed up at him with an expression that made it feel as though the nine worlds were empty and there was only the two of them.

Einer wanted to tell her that he would do anything for her and if she asked him to challenge his father to a duel to the death then he would comply. He would do anything for her. But Hilda already knew that, and she did not want his help, so he muttered the last thing he could think to say. 'I don't want you to leave, Hilda.'

They gazed at each other as they had not done in winters and winters; not since their second night together, before Einer's first raid. Her eyes were nothing like they had used to be. It was as if they had been wrenched out and replaced with burning embers. Hilda did not frown at him, as she usually did; and she did not find an excuse to divert her gaze or get angry with him, as he had expected. She matched his stare for a long while, and it felt like this was the first time in winters that they had understood each other without needing to speak.

They both knew she had to leave, or Einer's father would never understand how serious she was about the warrior path. If she left, he would realise that Ragnar would sooner have allowed Hilda to fight with the warriors from Ash-hill than leave them to fight without guidance.

That night, summers ago, they had talked about leaving together, her and Einer, to join crews elsewhere, but then Einer had joined the warriors of Ash-hill and they had both been so certain that Hilda would soon be accepted into their ranks as well. She had tried to leave back then too, he remembered, when she had first been refused, but he had stopped her then, as he was stopping her now, with promises about how they were supposed to raid together and how he could convince his father.

Hilda broke their long gaze. 'I should have left the first time,' she mumbled. The wind caressed her hair and the chain clinked at her side.

'I'm glad you didn't,' he told her, smiling at the thought of their first night together. 'I just wish we could go back to that time—'

'We can't,' Hilda interrupted, as she always did. Einer knew better than anyone that Hilda rarely listened to her heart, and perhaps, deep down, she did not love him as much as he hoped; as much as he loved her.

'I loved you before that night,' Einer admitted. 'But after that, I knew it had to be you.'

Einer could see from the curl of her lips that she was about to retort with one of her snappy remarks, that she would dismiss everything he had said, but he continued to speak and did not let her have the word as he usually did. 'Whatever it takes. To marry you is all I've ever wanted.'

Hilda's expression hardened. She was used to him giving her the word when she wanted it. 'Just because we had sex once doesn't mean we have to marry,' she snarled.

'Twice,' he corrected despite himself, and despite how angry it made her.

He waited for her to acknowledge it. The chain clinked from the blow of the wind and leaves were cast around them as they stood and stared at each other, like a deadly duel without swords.

If she did not love him in the way he loved her, then they were not meant to be, although Einer could not help but hold onto the belief that she did love him.

'It doesn't matter if it was once or twice,' Hilda finally said.

'To me it does.' He would not let her dismiss him again, not tonight. 'Those nights meant something to me. I thought they meant something for you too.'

Again, she was about to retort, but something stopped her.

Einer knew that he was asking too much of Hilda, asking her to listen to her own emotions and put her pride aside. He knew, but he had to ask. If she left, he knew she would never come back. They had once planned their escape together. He knew her.

'Stay,' he asked of her. 'Let me talk to my father. Come with us. This is your fight.'

The expression on Hilda's face was one he had never seen before.

'Do you know what I've been through?' she hissed. 'Not just the battle, but everything since.' She blinked her eyes furiously. 'And despite the odds. Despite the *gods*, I made it all the way here. On my own. And then your father dismisses me like that, and all you worry about is *marriage*?'

'Forgive, I never intended to tell you like this,' he blurted, and he felt that he was losing her. 'But I want us to be like we used to be. Especially with everything that has happened. You need me, and I need you,' he said at last.

'I don't need anyone,' Hilda said almost without thinking, as if she had said it a thousand times before, and she had. 'I don't need anyone.'

'I didn't mean it like that.' Einer had never been this honest with her before. For a moment, he had forgotten how she always contradicted anything she thought made her appear weak. 'Let's figure this out together. I love you, Hilda.'

His breath caught in his throat. His dilated eyes were fixed on Hilda and he did not dare move them. His entire being quivered, his hands trembled and his lips were suddenly dry.

For four full breaths, Hilda's bloodied ember eyes examined him, as if she were trying to find a reason to believe him. He held her gaze, smiled as best as he could, despite how nervous he felt, and gave her every reason to trust him. Finally he had said the words. Finally she knew for certain how he felt and why he always took her side and wanted her safe. His palms were sweaty from it all.

Hilda broke the stare, and walked away from him, dragging her horse along. As if he had said nothing at all.

'I always have loved you,' Einer said, wanting to say it all now that he had begun. He attempted to stay calm, although his heart pounded so loud that he thought all of Midgard could hear, and was equally terrified that his chest might burst. 'Let me help.'

'I don't need your help. I don't need *anyone's* help,' she said.

Einer took a deep breath. This was more complicated than he had thought. Whenever they were together nothing ever happened as it was supposed to, and Einer could not say anything that did not make her angry with him. He knew a lot of it was because he was the only family Hilda had, apart from her father. Since Ragnar had fallen ill, she could no longer be angry with him. So, whenever she had wanted to yell at her father, she had yelled at Einer instead.

'I don't have time for this,' Hilda sighed and mounted the horse.

'Wait, let me come, Hilda,' he said, before she could leave. He was saying all the wrong things and he did not know what the right things were anymore. 'Let me come with you.'

She bit her lower lip, considering it. 'You can't leave,' she decreed, and her harsh tone seemed to surprise even her. 'You have a ship. Responsibilities. Your father wouldn't allow it.'

'He's not the one I'm asking.' Einer knew there was nothing right for him to say. No matter what he said and how he phrased it, Hilda would find a way to twist his words around and pit him against her. 'You're everything to me.'

Hilda said nothing.

'At least tell me where you're going,' he pleaded.

'Wherever the wind takes me.' She smiled, as if it were a joke, but there was more to it than that. Hilda had a plan, or she would not be in such a hurry to leave.

'Where are you going?' he asked again, but she ignored him and pressed her lips harder together. 'Hilda, you have to tell me.'

'Why?' she asked. 'Why should I tell you?'

'So I can find you.'

'You won't need to find me,' she said. 'Not where I'm going.' Before he could say anymore, or before she could, Hilda turned on her heels and, as quick as the wind, she was gone again.

After a moment, he heard the sound of her horse gallop away.

BUNTRUGG

Chapter Thirty

BUNTRUGG GLIDED OVER the mossy forest-bed. The alf-made path was slim, and not built for giants, but he had travelled along it since morning.

Suddenly, a woman dressed in white, with short white hair, appeared on the path ahead of him. She stared at him for a moment, then, with a blink, she disappeared. All he had caught was a glimpse of the alf woman.

The alf had turned her back to him so quickly that had Buntrugg never before seen an alf, he might have fooled himself and thought that it had merely been his imagination, but Buntrugg knew the alvar well. Their curiosity was greater than any other part of them. That was why they knew everything worth knowing, and that was why he had entered their realm. He needed them to tell him which furnace to Muspelheim had been opened so he could find it and close it.

'I saw you, and you saw me. You will not get far,' he told the alf in his deepest voice, which shook the nearby trees. He closed his eyes and made himself a few feet taller; nowhere near his full height, but enough to frighten any giant-fearer.

The alf was nowhere to be seen when Buntrugg reopened his eyes. He had expected his firm threat to have startled the alf to reveal herself again. Perhaps she was not as young as her short hair had made him think. If that was the case, she would not be easily intimidated by a giant on his own. Or perhaps, she was not alone. Perhaps there were other alvar on the path. On their way to Midgard, to dance and enchant the short-lived, or off to listen to the secret conversations of the aesir and vanir.

Buntrugg closed his eyes and concentrated on his hearing. He could hear them breathing. There were many of them. Behind him, and in front of him, and off the path, hiding behind the trees.

They hid themselves from him by turning away and showing their invisible backs.

Frowning, Buntrugg listened for their leader: someone breathing steadier than the others.

He found her.

On the path, directly behind him. The controlled heartbeat of a leader seeking to help her people; a way to escape the threat that was Buntrugg, the giant.

Although their invisibility allowed them to leave without being noticed, the alvar were too curious to leave him standing there on their path. He was there, they had seen him; and before they left, they wanted to know why.

If Buntrugg closed his eyes and resumed his full giant form, he could reach out and grab their leader and force her to reveal her face. With her face and lineage revealed, she would have to tell him what he wanted to know, or face the possible of the annihilation of her kin. Threats was how most giants gained knowledge from the alvar, but, like his sister, Buntrugg refused to act like most giants.

He fixated on the leader so intently that he began to hear the mumble of her whispered thoughts, though not loud enough to make out any words. If she was not from the nearby halls, she would be more guarded; she must be from an island further inland, warier of giants than her peers, and less exposed to them.

With a deep breath, Buntrugg took in her smell and that of her fellow alvar. Like all alvar, the smell of moss and river-life was strong on them, and Buntrugg had to take three deep breaths to discern the subtleties that set them apart from other alvar. Reindeer; they came from deep within Alfheim, as he had suspected.

A clear alf voice disrupted Buntrugg's search. Other voices joined the first, and their song rose around Buntrugg. He shut his eyes. He knew the alvar hoped that their song might enthral him, although not as successfully as a dance, but with his eyes closed, he would not see them dance.

Their song was their second-best asset. If they enchanted him with their voices, they might force his eyes open and then they could dance until he lost track of time; dance him into the distant future where he would be no threat to them, and be too late to carry out Surt's orders.

Refusing to give in, Buntrugg made his body smaller. The smaller he was, the less room he had for other thoughts. If he concentrated on his sense of smell, he barely heard the beautiful song.

His next sniff gave him the final clue he needed. Beneath the smell of forest and moss and rivers, beneath even the smell of reindeer, was the faint scent of a quick colourful bird that only nested on one island in Alfheim; on only that one island, in all the nine worlds.

Buntrugg smiled and opened his eyes, unafraid of the alf song and dance. The education Surt had given him always proved useful when he was away from home. He knew who these alvar were now, and he would not be distracted, neither by their song nor by their dance.

The alvar danced around him. They spun and spun around themselves, revealed their features, so light that their faces were impossible to tell apart from their bright hair. When they turned their backs, they disappeared, and then appeared again when they faced Buntrugg. Their white clothes danced with them in the pattern of opening and closing flowers.

They danced and sang in the hope of enchanting him, a long-lived, in the same way they enchanted the short-lived. They would not succeed, and perhaps his smile gave it away, for as he opened his eyes, the alvar halted their dance and turned their invisible backs to him.

Buntrugg found the calm heart of their leader once more. He knew her name, and he was certain that she did not know his.

'Eignalysa, I have come to meet you,' he said, and fixed his eyes somewhere straight ahead where he thought she stood with her back to him. 'I seek advice from you and your people. I have travelled far to meet you,' he flattered, 'and I request your wisdom and knowledge.'

Even now that he had revealed her identity, Eignalysa did not show herself, but her curiosity forbade her to stay silent a moment longer, and so, she granted him speech. '"The wicked shall gain no knowledge from the alvar of Alfheim,"' she recited in a fair voice, both distant and nearby.

'"No giant with wicked purpose shall be allowed to enter the lands of Alfheim, so decreed Alf, and from that day forth, so it came to be,"' Buntrugg recited from the same story. Many times before, he had exchanged those phrases with alvar throughout Alfheim. 'Danger floods Midgard,' he revealed in hope that he could exchange information for information.

'As it floods every one of the nine worlds,' Eignalysa replied.

He wished that she would face him, so he knew where to rest his eyes, and so he could study her face and use his knowledge of the runes. He supposed that was also why she refused to face him; out of fear that his grip of the runes was greater than hers. Besides, Buntrugg also had the rage of the forefathers, and if she suspected that he was a giant, she would be more than aware of that.

'Look at me and learn who I am,' Buntrugg tempted.

'I do not need to know *who* you are,' the alf leader responded. 'I know *what* you are.'

'Are you certain?' he insisted.

Buntrugg's existence was not as simple as it might appear at first glance. His true form was giant, but he had lived near Muspelheim for most of his life, and his blood boiled accordingly. Those who did not know Buntrugg often thought that he was of vanir, or maybe aesir lineage, but certainly not that he was a cold-blooded jotun.

As long as he did not appear in front of them in his giant form, most were tricked by Buntrugg's warmth and his calm, which came from his control over the forefathers. Most giants allowed the forefathers to flow, for locking them away was both difficult and risky. The longer they were kept inside, the more they gained control when they were let out.

'Longer legs travel faster, and the Alfather is not a patient man,' Buntrugg said. Some aesir and vanir had the ability to grow, just as some giants had the ability to shrink.

Both statements were true. If he tried to lie, they would know from the sound of his heartbeat.

'You do not work for Odin,' Eignalysa said.

Her statement required an answer. Either Buntrugg kept his silence and agreed that she was right, or he lied, and she would know.

He smiled brighter. 'I *do* work for Odin.'

His heartbeat confirmed the truth. He worked for Surt and Surt had been given his task by the Alfather hundreds and hundreds, perhaps thousands of winters ago. So, his statement was truthful and his heartbeat steady.

With the confirmation that Buntrugg worked for the Alfather, Eignalysa revealed herself to him.

Likely, he was the first giant she had ever met. His own dark features were the opposite of hers; his dark hair short, his eyebrows heavy and his skin had been coloured by the sun. He had more in common with the tall trees in the forest than the alvar who lived there.

Eignalysa's body was so delicate, so tiny to look upon, yet, she was slightly taller than that of her peers. Not by much, but enough to distinguish her in a large crowd. She may have been altered by a skilled runemistress at birth, as a leader in waiting.

'Why are you here?' she asked, no longer able to contain the question within herself.

'To meet you,' he answered evasively to make her curiosity greater and make her more willing to share the information he sought.

'Why do you want to meet me? How do you know me?'

'I know every leader in the eight worlds.'

The events in Midgard passed too quickly to follow. Only Odin paid close attention to Midgard, and he had his two ravens to help him. The other eight worlds moved at a different pace.

'We have not met, so how do you know me?' Eignalysa asked, and by the tone of her voice, Buntrugg knew that her curiosity was piqued.

'I have heard about you and your people and of the colourful bird that nests nearby your halls.'

'A sight beyond any. The greatest bird of all,' she proudly said. His answer appeared to have pleased both her pride, and excited her curiosity.

Her alf followers, still keeping their invisible backs to Buntrugg, murmured their agreements with their leader. A few of them revealed their faces, wanting to see the foreign man who knew about their realm and the birds they held in such high esteem.

'Why are you here?' the alf leader asked for the third time.

Buntrugg did not possess much more patience; not in this small size. The forefathers already tingled at his fingertips, pleading to be released. 'I seek a dwarf forge,' he said and clenched his fists tighter. 'A dwarf-owned furnace was opened, but never closed.'

'Then why have you come to Alfheim and not gone to Svartalfheim to see the dwarfs?'

He had known that would be her first question. 'I don't know which dwarf I'm searching for.'

'And how would we know?' Eignalysa asked, fishing for another compliment.

The forefathers had little patience left. Buntrugg bit the inside of his lip so the pain would shadow their anger so he could continue this peaceful talk with the leader long enough to gain the information he sought. 'Because you turn your backs and hear every private conversation. You know everything worth knowing.'

'The dwarfs are not worth knowing. Their craft takes time and they rarely speak.' Her answer was immediate and not as playful as he had expected. Inland alvar, it seemed, were different from the ones with whom he usually dealt.

'But you know what has happened.' He attempted to sound calm, despite the anger that coursed through him. 'You know Muspelheim has been opened, and that demons have escaped.'

'*Now* we do.'

'You already knew. You were not present in Svartalfheim when they opened the door to Muspelheim for me, but the svartalvar were there, and other friends of yours were too,' he reasoned. 'You have heard about the laughter of Muspel's demons. You have heard how every dwarf left to check their forges so they wouldn't be blamed. So, you must know. Which dwarfs did not close their furnace?'

'We do not meddle,' the invisible crowd responded as one.

'I am not asking you to.'

'If we tell you who you are searching for, you will meddle, and then we will have meddled,' the leader of the alvar replied.

'Well then tell me *where* the forge is and I will not involve the dwarfs,' Buntrugg urged. 'If I do not involve them, I do not meddle.'

'We cannot tell you what we cannot know.'

'You cannot know it, but you do.'

'We do not meddle,' all the alvar repeated.

'The forge should already have been closed and locked. Surt commanded it,' Buntrugg insisted.

'All dwarfs in Svartalfheim checked their forges and closed their furnaces,' Eignalysa said, echoing what he had told her.

There it was. The slip Buntrugg had hoped for. The acknowledgement that they *did* know something. And that phrasing...

'All the dwarfs in Svartalfheim,' Buntrugg repeated, softly. 'What dwarfs are *not* in Svartalfheim?' Never before had he heard of a dwarf who did not live in their realm.

'Many dwarfs aren't in Svartalfheim.'

That was untrue. Dwarfs travelled and their forges were not all located in the same world as their homes, but their homes were inherited through generations, and great pride was taken in that fact. It could be possible that, in the same way that Buntrugg was not like most jotnar, there was a dwarf, perhaps a few, who were unlike the others. However, that would not be many dwarfs. If there were many such dwarfs, then Buntrugg too would have known about them.

'If not in Svartalfheim, then where do they live?' he probed.

'"All dwarfs live in Svartalfheim,"' Eignalysa responded.

'"...and some dwarfs spend their nights drinking,"' Buntrugg completed. With those words, and the final clue in his grasp, he retook his usual form. The alvar gasped and he sensed them scattering into the woods, leaving him the path. 'Thank you for your time, Eignalysa of Alfheim. May we never need to meet again.'

His head felt weightless and light in his large body. Suddenly there was so much room for his thoughts and the anger of the forefathers no longer bothered him. He turned back the way he had come from, carefully stepping *over* the large ring of alvar, who were watching him with great curiosity. Off he set towards the edge of Alfheim and the passages to the other eight worlds. His journey had barely begun, but already he had come far, and now, thanks to the alvar, he knew where to look next.

'"Some dwarfs spend their nights drinking,"' he whispered. 'And some dwarfs never return home.'

SIV

Chapter Thirty-One

SOMETHING STIRRED FURTHER along the Oxen Road. Siv glanced back to Tyra, who dragged her feet through the red leaves. Down the road, Siv sensed eight short-lived with six horses, undoubtedly on their way to Jelling. They had a foreign smell about them.

Somewhere up north, beyond the forests and fields lay Jelling where the Chief Harald, son of Gorm the sleepy, lived. Tingsmen called him Bluetan for his greed. Tyra and her had left the Oxen Road briefly to avoid the town on their way to Hedeby. Siv remembered Harald Gormsson from many summers ago, but he would not remember her; she had changed a lot since Jelling and Ash-hill had raided together. Bit by bit she had changed over the winters; the best way not to attract attention. Her hair had become lighter, a little more every summer, her eyes had changed colour too.

'Come, Tyra,' Siv called urgently.

Tyra rushed to catch up. The soft curls of her hair flowed behind her and her bow knocked against the arrows she carried on her back. Two furs were wrapped around her neck and shoulders, and along with the ragged hemline of her dress, it made her look like a wild animal.

During their long journey walking south along the road, they had encountered less than a dozen travellers. The Oxen Road was normally crowded in early winter. Few towns had been spared in the southerners' attack on Jutland, and the empty Oxen Road made that clear.

'What's happening?' Tyra whispered in a soft voice. She reminded Siv so much of Einer.

Siv took Tyra's hand. 'There are some people ahead of us,' Siv gave Tyra's hand a reassuring clench. Tyra's hand was so warm and small in hers. Siv smiled. She had always wanted a daughter.

The people Siv sensed came into view along the road. Two riders led a small retinue. The horses were tall like those of the south and their manes had been braided back. Behind the two riders followed a horse pulling a wagon, which was carved and coloured in fancy patterns from the east. A man steered while two women sat at the back, giggling. Behind them rode three more short-lived. The men bore weapons, all six of them; both axes and expensive swords.

Siv and Tyra approached. The men noticed them. Their hands flew to their expensive weapons, ready to draw them. An unease rose within Siv, but she continued on, dragging Tyra with her.

They were foreigners from the east so Siv had to avoid using her influence on them. Those outside of Norse lands tended to be more sensitive to her influence and become hostile to it.

As long as they continued to walk and did not make eye contact, it would be fine, Siv told herself to dismiss the creeping unease. Tyra too was nervous. Her heart rate grew faster.

Rain drizzled from the grey evening clouds down over the dark brown leaves on the Oxen Road. Siv hurried Tyra and her along, past the men. The warriors watched them as they passed. Siv felt their stares, and sped up a little until they were past each other.

Tyra's stomach grumbled. They had not had anything to eat, except for a handful of roasted chestnuts left over from last night. They had finished the last of their food reserves three night ago.

'Hungry?' asked a voice from behind.

One of the men riding at the back had stopped his horse to face them. He held out a bun of bread towards them, with a bite taken out of it that he was still chewing.

'Takka,' Siv forced herself to say with a smile without looking the man in the eyes. 'We're alright.'

With those words Siv turned away from him and forced Tyra to hurry away too. Tyra's stomach complained, unhelpfully. The clap of hooves followed them.

Siv stopped up and turned slowly back.

The man had followed them down the road.

'Are you looking down on me?' he asked in a dark voice.

The others had stopped further up the road, waiting for him to join them. The other five men still had their hands on their weapons, ready to turn their horses around and fight. The one in front of them leant forward in his saddle, smiling to Tyra. Siv forced Tyra to her back so the man couldn't look directly at her.

'I won't hurt you,' the man felt the need to say, but he was no longer extending the half-eaten bread bun towards them and he was no longer smiling either.

Siv was about to turn back to the road and keep him away with whispered runes to avoid a fight, when the man spoke again. 'We're men of the King,' he said.

They were men of the King, in Jutland where there were no kings. The retinue was headed north to Jelling, which meant that the self-proclaimed king who had weakened the old forces was none other than the coward chief Harald of Jelling. Finally, Siv knew exactly where Tyra and her were headed, and exactly how to make an entrance too.

With a simple phrase the six eastern warriors had become valuable to Siv and her plans. Unfortunately for them, they were worth more to her dead than alive.

The runes rustled around Siv's fingertips, ready to be used, but she did not need them.

She let go of Tyra's hand and allowed the anger to emerge. It tickled her feet and travelled up her spine, along her arms, making the hairs stand up, and tingled out to her hands. Her eyes widened with anger and settled on the horse.

The horse neighed and reared from the sight of Siv's forefathers. The man tumbled off its back. His horse bolted past the retinue. The other men dismounted. Their horses were spooked, ears darting back and forth, hooves marking the ground.

Meanwhile, the two women were busy talking at the back of their wagon. They were not alarmed, as if this had happened before.

The five men strolled down the road, hands on weapons, while their friend scrambled to get to his feet. He flattened his hair when he got up, and brushed down his tunic.

The ancient anger escaped from Siv's grip, up her arm, through her chest and out her mouth with the slight growl of a beast. The men fumbled to pull out their swords.

Tyra retreated two feet behind Siv, and Siv could feel Tyra's weight shift to peek from behind her back and watch the six men. 'Get back, Tyra,' Siv warned while she still retained control over her voice.

The earth beneath her feet trembled. Her eyes were blurred from anger that rushed through her and she could not feel her hands anymore from trying to suppress the urge. This was how jotnar went wild and turned into beasts.

'Continue on your way,' the man ordered, having suddenly changed his mind about stopping them on their way.

None of the others said anything. The two women on the back of the pretty wagon were laughing over something, watching Siv and Tyra through distant glances. Bravely the six men took a few steps towards Siv and Tyra and aimed the point of their weapons at Siv's throat.

Siv let her bloodline take over and let go of her own body. The spirits of her forefathers made her burst forward, growling and shaking from the power of their anger. Her seax hung sloppily at her side, despite her tight grip around the hilt.

With no more than six men, she could allow the forefathers to fight and have enough control by the end to shut them in again, before they noticed Tyra, or before she lost herself and went mad with rage. At least she hoped she had enough strength to stop in time. The forefathers had grown stronger since the last time she had let them out. Allowing them to take over reminded Siv of her childhood back in Jotunheim, and of her uncle who had succumbed to the anger; worse than a frenzied bear. She remembered when her father had killed him. It had not been a pretty death.

The men in front of her prepared to cut her down, and she rushed at them particular. The forefathers lent her their anger and strength.

The men swung their swords, coordinating their attack. One aimed for her feet, two for her neck, two others for her chest and the last aimed for her right hand in which she held the seax.

Siv stepped back and out of their reach. When the men tried to compensate by moving forward, while their weapons were mid-swing, she took another graceful step. Their swords clashed against each other.

Midgard seemed to slow before her. Siv saw the iron blades shake from the blow and the men's eyes widening in surprise, then closing tight as the jolt from their swords reached their arms and hit their shoulders.

The forefathers heightened Siv's love for the dance. She swirled around prettily, unnecessarily, flaunting her superiority to these men who no doubt called themselves warriors. A wicked smile crossed her lips, and still she had not lifted her seax.

The men struggled to regain control over their weapons as Siv moved in close to the man furthest to the right, and before he swung his sword, Siv poked him in the side, not with her seax, but with her little finger. The force made the man twist and he swung his sword wildly. Siv slid her feet back on the wet leaves and dropped to the ground, ducking his blow, then caught herself with her left hand, heaved herself up from the ground, and thrust the seax under the man's chin, up through his head.

The other five moved in to surround her, yelling as their friend collapsed to the ground. They hacked out after Siv's feet, and she pulled them in and stood straight. The five men were now at her back. Even without facing them, she could feel exactly where they were. The forefathers heightened her senses until she felt invincible; like a berserker.

She shuffled the seax into her left hand and ducked the next wave of attacks, counting each move. At the fifth attack, aimed at the vulnerable spot where her left shoulder met her neck, Siv shifted no more than the width of two fingers out of the way of the blow. She threw her right hand up to clasp her fingers around the sword. She helped the blade along, yanking the man's hand into reach, and clasped his wrist. Four men moved in with their swords as Siv dragged the round man forward and slit his throat with the seax in her left hand. The four men's swords tangled with their leader's blade as the round man fell to the ground.

The forefather's anger calmed with Siv's dance.

She avoided one blow and two before the remaining four men realised there was no use hacking out after a long-lived like her. Two of them cast down their swords and reached for their axes.

Siv did not move while they switched weapons, or even as they shared glances and circled her.

The first of them took a step towards Siv, and she slipped around him and slit his throat with a back-hand stroke. She was already shuffling towards the next one as he hit the ground, blocking his swing with her seax and crushing his throat with her free hand. Her hand came back wet with blood.

At that, the last two men lost any calm they might have had and charged at her, yelling. One of them was crying, and she ended him first, driving her seax into his heart as she ducked under his axe. The other had time to hesitate, to his regret, as Siv retrieved her seax, spun out of his reach and around to his back so she could finish him like the others. The man dropped at her feet, throat gushing.

Siv turned to Tyra.

The girl was gaping at the dead guards at Siv's feet.

Siv took a deep breath, not for air, but to force her forefathers back into the depth of her heart where they usually rested, along with her anger. They would not go back. Not this time. They had found another target. The forefathers had found Tyra.

'Run!' Siv yelled to Tyra.

The forefathers lunged after Tyra. With a loud roar, Siv lost herself to their anger.

The last thing she heard was Tyra scream.

SIGISMUND

Chapter Thirty-Two

HAD SIGISMUND NOT known to look for them, he never would have noticed Ash-hill's ships. They were moored close to the trees on the bank, their colourful outer planks hidden with leafy branches and the masts had been lowered.

Sigismund counted as they approached. If all the ships were as large as his own, there were fourteen.

Fourteen ships. Nineteen, including the *Storm* and the other ships from the far north who sailed with Sigismund. Hundreds and hundreds of warriors had gathered to fight the southerners. They had gathered at the mouth of the great Albis river. They had come from all over the north, not to protect Jutland or to retaliate against the southerners, but to fight for their way of life. Should they fail, there would be no more true Norse warriors in Midgard.

The paint chipped off Ash-hill's ships. They had not been cared for after the summer raids. The *Storm*'s summer journey too had been rough, and the dark pinewood hungered for tar. It would need repairs over winter, if there was anyone alive to sail it home.

Sigismund ordered his crew to moor on the starboard bank of the stream behind Ash-hill's warships. The other ships from Frey's-fiord and further north pulled in behind them.

While they secured their ships and unpacked, people gathered in the shade of the woods. Warriors who had half a hundred questions and as many compliments.

'Sigismund,' a familiar voice bellowed. Vigmer had gained new stripes of grey hair since they had last met. His grey eyes looked different from usual beneath the dark bushy eyebrows that he had not plucked since summer. His expression was grim, although he smiled. Everyone's expressions were grim, Sigismund noticed, as he gained the starboard bank to greet the chief.

They embraced each other.

'Is it true you worked on an Ulfberht blade up in Iceland?' Vigmer asked as they parted from their embrace, never patient.

'My teacher worked on one when I apprenticed with him.' There could only be one reason for asking. 'How did you get an Ulfberht blade?'

Named swords were rarely ever for sale. On the rare occasion when they were, the price was higher than a longhouse, and everyone with gold in the northern lands flocked to give an offer. With Jutland ravaged, there was no chance in the nine worlds that Einer's father could afford such a sword. He had not even bleached the fresh strands of his beard.

'I need a sword hilt,' the chief said, without acknowledging Sigismund's question.

Sigismund followed him away from the curious crowd of warriors.

They walked in silence through the woods and entered a muddy campsite. Sigismund hoped they would not need to stay there long. During the few weeks he had been back in Frey's-fiord after the summer raids, he had already forgotten the discomfort of getting mud everywhere: trudging through, sleeping in it. The weather was not in their favour. This would feel like a long raid.

Vigmer disappeared into a tent and re-emerged with a brown cloth bundle.

Carefully Sigismund took it and flipped back the cloth to reveal the shining weapon hidden inside. His reflection was clear as a mirror on the blade. It had never had a handle or pommel attached. It was like a newly forged weapon.

'A new Ulfberht,' Sigismund muttered.

There was no doubt that the blade was an Ulfberht, the weight of it alone was enough to know that it had been forged from the right metal, and it looked like it came straight from the flames, although to the touch it was cold as ice. 'How did you get it?'

'Hilda came with it.'

'Einer's Hilda?'

Ash-hill's chief nodded and watched Sigismund slide his fingers down along the fuller of the blade. It was sharp at the edges.

'Where did she get it?'

No answer was given, but he could see that the sword had been forged recently, and not lain around for some hundred winters waiting for a warrior to find it.

'They don't make these anymore,' Sigismund said. Everyone knew Ulfberht blades were relics of the past, passed down through generations of warriors, and if their production had resumed Sigismund would have known; any decent smith would have known.

'You need to make it taste blood,' he added. 'Ulfberht swords are tricky until they have tasted blood.' Some old tales said that the swords had a will of their own.

'It really is an Ulfberht, then?' asked Vigmer eagerly.

It was difficult to believe, but Sigismund trusted his eyes. It had a different tint from other swords, subtle, but present, and the weight was unique, as was the soft texture. It was not a forgery.

'Where did she get it?' he asked again.

Vigmer shook his head to indicate that he had not thought about asking.

'Where is she?' Sigismund asked instead.

'She left,' answered a voice behind him.

Einer stood behind them, eyeing the sword in Sigismund's hands. His eyes were swollen as if he had had been crying, and his voice was dark. He had always been tall, but he seemed taller now, than he ever had, and his height cast a long shadow over his father's face. 'She's gone.'

For a moment, Sigismund recalled the white snow, stained with blood, and Einer's face as he had looked down at the bloody trail of the white bear he had killed. There it was again, that lost stare. A chill travelled through Sigismund as he remembered what Einer had said once up in Iceland. "The gods didn't steer my hand. They let me go."

Vigmer backed away.

Sigismund grabbed the Ulfberht sword by the tang, and shuffled in between them. 'Einer, good to see you.' He pulled his old friend into a hug, then they pulled apart with a nod. Since Iceland, they had never quite returned to their normal ease around each other.

Next to them, Einer's father slithered away without a word.

'You found Hilda? She's alive?' Sigismund asked his old friend. 'Thora told me her corpse wasn't in Ash-hill.'

Einer nodded, face blank.

'Come with me to the ship? I need my tools for this.' Sigismund gestured to the Ulfberht blade and tapped Einer on the shoulder. 'Tell me everything.'

Einer did not speak while they pushed through the crowd, back out towards the ships, but gradually, Sigismund's old friend relaxed and came back to his senses, in the exact same way he had all those winters ago, after he had attacked that white bear.

'Much has changed since we last met,' Einer commented.

Their entire world had changed. With the southerners

mounting such a massive attack against Jutland, no one felt safe any longer, and although Sigismund's crew were not aware of the scale of the threat that hung over them in the way Ash-hill's warriors were, they understood that there was no other choice. They had to fight, or give up their beliefs. Midgard was not as free as it had used to be.

Together Sigismund and Einer legged onto the *Storm*. The sail had been bound up and covered with a tent cloth; two warriors remained on the ship, coiling the last ropes.

Sigismund removed the planks to the starboard side of the mast. Most of their things had already been moved to land; all that was left under the planks was a barrel with dried fish and the bag with Sigismund's tools. Einer helped him haul the heavy linen sack onto deck.

A gold bracteate hung over Einer's tunic. More wealth that Sigismund could not understand. Ash-hill had been burned and ravaged, yet Einer's father had an Ulfberht and Einer had a large gold neck-ring coin of old. Raiding was not that prosperous anymore. Sigismund had not seen that kind of wealth in many winters.

He dug into the coarse linen bag, searching for a triangular pommel. Four summers ago, his father's pommel had taken a blow and slipped right off the sword with the rest of the hilt. Since then, Sigismund always carried a few standard pommels and guards with him on raids, not that anything like it had happened since, but it made him feel prepared. Few of the raiders from Frey's-fiord fought with swords anyway, but those who did often needed their guards fixed.

Sigismund pulled out a pommel and the guards he had made last winter.

'She gave him that.' Einer watched the Ulfberht blade. 'All she ever wanted was to raid.'

'Hilda?' Sigismund asked, searching for the wooden handle he knew he had packed.

Einer neither confirmed nor corrected him, merely sat down

on the mast-fish and stared at the blade while Sigismund slid the guard and handle onto the tang.

'He shouldn't have accepted the sword if he didn't intend to allow her to come,' Einer stated, as if he wanted to find a way to justify how angry he was with his father.

The handle was two finger-widths too long for the sword tang. Sigismund made a mark in the wood with his nail where it needed to be trimmed.

'You haven't changed,' he noted. He glanced up at Einer, who seemed to snap out of some dark thoughts. 'Honourable even in the face of wealth like this,' Sigismund clarified. Back up north, too, Einer had refused to take as much as a claw from the white bear he had slain. He did not fight for silver and gold as most freemen did.

They both stayed silent as Sigismund fetched an axe and cut the handle. He checked it on the blade; slid on the guard, the wooden handle and the pommel. A perfect fit.

'Killing without remembering it is not an honourable deed,' Einer muttered with that empty look on his face again as he observed Sigismund go about his craft.

'It *can* be,' Sigismund said.

'*Can* be,' Einer repeated, dubiously.

Sigismund found his square hammer, lay the sword down on the mast-fish, and slammed the hammer into the tang. The sword rattled from the blow.

Einer watched as Sigismund hammered on, and they both knew he was thinking about the white bear up north.

Sigismund gave one last slam. Then he found two rivets that fit the pommel. He rolled them between his fingers and attempted to form the right words to help Einer.

Back in the day, the two of them had used to be so close, but Einer had not been the same since the white bear incident and Sigismund had not been able to accept that. He remembered what the girl Sigismund had liked at the time had said: "No one kills a white bear with nothing more than an axe." She had not talked about anything but Einer and his immense strength the rest of winter, and then well into the summer too, maybe that was why Sigismund had been so angry with Einer back then.

'The gods let you go,' Sigismund said, repeating what Einer had said back then.

A smile crossed Einer's face and all those long winters of barely speaking to each other were forgiven and forgotten. It felt as if they had never ceased to be the best of friends.

'I'm glad you're here,' Einer said. 'I've missed having a friend I can trust.'

Sigismund nodded as he secured the pommel with two rivets.

Indeed, he had many friends; everyone wanted to be friends with a chief's son, but he had few that he trusted with his darkest secrets as Einer had trusted him with the white bear incident. It seemed so obvious to him now, how Einer had struggled with that strength ever since, and Sigismund was ashamed that he had not stayed at Einer's side. 'I should have tried to understand.'

Einer's smile did not fade like Sigismund's. 'How could you? *I* still don't.'

All those winters, Sigismund had been convinced that Einer had simply restrained from sharing it with him. 'Can you forgive me for not believing you all this time?' he asked.

'All is forgiven,' Einer responded. 'And now you've come to our aid.' He smiled again and the tension that had settled around them as they spoke lifted, although they both knew this aid would lead either of them and many of their friends to the afterlife.

For a moment, they sat in heavy silence.

Most of the warriors who had gathered would die. This was not like most raids, where they would spend half their time in foreign taverns and laugh at each other around beach bonfires under the starlight, and only fight when the weather was favourable and the lands easy to take. This was a war. And people who went to war did not usually come back.

With Einer's help, Sigismund hammered the rivets flat; a few good pounds were enough. He grasped the hilt and lifted the sword. He would have liked to make a more beautiful hilt, but circumstances did not allow it. He balanced the sword on a finger, testing the weight. 'How did she get it?' he wondered aloud, once more.

Einer shook his head. 'She doesn't speak much,' he said and they both laughed at that. Hilda never had been very talkative. No matter how small her troubles were, she had always solved them all by fighting, even back when Sigismund had known her.

'She needed to leave,' Einer decided. As ever, he defended her. 'It wasn't fair of my father to refuse her.' Sigismund knew well the difficulty that followed from being the son of a chief. His father and he did not always agree about decisions concerning Frey's-fiord, but his father always had the last say, as Einer's father did in Ash-hill.

'Her eyes are... They're like embers... Like they're burning. She shouldn't have to be alone with that. Out there.'

'You did the most you could,' Sigismund said, confidently; it was Hilda they were talking about, and Einer had always done everything for Hilda's sake. If she asked him to jump from a cliff, or to kill half a hundred puppies, he would do it, only because she was the one asking.

Einer nodded and stared at the Ulfberht sword. Sigismund handed him the weapon.

'It's powerful,' Einer said, shifting the conversation to the shining blade. He turned it in his hands and tested the weight. 'Unlike anything I've ever seen.' He cast the sword from hand to hand and Sigismund could see that he was itching to swing it. 'Hilda had an axe that was just as beautiful. Better, even.'

The more Sigismund heard about Hilda and the gifts she had taken with her, the more he wished he had arrived earlier. He would have asked her how she had gained the Ulfberht blade. 'When did she leave?'

'Earlier,' Einer answered as he moved the sword this way and that, testing its swing. 'Just after the sunset.' Suddenly, as if he realised what Sigismund had asked, his hand stilled. 'You wouldn't be able to catch up,' he said. 'She has a horse.'

A horse. In southern territory where everyone had arrived by longship. Hilda continued to surprise. No wonder Einer had fallen for a girl like that.

Einer held the blade out flat in front of Sigismund, offering it back to him. When Sigismund reached for the cold metal, the blade cut into his palm.

They both stared down at the weapon and then the cut on Sigismund's hand. It was almost as if the sword had wanted Einer to shed first blood, as if it had chosen a wielder.

Sigismund returned the weapon to his lap and rubbed the blade with the sleeve of his tunic to remove the small blood stain, but no matter how hard he rubbed, the blood did not come off. It had sunk into the blade.

HILDA

Chapter Thirty-Three

LEAVES CRUNCHED SOMEWHERE among the trees. Someone approached. The Runes had been whispering to Hilda, but she hadn't been listening; instead, she had been thinking about Einer and what he had said.

The sounds came closer. She glanced over her shoulder and saw the hot figure and fylgja in the distance. The fylgja wasn't a bear. It wasn't Einer.

Bifrost won't stay open for long, the Runes urged. They had big plans for her. They wanted her to cross the gods' rainbow bridge, to leave Midgard, go to Asgard, and deliver her axe-offering to the gods. It was an honourable task, yet it felt like she was fleeing from a different kind of destiny. A destiny in Midgard.

The figure was a man, or a woman with wide shoulders, steadily catching her up.

He ran steadily; he was well trained. His fylgja was a big dog that almost reached his hip. If he had a fylgja, then he was from the north. He had to be one of the warriors from camp. Einer must have sent someone to convince her to come back. Though that wasn't his style; he had accepted her rejection and let her leave, and Einer never went back on his word.

The warrior came closer and closer. If she listened to the Runes and rode off now, she could make it away before the man reached her. Hilda yanked the chain to make the snow fox hurry along. The fox growled, but it didn't threaten to bite her as it did when she had first caught it a few days ago.

It listened to her now, walking obediently at her side, rarely tugging on the chain. Most of the time the fox was so calm that she forgot it was there. She had broken its spirit, exactly as she had told it she would. She wished she hadn't.

Half a day since she had left the camp—and Einer and his white bear—and she already missed someone to quarrel with. The Runes and her agreed on where they needed to go, the fox listened to her, even the horse obeyed her commands. Her Muspel sight had begun to feel comfortable too. No one and nothing opposed her anymore. She even missed her father's opposition. That frown on his forehead when he disagreed with her. The calm tone of voice he had used when he tried to teach her the right way to do things. Though she had never really listened to what he said, she missed his voice more than anything. The soothing sound of his storytelling. Those were the only times she hadn't been angry with him, at least in the end. She missed the old days, before his voice had become shaky and weak, back when he could make her laugh. Before he had made the chief promise never to take her on the raids.

She stopped up to wait for the warrior. She needed a good conflict.

The man hurried after her. The Runes made the wind rise to urge Hilda along, but the horse lowered its head to the ground, poking for something to eat, and Hilda hopped off its back. Her thighs already hurt from riding without a proper saddle.

She walked around the mare to face the man head on. The snow fox sat down on the dry leaves and seemed to lick itself like a bored cat. Hilda slackened the chain that held it, but even that didn't gain its attention.

The man and his tall dog slowed their run as they drew closer. 'I nearly gave up,' he said when he was within speaking range. He heaved from his run. 'It's been too many winters.' Hilda didn't know his voice.

'Too many winters?'

'Not since you visited Einer in Frey's-fiord.' He had a strange accent.

'Sigismund?'

His voice had become deeper, and he was leaner now than she remembered. He was taller than her, though not as much as he had been when they were younger.

'Einer asked you to stop me, didn't he?'

'Actually, he told me you couldn't be stopped.' Sigismund walked in a little circle, to cool down after his run.

'He's right.' Hilda watched as Sigismund caught his breath. If not because of Einer, she couldn't think of another reason he would have run like a crazed man to catch up with someone he hadn't seen in winters, and hadn't been that close with back in the day.

'I'm not going back,' she told him. She forced her snow fox to stand, gathered the reins and pulled the horse along.

'Are you leaving me here? I barely caught up with you,' Sigismund complained.

'I told you: I'm not going back.' She petted the horse's bright mane. At her feet, the fox yawned with a high squeak.

'I'm not here to ask you to stay.' Sigismund sighed, and she could hear him sit down on the leaves at her back. 'Won't you at least sit with me for a while? Just until I get my wind back.'

'Why did you run after me?'

'Come sit and I'll tell you.'

Bifrost won't stay open for long, the Runes said.

'I should be on my way,' Hilda said. She clapped the horse's neck twice in resolution, clicked her tongue and guided the horse straight ahead, hoping no thicket or tree were in her way. The mare moved with her, but its head was planted in the ground. It pushed aside fallen leaves with its muzzle and munched on some grass or moss beneath.

'Why the rush?' Sigismund called after her.

'No reason.' Hilda said, ignoring the rising wind. The Runes were nervous for some reason and they wouldn't tell her why. Her fox wasn't worried, though. She wasn't in mortal danger.

Hilda clapped the horse's neck and walked to Sigismund. He'd stopped heaving for breath and now sat with his legs folded. His fylgja lay down at his side; not a dog, but a wolf.

Hilda felt the ground with her feet, pushed away some leaves and sat down next to him. 'Why are you here?' she asked impatiently.

For some reason, that made him chuckle. 'I came with my warriors to help Ash-hill,' he said, knowing perfectly well that wasn't what she meant. He was silent for a moment before he spoke again. 'I have a question for you.'

'Then ask it.'

'How did you come to possess a new Ulfberht blade?'

Of course, he was curious. Sigismund had trained to become a smith, she recalled. Any smith would have given their life to learn what Hilda knew about the famous blades, and learn from Ulfberht, who she had killed in his own forge.

His question had the Runes more agitated than ever. *Bifrost won't stay open for long*. The wind swirled around her.

'Gods kill this wind,' Sigismund cursed, rubbing his arms.

Hilda snickered. She had become so used to the Runes' way that the wind no longer bothered her. Her hair slapped around her and got stuck to her lips and the bloody tears under her eyes. She felt it on her face, but barely noticed.

'I can't tell you how I got it.' The wind calmed and Hilda smiled to it.

'Why not?'

'They wouldn't like it,' Hilda admitted, knowing her words made no sense to Sigismund.

'The people who gave it to you?'

She nodded. It was half true. The Runes weren't people, but they were the reason she had gained that sword, and her axe too. They had found the metal and brought her to it. They had led her to the smith and his forge. All of it to appease the gods.

She looked up at Sigismund and wondered how his face looked now. If his beard had grown out better, or if it was still patched as it had been when they were younger.

'So, someone is making Ulfberht swords again?' Sigismund sighed.

The wind tore at Hilda's skirt and hair. 'I can't give you answers to your questions, Sigis.' She had used to call him that a long time ago. Now that he was a grown man, it carried a strange ring.

'I've come all this way,' he whined. 'Do me one last favour?'

She watched the heat within him boil around, and waited for him to ask his one last favour.

'Will you allow me to see your axe?'

Judging from the way the wind rose, the Runes were as uneasy about that as Hilda, but Sigis was an old friend. She handed the axe to him, alert in case he tried anything.

As Sigis reached for it, the axe slipped from her grip. Sigismund groaned.

'Forgive,' she said. It must have cut him.

'I know, you didn't mean to draw blood,' he eventually muttered. 'Neither did Einer.'

He didn't sound like he was hurt.

'Your axe is an Ulfberht too, isn't it?' Sigismund asked.

She didn't answer his question. He already knew too much and the wind was agitated.

'Two Ulfberht blades,' he mumbled and reached for the axe. His hands looked like he turned it to and fro; the light touch of a smith appreciating good work. 'It's a pretty weapon,' he said, and gave it back.

Hilda couldn't see it, so she was careful when she reached

for the weapon. She smiled to Sigismund, fastened the axe in her belt, rose and moved towards the horse. The fox followed, docile.

The mare was grazing. Hilda stopped in front of it, ready to swing up on its back, but for some reason it felt wrong to leave again. As if she were saying goodbye to her old life twice.

'Tell Einer I'm sorry for leaving him,' she said.

'Remember when we practised together?' Sigismund said instead. 'With Einer. You fought as if you were born with a weapon in hand.'

'My uncle sometimes said I slipped out with an axe in hand. Killed my mother from the inside.' A long time ago that had been funny. Since her father had passed on and with her uncle and aunt gone as well, the story that had used to make them all laugh had turned bitter.

'Remember what I asked you back then?'

She did, and smiled at the memory. 'To join your crew when we were both old enough to raid.'

'I stand by my words. It would be an honour to fight with you, Hilda.'

Hilda swirled around and stared back at Sigismund's hot fire. 'You want me to join?' she asked in disbelief. She was so used to her requests being dismissed.

'Hilda, had you asked, I would have followed *you* into battle.'

TYRA

Chapter Thirty-Four

'TYRA!' SIV CALLED for her, again.

Tyra made herself small, sitting in her tree. Her heart beat so fast she thought it might jump out of her chest. She hadn't slept all night. Every time she closed her eyes, she saw Siv launch at her, like a wild beast.

'Tyra, I know you're here,' Siv said. 'I wasn't myself. Can you forgive?' She was nearby. Tyra was well hidden in the yellow leaves of her oak tree, but she knew she couldn't hide from Siv.

That was why she had climbed the tree, like her father had taught her to do if a pack of wolves came chasing her. A bit like how Siv had helped her climb the ash tree back in Ash-hill to hide from the southerners. Siv had saved her life then.

'Are you yourself now?' Tyra asked aloud. She didn't like being scared of Siv. Not when Siv was supposed to be the only person left in Midgard who was on her side. Last night, too, she had been on Tyra's side, attacking those warriors because they had made Tyra cry. Tyra knew that, but she still shivered at the memory of being attacked.

'I am,' Siv answered, but that wasn't enough.

'Will you swear a promise to me, then?' Tyra asked.

'I will,' came the answer.

'Swear on your honour and your true name that you will never not be yourself around me.'

From the foot of the tree, Siv said the words. 'I swear it, on my true name, and my lineage, and on the honour I have earned, and all the honour I shall ever have.'

Tyra nodded. If that was it, then she could forgive. It would take long to *forget* it, if she ever would, but she could forgive.

'Will you come down from the tree, now, Tyra?' Siv asked. Not like her mother might have—in a commanding tone, that meant she had to crawl down immediately or be in big trouble—but like a friend who was sad that she wasn't included in some game. Tyra scooted off her wide branch and crawled down from the tree.

'What are we going to do now?' she asked, as she made her way down to Siv.

'We continue on our road,' Siv answered, but when Tyra had changed back into her blue dress and when they regained the Oxen Road and began to move along it again, Tyra noticed that they were going the wrong way.

'Why are we going back north to Jelling?' she wanted to know. It seemed stupid to walk into a big town like that with blood-stained clothes. Especially when they had travelled so far around the town yesterday, on their way south. People might misunderstand. People were usually good at misunderstanding, and bloodstains were difficult to explain.

There had to be a reason they were heading towards Jelling. Siv had a reason, for everything. Even for what clothes she put on in the morning, not that they had much to choose from anymore.

Siv didn't tell Tyra why they were going back north, just told her that it was better if she didn't know, but Tyra hated not knowing what they were doing, or why. She thought about what

Siv had told her in the runemistress' hut, and everything else she had ever said, and tried to figure out why they were walking to Jelling, when they had avoided the town on their way south. Somehow, everything Siv did, and had ever done, was connected.

Trying to understand it made her head hurt, and even if she guessed correctly, Siv wouldn't tell her anything. Tyra's father had always told her everything, even how hard his morning poop had been. Tyra giggled to herself at the memory, ignoring the uncomprehending stare Siv gave her. Sometimes remembering him made it feel like he was still there, and sometimes it just made her miss him more.

The clouds hung low. 'It's going to rain,' Tyra predicted, playing that she had Siv's skills. Siv could sniff the air in the morning and know, right then, if it would be sunny or rainy, and she would tell Tyra: "Put on another fur, it'll rain at high-day." And the weather always did exactly what Siv said. Everything in Midgard listened to Siv, even the clouds.

A raindrop hit Tyra's cheek. She tilted her head back and opened her mouth to gather all the raindrops she could. Her stomach growled.

A sudden thought entered Tyra's mind. 'Shouldn't we hide our weapons?' she asked.

Jelling wasn't much further, and the bloodstains on Siv's dress would be more obvious if she also carried her seax. The yellow dress Tyra wore was large on her and with her bow and arrows, it made her look parentless.

'A lot of people wear weapons in larger towns,' Siv said.

'I thought it was only guards,' Tyra pouted. At least that's how she remembered Hedeby, from when she had been there. The guards had carried these enormous swords and she and Hilda had very quietly slipped past them. She knew she had been to Jelling when she was younger too, but she couldn't remember how the town looked from the inside, or why they had been there. She had gone with her sisters though, a long time ago.

'You could just kill anyone who gets in our way,' Tyra told Siv.

Siv stopped up suddenly, as she only did when something bad was about to happen, or something unexpected.

'Guards.' Siv grabbed Tyra by the arm and forced her off the road, out to the forest to hide. They crouched down behind a wild thicket. Not long after, a dozen guards rushed past them on the road, looking about themselves as if they were searching for something, or someone.

Tyra waited until she couldn't hear the guards' steps anymore, and then she stretched to whisper into Siv's ears. 'They're looking for those two girls from the wagon, aren't they?'

The retinue had been rich and must have been expected somewhere. The girls had rushed off into the woods while Siv had fought the six warriors, and although Tyra had known she should have stopped the girls, she hadn't thought she could, not with a mere bow and arrow. In truth, she hadn't thought about it at the time. Unlike her sisters and parents, Tyra had no warrior instincts.

'The guards won't take long to find those girls,' Siv said.

Tyra didn't quite understand why that was important.

'They want to be found,' Siv clarified, but that didn't make much sense either. If the girls wanted to be found, and if Siv knew where they were, then why hadn't they gone after them to prevent any witnesses? The questions flooded Tyra's mind, as they always did whenever Siv told her something.

Like a good daughter, Tyra waited with Siv, crouched down behind the thicket, and didn't ask a single question though she had so many.

Half the day passed as they sat there, and all the silent mind games Tyra knew became boring and her stomach growled. The rain continued to fall and Tyra thought they might stay there until night, though she didn't know if she could stay seated all afternoon. The morning had gone by slow enough, and she wasn't the least tired, though she had stayed awake through the night.

Siv poked Tyra and pointed to the road.

The guards from earlier were walking back to their town, and with them were the two rich girls from the wagon. Even though Tyra knew the girls had slept in the woods if at all, scared of running into Siv, the girls looked flawless. Not a single stain on their dresses. Their hair was combed back and didn't in the least curl from the rain, as Tyra's did.

Siv elbowed Tyra and moved along the forest, following the two girls and guards to Jelling.

'Come,' Siv whispered to Tyra, then, and stumbled out onto the road. Right behind the guards.

She was going to kill them all.

'It's them!' Siv exclaimed in a strange accent, instead. She turned to Tyra and tried to drag them both off the road, but the guards had already seen them by the time they hid back in the forest. Two guards chased after Siv and Tyra. The rest rushed off towards Jelling with the two girls.

Tyra and Siv legged through the forest, but Siv didn't run as fast as Tyra knew she could. She ran sloppily, as if she had never run in a forest before. She stumbled over tree roots and twigs, and thickets caught her dress. Tyra tried to rush her along, but the guards were closing in and Siv was stalling too much.

'Hurry,' Tyra urged.

The guards yelled after them, and before Tyra could do anything, they had caught up.

Siv smiled to Tyra.

Tyra glanced around, hoping the guards wouldn't scream too loudly when Siv killed them, and hoping she would do it quickly.

Siv turned to the guards. 'Don't hurt us,' she cried, in that strange accent. Tears streamed down over her cheeks. The guards moved in and grabbed Siv. She tried to wrestle loose as she cried and repeated her plea: 'Don't hurt us.'

Tyra just stood there wondering what she should do, and then she turned on her heels, and off she ran. But before she could get further than five paces, the second guard caught her.

The guard pulled her back towards Siv, who continued to repeat her plea, over and over, and the more she pleaded, the more Tyra thought these guards really would hurt them, and for some reason Siv didn't have her usual strength, and it made tears swell up in her eyes.

'We won't hurt you,' the guard who had caught Siv tried to reassure them.

'You're with *them*,' Siv cried and shook her head so her hair swung out in front of her face and a few locks got stuck on her wet cheeks.

'Who?' he asked.

The tears continued to stream down Siv's face. 'They attacked us,' she whispered, as if afraid to say it out loud. 'Those girls and their friends.' She sounded like a foreigner when she spoke.

'The girls?' asked the guard who held Tyra.

Siv sniffed and stopped crying now that someone was listening to her. Tyra didn't know how she could lie so well. Even Tyra believed it.

'I don't know what they wanted.' Siv's lips trembled. 'This girl. She saved me.' She nodded to Tyra. 'I offered her some bread. And then they burst out from the forest and attacked us. There were so many of them. They killed my guards. I would have been dead if this girl hadn't taken me with her.'

Siv was so good at pretending. Tyra tried her best to pretend too, though it was difficult when she didn't know what Siv might say or do next. But she liked the idea of pretending to be the one who had saved them.

'We've been out here all night. I hoped he might send someone for me,' Siv continued, and she was so convincing that she made Tyra wonder who *he* was.

'You should have come to Jelling right away,' one of the guards said. He believed them.

Tyra was certain Siv had influenced them to believe her story, although the way she had told her story was convincing enough on its own.

'I thought they might have gone to Jelling,' Siv muttered and glanced up at the guards.

The guard's grip around Tyra's arm was not as firm as earlier. He returned a sympathetic smile to Siv. 'Don't worry, this will all be over soon,' he said. 'Come with us.'

They walked back towards the road. The guards let them walk on their own, and Tyra thought that Siv might attack them when they least expected it, but she didn't. The rain came down in heavy drops and the road was empty apart from the four of them. The other guards and the two girls from the retinue must have reached Jelling while Siv and Tyra were running away, because they were nowhere to be seen.

Jelling's outer walls were taller up close than when Tyra had seen them yesterday on the way south. It didn't seem to have been stained by a fight this summer; the southerners must have made a wide circle around the town when they had snuck up through Jutland in the summer. From the guards to the painted gates, Tyra already hated everything about Jelling.

The gates opened for them. In the town, wooden houses mixed with painted clay ones.

'Are you taking me to him?' Siv asked the two guards. The unnatural accent she spoke with was subtle but just enough to remind Tyra that they were playing a game.

'We expected you yesterday,' the guard said. 'King Harald asked us to bring you to his hall as soon as we found you.' Tyra's eyes widened, she had never met a king before. She wondered which part of the south this Harald was from; he couldn't be from too far south if his name was Harald. That was a name of the north.

The guards and Siv walked on in silence before Siv spoke again. 'What about…?' She looked down at the muddy ground without finishing her sentence.

'Those who attacked you?'

Siv nodded to confirm, and the guard carried on. 'The girls will be with him.'

'The others too? The men?'

'We only found the girls, but don't worry,' the other guard said. 'We'll be there to protect you.'

Siv said something in a foreign tongue Tyra didn't understand, but she supposed she had thanked them. The guards didn't seem to understand either.

The guards brought Siv and Tyra up a road Tyra imagined would be full of people on a less-rainy day. They passed another barricade and continued along a muddy path past a grassy lawn where apple trees grew and runestones had been raised on a long row. The ground had been marked and a few wooden planks readied for a house to be built, though there were no builders.

Behind that rose a large gravemound, taller than any grave Tyra had ever seen before, and it looked like a hill, but it was too round and perfect to be anything but a barrow, and huge runestones continued along the edge of the mound. Beyond that was a great longhouse, bigger than Siv's house back in Ash-hill, and that had been pretty big.

One of the two guards rushed ahead towards the longhouse, knocked once, and entered. The other guard made them wait outside, by the main door. The rain ran down from the roof and onto Tyra's head and shoulders, but Tyra didn't mind at all. Her dress was already soaked and her hair hung at the sides of her face, heavy with rain.

Tyra expected Siv to strike at any moment. Instead, the door swung open and the guard urged them inside.

'Whoever she is, she's lying,' a woman was yelling as they entered. The guard put a hand on Tyra's back, and on Siv's too. Tyra flinched away. It reminded her of the battle up at Ash-hill, but when she saw his face she realised it had been meant to reassure.

No shoes had been left at the little entrance by the door, and the guard did not remove his either, so Tyra proceeded onto the wooden floor with her shoes on, leaving a trail of mud behind her. Her mother would have yelled at her for that, especially since this was in a stranger's house, and there was a king inside.

Tyra stopped and waited for Siv when she was far enough around the corner from the entrance to look inside.

There were more than a dozen guards inside the hall, standing up against the walls, with their hands on their weapons. Tyra had never seen warriors act like this. It looked funny; as if they were dolls a little child had placed around the room.

'It's her,' one of the two women from the retinue yelled. She rose from a chair by a fire in the middle of the hall. She was alone; the other woman was nowhere to be seen. 'She's the one who attacked us.' She pointed at Tyra.

'That little girl?' asked a man, seated on a platform. He leant back in his chair, covered with warm woollen blankets. Tyra had to tilt her head back to look up at him, like she had used to do with Einer, who had always been tall. This man wasn't very tall at all, but the platform made him look a lot taller than everyone else. His clothes were pretty, blue and embroidered with silver threads.

'The two of them,' the woman from yesterday said. She wore the same clothes as then: a dark yellow dress with a strange round cut for the neck, and embroidered edges. She must have been really careful all throughout the night to have avoided stains on a brightly coloured dress like that.

'Lock them up,' she squealed in a strange accent, like the one Siv had put on out in the forest when they had run from the two guards. That was why she had sounded like that. It all began to make sense to Tyra, what Siv's plan had to be and why she hadn't killed the guards.

Acting shy and scared, Siv made her entrance into the hall. She kept a few steps behind Tyra. According to Siv's story Tyra had saved them both.

Tyra tried to act the part, and took another few steps into the hall, watching the man on the raised platform. He had to be this King Harald the guard and Siv had talked about outside.

He didn't look like a king. His face was ordinary, and if he changed into less expensive clothes, Tyra would neither have noticed him, nor been able to recognise him.

Tyra walked closer to the fire, while keeping her distance from the woman from yesterday, who was even now demanding that the King do something.

The warmth of the hall made Tyra feel cold. Outside, she hadn't noticed how frozen her hands had become. Now, her entire body shook from the cold of the rain soaking her.

'Who are you?' Harald asked Siv and Tyra.

'She's the one who attacked me,' the woman from the retinue yelled. 'I told you, I'm Tove, protector of Slavs and daughter of Mistivoj, leader of the Obotrites.'

Siv took a shocked step backwards, and as if all hope was lost, the tears streamed down her face once more. She covered her face with both hands and took a few deep breaths before she sweeping the tears away.

'Why are you crying?' Harald asked. He leant forward in his seat with interest, and Tyra was certain that if it hadn't been for the other woman, he would have run to Siv and pulled her into his arms. Siv had that effect on people: whatever she wanted them to do, she could make them do.

Tove Mistivojudóttir watched Siv, uncomprehending, and confused.

'I...' Siv sniffed and dried the tears and snot from her face gracefully with her wet sleeve. 'I didn't realise she knew my name.'

Finally, Tyra understood why they were there. Why Siv hadn't attacked the women, and why they hadn't gone to Jelling before the guards came back with the girls. Even Siv hadn't known the woman's name.

'*Your* name?' the woman from the retinue yelled. Now that Tyra saw her, Siv kind of looked like the woman. They had the same golden colour of hair and the same grey eyes, only their faces and noses were a little different—and, besides, Siv was a lot prettier.

'Don't you see she's lying?' the woman demanded, staring up at King Harald.

'How do I know *you're* not the one who is lying?' he asked. The look he gave the woman was full of reproach. Kings were all-powerful. If he discovered that Siv and Tyra weren't who they said they were, he could kill them, right there, without giving it another thought. He didn't have to do it himself, he could just point at them and make his guards slit their throats.

'She's wearing my dress,' Siv muttered, and then she burst into tears again.

'What did you say?' the King wanted to know, but Siv didn't repeat herself. 'What did she say?'

None of the guards seemed to have heard either, so Tyra took a brave step forward. She glanced back at Siv, hoping that maybe Siv could help her be strong, but Siv was crying a lot, and she didn't return Tyra's stare. Tyra had to be brave on her own. 'She said: that woman'—Tyra pointed to the rude woman from the retinue—'that woman is wearing her dress.'

King Harald and all the guards turned their attention back to the woman, who was yelling that Tyra and Siv were lying, that they were only doing this to take her wealth, that they had killed her entire retinue, but King Harald wasn't convinced by that explanation, for all it was the truth.

'I was out in the forest alone all night, hiding from them,' Tove Mistivojudóttir claimed. Tyra knew that was a lie, there had been her handmaiden. 'They murdered my guards. They're beggars. Look at them. An orphan and a wench.'

The words stung. 'You don't look like someone who has been out in the mud all night,' Tyra yelled, upset all the way down to her stomach. 'Not a single muddy stain. You haven't stayed outside all night in that.'

'She's lying,' the woman shrieked, already short of any explanation. 'An orphan like her would say anything to get food.'

'You're right,' Tyra retorted. 'I am an orphan, but you aren't

336

this great person you say you are. *This* woman'—she gestured to Siv—'had the kindness to offer me food. I might have been dead already if it wasn't for her.' All of it was true, a neat trick Hilda had once taught Tyra. Lying was easier if you didn't actually lie, and it couldn't be held against you either. At least that was what Hilda had once said, though Tyra was pretty certain that when you lied to a king, even if you didn't really lie, it could still be held against you. Right now, she was too angry to care. 'This woman saved my life,' Tyra said. 'Don't you dare make her out to be like you.'

Her heart was beating out of control, and she tried to calm her breathing. She still had Siv, she tried to tell herself, but she couldn't keep herself from thinking about her parents, and her sisters, and how happy they had been at Midsummer, and it made her go from angry to so sad she was struggling to hold back the tears. All because of this stupid woman who had called her an orphan and insulted Siv.

'My father can tell you who I am,' Siv suggested. She brushed the last few tears off her swollen face with the back of her hand and stared up at King Harald with that power in her gaze that Tyra knew well. Siv was definitely using her influence.

'My father is already on his way. And he wouldn't entertain something this silly,' the real Tove insisted. 'And what's going to happen to us while we wait? That woman might kill us all in our sleep.'

'What will happen?' King Harald asked and it was clear that he had already made up his mind about who to trust. 'She'—he nodded to Siv without taking his eyes off her—'will regain her rightful place at my side.'

'But she's lying,' the real Tove yelled. 'She's luring you in with her tears.'

'As for you,' King Harald said, raising his voice over the woman's protests, 'you will greet God.'

EINER

Chapter Thirty-Five

THEY WERE FOUR short of a thousand warriors.

Einer followed the other ship commanders onto his father's ship. He was almost surprised at how little it smelled of tar as he legged on board. The *Mermaid Scream* thirsted for tar. The shrouds remained sticky, but everything else, even the clue lines, were severely marked by the ship's summer voyage. The salty waters had faded most of the tar and paint, and like most of their ships, the *Mermaid Scream* needed thorough care.

Einer had spent all morning hoping Hilda would change her mind and come back, although he knew she never changed her mind, especially when she was hurting. He sat down on the mast-fish and looked around at the many new faces among the ship commanders. He had hoped they would have somewhere closer to twenty-five ships before they attacked. Not as many people had responded to their call of help as he had hoped, but hearing Thora speak, Sigismund had greatly helped gather warriors up north. Four entire ships had arrived with her from Frey's-fiord and further north. Strangely, the scouts they had sent overland from Ash-hill were the ones who had faced most trouble finding warriors and ships willing to join their raid. Every last Dane chief had to know how much of a threat the attack on Jutland posed to their own lands, but many had already made alliances with the asshole Harald who called himself king.

The ship commanders waited in awkward silence. Only Sigismund was missing.

'There he comes,' Osvif sighed.

Sigismund rushed ahead when he noticed that the ship commanders had already gathered.

Behind him marched Hilda.

Einer's heart raced at the sight of her. Somehow Sigismund had convinced her to come back. Already that was enough for Einer to feel so grateful that he swore a silent oath to make it up to Sigismund, somehow, some day.

Einer smiled to Hilda, but she did not meet his gaze, instead settled her ember stare on his father, ready to challenge him to a long-awaited fight.

'Go on to the *Storm*, Hilda,' Sigismund told her loud enough for the rest of them to hear. He pointed his ship out for her, three ships further up the row. 'I won't be long. The others will tell you what to do.'

'Wait,' Vigmer called.

All the warriors on the ships and on shore watched without as much as breathing. Hilda too.

'Why is she here?' Einer's father was all but stuttering, so clearly taken aback was he by Hilda's return. They all were, but no one else would have opposed it.

'Who? Hilda?' Sigismund answered. 'Don't worry, she has already packed. The *Storm*'s ready to sail out.'

Osvif, never subtle, burst out laughing at that, and two ship commanders from Odin's-gorge joined too. Everyone knew about Hilda the draugar, and the discord between Einer and his father over her fate; even the newcomers.

Vigmer had his hands pressed against his knees, not resting on his round stomach as they usually did; he was angry. 'I promised her father I wouldn't take her on the raids,' he explained to Sigismund.

Everyone liked Sigismund, and no one but Vigmer would challenge him on this, or anything else, for that matter; Sigismund never made a rash decision, and people trusted him. His reputation ran all over the Norse lands, from Hedeby to Birka.

'Then you've kept your word,' Sigismund said. '*You* aren't taking her on this raid, I am.' His voice was unwavering. 'Any southerner who sees her with the blood smeared across her face, the pale skin and those fiery eyes, is going to piss himself and faint before he can run,' Sigismund insisted with a laugh. He turned to Hilda with a reassuring smile. 'Go on, Hilda,' he told her and took his seat among the ship commanders. Sigismund managed to make Hilda look stronger than ever.

In the last moment before she walked away, Hilda caught Einer's gaze smiling. She glowed, and the blood on her face made her shine brighter. The happiness was echoed inside Einer, leaving him with a lingering smile that did not fail, even when Hilda was out of view.

His father rubbed his beard, darker at the roots where it had not yet been bleached, and tangled as if he had forgotten to comb and trim it. He grumbled something to himself, but none of the ship commanders asked him to repeat it, and had he not been the only chieftain present, they most likely would not have waited for him to start their meeting. 'Is everyone ready?' he asked, glaring at Sigismund.

None of the ship commanders responded. Since they were all there, they had to be ready to leave. The chief nodded and moved on. 'Food?'

'We're short,' Thora answered. 'We'll last today and maybe tomorrow, depending on the weather, but not much longer.'

'Same with the *Northern Wrath*,' Einer added.

'Us too,' Osvif said, and with firm nods, the remaining

commanders from Jutland revealed that they would also struggle with food. Those from Frey's-fiord and Odin's-gorge had brought some with them, but Ash-hill had not been able to bring anything. A thousand warriors were difficult to feed and they would have to stop to fill their stocks before they reached Magadoborg.

'Drink?'

'Will last us longer, but we'll need to fill up along the way.' No one added anything to that but the situation was clearly the same on all the ships.

'We're almost one thousand warriors,' Einer observed. 'The easiest would be to raid for food on the way.'

'You used to raid up the Albis river, right?' the chief asked a bulky man with black teeth who was the most influential of the three commanders from the Odin's-gorge area. 'Any suggestions?'

'Smaller crews tend to raid along the river. They avoid the big towns.'

'The first larger one is Hammaborg,' added one of the others from Odin's-gorge. 'A day's sailing from here.'

'We lost the chance of a surprise attack,' Vigmer said thoughtfully. 'Rollo's grandson will have sent word to his allies in Magadoborg, so they must know we're on our way.' Einer nodded, well aware what his father wanted to suggest. 'So instead of a quiet approach, we ought to hit strong and make them fear our arrival.'

'Announce our arrival and make them worry every day as they watch the horizon,' said one of the commanders from Odin's-gorge.

They easily agreed that it needed to be done. With Ash-hill's little food, they had no choice but to take at least one town to stock up, and that meant their arrival would be a well-known fact, no matter if Richard of Normandy had sent messengers to Magadoborg or not.

'How big is Hammaborg?' Einer asked.

'About the size of Alebu.' The largest town in northern Jutland was more of a city. Water channels and fortifications surrounded it and half a hundred boats and trading ships called its harbour home. The fight ahead would be tough, but a city of that size might not be prepared for raids. They would not have seen many.

'Guards?'

'We'll have to go in with shield-walls.'

'Perfect practice, then,' the chief declared. Good practice and a good introduction to raiding for Hilda, Einer thought. She would love it; after so many winters of training on her own, moving in a formation with a thousand warriors would be like a dream to her. If he found a moment to breathe on the battlefield, he would need to see if he could spot her among Sigismund's warriors. He would have preferred if they could raid side by side, holding their shields up against each other, like they had always practised but he trusted Sigismund to introduce her to the basics.

He tried to shake thoughts of her out of his head, but he continued to imagine how happy she would be after her first raid. They would finally fight together.

Osvif elbowed Einer with a laugh, and he looked around, confused. He had been so deep in thought that he did not quite have time to catch up on the joke, whatever it had been, but he forced a short laugh. He should have listened.

It felt odd not knowing what had been discussed, although he had been there through it all, and as far as he could remember it was the first time he had not been focused and come with suggestions while they planning an attack. The first time would have to be the last, and it would be fine now that Hilda was there, raiding with them. Just thinking her name made him smile as if he had already passed on and entered Valhalla.

'We should watch out not to waste arrows until we arrive at Magadoborg,' Thora said. She had always been practical in her approach to war. 'We'll need every throwing weapon we have at that point, and whatever other weapons we can pick up along the way would help.'

'Tell your warriors that they should try not to damage the arrows and spear launched at us too,' Einer's father concluded, back to his full sense and authority. 'Anything else we need to discuss?' He pushed against his knees and rose to his feet with a sigh, ready to conclude the meeting and sail off.

'That's it?' Thora asked, surprised that they had to meet like this for something so easily decided. Einer remembered how he too had always been surprised by the endless meetings when he had first become a ship commander, although that was a long time ago now. 'Are we not going to talk about how angry everyone is?'

The ship commanders sat back down but no one but Einer matched Thora's searching gaze.

'My crew are fighting over who lost most back in Ash-hill. They blame each other for not being angry enough. They blame me for not getting them to Magadoborg sooner. Last night I had to stop three fights on my ship before the crew went to sleep. All they do is talk about the slaughter in Ash-hill and blame each other for it.' Thora glared around at the other ship commanders from Ash-hill. 'My mother and father and little eight-winter old brother were killed in that fight. I'm as angry as my crew, and yet I can't tell them that we'll get our revenge and give our families the pride they deserve in the afterlife, because I, like them, have doubts about Magadoborg.'

'What do you really want to say?' Einer's father asked. His voice was rough and he scowled at Thora as if he had been betrayed.

'I can't tell my crew that we'll come away victorious from this fight,' Thora said although back in Ash-hill it had been her who had suggested that they attack Magadoborg. 'Magadoborg is huge, and I can't tell them that we'll find the revenge that we're looking for there, or that their loss will somehow be lessened if we do.'

'We had a Ting,' the chief snarled. 'You suggested this. We decided on it.'

'And I stand by my suggestion. And agree that we need to hit the southerners where it will hurt them as much as it hurt us. We need to make them know that they can't kill our families and get away with it. But that does not relieve my anger, nor that of my crew.'

'We're all angry,' Osvif agreed, and he was the last person Einer would have imagined to carrying anger around. 'I see my crew and friends fighting all day long. Most of the time they're ready to rip each other's skulls out.' He was right. Einer too had never struggled so much to make peace among his crew members. 'And a stop like that to raid for food does nothing to satisfy their rage. Nor mine. But I have two beautiful daughters waiting for me in Frey's-fiord, and their father promised them to come home to them after helping their mother pass on into the next life with dignity. Most of the warriors are not as lucky as me. Most of them don't have anyone they need to survive for.'

'I know they're angry,' the chief responded, staring at his hands, without looking at Osvif. 'But we can't do anything about that. We came here for a purpose. We need to strike the southerners' pride so we can have ours back, and in order to do that we needed food.'

'We all understand that,' Thora said. 'We understand that we need to stop to gather food,' Thora continued. 'The crews do too, but that doesn't help the anger.'

Neither Thora nor Osvif wanted to let the matter rest.

'Magadoborg will help the anger,' Einer's father insisted, no doubt feeling that his decisions were put into question.

'If we reach that far up the river before they start killing each other,' Thora said, and sat upright, ready to argue her case. 'They're angry at each other. They're angry at us. They're angry at the gods. We need to be able to tell them something to calm their rage.'

'What do you want to tell them?' the chief asked, as if he too had been thinking the same way, and for a long time. 'That we can't go around killing every last southerner? Because we can't. We aren't enough to kill everyone, not even enough to take Magadoborg for good, and that is not why we're here.'

Einer's father spoke with clarity, voice strong and powerful. He rose from his seat, looking around at each of them as he spoke.

'We're not here to kill every southerner in sight. We're not here to satisfy our own rage, or to do to them what they did to us. So you can all put your anger and your rage aside. It's of no use.'

He held a pause and just when Einer thought he was about to sit down, he continued.

'We're here to protect our lands and those we left behind, and if we are to do that, we need to take a stand. If we all die, then our gods will die with us. We need to make the southerners scared, and the only way we do that is by striking *effectively*, in unison. On the day we strike Magadoborg, if even one warrior strays from his task, then we fail. We have been wronged, but we are *not* enough to each go on our own killing spree, to satisfy our rage. That will only make us easy targets, and we're not here to die!'

Vigmer spoke with such conviction that when Einer glanced around, he saw that not only were the ship commanders startled to silence, but the warriors on land and on the other ships were all staring over at the *Mermaid Scream*, listening to their chief's speech.

'We're not here to die,' his father repeated. 'We're here to strike where the southerners least expect it, in a city where they think themselves safe. They will shit themselves when the bells of their precious churches announce our arrival. They will cry at the sight of us, see us in their darkest nightmares, and we will make them hate each other for what they have done to our families and what they have done to us. Their screams will be heard throughout the nine worlds, and when their cries ring through Valhalla's golden halls, our families shall know that we have avenged them. That is why we're here.'

Even the wind was silent for the chief's speech. Every warrior in earshot gaped at him. Not a single one of the ship commanders had anything to add.

As if he too had noticed the staring faces, Einer's father glanced around and cleared his throat. 'If we aren't going to act as one out in the battlefield, then this is a useless trip, and we might as well turn the ships around, sail back home to our burnt village, and wait for the southerners to attack again, next summer, when we've finally rebuilt.' He regained his seat on the oars and found Thora's gaze. 'You tell your crew whatever you need to tell them, Thora, but you make sure they understand this: we act as one or we die foolish deaths.'

He did not need to say that foolish deaths would not get anyone into Valhalla; they all understood what he meant.

'Anything else we need to discuss?'

Dazed, the ship commanders agreed that there was not, and made their way back to their respective ships with gloom hanging over them.

In a serious tone, the warriors gathered and raised the masts on all nineteen ships under respective instructions from their commanders. Einer's crew was quick to raise the mast and find their oars. Before the *Mermaid Scream* had put up their mast, Einer's sailors were ready to push out and row along the narrow stream leading back out to the Albis river.

Einer stared at Sigismund's ship behind them, searching for Hilda. He spotted a few blonde-haired warriors on board, but could not find her in the crowd. Then, just as the ship in front of them cleared the waters and Einer was about to give up and turn his attention back to his own crew and ship, his eyes caught her face. She was standing up, checking her grip on her oar, and for a brief moment, she glanced up. Einer waved to her and when her ember eyes met him, she smiled so bright that for a brief moment, he remembered how much she had used to smile when they were children.

There was less laughter among Einer's crew than usual. Staying there, in camp and safety for a few days had made them forget the true peril of their cause. Einer's father had reminded them.

This was their last stand. If they failed, all of them would die and no one would be left to raise their children. No one else would fight the changes to come. Their traditions would be forgotten, taken over by Christianity. Their children would be raised Christian. If they all died, they would never meet their children in the afterlife.

BUNTRUGG

Chapter Thirty-Six

THE DOOR SLAMMED behind Buntrugg, but the tavern was too loud for anyone other than the tavern owner to notice the new arrival. Even in his giant form, Buntrugg would not have stood out: the hall was tall enough for him to stand and there were other giants in the tavern. But Buntrugg did not want to give away his identity.

Freshly baked bread was served with shredded meat dipped in honey and the smell made Buntrugg's stomach grumble. The gods of fertility, as the vanir were known on Midgard, had an ease with cooking. A richer taste could not be found in any of the nine worlds, so it was no wonder that half of the houses in Vanaheim successfully doubled as taverns during the nights.

Buntrugg approached a table at the far corner of the hall, behind four alvar who sang and danced to the music of the vanir. Buntrugg sat down behind the alvar so he could watch the hall through their invisible backs. From the corner, he had a good view over the entire tavern, while no one would look past the alvar and notice him.

At the opposite end of the hall, three young giants played tafl with two dwarfs. From the expression on their faces the jotnar had the advantage, but the dwarfs would not give up until they came away victorious. Eventually, the dwarfs would win, and they would win big, because the jotnar were young, not much older than three centuries, and young jotnar lacked the wisdom associated with giants. Buntrugg excepted himself, although he was not even a century old: most giants did not leave the comforts of Jotunheim until they were well past their first century, whereas the first time Buntrugg had walked through into another world, he had been but thirty winters, and already Surt's servant. At half a century old he had travelled to all nine worlds, and several times too. No other giants could claim as much, except his sister, perhaps. In her younger summers, she must have come close, at least.

The tavern thrall rushed past the alvar towards Buntrugg, although the sight of them slowed the thrall's haste. Past the alvar, he settled his focus on Buntrugg and waited for orders.

Eyes fixed on the game of tafl across the room, Buntrugg leaned in over the table. 'When the dwarfs win, serve them a barrel of mead as a compliment from the tavern owner. I'll pay.'

He needed to find a dwarf forge that had not been closed and only a drunk, happy dwarf could tell him how to find it.

The thrall glanced over his shoulder, through the invisible backs of the dancing alvar to the table where the giants and dwarfs were playing tafl. 'The dwarfs are losing,' he said with a frown.

'For now,' Buntrugg replied. He leant back in his seat. The three jotnar laughed louder and louder, but the two dwarfs were quiet, no doubt sitting on a ploy to win the game.

'A barrel is expensive,' the thrall mounted the courage to say.

'It is.' Buntrugg dug into the outer pocket of his woollen coat, deep with coins. He grabbed one, placed the silver coin onto the table, swept his hand over it with his eyes closed, and at his mere will, the coin turned to gold.

The thrall's eyes went wide with wonder at the sight of one of Ymir's ancient coins. Few were left in the nine worlds, and Buntrugg's pockets were filled with them. Each coin had been forged and stamped in Muspelheim's heat, at a time only Muspel, Surt and a few other ancient beings remembered. The image fleshed into the coin was obscure despite the intricate details, and few people still knew how to read the letters that encircled the portrait. 'A barrel *is* expensive,' Buntrugg repeated. 'So, you can tell your master that you have made excellent money for him tonight.'

The thrall took the gleaming coin and rushed back to tell his master about their newest client and his deep pocket. The bald owner urged his thrall to serve Buntrugg food and drink, and soon, Buntrugg's entire table was filled with the best vanir bread, stews, meats, cheeses, fruits and half a dozen things he could not name, and in his hands rested a deep jug of mead.

The forefathers whispered through Buntrugg and made him tap a finger on the oak table in front of him. He took a deep breath to keep them calm, then sharpened his hearing.

The giants had not yet realised that they would lose. Loudly, they boasted that hnefatafl was a game invented by giants and played in all nine worlds. They bragged like most giants did, but the two dwarfs across from them remained unimpressed and focused on the game.

The dwarf at the board was beardless, and his hair was combed back in the latest aesir style, which even the vanir had yet to adopt. His friend had a smartly cut beard and his hair was short and just as precisely styled. One had a long nose, the other not, and they looked to be friends rather than kin; although perhaps more distant kin, since Buntrugg had once been told that dwarfs rarely mingled with anyone but kinsmen.

The three jotnar were growing patched beards and their clothes had greyed from their first long travel through another world. Once, Buntrugg's clothes had looked like theirs, colourless from harsh travels, but through the winters and summers he had worked for Surt, he had learnt the names of the runes that could keep the colour of his silk jacket from fading, and restore the soles of his leather shoes. These days, Buntrugg kept himself like a vanir, or an aesir, and his pockets were as deep with coins, if of the ancient kind everyone believed to be extinct.

Since Surt never left Muspelheim, he had no use for his wealth, and never had in centuries and millennia. Buntrugg could spend whatever he needed; never did he need to go anywhere on an empty stomach or travel with his own blankets to sleep under.

Just then, the faces of the three young jotnar flushed red and they banged their fists onto the table. Across from them, the two dwarfs smiled for the first time since Buntrugg had entered the tavern. Furious at their loss, the giants rose from their seats and loomed over the dwarfs, who remained seated, unfazed. The giant who had been sitting at the board cast the table aside as his two friends hurled their jugs of half-finished ale after the two dwarfs. The dwarfs ducked the blows while they counted their newly acquired gold, admiring the silver neck-ring one of the jotnar had gambled away when they had thought they had no chance of losing.

Buntrugg readied to intervene in order to protect his investment in the two dwarfs. The thrall stepped up to the giants, unafraid, and the tavern keeper shouted above the music that sore losers were not welcome in his home.

The jotnar assessed their odds. Vanir and aesir all around the hall glared at the giants with the hatred of centuries of war and disagreements; among them, dozens of dwarfs rested their hands on their weapons, ready to defend their own, if it came to it.

The eldest of the three jotnar enclosed the forefathers within his palm, with difficulty, and urged his friends to do the same. He smiled unconvincingly to the two dwarfs, and together the giants left the room with their sacks of clothes. The music accompanied them out into the night. Once more, aesir, dwarfs and vanir laughed and joked once more as if nothing had happened.

Buntrugg was glad to have taken on a smaller frame, since now he found himself the only giant in the hall. His eyes settled back on the two dwarfs who had won the game of tafl. They were pocketing their winnings and readying to leave the tavern with plenty of time to get home before sunrise. At their eagerness and relief at their winnings, Buntrugg knew that he had bet on the right dwarfs.

Just as they rose from their bench, pulled on their silk cloaks and prepared to brave the night, the tavern owner personally rolled out the barrel of mead Buntrugg had already paid for.

The two dwarfs stopped up at the sight of the large barrel and when the tavern owner explained that it was a gift to congratulate them on their victory, the dwarfs were torn about their decision to leave, and nearby tables stared at the barrel with long envious eyes.

The temptation of an entire barrel of mead, not ale and free of charge, was too much to refuse for the two dwarfs. They regained their seats, filled their large jugs and toasted to their own victory.

From afar, Buntrugg watched them as they counted their winnings, once more, and downed one jug of mead after the other. The clientele in the tavern changed as the night stretched. The dwarfs around the hall began to head back home and more aesir and vanir found their way into the tavern.

With all the time in the nine worlds, Buntrugg finished the many plates of food that had been put out in front of him, and right as he dipped the last piece of bread onto a herb-rich sauce, the two dwarfs poured themselves the dregs of the barrel of mead. Their hair, which had been so neatly combed earlier in the night, was in disarray, their voices much louder than the beautiful music, and their faces were flushed beyond recognition.

Buntrugg swallowed the last piece of bread and rose from

his seat at the far end of the tavern. He walked around the dancing alvar and to the table where the two drunk dwarfs were laughing. He smiled to them, asked to sit, and launched into pleasantries.

'Your heart beats funny, are you a vanir?' one of them wanted to know after Buntrugg had sat with them for a while.

'I am certainly no aesir,' he truthfully responded to avoid the question. The dwarfs did not question his identity again, and when they were both laughing at something else, and far too drunk to notice or care, Buntrugg began to gently probe.

'I have heard rumours that the dwarf lineages are dying out, is it true?'

There were no such rumours, and the dwarfs were quick to tell him. 'We're stronger than ever,' the bearded one stated.

'Sons and daughters in plenty,' added the other.

'So, no dwarf lineage has ever died off?' Buntrugg lured.

The two dwarfs looked at each other and snorted from laughter, so that mead flowed out their noses and made them cough and snort, and then laugh harder.

'There is only one dwarf family stupid enough to annihilate themselves,' the taller of the two shared when their snickering died down. They exchanged knowing smiles. 'The last of Alvis' kin got a little too drunk searching for him. They found him and died right there on the spot.' They both burst out laughing once more.

'Alvis' kin?' Buntrugg mused.

The story of Alvis the dwarf was told throughout the nine worlds; a proud story for the Alfather's dumb son, Thor. Everyone knew of Alvis, the stupid dwarf who had gambled for a marriage with Thor's daughter and won. Emboldened by ale, he bragged about his winnings to the father of the girl he had won. For all his drunken courage, he was then outsmarted by the dimwit Thor, and never made it home to Svartalfheim. Now all the beings in the nine worlds laughed at poor old Alvis who had been outsmarted by the dumbest aesir in the nine worlds.

Alvis' kin, however, Buntrugg had not heard about. This had to be the clan he was looking for: an annihilated dwarf clan with a hidden forge no one else knew about.

The two dwarfs finished their drinks, glanced up through the smoke-hole in the ceiling to see the signs of approaching morning. The stars were barely visible anymore and there was no moon; morning was no longer far away. The beardless dwarf licked his jug clean of mead and together they stumbled out of the tavern, still laughing about the fates of Alvis and his kin.

Buntrugg exited the tavern after the dwarfs.

Outside, like inside, the late night flourished with life. The lights from Vanaheim's many farmhouses and taverns shone like bright stars. The houses were scattered over the endless farmland, and from them, laughter burst out in steady song. Young girls squealed and darted off across a recently harvested field, towards the next tavern, to the drunken delight of the two dwarfs.

The vanir were well known for never sleeping. During the day, they tended to their farmlands and farm animals, and at night they drank until sunrise, when they could work in the fields once more.

The beardless dwarf turned to Buntrugg, almost falling over from the quick movement. He was taller than the other, and no doubt he was the most skilled at his work, for his friend deferred to him and followed his lead. 'Are you following us?' he asked Buntrugg in a slurred voice.

'I thought I would pay Alvis and his kin a visit,' Buntrugg answered with a wicked smile.

'Us too,' the beardless one answered, although clearly a visit to Alvis had not previously been part of their plan. 'Every dwarf in these parts pays the good old Alvis a visit on the way home,' he said as if to cover up his half-lie.

'Was Alvis that well-liked?'

'He was that well-hated,' the bearded one said. 'That well-hated,' he mumbled and laughed at his own clever response.

They travelled together across the farmlands. After the next tavern, over the hill, they encountered the first dead dwarf. Like a statue carved out of stone, he had been placed a little distance away from the tavern. Judging from the wooden handle in his stone hard grip, he had opened the tavern door and been turned. He had stayed away from Svartalfheim until morning, and sunlight had frozen him in place.

The jumble of petrified dwarfs thickened a few steps further along the path to Svartalfheim. Any dwarf petrified in Vanaheim was dumped out there for his or her kin to claim and bring the statue home. Most of the petrifications were recent, but a few were ancient, long forgotten. The two dwarfs edged their way through the tight tangle of dead dwarfs. They tapped the ones they had known alive on the shoulder, and expressed surprise that this or that dwarf had been stupid enough to be caught in the sun.

Buntrugg trailed after them, staring at the horrified expressions on the petrified dwarfs. Among them were a few peaceful dwarfs with their arms above themselves and curious expressions, as they'd watched their own hands turn into the same stone they had once been cut from. Dwarfs who had already led the lives they yearned for and had achieved what they wanted in this life, ready to turn back into stone and watch the ages and centuries pass.

'Alvis, Bafir, Andur and Lundir,' the beardless dwarf announced and pointed out four mossy stone statues at the middle of the jumble of forgotten dwarfs.

The eldest, Alvis, had known his fate before the sun had petrified him. His hands were reaching out to grab someone. The anger on his stone-face made it clear that he had been determined to take the dumb aesir who had done this to him with him into death. He must have succeeded at least in grabbing Thor, because three of his fingers had been snapped off.

Bafir, Andur and Lundir, however, had not known what

awaited them. Andur was examining Alvis' pockets for gold and silver. Bafir stood apart, in the middle of a yawn and a stretch, while the last one had a hand on Alvis' left shoulder and looked down at his feet, as though bored with the entire endeavour.

The beardless dwarf snickered. 'Do you know why there is so much moss on these four?'

Buntrugg admitted that he did not. The beardless dwarf, eager to demonstrate, lowered his trousers and began to urinate on Alvis. 'They stand the perfect distance from the passage grave,' he said. 'Right at the moment when all that mead and ale wants out.' He laughed and stared straight at Alvis' horrified expression as he pissed on the petrified dwarf. 'I hope they can still see.'

'And smell,' his friend added as he too let his trousers drop and urinated on the last of Alvis' kin. 'Do you know that Lundir cheated my mother into showing him grandfather's stone reserves?'

'That was Lundir?' his beardless friend exclaimed. He shifted to aim his piss onto the petrified dwarf in question.

'The sun is coming up,' Buntrugg warned, to hurry them along.

Startled, the two dwarfs cast their heads up to the brightening sky. They heaved up their trousers, eager not to end up in the same straits as Alvis and the last of his kin.

'You can always count on a vanir to be a good friend.' The beardless dwarf tapped Buntrugg on the lower back before they continued on their way home to Svartalfheim, where it would be night for a while longer. 'You're a friend now, so you can piss on them too,' he shouted over his shoulder.

Buntrugg smiled as he watched the two dwarfs leave and then he shifted his attention back to Alvis, Lundir, Andur and Bafir. The dwarfs had shown him to the only four people who knew the location of the open furnace, but these four dwarfs could not tell Buntrugg where to go next.

With a loud sigh, Buntrugg closed his eyes and regained his usual size to allow more complex thoughts. He knew of no runes that could undo petrification, and according to the legends of Svartalfheim, there was no other method either. It was impossible to revive a dwarf who had returned to stone. All of his tasks for Surt were impossible tasks, but this one seemed particularly hopeless.

The first sunlight climbed over the cliff and bathed the four dwarfs in the same light that had returned them to stone. No matter how difficult this would be, Buntrugg had no choice. No matter what, he had to find that furnace and close it. Surt would not allow failure.

Somehow, he needed to undo their deaths.

HILDA

Chapter Thirty-Seven

THE COOL NIGHT air woke Hilda. A gust travelled up the gaps between the oars she slept on and chilled her calves. Her shoulders were stuck between two men.

The Runes whispered incoherent words about a bloody war and endless battles. The snow fox's fur tickled her left ear. It lay above her, curled in around itself. The man next to her, a bulky man breathed heavily in his sleep. Further down the oars, someone snored, and Hilda's feet were so cold that she didn't think she could go back to sleep at all, no matter how much she tried.

Her eyes were hurting again. She grumbled and prickled a finger on her dagger. Blooded her eyes, and sighed in relief as the pain lifted.

She gazed up at the white world, and felt the rocking of the ship. Last night Sigismund had told the crew they would arrive at the first raiding grounds in the early morning. As she watched the sky, Hilda wondered how far away that was; probably not that long. Her body tingled with excitement over the upcoming fight. All her life, she had yearned for battles. Finally, it was time.

Hilda pushed herself up to stand on the oars. Blood from her eyes trickled down her cheeks. Careful not to fall, she fumbled for the fish-mast with a foot, stepped onto it and down onto deck. The snow fox sprang after her. She nodded to the warm bodies of warriors on watch—seated on the rowing thwarts, she assumed—and remembered to lift her feet high. Last night she had taken a fall because she hadn't lifted her legs high enough, and her knees were still scabbed.

Hilda felt her way over the slim rowing benches, all the way back to the stern, where a man sat with the steering oar. Sigismund, with his wolf at his side and his two helmsmen asleep at his feet.

'Too excited to sleep?' he asked.

'And a little too cold,' Hilda admitted and sat down next to him on the helmsman's bench. It was a tight fit for the two of them. She pulled the hat she had borrowed down over her forehead, and the snow fox settled on her woollen socks and warmed her feet.

'Tell me honestly, Hilda,' Sigismund whispered to her so as not to wake his helmsmen. 'Are you fit to fight?'

'I can hold an axe as well as any warrior on this ship.'

'Better than most,' Sigismund agreed. 'But you know that's not what I'm asking.'

She did know, but she didn't know how to give an honest answer. Being on a ship she couldn't see had presented more challenges than she cared to admit. Battle was more chaotic than life onboard a ship, and Hilda could see neither shields nor weapons; joining a shield-wall seemed near impossible to her. But there was no other option.

'I'd much rather die on the front lines than not fight,' she answered honestly.

'You deserve to fight where you want to, Hilda, but an unfit warrior endangers more than themselves. There's more than the front line in a battle.'

'I'm no healer, and I'm not standing guard on the ships.' She couldn't do either of those things even if she had wanted. She couldn't stand guard on a ship she couldn't see, and she couldn't heal wounds she couldn't see either. 'I either fight or I don't, what else is there?'

'A raid isn't the same as fight practice,' Sigismund told her. 'It's not a choice between the front line and nothing at all. There are plenty of roles.'

The wolf leads the way, the Runes whispered. They wanted her to heed Sigismund's advice. They didn't want her to fight on the front lines. They thought she would die, and she likely would.

'Like what?' Hilda asked.

'You could help Knut this time, and then we can see how it goes from there.'

'Help Knut with what exactly?'

'You'd be a fish,' Sigismund stated.

'A fish?'

'A helper. You swim through the ranks and help out,' he explained. 'If you were any other warrior, it's where I would have started you. You'll see the front line and witness the bloodiest parts of the battle.'

She wouldn't see *anything*, but she didn't remind Sigis of that.

'Everyone has been a fish at one point,' Sigismund said, though Hilda wasn't so certain he or Einer ever had.

'I can try that,' she agreed, and partly she felt relieved. She wasn't so certain that she was ready to die just yet. 'But I *will* fight on the front lines when we reach Magadoborg.'

She left Sigismund with those words, and with every step she took away from him, her heart swelled with relief. Thus far, she trusted the Runes and her fox to guide her, but a battle was different from walking through a southern forest or stealing a horse.

Hilda dragged herself back amidships where people slept on

the oars. She found an empty spot between two warm bodies, crawled up and wrapped a blanket around her shoulders.

The Hanged God will abandon you, the Runes threatened. *In the river, your corpse will rot.* The exact same words they had said up in Jutland by the runemistress' hut. The same words they had used to urge her to go south. *In the river, your corpse will rot.*

Trying to ignore the whispers, Hilda tried to lull herself asleep with thoughts of glory and battles.

BARELY HÁD SHE managed to fall asleep when noise woke her. Raiders talked and laughed about the fight ahead. No one slept at her side anymore.

Something was pushed into her hands. Hilda started away, until she felt the object. A bowl, filled with porridge no doubt. She took it and retreated away from the many warriors and their fylgjur. Two reindeer fylgjur watched her, but as soon as she matched their stare, they turned away. Hilda folded her legs and posed the bowl of porridge in her lap. The snow fox sniffed the bowl, but quickly lay back down, uninterested. It never ate anything, though Hilda offered, every time.

Hilda needed the food even if her snow fox didn't. She shovelled the plain porridge into her mouth, until the bowl was light in her lap.

'We should roll the oars back,' a warrior said somewhere to her right.

Hilda scowled up at him, too tired for any of the commotion, and with a deep grumble, she rose and walked along the mast-fish, behind seated raiders and fylgjur to regain the aft.

The warriors at the aft-ship were seated in a circle by the end of the mast-fish.

'Who's washing up?' Hilda asked. She held her empty bowl out above the head of a seated warrior, waiting for someone to take it.

'I'll do it,' she heard Bjarni say, almost as if he were apologising for something. The warm body she assumed was his took the bowl from her.

Hilda found the first rowing seat behind the circle of warriors and sat down, since none of the warriors made room for her. Last night, she had heard them whisper about her; they thought she was a draugar. Hilda had hoped she would be treated as warmly as any new warrior, but at the same time she felt proud that they were so afraid of her.

The snow fox settled in her lap. Hilda ruffled its ears. It had become affectionate since she had tamed its wild side.

'Finally awake.' Sigismund clapped Hilda on the shoulder. She hadn't heard him arrive. 'They were afraid to wake you.' He laughed. The raiders didn't laugh with him. In a serious tone, he addressed everyone at the aft-ship. 'We'll be using shield-walls in ship units. No throwing weapons. When we arrive at the edge of Hammaborg, the crew of the *Mermaid Scream* will decide how many ranks deep. Remember this is just a short stop on the way. What matters is that we get the food we need to continue to Magadoborg.'

Sigismund glanced around at them to see if they had anything else they needed to discuss, and when no one said anything, he walked past them towards the helm. 'Ready for entry,' he shouted.

'Ready at your posts,' the mid-shouter repeated to the entire crew.

With help, Hilda found her things below deck. She wrestled on her chainmail, strapped on her weapon belt and stroked the Ulfberht axe like a pet. She prickled a finger on it, and blooded her eyes before they began to hurt again.

The warriors rushed about the ship, found their places, grabbed their ropes and stood ready at the yard gallows. Hilda ducked under their swinging arms and tried not to trip.

'Hilda,' a man called and pulled her to the side.

His voice was old and worn, tall, but with a crooked back.

He only had one arm. No fylgja at his side. His was one of the birds that flew above the ship.

'You're my new fish,' he said and grabbed her, bringing her further aft. Out of everyone's way. Hilda stumbled over ropes and rowing seats.

Commands were shouted over their heads. People yelled at each other. Her mentor, Knut, spoke to her without minding any of it. 'Those tears make you easy to spot. You'll make a good helper. A good fish.' He was unafraid of her, like Sigismund. 'Today will be tough. It's a big city. But the perfect practice for Magadoborg.'

'I won't be a fish for that long,' Hilda assured him.

Any other crewmember would have pretended not to hear what she had said, but Knut wasn't afraid of her. 'Even so, it will be good practice.'

A battle horn was blown on a ship further ahead of them. Hilda leant over the side of the *Storm* and glared ahead. Warm bodies were running, and their fylgjur too. The first ships had arrived on land. Further in, people floated; they were standing on a hill. The floating people didn't have fylgjur: they had to be southerners. They looked like they were throwing something. Arrows. They were archers. It wasn't a hill, Hilda realised, but watchtowers.

Hilda had always thought she would be at the very front of the battle. That she would run up the steps to the watchtower, catching the arrows with her shield, and take out the first southerners by driving their own arrows through their skulls.

'Duck,' Knut yelled, pushing her down.

Something swished past her ear and a man screamed behind her.

'Lower the sail,' Sigismund commanded.

The warriors roared like there was no tomorrow.

More arrows swished over their heads, and a warrior behind Hilda fell to the deck.

'Don't we have anyone who can kill the archers?' she asked

Knut, staring at the dying sailor on the deck. His body was losing heat, and his friends were stepping on him to pull the ropes in the right direction.

'Didn't you hear the instructions? No throwing weapons,' Knut said, unbothered by the situation. 'Besides, they have the high ground. Even Ivald couldn't hit them from down here.'

Hilda stared emptily at the man who has been hit as his friends kicked his body out of the way. His body continued to cool; already, he was just a shadow.

The *Storm* creaked to a stop. The crew lined up at the fore of the ship, waiting to jump onto land.

There were no more arrows; the archers on the watchtowers had to be dead.

Knut elbowed her. She watched him bend down, heard him remove two planks at their feet and rummage under the deck. Hilda reached down, found his hands and helped him haul a large bag out from below deck.

'Everything we need. You take the bag, I'll cover you,' Knut told her and covered the planks again. The bag was heavy and difficult to carry alone.

Hilda looked up at Knut to ask him why *she* had to carry it, but then she noticed how he held up his single arm, his hand closed in a fist, as if he carried a shield, and she swallowed her question. She lifted the bag and manoeuvred along the ship with difficulty. The bag was heavy and the weight of it slowed her. Knut helped her over the edge of the ship, onto land.

Warriors in full gear with shields and armour bounded past them towards the fight. The front line began to form ahead, by what Hilda assumed were the town gates. They were so far away.

'You're our fish?' Einer shouted. He slowed his run when he reached Hilda and walked with her. His enormous white bear fylgja followed him. 'Thought you would be at the front line.'

'Me too.' She tried to match his speed, but the bag was cumbersome and she worried she would trip. 'Were you ever a fish?' she asked, to confirm her doubts.

'My first summer,' Einer said to her surprise. His bear groaned. 'Tougher than being on the front lines.' As always, he knew exactly what she needed to hear.

He reached in, brushed a lock of hair away from Hilda's face, and proceeded to arrange the sleeves of his own clinking chainmail as he walked with her. The great white bear walked at his side. Warriors darted straight through the bear as if it wasn't there at all.

'See you on the field, Hilda,' Einer said, and set out into a run. With long strides, he bounded past the crowd and caught up with his own crew. The enormous bear bolted after him.

Einer hadn't offered his help, she realised when his bear and him were long gone. She couldn't remember the last time that had happened. This was the first time he hadn't even offered. Even Einer didn't feel like he needed to offer his help; he thought her as capable as any other warrior.

The sweat rolled down her forehead and dripped from her eyebrows before Knut told her that she could put the bag down. They were standing on a patched field. Hilda dumped the bag and heaved for breath. Her tunic was drenched with sweat.

Other raiders had set up nearby: healers from the look of them.

Christian bells were ringing, somewhere ahead where the warriors were assembled in a great mass. So that was the city of Hammaborg. There were dots of warm bodies spread around in small clusters further away than the long row of warriors. Southerners inside the city. Most of the raiders were assembled in a long, deep shield-wall, but they didn't look like they were fighting, yet. More like they were readying themselves to charge the gates.

At the warriors' backs, to Hilda's left, two whole crews were watching the outer lands. Hilda spotted Einer. His bear was difficult to look past—on its hind legs it was taller than anything else—and Einer's heat looked warmer to her than anyone.

The raiders by the town chanted something in unison, down the rows in a wave of noise. They stomped their feet in the rhythm of the Christian bells' ringing.

Focused on the chaos of the battle lines in front of them, Hilda opened the bag and stuffed a hand into it. There were weapons and ropes and other strange things, and at the very top was a smaller bag. She opened that too, to find water pouches and bandages.

'Take that.' Knut nodded to something. Hilda assumed it was the small bag. 'Run to the front lines, and help.'

Hilda dried the sweat off her face and hauled out the smaller bag. 'Help with what?'

'Everything.'

She licked her teeth clean. 'Anything else?'

Knut hesitated to speak. He balanced from one foot the other. It made his crooked back more obvious. 'There is a place for everyone on a raid, Hilda,' he finally said. 'Even a blind girl.'

Hilda stared at him. She hadn't told Sigismund about her Muspel sight. She hadn't told anyone.

'We all know,' Knut said to her surprise. 'You stumble around the ship. Can't trust a stumbling girl on the front lines.' That explained Sigismund's suggestion to make her a fish. 'But prove that you can, and you'll fight at Magadoborg.'

Hilda lifted the small bag over her head.

In the river your corpse will rot, the Runes unhelpfully reminded her.

'Move low,' Kurt advised. 'The field from here to the town is flat. But beware; stay safe behind the shields, and don't get in the way.' He released a deep sigh. 'Ready to swim through the crowd to the front line?' He said it as if it were an old joke she was supposed to know, but she heard his voice quiver. Knut must have lost many young raiders in this way, but Hilda knew she was too skilled to pass on this early, despite what the Runes said.

'I've been ready since birth.'

She secured the bag so it hung in front of her, and sprang along the field, towards the warm figures massed around the city's barricades. The snow fox yelped a bark.

'Be a fish!' Knut yelled after her.

DARKNESS

DEATH, PAIN, AND fear.

Ragnar shivered from his last death. His sweaty hands clenched onto the distaff in his grip. The deaths did not become easier, and the Darkness was as frightening as it had been the first time he had opened his eyes to it. Even standing there, without saying anything, he was not safe.

In death, he had gone from being a skald to a runemistress who could see the future, and perhaps even change it. A watcher and observer, but one who could also influence the mind of someone as powerful as the Alfather. Ragnarok was in the future, and there was still time for him to change what he had done, to prevent Odin's death.

The thought gave Ragnar hope. Perhaps that was the reason he had opened his eyes to this Darkness in the afterlife. Perhaps he possessed the ability to change the premonition, and save his gods. Why else would he be there in the pitch-black dark? He had been expected in Helheim.

If he failed the gods would never rise from the bloody ashes of Ragnarok, to which he had fated them, and the nine worlds would fall, because of him. He had sentenced the Alfather to death. The harsh words echoed inside Ragnar's mind. He had sentenced the Alfather to death, but perhaps there was yet time to change the premonition.

Perhaps, in order to pass on into Helheim, he had to prove his allegiance to the gods.

Instead, on Ragnarok's grounds, he had doomed the Alfather to a horrid death, although he had not meant to do so. He had acted in hope to save his god. Besides, the death had been fated, nothing could have stopped it from happening.

This was all a test, Ragnar realised. He had let himself succumb to fear, but no more.

Ragnar attempted to comfort himself with the hope that if he saved his gods from Ragnarok, he might be sent to a nice afterlife in Helheim, where his wife and son waited for him.

Eager to escape the horrid Darkness and see a brighter future, Ragnar clenched onto the distaff and hoped that he would not go back to Ragnarok when he passed through the veil, but somewhere pleasant. Runemistresses chose which part of the future they saw; perhaps he could do the same.

Ragnar swallowed and tried to ignore his own heartbeat, which he could feel all the way up in his throat. His shoulders were heavy with responsibility. Both his hands clasped the runic distaff. Ragnar closed his eyes, wishing that it would take him somewhere nice and safe. Twice he tapped the distaff.

His distaff tore a veil into another world. A thousand knives sharpened against glass.

Ragnar passed through.

A warm breeze welcomed him. The grass was lush green and so perfect that it could been combed, and peppered with blue and white flowers that looked as if they breathed the breeze.

This *was* pleasant. Like a true runemistress, he had guided his visions.

The Darkness pulsated at the edges of what he could see, like a heartbeat. Somewhere above him, where the runic distaff's reach, birds chirped. Even day appeared as night to him. Ragnar's throat felt tight at the realisation that he was doomed to forever walk in silence and eternal night with a distaff as a torch, suffering painful deaths over and over, if he so much as took a loud breath.

Unless this was the path to Helheim, and he would finally pass on into the next world.

It didn't feel like the path to Helheim.

The smell of freshly trimmed grass and blooming flowers prompted memories of Midgard. He recalled how beautiful Ash-hill had been in summer. How happy people had been; how happy *he* had been. In Helheim, he would be happy again.

HILDA

Chapter Thirty-Eight

HILDA'S CHAINMAIL WEIGHED her down and slapped against her arms and her thighs. The snow fox yelped and hopped along at her side.

Hilda sprinted back into the midst of warriors, and ducked so as not to hit her head on the shields. The nearest warriors turned to her, startled. She moved at their backs, pushed further ahead through the heaving, sweaty rows to the front line. She tried to stay aware of where the shields would best cover her, like Knut had told her.

'Who asked for a spear?' she yelled as she passed. She clenched the spear in her hands, until someone demanded it, and took it. Then she turned in the crowd, looking for another task.

'Fish!' someone yelled after her.

The voice came from further into town. Hilda cornered past warriors trying to get across the narrow part of the front lines—Knut said it was a bridge.

The warriors banged their shields and shouted.

'Helper!' someone yelled again.

'Like a fish,' Hilda mumbled and scooped her way through the crowd. 'I'm here,' she yelled when she was close.

A short man two rows ahead struggled to turn and look for her. 'Your eyes are bleeding,' he yelled, forgetting, for a moment, why he had called for her.

'I always look like this,' she responded. 'What do you need?'

He took a moment to answer as he struggled against the crowd to hold his place. 'Help him,' he said, nodding towards the ground. 'He's not dead yet.'

Hilda followed his gaze.

He stood on top of another warrior, burning at their feet. People stepped on him, thinking he was dead, but Hilda saw his heat. She pressed through the crowd to reach him, bumped around shields and pushed warriors away. She crouched down by the man on the ground. Heavy warriors were standing on him. He was red with heat, and held a hand on his stomach.

'Runemis...' he mumbled hazily.

Hilda reached for his stomach. It was wet and sticky with thick blood. The wound was right under his ribs. A stab wound, and deep.

Hilda had never really learned to heal, but she needed to bind the wound before the warrior could be hauled out of the crowd and away to see a healer. She dug into her bag and brought out the bandages. She put one on his stomach and pressed down, and the blood soaked through immediately. She tried a second, then a third bandage, but she didn't have time to bind them up before they became as wet with blood as her hands and his stomach.

The dying man put a warm hand on top of hers. He didn't have the strength to clench, nor to speak; regardless, she knew what he wanted to say. They both knew what his destiny would be like if she bound him. For days he would suffer, and in the end, he would likely die anyways: not on the battlefield to be burned with other warriors, but in a bed, away from the clash.

Hilda looked down at the dying man, knowing what she

needed to do, as warriors clambered around them. They bumped into her back, and stepped over his bleeding body. They couldn't help it. It was too crowded to go anywhere else.

She put the bandages away, reached for her axe with one hand and his face with the other. Her fingers brushed over his broken nose. It had been smashed in. He was panting, scared.

Her hand travelled down his bearded chin, his neck, found his tunic and padded armour. She opened the armour at the shoulder with her axe, and moved her weapon down to his chest. She found his beating heart. It raced. Hilda placed her axe on top.

'In Valhalla, we shall meet again,' she told him, and placed her left palm at the back of the axe. She took a deep breath, ignored the clamour around them and smiled down to the man at her feet. Then she pressed down.

Her axe crunched through his rib cage. The blood splashed up her arms. The warrior's arm fell down at his side. Hilda's weapon was drenched in blood, her hands too.

She got up, and the crowd pushed at her. Raiders stepped over the man she had killed kicking his head about. His body cooled.

'Fish!' called a shieldmaiden from the front row.

Hilda turned away from the dead man, eager to forget. 'Who needs help?' she asked.

'Is it Hilda?' the shieldmaiden called, quieter this time.

'It's me,' Hilda confirmed.

'We're stuck here, but you can go.' The shieldmaiden's tone was commanding. It was Thora from Ash-hill. 'Tell Sigismund to check the ships,' Thora's loud voice was barely audible over the clamour. 'Something is wrong—it's too quiet here. Tell him to watch our backs.'

Hilda nodded, closed her bag, and with those words ringing in her head, she darted along the rows of warriors, searching for her ship commander. She hadn't passed his wolf on the way to Thora so he had to be at the back, waiting to get inside the town gates.

Somewhere down the ranks, warriors began to stomp and chant. 'Die, die, die!' Their voices resonated against the stonewalls. More joined the chant. The stomps grew louder.

Drizzle turned to rain as Hilda ran.

At the far end of the shield-wall, closest to the riverside, she found the *Storm*'s crew by their familiar fylgjur. The wind rose, and in the howl came the Runes' whisper, *The wolf will lead the way*.

Hilda came to a stop behind Sigismund's wolf. 'Thora said to watch our backs,' she blurted. The snow fox ran on, but Hilda yanked it back. It ducked in between the legs of the *Storm*'s warriors to avoid the rain. 'Said something's wrong and to watch our backs.'

'Einer and Vigmer are out watching the plains. Why did she send you to me?'

'She said to check the ships.'

At that, he turned to her. 'Hilda, you're with us now,' he ordered. He commanded his shield formation to turn around, then broke into a run back along the riverside. Hilda and Sigismund's fourteen warriors followed.

'Thora's right. They're targeting our ships,' Sigismund heaved as he ran. 'It was too easy to dock. They wanted us close.'

Hilda's snow fox leapt ahead, dragging her along; she struggled to follow and run across the bumpy earth. She shuffled the bag higher up on her back. Knut would be angry if he knew she was abandoning her position. She looked back up the way she had come, to where she had left Knut, but she couldn't see him among the healers, nor his crow fylgja.

The blood in her eyes clotted and the stabbing pain slithered back.

The wolf leads the way, the Runes said. So, this was what they had meant. They never quite shared their entire plan.

The warriors' chant at their back stopped. It had blended in with the pound of the rain and the rhythm of their steps through the mud, and with the chant gone, Hilda's heart beat faster. Sounds of the battle came in the wind. Hilda spotted Einer and his huge bear darting away towards the town; other warriors, too.

The rain continued to come down strong. Their run slowed, and Hilda was thankful for it.

There were no warm bodies in sight—no southerners, but no guards either, and they had definitely placed guards on the ships.

'Are they dead?' one of Sigismund's warriors muttered. 'Where are the rest?'

Hilda peered out from behind them, but saw nothing. Whoever the others were staring at, they were definitely dead.

Sigismund climbed onto the first ship. The warriors followed, and the snow fox leapt gracefully after them. Hilda watched them. She shuffled through the mud as close as she dared and reached out to the ship, and heaved herself over the edge, after the fox. With a relieved sigh, she fell in behind the others, her axe as ready to strike as to defend. Her chainmail rustled. She advanced slowly and lifted her knees high.

The warriors split into two formations and edged around the middle of the ship. Someone was lying down on deck. The heat oozed from him, fading fast. He couldn't have been dead for long.

Without a word, Sigismund pointed towards the other ships. In a long row, the warriors proceeded onto the next ship. Hilda followed, at the very back.

The guard on this ship was as dead as the first, and had been dead for longer; he was just a shadow to her sight. One of the warriors exited the row and moved down the length of the ship. The rest of them proceeded onto the next ship, and the next, and the next. The cold rain dimmed the heat of their bodies.

The rain came down harder and masked the sound of their steps, but the ships swayed under their weight as they crept. On each ship they found a guard dead, or sometimes two, dead.

They were faint shadows to Hilda, their bodies were nearly cold. She stepped on two of them, without seeing them.

One by one, the warriors left the row, each taking a ship, until all that was left was one warrior in front of Hilda. The snow fox was frenzied, barking madly the further they went, leaping this way, and that. It warned her of death. The wind pushed Hilda over the next edge. The last warrior in front of her moved down the length of the ship. Alone and shield-less, Hilda proceeded.

There were more ships further ahead, she knew. Nineteen ships in all. She had crossed fifteen.

She set foot onto the next ship. Her left hand fumbled for the rowing seats. It had permanent rowing thwarts, not removable; the ship was from Ash-hill. Hilda glanced down each way but couldn't spot the guard, not even a shadow. The snow fox darted over the mast-fish and barked, and Hilda followed, ducking under the sail and its many ropes. Her foot set down on something soft. Not rope—another carcass.

The ship stank of tar. This was Einer's ship, the *Northern Wrath*. There had to be two guards then, and that meant one of them was missing. Careful not to make a sound or rock the ship, Hilda manoeuvred over the rowing thwarts. The fox hopped over them with her. It didn't bark in warning. It didn't look anywhere specific. It didn't see the other guard either.

Einer's touch was all over the ship, and it felt as if he were there, following in her steps, hunting the second guard and the southerners with her. A breeze brought with it the sound of a soft knock against the side of the ship, as if something were floating in the water next to the ship and bumped against it. The other guard must have been pushed into the water; his armour would have made him sink.

Hilda looked down through ship's hull with her Muspel sight. There, by the aft of the ship: a faint heat. It couldn't be a corpse; it would have cooled too quickly in the water for her to see.

They were in the water. The southerners were hiding in the water.

She looked along the ships to Sigismund's other raiders and saw faint shadows in the water below them. They were in the water, she was certain of it. It's where she would have been too if she had wanted to sabotage the ships. Ruin the keel bad enough, and the entire ship was doomed.

Hilda tip-toed to the stern, shuffled over rowing thwarts until she felt the helmsman's bench and could see the faint shadow of a southerner below her. If she was lucky, he hadn't spotted her; but she wasn't usually lucky.

As carefully as she could, Hilda set her axe and the water bag down onto the bench by the steering oar. Then she grabbed the corner of her chainmail and, keeping time with the soft knocking against the side of the ship, wrestled the mail over her head and set it by the steering oar. She grabbed her axe.

'In the water!' she yelled, not caring that it might give the southerner below a chance to strike first. Likely, he had already spotted her, and knew she was coming.

She leapt over the side of the ship, watching the southerner's shadow as cold water enrobed her face. He moved towards her; she felt his movement in the water. Swung her axe and hit him. Her head broke the surface to breathe.

The southerner moved towards her. Her axe had hit its target, but the water had slowed her blow. His hand looked like he was holding a weapon, ready to strike. Hilda kicked with her legs to stay afloat and get a little further away from him and jerked to bring her axe back above the surface, but again the water slowed her. He moved in, ready to strike. Hilda kicked his leg and withdrew before he could cut.

The chain around her left hand tightened as she kicked herself out of his reach. The fox hadn't followed her into the water. She struck out at the man underwater, and kicked her feet to stay afloat. 'Come on,' she snarled to the fox, jerking on the chain. The rain splashed around her and the southerner lashed out. She felt a sting above her knee. Hilda kicked the man in the chest. With a stroke, she swam closer so the chain wasn't as tight.

The southerner moved back, away from her, and Hilda swam after him. He had Einer's ship at his back, she knew. Her eyes were on his weapon arm. He tried to lift it out of the water, but failed. He needed his arm to keep his head above water. Again, he kicked away from her, and his head knocked against the ship. Hilda struck, planting her axe deep into his skull. His feet stopped kicking and his body went limp. Like her father's once had.

Hilda put a hand against his face and jerked her axe free from him. She glanced around her for other shadows.

'Come on,' she urged the snow fox, pulling on the Ulfberht leash. 'I'll catch you.' The leash went limp. The snow fox looked like it was standing on the edge of Einer's ship, looking down. It tilted its head this way and that, considering. 'I'm here,' Hilda said. She didn't have much patience left. 'You won't drown.'

In the river, your corpse will rot, the Runes whispered. A cool breeze slapped her wet hair around, and the rain gained intensity. That was why the fox hesitated.

People splashed in the water to Hilda's right. The other warriors had followed her advice and jumped in too. She saw the red fires of their bodies and of their fylgjur in the water.

'We won't drown,' she assured the fox. Already she shivered from the cold of the river and rain.

There were more southerners for her to kill out by the last ships. She just had to swim to them.

Maybe she could tie the fox to something, but somehow, she knew it would escape if she did, and she feared to release it and be without a guide.

The pain in her eyes returned, strong as ever. It burned and made it impossible to think. Hilda raised her left wrist out of the waters and slashed it open with her axe.

The snow fox barked, and yanked at chain. 'Just jump,' Hilda hissed. The blood from her cut was washed out by river water and rain before she could get it into her eyes and soothe her pains. 'Come on,' she repeated and yanked on the chain. Again, the fox barked, as stubborn as her.

Something warmed the water behind her. Hilda kicked out, and her foot caught cloth. Something slashed at her ankle, another southerner. One of Sigismund's warriors would have recognised her and announced himself.

Frantically, Hilda swam towards Einer's ship. She glanced over her shoulder, and saw the warm shadow of a southerner following her. Her head thumped with pain as she struggled to pour the blood from her new cut into her eyes. The rain was too heavy, and without thinking she had put her wrist underwater and washed the blood from the fresh wound. The chain was tight. She could swim no further. Hilda spun to face the southerner.

Her head burned. The snow fox barked in warning. Hilda swung her axe, but struck nothing. She kicked out in front of her, brought the axe up again. Slashed open the soft skin by her left eyebrow. Blood poured over her nose, and ran into her eyes and down her cheeks. The pain retreated.

The chain splashed into the water. The snow fox had leapt over the side of the ship. The southerner yelled. Her snow fox had landed on him. He screamed as the fox circled his head, and tried to swim away, but too late. The Ulfberht chain tightened around his neck.

Hilda yanked the chain back. The man floated towards her. His hand groped for his neck, tried to loosen the chain's hold. Hilda brought her feet up to his chest and shoved the southerner away, pulling the chain taut as the snow fox wrestled the other way. The man flailed and Hilda yanked harder. His hands and feet forgot their struggle. His heat faded.

Hilda swam to the dead southerner and loosened the Ulfberht chain.

She turned her back to the fox and clapped her shoulder. 'Here.' The snow fox padded through the water towards her and scrambled onto her back, its claws digging into her shoulder. Hilda winced.

Her axe was difficult to fight with. It didn't move well through the water. She secured it in its clasp so it wouldn't fall to the bottom of the river and be lost.

With the snow fox on her back she took the first stroke towards the remaining ships, searching for the dim bodies of lurking southerners. Ahead she saw a shadow with no fylgja: a man with his back to Hilda, a few ships down. He seemed to be chipping at the hull of a ship with some sort of tool.

The snow fox sank its claws deep in her shoulders and pulled her hair.

The southerner's haste made it clear he knew they were there, but he didn't see Hilda, too focused on ruining the ship. He was as large as Hilda, and there was strength in his swing, but he wouldn't be as quick.

Slyly, Hilda swam to the next ship, felt the side of it with her hand and swam around. She lowered herself further into the water. The snow fox climbed onto her head, clinging to her wet hair, above water. 'Swim like a fish,' she told herself, and reached for her dagger with her right hand. She tried to hide under the water for as long as she could. Held the dagger ready in her right hand.

The man shifted his attention and noticed Hilda; he tried to wriggled his weapon free, but he was too slow. Hilda dived in and stabbed him in the back—twice, to make sure, and then once through the neck. The man coughed. Blood spilled over Hilda's hands, heavier than the rain.

There were no more southerners ahead. Hilda swam along the ship, until she felt the knotted ends of the shrouds amidships. The blood still poured from her slashed eyebrow, and kept the pain away.

Hilda grabbed the side of the ship to hold herself above

water. The snow fox clambered up her arm, and hopped onto deck, barking for her to follow. Hilda used the tarred shrouds to heave herself up after it.

She swung her legs over the side and stepped down onto a cold, dead body. Whoever it was, he had been dead too long for Hilda to see his shadow. There was a familiar smell to him, though.

Hilda glared each way down the ship, and when she had confirmed that no one else was there, she knelt down and felt for the warrior's face. He had a stiff beard, a wrinkled forehead, and he was old. She grabbed his shoulders. One arm.

Knut hadn't been out on the field when she had looked for him earlier. He must have realised something was wrong, and headed for the ships. Before any of them.

'Takka,' she told the dead man. 'For teaching me.' She stroked his cheek, rose from his side and followed the snow fox back across the ships to the *Northern Wrath* where she had left her things.

She trembled from the cold and struggled to lift the chainmail over her head. The blood from her eyebrow leaked down her face and kept her eyes freshly bloodied.

Some warriors moved across the ships, leaning over the edges to check the waters for more southerners. From afar, Sigismund and his wolf spotted Hilda and rushed to the *Northern Wrath*.

'Checked the last ships?' The burning light of his body had dimmed from the cold, like her own.

'Ja,' she answered and grabbed her bag with water pouches.

A horn was blown somewhere inland. It didn't sound like it came from the town, but outside the walls. The chief's horn, signalling for the last warriors who watched the outskirts of the town to join the battle. There was no fear of ambush any longer.

'We need to finish quickly if we're to join the fight,' Sigismund said when the sound of the horns died out. 'You go aft, I'll take the fore of the ship.' He nodded to her hand, and the bag in it. 'Knut will go in to help if needed.'

'Knut is dead,' Hilda revealed, and unexpectedly, she had to fight the tears back. 'He is on the last ship,' she said and moved in towards shore. Sigismund followed her.

'Your lips are blue,' her commander said, when he could have said so many things.

The cold made Hilda shudder, but the battle was already bloody and she had no time.

'You can finish here on your own. I'm not a fish anymore,' she responded and dropped the bag with water pouches at Sigismund's feet where she could see his wolf. 'I killed three southerners. I know I can fight, now. It's time for me to join the war.' She ran past her ship commander and his wolf, headed straight for the battle.

FINN

Chapter Thirty-Nine

SOUTHERNERS WERE SMARTER than most people gave them credit for; Finn had been certain they would have planned a decent defence of Hammaborg and the outlaying farmlands. But for once, he had been wrong. They had not been ambushed from behind as he had expected. Church bells rang, but the southerners had as good as abandoned the lands.

Half the warriors from the *Northern Wrath* and the *Mermaid Scream* had already run in to join the raiders outside the town's stone walls by the watery ditch. Finn too had an urge to run ahead, but he belonged to the Vigmer's shield-wall, and the chieftain was in no rush to fight.

Finn's shield dangled loose at his side, but his grip on the handle was firm as he restrained the urge to shout at the chief to hurry up so they could get some blood on their hands.

The rain ran from his helmet down his forehead and the length of his nose. Two younger warriors brought their shields up to block the rain, and Finn scoffed at them. That was not what shields were for; if anything, they ought to protect their shields from the rain instead. The fight in Magadoborg was ahead of them, and for that battle they would need strong shields, not rotten ones.

Three arrows planted themselves into the shield of the two warriors. Instinctively, Finn ducked, raised his shield to cover himself, and strode to Vigmer. The arrows rained over them, and Finn spotted a thick formation of southerners advancing towards them along the foot of the city walls. They must have left through one of Hammaborg's other gates, and waited for the warriors to assemble by the gates so they could attack from behind.

'Walls!' Vigmer commanded.

Despite the surprise, they banded together in their usual formation; Finn joined the second row of the chieftain's wall. In an outstretched arm, he held his shield steady over the shoulder of the man in front of him. Rain smacked onto his shield, ran over the edges and down over him. Instead of his sword, he wielded his battle-axe and made certain he held his part of the shield-wall so no southerner could break through.

Finn watched the advancing enemy through a slim gap of the shield-wall, Finn spotted the enemy who marched towards them. They had waited for the chief to abandon the outlook position so Ash-hill's warriors would have the water ditch that surrounded the city at their back.

There were more southerners, and they banded together in larger formations. For every warrior from Ash-hill there had to be at least three southerners.

A shield joined itself to Finn's, and he heard another shield-wall joining their length, though they were still outnumbered.

Arrows hammered into their shields like the heavy rain. Every moment the southerners did not charge was time Ash-hill used to strengthen their shield-wall. The arrows stopped when the southerners too realised that.

They charged.

Vigmer blew his horn again and had them rush forward with

the frightening speed they had trained last winter. The shield-wall held through the charge.

Their walls collided. The jolt resonated down the rows. The warrior behind Finn thrust his spear past Finn's helmet and shoulder, through the narrow gap between their shields. A southerner screamed. Finn twisted out of the way so the warrior behind him could use his long spear. His own axe was ready and his eyes searched for weaknesses in the southerners' wall.

The warriors on the front line grunted and crouched down, so that their shields protected the legs and feet of everyone behind.

Finn planted his feet in the mud to hold his end as blows rained down on his shield, and shouted to the two warriors in front of him, who looked up. Dan's red curls were easy to spot even beneath his leather helmet, and Holger was a recent addition to the team. Dan's friend Ketill had once had that place, but he had abandoned Ash-hill and allied with Harald Gormsson.

Finn nodded to them both, tightening his grip on his battle-axe. Dan and Holger opened the shield-wall, and Finn stepped out.

He only had one heartbeat to strike before he needed to retreat, and the southern formation was thick; their numbers were greater and shields were larger.

Too large to lightly move. An unlucky southerner shifted his shield to look through the gap in the exact moment Finn stepped out, and without hesitation, Finn hooked his axe around the man's neck and yanked it towards himself as he stepped back. The southerner's head rolled off and Ash-hill's shield-wall closed in front of Finn. Axes and swords hammered against their shield planks.

The southerners yelled, and Finn glanced down at Dan, crouched down by his feet. Together they burst out laughing and behind them their roars of laughter were echoed by other warriors from the *Mermaid Scream*. They had been craving a good fight. The southerners yelled louder, but Ash-hill's shield was solid.

Still laughing at the southerners, Finn nodded to Dan again. With a wide grin, Dan leant against his shield with his shoulder and glanced up through the slim gap between his and Holger's shields. Just then, an enemy spear came through the wall, planted itself into Dan's forehead and retreated before Holger could close the gap.

Dan fell forward onto his shield, and Finn crouched with a muddy knee on his still-warm back. His sword scabbard dug into the mud as spears and axes and swords battered against his shield. As he held the wall, Finn glanced up to Holger, whose frightened eyes were fixed on Dan.

'Eh,' Finn called to Holger. 'Ready?'

Holger swallowed nervously, rubbed the rain off his cheeks and forehead with his shoulder, readied his weapon, and nodded to Finn, who turned to the warrior behind Holger. 'Been this far up before?' he asked.

The man nodded, looked above his own shield, hurled his spear at the southerners and reached for his battle-axe. He focused his stare on Finn again.

'Your turn,' Finn told the newcomer, and as Dan had done a moment before, Finn leant against his shield and peered out through the slim gap in the wall.

A bloody spear was thrust at him. Finn shifted out of the way. 'Frozen snot face!' he cursed. The spear tore the padded armour on his shoulder, and the warriors behind him twisted out of the spearhead's way. Finn threw down his axe, grabbed the shaft of the spear and pulled it towards himself. When he felt the man on the other end let go of the spear, he thrust the shaft to smack into the southerner's face, then pulled it through the shield-wall on Ash-hill's side. The blunt shaft was bloody. A warrior behind him grabbed the spear and took it as his own, and Finn reached for his axe again. The shield-wall shifted to the left and Finn followed, stepping down from Dan's cooling body and into the mud. He looked through the gap between his and Holger's shields again.

The southerners' wall was solid at shoulder level. 'Feet,' Finn mouthed to the new warrior in his row, and with Holger he removed his shield and let the warrior through. The warrior swept his axe under the southerners' shields, hooked it around their feet and made no less than three of them fall. Finn and Holger shielded him again.

'Ahead,' Vigmer bellowed at the exact right time. They marched their shield-wall forward. Finn kept his stance low, and as he stepped over the fallen men, he gladly stabbed the worming southerners. The warriors behind him, took axes and swords from the dead bodies and took them as their own. Finn stepped over a warrior from the *Mermaid Scream* who had been stripped of his weapon in the same way.

The wall collided with the southerners anew; Finn put his weight into his shield.

'Shitting chicken,' Finn mumbled and glanced to his left. The chief held his bright Ulfberht blade. The southerners targeted him. Southerners always attacked the leader in a crowd, and thanks to his rich armour and weapons, the chief was easy to spot in their midst.

A mob of southerners burst through the deep shield-wall to Finn's right and forced them to retreat into horse-shoe formation with the city's river-ditch at their backs. In a moment's inattention, they had been flanked.

Finn was exposed. He moved closer to Holger in front of the chief and brought his shield out to his side to form a round corner. The rows further back shuffled around to engage.

All escape routes were cut off. They were trapped between the southerners and the water ditch surrounding the city gates, and the southerners kept pushing them back.

Finn exchanged his battle-axe for his sword.

He slashed out after the southerners, but they kept advancing.

Every southerner he hacked down left room for more enemies, and they closed in tighter and tighter, pressing Ash-hill's ranks back towards the slippery edge of the water, with sheer weight of bodies.

Vigmer cursed as too many blows swung wild; from the looks of it, he did not have full command over his sword. This was no fight to use a disobedient sword. But Finn knew the chief would not sheath an expensive sword like that during a fight, and nor would most warriors.

Under the chief's commands Finn pressed forward, with Holger at one side and Vigmer at the other. A desperate attempt to distance themselves from the muddy ditch. He smacked the back of the southerners' helmets, stunned them and stabbed them in the throat. At his side the chief attempted the same, but each one of his fatal blows missed; he hit shields and armour, never a neck, or arm or leg. His sword simply would did not listen to him.

Finn pushed ahead harder. Their wall was not as thick as earlier and they only had their own shields to rely on. Their feet were exposed, and the top of their heads, too. Finn readied to lift his shield above the chief's to protect him from harm, but he did not have time.

The chief collapsed at Finn's side.

An axe had cut through Vigmer's leg and made him fall. Finn attempted to push the southerners back so they could pull the chief away, but everyone knew it was already too late. Even the chief's gaze made it clear that he knew his time had come.

'Take the Ulfberht,' the chief hissed. He cast the Ulfberht sword away so it landed by Finn's feet, and then he reached for his old sword. An axe was hammered into his skull. Then another.

The southerners pushed Ash-hill's shield-wall back. Finn flailed to pick up the Ulfberht without letting go of his own sword. In the last heartbeat, he grabbed it with his fingers, holding both swords awkwardly in one hand, before he was pushed out of reach.

The southerners continued to push, forcing Ash-hill back

again. Finn could not find a solid foothold in the mud. The ground under his feet sloped down into the ditch.

'The chief...' Holger mumbled at Finn's side.

'Dead now,' Finn told him, insistent on not breaking away and to fight until the last breath. He sheathed the Ulfberht blade in his muddy scabbard and readied his own sword.

Ash-hill's warriors whispered about the chief's death at his back.

'We're not finished!' Finn bellowed, but their mid-shouter had seen the chief's fall and had already pulled out his horn. Four long, sad blows he made, and in his loud voice he yelled for everyone inside the city walls to hear: 'The chief is dead!' and then four additional long blows to erase any doubt. Their chief had passed on.

The southerners shouted to each other, and just as Finn found a foothold in the mud to resist, and push back, the southerners broke away. Finn stumbled forward.

Over his shield, he saw them protect their backs as they fled. Some of the *Mermaid Scream*'s warriors threw axes and spears after them, but the southerners were quickly gone. Their own shield-wall broke apart at the sight.

The chief had been trampled by half a hundred warriors. His tunic was stained with mud. His chainmail had been dragged off him, over his head, and his helmet taken. Even his weapon belt was gone. Finn touched the pommel of the Ulfberht blade the chief had given him in the last moment. At least the southerners had not taken the Ulfberht.

The rain had transformed to drizzle while they fought. Finn hung his shield at his back from its strap, removed his helmet and pressed the water out of his long braid. He glanced a few arm-lengths ahead to Dan's corpse; it was barely recognisable beneath the mud, but for a few locks of fiery red hair.

Behind him, the *Mermaid Scream*'s mid-shouter blew his horn and shouted again that Vigmer Torstenson had passed on in the battle.

The fight still raged in the town. One last time, Finn peered along the city walls to where the southerners had disappeared, before he put his helmet back on and marched towards the open town gates.

Faced with a thousand Norse warriors, the southerners had decided to flee out the back, leave half of their warriors to defend an empty city while the other half swung around to attack from behind. They had targeted the leader, the chief, and with his death they must have been convinced that the warriors would disband and sail each their own way home. They were wrong, and they would regret their error. Finn would make certain of it.

His wet tunic and trousers weighed him down and the mud slowed him. He rubbed the sweat and rainwater away from his face and concentrated on the town ahead.

A large part of the *Mermaid Scream*'s crew had reached the bridge over the ditch to the open gates, and were now waiting outside the town gates. The mid-shouter had fallen silent, the others too. As Finn approached, he heard Sigismund Karson tell them not to get any closer.

Finn broke into a run, pushing through the crowd towards the gates.

'Don't get close to him,' Sigismund told them all.

The crowd heaved and parted for a shieldless girl with blonde hair who could be no one other than Hilda. Finn darted after her and followed her across the bridge.

A yell emerged from inside the town.

'Stay back!' Sigismund warned, waving a handful warriors out through the gates.

Beyond the stone wall Einer raged, with his sword in hand. He had thrown down his shield and wrenched off his helmet, and now faced no less than a dozen southerners on his own. He broke their defence lines with brute force. As Finn watched, Einer hacked off one southerner's left arm and then both legs, roaring like a wild bear. His face and hands were drenched in dark blood.

The southerners ran from him as they might have run from a demon, yelling and scrambling over each other, but they had nowhere to run. Einer caught up with another of them and thrust his sword through the man's neck. With the man still caught on his sword, Einer yanked the southerner's left arm back so his shoulder blade popped out and his arm flayed loose, then wrenched him off the sword.

'The gods let him go,' Sigismund muttered.

Hilda stopped up next to Sigismund, Finn close behind them, and they all watched Einer's fury. He roared, and seemed even to swell in size.

Without so much as a frown on her face, Hilda slung her axe on her belt and walked straight ahead. Sigismund watched her, but made no move to stop her.

Finn followed her, to show everyone that he was afraid of neither her nor Einer, although with every step he took, his hands shook more wildly. He wrapped his fingers around his sword hilt to keep them steady.

She turned to face him. Her chainmail rustled and her lips were blue. The blood ran down her white cheeks, her fiery eyes were distant, and although her face was turned towards Finn, it felt as though she looked straight through him. 'Out of my way, hawk,' she hissed in a rusty draugar voice.

A powerful windblast lifted Finn off the ground and cast him back. He plummeted onto the mudded road, yet Hilda turned and calmly walked through the rising wind as if it wasn't there.

Her wet hair rose in the powerful wind, and it was impossible to take a single step closer to her; Finn struggled even to keep his eyes open.

Yet, unbothered by the wind and the warriors' yells, Hilda continued to walk straight ahead towards the unstoppable berserker who had once been Einer.

HILDA

Chapter Forty

EINER'S BEAR ROARED, five arm-lengths ahead of Hilda. It cast its head from side to side, tearing a man apart. In its frenzy, it attacked everything, hurling the bodies of southerners aside.

She couldn't see Einer. There were southerners preparing to attack. At her back were Jute warriors and their fylgjur, but not Einer. He was easy to spot; taller than most, and warmer too. Deep red, like his bear.

Another southerner launched at the bear. They shouldn't be able to see it. They didn't even have fylgjur of their own, yet they launched at the bear. At Einer, she realised. To her, they looked one and same, the bear and Einer.

Hilda had to stop it before it was too late. Sometimes, when warriors went berserk, they never went back. She walked towards the bear, and Einer. The Runes made the wind blow so strong that she could hardly move. Her snow fox barked.

'Let me go,' Hilda ordered the Runes. They were protecting her, thought she would be killed like the southerners who had come too close to Einer.

The enormous bear roared again.

Birds circled high above, but none of them dared fly as close as the hawk had. Hilda glanced back over her shoulder. Bears, oxen, deer and wolves. Hundreds of fylgjur and warriors stood in long rows, staring at her. Sigismund's wolf kept the others back with its barking and fierce growling. The fylgjur were fixed on Hilda, no longer Einer and his white bear. Each and every animal companion gawked at her from afar.

Einer and his berserker bear spotted her too. The bear rose to its hind legs. It was twice Hilda's size. The Runes' strong wind kept Hilda back.

'Let me do this,' she ordered.

The wind pulsated like a heartbeat. Hilda followed the rhythm with taps of her fingers against her chainmail, concentrated on it. When she had it, she let herself fall forward at the exact right moment, out through the whirl. Her stomach lurched, and her hand hit the ground and caught her weight. Her knees knocked against the hard ground.

'I can do this,' she told the Runes, and she asked for neither permission nor approval. The wind calmed. Hilda got to her feet and resumed her march.

The white bear bounded forward, lashed out at retreating southerners and roared at the watching warriors and fylgjur. It couldn't control itself; Einer couldn't control himself.

The chain rustled and the snow fox's fur pressed against Hilda's leg. She wasn't alone.

The bear was just a fylgja, she told herself. It couldn't harm her. Einer wouldn't harm her.

'Won't die,' Hilda muttered to the fox and to herself and to the Runes, and she hoped that it was true. 'You won't let me die,' she whispered to the wind and the snow fox. They had both saved her before, and they would again.

The enormous bear roared so powerfully that all the warriors' fylgjur behind Hilda began to howl and bark and yelp, and the birds above her shrieked and retreated.

'How do I calm him?' she asked the wind.

Everyone will be ripped apart.

'You're wrong,' she told them. This was not the first time she had seen Einer lose himself.

Last time was many winters ago, but she remembered the blank stare in his eyes and the murderous colour of his hands. Not a single one of the stable animals had survived the encounter, nor even the two thralls. Hilda alone had survived.

No one had understood back then how he could have torn them apart with his bare hands. And though Hilda had seen him plant his hands on each side of the first thrall's head, press the man's eyes out and tear open his skull, she hadn't understood either. Even when they sparred, she had never seen that kind of strength, neither before, nor since. But she knew now. It hadn't been Einer; it had been his fylgja. The white bear had killed for him then, as it killed for him now.

The bear roared, threw its head back and matched Hilda's stare. The short distance between them seemed to shrink.

It bounded forward on all fours, straight towards Hilda. The wind rose and pushed it back; the bear's teeth snapped down, a few fingertips from Hilda's nose. She felt the heat of its breath on her face, as the bear struggled against the rising wind. Its breath stank of iron. Einer's breath.

Now was the time to calm it. She had its attention; now or never. But she didn't know *how*.

The hundreds of warriors and their fylgjur were silent. Only the dying southerners on the ground screamed with the pain of their mortal wounds.

The bear's focus began to shift from Hilda, back to the screaming southerners. It rose to its hind legs again, and through the howl of the rising wind, Hilda heard the nearby slash of Einer's sword. Blood splashed on her skin, and she heard the southerners screaming. Most of the bodies on the ground were already fading shadows. By the time Hilda managed to calm Einer and the bear, they would all be dead.

Hilda reached for her godly axe, and while the bear was distracted by southerners, she dashed in. The bear saw her, and raised its claw to sweep her away. She was cast aside, not by the furred limb of a bear, but by Einer's hard arm. Hilda plummeted to the ground. The bear stood above her. Lifted its claws, ready to strike the fatal blow.

She bounded forward, axe ready, hit Einer at the back of the knee and dashed back out of his reach. The bear fell back down to all fours, but still lashed out after the southerners around it.

'How do I stop him?' Hilda whispered to the wind.

The Runes gave her no answer. They didn't believe she could.

The huge white bear crawled towards her. She would never be able to stop it with her axe. Certainly not knowing it was Einer. There had to be another way.

Last time she had seen Einer go berserk was so long ago. She racked her mind to remember what she had done back then, why Einer had never attacked her. The thralls had screamed in terror, and Hilda hadn't. Maybe he simply hadn't attacked her first since she hadn't gotten in his way. She must have done something else to force the berserker out of him. Must have said *something*. If only she could remember.

Everyone will be ripped apart, the Runes warned again, as if she didn't already know.

The white bear was much bigger than her. Every move carried incredible strength. It could outrun her, could strike her down in a single blow, if it wanted. Its only weakness— Hilda's only advantage—was the bear's size. She was smaller than either Einer or his bear, and if she was clever enough, she might slip past its grip and get close, but it would require all of her concentration, and even if she got close, she couldn't strike the bear down. It was her Einer.

For every heavy step the bear took towards her, Hilda took three steps away to gain time. Einer's mother would have known what do; she *always* seemed to know what to do. But Siv wasn't there to bring Einer back, and neither was the chief.

Nor had they been that time in the stables.

The thought sparked a myriad of questions. Einer had always stayed in Hilda's home during the summers when his parents were away, but sometimes during the winter, too. Why had he stayed with them on the nights when his parents were both home? Why had his mother so often arrived with him at their house, and spoken in quiet voices with Hilda's father? His parents had used to fight over it, she recalled. They had often quarrelled. Einer had used to say that his mother insisted that the best place for him was in Hilda's family home. Siv had never said why. She must have known about Einer's berserker-fylgja, as had Hilda's father. As a famed skald, he had known how to help.

The white bear bounded forward, and in the same moment, Hilda sprinted towards it. Her axe hung limp at her side. Her chain rustled as the snow fox darted ahead with her.

'Stun him,' she whispered to the Runes in the wind. She felt on the chain that the snow fox was ready. If the Runes helped her, she might have a chance of escaping Einer's attack with her life intact. The white bear raised its claw, but Hilda rushed on as if she hadn't noticed, and the Runes made a strong wind to drive the crazed bear's up to its hind legs. Fast, she slid past the white bear, and the snow fox darted through its legs, as she had hoped. She felt the Ulfberht chain wrap around Einer's left leg.

She and the fox ran on, pulling on the chain with all their might, but Einer was not as easy to overpower as the southerner in the river had been. They were stopped sharp at the end of the chain, and the white bear didn't even stagger. It turned its head and roared.

All they had done was enrage it.

She had no time to search for a way to calm the bear any longer. This was her last chance, and she was well aware of it.

Her father must have known how to calm Einer's inner berserker.

Memories of the winter nights when Einer had stayed with them flashed before her. On those cold nights, her father had made them recite Odin's high speech, no matter how well they knew it. Her father would tell stories, invent tales and entertain, but on those nights, they always had to recite Odin's words first.

Hilda rushed through the verses she hadn't recited in many winters. 'The more a man drinks, the less he knows his mind,' she said aloud, but that didn't seem like the right verse. All Einer had been drinking before he had gone berserk had been the water Hilda had delivered. The same water they had all drunk.

The bear's roar died down and its large head settled in Hilda's direction. She should have listened to the Runes and stayed at a safe distance with everyone else.

You will be ripped apart, the Runes panicked.

Again, Hilda rushed through the verses of Odin's high speech. From the top, unable to remember how far she had come. She would never find the words in time, but right then, as she thought there was no hope, she remembered what came after the verses about ale drinking, and she recalled how she had told Einer those same words, back in the stable so many winters ago.

'Silent and thoughtful a chief's son should be,' she told the white bear as she stared up into its heat, where she thought Einer's eyes were. 'And bold in fighting.' Those were the words. For a heartbeat, the white bear watched her without moving.

'Silent and thoughtful a chief's son should be,' Hilda repeated loud, in a steady and deep voice. The same one her father had used when he had told the ancient stories by the fireplace.

The many fylgjur around stirred at her words, in the same way Einer's bear did. 'Silent and thoughtful a chief's son should be.'

The great white bear fell down to all fours, and Hilda moved closer. The hundreds of fylgjur that watched her from a distance cried out and compelled their companions to listen as Hilda repeated the verse, and when she said the words one last time, a thousand warriors said them with her. 'Silent and thoughtful a chief's son should be.'

She reached for the white bear's head, and her hand found Einer's face, wet and sticky from warm blood. She wiped away the blood from his cheeks, and oddly she remembered how he had pressed out the eyes of that thrall.

She stared deep into the pulsating heat that radiated from Einer, and alone she completed the verse: 'And bold in fighting.'

The huge white beast groaned apologetically.

'Hilda,' Einer muttered. His voice came in a close whisper. 'Hilda,' he muttered again, and wrapped his arms around her in a tight bear hug.

SIV

Chapter Forty-One

VIGMER WAS DEAD.

The knowledge raced through Siv as she woke. She was rarely wrong about these things, and her heart ached with grief. She had thought his passing would be easier on her, given that she had already resigned herself to never see him again, but it hurt the same as the death of any husband.

Harald's bed was too soft for her. The pillows were too plenty and the furs too thick. As for Harald, he had farted throughout the night, again, and he smelled worse than any of her previous husbands, but Siv had not expected to like him, and she did not *need* to like him; she only needed him to like her, and that he did.

How a man who had been raised in the north could ally with Christians after what had happened this summer angered Siv beyond repair. Harald's surrender to the southerners and his decision to revoke his belief in the old gods, and his people's beliefs, rendered the rest of Jutland's sacrifice meaningless. They had fought for their safety and their beliefs; they had died

399

for it. And then Harald had decided to join hands with the southerners who had burned their lands.

As if his actions were not bad enough, his pride over the matter swelled by the day. Last night, he had declared that he had outsmarted the southerners to make them acknowledge him as king of the Dane lands.

Thinking herself elsewhere, Siv stared up at the smoke under the high ceiling of their room. She heard the rain tap against the roof, and wondered where Einer was now. She tried not to think about Vigmer. He had not been her best husband, but he had been hers. Had he died in the south or out east? Wherever he had died, it wouldn't be long before the news reached Jelling. A few weeks at most. It would be better if Siv could ensure that Tyra was at her side when the news came, no matter what they said, and who had fallen with him; it would not be easy to hear about their old life and have to pretend they knew nothing about it.

Since their arrival, Siv had only seen Tyra once. Harald was not ready to allow Tyra closer, but Siv needed to force him. She preferred not to use her influence on Harald, at least in the early days.

Harald rummaged on top of his furs, turning so his pale, naked body greeted the warm room and Siv. With a deep breath, she pushed back her doubts. Harald was not that different from her other husbands. He was just a man; just a short-lived she needed to seduce and influence.

She wriggled closer to him, kissed his upper hand and watched his eyes flutter open. 'Awake at last,' she whispered into his ears with the subtle eastern accent she had to speak with now. She pushed her revulsion at Harald's lack of honour aside, and kissed his neck.

'Missed me?' he grunted, eyes still closed. He twisted his head towards her. Despite his foul breath, she planted her lips on his. 'If you missed me this much, you could have woken me,' he told her when their lips parted, exactly like Vigmer had told her after their first night together.

'You slept so well,' she said like she had back then, and smiled, but unlike that time with Vigmer, her smile was forced, and she did not love the man at her side as she had once loved Einer's father.

Harald leaned in for another kiss and caressed her bare skin, up and down along the hip-line.

'I've been thinking while you were sleeping,' she said and eyed his body, waiting for him to prompt her.

'About what?' he asked with a wicked smile.

She rummaged a little closer to him, placed her head on his strong chest that reminded her of her third husband, and hugged him tight. 'About that girl who saved me.'

For a little while neither one of them said anything. Siv could feel him pondering how he could avoid this conversation, but she would not let him. 'Tyra,' she said.

'...Tyra,' Harald repeated. 'What about her?'

'I want to keep her close.'

'Good. We'll make her your handmaiden,' he said, misunderstanding, as Siv knew he would.

'She saved my life.' Siv tilted her head backwards to gaze up at Harald, and rested her chin against his hairy chest. Harald peered down at her. She could see his will crumble at the sight of her. His resolute mind softened under Siv's stare. 'She brought me to you. She deserves more.'

'Gold?' Harald suggested, twisting to the possibility of rewarding Tyra, but not in the way Siv wanted him to do.

'Gold won't mean anything to a young girl like her,' Siv said. 'I want to give her a family.'

She felt him nodding, but his mind was at unease, and she knew he would try to dismiss what she suggested. 'We'll find a nice family for her.'

For a moment Siv lay and waited for his mind to settle and for him to believe that he had won, and then, when he was off-guard, she looked into his eyes. 'I want to keep her closer. I want to take care of her.'

His looked away. He knew exactly what she meant and was clearly trying to come up with some excuse not to adopt Tyra.

'I want her to be our daughter,' Siv said plainly.

Harald's mind was rock-hard in opposition. If she wanted to sway him, she would have to force her way into his mind, and Harald would notice. Instead of her influence, she had to rely on well-placed words and winning arguments. 'Here she would have siblings to play with and parents who care about her. We owe her more than we can give,' she said, with an emphasis on the word we.

'She is parentless.' He said it like an insult.

'Exactly,' Siv answered and manoeuvred a little further away from him to make him see the distain on her face at what his tone suggested.

'If she hadn't saved your life I would have outlawed her.'

'But she did save my life.'

'And I am grateful for that,' he said and tried to bring her closer to him, but Siv moved out of his grasp and sat up at the side of the bed. She reached for his mind, but found it shut to new ideas, and she did not want to risk breaking through and being discovered as a long-lived.

'It's not enough,' she insisted, and then another argument presented itself. 'I don't feel safe here without her.'

'You're safe here, with me.' He smiled to her, trying to reassure her.

'So, you've caught the men who attacked me? The ones who killed Harlin and Gavyn and Bick the Hairless?' She forced tears into her eyes when she looked back at Harald and hoped that he did not know the names of the guards who had protected the real Tove; the ones the forefathers had helped her kill.

'We will catch them,' he said.

'What if you don't? My guards didn't save me when they attacked. That girl did.'

'You were both lucky to get away.'

'You weren't there,' Siv hissed. 'It was more than luck.' At that she rose from the bed, knelt by the wooden chest of clothes and pulled out a yellow dress that she slipped on in silence. 'I can't marry you if you can't honour the person who saved my life,' she said after a while, as if she had considered these words with great care.

She made an angry frown as she marched to the door where the coats hung. Elegantly she slipped on one of the three outer-gowns Harald had bought for her yesterday.

From the bed, Harald watched her, his mouth gaping open. 'The marriage has already been decided. Your father and I have agreed.'

'My father doesn't dictate my life,' Siv hissed in the same way she had, hundreds of winters ago, when her real father had promised her away. 'I make my own decisions. And I won't abandon the person who saved my life.'

'I don't want you to either,' Harald said, dumbfounded and desperate to keep her there, in his warm room. His mind was crumbling to the influence of her words, and with another push he might do whatever she asked, but he was not convinced, yet. 'Make her your handmaiden and she'll always be close. Give her gold as thanks. Give her dresses.'

'You know, while I was lying there, waiting for you to wake, I was actually thinking about all the ways in which this might be good for *you*,' she said scornfully and turned to face him, readying for that next push. 'As King, you would show yourself to be generous.' She counted the reasons on her fingers as she spoke. 'You would make me happy and love you more. You would give your children someone new and exciting to play with. You do know they haven't done anything but ask about that girl since I arrived, right? And as if all of that isn't enough, you would gain yet another daughter to marry into alliances abroad, like my father wants me to marry you.'

Harald tried to protest and tell her why he could not accept Tyra into his home and family. 'Tove. Listen,' he pleaded, but his resolution was crumbling and Siv did not let him say more.

'I'll leave with my father when he gets here,' she said as she imagined a woman like Tove would.

Ignoring Harald's continuous pleas for her to listen to reason about gold and servants, she left the room, remembering to frown on her way out. Guards waited in the main room of the house, exactly where Siv had thought they might, and when she met their gaze, they lowered their eyes.

She crouched by the side of the door and slipped her feet into a pair of shoes a little too large for her feet.

'Is there a decent inn in town?' she asked the guards who refused to look at her.

'Ja,' one of them responded, staring down at his toes instead of up at Siv. 'The Blue Horse.'

The four guards avoided her gaze and she knew they had heard every word she had spoken to Harald, exactly as she had planned it. If she had not instilled enough worry in him about her leaving, the stares these guards would give him when he left his sweaty bedroom would be enough to sway him.

She set for the door. 'Stay with him,' she told the guards when two of them followed her across the room. 'You don't need to protect me, I'm not his anymore,' she declared and marched out of the longhouse into the morning rain.

Harald had neither been eager or prepared to allow Tyra into their family, but Siv would do what needed to be done; she would not be parted from her daughter.

The door swung open behind her.

'You can't leave,' Harald desperately called after her.

'I will be staying at the Blue Horse until my father arrives or until you find some decency,' she said without as much as slowing her walk. 'You can come and find me, there, in person, when you've decided how to reward my life saviour.'

'Fine,' he yelled after her.

Siv stopped up and faced him. He was standing half-naked on the wet grass, desperate to keep her from leaving. She watched him with crossed arms and waited for him to say more.

'I'll adopt her,' he said. 'After the wedding.'

'Before, or there will be no wedding.' To reinforce her point, Siv turned back and kept walking. As all men did, Harald too would crumble at her will.

EINER

Chapter Forty-Two

EINER WAVED A fly off his cheek. His father lay at the top of the funeral pyre and the winter flies buzzed around him. The southerners had stripped everything from him. Ulfberht swords were famous even in the south, so that was understandable, but they had taken *everything*, even the simple weapon belt Vigmer had worn since his first raid. It had not been worth anything, but it had meant a lot to his father, and it had been stolen from his warm corpse.

The eighty-nine brave warriors who had passed on with the chief lay in a circle around him. Enough had passed on to form a crew for a large longship, and had they passed on at a different time and place, they would have been sent on their way on a burning ship, but the battle with Magadoborg was close and Einer had insisted that they could not afford the sacrifice, although his father deserved to sail to Valhalla. Instead he would have to walk into the afterlife with his warriors.

At least, there had been time to heave the corpses free from Hammaborg as they made their escape, and that was something for which to be grateful. After seeing Einer go berserk, the southerners had kept a distance that had allowed for a safe retreat with both food provisions and their fallen.

The stubborn fly settled on his cheek. Einer brushed it off again, but as soon as he lowered his hand, the fly came back.

'The chief will understand,' Osvif reassured Einer and tapped him on the back so the fly flew off. 'He would have done the same.'

Osvif was probably right.

'At least the southerners won't attack,' Einer said. 'They went straight for my father. They hope his death will scatter us.'

They had gone for the ships too. They had not been able to sail far up the river in their escape. The *Northern Wrath* had been close to sinking when Einer had given the order to dock along the river.

The time had come for Einer to assume the role of Ash-hill's protector and to show that the warriors and other ship commanders could trust him to keep his father's word and lead them into battle in Magadoborg against the Christians. Assuming they were willing to follow him, after his recent berserker outbreak. In one day, people who used to joke with Einer had begun to fear him, and Einer knew exactly who had fuelled the gossip.

'Do you know where Finn is?' he asked his friend.

'Out on the *Mermaid Scream*, I think,' Osvif answered. 'Why?'

'I have something for him.' Einer turned away from his father's funeral pyre.

He headed for the river and the long row of ships, splashed through mud and blood puddles from where they had dragged the corpses. It reminded him of the last time he had seen Ash-hill.

The wind was cold by the ships. The sound of the ropes slapping against wood and the howl of the wind was welcoming. It almost felt as if everything was as it always had been, except Einer knew that nothing would ever be the same.

The *Northern Wrath* was filled with chatter. A dozen ship builders were on board. The ship repairs were in full work. Had Sigismund and his warriors not hurried to the ships during the battle, the damage would have been much worse, and most of the ships would never have sailed again.

Out of all the longships, the *Northern Wrath* had taken the most damage; hearing the older men talk, everyone seemed to think the southerners had targeted Einer's ship because it was the largest and most impressive of the lot. They must have thought it belonged to the chief.

Einer proceeded down the row of ships to the *Mermaid Scream*. Many warriors worked on his father's old ship. Finn was standing amidships, laughing and joking with the men. He noticed Einer, diverted his gaze, pretending to be busy tying ropes.

Einer sighed and jumped onto the *Mermaid Scream*. With a smile, he walked past his father's warriors to the midship, and to Finn.

'Hei, Finn,' he said, receiving no answer. 'The *Mermaid Scream* is part of my inheritance.' Einer peered down the length of the ship. It would take time to accept that his father would no longer command it. 'You deserve this ship, so I gift it to you, Finn. You'll be a ship owner and commander from today on.'

Finn scowled up at him with those cold eyes, but said nothing.

'My father trusted you greatly. Will you hold the sacred mead?' Einer asked, offering Finn the highest honour he was in a position to give. 'My father would have liked a good friend to have the honour when we send him on his way.'

'Your father didn't consider me a friend,' Finn snarled, as if Einer's proposal had been a taunt.

'He would not have chosen you as his steersman if he didn't,' Einer said, but Finn's glare did not soften. 'The ship is yours,' Einer said. 'I'll inform the other commanders. See you at the funeral.'

With a decisive nod, he left Finn and the warriors on the

Mermaid Scream and strolled back towards Hammaborg's stone walls and the pyre they had built outside the city gates.

Ragnar Erikson's funeral had been more impressive. Although Einer had given all the silver and gold rings he had, the funerary gifts were few and the send-off left much to be desired in the next life. The only riches Einer had kept was the gold bracteate that his mother had given him, with clear instructions to never part with. He was convinced the bracteate was what had saved him from the mortal wound Finn had inflicted. He had no other explanation for his quick recovery, and whenever he was hurt, the bracteate warmed his chest, as if to give him strength.

There was still time before midday when the funeral ceremony would begin, but some warriors had already gathered around the simple pyre. When Einer joined them, Old Hormod walked to the pyre. His long grey and white hair had been combed away from his face with grease to hold it in place. He walked to Einer's father, and pulled off his own silver arm-ring.

Half a hundred summers ago, Hormod's grandfather had gifted it to Hormod's father, and a dozen winters ago his father had given it to Hormod before passing on himself. That ring was the most precious object Hormod owned. With a proud smile, he lifted it above his head so Odin's two ravens might see. Then he slid the silver arm-ring that had been in his family for as long as anyone could remember onto the chief's wrist. A present for the chief to pass onto Hormod's son in the after-life.

After Hormod, a long row of warriors approached the pyre one by one. In their hands, they each held a drinking cup and together they lifted their gifts above their heads to display them to the gods and show how well loved these fallen warriors were. They placed a cup by each one of the ninety fallen warriors. After them, came Osvif and lifted a jug with the wine from the barrel they had raided in Hammaborg. He served the expensive wine to the chief, and then walked around to fill all the cups.

Despite the limited wealth of Ash-hill's warriors, the pyre filled up with hundreds and hundreds of gifts, as each person in attendance left a present with one of the ninety warriors. Although the pyre had been empty that morning, by midday it overflowed with wealth. The armour and weapons Einer had scraped together were the least of the gifts.

Nine-hundred warriors gave nine-hundred gifts. Their generosity would ensure that the ninety fallen would become wealthy men in Valhalla and their investment would show itself in the afterlife. Einer knew his father would not forget a single person who had raided with them on the way to Magadoborg, and when the warriors began to arrive in Valhalla, they would be warmly welcomed.

Finally, Hilda arrived and with her came the thirty warriors from Sigismund's ship. They came into the funeral circle two by two and each pair struggled to carry a large rock between them.

Hilda and another shieldmaiden lumped towards Einer with the largest rock between them. The warriors took their stance in formation around the pyre, making the outline of a large ship, and placed down their large stones.

In generations to come, thanks to these stones, people would know that great warriors had fallen and been honoured here, and Einer wondered how he had not thought of it himself. Many of Ragnar's stories had used to end with the funerals of great warriors, and in many of the stories stones were placed around the pyre in a ship formation to symbolise a warrior's worth, like the graves up in Alebu. Perhaps Hilda had been the one to think of it; after all, no matter how little she liked her father, she *was* the daughter of a skald.

Hilda smiled to Einer and walked to stand behind him, where only the closest family were allowed to stand. She leant in and whispered into his ear. 'Do you want me to hold the sacred mead?'

Her question made Einer smile, truly smile, because anyone else in Hilda's position would have made a comment about his father and relayed their sympathies, but Hilda and he knew each other so well that no such words were necessary, and he hoped they never would be.

'Nej, I asked Finn,' he responded. 'I'm glad you're here. At least for the eighty-nine others.'

'Einer.' Only she could say his name like that, as his mother would have, and with a voice that carried more than a dozen summers worth of memories. 'Your father was a great man.' She blooded her eyes, and watched him with her piercing ember stare. 'I was angry with him,' she admitted, 'as were you, but I never stopped respecting him.' She was the last person he would have expected to speak like that about his father.

He thanked her with a smile.

The blood bowl and the mead bowl were brought forth and people parted to make place for the animals, which would be sacrificed.

Uneasy, Einer scoured through the thick rows of warriors for Finn, but could not find him. The task of carrying the mead and blood bowl came with great honour and Einer would have thought Finn would have rushed to be at the funeral in time, but he had not arrived yet.

The crowd waited; ready to stomp and sing and show their support to those who had passed on. A tall man from Odin's-gorge entered the circle of warriors. In his hands, he held hammer and chisel, and by the large stone Hilda had brought, he knelt. With fluid movements that were the work of dozens of winters, he brought forth the chisel, placed it at the very centre of the flat side of Hilda's rock, and then he hammered.

Clang, clang, clang. The sound of the rune carver's hammering resonated around the otherwise quiet funeral grounds. With the ninth clang, the warriors around the pyre stomped to the rhythm of the man's hammering. A hum emerged among the warriors in a dark tone, and in the crowd to the east of the pyre, Thora's shieldmaidens began to sing, and others picked up their chant, while the tall carver hammered the lightning-bolt shape of the rune of honour and success deep into the stone.

More warriors joined the chant and they sang to the hopeful tune of the story of creation. Nine hundred warriors stomped and sang and hummed along, and accompanying them was the clang of the rune carver's hammer hitting his chisel.

At the opposite side of the pyre from where Einer stood, some shieldmaidens stepped aside to allow Finn to pass through and stand at the innermost part of the circle.

'Finn,' Einer mouthed, not to interrupt the beautiful chant, and with a smile he waved Finn towards the place of honour in the ceremony.

Finn took a step forward and glared at the singing people so a few of them stopped and the song trailed off. Coldly he settled his scowl on Einer.

'Why should I hold that heavy bowl just because you want me to?' Finn hissed.

The few warriors who still stomped and sang stopped, and even the tall rune carver raised his chisel to look at Finn.

'You might have been the son of a chief, Einer,' Finn spat, loud enough for all the nine-hundred warriors to hear. 'But now you're only a freeman, like the rest of us. You aren't my leader. And neither is your father.'

BUNTRUGG

Chapter Forty-Three

In Yggdrasil's shade, Buntrugg waited for the only being in the nine worlds who could help him revive a dwarf. The only one who could help him finish his mission for Surt, and close the opened furnace before Muspel's fire demons escaped into Midgard.

The wind scurried across Asgard's plains. It played with Yggdrasil's dark green leaves and released a wave of dancing hawk-wing-seeds. Large like a mountain, Yggdrasil's trunk stretched on either side of him. Buntrugg lay with his back against the tree trunk and watched the huge branches above him. He tried to look at ease there, but unaccompanied giants were not welcome in Asgard.

Soon autumn would reach Asgard and people from the seven common worlds, all except the worlds of fire and ice, would gather around the ash, waiting for spring. A mere day after Yggdrasil's last dark red leaf fell to the ground, the first new buds appeared. The first few winters Buntrugg had worked for Surt, he had assembled with hundreds of thousands to watch winter pass, and cheer at the beginning of spring. An event celebrated throughout the worlds, for it meant that the longest winter was not upon them yet. These past few Asgard autumns he had been engaged with tasks for Surt and been unable to attend or celebrate. Hopefully, this winter would be different.

'You will not again experience Yggdrasil's change from autumn to spring, Buntrugg,' a coarse voice wisely said. 'Not this autumn and not any future.'

Behind Buntrugg's feet stood the woman he had waited for all morning. Her hair was hip-length and braided intricately to highlight its many shades of red. Her eyes were blank and dotted with stars. Naturally, the veulve knew his name, although they had never been introduced, nor met.

'Then I have been lucky to experience it in the past,' he said after a good moment of silence.

'Most are not as lucky,' the veulve agreed.

In the past, during Yggdrasil's autumn festival, he had seen her, far, far away, over the heads of hundreds of thousands of people, but never before this close. Up close she was more beautiful than he remembered. Her eyes were as mesmerizing as an alf dance and elegance shone through her. Her robes, coloured in the ash's dark green, flowed off her perfect form.

'For springs and summers I have prepared for your arrival, Buntrugg.'

Somehow, the veulve knew why he was there, although Buntrugg had not known that he would come until he had seen the four dead dwarfs in Vanaheim and found no solution to his problem.

'I've prepared for your arrival since before you were born.' Something about her voice reminded Buntrugg of Surt. Perhaps all beings as old as the veulve and Surt eventually gained the same coarse voice, and spoke not for themselves but for the nine worlds.

The veulve held out a closed flask. 'Keep it safe while you climb. Then rub it onto the dwarf's stone-hard skin,' she said as Buntrugg placed his large hand down in front of her. She dropped the dark blue flask into his palm. 'Every crevice. You rub it well enough and the dwarf might live.'

Buntrugg made the flask roll along his palm to examine it. The glass was strong, forged in Muspelheim's dearest heat, where Surt fought demons. The flask had been large in her hands, but in his, it was tiny. He slipped it into his inner coat pocket along with Ymir's ancient coins.

'As I climb?' he asked.

'You must climb the first tree of the nine worlds and tap its sap,' the veulve ordered. Once more she held something out for him to take: a wooden spile to tap honeyed sap from the tree. Buntrugg took it and rose to his feet. His giant form did not make the great Yggdrasil look any smaller, as it did most things. The proud ash was so wide and tall that it would take half a hundred giants to surround the trunk, and in height it was all the greater. It would be easier to tap the tree's sap by the roots, where the sap flowed in abundancy.

'Down here the sap will never cease to flow. Yggdrasil would die, and all nine worlds with it.' The veulve had a reason for everything and an answer to every spoken or unspoken question. She did not always give her answers, but when she did, they were always right.

'Why me?' he asked. She had prepared everything else for him, and if she had been preparing this mixture since before Buntrugg's birth, it seemed strange that he had to tap Yggdrasil's sap himself.

'The Ginnungagap asked for you by name and lineage,' the veulve said. 'The nine worlds have plans for you, Buntrugg.'

Surt sometimes told him that, too. Buntrugg did not know what it meant, and the veulve, like Surt, did not explain. What mattered was that Buntrugg needed Yggdrasil's sap to revive the dwarves who could show him to the furnace Surt had tasked him to close.

Buntrugg gaped up at the large tree. Some of the outer

branches sagged low enough for him to reach, but the ash was taller even than some mountains in Jotunheim.

The lowest branch sprang from the trunk so far up that Buntrugg could hardly see it; to even begin climbing, he would first need to climb up a low-hanging branch from its end, and to then reach the top of Yggdrasil would take him days. But if that was what he needed to do in order to revive the dwarfs, to be shown to their forge and close their furnace, then he did not have a choice.

'How far up?' he asked.

'Ratatusk will show you how far,' the veulve answered, and right as she named him, the little red squirrel who lived in Yggdrasil climbed down the long slender branches towards them. The veulve's star-dotted eyes followed the squirrel's movements. 'Ratatusk will open the bark for you,' she continued. 'Fill the flask.'

Once again, Buntrugg stared up at the enormous tree. His height would allow him to grab the lowest hanging branches, but with it also came an incredible weight, and Buntrugg doubted Yggdrasil's outermost branches would carry him in any form heavier than that of a piglet. No mistakes could be afforded; if he broke so much as a small branch, he knew the disastrous results that would follow. Somewhere in the nine worlds an ash-tree would die, because of him. All ash-trees came together on Yggdrasil. Every smallest branch was an ash on its own somewhere in the nine worlds, and every ash-tree, no matter how little, was significant.

'Listen to the silence of Ginnungagap,' the veulve advised. 'You change your form almost as easily as your sister. You will not allow Yggdrasil harm.'

'You knew Glumbruck?'

The veulve ran two fingers through her braided hair. 'I know her still,' she mysteriously responded, and as with Surt, Buntrugg knew not to ask more.

Of course the veulve knew his sister, and truly that was not what he meant to ask. He wanted to know *what* she knew about Glumbruck. No one at home ever spoke of his sister.

Warily, he watched the wise Veulve and her deep star-dotted eyes. The veulve did not help anyone who did not deserve her help, and for centuries, ever since the Alfather had abused the favour she owed him, she had neither accepted nor given a single favour. Yet, she had prepared everything for Buntrugg, before he had been able to ask for her help.

'Before the nine worlds, we all listened to Ginnungagap's silent song,' she said, echoing the words Surt sometimes employed.

Ancient beings like the veulve and Surt remembered an age without worlds and time, where the oldest forces were free to create. An age that Buntrugg could not imagine: a place without ground to walk on, and with no star-light to see, or noses to smell. An age that only the eldest beings knew and recalled. At some point, Surt and the veulve, and the few other elders of the nine worlds, had taken it upon themselves to preserve what little was left of the runes and Ginnungagap. They had ceased to live for themselves and begun to live for that age they recalled, of a time without time; a place without place. In many ways Surt and the veulve were alike. They acted as one, and followed the wishes of the Ginnungagap.

Often, Buntrugg thought about that old age that he could not imagine, no matter how hard he tried. Surt never shared much about the time that had used to be, but every few winters, something slipped; some detail that Buntrugg held onto and cherished, as much as he cherished the nine worlds.

'Your sister and you are not that different from us, Buntrugg,' the veulve told him.

The compliment made him smile. Buntrugg twisted around to see the veulve, and thank her, but when he stared down at the grassy ground by his large feet, where she had been, there was nothing to see. The veulve was gone, and like Surt, she had left him with another impossible task.

At least this time, he had been given specific directions as how to accomplish his task.

Readying for the difficult climb ahead, Buntrugg closed his silk coat and ran out to Yggdrasil's outermost branches. Ratatusk noticed him move, and settled on a higher branch to wait for him.

Buntrugg stopped below a low-hanging branch and reached up. His left hand grazed the branch, but it was too fragile for him to put his giant weight on. Buntrugg took a deep breath. Every time he took on a small form, he was reminded of his sister, and his awe increased. Such an ease she had with the runes that she had assumed a near-perfect form of a short-lived, taking the name Siv. As far as he had heard, she had only taken giant form once during this past century, and had otherwise confined herself to a short, awkward body the size of a new-born giant.

Unlike her, Buntrugg was unable to shrink without closing his eyes first. His focus needed to be complete. His parents insisted that using the runes became easier with age. Already Buntrugg knew that he was better at managing them than anyone else under a century old; even some twice that age could not control the runes as well as he.

When Siv had been his age, back when she had been called Glumbruck, she must have been skilled at handling the runes too. Otherwise she would never have managed to live among the short-lived for so many centuries without revealing her lineage.

Buntrugg closed his eyes and imagined himself shrinking. He held himself up with a grip around the branch above him, and felt his feet lift from the ground. With all the strength in his overarms, he pulled himself up. The branch creaked under the pressure of his weight, and Buntrugg continued to shrink in size. When he opened his eyes, and got to his feet on top of the branch, he was not much bigger than Ratatusk and the branch he stood on top of was wide as a road.

A breeze wheezed past and nearly blew him off the branch. On all fours, Buntrugg climbed up the branch. He was so little that he used the leaf stems as hand and foot rests. His small size made Yggdrasil look much larger. By the time he reached the spot where the red squirrel, Ratatusk, waited for him, it was already midday, and sweat dripped off him onto the leaves and ran down the branches he had climbed.

How nice and easy it would have been to ride to the top of Yggdrasil on Ratatusk's back, but the animals that lived in Yggdrasil's crown and foliage were proud beings much more honourable than a simple giant like Buntrugg.

The leaves became scarcer as he travelled up after Ratatusk. Buntrugg increased his size to move quicker, and the leaf stems bent when he stepped on them, threatening to break. He tried not to think about how a single wrong step would make him fall and fall before this small body would shatter on the ground beneath. Even if he somehow mustered the calm to make himself larger as he fell, he still would not survive the fall.

The closer he came to the trunk, the larger Buntrugg made himself, as the branch grew thicker. The forefathers did not bother him during his ascent. It almost seemed like they wanted him to succeed the impossible climb. Indeed, he could feel them focus his thoughts.

Relentlessly, Buntrugg climbed. The sustenance he had bought in Vanaheim with Ymir's coin carried him, but eventually he would need to eat.

The evening approached and light disappeared as Buntrugg reached Yggdrasil's middle layer of branches and leaves where the ash's four deer grazed and ran about. By that time, Buntrugg was so practised at changing his form that he no longer needed to close his eyes to do it, and he had climbed up the ash-tree with a speed that nearly matched the squirrel.

Giant and squirrel paused by the middle layer, above the clouds, and with Yggdrasil's four deer they watched the dance of bright lilac colours across the sky as the sun lowered in the horizon. The last of the evening sun cast Yggdrasil's shadow so long and far that it covered every part of Asgard. Fields and forests and great halls and houses and rivers were hidden in the shadow of the first ash.

Then, once more, Buntrugg and Ratatusk climbed. They clambered and jumped and heaved themselves up throughout the night, and when the night was at its darkest, Buntrugg had finally risen himself far enough up to glimpse the top of the ash.

Ratatusk planted his teeth to the bark of a large branch, chopping away, carefully and gracefully. Finally, they had reached their destination, Buntrugg realised. He sat down and made himself as big as he dared, so he could think properly.

At Ratatusk's prompting he planted the spile into the hole the squirrel had dug for him, and out dripped Yggdrasil's precious sap. Buntrugg reached for the flask the veulve had given him and opened it, careful not to spill the thick contents within. A vile stench emerged, of wet fur and rotten eggs, and an overpowering floral smell that made him sneeze.

He held the flask up to the spile. The honeyed sap poured into the dark blue flask and mixed with the smelly ointment the veulve had made, before spilling out over the top of the flask and dripping over Buntrugg's hands. Buntrugg secured the cork on the flask and for a moment he lay down, exhausted. The way down would be long and much more dangerous, but he had come so far, and that in itself was something to celebrate. Even the Alfather had never climbed to the top of the tree. Odin had only hung himself the height of four jotnar into the air.

'Takka,' Buntrugg told the ash-tree, and the wind, and the little red squirrel.

Ratatusk hung onto the tree above the spile with his head down and drank Yggdrasil's sap, then he twisted his furry red head in Buntrugg's direction as if to tell him to drink too, and replenish his strength. Easily convinced, Buntrugg lay down on the bed of leaves below the spile and let the sap drip into his open mouth. The honeyed water tasted sweeter than the Alfather's famous skald mead, and Buntrugg felt all the more thankful that Yggdrasil allowed him to taste its healing sap.

Content with his climb, Buntrugg watched the myriad stars sail above him as the sap dripped down his throat. His muscles complained, his stomach growled from hunger, his forehead was wet with sweat, his tunic and coat both stank of it, yet Buntrugg had never felt more serene. As he lay there and watched the stars blink their hellos and goodbyes, and felt the cool night breeze, and both heard and sensed Yggdrasil dance with the wind, a foolish smile crept itself onto his lips. Right then, he heard the complete silence of Ginnungagap, sensed the insignificance of his existence in the face of the great void and oldest force in the nine worlds. And he knew and understood, for a moment, the unspoken truth Ginnungagap allowed him.

SIGISMUND

Chapter Forty-Four

FINN'S OPPOSITION TO Einer had shaken Ash-hill's warriors and the night had been loud with chatter. Sigismund had ordered Frey's-fiord's warriors to refrain from drinking their minds away.

Last night had offered rich opportunity for the southerners to take them by surprise. With their ships damaged, they were vulnerable and they had been forced to dock in riding distance from Hammaborg, but no southerner had come near them since they had made camp two days past. Not even a trading ship had sailed along the river. The southerners must have thought they had obtained victory by killing Einer's father, and under the circumstances of a regular raid, their reasoning would have been right, but this was no ordinary raid.

'We have the advantage now.' Thora stared at Sigismund with her kind brown eyes. She read his expressions better than his own crew and knew exactly what he was thinking. Their decision to carry on with the raid despite the chief's death might come as a surprise to the southerners.

'Somewhat,' Sigismund said, hugging her from behind and resting his bearded chin on her shoulder. Together they watched six warriors set fire to the last unburnt remains from the smoking funeral fire. Crows had settled on the tattered corpse-flesh, but the warriors furiously waved them away.

The rising smoke was black and the smell was heavy and grim. Thora twisted to see Sigismund and study his expression. Her brown hair was gathered in the braid he had made for her that morning.

'Worried about Einer?' She did not need an answer to know that she was right, again.

'And Ash-hill,' he admitted. 'Just look at Finn yesterday. You need a chief, or the warriors won't be united on the field.'

Thora sighed and returned her gaze to the remains of the funeral pyre. 'So, the southerners were right to target Vigmer. His death has strengthened our resolve, but also weakened our unity.'

Dozens of warriors with shields and weapons came up from the ships towards the remains of the funeral pyre to gather for the Ting. Thora's warriors were the first to gather and sit down on their shields by the burning remains, too worried about the verbal beating they would take from their commander if they were late.

The gathering was not as large as for the funeral; they were just a few hundred warriors. The election of a new chief fell to Ash-hill's warriors. Sigismund and the other ships' commanders were merely present to confirm their support for the new chief and the continuing raid.

The crowd quieted as people assembled. The ship commanders took the inner-most positions. Sigismund lay down his shield and settled on top so he did not have to sit on the cold ground.

A tall girl faced the smoking remains of the funeral pyre, in the eye of the crowd. Her bright red hair hung free and she batted her eyes to avoid the smoke-heavy air. She lifted her arms to the sky. 'I now declare the Ting open.' Her voice resonated against the town walls.

For a girl of no more than fifteen who had never intended to become a warrior, Dagny had proven to be braver than most. Not only had she, in Frey's-fiord, decided to sail south with Thora again to avenge her father's death, but according to Thora, although Dagny was not a trained warrior, she had stayed calm through the fight and done what had been asked of her.

'Our chieftain, Vigmer Torstenson, has passed on to meet the gods.' Despite her young age and inexperience, her voice carried far. 'His passing leaves us many choices, and a void that needs to be filled. We need to elect a new chieftain to claim Ash-hill's chieftaincy. According to law, all nominations need to be made with the support of twelve freemen, none of whom can be a close kinsman of the nominated.' Confidently, she proceeded to recite Ash-hill's laws, first on blood-ties and then on chieftaincies.

Sigismund doubted that Frey's-fiord's own lawmaker knew the special clauses in their law as well as Dagny knew those of Ash-hill. Not with a single word did she hesitate or stumble. The more complicated the laws became, the clearer Dagny's understanding of them was.

'All nominations will now be welcome,' Dagny declared.

A group of warriors rose to the take the ring. Thora joined them.

An old man from Einer's warship took the word. 'I, Hormod Bjornson, nominate Einer Vigmerson for Ash-hill's chieftaincy.' Thora seconded Hormod's nomination, and one by one ten other warriors did the same.

Next, Einer rose from his seat and took the inner circle. The gold bracteate he wore made it clear that he was a man of influence. 'I, Einer Vigmerson, nominate Thora Torvaldóttir for Ash-hill's chieftaincy,' he said and gave a reassuring smile in Thora's and Sigismund's direction.

Where Sigismund had always wanted to take over after his father someday, Einer had never expressed an interest in becoming chief; not even when they had been children. If Einer supported Thora to take over after his father, then no one could doubt her abilities.

A dozen warriors assembled in the inner ring after him to support Thora's nomination.

A smile crossed on Sigismund's lips, although he tried to contain it. He had told Thora someone would recommend her for the chieftaincy; she had many supporters and admirers.

'Trust me, you'll do great,' Einer whispered to Thora before he regained his seat. When they had talked about it, Thora had not mentioned that the one who wanted to nominate her was Einer. An important detail to leave out, even if she had not wanted Sigismund's advice to be influenced by his friendship with Einer. Regardless, he had told her that she would be a good choice, and he meant it as whole-heartedly as Einer did.

As Sigismund watched Einer regain his seat with that calm smile on his face, everything fell into place; Einer intended to resign his nomination and allow Thora to become chief. That was why he showed his support for her; he knew as well as most of the other warriors that she was a good choice and that she would be as skilled a chief as she was a ship commander. Einer could not stop his warriors from nominating him, but he could find grounds to withdraw if there was another worthy candidate.

A young blond warrior gained the inner circle and took the word. 'I, Holger Egilson, nominate Finn Rolfson for the chieftaincy of Ash-hill.'

A mumble went through the crowd. What Ash-hill needed was not an ambitious chief like Finn, but one who would put the needs of many before his own, like Einer, or like Thora. Sigismund was not the only one with those thoughts; an uneasy quiet settled over the hundreds of gathered warriors as eleven more freemen backed Finn Rolfson as a candidate.

Chatter rose from the ranks and Finn's name was whispered everywhere. A cold breeze swished over the assembly and crows cawed.

No more warriors took the circle to nominate another candidate, so Dagny demanded for calm to fall over the Tingsmen. 'Let the candidates join me,' she said.

Finn sprang up, rearranged his faded red tunic and smiled to the warriors who had nominated him as he passed them by and took his place at Dagny's left. Einer took a stance next to him.

With a heavy sigh, Thora rose from her shield and gained the inner circle too. Strangely, she seemed not to like the idea of becoming chief, although Sigismund thought the title would suit her well, almost as well as it would suit Einer. Lack of ambition could be an advantage: it made for trustworthy chiefs.

At this rate, Thora would likely end up as chief of Ash-hill. Einer had many supporters, but his berserker rampage had scared a large part of the warriors. Thora held many of the same qualities as Einer, but her fear of responsibility held her back. If she was willing to overcome that fear, Sigismund knew she would be the kind of chief whose exploits would go down in legend.

'I wish to withdraw my nomination,' Thora declared, glaring at the wide-grinned warriors in the crowd who had come up with the brilliant idea to nominate her.

'Due reason needs to be stated and acknowledged to withdraw as candidate before the vote,' Dagny responded, reciting a long list of possible reasons. Sigismund could not find a single one that could be associated with Thora, who was young, healthy, and had proven herself a capable warrior and ship commander.

When Dagny was done, Thora said nothing for a while, and instead stared at Einer. They both knew what her resignation would mean; Einer would have to assume the responsibility and take on the role he had always intended to reject, or Finn would be their chief by default. Einer gave Thora an approving nod. He was already acting as a chieftain and he was respected as such too, or Thora would not have bothered to ask for his approval before withdrawing.

'I voluntarily withdraw my nomination on grounds of divided loyalties,' Thora stated.

'What evidence do you provide for your divided loyalties?' Dagny asked on behalf of them all.

Thora wet her lips with her tongue, and although her eyes flickered over the crowd, she looked confident as ever. Her clothes hung loose, the sleeves of the green tunic she wore were too long and her trousers hid her shoes. The clothes belonged to Sigismund, but he doubted they would ever look as good on him as they did on her.

Thora took a deep breath and matched Sigismund's gaze. 'I'm pregnant,' she declared.

Thora was pregnant. The words rang inside Sigismund's head, and he searched her brown eyes for the truth, to assure himself that this was not a lie to help her renounce the chieftaincy, although lying was not her usual manner. Her smile rinsed away any doubt. Thora was pregnant.

'How does your pregnancy divide your loyalties?' Dagny asked.

Thora's eyes rested on Sigismund, and it felt as if she spoke straight to him, although several hundred people were watching. 'The father is from Frey's-fiord and a contender to their future chieftaincy. Should the father acknowledge the child, my loyalties will forever be divided between Ash-hill and Frey's-fiord. And should he choose *not* to acknowledge the child, I cannot guarantee that any future dealings with Frey's-fiord will not suffer under my chieftaincy.' Thora removed her brown eyes from Sigismund and stared out over the large crowd. 'Therefore, I would like to withdraw my nomination.'

Despite complaints and protests from the excited crowd, Dagny granted the resignation, and Thora returned to her shield. A mysterious smile brightened her face as she sat down next to Sigismund and began arranging the long sleeves of her tunic, as though she had all the time in the nine worlds.

Sigismund's stare followed her every move. 'You're pregnant?' he asked, unable to wait any longer.

'I didn't want to say anything until we were sailing home,'

she said and her light brown eyes settled on Sigismund's to judge his feelings. 'Not before I was certain all three of us would survive.'

Sigismund leant in closer. 'You're pregnant?' he asked again, and his lips curled up into a smile beneath his beard. 'Thora, you shouldn't give up the chieftaincy because of this.'

'I'm not,' Thora responded and grabbed Sigismund's tunic to stop him from jumping to his feet. 'I've never wanted to be a chieftain,' she whispered to him. 'I like to fight, I love sailing, but I hate making decisions for others.' Her calm voice put Sigismund's worry to rest.

'You'll have to make decisions for the child,' he chuckled, leaning in for a warm kiss.

'I can handle that much,' she mumbled and kissed him back.

The news still rang in Sigismund's head, but Thora must have known for at least a few days, maybe longer, because she moved her attention back to the Ting easily and cast her vote for Einer.

Sigismund took a few deep breaths to calm his racing heart and returned his own focus to the Ting, although he continued to watch Thora out of the corner of his eyes as the warriors of Ash-hill cast their votes.

Many kept their silence; neither voted for Einer nor Finn, and the count was too close for a clear decision to be made.

'I see many who are undecided,' Dagny said. 'Voice your concerns and we shall resolve them.'

'Thora withdrew.' A warrior somewhere in the seated crowd reminded everyone. 'But you have more reason to withdraw than her, so why do you insist on keeping your nomination? A berserker can't be trusted to make decisions for us all.'

'Ja, Einer,' Finn teased in a low voice. 'You have no right to stand here.'

His mockery was heard. 'Both of you have more reasons to withdraw than her,' the man from earlier shouted. 'You've always been after Einer, and tried to create issues when there weren't any. And everyone here knows about your falling out with the old chief.'

People murmured in the crowd. Clearly everyone had *not* known about Finn's falling out with the chief, but now they did.

'We're all Tingsmen here,' Dagny scolded the crowd. 'If you want to speak, you claim the word.'

The crowd calmed and Osvif's helmsman stood up. 'Your dislike for each other has deep roots. No matter who is chosen, I doubt that Einer will accept Finn as his chief—and certainly you, Finn, will never accept Einer as yours,' he declared and turned to the crowd. 'These two will always find a way to oppose each other, just as the giants and the aesir will always be at war.'

'That does not mean that either one of them is unfit to be chief,' a shieldmaiden yelled, and Sigismund twisted around to see who had spoken. Three rows behind him, Hilda stood and shuffled past the rows of warriors to entered the circle and speak. Her posture had gained a calm from these past few days of raids.

Despite the unease of the warriors, Hilda did not need to spend a single moment quelling the crowd to remain quiet; the dried blood on her cheeks and in her hair, the bloody tears under her glowing-ember eyes, silenced everyone who could see her.

'Both of them are more than capable of being good chiefs,' Hilda said. 'You all hesitate, because the events since summer makes you doubt if they can be trusted. This autumn was difficult for us all. Don't you think that you have shown different sides of yourselves too? You hesitate, not because you doubt their capabilities to lead, but because you don't want to choose one and offend the other.'

A warrior a few rows out rose to speak. 'Nej, we hesitate because—'

Hilda cut him off: 'I have more to say.'

The large warrior shut up and sat down on his shield with the expression of a puppy that had been kicked for the first time.

'Finn started out with nothing when he first joined the raids,' Hilda declared. 'And luck alone did not lead him to become steersman on the *Mermaid Scream*. Regardless of what quarrels they might or might not have had, Vigmer trusted Finn to steer his ship and protect him in battle. Finn is an ambitious man and he will confidently lead Ash-hill.'

Hilda turned around herself as she spoke so everyone in the crowd had a chance to see her fire-like eyes and blooded face.

'As for Einer, he has been a crucial war-leader over these past many summers and he has proven his skills and strength in battle more than once. You know him as a generous man who gives to others before taking himself. Those of you with farms will know how he walks from farm to farm during the harvest season and helps where needed. Has he ever asked to be paid? Has he ever complained? Nej, he helped you willingly. Last winter you would have chosen Einer as your chieftain without blinking. What stops you now? You've witnessed, all of you, how strong he is in battle—how he can tear a man apart with his bare hands—and his strength frightens you.'

'He's not himself when he is like that,' Finn hissed. 'Nothing can stop him from killing.'

'*I* stopped him,' Hilda retorted and faced Finn straight on.

'Finn's jealous because *he's* not a berserker,' someone in the crowd yelled.

'A berserker? How can we trust a berserker to lead us?'

This time Osvif rose to defend Einer. 'A berserker is not much different from any other warrior. Einer could have torn Hilda's head off, but he didn't. Even when he goes berserk, he is still the same.'

'How can he be the same?' another of Finn's supporters protested.

Sigismund had heard enough. He rose to his feet to defend his childhood friend and say what Einer would never admit himself. 'Einer has always been a berserker,' Sigismund revealed to the crowd, and although he was not from Ash-hill and should not have been allowed a say, the crowd stopped and listened.

'When Einer was twelve winters old, I witnessed him kill a white bear. No other boy of twelve could have done that. He has always been like this, but he has never let it show because he worried you would react in this exact way. That you would be scared of him, no longer trust him. Einer has not changed, even if your opinion of him has.'

That silenced the crowd for a long while.

An old white-haired warrior rose. 'It comes down to a question of what Ash-hill needs: a generous chief, or an ambitious one? In these times of war, I vote for an ambitious chief.'

A clamour of agreement rose among the warriors, but not long after came the protests.

'Nej, we need a chief who will keep us unified.'

Dagny called for another vote, and although more people voted, the difference between Einer's supporters and Finn's supporters was not great enough.

'We're clearly undecided,' Dagny announced. 'We can continue to sit here, close to our enemy, and debate, or we can settle this in a different way.'

Finn and Einer appeared equally tense at that. They held their breath and stared at Dagny. Apart from a vote at a Ting, few ways could decide a chieftaincy. 'Let the gods decide,' Dagny stated, and Sigismund held his breath at what he thought she suggested. 'Let it be decided by holmgang.'

Her proposal stunned the crowd into silence. A duel to the death.

The warriors settled their tense gazes on Einer and Finn.

Einer was larger and stronger, and he was skilled in battle too, but Finn had the advantage of a longer raiding career, and a slimmer build, which would prove important in the narrow fighting ground of a holmgang. Even so, it seemed to

Sigismund that there was no doubt whatsoever about who the winner would be. Einer's brute might was evident.

The hundreds of warriors examined their two potential chieftains as Sigismund did. Out of fear of losing their reputation, neither Finn nor Einer could back away from the deadly fight. A holmgang they would have. The gods would choose one as their champion, and the other would die.

TYRA

Chapter Forty-Five

TYRA LIKED SVEND's secret gravemound. Sitting on top of it, in the drizzle, reminded her of home.

'Tove says you're a warrior,' Svend said with admiration in his voice. 'That you've already been tested in battle. What's it like?'

Although he was the son of a king, Svend had never raided, or been in a fight. His blue eyes were fixed on Tyra, waiting for an answer. He didn't know how her parents had died. Or that she was in Jelling now because of the stupid southerners who had killed her family. He didn't even know that she had any sisters.

'Not like the stories,' Tyra admitted, although she hadn't really wanted to say anything at all. 'The stories always say that you'll find glory in a battle. But you won't. You find it afterwards.'

Svend ate up her every word, and Tyra shifted to sit to face him, glad to teach him something he didn't know. 'Everyone stinks of sweat, and there's no room to breathe, but the brave ones give strength to everyone else. So you have to find a place next to someone really brave.' Someone like Siv, she thought, though she didn't say it aloud. 'And you have to have good shoes because the ground is slippery with blood. And you shouldn't look down at the corpses because there'll be people you know.' Her excitement at teaching him about battles stopped right then as she remembered how she had tripped over a body as Ash-hill was burning and how she had glanced down and stared into her mother's dead eyes.

She shifted away from Svend, but he had caught on. 'Did your parents die in that battle?'

She nodded, pressed her lips together not to cry as she tried to shake the image of her mother out of her head and forced herself to stare back out over farmlands.

'How did *you* survive?'

'I fought next to the bravest person on the battlefield.'

'And he saved you.' She didn't correct him and tell him—that it was a *she*, Siv, who had saved her, not a *he*—not that she could have told him that even if she wanted. When she tried to say something, her lips sealed themselves shut and she couldn't say anything at all. She knew it was Siv's doing.

For a moment, Svend repeated the advice Tyra had given him, and then stared back up at her, hungry for more. 'Did you kill many people?'

'I did.' His admiration was clear, and Tyra felt pride tingle up somewhere inside her chest.

'Some of the warriors say you never forget the face of the first person you killed,' Svend said as if he wanted to show her that he too had some knowledge about battles. 'They told me to make sure the first man I kill isn't an ugly drunkard.'

Tyra chuckled, and Svend smiled brighter.

'That's funny,' she admitted. 'But it isn't true. I don't think I even noticed what the first one looked like, or any of them.' She didn't remember how many lives her seax had taken, and parts of the battle were all blurry and she couldn't make out the details. 'I don't remember their faces. But I remember every single person *they* killed.'

She didn't tell him anything else, but Svend appeared to understand what she meant. He watched her with a kind stare that reminded Tyra both of her sister Ingrid and of Einer.

Svend scooped closer to Tyra so their legs touched. He stared down at the hem of her dress, as she fiddled with it. 'Your parents will be waiting for you in Valhalla,' he whispered so quietly Tyra had to take a moment to ensure that she had heard right. It was exactly what she needed to hear. 'That's what Tove said,' he whispered and diverted his gaze before his cheeks flushed in embarrassment, but from his gaze, Tyra knew that he believed it as much as her.

She hadn't expected a Christian like Svend to bring up Valhalla and the old gods, especially not after how angry King Harald had been at Tyra for mentioning Odin that same morning. 'They saved me a seat,' Tyra agreed to let him know that she believed it too.

He smiled to her and matched her stare. 'At Odin's high table.' King Harald would be furious if he ever learnt that his eldest son had mentioned Odin; and in this way, with longing.

'At Odin's high table,' she repeated. And Tyra felt as if with those words and their shared gaze, they both acknowledged the gods and agreed that they would share them in secret. His eyes had the same kind, sorrowful shape as Einer's eyes, but their colour was more similar to Hilda's, and when Tyra stared at him, Svend reminded her a little bit of everyone she had ever loved.

He coughed and looked away. 'You know, sometimes, I feel like someone is inside this grave, watching me,' he said.

'*Is* there someone inside?' Tyra wanted to know. She twisted around in the high grasses to see the entrance, but it was at their back, and she couldn't see it. Maybe a curious draugar lived there, or maybe some animals had taken shelter inside the jotun passage grave. Whatever it was, she liked the idea of someone living inside a passage grave.

'I've never gone inside,' Svend confessed, and he seemed a little embarrassed to admit it. 'It feels like I shouldn't go in.'

'Well, today we're going inside.' She knew well that he would do it if she did. In that he was like Hilda, except Hilda would have been the first to suggest going inside, and also the first to do it.

Tyra got up and her heart began to pound as she raced down the slope of the grave and walked around through the tall, uncut grasses to the front. She felt something stir in her heart at the sight of it, and she understood why Svend had never gone inside. Weeds and wild herbs grew around the gravemound, and the grass was high, as if neither pigs nor goats dared approach the ancient passage.

'The gods protect this grave,' Svend whispered to her from the top, as if he didn't dare to speak any louder.

'Come,' Tyra said and waved him down towards her.

'Are you really going inside?'

Tyra was older than him, and thanks to Siv she knew more about the nine worlds than most. Sometimes Svend didn't dare to follow her. Sometimes he was scared when she wasn't. That was why he had begun to call her *fearless*. He wasn't coming inside with her, Tyra knew, but equally she knew that she had to. 'I said I would, so I will,' she said, stubborn as Hilda.

A wind pushed at her back, sending her a few steps further ahead. She thought she heard a faint, voiceless whisper that called her to approach and enter the grave. With certain steps, she walked closer, aided by the wind at her back, and the voiceless whispers from the darkness. She ducked and walked out of the drizzle into the damp, mossy passage.

She narrowed her eyes to better see. Someone was in there.

A small woman with long golden hair braided in the ancient style. Her dress was bright red and new, and too large for her size. Her palm bled, and she held a seax in her hands. The small woman glanced back to Tyra over her shoulder. And before her face was revealed, and despite her height, Tyra knew that it was Siv.

For a moment, they stared at each other. The passage grave shook, and the earth trembled. The back stone of the passage rolled away behind Siv to reveal a pitch-dark corridor of stairs.

'Come out, Tyra,' Svend yelled from outside the grave.

Her heart beat all the way up in her throat. He couldn't know about Siv. He couldn't see them both in there. She heard him walk through the high grasses, and his voice came closer. 'Tyra!'

Siv glanced to the high grasses outside the grave, where Svend was. Then, in a moment's decision, she grabbed Tyra's wrist. 'Come with me,' she said and walked through the dark opening at the back of the grave.

Tyra let herself be dragged through, half excited and half worried about Svend, outside.

The stone that marked the passage's back wall rolled back in place and shut them in. It blocked out all fresh air, and all light, and all sound but their breathing.

'Where are we?' Tyra asked. It felt like that time she had crawled into the ash-tree during the battle back in Ash-hill. She had the same strange feeling.

'In a passage between worlds,' Siv responded.

A flame appeared in front of them. It floated in the air, and had appeared from nothing, like the fire Siv conjured when they needed to light a bonfire. The floating flame lit the way. There were many steps beneath, so many that Tyra couldn't see the last one. And she couldn't hear an end to the passage either.

'Svend...' Tyra said and stared back at the stone behind them. The passage grave echoed his name back to her. She didn't want him to think that she had left him.

'Svend won't wait for long,' Siv said. 'In here, time is just a word.'

Tyra nodded at that. Time was strange. Sometimes it went too fast, and sometimes so slow that she wondered if it went by at all. This had to be one of those moments.

Siv removed leather shoes that were too large for her newly

small feet. Without a word of explanation, she posed the shoes on the top steps.

'Why are we here?' Tyra asked.

'You're here so I can introduce you,' she said and took the first step down.

That was why she had taken Tyra with her, but that wasn't why Siv was there. She had already been inside the grave when Tyra had arrived, and couldn't have expected Tyra to show up.

'Why are *you* here?' Tyra asked and followed Siv down the stairs.

'Because I need the help of the one I'm introducing you to.'

'Who is it?'

'Someone who can help you—if, someday, you need him to.'

'Help me with what?'

'Anything you need.'

That was a good person to know, but it also sounded like a scary person. If someone as powerful as Siv sought his help, then he had to be more powerful than Siv, if that was even possible.

Tyra hurried down the steps after Siv, who walked a lot faster than Tyra, though she was not as tall as Tyra now. Help you? With what?'

Siv laughed at Tyra's endless questions, but she answered them anyways. 'With the wedding.'

'To King Harald? Because the real Tove's parents will know you aren't her?'

'You already know the answers, and yet you ask.'

'I just want to make sure that I have the answers right,' Tyra said, and her heart felt strange from all the answers Siv gave her. She didn't like it. To begin with, Siv hadn't told her anything. She hadn't answered any questions, and sometimes hadn't allowed Tyra to ask any. Now she answered them all, even the obvious ones. It didn't feel right. It felt like Siv was preparing Tyra for a future when they wouldn't be together.

'Will I ever go to Valhalla?' Tyra asked and struggled to hold back her tears. She didn't even know why she felt like crying.

'The valkyries would be foolish not to give a brave girl like you a place,' Siv reassured her. 'And the valkyries are not foolish.'

'But, back at the runemistress' hut, you said the nine worlds would no longer be together and that the runes would disappear, so if I die after the runes have disappeared, then I'll just disappear too.'

'Tyra,' Siv said in her old soothing voice that always calmed Tyra's worst fears. 'For as long as I live, I won't let the runes disappear. You *will* see your parents and sisters again.'

'How can you be sure? What if the runes disappear first?'

'You and me'—Siv looked Tyra straight in the eyes as they walked down, and her gaze felt important to match—'we know about the runes and the nine worlds. Together we will ensure that the runes don't disappear. We will save the nine worlds.'

'You and me?' Two people seemed like too few to save nine whole worlds from falling apart.

'You and me,' Siv repeated and her certainty reassured Tyra a little.

'How?'

'Do you know why we came to Jelling?' Siv asked.

Determined to guess correctly Tyra racked her mind. 'Because King Harald has become Christian,' she muttered. 'He has abandoned the old ways.' She was still short as to why that meant the nine worlds were falling apart, but it was the only reason she could come up with.

'That's right,' Siv said. 'Harald has abandoned the old ways. The runes don't mean anything to him anymore, and he is abandoning the old traditions one by one. The old traditions are what keeps the runes here with us, and what binds Midgard to the other eight worlds. If everyone who lives in the lands that Harald rules suddenly stop caring for the traditions, the runes weaken.'

At once Tyra understood what they needed to do. What her life mission would be. 'And if enough chieftains also abandon their ways and their people do too,' she whispered, 'then the runes will disappear completely.'

'Exactly,' Siv praised. 'So how can we—you and I—save the nine worlds?'

'We have to ensure that people keep the old traditions. Then the runes won't disappear anymore and the nine worlds won't drift apart!' Suddenly she understood why they were in Jelling, and why Siv had assumed Tove's place. 'We need to make King Harald change his mind,' her words echoed down the steps.

That would be difficult to do; King Harald was stubborn and more than anything he was proud of his recent decision to become Christian. But if they managed, then the wrongs would be righted and the runes would return.

'Siv,' Tyra grabbed the skirt of Siv's dress to stop her quick walk down the steps. 'What about the others?'

'What others?'

Tyra searched Siv's grey lynx eyes for the sadness she knew had to be there somewhere. The same sadness Tyra had when sometimes she sat on Jelling's gravemound and waited for her parents and sisters to come find her. 'My family passed on,' she whispered. 'But Vigmer… And Einer. They're still in Midgard.'

'Einer will be safer with us here.'

Tyra didn't like how Siv hadn't included Vigmer in her answer. Something must have happened, and Siv would know. 'Will we ever see them again?'

'Not in this life,' Siv responded straight away, and she sounded so sure.

'In Valhalla,' Tyra said.

Siv nodded. 'You'll see them in Valhalla,' she agreed, and Tyra couldn't help but notice how Siv had said *you* instead of *we*, but, for once, she didn't want to ask why, because if her fears were real and Siv and her were to be separated in death, then she didn't want to know about it.

In silence, they marched down the endless steps and although Tyra was neither hungry nor thirsty, she didn't doubt that they had walked an entire afternoon. The little light from the floating flame fell upon the last step. At this end too, the passage was sealed by a large rock.

'He should have been here by now,' Siv muttered when they reached the rock, more to herself than to Tyra. For a long moment, they stared at the large rock, and Tyra wanted to ask what they were doing, and why they waited like this, but Siv had already told her that they had come to meet someone, so she supposed that was why they waited.

'We're going through,' Siv said after a long time had passed, and loudly, as if she needed to say it aloud to convince herself that it was the right decision.

She put a finger to the sharp seax she held. Tyra wrinkled her nose, afraid of what might happen. A few drops of blood trickled out from the cut and Siv smeared them onto the dark rock wall.

The cave trembled. The large rock rolled to the side, and a blinding light appeared. Beyond, everything was white, and a cold north wind blew snow into the dark of the grave.

Together they walked out of the passage. Tyra shivered from the cold. Her shoes were not thick enough to protect from the coat of snow, but Siv walked barefooted and she didn't shiver.

Snow fell so heavily that Tyra could barely see six feet ahead and she certainly couldn't see the sky above them, or any landscape, or much of anything at all, really. The snow froze her cheeks, and settled like stars in her hair. She took a few steps back to take cover inside the dark passage, but, behind them, the stone door had rolled back into place, though Tyra hadn't felt the earth shake.

Siv walked away from the passage, and Tyra hurried to follow, so she wouldn't be lost in the snowstorm. They had taken no more than ten steps away from the passage before Siv stopped up and Tyra bumped straight into her.

In front of them a large foot was planted into the snow. For a moment Tyra thought it was one of those immense statues she had heard about from the ancient south, but then the toes wriggled.

Gaping, Tyra gazed from the foot and up the vast legs, clothed in brown trousers. She could see as far as a sand-coloured tunic above, but then the snow was too thick to see any further.

Siv also stared up at the large giant, but she wasn't scared, or in the least worried. She held out her hands, palms up. A strong wind blew the snow away so it circled around them—her and Tyra and the giant—but not between, and Tyra just knew it was Siv's doing. Even the wind did what she asked.

The jotun in front of them stared down at Siv and Tyra. His hair was dark and his face was sharp. His jaw was angular, his nose straight, and his green eyes shone, as if the light sprang from inside his eyeballs. The giant's broad shoulders made him look taller than he was, and he was already tall.

Seeing the giant's face, Siv took a single step backwards.

Tyra didn't know who he was, but Siv's unease told her what she needed to know. He wasn't the man Siv had wanted to introduce Tyra to. He wasn't the man who could help them.

Tyra reached down and took Siv's hand, not because she was scared, but because she sensed that Siv needed her to. In reassurance, Siv clenched Tyra's hand. They shared each other's strength. Tyra's body warmed from holding Siv's hand. Even her eyelashes unfroze.

'Where is Buntrugg?' Siv demanded to know.

The giant wasn't startled by Siv's persuasion, as most people were, and he didn't answer her question. Tyra had never seen anyone avoid one of Siv's questions. Everyone listened to Siv, and everyone always did what she wanted them to do. Except this giant seemed to know Siv's tricks and it didn't look like they would work on him.

He scoffed at Siv and her question. Tyra clenched Siv's hand tight and scowled up at the large jotun. She thought of Hilda and how Hilda would have acted in the presence of such a scary being, and just thinking of Hilda was enough to take her fear away, and for her to stand up tall, and glare at him, despite her tiny size.

His stare pierced her, but Tyra matched his eyes and decided that it was a stare-duel, like Hilda would have done. She wouldn't be the first to look away.

'Who is this, Glumbruck?' the giant asked Siv.

'My daughter,' she answered in a cold voice. The same cold voice she had used before she had killed those guards outside of Jelling.

The jotun closed his eyes and sniffed the air. He took three deep breaths, and then he opened his eyes, suddenly, and watched Tyra. 'You shouldn't have brought her here.' His voice was as cold as Siv's, and as powerful. 'Her clothes smell of Midgard. She doesn't.' His sight settled back on Siv, and in a scary and deep voice that made the snow shake, he said: 'Did you steal her too?'

'Where is Buntrugg?' Siv insisted. Despite their obvious difference in height, and despite the jotun's imposing voice, Siv wasn't shaken. 'Where is your son?'

'You shouldn't have used the passage. The high court can do worse than a fair banishment.'

'Jotun courtrooms have never been fair.'

'You lied.'

'And you banished me.' She didn't say it with resentment or anger, but stated it as a simple fact. 'Where is Buntrugg?'

The giant wavered at Siv's insistence. They all knew, even Tyra, that Siv wouldn't let this rest until she had an answer. She wasn't unlikely to kill either. Like she had taken out Tove's guards outside of Jelling. That sheer power could kill a giant, too, Tyra was certain of it. But Siv didn't attack, at least not yet.

'I *will* allow the forefathers to kill you unless you answer,' Siv said. 'I have greater control over them than you.'

The broad-shouldered giant didn't contradict her. 'You'll regret it.'

'I won't.' Her voice carried no doubt.

Despite his height, Tyra didn't think the jotun was as strong as Siv. It almost looked like he feared her. As if he, too, knew how powerful and convincing Siv could be.

Finally, he gave in. 'Buntrugg is on an errand for Surt.'

'Where?' Siv wanted to know.

'Nowhere you can go.'

'I'm here. Where did Surt send him?'

'He is in Asgard.' He closed his eyes, and sniffed the air. Five deep breaths he took. When he opened his eyes again, they were fixed on Tyra. He cocked his head to one side, and mumbled something to himself as he turned away.

Siv released her grip on the wind and allowed the snow to fall between Tyra, Siv, and the giant. Tyra watched his heels disappear into the snowstorm, and then she hurried to follow Siv the few steps back to the passage grave.

'Who was that?' Tyra asked when the passage had closed behind them. She had barely dared to breathe in his large presence.

'My father,' Siv answered. She began up the stairs.

That wasn't at all how Tyra had imagined Siv's father—not that she really knew how she had imagined him to be, but certainly not like that. They didn't look alike, and besides, he wasn't kind like Siv, and he hadn't sounded like he cared for Siv at all.

Tyra's own father would have moved all of Midgard if that meant that he could help Tyra. She didn't like to think that some people had fathers who hated them, or had banished them, like Siv's father had her, but she knew that some people did. Harald wasn't the best father either.

They had walked far up the passage before Tyra decided to gain more answers. 'Will you go to Asgard now?' she asked, and somewhere deep down she hoped that Siv would say yes and would take Tyra there. Maybe they could visit Valhalla so Tyra could see her parents and her sisters.

'I can't go to Asgard,' Siv said.

Tyra knew she shouldn't have hoped for anything. 'Because you were banished,' she completed.

'Nej.'

Tyra wanted to ask why Siv couldn't go to Asgard, but Siv likely hadn't told her because she didn't want Tyra to know. 'Then how can he help us?' she asked instead. 'Buntrugg, I mean?'

'He can't,' Siv said. Absentmindedly, she stared down at her bare feet as she continued up the steps. 'If he is in Asgard, then he is the one in need of help.'

Tyra didn't know what she should say to that.

For a long while thereafter they walked and walked up through the dark passage. At the top, Siv smiled to Tyra and smeared blood onto the stone. 'Svend is waiting,' she said, right before the passage shook and the stone rolled away.

Tyra stared up at Siv for permission. Like a true mother, Siv nodded to her and smiled, and like that, Tyra darted out of the long passage and out of the grave, straight into the drizzle.

Svend circled the grave, and smiled when he saw her run to him. He hugged her tight, and refused to let go. 'Tyra! Where were you? I looked inside, but you weren't there.' The words streamed from his mouth. Some time must have passed for him, after all, while she had been gone.

'Someone was in there.' She wanted to share it all with Svend, though she knew she could never tell him about Siv. Or rather, about Tove, because that was the name Svend knew her by. Like how Tyra called her Siv and Siv's father called her Glumbruck.

Svend let Tyra's escape the tight hug. 'In there?' he asked and stared into the dark of the passage grave, half brave and half scared. 'Who?'

'A jotun,' she answered and that made Svend stare and frown even more. If Tyra hadn't known Siv, it might also have been difficult for her to understand how a giant could fit inside such a small place, but she knew Siv, so she knew how.

'Let's go,' Tyra said. She took Svend's hand and dragged him away from the passage grave to give Siv a chance to leave. 'You were right. We shouldn't go inside.'

Together they pushed through the high grasses of the clearing. The rain drizzled down over them and wet Tyra's hair and clothes again. Svend didn't comment on the fact that her woollen dress had dried during the short time she had been inside the grave, though she knew he had noticed. Maybe he didn't dare ask.

They reached the edge of the clearing, and there, by the first bushes, stood two ragged wolves. They were tall and held themselves with a royal posture. Their fur was dark grey and they stared straight at Tyra.

'Geri and Freki,' Tyra whispered their names, so as not to startle the wolves. They didn't growl, or show their teeth, and there was just the two of them. Wolves always travelled in packs.

'Odin's wolves?' said Svend.

The wolves didn't in the least startle at the sound of their voices.

'They're here to see you,' she told Svend. 'The son of a king. The gods are watching you.'

'Nej,' he said and he sounded so certain. 'They're here to see you, Tyra.'

MUSPELDÓTTIR

Chapter Forty-Six

ONE, TWO, THREE, four, five, six, seven, eight, nine.

Muspeldóttir waited for her chance, readied and reared her hot red fire. She charred her host's eyes to gain vision. In the forge, she had entered this way; burned herself into the female host.

Since then, the host had regained control, casting Muspeldóttir into ice. Now, Muspeldóttir struggled to live.

One, two, three, four, five, six, seven, eight, nine.

She battled to regain some vision, and peer out through her host's hot eyeballs.

Spirit animals roamed around, following the warriors they served. The heat oozed out of the perfect hosts, every single one better than this. Perfect for a fire demon: hot and cosy and obedient. The snow fox was much too cold for her.

One, two, three, four, five, six, seven, eight, nine.

A warrior stopped in front of her. She watched heat escape out through his mouth. The man talked to Muspeldóttir's host, but she was unable to hear him. His spirit animal was a hawk, and it screeched to her as she watched it. What a perfect host he would have been.

She would give anything for some heat.

One, two, three, four, five, six, seven, eight, nine.

Her fiery fingers were cold and stiff, as if she had entered Niflheim.

If she had been a little wiser, and not in quite such a rush to leave, she might have caught a much warmer soul, and then set flames to all of Midgard and turn Odin's followers to ash.

Muspeldóttir's host felt her presence. Startled and afraid, she held her breath.

One, two, three, four, five, six, seven, eight, nine.

The host wet her eyes with frigid blood, that seeped through the eyeballs like poison.

Screaming, Muspeldóttir retreated, relinquished the newly gained vision, and curled up around her fiery self. Her blue flame flickered dangerously. The host was so set on killing her.

Muspeldóttir focused her hearing.

One, two, three, four, five, six, seven, eight, nine.

The ice-cold blood froze her outer flames, turned them from blue to red to ice white. A finger broke off her frozen hand. Ice shattered into a thousand shards.

The blood extinguished her bright fires. Only long-lived had cold blood like this. Cold blood that could kill Muspeldóttir. If she did not escape, she would die.

One, two, three, four, five, six, seven, eight, nine.

Wide would she throw Muspelheim's great gates. Such a feat would require great strength, and a blazing heat she did not have. A heat this cold blood had robbed her of, but once she freed herself from this host, she would rekindle her precious flames, and would secure her kinsmen's freedom.

Together, they'd set Midgard ablaze.

HILDA

Chapter Forty-Seven

'HAVE YOUR BALLS turned to frost, Finn?' Hilda said, tired of his constant complaining.

The wind whipped around her, and she rubbed blood onto her eyes again. They itched, as if they had been scratched on the inside, and were sore too, but they often were when she forced blood into them. She blinked until the worst of the pain receded.

Finn grumbled incoherently. He was angry, and scared, and he was right to be, but she wouldn't tell him that. The sooner this issue of chieftaincy was settled, the sooner they could sail on to Magadoborg. Everyone knew this fight had to happen, or matters between Finn and Einer would never rest. This feud needed to end with a mortal wound.

'I didn't think you were a coward,' she said. 'Until now.'

'I'm not a coward!' Finn snapped, louder than needed. The warriors by the cooking fires stopped what they were doing to watch Hilda and Finn. Not that they hadn't been watching them before Finn had yelled. Now they simply had an excuse to stare.

'Why are you angry?' Hilda asked in a lowered voice, so as not to embarrass Finn further. 'You always talk as if you're the best warrior in all of Midgard. Now's your chance to prove it.'

'Einer is bigger than me!' He turned his head this way and that to scowl at the people who stared. 'He has the advantage.'

'And what do you think the southerners have right now?' she asked him. 'We're still here to fight them. So, are you going to back down like the coward who has taken your tongue? Or are you going to fight, and either prove that you are the better warrior, or die a worthy death that will seat you in Valhalla?'

He chewed on that for a moment. Finn had nothing to lose; if he won the fight, he would become chieftain, and if he lost, his afterlife would be secured.

With a loud sigh Finn brought his hands up to his hair, which she remembered was long and well-kept, and combed a hand through it. 'Be my shield-bearer,' he said. 'Give me a chance to survive.'

'Nej,' she replied. 'You'll have to fight your own way out of this.'

She shook the Ulfberht chain in her hands to rouse the snow fox, and started back towards camp, eager to leave Finn behind. She glided past hot bodies of warriors stopped dead in their tracks.

'You think it's that easy?' Finn yelled after her.

Anew, everyone turned their heads to watch her. Hilda felt the stares. If she left like this, without saying anything, Finn would win the argument. She hadn't intended an argument, but that was what it had become.

'Fine,' she hissed, twirling around to face him.

He had followed her away from the cooking fire. Hilda licked her lips clean as she examined her audience. The warriors kept a respectful distance. They were right to respect her; Finn ought to as well. The chain in her hand rattled. The snow fox pressed against her left leg in support, and the wind brushed past her and reminded her of its presence.

'Easy?' Hilda repeated. 'I fight blind! So, ja, next to that, dying an honourable death is easy.'

With a final nod to Finn, she clicked her tongue for the snow fox to follow and stumbled along the plain quickly enough so that Finn had no time to think of a remark, if he even could.

If he wanted her to be his shield-bearer during the holmgang, he shouldn't have insulted her. Finn had suggested it to her as if it were a great honour, and normally it would have been. But Finn only wanted her to do it because it would rattle Einer to see her on Finn's side. Well now, he needed to find another shield-bearer, and another way to rattle Einer.

If he had asked, Hilda might have acted as Einer's shield-bearer, but certainly not for Finn.

The Runes whispered some nonsense about a storm. *On the river, your storm shall rise*. Hilda ignored them and spat on the muddy road. The snow fox strutted at her side.

The camp was easy to see with the hundreds of fylgjur flying above and the hundreds of more on ground. There were so many that even Hilda was able to find the tents without walking into a tree, or worse. It helped that they had made camp at the edge of the woods by a plain.

'Hilda,' someone called. Hilda narrowed her eyes and focused on the voice. There were so many warriors and she only had their fylgjur and their voices to differentiate them. Einer was easy to spot—he was at the edge of camp, burning hot—but everyone else was more difficult.

'Hilda,' the warrior repeated. She couldn't place his voice.

A warrior stopped up in front of her. His fylgja was a dog. There were a lot of fylgja dogs.

'I was looking for you,' he said, and then she knew him: Einer's old friend, Osvif. His casual tone gave him away. 'It's about the blessed ropes.'

'We don't have any blessed ropes,' said Hilda.

'That's why I'm here. We thought you might bless them.'

Hilda frowned at him. Without a runemistress, her father

might have said the words back in Ash-hill, but Hilda was not a skald like her father, nor had she ever cared to become one.

'We're down by the river,' he said, and began to walk, turning his head turned back to look at her.

Hilda had nothing better to do, so she followed him across the muddy plain.

She noticed the crowd of warriors, on land, not one of the ships. Eyes fixed on the ground as they eagerly discussed what to do now It had to be the ship builders. With timber from the trees they had felled and split, they had repaired the ships and built river traps for their retreat, she had heard. Now they had to be working on the holmring.

Hilda and Osvif set off towards the group.

'Who will you cheer for?' Osvif asked when they were a few good strides away from anyone else.

'The gods will choose their champion.'

'And who will you ask them to choose?' he insisted.

'The gods don't listen to me.' If the gods listened to her, she would have started raiding the same summer as Einer, or at least no more than a summer or two later. She wouldn't have had this Muspel sight either, and Ash-hill would never have been attacked. The gods had never listened to her. She doubted they would start now.

'Have you and Einer spoken since his father passed on?'

Hilda tried to ignore the question; she didn't like to admit that they hadn't. Einer always came to her before, but he had stayed away, busily surrounded by warriors. It reminded her of this summer when her own father had passed on; they hadn't talked much back then either.

This time it was different, though. The warriors might misunderstand, like Osvif, and think that she supported Finn, when Einer clearly needed to win the fight. To escape Osvif's question, Hilda pressed two blood-soaked fingers against her eyeballs, and sped up across the plain as much as she dared.

The wind rose around her and Osvif, announcing their

arrival. The Ulfberht chain rustled at her side as Hilda pressed into the circle of ship builders. Their talk slipped from their minds at the sight of her.

'What are you looking at?' she asked

A man next to her cleared his throat. 'The holmgang platform.'

'Platform?'

Holmgrounds were usually made of a skin laid on the ground, edged by four hazel poles, bounded by the holy ropes. A holmgang could be had anywhere as long as holy ropes enclosed the edges of the area, but Hilda didn't understand why they would have it on a platform.

'Why a platform?' she asked. Maybe the ground was too uneven, but it didn't seem that way to her, and it shouldn't matter either.

'It'll be secured out on the river,' the warrior replied.

'You want them to fight on the water?'

'We didn't decide it,' Sigismund said. She noticed his wolf, but couldn't pick him out in the crowd. 'Einer and Finn did.'

She didn't need to ask who had suggested it. It had been Finn, and conveniently he had left that out when he had asked her to be his shield-bearer.

Finn must have hoped that he could push Einer off the platform, so Einer would drown and die, and swim to Ran and Aegir's hall in the afterlife. Finn knew he couldn't beat Einer in a straight fight—his best chance of becoming chieftain was to push Einer out of the holmring—but as long as Einer was alive, he posed a threat to Finn. Fighting on a floating platform on the water made it a matter of balance, and Finn had sailed his entire life. For a lot longer than Einer. He had an advantage. And he was smaller besides.

'We brought some ropes out for you,' Sigismund told her.

The Runes repeated the words they had chanted all day. *On the river, your storm shall rise.* Hilda had deemed it nonsense, but all day they had been whispering about the duel that would take place on the river. She just hadn't realised until now. They could have tried harder to make themselves understood.

Hilda followed Sigismund around the crowd. His wolf glanced back to confirm that the snow fox was following. Abruptly, he stopped up and pointed to the ground.

She knelt down to where he had pointed. Never before had she blessed anything, and never had she thought she would. Sigismund and a dozen other men gathered at her back and watched.

The rope had been laid out on blankets. Hilda felt the lengths of it. It was formed of many smaller ropes, spliced together.

'Are these southern blankets?' she asked to confirm her suspicions.

'Didn't seem right to put the ropes in the mud,' a man said at her back.

Good intentions, but wrong conclusion. The blessed rope at home had always hung on the wall, and never touched the floor of the house.

'The rope shouldn't be put down on Midgard's ground at all.' Hilda pointed to a few of the working men who had gathered around her to watch. They moved in and picked up the large bundle of rope. 'Spread it out,' she ordered.

They hurried to comply, eager to learn and help, like children at their first blót. Most of them had never seen a runemistress bless anything. Neither had Hilda.

With the men holding up the rope, Hilda could see exactly where the rope was and how long it was.

Wealth. Strength. Warrior. The Runes began, eager to help, and then they continued to list every property of every single rune, in a mysterious order.

Hilda followed the wind's words. She named the properties of the runes, once and twice. The men watched her. When she began to recite the runes a third time, the Runes made the wind dance down along their hands, down the length of the rope. The rope-holders' awe was clear from their gasps. Hilda smirked at their surprise. Those who didn't respect her already soon would.

She continued to name the runes in order. The wind settled when she reached Isa, the last rune. The bystanders began to clap, but the work was not yet done. The Runes swirled around Hilda and made her hair rise with their instructions.

Hilda took a deep breath and said the last words. 'From Midgard you were. In Asgard you shall be seen. In Vanaheim you shall exist. In Svartalfheim built, and judged in Alfheim's courts.' She nodded to say that now the deed was done, and once more the many bystanders burst into applause.

When the echoes of clapping died, Hilda gave the men the last instructions. She would have told Sigismund, but she didn't know which one of them was him. 'Once you attach the holy rope to the hazel posts, no one can go inside the holmring until the holmgang begins.'

With that, she left them. All the awe-struck warriors, all their staring fylgjur. Her snow fox was as proud as her, strutting at her side as they walked back up towards camp.

Osvif was right. She ought to see Einer before the fight. With the holmring being a float on the river, Einer's victory was no longer as certain. There was no more reason to hide her true loyalties. The wind pushed against her back in agreement, hurrying her walk across the plain. *On the river, your storm shall rise*, the Runes whispered. It sounded like they wanted Hilda to use them to decide the outcome of the holmgang.

'The duel will play out,' she told the Runes. 'The gods will decide.'

Ignoring the Runes, she entered camp and slowed. There were many people and fylgjur and it took Hilda a moment to get her bearings and find out where the tents were and where the path between them had to be. She headed to the inner edge of where he and most of his crew had slept the night before. All day she had seen him there, preparing for the holmgang.

Hilda had slept down on the *Storm*. A lot of people slept on the ships, despite the cold in the nights. An unease followed Hilda when she was away from the ships. A deep worry that the southerners would attack the ships again and no one would be there to stop them this time.

She found the fabric of the tent where Einer was, followed it around, flapped the tent open and entered.

Einer sat on the ground opposite the opening. His white bear had curled up next to him. It peered up at Hilda and shifted to rest its heads on its paws. The wind entered with Hilda, making her presence known. Einer looked up from his things and over his shoulder, to her. She was certain that he was smiling at the sight of her. He always did.

She missed his smile.

'I heard you declined Finn's offer to be his shield-bearer, and about the ropes. I'm glad.' Einer focused back on his things. Of course, he had heard. Einer always knew everything that was happening.

'You shouldn't be alone,' Hilda said.

She heard a wooden chest slam shut. Einer sat down properly on the ground, facing her, arms on his kneecaps. For a moment he just sat there.

'Einer, you can't be alone before the fight,' she insisted.

'I'm not afraid of him, Hilda.'

'Leif wasn't afraid either,' she said. Her brother had died for the exact same reason. He hadn't been careful before his first holmgang and he had died in bed, deprived of glory and of Valhalla.

Perhaps Finn would find the courage to only act once they were inside the ring and ready to fight, but it was not worth the risk.

'I'll ask Osvif to stay with me,' Einer agreed. 'I have a request.'

Part of Hilda had known that he too would ask her to be his shield-bearer if she saw him before the holmgang. There had been a time when she would not have hesitated to agree. However, even though Hilda knew she couldn't, everyone else

456

thought she could influence the gods. If she picked a side, either Finn's or Einer's, the other would fail from a lack of hope alone.

Yet, it was Einer who asked, so regardless of what anyone might think, she would stand by him.

'Will you fight at my side at Magadoborg?' Einer asked.

It was not what she had expected. 'You'll have to ask Sigismund that,' she blurted.

'He will agree if you do. Will you fight with me?'

She took a step further into the tent, and towards him. Einer still watched her. He knew her well enough to guess her answer before she said it aloud.

'If you win,' she said.

'If? We both know how this will end,' he joked lightly.

'Don't underestimate him, Einer.'

'I won't.' Einer nodded, suddenly serious. 'He's a seasoned warrior. But holmgang has rules. It's not like war.' The same argument Hilda's brother, Leif, had once employed. Before he had been poisoned in his sleep. 'Within the marked area, he can't use his usual tricks.'

'You mean aboard the float.' She was angry with him, she realised, when she heard her own voice ringing. Angry at him for agreeing to put himself at a disadvantage. For allowing Finn to dictate how the duel would proceed. And scared, too, that he would die in the same way her brother once had. 'Why would you agree to that?'

'It doesn't matter where we fight.'

How could it not? If either of them fell off the float, their heavy armour would make them sink. They would not only forfeit, they would drown, and never go to Valhalla.

Nonetheless, she nodded to say that she understood.

Her mind was empty of words, so she nodded again, and fumbled to find the tent opening.

'Hilda,' Einer called before she could go.

She rested her hands on the tent-frame and twisted her neck to see him. She half-knew what he would say. He had said the words half a hundred times. Before he left to raid, or before a hunt, he always left with the words; "I will wait for you in Valhalla."

At least he had used to, before they had drifted apart. Before their second night.

She smiled, waiting for him to say it. But when Einer spoke, that was not what he said.

'I won't die like Leif,' he assured her. 'I won't leave you like your brother did.'

And that worried her more than anything. He would be slaughtered before the holmgang even began, exactly as her brother had been.

BUNTRUGG

Chapter Forty-Eight

Buntrugg waited for the last rays of hot sunshine to fade so he could revive the dwarfs. He sat with his legs folded and stared at Alvis and the last of his kin. The salve that the veulve had given him rested in his palm. There would not be enough for four dwarfs, but enough for one, perhaps two.

Buntrugg examined the four petrified dwarfs, trying to choose. The eldest and most famous, Alvis, had been turned to stone before the other three, and perhaps the forge Buntrugg needed to close had not belonged to Alvis, but to a rival kinsman; besides, the stories about him did not flatter his intelligence.

It needed to be one of the three younger dwarfs. The two dwarfs Buntrugg had followed from the tavern had revealed that Lundir was a thief; if so, it had to be one of the other two. On the other side of Alvis stood Andur. His long fingers reached into Alvis' open pockets. A greedy dwarf, but not too smart either, since he believed that he could gather gold and silver from the open pocket of a petrified dwarf, and he could not be too trustworthy either, to steal from an old kinsman.

That left Bafir, who stood apart from the others, in the middle of a good stretch and a long yawn. Not much was known about this dwarf, and that was both good and bad.

The last sunlight disappeared below the horizon, so that only the slim slither of the moon lit the path. Soon the path would flood with tired visitors from Svartalfheim, come to celebrate the day's victory and drown its losses.

Buntrugg made himself dwarf-sized with barely a thought; his climb up Yggdrasil had been good practice. He uncorked the bottle, releasing the horrid smell of rotten eggs, wet fur and sharp herbs. He wrinkled his nose. 'Every crevice. Rub it well enough and he might live,' he whispered to himself, in the veulve's stern words.

It would take him all night to revive the dwarf, but he had to be finished before the next sunrise when the strong light would transform any living dwarf back to stone, and cast them into their afterlife.

Buntrugg rubbed the thick salve between two fingers and begun with Bafir's head. The most important part had to also be the best place to start. He slapped the salve onto the yawning dwarf's forehead and rubbed it into the frown-lines, and then into the first strands of hair. And the more he rubbed, the more it seemed as if the yawning dwarf regained colour. The forehead was red and his hair dark, much the same tone as the stone, but a little more colourful. The skin and hair softened at Buntrugg's continuous touch, or rather at the touch of the salve.

Soon after Buntrugg had begun, the night's first dwarfs arrived, and stopped and stared at him. They knew they had been the first to leave Svartalfheim, so they also knew that Buntrugg was not a dwarf, despite his size.

'Didn't make it home last night,' Buntrugg told them. 'Spent the day with the vanir.' Both statements were true and they would be able to hear that on his heart. Hopefully, his size would be enough of a trick for them not to question his lineage or ask anything of him. As long as they did not notice the colourful hairs on Bafir's head, now ruffling in the night breeze.

The dwarfs grunted in response, a few of the younger ones chuckled, and then they moved on.

Buntrugg sighed with relief and continued to rub salve onto Bafir's head.

'What are you doing?' A dwarf stopped up on the path behind him and watched Buntrugg work the salve into the crown of Bafir's hair.

'I hope they can still smell,' Buntrugg grunted. He swept some revived hair to the side to reach the stone-hard ones beneath, and hoped the onlooker would not notice.

His comment made the dwarfs laugh: not just the one who had stopped up to watch, but all those close enough to hear his answer and smell the salve.

'I hope you're right,' said the dwarf who had asked. He tapped Buntrugg on the shoulder and continued on his way, and it was a long while before another dwarf stopped to ask the same question.

Each time someone did, Buntrugg answered in the same way, and each time, the dwarfs moved on with loud laughter. Most walked by without as much as glancing at Buntrugg, too taken by their own conversations or their stomachs' rumbling demands for ale.

The crowd began to thin out, and Buntrugg continued his work uninterrupted.

From the hair and the forehead and the ears, he moved his way around the temples and down to the cheeks. The jawline came next, followed by the chin. He rubbed Bafir's closed eyelids with the salve, and applied some on the bridge of his nose too. He even put salve on his little fingers and stuck them up the dwarf's nostrils. He rubbed the salve on as well as he could, until he felt the stone crumble away and the skin inside the nostrils soften.

Air was blown onto Buntrugg's fingers and Bafir's eyes

blinked open, as if un-stoning the dwarf's mouth and nose had restarted his heart.

'Bafir,' Buntrugg said. 'I'm here to free you from the afterlife.'

Bafir's eyes darted around, and then settled on his two brothers turned to stone.

Knowing that he did not have the luxury to halt his task, Buntrugg continued to rub the salve in. 'Don't bite,' he warned, as he introduced a hand into Bafir's open mouth. With steady speed, he rubbed the salve into Bafir's tonsils and onto his tongue and palate and teeth. He retrieved his hand as soon as the teeth regained their yellow colour.

Bafir smacked his lips a few times to test their use. The dwarf's eyes were fixed on his brothers' petrified faces. 'What about *them*?' were his first words.

'I had to choose one of you,' Buntrugg honestly responded.

'You chose well. What will it cost me?' was his next question.

'A guided tour,' Buntrugg answered and proceeded to rub salve into Bafir's neck. His hands worked quickly and he soon moved onto Bafir's shoulders and the dwarf's questionable choice of tunic. For a long while he worked, in silence, while Bafir watched him, deep in thought. He had freed half of Bafir's left arm before the dwarf addressed him again.

'What exactly is it that you need me to show you?' Bafir narrowed his eyes suspiciously at Buntrugg. 'Why would you trouble yourself with this?'

'Muspel's demons have escaped,' said Buntrugg while he rubbed salve around the dwarf's pointy elbow. 'Through your furnace.'

'Impossible.' Bafir's forehead wrinkled with confusion. 'Fire demons can't escape Muspelheim.'

'They don't care about what they can or can't do,' Buntrugg answered. The stone crumbled away under the touch of the salve on his sore fingers. 'Someone has been into your forge and opened the furnace. I need to close it.'

For a moment longer, the dwarf mused on those words, and

searched for a way out of the situation. A dwarf's forge was more sacred and important than a horse's weight in gold. 'How do you know it's mine?'

'Dwarf furnaces are the only direct opening to Muspelheim, and the only dwarf forge that cannot recently have been visited by its owner is yours.'

'Except it could have been.'

'What do you mean?' Buntrugg asked, suddenly certain that he had found the right dwarfs.

'My brother had an apprentice,' Bafir willingly shared. 'Then he outlawed him. He shouldn't have done that.'

That explained how a dwarf furnace could have been opened after Surt's warnings. A banished dwarf in a forgotten forge…

Bafir wriggled his nose with a decision. 'I promise to close the furnace,' he said.

The answer was far from enough. 'You'll take me down into your forge and I will lock away Muspel's kin myself,' Buntrugg insisted, as he rubbed salve into the crevices of the dwarf's plump fingers. 'Or you can try to close it on your own and be burned alive by the flames of Muspel's children.'

The sincerity of Buntrugg's words baffled Bafir into silence. The dwarf folded and unfolded his fingers to regain control over his stone-like limbs. 'Who are you?' asked the dwarf at last.

'I'm the man rubbing disgusting salve onto you to bring you back into this life, Bafir.'

His answer did not appease Bafir's curiosity. 'You're a giant,' the dwarf remarked. 'You've changed your size.'

Buntrugg saw no reason to deny the truth. The more the dwarf guessed on his own, the more confident he would become, and hopefully, the more he knew, the more curious he would become. All creatures were curious about certain things, but to arouse the curiosity of a dwarf was no easy matter.

With his newly freed hand, Bafir reached for some of the veulve's salve to help. The stench made him wrinkle his nose, but he dipped a fat finger in and scraped out some salve to rub into his left armpit.

'So, I picked the wrong brother,' Buntrugg joked. 'The yawn suggested you'd be less observant.'

'The sunrise has poor timing,' grumbled Bafir to save what little remained of his honour. He began to rub salve onto his crotch. 'Did people laugh at me?'

'That moss at your feet,' Buntrugg pointed down to the yellow and green moss that covered the dwarf's legs. 'I'm not touching it.'

'That's what that smell was,' Bafir complained. His eyes rose from his own feet and settled on his brothers Lundir and Andur, who stood on either side of Alvis. The sight of the moss that covered his brothers to the hips made him laugh. 'Thieving Lundir caught at last,' he chuckled and continued to smear the thick salve onto his trousers.

The dwarf began to whistle as he worked, glad to be better off than his brothers. 'You're lucky you didn't choose to revive Andur,' Bafir said. 'He never would have taken you. And Lundir would have robbed you of that gold in your inner pocket.'

Buntrugg resisted the urge to touch his pocket filled to the brim with Ymir's coins. Bafir was watching him, and Buntrugg knew that confirmation of his wealth was exactly what the clever dwarf hoped for. 'If I was wealthy, I wouldn't work like this,' he said instead. His heart beat true: the work he did for Surt was the only reason he had any wealth at all.

'It shouldn't be possible,' Bafir mused. 'What we're doing.' He glanced over his shoulder at Buntrugg, now rubbing the back of his legs. 'How is it possible?'

'How is life possible at all?' Buntrugg asked in answer. The veulve, like Surt and the other ancients, knew things he never would. Things that he could never comprehend. 'What was the afterlife like?'

Bafir considered the question and stared up at the night sky to find a way to phrase it. 'Long,' was his answer. 'Different.'

He focused back on the salve and his stone feet. The flask was nearly empty, but Bafir scraped the inside for enough salve to free his feet.

With a loud sigh Buntrugg finished reviving Bafir's heels so only the front of the dwarf's feet remained. The veulve had known exactly how much salve was required, and Buntrugg had timed it well. Soon the first dwarfs would begin to head back to Svartalfheim after some good hornfulls of mead and ale, and Buntrugg and Bafir would be on their way to another world and no one would notice that the third brother and last of Alvis' kin had disappeared.

Buntrugg lay down on the grass and stared up at the blinking stars above. The longer he stared up at the sky, the more stars he saw. The night-view was so different there from back home. All the nine worlds had different skies and yet somehow, they were so familiar. He felt Bafir watching him.

'Why do you ask about my afterlife?' the dwarf mused. 'Yours will be different from mine, giant.' For a dwarf, Bafir was especially talkative.

'We'll see. I still have many centuries to live.'

'Oh, you're one of *those*.' Bafir rolled his eyes so obviously that Buntrugg could see it from where he lay on the grass. 'You don't think my ancestors tried to change *our* afterlife?'

Buntrugg left a long enough silence for his words to hold weight and meaning. 'My afterlife has quite different premises from yours.'

'Are you saying my ancestors gave up too easily?'

'Ja, they did.'

'Dwarfs don't pursue impossible tasks.' Bafir's tone was almost sympathetic to the inevitable fate of all giants. 'Forget it. Your afterlife will never change.'

Buntrugg was not as certain as the dwarf, and unlike Bafir who had been to the afterlife and back and did not appear to hate the idea of dying again, Buntrugg had to keep the hope that things could change. Someday the afterlife would claim

Buntrugg, too, but until then there were yet many corners of the nine worlds to see and many impossible missions for him to solve, should his fate allow it.

Half scared of the anger that transformed giants in death and half excited about the time he still had left, Buntrugg searched the sky for any star formations he might recognise from home, but he found none.

'The afterlife can't be changed,' Buntrugg muttered, and then he smiled to himself. 'And dwarfs can't be brought to life once they have turned back to stone.'

EINER

Chapter Forty-Nine

EINER LIFTED HIS mail over his head and struggled to push his arms through.

'You shouldn't wear your mail,' Osvif warned, again, as he helped Einer arrange both mail and tunic. 'Finn won't be.'

'Then the gods will deem him unworthy and choose another champion,' Einer responded, and smiled, remembering it was Hilda who had taught him that.

Einer strapped on his weapon belt, and tested his sword grip. He arranged his hair and put on his helmet, aligned the nose protection and strapped the helmet on under his chin. He turned to Osvif, arms spread to show off his war-ready appearance. His friend displayed a sad, bitter smile, but forced himself to replace it with the kind of beaming pride a father might show.

Together they exited the tent. The camp was quiet and most of the tents had already been taken down and packed on the ships. There were less than a dozen left.

Morning rain had revived the stench of blood and smoke

from the funeral, and right by the edge of camp, by the last tent stood Finn Rolfson, as if he were waiting for Einer to emerge, wearing his helmet, padded armour and fighting gloves. With Finn was his shield-bearer: big Stein from the *Mermaid Scream*.

Stein was not as tall as Einer, but he was much larger around the stomach than anyone else, and he had the strength of three bulls. No one got in Stein's way, not even Einer's father. He was notoriously surly, but Einer supposed that even a man like him could be flattered into being a shield-bearer, if the reward was great enough. He wondered what Finn had promised him.

Without exchanging words, the four of them left the camp and walked down towards the river where everyone waited. Throughout the night, as he lay awake, Einer had heard activity down there: the hammering as the holmring was built, and the commotion of gathering people.

Nine hundred Jutes had gathered, and like this, on either side of the river and on the ships, their numbers looked even more impressive. By now, they had noticed Einer and Finn. A few warriors pointed up at them and a complete silence swept over the crowd. Birds screeched and flew low over the silent crowd, dark clouds rested above them, and the air smelled of imminent downpour.

Out of habit, Einer searched for Hilda. His eyes travelled over the banks and then over the ships, but he did not see her.

Down by a small southern river-boat Ralf had found, which would take them to the holmgang, waited Sigismund with Einer's three shields. Einer could have designated no other to be his shield-bearer; not because they were old friends, but because Sigismund was the only warrior everyone respected, and knew would never interfere in a fight. Every warrior recognised Sigismund's honour and worth, no matter if they were from Ash-hill, or Frey's-fiord, or Odin's-gorge, or Tyr's-lake, or elsewhere.

Next to Sigismund stood their lawspeaker, Dagny, and the other ship commanders. Without a word to any of them, Finn leapt onto the small boat and sat down on the middle bench. Einer smiled to each ship commander before Sigismund and him followed Finn and Stein. Einer still could not find Hilda. All the blonde heads caught his attention, but none of them was hers.

They rowed the small boat out onto the river and upstream, so the current tugged them down towards the holmground. The water foamed around the platform and pushed it up so that one end rested higher than the other. They would both have to fight for the high ground, with the stream at their back, and for Einer that fight would have more urgency since he was heavier and taller than Finn. No doubt Finn had chosen Stein as his shield-bearer for his weight, and Einer was convinced that Finn had urged Stein to stand on Einer's side of the platform, to shift the weight further in Finn's advantage.

The boat bumped against one of the poles tethering the platform in place.

Dagny rose to address the crowd and the gods, and to announce the fight. 'Aesir, vanir. Before you we stand, ready for a holmgang that will decide the chieftaincy of Ash-hill. May the gods choose their champion and guide us with their choice.'

Under normal circumstances, an announcement like that would have been met with roaring applause, but not today. Nearly a thousand warriors waited on the ships and on either river bank, but no-one made a sound.

'There was no challenger, so they shall enter the holmring under equal obligation. First, the eldest, Finn Rolfson, shall enter the ring with his shield-bearer, Stein Bjarneson.'

Finn glared at Einer, fumbled for the blessed rope and stepped under it. Both boat and platform rocked under the movement. Behind him, Stein transferred Finn's three shields from the boat onto the platform, and then he followed, splashing water onto the planks, washing away the chalk marks at the edge of the ring.

'Now Einer Vigmerson, shall enter the ring with his shield-bearer, Sigismund Karson.'

Einer walked to the middle of the boat, reached out and leapt over the blessed ropes, keeping a cautious eye on Finn. No matter the rules of a holmgang, Finn was more than capable of cheating, and taking his chances at a ting later to feign innocence of his crimes.

Einer's shoes were slippery on the wet planks of the holmring. He had forgotten to tar his soles, and cursed himself for it. He received his three shields from Sigismund, laid them down on the wet platform, and helped his old friend into the holmring.

The boat pulled away from them, while Dagny resumed speaking. 'Let it be known to gods and freemen that both champions have been made aware of the rules surrounding a holmgang, and have sworn before the gods to honour the laws.'

Einer picked up one of his shields and Sigismund took the other two. One of them Sigismund readied so it could quickly be passed to Einer, if needed, and the other he slung on his back.

At ease, Einer took stock, taking his time. His shoes were slippery, and he would need to remember that during the fight, so as not to be caught off guard, but otherwise everything was in order. His chainmail hung nicely, his helmet was secure, his trousers were straight, and his weapon belt was in perfect position.

He balanced his weight from one foot to the other. The platform shook, and water splashed up over the sides, although not as much as he had feared. It was well secured between the poles.

Stein stood in a corner of the holmground, with the current at his back. His weight pressed the platform close to the foaming waterfront. Finn stood next to Stein, right between the two poles and Einer placed himself on the chalk line nine feet away, with Sigismund navigating on the three feet of planks behind Einer, so as not to tilt the weight too much to one end of the platform nor the other. Every movement could be felt on the Holmring, and every shift of weight counted.

Finn looked ready to attack with his shield held high and Stein, who bore no armour, not even a helmet, held a spare shield up to protect himself, as if he too was going to fight. A shield-bearer with no armour on a holmring suspended on a river. No doubt Einer would need to be as wary of Stein as he was of Finn. Where Sigismund would never interfere in the fight, he doubted Stein held the same reservations.

Einer was well prepared, and Finn's plan was too obvious. Had Einer worried about the outcome of the fight, he might have taken off his chainmail and thrown off Finn's plan, but there was no need. The outcome was obvious. The gods would really need to *try* if they wanted to change it.

'Your blood-line will die with you, Einer,' Finn said. His tongue was busy, hoping to intimidate, but his eyes were filled with terror and fear. Finn knew this was how he would die. Just as the horse at Ragnar's funeral had known.

'In the afterlife we live on,' Einer reassured.

The crowd was far away, and the boat was heading for the bank. They were all alone, and Finn and Einer both spoke in lowered voices. No one inland would hear.

'Let both champions take their first weapons,' Dagny shouted.

Einer reached under his shield for the sword at his left hip, eyes fixed on Finn. His opponent had two swords to choose from, one at each hip, but he unsheathed the sword on his left hip first, the one he had begun raiding with last summer. Einer's stare lingered by Finn's right hip for a moment longer. Finn even carried his old battle-axe. Einer carried no other weapons but his sword, but Finn had enough weapons for three men.

'Didn't know you owned two swords,' Einer commented, impressed at how quickly Finn had gained such wealth.

'There were many pickings in Hammaborg,' Finn responded with a sneer.

Better perhaps than anyone, Einer knew how little pickings there had been after the battle for Hammaborg. There had not been many worthy weapons left on the battlefield. Although he had searched through the remains until the moment they had sailed on for decent weapons and armour for his father and the many warriors who had passed on, Einer had only found two swords.

Finn had a plan. For a moment Einer's heart raced at the thought that he had been wrong about Finn and that the look in his eyes was not fear at all, but excitement. He worried that Finn had some hidden trick, certain that the gods had chosen him and not Einer.

Einer turned the shield in his hand. He concentrated on himself to regain his calm.

Finn could not win.

Einer held his shield so only his eyes showed over the top, well aware that his legs were exposed. He held his sword out, ready to rap it against the shield and begin the match as soon as Dagny finished reciting the rules.

Finn lifted his shield and prepared his sword in the same manner as Einer.

'May our gods have gathered and opened their high court. May they look upon us fairly and begin this match,' Dagny announced from the starboard bank.

Finn and Einer tapped their shields three times, and waited for the gods to give their sign that their holmgang was acknowledged and would be judged fairly.

Einer examined Finn from the top of Finn's shiny helmet down to the tarred soles of his shoes. Finn's padded armour was not as heavy as Einer's chainmail, but below his arms the armour was cut poorly and restricted Finn's movement. Not much, but enough for Einer to notice.

The shield Finn held in his hands was not his own. It was larger than Finn's usual one and of fine build, but it was no longer new. The animal skin over its edges was worn down from use, and the shield boss had been dented many times. The second shield, which Stein held up to protect his face, was not Finn's either. From the familiar way in which Stein clasped onto it, Einer assumed that it belonged to Stein. The last one, on Stein's back, was Finn's own.

Finn planned to survive until the last shield.

Einer held his own shield in his hands. The grip had formed to his fingers from summers of use, the boss had been replaced last summer, and the thin leather that protected the front of the shield was bleached by the sun and stained with blood.

The two shields Sigismund held were shields with no owner that Thora and Sigismund had brought from Frey's-fiord. Both, he had tested last night and chosen among many presented to him.

On his right hand Finn wore a silver ring; a last resort, in case he fell into the river and drowned, and had to buy his way into Aegir and Ran's halls. Beneath his chainmail and tunic, Einer felt the cool gold of his bracteate. Until now, he had not thought of it, but he supposed the gold bracteate would buy him a good seat in Ran's hall, if it came to it.

With a loud shriek, two ravens dropped out of the thick clouds above the crowd and darted down towards the holmground. The sign from the gods.

One heartbeat Einer allowed himself to glance up and confirm the sign. One heartbeat, and he skipped ahead and attacked. His breath was steady, his heartbeat slow. Finn let out a grunt and stopped Einer's powerful swing. Their swords clashed.

Einer filled his lungs with fresh air. Without hesitation or strain, he pushed against Finn's sword. The tips of their blades pointed to the sky and their sword-guards clanked. Einer put a finger over Finn's guard to keep it in lock. While Finn was occupied with the thought of freeing his sword from Einer's strong hold, Einer took another deep breath and thrust his shield forward into Finn's, which in turn knocked Finn's helmet and stunned him for half a heartbeat.

Einer unhooked their weapons, letting Finn's sword swing harmlessly at the timbers beneath their feet. Calm as ever,

Einer raised his sword and struck Finn's shield at a spot where two planks met, poorly concealed beneath the worn hide. His sword might get caught in the shield. He would need to strike strong. His sword carved straight through the long shield and parted it in two, right down to the shield boss. The top of the shield flapped down and hit Finn over the toes. He swallowed a grunt of pain and surprise. Even under the shadow of his helmet, his shock was evident.

Before Finn could raise his sword and reciprocate, Einer stepped back so he stood exactly where he had been when the combat had been announced. Once, he tapped his sword against his own shield in honour of the laws of holmgang, and out of respect.

Big Stein gaped at Einer like a child seeing a being from another world.

Odin's two ravens circled the holmgang.

Shaking from shock, Finn picked up the top of his ruined shield and threw both pieces over the blessed ropes and into the water. The planks landed flat and floated down the river, past their many warships. He hissed at Stein for his next shield, and Stein reluctantly let go of his own shield and fumbled for Finn's shield on his back.

Finn wiped his face on the arm of his tunic, and Einer could not quite tell if it was cold sweat or tears that he wiped away. Finn was still shaking like a leaf in the wind at the thought of dying.

Einer held his ground, and at the corner of his eyes he saw Sigismund behind him. His friend had not moved the length of a fingertip since they had taken their stance on the float. Opposite him, Stein had moved from his corner, shifting the platform to Finn's advantage.

Finn took a few deep breaths to stop his hands from shaking. Finally, he tapped his new shield.

The fight resumed. Einer matched his opponent's nervous stare. The padded armour had already begun to annoy Finn. It rose with his movements and dug into his armpits. Finn rolled his shoulders to straighten it, and had Einer had any intention of attacking first this time, that would have been the perfect opportunity. Yet, Finn's annoyance at his armour almost seemed like too obvious an opening.

Einer breathed deep to fill his lungs, and only expelled half the air again. His heartbeat was steady and he felt the blood pump out to his fingertips.

He had watched Finn fight enough time to know how Finn would attack. Last their swords had clashed, so this time, Finn would move in with a blow of his shield in an attempt to unbalance him.

Einer fixed his eyes on Finn's face. In battle, a facial twitch before attacking meant nothing; but in a duel, that little twitch was everything, and Finn had never been an expressionless fighter. Never before had he needed to be, since his biggest strength was in a shield-wall.

Unlike most warriors, Einer knew the holmgang well. As a boy, he had looked up to Hilda's older brother, Leif. Together the two of them had raised a dream of becoming holmgang champions, although it had mostly been Leif's dream, and it had died with Leif.

Einer took another controlled breath and listened to his own heartbeat. His gaze was locked on Finn, who still had not moved, though he looked impatient to launch back into the fight. A soft wind danced around the platform, making the braid of Finn's hair slap at his back and caressing Einer's calves.

Briefly, Finn's lips stretched into the twitch Einer had waited to see. Exactly as Einer had expected, Finn attacked shield first.

Ready for the blow, Einer kicked the shield off course, and countered Finn's sword-stroke with his shield. The blow diverted, Einer launched another kick that rattled his opponent. Again, he hacked Finn's shield to pieces, a clean cut through the middle, all the way to the shield boss. A move like that might have trapped his sword, but Einer was quick to twist it free. He had not yet moved from where he had stood when the holmgang had begun.

Stein stepped in to protect Finn and push Einer back, although that was not his role as shield-bearer, and although Einer had no intention of attacking any further. He, unlike Finn, intended to follow the rules of a holmgang; to honour the gods, but also to honour Leif's memory.

Finn retreated behind Stein to the corner of the holmring, and rearranged both his helmet and padded armour. Never before had Einer seen nor expected to see Finn like this, terrified of a fight.

Einer tapped his own shield with his sword once, to call for a break while Finn discarded his second shield and collected his last one.

Ready once more, Finn pushed Stein out of his way, and twisted his shield in his hand to test his grip. This was his own shield, and it rested better in his hand than the other two. His grip on it was steady. His stare did not quit Einer.

He had his own shield, his last. He ought to announce the continuation of the fight, with a tap, like Einer had announced a pause, yet Finn continued to stand there and glare.

Above them, the ravens began to caw, and one of them dashed overhead of them. The wind of its wings cooled Einer's neck. It cawed and circled around them.

Finn stepped towards his shield-bearer, up on the high-ground of the platform. His shield-bearer, who had now fulfilled his legal duties and stood without a shield, shuffled behind Finn, exchanging places. All the while, Einer held his ground. His shoes were slippery; too much movement might make him lose his foothold. Besides, no tricks could change the end result.

Finn arranged his padded armour, and then his helmet, and his trousers. He took his time, and ignored Einer, and Sigismund and Stein, and the hundreds of people who watched them inland. His hands were shaking again.

Finn grimaced and twisted the shield in his hand. A bindrune was painted in a dark brown colour.

Suddenly, Finn tapped his shield, and rushed ahead. He threw himself into a head-butt. Their helmets clonked together. Finn had his sword ready to drive up through Einer's neck, but Einer countered the move, and hacked out after Finn's last shield.

The edge of it shattered under Einer's blow, but Finn was not thrown by the prospect of fighting without a shield. He threw it away and then his shield-hand clasped around the hilt of his second sword. The one at his right hip. A wooden hilt that Einer knew well. Mere days ago, he had helped to put that hilt on its sword. As Finn pulled the sword free from the shabby leather scabbard and revealed the blade, Einer and Sigismund both breathed the name of the sword: 'The Ulfberht.'

In a last desperate move, Finn pointed the tip of the sharp blade at Einer. The inlay shone, as if the sword carried its own light. Above them the two ravens cawed louder than ever.

At loss for words, Einer stared at the sword, not knowing what he ought to do or say. It had never occurred to him that it might not have been southerners who had looted his father's corpse.

Although Einer found no words, Finn, as ever, knew exactly what to say. 'Your father chose me.' The confidence of his words did not carry over to his shaky voice. 'With his dying breath he called for me, and as his last action, he gave me his sword.'

'You're not worthy,' Einer roared. The old anger flared inside him, and for a moment, he thought the gods were letting him go, but then the anger settled inside his hand, and with a strength he had never known before, he swung his sword.

Finn's heavy shield-bearer ran forward. Stein threw himself under Einer's shield, and grabbed Einer's legs, to pull him off the platform into the cold river. Einer glided backwards, unable to find rest under his worn soles. Stein had a firm grip around his feet, and Einer's blow fell wide. Einer's hand slipped from the hilt and the sword fell. Stein staggered under his own weight, and slipped under the holy ropes into the water.

Just then, Finn kicked Einer's back, and as he fell, Einer met Sigismund's pained stare. As the law required, Sigismund stood back and did nothing, as the honourable shield-bearer he was, and as Einer's feet lifted from the platform and he fell out over the side of the holmgang, he caught a glimpse of Finn. Even he seemed surprised at his own success.

Einer fumbled after the blessed rope as he fell, and caught it with his free sword hand. An unknown strength flooded Einer's arms and made him kick a foot against the platform. His shield knocked against one of the corner poles, and although he knew it to be impossible, by the gods' will, he caught himself. His left foot found the edge of the platform, the shield in his outstretched arm held his weight against the pole and with his right hand he steadied himself with a grip around the blessed rope.

Einer's body acted on its own, without his commands, and heaved itself out towards the pole so he could steady himself better. When he was close enough, he discarded his shield to gain a better grip.

According to the holmgang law, discarding a shield meant that Finn had to pause the match, but Finn did not follow the rules. Fear of death made him rage ahead, swinging both swords. The Ulfberht blade carved through the blessed ropes, and cut off Einer's last life-line, and yet, the gods did not let him die. An old force took over his body and moved for him. With unfamiliar agility, he ducked away from Finn's blow. A strong wind blew at his back and pushed him back onto the platform.

A new shield was in Einer's hand before he could look at Sigismund and ask for it, right in time to block Finn's next blow.

'The Ulfberht doesn't belong to you,' Einer said, blocking Finn's double blows with his shield as easily as if he fought a child.

Although he had no weapon, Einer moved in. He attacked with his shield. Thrust it at Finn's face and moved around Finn's desperate blows.

By command of the gods, the sun shone through the thick

layer of clouds onto the platform, blinding Finn into retreat. Backwards he stumbled, as Einer smashed the shield into Finn's face. Finn took a step back; no more than a step, but a step too far. Finn's foot slipped off the edge of the platform. His back smacked against the water.

Einer cast away his second shield and threw himself forward, stomach onto the platform. His mail bit into his chest as he landed, and yet he neither gasped nor groaned, only reached his arm out over the waters, towards Finn.

Finn's padded armour kept him afloat for a moment. If they both reached, Einer would be able to grab him and save him. Yet, even knowing that, Finn hesitated.

'That blade belongs to my father,' Einer said and stretched as far out as he could. 'Don't you dare take it with you.'

He caught Finn's thick braid and hauled him back.

'I won't allow you the honour of Aegir's company,' he grunted. He grabbed hold of Finn's padded armour and heaved Finn onto the platform, despite his struggles to escape, eager to drown with the Ulfberht blade in hand.

Einer dragged Finn onto the platform with one hand, and held him down with the insistent pressure of a knee on the back. Like a fish out of water, Finn struggled to free himself from Einer's grip, and when finally he gave up, he stretched his neck and stared up at Einer. His expression was resentful, and rightfully so.

Einer removed the axe from Finn's weapon belt and threw it out of reach. Lightly, he heaved Finn's wet body around onto his back. The Ulfberht sword was still in his grip. Einer locked Finn's hands in place, and wrenched the Ulfberht sword free. Finn yelped for his life. Einer closed a fist and punched Finn's nose bloody to shut him up.

Finn had no shield left, his shield-bearer had fallen into the river and swum to shore, but legally, Einer had no reason to halt the fight. Einer pressed a foot over Finn's two hands on his chest, and stood up tall over Finn.

The two ravens cawed as they circled far above. Sigismund watched from a safe corner of the platform. The audience on land was quiet and watchful.

As he had fallen, Finn had held onto the rope Hilda had blessed, so although he had stepped off the platform, he had not left the holmring, which meant that by law, he had not fled from the fight. Einer knew the rules of holmgang well, and in order to put an end to it, there was only one thing to do.

Einer placed the tip of his father's Ulfberht blade above Finn's heart. Water trickled out from Finn's padded armour under the pressure.

Loud enough for everyone in the nine worlds to hear, Einer roared: 'Now, for the mortal wound...'

DARKNESS

A SONG FILLED Ragnar's ears, but it was not the comforting song that helped people pass into Helheim. It was another song that Ragnar knew well; Loki's song.

Birds sang along to Loki's hum, and then the giant appeared at the edge of the Darkness. His steps left heavy prints on the flowery lawn.

'Don't they hunt on their own?' Loki asked in a raised voice, staring straight ahead, past Ragnar, as if he was watching someone there hidden in the dark. 'The wolves,' he added.

Right as he said it, a wolf emerged from the Darkness. Ragnar flinched out of the beast's way. The memory of Fenrir at Ragnarok was still vivid within him.

The wolf snarled at Loki. An old man cackled with laughter. Keeping his distance from the wolf, Ragnar took a few tentative steps ahead.

The old man had long grey hair, combed to wave out over his shoulders. It was the same silver grey as the brooch that closed his coat. His attire was night blue from the socks to his long coat. The wool was decorated with silver. Laughter escaped through thin lips. The old man's single eye rested on Loki, and shielded behind his silver hair was the black hole where his other eye should be.

Ragnar gaped up at Odin's slim figure. It was not the same as seeing him at Ragnarok, with the urgency of saving him from death. Then, he had not had time to fully realise that he was in the presence of the almighty Alfather.

Odin slyly watched Loki. 'They're spoiled.' His voice was rough like the growl of his two wolves.

The two wolves barred their teeth at Loki, but at Odin's command, they stopped.

Back in Midgard, Ragnar had always struggled to understand how Odin and Loki had become so close allies, especially given that their friendship would cause the downfall of both gods and giants. Odin and Loki were alike in many ways, but as Ragnar watched Odin's wolves growl at Loki, he could not help but think that the Alfather and Loki were not as close as the stories told.

Only through a blood tie could gods and giants ever hope to find peace. If Ragnar united Odin and Loki in the famous blood tie, then perhaps he would prove himself worthy to be welcomed into Helheim.

Ragnar remembered how puzzled Odin had been at his own actions during Ragnarok, when Ragnar had forced him to run. He could not simply place the thought in Odin's mind. This needed to feel genuine to Odin, and for that Ragnar needed to convince him through good arguments.

One of Odin's wolves snarled. Its sharp teeth were clenched around a small bird.

'What have you got for us, Freki?' Odin asked and crouched down at its side. 'Let go,' he said to the wolf. 'Freki, let go of the swallow. What about you, Geri? Did you also catch something?'

Chuckling, Odin reached out a slender hand and patted his

wolves. His wrinkled hand bore nine gold rings, each twisted and dotted in the ancient style. The other gods eagerly ate from the apples of youth to stay young, but Odin ate only enough of the apples to sustain him, not to make him young. In age, he and Loki were not far apart, but Odin looked significantly older.

Even after leaving one eye at Mimer's well to observe, Odin was always in search of more knowledge. Perhaps he wanted to appear wise as well, Ragnar mused. Wise as an old man. Even if the Alfather could sit in his hall and know everything happening in the nine worlds, he might not be satisfied. Perhaps this was how Ragnar could convince him to trade blood with Loki.

'Your eye rests with Mimer in Vanaheim,' Loki said in response to Ragnar's thoughts, and Odin appeared surprised that Loki knew it.

'You can see the vanir move from there,' Loki continued. He rubbed the thin line of a beard on his chin, combing it through with his fingers. Ragnar did not need to assert his influence for the giant to catch on. 'And with the eye in your skull, you see Asgard. Nine worlds, but only two eyes.'

Odin smiled as Loki worked through Ragnar's given thoughts aloud. The Alfather seemed to be impressed by the giant's observations, and Ragnar felt he shared some credit there.

'You want to send the wolves off into one of the other seven worlds.' Loki was not asking.

The Alfather cackled with laughter. 'You're perceptive.'

'But the wolves won't make good scouts. Unless you bind them to you with runes.'

Odin nodded, and ruffled his wolves' rigid fur.

'You've tried,' Loki observed. 'That's why you no longer eat. Your wolves eat for you.'

For some reason, the Alfather became wary at that observation.

'A bird would be a better scout,' Loki continued, sensing Odin's unease. They stared down at the dead swallow Freki had caught. Loki crouched by the bird, and pushed its small beak this way and that. 'Swallows aren't that clever,' he said.

'Ravens are better birds,' Odin agreed. 'A perfect scout.'

Two perfect scouts, Ragnar corrected, and thought about Odin's two ravens, Hugin and Munin, who always flew together and explored Midgard. They had used to love to sit in the ash tree back in Ash-hill and look over the villagers. Yet, despite how long the birds stayed in Ash-hill, they still managed to fly across Midgard's lands and return to Odin when the day was over.

'Two birds would make better scouts,' Loki prompted. The giant was a lot more subjectable to Ragnar's influence than the Alfather.

A wicked smile grazed both Loki's and Odin's lips. They both knew the other could grant them what they wanted: Odin wanted scouts, and Loki wanted to be accepted in Asgard.

Loki rose from the swallow's side and brushed his knees clean of grass stains. 'It's a difficult thing to bind a mind to a being,' he said. 'We aren't kin, you and I. I could end up killing you.' He laughed, as if to dismiss this whole conversation, but from the way he watched Odin, Ragnar was well aware that Loki wanted anything but for the Alfather to dismiss it.

Odin too rose, and his wolves darted up ready to dash through the forest and play again, but the Alfather no longer watched them. They had lost their value. It seemed unlikely that anyone could trump the great Alfather, but Loki navigated past Odin's suspicions, with a little help from Ragnar.

Giants and gods had a different air about them. Both argued their cases convincingly, and these were likely the two cleverest men in the nine worlds. In a way, they were much alike; sly and careful, and always ahead of everyone else. But where Loki hid in the shadows, Odin bathed in light praise, and he had the real talents of a leader.

The Alfather needed another push in order to suggest a blood exchange with Loki. Ragnar scoured his mind for that last argument. Anything that might sway the great Alfather. Mixing blood with a giant would prove Odin's superiority to the other gods. No matter how little the other gods liked Loki, if Odin said they needed to accept the giant among them, and if they listened, then it would establish the Alfather as an even more powerful god than ever before.

Ragnar watched Odin's lips twist into a wicked smile and knew his thoughts had been heard. Urged by Ragnar, the Alfather pursed his thin lips. 'What if we mingled blood?'

FINN

Chapter Fifty

WATER TRICKLED OUT of Finn's ears. He was pinned down. Einer had a foot on his chest, the Ulfberht blade in hand, and Finn's padded armour was heavy with water from his dip the river.

'Now for the mortal wound...' said Einer, raising the Ulfberht sword over Finn's heart.

Fear flashed through Finn. He recalled how his sword had pierced Einer's stomach at the beginning of summer. How the blood of a kinsman had stained his sword. How it had stained his hands, his tunic. How Einer had looked up at him with that expression of betrayal. With that surprise and horror. That same horror Finn felt now. That same betrayal.

The wound would be deep. Fatal, but a slow death full of agony. For days, he would suffer, before he passed on. For days, Finn would struggle against death. For days Einer would tarnish his honour as Finn lay dying. Just as Finn had done, when it had been Einer with the mortal wound, but Finn did not have the gods watching over him as Einer did.

With a dark look on his face, Einer lifted his sword to the skies.

The clouds were black at Einer's back, but a ray of sunshine broke through and blazed off his helmet and chainmail. The two ravens glided at Einer's back. The gods had chosen him.

Einer lifted the sword and thrust without a breath of hesitation.

Finn yelped and thrashed, but Einer had him bound with a foot on his chest.

Finn wailed from the pain that shot through his entire body. His blood pounded with it. And then the realisation hit him: Einer had not struck his heart. Nor pierced his stomach, nor severed his head, nor punctured his lungs.

Panting to control the pain, Finn lifted his head and stared down at himself. The sword was planted in his left thigh.

He glared up at Einer, who matched his stare. Einer had let go of the sword, leaving it impaled through Finn's leg and into the platform. Every slightest movement tore at the wound.

Einer neither smiled nor acknowledged Finn's suffering. He regarded him as he might have a lifeless rock. 'Will this be acknowledged as a fatal wound?' Einer asked the crowd and gods. He stepped off Finn with his foot, but the sword held Finn down.

Finn let his head knock back down against the platform. His left leg throbbed with pain. His lower leg was already half numb. 'Will you—' He broke off and gasped. 'Remove the sword?' he begged.

His head spun. Murky river water trickled out of his padded armour. His entire body was heavy and worn down. His eyes rolled back, yet the pain kept him lucid, and when he looked up at Einer again, he saw one of the two ravens circling above him. Its black eyes stared down at Finn and it cocked its head from one side to the other, judging him.

'The sword—' Finn begged.

Einer did not acknowledge Finn. 'Is the wound acknowledged?' he asked again.

'*Aaack—Wound*,' the raven croaked with him.

'Einer, the sword,' Finn mumbled again. Lying still was impossible, but every wriggle hurt as if he was being stabbed all over again.

Behind Einer, Sigismund Karson stared at the two ravens as if he was worlds away and could hardly believe what he saw. 'The wound is legal,' he announced for the crowd on land.

'Sword…' Finn pleaded to either of them.

'With a fatal wound Einer Vigmerson has defeated Finn Rolfson in holmgang,' he heard Dagny shout from a distant place.

With a fatal wound. A stab to the leg would not be fatal. Einer should have left him to drown. That would have been worthier. Instead, with one stab, Einer had taken everything from Finn: his hope of the chieftaincy, his hope of glory, his unsoiled reputation as a warrior, and his future as a ship commander. A wound to the leg might make it impossible for him to fight as before. If he could not fight, he could not lead other warriors in battle. Everything he had ever earnt, everything he had hoped for, had been taken from him.

Finn strained to wriggle his left foot, he groaned from the pain. He could still move his foot, but Ragnar Erikson had been able to move his foot too; and he had lived with a limp so severe that he had never again gone to battle. All from a wound to the thigh. A mortal wound, not to Finn's life, but to his future. The shield-walls would be inaccessible to him. In a duel he might yet die with his honour intact, but with a limp like Ragnar's he would never again be on the front lines in war.

Finn clutched the edge of his tunic to fight the pain, and his jawline stiffened. 'I'll show you "fatal wound,"' he hissed and pushed his shoulders up from the wet platform; he was heavy and it made his thigh hurt even more. His back muscles ached and he could not sit up. His leg quivered and his head pounded.

Although he flailed, Finn could not reach the sword to free himself. 'Get your sword. We're not done!'

Einer did not even spare him a glance. He was a chieftain now.

The warriors on either bank clamoured and cheered for him. Their new chieftain. They acknowledged him with songs and war cries, and then the cheers died down, and Finn heard the ship commanders, one after the other, pledge their allegiance to Einer.

All the while, Finn struggled to try to get to his feet again. This was not the end. 'I am a ship commander too, and I will *not* acknowledge you!' Finn snarled, but Einer did not care. No one cared.

Sigismund pledged Frey's-fiord's ships to Einer's cause, and then he stood back.

'Sigismund,' Finn called to get his attention. 'Sigismund. Sigismund, you know the rules. Fight until death. I'm not dead. Tell him to fight.'

'The holmgang is over,' said Sigismund.

'I'm not dead,' Finn howled.

The boat arrived to take them to shore, to join the clamour of happy warriors on either bank. Dagny addressed the crowd. 'The gods have chosen to pass Ash-hill's chieftaincy to Einer Vigmerson.' Her voice carried over the cheering.

Einer knelt to their lawspeaker, and the ship commanders, and the warriors.

'We're not done!' Finn insisted, still trying to worm free. He stretched as far as he could to reach the Ulfberht and pull it out of his leg.

'You have chosen me, and as chieftain, I shall serve,' Einer said the sacred words. The crowd fell as their new chief spoke; the ravens glided over the crowd.

'Not... done.' Finn grunted. His fingers grazed the blade.

Having said the words, Einer rose to his feet. The platform rocked under his weight. Dagny and the warriors on the small boat watched him with proud smiles.

'As chieftain, I demand an immediate Ting,' Einer said.

'A Ting? On what grounds?' asked Dagny.

They spoke as if Finn was not there, as if they did not hear him or see him. 'Einer,' Finn said, and this time, Einer granted him a look, glaring down at him with unfamiliar rage.

'I, as the sole heir of Vigmer Torstenson, accuse Finn Rolfson of theft and treason.' His green eyes seemed to bore through Finn with a hot fire. His words rang inside Finn's skull: *theft and treason.* 'He stole the Ulfberht from my father's corpse.'

Since Einer had spoken first, nothing Finn said could rectify the accusation. No matter what Finn said, no one would believe him. The truth mattered little when it came to trials, only the evidence mattered, and no one would believe Finn's testimony. With the Ulfberht sword as evidence, and all warriors as witnesses, Einer was set to have it his way. The law-deciders rarely ruled in favour of the accused if there was evidence. Finn's statement alone would not be enough to sway the crowd.

Desperate not to lose any more, Finn begged, 'I acknowledge you as chief, Einer. You don't need to do this.' Whatever it would take, he needed to come out of this victorious. He could not lose anything else. Already he had lost too much.

The boat knocked and rattled against the holmground in the current. 'We need to leave this town as soon as possible, Einer,' Dagny said quietly, so those inland could not hear. 'You said so yourself.'

Finn squirmed with the pain as water dripped into the wound from his wet clothes. He watched Einer, silently pleading for him to agree with Dagny; the longer Finn had to prepare for the Ting and trial, the better his chances would be, and with a little distance, none of this would seem as bad.

'This needs to be settled before we sail away from my father's grave,' Einer responded, 'but it won't take long.' And with those words he wrenched the Ulfberht sword out of Finn's leg.

Finn roared from the pain and curled in over himself, incapable of moving. Once again, Einer did not in the least acknowledge his suffering, but dried the blood off the Ulfberht and addressed the crowd at either bank.

'We can't stay here any longer. There is no time for a trial. But the facts are clear: Finn stole this. You've all seen the evidence.'

Finn uncurled to glare at the warriors, but saw many eyes looking to Einer. He was a chieftain now, Finn realised. Everyone wanted to help him and do him favours. Even more so than when he had been a chieftain's son.

Not only was Einer chieftain, he had also regained the little honour he had lost with his berserker rage.

Desperate to regain some honour too, Finn shouted to the riverbanks. 'I fought alongside the chief when we were ambushed. After his own son had run to the town to fight,' he glanced back up at Einer to plead for mercy. This was not what he had intended. 'I fought shoulder to shoulder with the chief when the southerners broke our shield-wall. When they killed the chief. He spoke to me, right before he passed on. He held onto me, and he gave me the Ulfberht blade. Told me to have it.'

'To protect it from looting,' Einer completed in the tone of a chief. 'And had you given it back to him at his funeral, we would not be here.'

Without waiting for the crowd, or for Dagny, and without acknowledging Finn any further, Einer took the lead. 'Sigismund, you're a respected smith. To your knowledge, what is the price of an Ulfberht blade?'

Sigismund seemed flustered, but he answered all the same. 'Fifteen marks of silver.'

Finn lay down flat and stared up at the dark clouds, where the two ravens circled far above.

Fifteen marks of silver. Four-thousand-and-eight-hundred arm-lengths of homespun. The price of three houses and associated farmland. *None* of them had that kind of wealth; even Einer would not have been able to conjure fifteen marks of silver.

A raven cawed and circled closer. In disbelief, Finn glared down at himself and his injured leg. How could this have happened? How could it have gone this far? Fifteen marks of silver was more than he had ever owned and more that he had ever hoped to own, in this life or the next.

Fifteen marks of silver. Just the sound of it was daunting. Everyone was watching, but Finn didn't care. They couldn't do this to him.

'I didn't steal anything,' he insisted. 'It was handed to me. *Given* to me.' He closed his eyes and focused on his breathing. His thigh hurt. He could no longer feel his leg, and his entire lower body throbbed. He needed treatment.

No one listened to him.

Dagny declared that Finn was guilty of theft, guilty of treason, and that he would have to pay fifteen marks of silver. None of them knew how Finn had been looked down upon and ignored because he was the son of a farmer, because he had been born with less than every other warrior. As if his poor heritage somehow stained his honour, and as if he was unworthy of the mere possibility of winning glory through battle, since he could not pay for a decent sword. It had taken him his entire life to earn a sword of his own. It had cost him four-hundred arm-lengths of homespun, and his wife had hated to part with all that wealth for mere iron.

None of the others came from such beginnings. None of them had spent summers begging their parents to set aside enough wool every sorting to make their own padded armour, but Finn had. During the days, he had worked on his parents' farm until sundown, and at night had spun wool, and when he had enough string, he had woven, throughout the nights. Two winters it had taken him to sew it, and even then, he did not have any shoes to bring, or any fighting gloves. Shields, he made in plenty, when he did not have to work on the farm or on his armour, but leather shoes were a luxury in his family.

None of these people who dared judge him had ever struggled in that way. None of them had worked as hard as him.

'The appropriate penalty for theft at this scale is outlawry,'

Sigismund announced right there for everyone to hear and think about. The most honourable and well-respected warrior of them all.

The mere thought of outlawry, of being hunted by everyone he had ever known, hit Finn like a thunder strike. If Einer wanted to, he could take Sigismund's suggestion and outlaw Finn for not being able to pay what he owed. At least Finn's parents were not alive to see him like this. At least they had already passed on with honour, knowing that their son had become a proud warrior, and so had his wife, but that also meant that he was alone. No one was there to support him, or worry over his fate. It was just him, against hundreds of warriors who had already decided that he was worthless.

'How are you going to pay, Finn?' Einer asked, and they were all watching him; Sigismund and Dagny and the warriors inland.

'I will pay with the *Mermaid Scream*.' The words were difficult to force out. Never had Finn thought he might give up the position he had gained only yesterday, but there was no other option.

'The *Mermaid Scream* should be worth nine marks of silver,' Einer agreed. It was a generous price for an old warship that had sailed too long in rough waters. A generous price for a ship that had been part of Einer's inheritance yesterday. Even Finn recognised that.

'That leaves six marks of silver,' Dagny said and once more her sight settled on Finn, waiting for him to conjure up the remaining debt.

All eyes were on him, exactly now when he did not want them to be. Einer looked at him expectantly. 'I don't have that much wealth,' Finn stammered. He did not know what to say, or how to pay the fee. Unlike Einer, he did not wear a gold neck-ring; he had not grown up rich. 'Confiscate my house.'

'Your house burned down,' Einer said in the voice of authority his father had once employed. 'Your house is no longer worth what it used to be. Even before, it was never worth six marks of silver.'

'I own a pig,' Finn stammered desperately, anything to settle his debt. 'I own two. And a goat, and twelve sheep.'

'Not anymore.'

'I have guarantees on my lands.'

'None of us have guarantees on our lands anymore.'

There had to be a way. Last summer he might have conjured up four marks of silver if he had sold everything he owned, apart from his farmlands, and if Einer had accepted a guarantee on his lands, and even then, it would have taken him, at the very least, nine summers to repay the full amount. None of that was possible anymore, but *still*, there had to be a way.

'There is only one way,' Einer said, and they both knew what he meant.

Finn fought back the tears and shook his head, afraid his voice would break if he tried to speak.

Any payment would do. Poverty did not frighten Finn; whatever he had to do without, he would. He would give up gold and silver and clothes, and would walk around naked without a sword or even a pair of socks, if that was what it took. Anything but what Einer was about to suggest. Anything other than this.

'Unable to pay his penalty, I, Einer Vigmerson, declare Finn Rolfson debt-bound to me.' Einer did not look at Finn as he said the words. He did not smile triumphantly, as Finn had feared, but looked straight through him as if Finn no longer existed. 'With all of you as witnesses, through his debt of six marks of silver to me, I hereby buy Finn Rolfson, and declare that from this moment on, he is no longer a freeman.'

Finn buried his face in his hands. He focused on his breathing, and on the pain in his leg. He tried to shut out the sounds of the crowd, and Dagny's voice that took over for Einer to announce the conditions of the arrangement. Three deep breaths, Finn allowed himself, with his face hidden behind his palms. He blinked the tears out of his eyes, and then he made his hands glide down his face to smooth his beard.

'His lineage is removed,' Dagny announced. Her voice penetrated like a sharp dagger through Finn's thoughts. 'Henceforth he shall not be known as Finn, the son of Rolf, but as Finn the thrall.'

His father had not been a well-known man, not in death and not alive, and yet the loss of the last thing that connected him to his parents; his name, sent a shot of grief through Finn.

'He shall hold none of the privileges that freemen do, shall be helped by no one. Cattle and the children of thralls shall be higher-born than him. Any freeman who assists this debt-thrall shall have to pay fines to his master, Einer Vigmerson.'

His master. From now on Finn was no better than a dog, to be kicked if he barked at the wrong time.

'All work he does shall be payment towards his debt. When half his debt has been paid back, his master may choose to return his freedom and lineage to him. Until such a day as his freedom is given to him again, he shall serve his master as a thrall, and if he strays from his position, he shall be outlawed, and never again be allowed to set foot in Jutland.'

Finn did not know which was worse, between thraldom and outlawry. If he were outlawed, everyone he knew would legally be allowed, and worse: expected, to kill him on sight. An outlaw had less rights than a thrall; at least a thrall was not hunted, at least he belonged somewhere. Even if it was to Vigmer's boy.

Confident, with the support of the hundreds of Jutes who watched them from the riverbanks, Einer turned to Finn. The holmground rocked at his steps and water splashed up onto the deck. He crouched down and leant in so close that their noses nearly touched.

'I could accuse you of manslaughter,' Einer said softly, 'and have you branded and outlawed. And with this evidence,' he tapped the Ulfberht sword he had sheathed by his left hip, 'I would win that case.'

Never before had Finn felt so small in Einer's tall shadow, never so powerless. 'Why don't you?'

'Because I don't do this to destroy you, Finn. I just want to honour my father.' That was what Einer said, and yet those words destroyed Finn more than anything.

After everything he had been through. From a poor farmer family, he had become a steersman, and on the chieftain's own ship, no less. At Vigmer's death, he had been gifted that ship; Einer himself had been the one to give it to him. A humble farmer's son, risen to a ship commander; to a candidate for the chieftaincy.

That had been yesterday, and somehow, Finn was there, on the river now, stripped of honour, stripped of freedom. Lesser even than when he had been born. His life was worth less than a cow.

'You robbed him of an Ulfberht blade in the afterlife, Finn,' Einer continued, although he did not need to. 'You have to pay for that so my father can regain his honour, and so when I pass on, I can give him back the blade that rightfully belongs to him.'

Einer rocked back then, as though their talk was done.

'This does nothing to honour your father,' Finn hissed. The tears swelled up despite him, and he stopped trying to keep them back.

Ignoring Finn, Einer addressed the crowd. 'Ready the ships to sail out! We leave as soon as everyone is packed.'

But the crowd did not part, even at their chief's command. They wanted to watch Finn's humiliation. They wanted to watch as he lost the last part of his dignity.

Einer sighed. Still crouched at Finn's side, he removed Finn's helmet and lifted Finn's braided hair in one hand, drawing the Ulfberht blade with the other. The cold metal slid against Finn's neck.

Finn closed his eyes. Heard the rasp of the blade through his hair, felt his head become lighter. His freedom to choose was taken from him: even his hair was no longer allowed to grow. Even his beard would be cut.

The breeze played on his neck, and Finn felt colder than he ever had. Even colder than his first night on board the *Mermaid Scream* when the wind had howled and he had not even had a blanket to warm himself. Tears streamed down his cheeks, and he let them.

This was not where he was supposed to be. This was not the destiny he had expected. It was not the future he wanted. The gods were punishing him, and Finn did not understand why. They had already taken so much.

TYRA

Chapter Fifty-One

EVER SINCE SHE and Svend had gone to the grave, Tyra had wanted to go back. But with all those guests who gathered in Jelling for Siv and Harald's wedding on Winter Night, there hadn't been much opportunity to go back.

'A rainstorm's coming,' Svend said, as they sped through the western forest.

'We can take shelter inside the grave.' Tyra raised a daring eyebrow in Svend's direction.

'Was there really a giant in there, last time?' This wasn't the first time he had asked, but it didn't seem like he didn't believe her either. It was just that he couldn't understand how there could have been a giant inside such a small grave.

'There was,' Tyra said, but she didn't tell him anything else, certainly not who it had been.

Soon the forest drummed with heavy drops of rain. The downpour made Svend and Tyra speed up until they saw the old grave in its clearing. They both went quiet at the sight of it. Svend reached for Tyra's hand, and together they crawled through the last thicket and approached the ancient grave.

The rain fell freely in the clearing, but the storm didn't make them rush to take shelter. Something about the grave demanded full respect and attention.

Tyra thought she heard a faint voice emerge from the gravemound, despite the loud downpour over the high grasses around them. 'Do you hear that?' she asked Svend.

He tensed at her question and squeezed her hand. After a moment of careful consideration, he shook his head. 'There's nothing but rain.'

Tyra was certain she heard something. Maybe not quite voices, but a kind of silent call for her to approach. It wasn't so much something heard as something *felt*, like a warmth in her chest and in her stomach.

The darkness of the grave, like the darkness in the tree, wanted to retrieve her. It had made her come out there, she realised. It hadn't so been her own curiosity, but a summons.

Quiet, like thieves, Tyra and Svend crept closer to the gravemound. Tyra led the way and tried to reassure Svend with the occasional hand-squeeze. She knew what was inside the grave, but Svend didn't. All he knew was that Tyra had disappeared when she had gone inside last time.

Tyra swept the last high grasses away, and ducked to peer into the grave. She half expected to see Siv, like she had that last time.

'There's no one here,' Svend let out in a relieved breath as they went inside. His entire body relaxed, he let go of Tyra's hand, and then he sat down onto the stone bench along one wall of the grave.

But Svend was wrong.

Tyra stared into the dark corner of the grave. There *was* someone inside. Not that Tyra could see anyone—and it wasn't Siv, because she was in Jelling—but Tyra knew there was someone there. The silence of the darkness that seeped out of the grave told her. A presence was there, inside, with them.

'We aren't alone,' she said. 'There is someone in here.' She smiled wickedly to Svend, ready to really impress. 'And I'll bet the full length of my life-thread that I can name them.'

'I'll take that bet,' answered a coarse voice from the darkest end of the passage.

Tyra's heartbeat caught in her throat. She had said it for fun, to impress Svend and tease him with how much she knew about the nine worlds, but there really was someone inside, and her bet had been taken, and now she was bound to her tongue.

Tyra gulped down her fears, and took one deep breath to calm herself, like Hilda had once taught her. 'What will you offer if I win?' she asked into the jotun grave.

Someone sighed and then a second voice, deeper and scarier than the first, spoke. 'We don't have time.'

'Do you know how long it's been since I was offered a wager?' said the first voice.

Tyra heard another sigh.

Neither of the two beings revealed themselves. The grave remained as empty as when they had first entered, and yet she had not imagined the voices. Svend sat half petrified at the edge of the grave. His sight was fastened on the stone wall at the dead end of the passage.

'What do you want if you win, short-lived?' asked the coarse voice that had spoken first.

To show these people—whoever they were—that she wasn't scared, Tyra took a step forward. She wondered what Siv would have wanted. 'A favour.'

'A favour,' the voice acknowledged, 'against your life-thread.'

Svend grabbed Tyra's sleeve. His face had turned pale like goat cheese. He threw his head urgently at the doorway, and the pouring rain outside.

Tyra shook her head. 'I'm bound by my word,' she said.

Svend urged her to forget about it and leave, but he knew as well as her that they couldn't. It wasn't exactly as if whoever was hiding in the dark would allow them to, either.

'We're King Harald's children,' Svend hurried to say, so as to make it clear that if Tyra or him disappeared, they would be missed, and there would be retaliation.

The two voices said nothing in response. Tyra prised Svend's fingers off her sleeve and smiled reassuringly to him, like Siv had smiled to her so many times. Svend's desperation settled, and Tyra redirected her gaze to the dark of the passage grave where she supposed the owners of the two voices watched her.

'Are you here to see...?' she glanced at Svend. She couldn't say Siv's current name, or he would know who Siv really was, and it wasn't Tyra's place to tell him about Siv and what she could do. She supposed the name Siv didn't mean much this far south, either. There had been another name. The giant down in the passage grave, Siv's father, he had called her something else. '...Glumbruck,' Tyra recalled. 'Is that why you're here?' she fearlessly asked. 'Because of Glumbruck?'

'No questions,' grunted the coarse voice that had taken the bet. 'Give us a name.'

The other person was so silent that Tyra was almost certain he held his breath, and that probably meant he knew who Glumbruck was.

It wasn't Siv's father. His voice had felt like the earth, but these voices didn't. The first felt sort of *rocky*, and the second almost like fire. Tyra didn't know many jotnar names, and she supposed they were jotnar, like Siv, since they came through this grave. In fact, apart from Siv's name, Tyra knew only one other jotun name. 'You're Buntrugg,' she said.

'You mention dangerous names as if the owners were friends,' said the dark voice that reminded her of fire. His tone was deeper and scarier than Siv's father's voice had been. It made Tyra shake all the way through to her bones.

But his response told her that she had guessed right; had she been wrong he would have said so. 'I'm right, aren't I?' she pressed.

'So that's your name,' said the voice who had taken the bet. He chewed on it. 'Buntrugg.'

'I win,' Tyra hurried to say, eager to finish the bet. 'You owe me a favour.'

The coarse voice laughed. 'Nice try, short-lived, but that's one name, and there are two of us.'

Tyra thought long and hard about a way to escape this. She hadn't intended to give up her life for a stupid wager, but she had said the words aloud and her wager had been taken, so she couldn't back out. Somehow, she had to find a way to win, though she didn't know any more jotnar names. Just the ones from the stories, and she didn't think the man who had taken her wager was a famous jotun like that, or he wouldn't have dared to take the bet.

'No guesses?'

Tyra went through the little information she had. The man had taken the wager right away, so he was fond of gambles, but many people were, and that wasn't a very good clue.

The voiceless whispers of the darkness drew Tyra's concentration to a faint knock against stone—so subtle that she might have missed it, had the voiceless darkness not grabbed her attention and drawn her in. Stone against stone, over and over like a heartbeat.

An old story swelled up in her mind at that thought. A story of a being who had loved a wager; the famous dwarf Alvis who had taken one wager too many and had been turned into stone for his greed.

'You're stone,' Tyra said aloud. His voice, too, was coarse like that of a rock. 'You're Alvis' kinsman.' Her voice shook as she said the words, and she just knew that it couldn't be the right answer, but she had no other guesses, none more precise, and her father had always said that a bad guess was better than no guess. Siv's brother, Buntrugg, had to be a jotun, so maybe at least guessing that the other man was a dwarf would be enough to save her from trouble.

Deep, loud laughter rang out of the passage grave. Not the same grating laughter as before; it was smoky, almost burnt, like that of a large man who had sat too many nights by the fire.

The other man grumbled.

'She has you cornered, stone kinsman of Alvis,' said Buntrugg when he had controlled his humour. 'Better give her what you promised.'

'At least I know *your* name now,' the dwarf grumbled. 'Very well, short-lived. Tell me what the favour is.'

Tyra's luck was good, exactly as her mother had used to tell her. To win a bet against a dwarf—and to have him admit it, too—was no easy matter.

'I think I'll save the favour for another time,' Tyra said.

'So be it,' the dwarf answered, but he didn't reveal his face, and neither did Buntrugg.

'I have guessed your names and lineages, so you can reveal yourselves now.' Tyra glared at the dark end of the passage grave. She was curious as to how Buntrugg looked. Siv had wanted to introduce Tyra to him. Now she had introduced *herself* to him instead. Well, she hadn't exactly told him her name, but she had shown him that she knew his.

Neither Buntrugg nor the dwarf revealed themselves to her and Svend, though, and Tyra wondered what Siv might have done in here place—and then she knew how to act. Calmly, as if she had all the time in the nine worlds, Tyra sat on the stone bench next to Svend and stared into the dark of the cave where she thought their faces would be, and pretended that she *could* see them.

'Can you see me?' asked the coarse voice of the dwarf, exactly as she had hoped he would.

Again, Buntrugg sighed. Between the two of them, Buntrugg was obviously the smarter. Tyra wondered if that was how it felt for Siv to travel with her, because she didn't know as much about the nine worlds as Siv. At least, she didn't *yet*, but someday she intended to know everything.

'You're not like other short-lived I've met,' Buntrugg's deep, fearsome voice announced. 'Who are you?'

A face appeared on the bench next to Tyra. Green eyes shone beneath dark bushy eyebrows, half hidden behind long dark hair that matched his skin. Had Tyra not met Siv's father, she never would have guessed that the man who sat next to her was Siv's brother. They looked nothing alike, though their way of speaking felt somewhat similar. She wondered if this was how Siv really looked. She knew that Siv could change her appearance. Her nose had changed shape since they had left Ash-hill, and her jaw had changed a little too.

Behind Buntrugg appeared the dwarf's face, outlined by a sharp jawline that looked as if it had been cut straight out of rock—which of course it must have been, many centuries ago.

The dwarf and Buntrugg were both almost as tall as Tyra, but they were grown men.

'Dwarfs,' Svend breathed. Buntrugg matched his stare and Svend ducked behind Tyra.

Tyra knew better. Buntrugg was a jotun. He had to be, if he was Siv's brother. Besides the men's proportions were different: Buntrugg had longer legs and he was slender to look upon. He also felt different, a lot like Siv, and the dwarf didn't feel anything like that.

'How do you know Glumbruck?' Buntrugg's voice made the passage grave tremble of terror.

'I'm her daughter,' Tyra responded, unafraid.

'I thought you said you were some King's children,' said the dwarf and narrowed his eyes at Svend who sat further out towards the exit.

'We are,' Tyra responded before Svend could say anything. 'But I'm also Glumbruck's daughter.'

Buntrugg sniffed the air, as his father had when Tyra and Siv had gone through the passageway and into the snowy landscape. 'You aren't her daughter.'

'Not by blood,' Tyra specified and she watched him as he sniffed the air again, exactly like his father had done. Almost as if he could smell who she was. 'How else could I know her name? And yours?'

A third time, he sniffed the air and narrowed his eyes at her. 'For you, there is a way.' He watched her as if he expected her to say something then, but Tyra didn't know what he wanted her to say. Then he continued, 'But you speak the truth, daughter of Glumbruck.'

His voice soothed Tyra, like Siv's voice often did, and she felt strangely safe with him, despite knowing that he was a jotun.

Buntrugg leant forward to stare at Svend. 'You can't be Einer.'

Unlike her, Svend was *terrified* of Buntrugg and the dwarf. He cowered from them, his eyes were fixed on their feet.

'Einer isn't with us anymore,' Tyra hurried to answer.

Buntrugg enrobed himself in his cloak so only the top of his head with his furrowed brows and his piercing eyes was visible. 'Tell Glumbruck that I look forward to our next meeting.'

With those words, he rose from the bench and walked past Svend and Tyra into the rain. The dwarf hurried after him and then took the lead through the high grasses.

Outside of the grave Buntrugg stopped and turned back to Tyra and Svend. 'You two would be wise to stay away from this grave,' he warned in a voice that burned itself straight into Tyra's heart as Siv's words sometimes did. He pulled his hood over his dark hair, and then Tyra couldn't see him anymore, although the high grasses moved where he walked.

Svend sighed loudly with relief. 'I thought they were going to claim our lives.'

'Me too.' Tyra rested her head against the stone wall. 'I'll never, ever, gamble again.'

'How did you know their names?' Svend asked in a whispered voice.

'I know many names,' she said and hoped she sounded as mysterious as Siv and Buntrugg and other giants.

She looked back to the dead end of the dark passage, and she could almost see the darkness emerge from it. The same darkness as the one inside the ash-tree where Siv had hidden her away during the fight. She could hear it whisper to her, call her closer.

Had it not helped her and given her the last clue, Tyra would have been forced to give up her life to the dwarf. The grave had saved her. Darkness had saved her. A second time. And Tyra knew there would be a price to pay.

SIGISMUND

Chapter Fifty-Two

'THE PLAN WAS to strike quickly and retreat,' Sigismund argued, as he had so many times already. 'We don't have the numbers for a siege.'

Once again, they arranged the warriors on the hnefatafl board, in long rows, to show how many berserkers and how many regular warriors were available.

Old Aslak stroked his long white beard and smiled at yet another easy success. The ship commanders had risen from their seats and were bent in over the gameboard, even Thora and Osvif, who both hated the game.

Every single ship commander had a different idea as to how they ought to attack Magadoborg, yet none of them had succeeded in defeating old Aslak who was a master at tafl.

'They won't attack us on their own,' Osvif said, and he was right. 'They have no reason to send anyone after us. They can just stay safe behind their walls and wait for us to run out of food. We need to provoke them to attack.' His deep voice and thick red beard gave his words more weight.

'We can trick them into thinking we're not much of a threat,' Thora said.

'And that still won't make them attack us,' Osvif argued, pounded his fist on the poor tafl table. 'They have no *reason* to attack us first.'

Everyone's frustrations showed, in the circling conversation and the commanders' grim expressions. More than once, Sigismund and Einer had forced people to return to their seats.

'Sigismund is right. We aren't here to die,' said Einer. He gestured to the board where Aslak faced Lindorm in their fifth game of tafl. 'But it's true that they're never going to open their gates and send out an army to attack us.' As a chieftain ought to, Einer held the true tone of authority and reason. His clothes were humble compared to the strong colours and heavy jewellery most chiefs sported, except for the gold bracteate, yet even in plain clothes, no one could possibly doubt that he was a chieftain. The job was well suited to him.

Einer reached in over Lindorm's head and took one of Aslak's green warriors and one of Lindorm's red warriors. In the midst of old Aslak's set-up, he planted the bright red warrior. 'We need to infiltrate them.'

The ship commanders fell silent, their eyes searching the tafl table for new possibilities and solutions.

'How?' Thora eventually asked.

Einer smiled up at her. 'That's the problem.'

'We send our berserkers in first.' Lindorm grabbed the five tallest red stones and marched them straight up to Aslak's set-up in the middle of the oak board. 'During the night, our berserkers crawl up over the city walls and open the doors for us.'

'Too risky,' Einer decreed. 'As soon as anyone from Magadoborg sees our ships approach, they'll be on high alert. No one will make it across the wall, and we aren't here to die,' he repeated.

'We disguise ourselves like Chief Frode did when he spread the false rumours of his own death,' Lindorm continued.

Suddenly, they were full of good ideas. 'Dock far enough away from the city, pretend to be one of theirs and walk straight in.'

'It's the best we have so far,' Sigismund agreed. 'But realistically we can't disguise hundreds of warriors as southern farmers. Maybe a dozen, if we're lucky.'

'Good, we can work with this.' With that simple praise from Einer, the ship commanders beamed.

'Who has been to Magadoborg before?' Sigismund asked.

Osvif, Lindorm, and one of the other ship commanders from Odin's-gorge indicated that they had been there.

'How many people do we need inside to open one of the gates?'

The three men sighed and looked at each other to agree on an answer. 'I'd say thirty, for a chance,' Osvif said.

'More,' Lindorm added. 'They don't have that many guards by the gates, but they can quickly call upon more.'

'Fifty warriors ready to die for the cause?' Einer estimated.

All three men nodded their agreements.

'That's more than we can hide in the small crowds,' Thora stated.

'Refugees,' said a hoarse voice, and into the tent came Hilda, with the cold wind howling around her, as it always did. The blood had long dried into her cheeks, and the iron chain in her right hand clinked and floated around her legs.

'Don't attack Magadoborg,' she said. 'Attack the surrounding villages. We can hide among the refugees. As long as the ships are far enough away so the southerners don't suspect anything.'

She shrugged at them, as if to say that it was the plainest of ideas and that she really did not understand how they had not thought of it for themselves.

For a moment, she turned her burning ember eyes on each of them, and although Sigismund knew that she could hardly see, she ended on Einer's direction, as if she knew exactly where he was standing. 'The wind has turned in our favour. We need to leave.'

DARKNESS

'BLOOD-BROTHERS.' LOKI tasted the word on his slim lips.

Ragnar glanced back the way they had come. Odin's and Loki's steps parted the ankle-high grasses, but Ragnar's own steps left no trail through the frosty grass, although his trousers were wet from melted frost. At Ragnarok, too, no one had noticed him, until the wolf had arrived.

'We're here,' Odin whispered.

The tall woods dispersed to reveal an oat field at the edge of the Darkness. The crops were bright yellow, not unlike rye fields. each straw grew perfect.

Odin whistled and out of the forest behind him came his wolves. Their tongues hung out wide in exhaustion and their fur was wet with sweat. On command, they fell in on either side of Odin, and moved into the field with him. Loki fell in behind and Ragnar trailed after them, watching the ground for adders. His hands hurt from holding the distaff in such a tight grip, but he was on edge, worried at each step that something would burst at him out of the Darkness.

The birdsong was gone, Ragnar realised. On the plains and in the forest, birds had been singing, but here on the field, there was only a breeze, ruffling the oats.

Odin walked out of the field, onto a lawn. The wolves snuck after him, Loki followed out of the field in the Alfather's exact footsteps. Ragnar was careful where he stepped, until he stood with both feet on the short grass.

Out of the Darkness came a house built of darkly coloured wood. Runes were carved in a long line on either side of the door, into which a flying serpent had been engraved. Ragnar approached the house and touched a hand to the dark wood. It was sticky. as if soaked in tar, but a stench of iron clung to it, and when Ragnar pulled his hand away, it was red with blood, like the grass at Ragnarok.

'Is this where she lives?' Loki heaved. 'The veulve?'

The Alfather stopped in front of the door and raised a hand to knock. Before his knuckles touched the blooded wood, the door was flung open. Beyond lay a room hidden in shadows.

A woman's deep voice reached out of the dark house. 'Finally we meet, Loki,' she croaked.

The Alfather took a cautious step into the dark house and Loki followed, but the two wolves stayed outside, growling softly at whoever, or whatever, was inside. Swallowing his fears, Ragnar also stepped over the threshold, into the house.

'I know why you're here,' the woman said, as the three of them approached. The fireplace in the middle of the room suddenly burst into flames. It lit the muddy feet of the woman who stood on the other side of the fire.

Her red hair reached her hips and had been braided over and over into larger and larger braids. Her clothes hung elegantly from her shoulders and it seemed as if she had wrapped herself in one long piece of dark green fabric. Her arms bore no rings, her ankles were free too, and her eyes were dark and dotted with stars and seemed to pierce through the nine worlds, seeing all there was.

'I've been waiting,' she said. 'I've been preparing.' Her lips were charred and barely moved as she spoke, but then they twisted into a broad smile that sent a chill through Ragnar.

The entire house made him uneasy. It was empty. No tables, no chairs, not even a sleeping bench. The walls were blooded, the same as outside, and the beech floor was dotted with blood too.

Two dead ravens lay on the floor behind the veulve. Their black eyes were wide open, and their feathers were in disarray.

'You've caught two ravens,' Loki muttered. 'How did you…?'

'She knows everything,' Odin whispered.

The veulve knows all, Ragnar recited in his head, *not even gods can change the truths she knows*. She did not look anything like what he had imagined the most powerful runemistress in the nine worlds would look like. He had always imagined the veulve and great fortune-seer to be an old lady, wrinkled and worn, or maybe a burnt corpse, but although her voice sounded worn, she did not look it.

Odin and Loki both stared at the two ravens.

'I asked the wind for help, and then it blew. And these two fell onto my field as if they knew.' The veulve seemed to look at no one as she spoke, only stared ahead, at the air between Odin and Loki, where Ragnar stood.

Ragnar jerked around to see if there was something behind him, but he could not see anything worth noting. There was just the veulve's bare house, and beyond that, the Darkness.

It almost seemed as if the veulve watched *him*.

HILDA

Chapter Fifty-Three

THE NEARBY WARRIORS had spotted Hilda, and their fylgjur made it obvious they wanted to talk to her. These days everyone demanded her presence. At Tings and when the ship commanders met, Hilda was invited to have a say. They listened to her, though she didn't own a ship.

'You're coming?' a warrior asked. He almost seemed scared to address Hilda, hesitant to approach, but he did. His small bear of a fylgja stayed at a respectful distance. It feared her, Hilda realised. As did the man.

'I'm not coming. The gods have different plans for me,' she said. Einer had offered her a spot as a refugee berserker, knowing what being on the front lines meant to her, and though she was glad to be asked, Hilda had turned it down.

The warrior was wary of her, his bear was too, but he didn't leave.

'What do you want?' she asked, eventually.

'I have questions,' he said in a hushed voice.

'Questions?' Hilda crouched to pet her uneasy snow fox.

'You know about the gods,' he said. 'About the afterlife.'

Hilda nodded. Her eyes were sore, and began to sting. They blazed hot like a fire. The pain bit into her core, but Hilda didn't blood her eyes. In the fight, she would have to slash up her eyebrows again, so she could focus. That drained a lot of blood. Up until the fight she couldn't waste any blood.

She groaned to supress the pain. It made her dizzy. She sat down on the grassy ground and continued to pet the fox to focus on something other than the pain. The fox didn't want to be petted, wriggled out of her grip, but she tugged on the chain and held it close.

The man and his bear watched Hilda. He took a tentative step forward, but then thought better of it and stepped back again.

'Ask your questions,' she ordered, eager to think of other things than the bite of fire in her eyes.

He sat down across from her.

'I like fighting, but I'm quite a good fisher too.' He whispered it like a secret. 'With spear, more so than with nets. Lured and caught a porpoise last summer,' he boasted.

Hilda just wanted him to get to the point. Her snow fox calmed at her constant touch. But its body shook with energy.

'The stories of Valhalla are all fighting and eating. Isn't there time for other things too?' the man finally asked.

'Of course. Why wouldn't there be? It's just another life.'

'Another life?' He clearly hadn't thought about it like that. 'So, people age in the afterlife? I can die again?'

So many useless questions.

'If you die, the valkyries will wake you up.'

'On Odin's battlefield, but what about the people in Helheim? The valkyries don't wake them.'

'If you die in battle, you won't go to Helheim.' Worrying about useless things served no purpose. The Alfather had said something similar in his high speech.

'Tak,' said the man, and left.

His bear puffed with relief. All the fylgjur were uneasy around Hilda and her snow fox. They knew she could see them. Just by glancing at someone's fylgja, she knew more about them than their closest friends. Knew who they were, all the way into their core.

Einer's white bear was the only fylgja that kept calm around Hilda. *A white bear will lie in a lake of blood,* the Runes reminded her, as they did lately, whenever she thought of Einer. As if they wanted her to know that his destined time was up. She knew they didn't like her joining the warriors and the battle— she knew she needed to deliver the axe to the gods—but the Runes had agreed to let her fight at Magadoborg. Afterwards, she would leave for Asgard to deliver the god-worthy axe.

Someone else approached. A cow for a fylgja, not quite as scared of Hilda as the bear had been.

'Can I ask you something?' The shieldmaiden the cow belonged to had a deep voice, almost like a man's. Her shoulders made her look like a man too. 'They gave me these.' She held a hand out.

It seemed like such a simple thing to look into someone's hand and see what they held, but Hilda no longer could. Hilda tilted her head and looked up at the shieldmaiden. 'What did they give you?'

'Fury caps. For when we go berserk.'

'Take them a few moments before you attack.'

'I know how to take them,' the shieldmaiden responded. 'But I've never been in a berserker frenzy before. Not in battle.'

'It'll give you clarity,' Hilda assured, though she had never taken fury caps either. She hadn't been in as many battles as this shieldmaiden either. Not yet, anyways.

'What if I take them, and die in the berserker frenzy?'

The shieldmaiden didn't elaborate and clearly expected an answer, though Hilda had no idea what it was she wanted to hear. 'Then what?'

'Will I always be in a berserker frenzy in the afterlife?'

'The effects of the caps wear off.'

'Even in the afterlife?'

'Ja.'

It sounded like Hilda's answer came as a surprise. 'I always thought you live out the afterlife in the state you died,' said the cow shieldmaiden. 'Never age or change from your moment of death.'

'Why?'

'In the afterlife we just have to fight, over and over. Besides, the gods don't age.'

'Because of the golden apples,' Hilda specified. 'You think they give out gold apples every morning in Valhalla and Helheim so you can always be young and beautiful? Your gods must be different from mine, then,' she joked.

'The effects will wear off?' the shieldmaiden pressed.

'Ja,' Hilda answered again, bored with this shieldmaiden's incomprehension. Her question was not so different from that of the warrior from earlier. Both shared a lack of faith in the possibilities of the life that came after this one.

Her answers must have pleased, for the shieldmaiden thanked Hilda and walked off. Her fylgja was more content than before. At ease, almost, with the prospect of dying a berserker death.

Hilda noticed the tension in the crowd. All of them were volunteers, but they weren't the berserkers Hilda had expected them to be. She had looked to see fylgjur like wolves and bears following berserkers, but this crowd was different. A few were indeed wolves and bears, but most weren't. There were two deer, a hare, and quite a lot of birds too. There was even a seal, and Thora's beaver, of course. Not the usual predators who charged first in battles.

Many would pass on with this mission, as the Runes had warned her. They would fight, wild like berserkers, to open the gates. What a way to pass on: to die together, and knowing that their death would save all those who survived. That was the greatest honour of all.

For Thora, it was different. She was pregnant. Her bump had begun to show. Few women showed so early on. Her fylgja wasn't alone anymore either. A bird waddled around next to Thora's beaver; it looked like a seagull.

As if her fylgja had told Thora that Hilda was watching her, she approached with her beaver. The seagull took flight. Sigismund and his wolf came too. 'Hilda, Einer told me you aren't coming,' Thora said, and not like an insult, but with curiosity.

'He only offered to be kind. My hair is the wrong colour to pass for a southerner,' Hilda said. Her burning eyes wouldn't help either.

The seagull flapped down to sit next to Thora's beaver, who kept watching Hilda, reluctant to approach her, though it never had been before.

'What's your question, Thora?'

For a moment, no one said anything.

'I don't have anything to ask, Hilda.' Thora's tone held a hint of discomfort.

'You do. Your beaver does.'

'What?'

'Your fylgja looks like you have a question.'

'You see my fylgja?' For the first time in all the winters they had known each other, Hilda sensed unease in Thora's voice. The same worry of death Hilda had faced the first few times she had seen her snow fox.

'As long as *you* don't see it, there's no danger,' Hilda reassured.

Thora's and Sigismund's burning bodies shared a long gaze.

'What do you want to know, Thora?' Hilda asked.

Thora hesitated to speak. 'Will I always be pregnant?'

'What do you mean?' The hesitation and questioning was so unlike the glory-found shieldmaiden, sailor and ship-commander that Hilda knew Thora to be.

'If I pass on—I mean, what happens to pregnant women in the afterlife?'

'They give birth,' Hilda answered, without having to think about it.

Her quick answer made Thora's fylgja relax. 'So, the child will be born. Even in the afterlife?'

'Ja.'

'How do you know?'

'I see it.' The child already had a fylgja. It would be born one way or another. 'Your child will be a great sailor.'

'A sailor? How do you know?'

'It's pretty obvious to see.' With a beaver as a mother and wolf as father. The child would be adventurous. Besides, seagulls travelled far distances, and always over water.

'How do you know all of this, Hilda?'

Hilda shrugged. It all seemed too obvious to her.

'The gods have chosen me.'

BUNTRUGG

Chapter Fifty-Four

ALL NIGHT BAFIR and Buntrugg had walked through Midgard. Their hoods were raised so no short-lived could see them, and the dwarf refused to answer Buntrugg's questions. Every long-lived knew that Midgard had no direct openings to the other worlds, yet Bafir continued to insist that the forge was there.

The idea of being fooled by a dwarf made Buntrugg's muscles clench. 'It isn't wise to test a giant's patience,' he said.

'I've already been turned to stone. Death doesn't scare me.'

'A death at the hand of our forefathers is not as graceful as a being turned to stone.'

The anger in Buntrugg's voice made the dwarf stop in his tracks. He held his hands up to show Buntrugg that he was without a weapon. 'I never said the furnace was in Midgard. But the path to it is,' said Bafir. Slowly he backed away from Buntrugg. 'Calm your ancestors, jotun.'

The dwarf was right to blame it on the forefathers. Their anger continued to mount. Buntrugg took a deep breath and steadied his shaking fists. 'Why are we walking in circles?'

'We aren't. We're nearly there.' The dwarf pointed past the last earthed fields towards a hill. On top of it a gravemound had been built, half hidden in the hill's high grasses.

'A passage grave?' Buntrugg asked. The sight of it almost disappointed him.

'You'll understand once we're there,' said the dwarf.

Together they proceeded along the rocky road, across the earthen fields towards the hill. The night sky thundered above them, and lightning danced. The slope of the hill was steep. The entrance was narrow, like those of most jotun passage graves, but this one was so small that even a dwarf would need to crouch down to enter.

Buntrugg kept a wary eye on Bafir as he approached the grave to examine it. Usually, when he approached a grave, he could sense the passage. It produced a sort of heaviness in his chest, but the feeling here was different.

'This isn't a jotun passage grave,' Buntrugg said and stroked the walls of stone. His fingertips glided over the rocks that had once been smoothened not by touch or tools, but by rivers and ages of lying in dark forests. To his knowledge, ancient jotnar had used axes and other tools to cut their stones.

Bafir looked pleased. 'You think your ancestors were the only ones who could make passages between the worlds?'

'Dwarfs built this?' Buntrugg examined the craft. Dwarfs couldn't have made something like this. The knowledge was not something they had ever possessed, but some of the ancient tales said that svartalvar and jotnar once worked together. Besides, this grave had an old smell of moss that belonged only to the darkest forests of Svartalfheim. 'This isn't dwarf work,' Buntrugg concluded. 'Ancient svartalvar conjured this place.'

As he had often before, Bafir chewed on Buntrugg's name, 'Buntrugg, Buntrugg...' The name could not mean anything to him, for he had been turned to stone long before Buntrugg had been born. 'How can such a young jotun know so much?' Bafir asked in a quiet voice, perhaps in hope that Buntrugg would provide a clue if the question wasn't given in too obvious a manner.

The flattery made Buntrugg smile, but he did not address it. Instead, he reduced his size and urged Bafir to go first into the dark of the grave.

It was strikingly similar to a jotun passage grave, except for the subtle smell of old moss, the cut of the stones and a feeling that grew somewhere within Buntrugg. He had felt it when they had taken the passage into Midgard as well, almost as if something inside the grave called his name. Not a draugar, Buntrugg had dealt with plenty of draugar. This was different.

The dwarf walked to the back wall of the passage. He had picked up a thick branch to use as torch and conjured a flame. 'Someone has been here,' he whispered. 'Not just Lundir's apprentice.' He placed his nose up close to the stone and took a sniff. 'Impossible.'

Buntrugg closed his eyes and focused on the scents inside the grave. The old moss of the svartalvar who had built it, the moist wet rocks and the dusted smell of dwarfs... and then he found it, the same smell Bafir referred to: a short-lived had been there.

Fresh blood splatters covered the back stone. Not today or this week, but within the past moon. Buntrugg placed his nose next to the fresh blood. A short-lived had passed by, or perhaps not. There was a hint of something else.

'I know that smell,' said the dwarf before Buntrugg could attempt a guess. 'Norn blood.'

'A fate-teller?' Buntrugg had never met a norn other than the veulve, and even he thought it strange to never have met one, for he had travelled all throughout the worlds, and apart from the three great nornir who spun fates and the veulve, most were as well travelled as him.

'Not full-blooded. Now we know why the furnace has been opened,' said the dwarf as he blooded his finger. He touched the back wall above the half-fresh blood. 'Ulfberht got a client.'

The passage grave shook and the stone rolled away to reveal a dark passage.

Somehow the passage was darker than any grave Buntrugg had ever passed through, and the forefathers within him stirred at the sight of the Darkness. With cautious steps he approached the deep dark, and sniffed the air. He smelled fire and ice, cool and heat. The nameless whisper of the passage grave was stronger. Buntrugg stepped through and took another sniff, to be certain. 'Your passage grave leaks.'

'Nothing to worry about,' said the dwarf. 'It has always been like this.'

That did not put Buntrugg's mind to ease, and he knew that this was information that he needed to share with Surt when he finished his mission. A leaking passage grave that no one intended to repair could cause problems in the other eight worlds.

Bafir, too, stepped through, with a burning torch in hand. The passage grave began to shake.

The forefathers stirred with unprecedented thirst. They flourished inside Buntrugg, and he failed to make them retreat, and failed to calm them, as he never had before.

The silence of the grave seemed to speak to him as the Ginnungagap at the top of Yggdrasil had. It made the forefathers rise, not with their usual anger, but with a strange worry. Never before had the forefathers presented any emotion other than rage.

'Wait, something's wrong,' Buntrugg shouted. He launched himself towards the narrowing exit. With a loud clunk, the passage grave closed, and Buntrugg's neck snapped backwards. Of a sudden, his mind was light to carry like never before. All the rising confusion inside him from the forefathers' strength disappeared. Their presence was lifted from him.

Buntrugg searched his heart and the deepest corners of his mind for a trace of the forefathers, but they had left him, almost as if the passage grave had locked them outside. Then he heard it: a rush of air, and the rise of a deep dark laughter.

'What is that?' Bafir asked, his voice shaking.

'You hear them?' Buntrugg asked. He feared to see where the voice came from, because partly, he already knew.

The dwarf wielded his burning torch. Long shadows danced around the flame, but somehow, they were more than shadows. They were warriors, equipped for war, muttering the words of war in all the known languages of the nine worlds, and laughing at the thought of victory. Their shadows carried weapons and shields, worn from battle. They were more than mere shadows, and Buntrugg recognised their faces.

A chill travelled down his spine to his heels, at the sight of them. Never had he thought this to be possible, and without the forefathers' usual anger within him, he felt tiny in the face of danger.

'Who are they?' asked the dwarf. His voice was barely audible above the silence of the grave.

The shadow warriors laughed louder at the dwarf's question.

Buntrugg stalled to answer, terrified to break the silence and the shadows' crazed laughter, for he knew well to whom they belonged, and he did not want them to be aware of him, for he had never before had to face them.

'They are my forefathers.'

EINER

Chapter Fifty-Five

ALONE, EINER WALKED to Magadoborg's south gate. With the sun hanging so low, the tall gate cast enormous shadows. Even with a thousand warriors, and with the gates opened by the berserkers inside, Einer was well aware that the fight to come would be a difficult one.

The day's last sunlight hit the spotless helmets of the many guards who watched Einer from atop the huge wall around the city. Their spears and bows were raised and ready to kill.

Einer walked on. He wore no helmet and no armour. His tunic was newly washed, and he had bound his trousers with an embroidered strip of linen. He had trimmed his hair and beard and plucked his eyebrows in preparation for the night's festivities.

The guards fretted and shouted, both to each other and to him, but Einer kept walking. Only when he stood so close that he could see their faces and could count every stone and plank on their tall barricade did he stop up.

The southern guards took their aim and released their arrows.

Iron shot straight towards Einer, but he held his ground. He had calculated his distance well. If one of them could shoot this far, they almost deserved to wound him, but none of them did, and none of their arrows came close. Unafraid of them, Einer calmly observed the city.

The information Osvif and Lingorm had provided spoke truth, although neither of them had seen the Christian city in recent summers. Nothing much appeared to have changed. The city had no more than three large gates: to the south, to the west and to the north. To the east was a closed harbour that connected to the river, but to sail into foreign territory with their precious ships was too dangerous. The city walls were surrounded by a deep canal, so the only passage in and out was through the gates. The southerners had the high ground of their barricade.

'The corpses are ready,' Finn said, approaching from the back.

Somewhere behind those walls, some of Einer's best warriors waited to strike, unless they had been discovered already, but Einer was sure he would have known if the fifty-three berserkers had not succeeded in infiltrating the southern stronghold. Perhaps a few of them would have escaped and found Einer, or the Christians would have bragged in misplaced hope to scare off the hundreds of remaining warriors still outside the gates.

Finn hadn't left. 'I want to fight,' he said.

'I'm sure you do,' Einer responded.

The southern guards sent off a few more arrows, which landed in the grass about six feet in front of Finn and Einer, neither of whom so much as flinched at the southerners' shouts and attacks.

'You have plenty of warriors who would rather carry out the wounded and dead than be on the front lines. Plenty of young inexperienced warriors who will be better off at the back.'

Einer nodded. 'And they will be at the back, where they belong, and so will you, Finn.'

'You need all your best warriors up front,' Finn continued to argue, but Einer had already decided how it would be, and nothing could make him change his mind.

'If you would rather be outlawed, I can grant that wish. You're not a freeman, Finn. No longer a warrior,' Einer reminded him. In truth, Finn did not have the right to speak unless spoken to, but Einer had no intention of punishing Finn for the indiscretion.

The southerners conjured up someone with minimal knowledge of Norse. 'What you want?' the Christian shouted in their tongue. Einer ignored him.

'I'll soon buy my freedom,' Finn hissed. 'I've been gathering silver.' Then he went very quiet, and made it rather obvious that he had not intended to say as much.

'Good,' Einer said in response. 'We'll need a lot of silver to rebuild Ash-hill when we get back.'

As always, Einer's honest comeback made Finn lose his wits.

'You'll have to release me and let me fight then.'

'When you've paid back half your debt, I'll gladly return your father's name to you,' Einer said and turned away from Magadoborg's gate. 'But until then, Finn, you do as I say.'

The southerners shouted after them in poor Norse, but Einer did not even glance back up at them as he left. Finn fell in at his side, already accustomed to his position as a follower. Finn had always been a follower, even if he refused to realise it.

Together they walked away from Magadoborg's south gate, across the bare fields.

At the edge of the fields, the warriors had gathered for the evening's celebrations. Since high day, their pots had sizzled with fish soup, ready to be consumed before they moved into battle formations. Firewood had been piled up in large stacks as tall as funeral pyres. The warriors had installed woollen blankets and furs around the unlit fires.

Finn took his leave, both of Einer and the festivities, and walked off into the early night, to accomplish his chores.

All eyes fell upon Einer when he approached the large pyres, and the chatter died out.

'A few practical things, first,' he said as his mother had used to before his father made the fun to announcements. 'There's midnight fish soup for everyone.' He pointed out the small fires at his back to whoever might not yet have noticed them. 'Remember to take your blankets and bowls with you and pack them *under* deck on the ships. When you go down to put on your gear, take what you can carry down with you. Anything we forget to take with us will be left behind. And cooks—' he found the *Northern Wrath*'s chief of provisions and locked his stare. 'Takka for the feast and remember your pots.'

He moved onto more important matters.

'Shield-walls keep the guards busy while the rest of us go through the houses. No plunder allowed; ravage and kill. Make certain you're seen and leave the weakest alive.' He had given the instructions many times before, but he needed to make certain that the warriors understood and remembered why they were there. It would not be a pretty fight. 'No looting,' he repeated. 'We're here to make them fear us. Remember your rage. Nurture it. Your wrath is sacred.'

A few warriors stood ready with torches and Einer nodded to them before he proceeded. 'Let us light the fires and sing our way into the Winter Nights,' he announced. 'Under the watch of the full moon we will hold our blót! Sacrifices not in goats or pigs, but in southerners.'

The warriors clamoured and yelled and hooted at the thought of their final revenge.

'Most of us will not come out of this alive,' Einer continued. They would be lucky if *any* did. Magadoborg was larger than he had thought. 'But we shall meet and feast together in Valhalla.'

The crowd took his warning seriously. Most of them were not yet ready to die, but they had come this far and there was only one way out with honour.

'Fight until death, and fight again on Odin's battlefield.'

They roared their agreements. Thus, their feast began.

The ship commanders waved Einer over to them. They had saved the honour seat in their midst for him. Aware of what was expected of him, Einer joined them, although his heart yearned to sit among the warriors on his own ship.

To sit with the ship commanders was probably best. His presence might be a burden to the warriors now, since he was their chief, although he wished it would not be. Perhaps when everyone was used to him as being chieftain, they would not shy away from his company. At least Osvif and Thora and Sigismund did not treat him any different. Osvif and Thora were not there. They had both entered Magadoborg as berserkers and might never make it out again. He hoped they both would.

The warriors watched the great pyres catch the first flames with wonder, but Einer watched on with a heavy heart. No old pigs or sheep would be sacrificed to the alvar and goddesses and roasted tonight, as they were meant to be. They had no old stock to offer, and none to feast on. Nor could they afford to drink tonight, on the first of the three Winter Nights, and Einer carried the heavy responsibility on his shoulders. As chief, he was supposed to guarantee these things for the freemen of Ash-hill, and yet he could not.

The unusual lack of festivities would last for a while. The Yule drinking in two full moons' time would be as scarce as these Winter Nights, as would the Midsummer feasts, and he suspected that times would be tough until harvest, likely far beyond then.

Fire clung onto the foot of the pyres and burned itself to the top, and the warriors began to sing so loud that all the southerners in Magadoborg would hear them. They skipped right past the song about the animals they had sacrificed, since there were none, although some loud warriors two pyres inland insisted on singing the one about pigs since "that was what the southerners were." Instead they went straight to the song about winter and, as if called upon, a northern wind began to rise.

Even without a chanter to lead them through the verses, they all remembered the words.

North winds blow through the trembling wood,
On Winter Nights.
Ancestors fall, red from their ash,
All shall change.
Remember those from our childhood,
On Winter Nights.
Thor's clouds rumble with lightning flash,
All shall change.

The full moon peered over the horizon as they sang. Einer scanned the gathered faces, and his eyes stumbled over Hilda, sitting across from Einer with her eyes closed. In a loud rough voice, she sang, and Einer could not help but think that it was she who invited the northern wind.

He rose from where he sat with the ship commanders, and walked around the tall pyre, towards her. 'Hei,' he said to get her attention, and when she saw him, she scooped over to make place for him on her blanket.

'Are you ready for tonight?' he asked to make conversation.

'Not really,' she unexpectedly replied.

Her answer baffled him. 'Why not?'

She pursed her lips, as if she did not know how to answer his question, or if she even ought to answer it. 'I'm beginning to understand why my father chose Helheim.'

Einer stared at her, hoping that she would explain what she meant.

'He wanted to go to Helheim to meet my mother. I bet your mother, too, will want to go to Valhalla to meet your father, when she hears how he passed on,' she said.

'If she's alive,' he answered and hoped it to be true. He had not allowed himself to think much about it, but he had not seen her corpse among the many they had burned. If she were alive, he did not understand why she had not come home to Ash-hill after the battle. 'If she is, she probably already knows that he has died,' he dismissed. 'She knew about Leif.'

Hilda focused down on her hands. Every hint of a smile faded, as it always did when she thought about her dead brother. 'I thought my father had paid someone to ride back to Ash-hill ahead of us.'

Einer shook his head. 'We were eating outside, at high day, when my mother suddenly got very sad. Then she announced that your brother had passed on, before his first holmgang, and that we needed to prepare for his funeral so Ragnar wouldn't need to when you came back.'

Hilda bit her lip. 'Leif isn't in Valhalla, you know,' she said.

'You can't know. Maybe the valkyries chose him anyways. He died close to combat.'

'He died in bed, Einer. The gods weren't even watching.'

He didn't question how she knew.

'My mother is in Helheim too, and my father. If I die in battle I'll be alone in Valhalla.' She was trying to sound matter-of-fact about it. She examined her nails, brushed her blonde hair back and scratched some dried patches of blood on her cheeks. Einer watched her all the while; she was trying to ignore her worries, like she always did, and it was not right.

'Your uncle and aunt are there,' he said to reassure her. 'Jarn, and Gunna, and Ingrid and Astrid and Yrsa, and there's my father, and everyone here will go to Valhalla. You won't be alone. There'll be plenty of people you know.'

'But not my parents,' Hilda completed.

At that, Einer understood what she had meant. Towards Ragnar's end, when his death had been imminent, Hilda had begged him and begged him to stand up and fight and die in battle so he would pass on into Valhalla. At the time, Einer had not thought much about it, but now he understood why she had been so insistent. Hilda wanted to die in battle, but she also wanted to see her family in the afterlife. Her mother had left for Helheim, but then, Hilda had never known her mother. At the very least, she had wanted her father to go to Valhalla, and wait for her to join him. She didn't want to be alone in the afterlife. Ragnar must have known that.

'When the time comes, we'll go together,' Einer said to reassure her.

'I'll go on my own.' As always, Hilda ignored his offer.

Einer smiled. He didn't know what he had expected her to say, but he should have known it would be something like this. They both resigned themselves to the continuous songs about those who had passed on before them. Through the songs Ragnar had created, they spoke the many names of their forefathers and remembered their deeds, but there were no songs about the brave ones who had died this summer.

> Honour the dead,
> Remember their names,
> See their faces,
> And speak of their ways.

Not once did Hilda blood her eyes as they sat there and sang. Her breathing was heavy and her eyes blazed like the fires in front of them.

'Fine,' Hilda said, after they had sung for half the night. She avoided his gaze as she said it, and although Einer searched through their last few conversations, he could not think of a single thing she might be responding to.

'But I have conditions.'

Blankly Einer watched her, and his thoughts raced trying to work out what she was talking about. He could not just ask her, because Hilda clearly expected him to know and she tended to get angry at him if he did not follow along. He nodded to urge her to continue and present her conditions.

'The kids will be mine,' she said very seriously. 'Like Gunna and Jarn.'

Einer's heart skipped a beat at what he hoped she meant, and his mind failed to find any other possibility no matter how much he tried and no matter how unlikely it seemed.

'They won't be chief Einer's children, they'll be Shieldmaiden Hilda's children,' she continued without a hint of amusement. Her harsh stare found his gaze, although he did not think that her fire-like eyes could see him.

Einer's jaw dropped open as he stared at her, and then he melted into a foolish smile and his heart galloped away and tears swelled up in his eyes, because he had long given up any hope that they might ever have this conversation, or that Hilda might even consider his proposal, and yet she had.

'You're a chief, but we'll be equal.' By that, she meant that she would make all the important decisions, and all the unimportant ones too, but Einer didn't mind at all. He had expected as much.

Eagerly he nodded for her to name any other conditions she had, because he would agree to them all.

'If I want to go raid, then I go raid.' She counted the conditions on her fingers. Satisfied with their number, she matched his gaze with her fiery eyes and Einer understood that now it was his time to answer her.

'Fine,' he answered like she had, and smiled to her, only her. No one else mattered. 'Have I told you that I love you?'

'You have,' she said.

'Well I do.'

She halted for a moment and then she nodded. 'I know.'

With slow movements, so as not to startle her, Einer placed his palms on her cheeks, as she had done to him when she had calmed his berserker rage.

Einer had always thought that if anyone other than his mother could love a boy like him with a berserker rage he couldn't control, someone even the gods could not control, then it had to be a strong shieldmaiden like Hilda.

For some reason, his hands on her cheeks, and the warriors'

loud song, made him remember the horse they had sacrificed at her father's funeral. It had known that death was near and it had laid its life in Einer's hands because it had no other choice.

'Hilda, are you certain?'

He had to know that she would not suddenly change her mind, and that this was not some result of her worry about tonight's fight in Magadoborg.

At his question, Hilda leant in, slowly. Right on the lips, she kissed him, exactly as he had always hoped she would, and exactly as he had always thought she never would.

The blood coursed through him when their lips parted.

'I love you, Hilda.'

'You've said that already,' she mumbled, and into his ear she whispered the words he had spent a lifetime longing to hear: 'I've always loved you too, Einer.'

MUSPELDÓTTIR

Chapter Fifty-Six

MUSPELDÓTTIR'S STRENGTH SWELLED with new heat. Her host body had begun to warm. A fire of passion swelled inside. The warmth fed Muspeldóttir's deep fire. It made her regain her lost forces. It made her swell in size and focus. Few fires were fierce like profound love.

One, two, three, four, five, six, seven, eight, nine.

More easily than before she took. Her host's vision was easy to take. Effortlessly she regained her sight, much quicker now than ever before.

With Muspeldóttir's new surge of heat, she felt her brothers' distant presence. The furnace from which she had crawled out was still wide open, somewhere out there.

One, two, three, four, five, six, seven, eight, nine.

All parts of her flaming self felt it. Her brothers' furnace was still open, but they possessed no short-lived bodies; no means of escaping their homeland.

Soon she would melt her way out of here, and anything that came in her way, she would burn at the stake and feed on.

One, two, three, four, five, six, seven, eight, nine.

Soon her brothers would be free like her. Soon they would destroy all of Midgard, and burn all of Odin's followers.

SIV

Chapter Fifty-Seven

THE FOREFATHERS BEGGED to be let loose. Siv allowed them to tingle out from her fingertips, up her arms and neck and down the length of her body, but always she kept them inside, where they could not be seen. At every moment, her fingers were ready to close the forefathers back into her fist.

Despite knowing what waited for her back in Jelling, she did her best to smile and keep the forefathers ready to act.

Bathed in evening light, Jelling's tall gravemound peeked up from behind the last hill and when Siv walked closer, the barricade around Harald's courts appeared too. The Oxen Road turned north and south; sometimes Jelling was easy to spot and other times hidden behind small hills and trees at the edges of the fields.

'My queen, your parents arrived,' a guard shouted down to her when she reached the barricade. He smiled foolishly at the sight of her. A bit of red hair escaped from under his helmet.

'Takka, Thorvald,' she shouted to him, and walked through the gates.

She listened for his heartbeat and that of the other guards. They liked her, she knew, and unlike Harald, she knew all their names. Someday her effort to acknowledge them would ease their decision to stand with her against Harald.

Siv proceeded out towards the longhouse where Tove's parents waited for her. As soon as they saw her, they would know that she was not their daughter, and alert Harald. Their arrival prompted Siv to act quicker than she would have preferred.

She concentrated on her smile to show all the people in town how excited Tove was to see her parents again.

The town was loud with voices and laughter. All the nearby farmers had put on their finest clothes and come to the heart of Jelling to celebrate the nearing of winter and watch the mounting festivities for the last of the three Winter Nights, when the wedding would be held.

The backdoor to the longhouse swung open. Tyra emerged, and caught sight of Siv.

Siv closed the forefathers into her fist.

Tyra rushed to her, agitated. 'They'll know you're not her.' She stared up at Siv with her large doe-eyes.

'They won't,' Siv said, although Tyra was right. 'Stay here.'

She put a reassuring hand on her daughter's shoulder, but it did not work as well as usual.

Tyra looked at Siv's closed fist, with which she kept the forefathers' anger inside. 'You're not going to be yourself, are you?'

Siv did not need to answer, they both knew what she had to do.

'You promised you would always be yourself around me. That you wouldn't do it again.'

'That's why you should stay here,' Siv repeated. She had to solve this, and the only way was with the help of the forefathers. Even if it meant risking her own long life. Even if it meant that she may end up like her uncle, mad with anger and killed by friendly faces he no longer recognised. If there was the slightest chance to save the nine worlds, and to save Tyra, then Siv had no choice. She had to do it.

'You promised.' Tyra was terrified. She was trying to keep from crying and trying to find a way to stop Siv, but they both knew what had to be done, and there was no time to wait.

Siv gave Tyra one last tap on the shoulder.

'Svend is inside,' Tyra begged as Siv began to walk away.

Siv did not respond. All she hoped was that no one inside the hall had heard her exchange with Tyra. All she hoped was that she could keep the forefathers under control so she would not go mad.

Outside the carved door to the longhouse, Siv reached out with her mind to sense the short-lived inside. The foreign ones stood out to her, but they were difficult to separate from each other as she was not yet familiar with them. The easiest short-lived to identify was Harald's impatient heartbeat, and then the excitement of his two sons, Svend and Hakon. Harald's eldest child, Gunhild, and his youngest, Sigrid, were inside too. There were guards and thralls, too, but their smells did not stand out as clearly to Siv.

Last, Siv concentrated on the foreigners. One of them shone with confidence, and she guessed the rapid heartbeat belonged to Tove's father, Mistivoj, whose voice Siv could hear outside. The short-lived whom Siv deemed to be the mother was harsh and confident as well, but not as loud. However, Siv sensed the woman's closed heart and ears; the mother would not readily accept Siv as a substitute for her own daughter.

Two more short-lived were seated at the table as well: Tove's siblings, Siv guessed, for next to their parents they were quiet, though they sounded stubborn, like their mother.

Siv took another deep breath to prepare herself for what was to come. She released the forefathers to test their anger and power, and then locked them away again.

Their bright faces watched her, and although they had once known each other well, Siv could hear on their heartbeats that they were scared of her, and of what they were about to attempt. The smell of moss on them was strong to Siv's sensitive nose, but a short-lived would not notice it, nor would they know what it meant.

'Keep your backs to them at first. Harald needs to introduce me, then you may begin,' she told the three edgy long-lived, and barely had she said it before she pushed open the door.

The conversation inside the longhouse stopped as Siv slammed open the door.

Her sight settled on the long-table were Harald and Tove's family were seated, and she smiled, as she had often seen her own children smile when they had come home after a long journey away and saw their parents.

'There she is. Finally,' Harald exclaimed. The strain of the conversation with Tove's family made him smile awkwardly and his eyes begged for help. His children, too, appeared relieved to see her. Svend and Hakon both looked ready to sneak out of the longhouse after Tyra.

Tove's father wore a deep frown of annoyance at being interrupted in the middle of a serious political discussion. His wife and their two older children were indifferent to Siv's arrival, and she knew why. They probably thought she was a thrall or a paid servant girl Harald had called upon to entertain them while they waited for Tove to arrive.

'What took you so long, Tove?' Harald asked her.

That was it, the name had been mentioned, and the mother and brother and sister met her stare, and Mistivoj frowned deeper, unable to recognise his own daughter. They stared at her in confusion, unable to understand why she was introduced by their daughter's name.

An enchanting song and melody emerged from behind Siv. She took a few steps into the longhouse, to allow the long-lived behind her to be in full view. Anyone who looked her way, would see the alvar at her back, and be enthralled by their dance.

She watched it happen. Svend and Hakon were the first to lose their will to the beautiful dance of the alvar. Young boys were usually the easiest to influence. Young Sigrid was no more than half a heartbeat slower, and only because she had been looking at her feet when the alvar had begun to dance. Her face shone with marvel and wonder at the sight of them. Tove's proud father, and Harald too, were almost as quick to fall into a daze. Gudrun swung along to the beautiful song, and Tove's brother and sister soon lost themselves to the music as well. For a moment, the mother narrowed her eyes, but then she too accepted the wonder before her.

The guards and thralls took the longest, because they had tasks to focus on so their eyes did not immediately fall upon the alvar, but as soon as they saw the alvar, and listened to the foreign words they did not know and yet still understood, they were swaying along to the music with wide smiles on their faces. Smiles that would fade as soon as Siv began her task.

The alvar enchanted the crowd so none of them would remember this moment.

Once again Siv tested her hold on the forefathers. She allowed them to escape up her arm and course through her, and then she closed her fists and locked them away.

'Just like last time,' she told herself, although she had lost herself then, and this was a lot more dangerous. Once she let the forefathers go, they would be in control; and Siv was not certain that she had the strength to capture them and cast them back into the shadow of her heart where she kept them locked away.

She opened her fists, slowly, so the forefathers would not rush out too fast. Up through the hot veins in her arms she allowed them to escape, and into her mind she allowed them to come. They flooded up through her, made the anger inside her rise, and the ancient urges to kill too.

At her back, the alvar continued to dance, and the many people in front of her were too taken by the alvar to notice Siv's changing expressions.

Out they flowed, until her fists were empty of forefathers. Siv gained a certain calm as her mind retreated from her body to allow the forefathers to take over. With the new calm, she subdued the forefathers' anger, whispered soothing words to them and names of old, and when she closed her fists, there were no forefathers inside to lock away; instead, she locked away their retreat, so they were forced to stay with her, in the foreground of her being.

The forefathers emerged from every limb of Siv's body to demand more room. They crawled beneath her skin, desperate to burst out and escape their long and tiresome afterlife.

The longhouse darkened in the presence of the forefathers, and the contented smiles of those enchanted by the alvar faded. Even without a physical presence, the forefathers dampened every light.

Siv fought her way back to the surface of her own mind. Over and over, she mumbled the old names of the forefathers she had once known, to remind them that they were inside *her* body and under *her* control. She named her uncle and grandparents and her grandparents' parents and every other forefather she knew. With their names she forced herself to the surface. She allowed the old forces to reach out of her body and lean over Tove's family. Like long shadows of their past glory, the forefathers shrouded everyone in the longhouse. They whispered to be let inside short-lived bodies and take over.

Their whispers were loud inside Siv, for through her they gained a voice. With their force and insistence and centuries of knowledge and control, she spoke for them. 'I am Tove,' she said, and her voice resonated in the forefathers' whispers around the longhouse.

Her control over them, her knowledge of their names, made them forget their own whispers, and repeat hers instead. They gave her words gain force and they fuelled her insistence with their ancient knowledge of the runes.

'I am your daughter,' Siv said to Mistivoj, and to his wife.

'I am your sister,' she said to Tove's brother and sister, whose names she did not yet know. Her words were echoed by the forefathers and her commands give force by millennia of anger and frustrations. 'You recognise me from home,' she continued. 'You've known me all my life.'

The forefathers found strength in the new purpose Siv had given them. Siv struggled to keep her fists closed and her control over the forefathers. They tugged at the very core of her being.

The guards provided easy targets for the forefathers. Their attachment to the real Tove was not great. Although they had known her, none of them had been friends with her, or been anything more than watchful shadows in the back of her father's hall. Soon enough their faces became peaceful as they accepted the truth that the forefathers whispered into their minds.

Many of the others also gave into the forefathers' whispers and Siv's commands. Svend's and Hakon's smiles returned, as did Sigrid's and Gudrun's. Even Harald once again drooled over the alvar's beautiful dance.

Tove's younger siblings needed more convincing, but their strain too began to ease.

'I am Tove,' Siv repeated to remind the forefathers of the purpose she had given them.

She struggled as their shadows leaned out of her body. The ancient forces threatened to tear her body apart. Under her skin, the forefathers gnawed at her veins and attempted to bite themselves free, should Siv allow them half a heartbeat of opportunity.

Tove's family held onto the memory of her for much longer than Siv had hoped. She did not know how long she could keep the forefathers under control, and convince them not to kill. Already, she tasted blood in her mouth, and her head pounded with the thought of murder.

'I am Tove Mistivojudóttir,' Siv shouted, to shut out the forefathers' demands from her own mind, and to keep them in check. 'Protector of Slavs, and daughter to Mistivoj, the leader of the Obotrites. You recognise me now.'

The forefathers whispered her words furiously. Their voices came so loud and so fast, that had Siv not said the words first, she would not have known what they said at all.

Her short fingernails dug into her palms and her precious blood trickled out. The forefathers' blood-lust worsened.

'You know me,' Siv yelled. The forefathers echoed her words. 'Say my name.'

'Tove,' said Tove's father, and brother, and sister, and Harald and Svend and Hakon and Sigrid and Gudrun, and all the guards and thralls. All of them said her new name, and all of them, knew in their hearts that Siv was Tove; the same Tove most of them had known since birth. She listened to their hearts beat with the truth. All of them accepted her new identity. All but one.

Tove's mother clutched onto the memory of her real daughter. Her expression was strained. Her yellow teeth were clamped together. The veins popped out at her temples and at her neck, and her deep dark brows wrinkled her forehead. Her eyes did not blink, consumed by the alvar dance, and tears of exhaustion rolled down her cheeks.

'I am Tove,' Siv said again, and the long shadows of the forefathers whispered and whispered the words around Tove's mother. Her face turned red from the effort of holding onto the memory of her real daughter.

'I am your daughter.' Siv's palms stung. Her ancient blood dripped onto the wooden floor of Harald's longhouse. The forefathers strained from Siv, so that she could barely hold them.

And then, one of them broke loose.

Siv grabbled after it with her mind, but it evaded her every move. She sensed its shadow floating around Tove's stubborn mother, who refused to let go of her daughter's memory. It stole her attention, and fuelled by Siv's concentration, the lone forefather attacked. It plunged into Tove's mother's very heart.

Her shriek cut through the early night, and all those outside the longhouse must have heard.

Taking the mother's life, the escaped forefather floated along to the next short-lived: Svend.

Siv took a quick breath and focused her mind on the forefather. She opened her fist far enough to reach out after the shadow. She caught him, heaved him into herself and closed her mind off. The forefathers released their hold on everyone, and right there in their midst, Tove's young mother collapsed onto the floor into a lifeless bundle.

Outside, Siv sensed the guards stirring and flocking towards the longhouse. Soon the door behind her would swing open, and by that time, this had to be over.

Siv closed her eyes and forced the forefathers to retreat. They glided down the length of her arms, and despite their fury, they snickered at their final victory. In one last effort, Siv closed her fists and locked the forefathers back in the corner of her heart where she kept them safe.

'Your debt to me is paid,' she said to the dancing alvar at her back.

FINN

Chapter Fifty-Eight

THE *NORTHERN WRATH* creaked. The night was cloudy. Finn struggled to see as far as the fore-ship. Although he squinted, he could not spot the *Wave Crusher* in front, but he felt the jolts of the sailors' oar strokes.

Every rowing bench on board the *Northern Wrath* was filled with dark figures, half dressed, their heads hanging low. From afar, they looked like rowers, although the *Northern Wrath* had no oars in the water. There were no oars on board at all, and the mast had been removed. The yard had been taken elsewhere too, as had the sail and all of the ropes. The ship had been stripped of everything that made it a ship, even the deck had been taken up and used for river traps. Left was only the ship's bare hull and a ballast of stones and corpses.

At a slow pace the ship moved up the river, dragged by the *Wave Crusher*'s strong rowers. A ship as beautiful as this was not made to be towed. No ships were, but least of all the *Northern Wrath*. It had been built by Jutland's best ship-builders, and every plank had been perfect, as if the gods themselves had gifted them. The southerners had ruined it. They had ruined everything.

Finn watched over the corpses like a helmsman bound for Helheim.

Fate was cruel.

At last his dream to serve as a ship commander on Einer's ship had come true, but not in the way that he'd imagined it. He led a crew of corpses, and the stench of them snuck back to the aft and enveloped him. Finn was only there to stand watch over the corpse ship.

Earlier the warriors had attacked the outlying villages around and dragged the dead away, and south of Magadoborg, warriors were celebrating Winter's Night with fires and song. The corpses from the villages were to be assembled around them so it would look like all the Jutes were celebrating, and the southerners would not suspect an attack in the night. Certainly not from the north, when they had built their fires south of the city.

The rowers' strokes were quiet as they sailed under the bridge that crossed the river. Quiet so no guards would notice them. With their mast down, the ships slipped past the low hanging bridge, unnoticed. Most ships were too tall to pass without making themselves heard, but with their masts down, the *Wave Crusher* and the *Northern Wrath* were the perfect height.

The two strands of the river joined again. The night was dark and the song from inland made it clear that they were close to the shore south of Magadoborg, where the warriors were celebrating Winter's Night. Their song rang out like an echo among mountain tops.

Inland, Finn spotted the lit pyres. Warriors were dancing and celebrating, on the first Winter Night, while Finn was on a corpse-infested ship, towed like a cattle barge, and alone.

By law his lineage had been taken from him, so he had no right to celebrate on Winter Nights, because he had no ancestors to celebrate, in the same way that he was not worthy to fight during the battle, as if legally removing his name somehow removed his claim to revenge. Like everyone else, Finn had lost his family back in Ash-hill. His wife had died, his parents had died, and yet among all of these warriors he was the only one who would not be allowed to take revenge, though he had lost more than most.

The ship's course changed as the *Wave Crusher* moved in towards the river bank. The pace slowed. The strokes of the oars grew less frequent, and then stopped.

Finn heard the shuffle of warriors on the other ship. He leapt forward to cast the aft mooring rope. A warrior shouted for him to hurry. Finn cast his rope and rushed out to the fore of the ship, hopping from rowing thwart to rowing thwart, careful to step between the corpses and not miss a step, for fear of tripping below deck.

Before the ship was properly moored, warriors were leaping on board and throwing corpses onto land. least everyone acknowledged that this was an important task and needed to be accomplished quickly, so Finn was not alone in the task of carrying corpses.

Remember their faces,
They smile to me and give me strength.
Remember their voices,
They call for me, as I call for them.
Remember their names,
Those who have left, linger forever.

The warriors sang as they unloaded the dead ballast. Four of them had the audacity to laugh. None of this was funny to Finn, and he did not feel like singing about some glorified past. Scowling at them, he hopped off the *Northern Wrath*.

Two carts had been put out by the riverside. The warriors had already loaded one of them with half-naked southern corpses. Eager to move on, and away from the sad sight of the *Northern*

Wrath's reduced glory, Finn took the cart and began to wheel it inland towards the Winter Night pyres.

'Where do you think you're going?' asked a blond warrior from Odin's-gorge. Since Finn's hair had been shortened, everyone thought they could order him around.

'Chief Einer told me to let you unload,' Finn said, although Einer had said nothing of the sort. He proceeded to roll the cart ahead and ignored the warriors questioning his work.

Unlike him, they would not have to walk the long way around Magadoborg to the north gate while others fought inside the city; they would sail the ships down the river to the north gate. Finn had other things to do.

The cart was heavy to push over the bumpy field and no one arrived to assist Finn when he came close to the pyres. The singing warriors looked at him with disdain, annoyed that he ruined their Winter Night party with the stench of southern corpses.

Many warriors still stomped around the fires, bellowing the words to the old songs, but a few dozen were hammering scraps of the oars from the *Northern Wrath* into the ground by the pyres, timing their hammer blows with the dancers' stomps.

One by one, Finn dragged the corpses off the cart and secured them onto the oar poles around the first pyre. To give the best illusion from far away, he arranged the corpses so some were standing and others sitting.

As his work began, the half a hundred warriors dancing around the first fire, retreated away from the rotten stench to join the circle around the next pyre and continue to sing and celebrate.

All of the fights that had ever come before appeared pointless next to the revenge and glory that would be served and found tonight, on the night when the ancestors watched. Of all the fights Finn had known, this was the one he was most desperate to join, and yet he could not. If he joined the fight, and disobeyed Einer's orders, Finn would be outlawed and no doubt killed by a Jute, or worse; he might be left all alone in these damned southern lands, while the rest of the survivors sailed home to a coast he would never again be allowed to see.

Finn had so much to fight for. His mother had died without ever seeing riches. The cold hands of her corpse had been rough like those of a thrall, like Finn's hands were now, worse than a rower's. His parents had never complained about how little he had given them in return for the many winters they had raised him. They had supported his decision to become a warrior, although it had meant that he was away all summer and could not help around the farm. They worked more than most. Their lands were too scarce to hire help from outside and yet too large for them to manage on their own, especially the last few summers after his father had broken his ankle.

Finn ought to have bought them a thrall, or at the very least to have set aside enough money to hire a farm boy for the summers when he was away, but he had bought a sword instead and it was too late to regret. They would never know such luxuries now.

Nor would his wife. Despite her parents' protests, she had married Finn and suffered for her choice. He should have taken better care of her. He ought to have realised that she only nagged him because she loved him, as he had once loved her. Instead, he had taken her presence for granted. When he was gone, she had helped his parents. She had worked twice the shifts and still managed to keep their own household and care for their sheep.

Finn raised another corpse and secured the southern man's tunic over a broken oar, so it would hold him up, and then he pushed his corpse-filled cart along to the next great pyre.

Some of the dancers saw him arrive and stopped the festivities to help Finn raise bodies, and those who did not, formed a long chain and danced around the corpses Finn had put up around the first pyre and then danced back inland towards the next pyre that he had yet to reach.

More warriors assembled to help him, and they worked swiftly, eager to start the fight. Those who did not look forward to the battle, at least looked forward to getting it over with, to returning home and rebuilding their old lives. They seemed to have forgotten that no one waited for them at home.

Abroad, it was easy to forget, but once they returned to Jutland's coast, reality would set in. Nothing could ever be as it had been. For Finn, there was nothing to gain at home. At least not for the first few summers and winters, while he worked to pay off his debt to Einer.

Home in northern Jutland, Finn expected that Einer would make him work harder than anyone else on the building works, and out in the fields too. The rings and coins Finn had gathered would not be enough to buy his freedom for at least another dozen summers, if not two, unless he could convince others to help him buy his freedom. He supposed that the task would be easier back in Jutland, when everyone had fallen back into old habits, and remembered Finn, not for the new length of his hair, but for who he had used to be.

As the work proceeded, many of the warriors moved down to board the ships to sail back down the river, so they could reach Magadoborg's north gates and prepare for the fight.

The warriors who stayed behind sang louder to make up for those who left on the first ships, and every warrior who was left, helped Finn raise the last corpses.

The crowd thinned out as more warriors left onboard the ships, but a group of twenty helpers and healers stayed behind with Finn to feed the fires and together they sung loudest of all so that inside Magadoborg it would sound like hundreds of people singing.

As the snow falls and melts again,
As the river changes course and dries out,
As trees are cut and mountains rise,
Good deeds, remain carved in stone.

THORA

Chapter Fifty-Nine

THE WINTER NIGHT song echoed down the streets of Magadoborg. Thora kept a protective hand on her belly as she hurried down the dusty road towards Magadoborg's north-most gate to take her stance and fight with the other berserkers. Together they would open the gates for the warriors outside.

A door opened down the road. A scared southern face peeped out to assess the situation. His eyes caught her, and Thora picked up her pace. The man addressed her in the southern tongue. Thora caught only one word: *safe*. She shook her head, and did her best to appear really scared, cradling in over herself, as she ran down the road.

The southern man watched her, and when she had passed him by, she heard his door slam shut.

Thora's gaze was focused on the road ahead, and she hoped no one else would ask her anything, not while she was alone. She had not spoken a single word since they had entered Magadoborg. There were others who knew the local tongue, and when they walked in groups during the day time, she could slip away without needing to say a word, but they would attract too much attention if they walked in a group at night, especially on this night.

The southerners were scared. They barricaded themselves inside their small homes, but the loud song from outside the south gate kept them awake, and terrified.

Thora peered ahead to the last corner leading into the small square by the north gate. At the corner of a house she saw Karl, Thorbjörn and Heidi, ready in their places. They greeted her with respectful nods, but Thora pretended never to have seen them, so that if a southerner was watching her, she would not give away their position, for their role was the most important. Among the fifty-three Jute warriors in Magadoborg, those three were the only ones who would not take berserker caps. They needed their full wits in order to charge at the right moment and pry open the north gate.

Thora passed by them as if she had never seen them. With both of her hands resting protectively on her stomach, she strolled across the square towards a road running between the barricade and the first crooked houses. Up that road, at the edge of the square, was where she had to take her position.

Thora's heart beat with worry of being discovered. She hoped that with her confident walk she looked as though she belonged there.

She allowed herself a quick glance to the top of the gate to count the guards. A few of them watched her and she diverted her gaze. She managed to count eight guards, and from having kept watch over the guard shifts these past few days, she knew that there were at least five more that she could not see from this position. On the barricade, further down from the gates, there would be more guards, but other warriors would take care of them. All Thora needed to worry about were the guards directly above the gate, and there were fewer of them than she had feared.

She reached the far side of the square, glanced over her

shoulder to see the positions of the guards behind her and found a good place to sit at the start of the slender road. She let out a heavy breath. Her heartbeat raced around her body, and she rubbed her belly to reassure the baby inside that all would be well.

At least their odds were decent.

Magadoborg's guards had concentrated themselves around the south gate, outside which the pyres had been lit. Exactly as they had hoped.

The loud ring of a song about Ash-hill's ancient ancestors calmed Thora's heart and made her regain her focus. It would be a while before the attack, or at least it might be. She could not be certain how far Ash-hill's warriors were outside of the gates. Their signal would come through song.

She glanced into the square and up the dark roads to spot her fellow warriors, but they were as well hidden as her, and she found no one. A good sign, and yet it made her nervous to sit alone and wait.

The longer Thora listened to the song, the more certain she became that the loud taps were not the sound of a hundred warriors stomping, but that of the back of axes hitting tree trunks. She hoped she was right, because then the warriors outside were close to assuming their positions in the far shadows outside the north gate, and she would not have to wait much longer. She felt exposed with her axe hidden under the skirt of her dress, and with no armour or shield.

For summers and summers, Thora had fought both against northerners and southerners, but during all of those raids when she had fought and gained a good reputation, she had fought with a helmet, armour and shield. This would be her first fight without any of that, and a big part of her feared that it would also be her last.

The rhythm of the song changed.

Three long stomps and then two short ones; the berserker song. Thora reached into the pouch on her belt and dug out the small pieces of dried berserker caps. The bright red and dotted caps rolled around in her palm. They had been given to her with the promise that they would give her enough strength to accomplish her task. There had been no promise of a safe return, and wherever there were berserkers in a fight, no more than half could be expected to make it back at all. Even then, only a third of the survivors recovered from their wounds.

Thora stirred the bright red pieces of caps in her palm, and recalled how she had found her little brother's torn body in the embers of Ash-hill. He had not even reached her to the hips, and yet the southerners had hacked off his arm and killed him.

Blinking back the tears, Thora cast the bright red caps into her mouth, chewed them well, so they would work quicker, and then swallowed them. They had been honeyed; the taste reminded her of summers at home, when little Björn had used to beg their parents to be allowed to sprinkle honey on his flatbread. The memory helped her nurture her wrath. The rage would get her through the night. Their rage would get all of them through, no matter if they died or lived. Their wrath was sacred and well-guarded.

Amongst the loud noise of the berserker song emerged the sound of steps down the road. Startled, Thora glanced over her shoulder, up her road. She recognised Osvif's ragged walk and exhaled.

He crouched down next to her. For a moment, she had thought that he was late, and that she would have to go up on her own, but his sudden appearance allayed her fears. As long as he had taken the berserker caps, everything would be fine.

Before they had entered the city, Osvif had complained about having to take them, but she needed him to enter the craze like her, or they would never be able to overpower the dozen guards on top of the barricade.

Two other warriors had been positioned at the other side of the gate. On both sides, a staircase led to the top. The dozen guards on top were theirs to take: her, Osvif and the two warriors opposite her. Chances were that at least one of them would not survive to the top of the stairs, so, most likely, there would be no more than three of them to overrun a dozen warriors. The guards had full armour on, and spears and axes and arrows. If all four of them did not go into a berserker rage before they mounted those stairs, they would never make it to the top, and they would have no chance of taking out the guards, and then every Jute down in the square would perish.

'Have you eaten the caps?' Thora asked Osvif as he sat down with his back against the barricade.

Osvif showed her his empty pouch and nodded. She showed him hers.

From then on, they waited in silence. Thora's stomach tied itself into a knot. The baby knew that a fight was coming, and her insides stirred with the knowledge.

The berserker song seemed to never ever end, and the red caps had not begun to work. Thora had heard about it before; sometimes they did not work as they were supposed to do. Perhaps they had not been dried properly, or perhaps they had been too honeyed so the effect could not penetrate, or perhaps she was immune to them, somehow. Still she waited as the berserker song mounted and gained pace, and nothing happened, at all.

Thora fiddled through her pouch. Perhaps she simply had not taken all the caps and that was why they were not working, but her hands emerged empty from the pouch and she knew she had chewed everything she had been given, even if that had proved to not be enough.

Next to her, Osvif looked normal as well, or almost. He had darkened his hair to look like a southerner and he looked different without his bright red locks. Even his daughters wouldn't have recognised him. He stared down at his nails. Had Thora not known him, she might have thought that he was calm about this whole thing, but Osvif did not have a habit of cleaning his nails.

The berserker song rang through the town like a distant herd call. Granted, Thora had not often sung the berserker song, but she had not thought it would last this long. At any moment now, it would end, and the berserker caps were still not working.

Her blood pounded loudly within her, and the town seemed to stir with noises. Night birds on the roofs, mice in the town square and up the road; Thora even felt that she could hear the heartbeats of the guards on the walls, and the snoring of the southerners hiding safely inside their houses. They would not be safe for long, and the thought made her chuckle.

The long wait was making her sweat, and her mouth watered. 'Are the caps working for you?' she asked Osvif and for some reason the question made her giggle like a little girl.

Osvif shook his head, and kept his eyes fixed on his clean nails, and he too giggled, like her.

Thora did her best to try and stop, but holding it in was difficult, and the more she thought about it, the funnier it became. And Osvif laughed in a funny way, and he drooled too, so his saliva dripped down onto his stomach, which made her giggle even more.

Determined to focus herself, Thora brought her axe forth, so she held it in a hand, still hidden in her skirts, not to rouse suspicion if someone walked by and saw them sitting there.

Sweat dripped from her eyebrows and down onto the skirt of her dress. With her back hand, she dried the sweat off her forehead. There was so much of it, and her tongue swam in water too, she almost drooled like Osvif.

Osvif began to cough. Alert, Thora watched the road and the square, worried that a guard might have heard and come look, but only a hungry rat moved, and when her eyes settled on Osvif, she realised that he was not just coughing. He vomited up against the wall. White and red pieces of chewed caps stuck to the stone wall, and the mere sight of it made Thora's stomach turn.

Before she could stop it, she gagged and the sweetened pieces of caps came rushing up. Osvif giggled at her and tapped her on the back as she threw up, but once the caps were all up, the urge stopped, and all that was left was a foul taste in her mouth and the mounting sweat on her forehead.

At least the caps ought to have been in her stomach long enough to give effect, although so far Thora did not feel as if they worked at all, and at any moment now the song would stop and she would need to race ahead and up the stairs to the top of the gate and fight for her life and that of the baby.

She rubbed her stomach and spat to the side to rid herself of the foul taste in her mouth. The spit mounted quickly and she spat again, and she was hot all over her body, and then, as she watched a southern guard crossed the square, slowly almost like a snail, *in that moment*, she felt it. That irresistible urge to dart forward and after him. He walked so slow and he was no match for her, even with his armour.

Determined to stay put as she had been instructed, she pressed her hand hard against the ground and gritted her teeth, and she suddenly understood why berserkers bit into their shields before a battle. Never before had she had so much trouble holding back and waiting.

Her eyes felt as if they were popping out of her head with the need to launch into action, and everywhere she looked, she saw the flames of Ash-hill burning and the corpses of her parents and her little brother. The southerners would not get away with it, not after everything they had done, but there was the music, and the singing and she recalled she had to wait for the berserker song to finish, and stayed put.

She sharpened her ears to hear the song, but she only heard the fabric of her dress rub against the stone wall as she rose to her feet, and then some distant yells. The song had stopped.

Thora leapt out of hiding, axe in hand and ready to slice. She rushed ahead, and the world bumped up and down around her. Her eyes fell on the staircase. She bumbled towards it, and mounted the steps. Somewhere nearby she heard southerners shout, and she roared in response.

Arrows were shot at her, rattling against the wall in front of her. An arrow struck her left arm, thrusting her against the wall. The wound barely hurt, their arrows were soft like wool.

The first southerner appeared before her. He had descended one flight of stairs to reach her and positioned himself on the high ground.

Thora roared, and invincible she ran at him, swinging her axe. She ducked under his blow, as easily as if he was a child, and shouldered him to the edge of the stairs. With a single axe-blow she made him fall over and down, down, below.

The sight of him fall made her giggle anew.

Something bumped into her back. Axe out, she swung around. Osvif ducked under her blow. He pushed her along and together they leapt up the last few steps to the top of the barricade, laughing. Three guards were at them, and another arrow caught in Thora's arm. It made her stumble backwards, close to the edge. Another one hit her, this time in the leg.

Thora grimaced at the blood, and yelled at the southerners. She swung her axe and yelled that they were cowards to shoot arrows at such close range and that they could shoot all they wanted because she would kill them regardless, but everything she yelled came out in loud bear roars.

Her axe tore through the neck of the closest southerner. She ran towards the next one and bumped into his shield so he backed away. Laughing, she ducked down so he stumbled over her little body, and Thora chopped his legs into fine pieces.

Below them, the gates were being opened.

At her back, Osvif was yelling equally incoherently and roaring like a wild animal, which made her laugh. The arrows shot over her head, and when she was finished hacking into the southerner's legs and rose to look at Osvif, she saw that he had arrow wounds across his chest, and his thighs, and still he was roaring and yelling and throwing his axe around. There were two dead southerners at his feet, and he gladly balanced on top of one of the corpses, while a third southerner attacked him.

The southerner's spear pierced Osvif's chest.

Osvif's back hit the short wall of the barricade, and the southerner pushed him. Before Thora could join the fight, Osvif staggered, roared, and fell off the barricade, into the void below.

Thora came flying in towards the fight. With a solid kick to the balls, she made the southerner stagger, and then pushed him off the barricade, after Osvif.

An arrow pierced her thigh, again. Annoyed, Thora looked down at herself and broke off the two arrows in her thigh, and then the two in her left arm too. Then she darted straight towards the archer.

He pissed himself from fear, fumbled with his arrows. Seven large steps to reach him; he loosed one last arrow, which pierced Thora's shoulder.

She growled at him. As he fumbled for his spear, Thora tore the arrow out of her shoulder and planted the southerner's own arrow in his eye.

Her hands were bloody, so was her dress, and the smell of iron made her hungry for more. She cast around herself for the next guard. For another southerner to kill, and roared for them to come forth.

Every last one of them would die.

EINER

Chapter Sixty

A PIERCING BERSERKER cry echoed over the dark fields. A ringing silence followed. If they heard the cries out in the fields, then guards all over in Magadoborg would certainly have heard them too.

Einer glanced to Hilda, who was fiddling with the edge of her shield. She could have been inside with Thora and Osvif and the others, but he was thankful that she was not. If the plan failed and the north gate did not open, then the berserkers would be on their own inside Magadoborg. At least their berserker rage would make their passing easier.

Someone tapped their shield: Magadoborg's gate was opening. The berserkers had accomplished their task. Einer saw it too, tapped his shield and burst through the dark field.

The warriors followed his lead. Hilda's shield knocked against Einer's as they ran, and his father's Ulfberht sword bumped against his thigh. He needed it with him when he passed on, so in the afterlife he could return it to its rightful owner.

None of them yelled or roared as they usually did when they

attacked. The longer they could go unnoticed, the better.

The first arrow flew over the crowd. Another caught in Einer's shield and he heard the whisper of arrows over his head, the grunts of warriors behind him.

The gates creaked open wider. A berserker burst out of it with a bear's roar and began to laugh. Her back was covered in arrows, her shield hand had been chopped off. She stared at it as she laughed and shouldered the gates wider open.

Southern guards hacked out at the berserker as the gates opened. She ducked their blows, laughing all the while. The southerners were already dead with fear. One caught sight of the hundreds of warriors rushing at them and let out a yelp. Einer burst out from the dark, ran the five paces to the bridge and the gates, knocked the southerner's shield out of the way and planted his sword into the man's screaming face. The blood ran down Einer's blade onto his hand as he tore the blade free and looked up to see Hilda had finished off two other southerners with axe blows.

She smiled, showing bloodstained teeth, and together they burst through the gates, into the town. Three southerners charged at them. Jutes leapt past them into the town, shouldering two of the defenders out of the way. Einer smashed into the third with his shield, and Hilda stepped over the man's legs, cut off one arm with her axe and focused on the next southerner. Einer stabbed the soldier through the neck.

Hilda kicked the next southerner on the shield so he fell, stepped onto his shield to pin his axe arm and severed his neck. The blood splashed up her legs. Smiling, she stepped over the southern corpse and they joined the flood of warriors rushing into the town. Einer stayed at Hilda's side.

Smaller fights broke out around the square beyond the gates, and berserkers raged against friends and foes alike. Einer cast around for a fight to join. Hundreds of Jutes ran with them, around them, behind them, ahead of them.

'Blót!' Einer roared.

'*Blót!*' hundreds and hundreds of warriors clamoured. The southerners were their Winter Night sacrifice to the gods.

Broken southern bodies lay in bundles along the walls, fallen from atop the gates. A few berserkers, too. Einer's eyes fell on Osvif. Someday his daughters would take vengeance for him. Hilda and Einer darted off along the walls. The noise of battle was deafening. More defenders would soon arrive through the streets.

Einer glanced over his shoulders. Two dozen warriors from the *Northern Wrath* had found him in the crowd and followed his and Hilda's lead. Most of them had blood down their faces, where they'd slashed open their eyebrows to match Hilda.

'First road, shield formation!' Einer roared to his warriors, and they darted along the street. They followed the outer walls, clearing the path for warriors to follow and ravage one house after another. A woman's scream rang out from a crooked house, where a berserker raged inside.

Einer proceeded warily, scanning every forked road they passed, and then he saw the heels of a southern warrior down a road into the centre of the city. Hilda kept a hand on the outer wall and set after the southerner.

He gestured for his crew to follow. They hugged a wall and peered around the corner, to see two dozen guards forming up around a large house. In their midst, their leader was talking to someone richly dressed. They thought it was a siege, or an attack to take out their leaders, like they had gone after Einer's father down in Hammaborg.

Einer smiled to his warriors, as more Jutes ran up the street behind them. If the southerners concentrated all their efforts around people of influence, that gave Ash-hill an advantage. They could freely ravage the city, instil terror in the townsfolk. The southerners would protect their leaders, while common freemen were torn apart. For weeks, and moons, and winters, and summers, fear of the Norsemen would reign in Magadoborg and every southern city would know the horrors that had transpired there. Every southerner would fear them.

A guard spotted Einer peering around the corner, and yelled. Others turned.

Without hesitation, Einer darted out onto the street with their runemistress and a dozen warriors at his back. Roaring, shield high, he smashed into a man's shield, and kicked him in the groin. The southerner bent over himself, and Einer hacked through his neck. Peered around for the next one. He towered over them all, southerners and northerners.

More Jutes arrived at his back to fight. More southerners came, too, retreating into a shield-wall, which grew deeper.

Ash-hill's warriors feel back into another shield-wall, Einer holding up the upper part, with Hilda holding the shield below his. They waited for the southerners to make the first move. They knew their task: keep the defenders busy, keep them there while others raged through the city.

The southerners backed away towards the large house. They tripped over each other's toes in their haste, and half of them abandoned their shield-wall to turn and run inside.

'Follow!' Einer roared, stepping ahead.

The scared southern guards scrambled into the house, yelling to each other. Einer's warriors played along. They roared and tried to chase the southerners inside. Hacked against the door as it closed. Banged on it, too.

Hilda roared for a godly sacrifice. 'Blót!'

Others did the same. '*Blót! Blót! Blót!*' they yelled, and the blood ran from their eyebrows over their noses and cheeks.

The southerners barricaded themselves inside their house, peering out from wind-holes on the top floor.

'We need to keep filling this street,' Einer told his warriors. 'Keep them busy, and anyone who can, start going through the houses.' He looked around at them and repeated his battle instructions for the hundredth and twentieth time: 'No looting. Only blót and fear.'

'*Blót! Blót! Blót!*'

He looked to Hilda. She waited for him to finish his speech, and as soon as he looked to her, she beckoned for him to follow her. They raced up the street, further into the city. Jutes ran around the town in groups of four and six. Bigger groups concentrated around the buildings where southern guards were cowering.

Hilda and him went alone. Out of all the warriors they were among the most frightening: Einer, tall as a bear, and Hilda, a ruthless shieldmaiden with bloody tears.

Einer moved to the door of a small house and Hilda followed. He kicked the door in.

Someone inside screamed. Hilda entered first, slammed her shield into something to the right of the door: a southerner, hidden in shadows. The man staggered back. Einer followed Hilda in with his shield high and sword ready.

Two men were inside. The one Hilda had struck retreated to stand with an older one behind him. The men were both shivering and backing away.

'Why don't they fight? They're just—' Hilda trailed off, but the shock was evident from her voice.

'I know,' Einer said and lowered his shield. 'I know.' His voice didn't shake but in his heart, he saw all of those farmers and children slaughtered at home. He didn't want to give anyone else that pain. 'It's necessary, Hilda,' he said, as much to convince himself as her.

She let out a ragged breath and nodded. 'I'll get the others.'

It hadn't occurred to Einer that there were others in the house, but of course there had to be women. Hilda was already off searching. Chairs screeched across the floor as she forced them aside.

Warriors howled in the street outside. Berserkers roared. Children screamed and cried.

The two terrified men huddled close together. The younger one made to follow Hilda. Einer took a step ahead and held his sword out, blocking the way. They glanced to him. He shook his head and pointed to a corner of the room. Obediently, they both stepped back.

They shouldn't have to die for this. During a normal raid Einer would hardly have looked at them. They had done nothing wrong. They were not the ones who had attacked Ash-hill, but they were southerners, and they were as innocent as Ash-hill's farmers and children. Their deaths would be felt, and that was all that mattered. At least in their afterlife, they would be together.

Hilda came back pushing a woman and two children in front of her. The youngest was a boy of no more than three. His sister couldn't be older than six. Crying, they ran into the arms of their grandfather, and their mother hurried after them. They were so little.

'Nej,' Einer whispered when he saw the children, and this time his voice *did* break. He brought his sword hand up to rub his beard. He blinked his eyes fast to keep back the tears. 'We can't.'

'We have to,' Hilda said. 'If we don't retaliate, they will attack again, and it will be *our* kids, then.' Her ember eyes rested calmly on Einer, but her hands were shaking. 'The sooner we do this, the sooner we can forget.'

'Hilda,' he said softly. 'We're never going to forget this.'

She cast her head back at the terrified family. Her blood tears had thinned with real ones. She knew he was right, and her voice broke when she spoke again. 'Maybe the kids will run.'

'Maybe.' He hoped that she was right.

Had they been alone, neither Hilda not Einer would have gone through with it. Even standing together, Einer could hardly make himself ready his sword. At least, together, it was easier to remember the stakes. He looked at the little girl. Now was the time for her and her little brother to run for their lives. Now, before Einer had to attack them too.

'For our children,' Hilda said, and then she struck the children's father.

All they could do was make the deaths quick, and they did. In one breath, Einer had sliced the mother's throat, in the next she was dead. Their father died as quickly.

Einer shifted his head slightly to the right, to the door. No more than a slight movement, almost a tic, but the little girl understood. She grabbed her brother's hand and ran. He let them run. At least this way the children had a chance, no matter how slim.

Only the old man was left, and he was sobbing silently. *Leave one alive.* At least they were done. At least the kids had run. Einer's breaths were ragged as he cleaned the blood off his sword. He knew these acts would haunt him in his nightmares.

'We had to,' Einer muttered as he left the house, rubbing the tears off his face. In silent shock Hilda followed him out of the house.

The same chaos as earlier prevailed outside. Screaming southerners, Jutes chasing them, chanting: '*Blót! Blót! Blót!*'

Einer scanned the corpses on the street. The children they had allowed to flee were not among them.

Hilda proceeded up the road to the next house. Einer stared down the road to the big pretty house in which the southern guards had barricaded themselves. Three dozen Jutes mobbed the doors, banged on them, keeping the southern guards penned.

'Let's join them, again,' Einer said. He did not want to experience that again; once was more than enough. 'They'll get the doors open soon. We can fight the warriors. Fight in the shield-wall.' They were both shield-wall warriors; no one would even flinch if they decided to stay there and wait for the door to be breached, for a true fight between warriors to erupt again. It played to their strengths. It was not a cowardly choice.

'We need to do this,' Hilda insisted. She was still crying, but for all the tears, she was stronger and more resolute. 'This is why we're here.' She stared straight ahead. Did not even glance to the side, or start when three warriors burst out from a house to their right.

'Hilda, we don't need to. The shield-wall needs to be manned too.'

'You're a chief, Einer, are you going to let anyone else do this for you?' She was right to call him out. Hilda always knew what needed to be done.

Einer's stare hardened like hers.

DARKNESS

'SHALL WE BEGIN?' asked the veulve, wielding a runic distaff like Ragnar's. Hers was not made of narwhal tusk and metal, but of wood, darkened by blood, like her house.

'Hands,' the veulve said. At her command both Odin and Loki raised their right hands, palms facing up. The veulve brought her distaff out so it faced their open palms and then she said a single word, the name of the warrior's rune: 'Tiwaz.' A gash opened in a straight line along both Odin's and Loki's middle fingers and carved down to their wrists.

Ragnar gulped at her control over the runes. Naming one was enough for her to carve open their palms. She smiled as she watched Odin and Loki reach out for each other's bloody hands, not touching yet.

'The bond that will bind you will have no equal,' the veulve said to begin Odin's and Loki's vows. 'And no end. You will be brothers, more than in lineage. You will be brothers in blood, and where one goes, the other will follow.'

The room went quiet. The fire no longer gave any sound, the

wind no longer touched the house, and all nine worlds seemed to slow and wait for Odin's and Loki's blood promises to be exchanged.

'Naudir,' the veulve said. Her mention of the rune of necessity spun a white thread surge out from the hollow part of her distaff, wrap around Odin's and Loki's bleeding hands, still the width of two fingers apart. 'When I drink, you will drink, and neither shall sit with an empty cup,' the veulve said.

Odin and Loki recited her words, and, as they did, the white thread settled around their hands and bound them to their words.

'Kauna,' the veulve said. The fire surged up high at the mention of its rune. 'When one is warm and the other is not, the heat shall be shared.'

Again, the Alfather and the giant recited her words, and a second thread, bright red like fire, surged out from the veulve's distaff and around their hands, binding their promise.

And in this vein, the veulve called twenty-three runes, and Odin and Loki said their vows, and when there was only one rune left, the shining threads of promises around Odin's and Loki's hands tightened until their bloody palms touched. They clenched each other's hands. The blood on their palms mixed, and the threads shone brighter.

'Odal.' One last time the veulve pointed her distaff to their hands as she named the rune of family; the last rune. 'From this moment on you will be bound together stronger than any family. You will be two parts of one, and never alone.'

A thread as red and dark as blood spun from her distaff and wrapped around their hands. Around and around, until it shielded all the other shinning threads, and Odin's and Loki's hands could no longer be seen.

'No vow shall be greater. No promise of more value, and neither shall ever be alone. You are one and you are two, bound in blood, promised in blood, born in blood.'

The blood-red thread around Odin's and Loki's hands tightened, and giant and god, both clenched their teeth so as not to scream from pain. Ragnar winced at the sight of the sweat on their foreheads and the creases on their faces. The red thread continued to crush their hands together.

Smiling, the veulve stared at their hands, her dark star-plucked eyes wide in anticipation. The red thread could no longer be distinguished from the solid grasp of Odin's and Loki's hands.

Their faces relaxed. The red locks of hair from Loki's temples were drenched from sweat, and Odin heaved for breath. They did not let go of each other. Their hands were red, and thick drops of mixed blood splashed out over the floorboards. The Alfather smiled and watched his new brother with pride gleaming in his single eye. Loki smiled too, and his protruding chin made him look wicked. They both looked wicked; the one-eyed man and his trickster brother.

The new brothers pulled each other in for a hug and slapped each other on the shoulders, acknowledging each other in a new way, now that they were brothers, one and same.

Until this very moment, Ragnar had never understood why their bond was so sacred, but being witness to it; seeing the threads wrap around their hands, binding them to their words, and witnessing the veulve's incantation of runes, made him understand. Exchanging blood to become brothers was more than an act before gods. This exchange between Odin and Loki was an exchange before all the nine worlds. Even death would bind them to their vows.

And Ragnar had provoked it.

'About those ravens.' Odin gave Loki one last squeeze before they parted from their hug.

Loki rounded the fire to the birds. He scooped down, picked up the two ravens and brought them back to lie at Odin's feet. 'I need you to sit down, old man,' he said. 'Hold a hand on each bird, and don't let go until it's done.'

Obediently, Odin touched his hands to the dead birds. Their beaks were half-open and their black eyes were distant. Loki smiled at the Alfather's gesture and crouched down by the ravens. He petted their feathers, muttering to them, and when they were sleek and perfectly composed, Loki called on the runes, much as the veulve had done. Watching Loki work was like watching a mad man call for the gods.

Ragnar stood back, tip-toeing to see over Loki's shoulders.

Something grabbed his distaff. Ragnar spun around.

The veulve had moved around the fire without him noticing, and was staring straight at him. Her hand went straight through the distaff, but she grasped the air around it and used her runes to hold it still. Ragnar shivered at the sight of her. His legs felt weak and unable to hold him. His distaff was locked in place by her runes, and he did not have the strength to pull it away. Her night-sky eyes looked directly at him.

'I feel you using the runes, story-maker,' she hissed, so softly he was certain neither Odin nor Loki heard. 'The skald who hides silently in the dark.'

Ragnar shuffled as far away from her as he could without letting go of the distaff. His heart beat in his throat and yelps of fear mounted up inside him.

The veulve did not follow him with her eyes, but still she held his distaff in place. 'Their presence burdens the Ginnungagap,' the veulve croaked. She released her grasp on the runes, and Ragnar fell backwards. 'Free them,' the veulve said as Ragnar fell. 'Free them all.'

He hit the floor with a loud bang, and although neither Odin nor Loki seemed to have noticed him or heard, Ragnar was well aware that something had. He sobbed, waiting for the Darkness to come, and it did.

A sword slashed into his ribs, shattering them. Ragnar sobbed and screamed. The sword carved through his body.

Death, pain, and fear.

THE COLD DARKNESS settled on his shoulders and wrapped around Ragnar.

As if complete darkness was not bad enough, he had to suffer countless deaths too, and the veulve... She knew, she had seen him, she had grabbed him and made him die anew, and still the Darkness did not re-open the veil into Helheim.

Trembling, Ragnar clasped the distaff in both his hands, leaning on it for support. He just wanted it to end. He wanted to pass on into the afterlife of Helheim as he had been supposed to do, and he wanted to get away from this Darkness and this pain in his chest and the constant fear and the deaths that waited for him. The last thing he wanted was to tap his distaff and see the veulve again, but going back in was the only hope he had to find a way out of the Darkness.

In a sort of trance, he tapped the distaff and made the sounds in his head. The shriek pierced through the black void, the thread spooled from his distaff, and the veil opened. Even the now-familiar shriek did not pull him out of his daze as he hurried through the opening.

Ragnar glared around, searching for the veulve, and there she stood, right behind Odin, watching Loki work. The veulve did not address him, or even look at him, but Ragnar watched her anxiously. Uneasily, he watched Loki mutter the names of the runes as he conjured them and knotted them around the two birds. The giant grunted from effort and used all the strength in his arms and shoulder to wrap the runes around the two birds and Odin's hands, binding them together. The Alfather had closed his single eye and his forehead lined with the effort, his hair a sweaty tangle.

Loki's song went quiet, and Odin opened his single eye, staring down at the two animals.

They twitched, opened and closed their beaks, and blinked. Odin cackled with laughter, and when Ragnar focused on the birds he could see their chests pump with breaths. The runes settled around Odin's hands and the birds' feathers.

Loki stood up tall. 'Meet your new scouts: Hugin and Munin.'

'Hugin, Hugin,' one of the ravens croaked. It twitched, flapped its dark wings and hopped closer to Odin on its twig-like legs. The other took longer to get up and flap along with its raven brother.

'They speak,' Odin whispered.

Hugin flapped its wings again and flew up to clasp his long claws around Odin's wrist. The other bird, Munin, cocked its head to one side and stared up at the Alfather.

'Well done, brother,' Odin muttered, patting Hugin on the head. The two birds cawed and croaked, and as Odin rose to his feet, Munin took flight and settled on the Alfather's shoulder. 'They'll be good companions,' Odin said.

The veulve approached the fire. Ragnar watched her as she brought her hand out over the flames and extinguished them. The room went dark and she disappeared into the shadows. Odin and Loki walked out of the house to the two wolves on the lawn outside, who waited for their master to emerge.

Ragnar backed away from the shadows where the veulve was, and followed the giant and the Alfather, bracing for a death at the fangs of wolves or at the beaks of ravens, but before he could reach the open door, it shut.

The veulve's house felt like the Darkness itself.

'The Ginnungagap is not finished with you, story-maker,' the veulve said. 'Go make your stories.' The blood-painted house was pitch dark, and no matter which way Ragnar propped his head, he could not see the veulve, or hear from which direction her voice came.

'Kauna,' he heard her say, but the fireplace did not light up at her command.

Ragnar scratched an itch on his left wrist. Another emerged on his right and then at his ankles, and as he looked down at himself, flames erupted up his body. They burned his hairs and melted his skin. The searing pain arose so suddenly and intensely that Ragnar could not hold in his high shriek. Fire burst up his body, lit the house, leapt into his eyeballs, and melted everything in their way. And through the flames, he saw the veulve with her distaff. Her distant starry eyes were fixed on him.

Death, pain, and fear.

HILDA

Chapter Sixty-One

HILDA RUBBED HER eyes. The pain had begun to return. The blood had thinned from her tears.

Einer came into the house to check on her. His bear stood tall at his back. He had finished his own house, and was waiting for her to move to the next. 'You good?'

'It's necessary,' she said, again. She had repeated those words over and over to herself. She needed to be strong for their children. Just one night of horror. One night.

Hilda dried her runny nose with a backhand and joined Einer outside. There weren't any Jutes on the streets anymore. She didn't like the quiet: the stillness. She kept her shield high. Her snow fox yelped. It worried, like her.

Einer watched their backs. 'Something's happened,' he said, and he was right. There had been many Jutes still on this street when they had entered the houses—at least a dozen.

'What are you thinking?' she asked.

He shushed her. She went quiet, glanced around her white Muspel sight. No one was there. Southerners crouched and sobbed alone inside their houses, surrounded by fading bodies, but there were too few Jutes and no one running between houses. Something was amiss.

Battle cries erupted from elsewhere in the city, and Hilda turned to look. There were many hot bodies some way down the road.

'They must have gained reinforcements,' Einer said. 'While we were inside.'

'Down by the house,' Hilda said.

Another raider emerged from a house near them, and glared around, as confused as them. A bird fylgja flew above him. Einer called him over, and they hurried down to the large barricaded house.

The clashes of battle grew louder as they approached; half a hundred brave defenders had re-emerged from the house. More had joined them from elsewhere too and a deep shield-wall had formed across the street.

The southerners had advantage in numbers and terrain. They knew this city and its short-cuts.

With a chieftain's heart, Einer urged Hilda and the other warrior ahead, and joined the back of the Jute formation. He pushed for the middle of the wall, where the fight most desperately needed a commander, and let his shield fall from Hilda's side.

For a moment, she thought that he had left her at the back, but then reached back towards her, and warriors around him turned to see her and let her through. She rushed up to the front lines with Einer.

A southerner broke through the line, and Einer hacked him down and kicked his dead body away. There was no room to move. This was the fight Hilda had craved.

It would not last long.

If the southerners were coming out of their houses, it meant that they trusted that reinforcements were on their way. It meant they were confident; they never chose to fight if they weren't sure of victory.

Einer knew it too.

He blew his horn once, a signal for them to prepare to retreat. All they needed was to hold the wall long enough for the Jutes to pull out of the homes around them, then they could haul their dead out of the city, and shake the berserkers out of their craze. They needed to hold the wall long enough to retreat. It would not be easy, but no fight ever was.

Einer ordered them into formation. His commands were loud, and even the warriors of Frey's-fiord understood and obeyed.

The line pushed; not chaotically, like back in Ash-hill, but every movement with purpose. Every breath calculated. The most disciplined fighters were assembled in the shield-wall, and Hilda was among them.

She steadied the grip on her shield. Back when she was training, it used to be heavy in her hand, but now she barely felt the weight of it, and the battle screams were muddled by the clamour of her heart.

Hilda planted her feet on the street, and found room to force her shield into the wall. To hold her own end next to Einer. Finally they were together on the front line, as they had both dreamed about for a lifetime.

BUNTRUGG

Chapter Sixty-Two

THE FOREFATHERS DID not grow tired of their own laughter. All the way through Buntrugg's and Bafir's long descent in the leaky passage grave, the forefathers howled with laughter. Every now and again one of them would get close to Buntrugg, a fingertip from his face, to scare him, which they did, for he knew of what they were capable. He also knew that he could never allow his fear to show, so he kept it locked away, as he had once kept the forefathers locked away, when they had been within him and not without.

Bafir was not as skilled at hiding his fear. He clutched onto his dagger as if it were a sword.

This far down in the passage, the grave leaked so much that Buntrugg marvelled at it. One wall was visibly frosted with ice while heat poured off the other. Bafir insisted that the grave had always been like this, but it did not feel natural.

They reached the end of the passage, sealed by a large rock, and they both halted. A hiss came from the far side of the rock; they held their breath and listened, and the forefathers gathered around to lend their ears to the noise.

Fire demons crackled and hissed behind the rock, but their voices interlaced with each other in chaos, and Buntrugg could not make out their individual snaps. They were furious, though, and through the open furnace, they had the full strength of the fires of Muspelheim to draw on.

The longer they waited, the stronger the escaped demons grew.

Buntrugg looked at Bafir. 'Do you still doubt that your furnace is open?' He reached over and prickled his finger on the tip of Bafir's dagger, and then brought his hand up to the stone exit.

Before his bloody finger could touch the stone, the dwarf grabbed his arm.

'What are you doing?' Bafir hissed. 'You can't open it. Don't you hear them?'

'We can't close the furnace from out here,' Buntrugg answered, although he too, did not feel confident that opening the passage to the full wrath of Muspel's escaped demons was wise. But Surt had given him a mission, and Buntrugg was more afraid of what would happen to him if he reported back without having closed the furnace, than he was any number of fire demons.

Bafir and Buntrugg stared each other deep in the eyes, both holding their breath. 'You can really close it?' Bafir finally asked.

'I'm willing to try.' Buntrugg wrestled his hand free of the dwarf's grasp and touched his bloody finger onto the stone.

The forefathers scurried away into the dark of the passage. The dwarf whimpered, and when the passage grave began to shake, Bafir scrambled up the stone steps.

The stone exit rolled away, and heat gusted out, melting on the left wall and blurring the forge. The demons within cackled with laughter and excitement, and Buntrugg heard their fires speak.

'Our sister's back,' one fire demon cackled.

'As she promised,' another snapped.

'Returned with bodies.' And they all laughed, so that the heat burned itself into Buntrugg's ears, and they snapped their flamed fingers.

Their heat made it difficult for Buntrugg to breathe. He closed his eyes, and as hard as he could, he called for the rune of ice, Isa. He imagined his body cooling as though he stood in Niflheim itself, and he imagined that no fire could melt the ice that surrounded him; but the heat only mounted.

The rune did not obey him. Hurriedly, Buntrugg concentrated on Algiz, the rune of protection. He put forth his hands to shield his face from the intense heat, and called for the rune, but it did not come to protect him.

The runes weren't with him. They had left with the forefathers.

Buntrugg gulped and opened his eyes to the fiery forge. Defenceless, he watched the blurry fires of Muspel's demons laugh and dance. He clenched his fist, but he knew the forefathers were not within him. He called for all the runes, but none showed up. Without them he could neither increase his size, nor strengthen himself.

His eyes teared from the heat as he peered into the blazing hot forge. Somewhere in there, in the chaos of Muspel's demons, was the open furnace. The one he needed to lock.

The passage grave shook again, and the rock began to move back into place. Buntrugg stepped through, into the blaze. Demons danced around him.

'A long-lived,' they whispered, and made their fires tall, in the same way the forefathers had sought to intimidate him, up in the passageway.

'A challenge,' said another of Muspel's children.

They had taken over the forge as completely as they had taken over Surt's mountain back in Jotunheim. Buntrugg narrowed his eyes against their light and set eyes on the furnace. Even if he managed to close it now, so many demons had escaped into the forge that there would still be work to do. And Buntrugg no longer believed that he could close the furnace and hope survive to capture the escaped demons. Without the runes and the forefathers to help him, he was as powerless as a valley giant.

The passage gradually closed behind him.

In one last act of desperation, Buntrugg addressed the forefathers. 'Surt sent us here,' he said aloud. Never had the forefathers begged to be let free in the presence of Surt. Never had their anger flared when one of the ancients were around.

Buntrugg's sister had to be the only being in the nine worlds who had ever opposed Surt, something even the forefathers and the Alfather had never dared.

'Help me do this,' Buntrugg pleaded with the forefathers, uncertain that they could hear him, or even understand his words. Never before had he spoken directly to them, but whether they understood the words or not, he supposed that his wishes would be conveyed. 'Use your anger. Push them back. I'll close the furnace.'

A blast of wind made Buntrugg stumble forward. The demons' lights became bearable to his eyeballs, and he found new air to breathe. The fires of Muspel's sons were dimmed by the arrival of the forefathers. From the passage grave, they had come, just as the exit sealed.

Fearing Surt's wrath, the forefathers had come to help, and their fear fuelled their anger. Their shadows surrounded Buntrugg, protecting him from the miserable heat of Muspelheim's beings. Their faces flashed with anger, retreating beyond the forefathers' shadows, assessing this new threat. Even Muspel's own sons knew about the forefathers, and that their strength was not to be taken lightly. Every long-lived knew that.

The forefathers circled Buntrugg, their dark, worn faces peering down at him. Hundreds and thousands of faces and destinies watched him, and then, all at once, as if with one mind, they turned away from him, and their weapons flashed forward, and their shields were raised high.

A roar shook the fragile forge. A roar that Buntrugg had felt within himself thousands and thousands of times, whenever the forefathers were too consumed by their anger to listen to reason, but it felt different outside of his body. Scary as if he might die merely from standing in their presence.

The fire demons shrieked, their flames crackling and smoking where the forefathers hit them with weapons of old. The weapons cooled the demons' fires, turned their fingers to smoke, dulled their arms from purple to soft yellow.

Buntrugg took a step ahead into the chaos, eyes fixed on the furnace, and he advanced towards it, careful not to make himself noticed by the few demons not engaged in fights.

The forefathers' anger and fighting techniques made the demons surge back towards the furnace, to reach into the true heat of Muspelheim. They gathered around the furnace and warmed their cooled fingers and heads and arms and legs, and shrieked. The forefathers kept pushing. They slashed about themselves with their ancient swords and axes, and with their spears, they pushed one demon after the other back into the flames of Muspelheim.

Buntrugg braced himself against the extreme heat and stepped forward. The furnace did not merely open to Muspelheim, but into the very heart of that world, where the hottest fires burned.

His clothes fell off his body as ashes.

The forefathers amassed by the open furnace. They shrieked from effort as they pushed demons back into the furnace, and kept them from crawling out again.

A long blue tongue of flame reached out from the furnace and clasped around Buntrugg's left wrist, holding him tight.

'The era of Muspel's sons has arrived,' rang a rusty voice; the voice of Muspel himself. The words were not said aloud, but found Buntrugg through the flame. They burned themselves into his head and scratched at the insides of his eyeballs. 'You cannot stop us.'

The voice made Buntrugg's ears burst into flames. The skin at his temples melted. He tried to put the flames out, but they danced up along his arms. He screamed from pain, and as he did, the flames entered his mouth as well; they travelled down his throat and set him ablaze from the inside.

'*Feed the fire*,' a thousand demons cackled.

Buntrugg watched the furnace. His arm was drawn towards it by Muspel's blue flame.

'Feed the fire,' chanted the dark voice.

The furnace was right there, ahead of him. Surt's mission was within his grasp. Around him the forefathers fought with all their might and fury to contain the demons within the furnace.

Through his pain, Buntrugg found the strength to persist.

His eyes were melting, yet he still saw the blaze of Muspelheim from the furnace, and despite his melting ears, he heard the chanting and laughter of thousands of demons gathered to watch: *Feed the fire. Feed the fire.*

Buntrugg reached for the metal door. His palm burned into the metal, but the pain was nothing compared to that of the blue flame on his arm and the fire within him, and with one last effort, Buntrugg slammed the furnace shut.

Muspel's flame unclasped from his arm.

A last scream of agony escaped from Muspelheim as the door closed. It set the ground ablaze, sent Buntrugg tumbling backwards. He splashed into water and sank into depths. Steam rose from his body, and bubbled up all around him, and through his half-melted eyes, Buntrugg watched the surface of the water above him.

Bright fire raged through the forge, and then the glow faded. The furnace remained shut. He had succeeded. His last mission for Surt was done. Nothing else mattered. He had succeeded in his task, even though his body was burned beyond saving, and he was drowning.

His lips had melted away, and Buntrugg could no longer smile, even if he wanted to, but none of that mattered: he smiled within. The nine worlds were safe, for now.

With that knowledge in mind, Buntrugg accepted his fate.

MUSPELDÓTTIR

Chapter Sixty-Three

A SURGE OF HEAT reached Muspeldóttir.

All the way from home, her name was called. Muspel's sharp cry stoked her weak flames, fuelled her fire with strength and heat. The surging heat she had been missing. She regained the fury, she had lost.

But as quickly as it had arrived, Muspel's scream faded and disappeared.

One, two, three, four, five, six, seven, eight, nine.

Her father and brothers were locked up. Muspeldóttir was their only hope. The time had come to leave this body; either escape or be extinguished.

One, two, three, four, five, six, seven, eight, nine.

Muspeldóttir took back her vision. She gawked out through her host's bloody eyes, and searched for this body's fast fylgja.

With the fylgja's death, she would escape. The white fox was still tied to that chain. That meant it would be easy to catch.

All she would have to do was reach out. Her flames were both eager and ready.

One, two, three, four, five, six, seven, eight, nine.

With all her might she leapt at the fox. Her fingers grabbed its tiny, soft neck, squeezed as it wriggled under her hold.

She fed on the fox's yelped pain. At last, she clenched with her flaming hands. The fox collapsed, dead from her wild flames.

Nothing could tie Muspeldóttir to a body without a destiny.

One, two, three, four, five, six, seven, eight, nine.

The girl's body was as good as dead, no more than a corpse waiting to die.

Nothing could hold her back anymore.

So, Muspeldóttir slithered away, scurried along to find a new host, laughing, cackling at her own success. This time, she could afford to be slow, when she searched for a suitable host.

One, two, three, four, five, six, seven, eight, nine.

Her fire blazed like never before.

HILDA

Chapter Sixty-Four

HILDA SCREAMED IN pain. Down her cheeks burned a thick fluid that was either clotted blood or her own eyeballs. She didn't know which, but it seemed to burn through to her skull.

She slashed open her eyebrows and fresh blood trickled down. With the back of her hand she rubbed her eyes, until her hand began to sting as much as her face. She burned like she hadn't since the forge. As if her eyes were in flames. Blood ran fresh over her cheeks, but it didn't soothe her.

She couldn't see anything. Everything was white: no burning fires, no people, no fylgjur, although she was in the midst of hundreds of warriors. Just white. Her Muspel sight was gone. Her entire being throbbed with heat and pain.

The battle clamour rang around her, and Hilda tried to focus on the sounds. A southerner fell hard against her shield, and she put all her strength into it, pressed with her shoulder to hold her part of the wall. Warriors pushed at her back and side; she couldn't see them or their fylgja. Her breaths were short and loud. Her heart raced.

'Hilda!' Einer was shouting to her, and when she focused on his voice, she realised that he had been shouting for a while. 'What happened?' he asked. 'Are you good to fight?'

Hilda shook her head. She didn't know; she didn't know *anything* anymore. Not even where Einer was. She couldn't even see her own snow fox, or hear it over the throbbing pain in her head.

'Hilda, what is it?' Einer shouted at her back. He stood behind her. 'Did you see something?'

'You need to take over for me,' she told him.

'What?'

The clashes and shrieks of the battle broke through. All the noises Hilda had supressed. Her breathing was panicked, as if she had never been in battle before.

She couldn't see anyone.

'You need to take over for me,' she shouted to Einer over her shoulder. 'I'll be back,' she assured, uncertain that she would. The pain left little thought for anything else.

'Your eyes...' Einer muttered.

'Einer!' she yelled, to snap him out of it.

'What do you need?' he asked.

'I need to go.'

'Then go,' Einer agreed. 'I'll be there soon.'

'I'll come back,' she repeated.

Einer shouldered past her, and crouched into place. Hilda wrestled her shield free of the wall and cornered backwards through the crowd. She packed her axe away and secured her shield onto her back. Touched her helmet, to make sure it was tight and her neck didn't show. Then she found the wall of a southern house and followed it away from the noises of battle.

'Hilda! Where are you going?' Einer yelled after her.

She didn't know what to answer. She would be back.

The chain in her hand was stiff. She had to drag the snow fox along.

'Come on, I need you,' she begged, but the fox didn't move. It wasn't barking anymore either. It wasn't just that she couldn't hear it over the dunking pain and clashes of war.

Hilda dragged the snow fox closer. Her fingers brushed its fur coat. The fox didn't react. It lay on its side, its neck tilted at an awkward angle where the Ulfberht chain was tied to it. Her fylgja lay lifeless at her feet.

Her fox had saved her more than once. It had helped to guide her. It was not just a warning of death. To Hilda, it was a guide. A guide that had once belonged to her mother. The only piece of her family that she still had, and the only hope for a future. It *couldn't* be hurt.

She scooped it up and it lay lifeless in her arms. The fox could no longer help her, the Runes were silent, her eyes burned like fire itself. She needed help.

'Fish! Fish!' Hilda yelled. 'Fish!'

'What do you need?' asked a man. His voice was close.

Hilda stopped. 'Are you the helper?'

'Ja,' came the answer.

'You have to bring me out of this town,' she ordered. 'Take my arm and guide me.'

At her command, a cold hand clasped her forearm, and dragged her along.

With the Runes' rising wind at her back, and the warrior leading her. Hilda sprinted from the battle, down the long street past houses of wailing children and women.

She cradled the fox in her arms. Its body was stiff, but its neck and chest were warm and its fur smelled burnt.

'Wake up, wake up,' Hilda muttered as she ran through Magadoborg with the fish, away from the battle she had always wished to join. She was led out through the gates and to the fields outside the city, where the fish and the healers were gathered.

One in their midst, out of range of arrows, the fish leading her slowed down. The snow fox's body had begun to cool at Hilda's touch, despite her close embrace.

'We need a healer,' cried the man.

'I don't need a healer,' she told him. He didn't move. 'Tak. You can go back now,' she added, pointedly. She wrestled her arm free of him and took a few steps away.

She crouched down into the mud, removed her shield, and she lay her fox onto it.

Her fylgja was supposed to warn of her death, not die itself. It was supposed to always be there, and guide her to make the right decisions, in battle and in life. Its luck was supposed to steer her hand. A dead fylgja was more than a mere bad premonition; Fylgjur were supposed to live forever, to grant luck and good fortune and to protect as a mother would.

She was uncertain what to do now. Sweat tickled against the iron of her nose guard. Hilda removed her helmet. Next, her hands reached for the Ulfberht chain, and untied it from around the fox's neck. Its long fur was hot and brittle as if it had been burned.

Hilda cast the chain aside and focused on her fylgja. She nuzzled its ears, as it had always liked. Massaged its chest where its heart was supposed to beat. Whatever she tried, the snow fox lay motionless on her shield, still cooling.

Fylgjur weren't supposed to die. The thought echoed in Hilda's head. Yet somehow, her fylgja that wasn't supposed to die lay lifeless before her.

The Winter Night wind froze her ears, though the Runes didn't speak. They were being too silent. Her fylgja had not run away, as some people's supposedly did. It was dead. There was something bigger going on.

'Hilda, why are you here?' Finn's familiar voice and the shriek of his hawk interrupted her thoughts. 'Should I call a healer?'

'Leave,' Hilda coldly answered. She had no time for him.

'Your eyes—'

The wind picked up with Hilda's anger, and pushed Finn back. She heard his hawk shriek.

Hilda stroked the snow fox's fur, all the way from its ears

to its thick winter tail. 'You'll tell me how to undo this,' she ordered the wind. 'Whatever you need me to do, I'll do it.'

The wind stirred around her and tugged her hair out of its braid, but it didn't speak. It caressed her arms and flew around her, and she heard the Runes whisper faintly to themselves. It was always when she most needed their help that the Runes refused her.

'You want something from me,' she urged. 'I know you do.' Every word the Runes spoke to her had a purpose. They must have chosen *her* for a reason. Like the gods, the Runes had plans for her.

'I'll give you whatever you want. I'll sacrifice everything I have. Anything! Just tell me how to undo this!'

Hilda knew that the healers, and the fish, and Finn, all heard her talking to the wind, but she didn't care about any of them.

'You didn't want me to get into this battle,' she argued with the silent wind. 'You can't possibly have wanted my fylgja to die. So, help me undo this death.'

It has passed through. We cannot heal it. The same as when she had first asked them to heal her eyes. But if there was *nothing* to be done, then they wouldn't have stayed silent this long. They could have told her straight away that it was impossible, but they hadn't. They knew how to undo this.

'You know there is a way,' she told the wind.

You already owe us a night for your Brisingamen.

'Then I'll owe you two nights. Two promises,' she said, desperate to get her way. If she didn't have her fylgja, she was as good as dead anyway. Death would seek her again and again, and if her fylgja wasn't there to warn her, death would take her, and she had still not seen a proper raid. These past few weeks had only been a taster, and they had not been enough. She wanted this life. She wanted to fight. 'I'll make whatever sacrifice is needed.'

Her father had taught her that all sacrifices before the gods were rewarded. None was too great if it could revive the fox, for only the fox could keep her from being wrenched away from this life.

Twice you have asked for favour. Twice you owe us.

'I keep my promises,' Hilda answered the wind. 'I'll do what you ask of me.' She meant it. Whatever the Runes wanted, she would give it to them.

She had used to be scared of the fox—back in Ash-hill, before she had the Runes—but over these past weeks, she had grown fond of it. In turn, the snow fox too had grown fond of her. It had allowed her to pet it, and had followed her wishes. It protected her.

Hilda stroked the snow fox's stomach. Its body was now ice-cold. Even with her Muspel sight, she would not have been able to see it anymore. She placed her right hand onto the fox, right above a heart that no longer pumped. Though she hoped that she was right, and the Runes could mend this, part of her also feared what it might cost. Bringing back the dead was a tricky deed; she didn't have to be a runemistress to know that much.

'Tell me what to do,' Hilda insisted, and the Runes obeyed. The wind picked up, as if it wasn't already strong enough. Then came fast whispers and low murmurs, and before Hilda knew what to do, she was chanting along to the Runes' fast hum. Words she didn't know flowed out of her mouth, as the Runes spoke through Hilda and made her act.

'Kauna, may my heat be yours.' Her free hand brushed the snow fox, and she felt something, like a solid thread, bind her right hand to the snow fox's body. A kindred sense linked the two of them. As if they were one and same.

Suddenly, the wind's cold gust made her shiver, and her hands turned to frost. Though she began to feel cold, she felt the snow fox's body warm.

'Naudir, you shall eat in my stead.'

The little hunger that had installed itself in her stomach from the fight disappeared. The Runes made her pass her hand over the body of the snow fox again. Again she felt a thread settle around the snow fox and her right hand.

Through Hilda, the Runes called their own names and made promises and conjured threads. With every thread, the bond that tied Hilda's hand to the snow fox, tightened, until it began to hurt. The bond cut into Hilda's skin, so blood flowed out over her fylgja's long fur.

With every named rune, Hilda felt a little part of herself hurt and fade, and for all that she'd lost, sweat trickled out on her forehead from the effort. Soon it would be over—more than twenty Runes had been named—but that thought didn't soothe Hilda's pain, for the Runes never halted nor stalled for her to regain her forces.

Hilda yelped as the last thread wrapped itself around the snow fox and her hand. It hurt as much as her eyes. It crushed her hand to the fox's slender body, and bound them so close that Hilda felt as if she were being strangled.

She clenched her eyes shut, to keep the strength to finish.

Under her right hand, the snow fox stirred. Its heart pumped, slowly at first, then faster and faster. Its body began to wriggle and its warm wet tongue licked the blood from her hand.

The pain rose from Hilda's eyes. She had forgotten what it felt like to be painless. Bliss.

The snow fox barked at her.

Smiling, Hilda opened her eyes to it.

Long white fur waved in the wind, blooded at the tips. Hilda's own hands were dark red with blood, and the rest of her skin was pale. Her shield had colours: green like a forest, with a black bindrune on top. The grasses were brown with mud, as was her dress.

She could *see*. Could see it all.

Her fylgja radiated life.

Once more her snow fox barked. It showed its teeth, snarled, ready to launch back into battle.

Eager to comply, Hilda put her helmet back on. She secured

the Ulfberht chain around her waist; she and the fox were bound far closer by the Runes. They didn't need a chain.

Finally, Hilda picked up her green shield, and drew her godly axe. It glistened with blood. Everything felt light in her hands. Strangely so, considering how tired and worn she had been a moment before, as the snow fox had gained life.

Its long white winter coat was beautiful.

The high ones never return gifts, the Runes reminded her. But she didn't want to get anything back. She had all she wanted. Her snow fox barked and looked up at Hilda for a command to follow.

Healers and helpers had gathered around her. Their fylgjur stared at her, beasts baying and birds screeching. Hilda walked through their midst back towards Magadoborg to join the ranks again, as she had promised Einer.

Although night shrouded the lands and the night sky hidden by clouds, Hilda had never before seen so many shades of colours. She glanced around with new understanding. Everyone's fylgjur were so clear, like they had been to her Muspel sight, and the colours all around her were stunning. A sky that she might once have called black, she saw now was a multitude of blues and purples, blending together in the clouds.

Maybe it was because her fylgja had given her new hope that her Muspel sight had lifted. Maybe it was because tonight was the first Winter Night, the night of the forefathers, and the gods were watching. Whatever the reason, Hilda had never experienced the world like this before, and with the Runes at her back, and the snow fox running with her, free of the Ulfberht chain, Hilda held her shield high and set off towards Magadoborg's gates.

She could see the gates. She could see the roads. She could see the town. The corpses on the ground, the blood and mud. The white frost of winter.

No arrows were shot after her, but she kept her shield up regardless, and pushed ahead. Ran up the streets towards the town centre, taking in every detail. Every mossy stone. Every drop of blood. Severed heads and arms. Broken doors and screaming folk.

Corpses, southern and northern, filled the roads. Houses had been raided across half the city. Children and old men wailed amidst the devastation. Their purpose had been met. Now they just needed to hold the shield-wall for as long as they could. The longer they stayed, the longer they would be feared.

The organised chaos at the front line was familiar. Stable as they would have been on a real raid. The sight of it made her cry. She had missed it all, had missed *them* all so much. The warriors. Her kin. Friends. Home. She missed Einer most of all.

She pushed through countless raiders and their fylgjur and searched over the tops of their heads and shields for Einer and his great white bear.

Old Hormod held up the middle of the wall, and a younger warrior stood behind him.

Hilda searched for Einer, but he was nowhere. His bear should have been easy to spot.

'Where's Einer?' she shouted to Hormod, but gained no answer. She tried to push ahead but no one made room for her to retake her old place. It made no sense for Einer to have left the shield-wall to lesser commanders, unless something had happened. Something bad.

'Where is Einer?' she tried again, addressing one of the younger warriors at her side. He had bloody tears running down his cheeks, like her. He didn't answer. None of them gave any indication of having heard her question.

Hilda raised her shield high, and glanced around for Einer. Maybe he was raiding through the houses again. Nej. Like her, he wouldn't have left the shield-wall unless it was serious, unless he had felt that he had no choice. Einer was in danger.

EINER

Chapter Sixty-Five

EINER RACED THROUGH Magadoborg's gates, out to where the wounded were, out where Hilda had gone. There were many injured warriors, and not enough healers, and among the wounded were just as many corpses being transferred from the battlefield back to the *Northern Wrath*.

They were nearly ready for the last retreat and the journey home.

The gold bracteate knocked against Einer's chest, but it did not burn his skin as it had done at Ragnar's funeral. It beat in a strange rhythm that made Einer acutely aware of a deep sorrow mounting within him.

It had begun after Hilda had left the front lines. He had no words for the sudden arrival of the sorrow, but it was there: something had gone wrong. His chest tightened and his hands and toes burned with strength and anger. The same anger that had taken over for him back in Hammaborg and up north in the ice. At any moment, he might no longer be able to contain it. He could not be fighting in a tight shield-wall when it happened. When he went berserk, someone else took over, someone who didn't know kinsman from enemy. He could end up killing them all.

Einer searched through the crowd of wounded warriors and healers for Hilda, and then his eyes fell on his debt-thrall, coming back up from the river with an empty cart. Their eyes met, but Finn immediately looked away.

He waved Finn towards himself with his shield. 'Finn, have you seen Hilda?'

Finn abandoned his cart and approached, but he avoided looking at Einer. Berserkers roared inside Magadoborg; soon they would need to calm the few survivors from their rage and bring them down to the ships. Soon the battle would be finished. Einer had no time. He needed to find Hilda before then.

'What's wrong?' Einer asked, and searched this way and that looking for Hilda. 'Where is she?'

Finn kept a cautious distance from him. 'She was praying to the gods.'

Arne and the other healers, and the injured warriors who had enough strength to sit up, watched the exchange. They held their breaths as they watched, and their expectant staring did not comfort Einer's worries.

He threw his shield onto the dirty ground. 'Where is she?' he asked again, trying to keep his calm.

His eyes roved over the crowd of injured warriors lying on the ground, searching for her bright helmet or her blonde hair, and then at the very back of the line, he saw her. Her helmet had been removed to reveal her messy hair. Her skin was pale, her bloody tears were blackened and clotted, and her eyes were shut.

The injured warriors wormed out of Einer way and left him a wide path through their midst towards Hilda.

With more calm now that he had found her, Einer walked towards her.

His heart raced. The battle cries faded into echoes.

She did not lie on the same row as the warriors who were being treated, and she did not lie on a blanket as they did. Instead, she had been lain on top of her shield, and Einer knew what that meant, but he pushed it aside in his mind, for he did not dare to admit the truth to himself.

'There were no cuts to treat,' one of the healers said as Einer walked past. 'She had no battle wounds. She just... collapsed.'

'The gods reclaimed her,' someone in the crowd muttered, and the phrase was passed around in the crowd. 'The gods reclaimed her.'

With every word, the anger mounted in him. The rage slithered up from his hands and feet, and raced around his mind, but he kept it at bay as he took the last few steps towards Hilda.

She was smiling.

Einer crouched down at her side. He swept the loose strands of hairs from her braid away from her face. Her skin was cold and clammy to the touch.

Barely had she accomplished what she had always dreamt of, and the gods took her. She would not have left willingly.

Somehow, she did not look like herself. She was too still and unresponsive, and as Einer stared at her face, he half expected her to open her eyes and frown at him for having worried about anything at all. If he just stared at her long enough, she might open her eyes, she might come back, and laugh at him, or scold him for having left the fight to search for her when she had told him that she would be back.

She had promised she would be back, and yet there she was, among the corpses of lesser warriors.

Tears streamed down Einer's cheeks before he even acknowledged the sorrow in his chest, and he did not dare to lean in and touch her cold skin again for fear that he was right and that the gods really had claimed her, right when she had been happy.

The happiness flowed from her, even there, sprawled out next to the other corpses. She was smiling.

He remembered how she had used to smile whenever she had gotten him into trouble, which had been often. Especially that once, when Hilda had somehow managed to get one of Tormod's cows up onto the roof of his barn and called Einer over to see, right as Tormod had arrived. The moment the angry farmer had appeared, Hilda had vanished, leaving Einer alone on the roof with the lowing cow and no explanations. For weeks, Hilda had laughed at him for getting caught, with the exact same smile on her lips as she wore now. The same smile she wore to her death.

He had promised her so much. He had promised her raids, marriage, and sons named after her. He had promised her everything he had, and everything he would ever gain for himself, for the both of them.

The gods were to blame for this, and he would make them pay for taking her. The ancient rage begged to be let loose. That familiar fury boiled up inside him. Although he had no recollection of any of the times it had taken over, he had felt it often. He knew the anger well.

Einer dried his tears with the back of his hands, although they streamed down his face regardless. The deep repressed northern wrath surged up his arms and through his body, and Einer welcomed it. As the tears dripped from his chin, Einer turned his attention back to Magadoborg, and urged the ancient forces within him to take over and lead him to oblivion.

HILDA

Chapter Sixty-Six

Despite how her arm-muscles hurt, Hilda held the upper part of the shield-wall. Einer still hadn't returned.

Lingorm ordered their shield-wall to back away into the square. At last, Hilda saw Einer's white bear. It rushed across the square, wild with rage. Einer raced down a road to Hilda's left, straight to another shield-wall. Sigismund and his wolf were there. Einer disappeared into the crowd, behind the southern houses, and then Hilda heard the blast of a horn.

One long blast to signal their final retreat. They had raided the houses they needed to raid. They had killed all the children and men and women and old folk they needed to kill. They had installed fear. Their cause had been met. For those who were alive, it was time to go home.

The last corpses of fallen comrades were heaved free of the crowd in Hilda's shield-wall. Hilda grabbed a yellow blooded tunic with her free hand and, shield held high, dragged the corpse across the square, where carts were being brought out.

Her snow fox clasped its strong jaw around the fallen

warrior's upper arm and helped her drag. Hilda smiled at the sight of it. She didn't know what she would have done without her fylgja, and if she would even be alive now.

The thought raised an unexpected worry. Her fox had died and she knew a price had to be paid, a high price, to pay for a life. The Runes had stayed silent since they had helped her heal the fox. Once in a while the wind would blow harsher, but the gusts brought no commands or warnings for her as they had used to do. Was their disappearance her price? The price had to be greater than that.

She hauled the pale body along the road as the shield-wall retreated, all the way to the square by the gates, where she let go of the corpse. The large warrior who was supposed to carry it away on the cart just stood and stared down at the corpse, petrified. Her snow fox snarled and let go of the dead man's arm. Finally, the warrior seemed to come back to his senses. He grabbed the corpse and threw it onto his cart with the others.

Most warriors at the back were already on their way down to the colourful ships to ready the oars and take their places. In a steady stream, they broke free of their shield-walls and hurried out the gates, down to the river. Vivid tunics drenched in blood rushed past her.

At the gates, Hilda waited for Einer and watched the last fighting crowds. The warriors' fylgjur were so obvious in the early morning light. Clear like never before.

All the shield-walls had retreated to the square. The warriors backed away towards the north gate in a slow, controlled step.

There were so many colours. So much to see, but there was one thing that Hilda didn't see. She searched through the jumble of warriors and fylgjur in Sigismund's shield-wall where she had seen Einer run off. A large white bear ought to be easy to find, even at a distance. Yet, she couldn't set eyes on it, for there were too many fylgjur around her and too many warriors.

As the shield-walls merged and withdrew, smaller bands broke away. Warriors rushed past Hilda and out of Magadoborg with their shields at their backs.

'Has anyone seen Einer?' she asked the many warriors who darted past her. None of them answered her. They almost seemed scared to answer it. Some were terrified. Not the usual war terror that trained warriors carried away from a battle, a different sort.

'Did you see?' Warriors who broke away from Sigismund's wall whispered.

'Not a berserker. A beast,' they whispered. Scared to speak aloud.

'He's gone.'

Hilda asked them to explain—they had to mean Einer—but no one stopped to talk to her. No one addressed her at all, or acknowledged that she was there. The Runes did not speak to her either.

Sigismund came rushing past her, dragging Thora's body, pierced with arrows. Blood had darkened her brown dress. Sigismund's grey wolf helped him haul the body along, and then Hilda saw the beaver and when she looked up to sky, she saw a seagull circle them too, and the sight made her smile. Corpses didn't have fylgjur. Although she looked it, Thora wasn't dead.

Hilda searched through the large crowd of southerners for a sign of Einer. Finally, her eyes found his white bear, further into Magadoborg than any other fylgja.

Her new vision was so bright and clear. She struggled to focus anywhere, because she saw everything. All these full colours that she had never known before. But now that she had found Einer's bear, she didn't let it leave her sight.

His bear was mad with rage. It lashed out around itself, and roared so loudly that Hilda felt pain in her heart. 'Einer needs me,' she muttered, and tightened the grip on her axe.

A strong gust pushed Hilda back to the gates. At last, the Runes broke their silence. *A white bear will lie in a lake of blood.*

Hilda watched Einer's white bear from afar. It was in a frenzy. It drew further and further away from her, and she knew that even with her skills and clear sight, it was unlikely that she would survive to the centre of Magadoborg and catch up with him. She would fall before then. She might not be able to calm him, even if she did reach him.

The wolf will lead the way. The Runes wanted her to follow Sigismund to the ships.

Einer was strong. With his berserker rage, he yet had a chance of making it out of Magadoborg.

'Fine,' she whispered to the wind, and reluctantly, she turned away from Magadoborg, covered her back with her shield, and with the last few warriors, she ran out over the plains outside the city and down towards the ships.

The dark of the night made other warriors stumble, but Hilda saw clearly. The ground was lit by the starlight, despite the clouds. She sprinted over the burnt fields with the snow fox running and barking at her side. It felt good to run again.

Warriors parted for her where she went. Their fylgjur were alerted by her snow fox's barks.

Down by the ships, the crowd was thick. Many had already boarded their ships, while others helped to pile the last corpses onto the *Northern Wrath*.

Hilda pushed through the crowd to see Einer's old ship. The *Northern Wrath* looked worn and winter tired, yet in the early morning, the ship's colours shone, greens and yellows and reds. Dead warriors had honourably been lain out on their shields all over the ship. No fylgjur down there.

In their midst, Hilda noticed a man crouched down by one of the corpses. He wasn't dead. Two wolf fylgjur were at his back. The man rose to his full height. He was tall like Einer, but slender and old. Long silver curls of hair travelled down his back.

Hilda knew exactly who it was. Eyes fixed on his back, Hilda waited for the Alfather to turn around. She wanted to see his face, and his famous single eye.

The Runes made the wind rise around her. *The Hanged God will abandon you.*

Out of the crowd on shore came eight spear-women, who joined the Hanged God on the *Northern Wrath*. Women with gold shields on their backs and weapons in hand, and the fierce stares of shield-maidens. Fylgjur accompanied them, crows and ravens, all of them. Like Hilda's father's.

None of the bystanders saw them. Only Hilda did. In a trance, she stared at her idols. They were exactly as she had hoped they would be, fierce and strong. Their armour was tight and twinkled in the night. They wore short sleeves and their muscular arms were bare. Their helmets weren't bright, but old and blooded.

Her mouth hung open as she stared at them.

The eight valkyries focused on their task. They followed the Alfather, and by every corpse he designated, they knelt down and whispered into the corpse's ears to guide the fallen to Valhalla.

Three of them carried axes, but the others walked through the corpses using spears as walking sticks. They balanced lightly on the rowing thwarts.

The Alfather had even more grace. Barefooted, he trod through the corpses, yet even without shoes, he looked rich. Even without a coat, he looked warm. The warmth practically radiated from him, and his skin shone like gold in sunlight.

The crowd began to thin out. Warriors and shieldmaidens boarded their ships. Hilda pushed through the last crowd to get closer to the *Northern Wrath* and to Odin.

The Hanged God will abandon you, the Runes grumbled. *We gave you your Brisingamen, now give us a night.* This was the first price she had to give. She had promised to grant two wishes for the Runes. This was the first. The Runes wanted her to leave with Sigismund. The wind swirled around her as she approached the *Northern Wrath*.

The Alfather glanced into shore. At once the wind died, and

the Runes scurried away. Hilda stared into his single eye. Silver like his hair, sharp like a blade.

Odin didn't notice her. There were too many warriors around. The valkyries joined his side, and the Alfather turned back to the corpses at his feet.

The wind picked up as soon as Odin's single eye looked away. *The Hanged God will abandon you.* They had told her that up in Jutland too, after the attack on Ash-hill.

The last warriors on shore pushed the *Northern Wrath* out onto the river. Hilda pushed with them.

We gave you your Brisingamen, now give us a night, the Runes repeated.

'I hear you,' Hilda told them, her eyes fixed on Odin and his valkyries. 'I gave my word. I'll leave with Sigismund.'

Her heart yearned to walk up to the Alfather and the valkyries, hand over the Ulfberht axe and greet them. Or at the very least, to stay behind and keep watching them, but the Alfather and his valkyries had not come to speak to her. They had come to gather the slain. Someday Hilda's turn would come, but it was not today.

She backed away from the scene, wrenched her eyes away from Odin's silver hair, and rushed along the bank to find Sigismund's ship.

She didn't need to go far. Three ships further down, she spotted the *Storm*. Already the warriors were pushing away from shore. Hilda leapt onto the ship in the last moment.

'Hei?' Turid called and for some strange reason she wasn't looking at Hilda. Instead she stared at the exact spot where Hilda's snow fox was standing.

If Hilda hadn't known better she might have thought that Turid could see the fox, but Hilda knew that no one could see the many fylgjur, apart from her.

'Come on, you can't stay here.' Turid clicked her tongue at Hilda as she would to a dog. Though Hilda knew from Turid's hesitant smile that it was a joke, but she didn't laugh, nor did she comply and rush onto one of Ash-hill's ships. She sat down on her usual rowing seat with her fox. It snapped out after Turid, and Hilda petted it to keep it calm.

Turid didn't question her decision again, and found her own rowing seat as well, though she kept glaring across the ship, in Hilda's direction.

They rowed out to the middle of the river. The wind howled at her back, eager to make Hilda leave this place. The Runes made the wind pick up so they drifted quickly down the river. The order was given to pack the oars away. They had been supposed to row all night, but the Runes made the wind favourable to set sail.

Off-duty tonight, with the others who had been at the front lines, Hilda walked aft so as not to stand in anyone's way when they raised the sail. Their best sailors scurried around her. Hilda leant out over the side of the ship and peered back up the river. The last ship from Ash-hill rowed out onto the river, and when they were far enough away from shore, they came to a halt.

Fire arrows were sent off. Nine arrows, one for each world.

The *Northern Wrath* caught on fire. In the smoke, Odin and his valkyries continued their work, as easily as if they stood in mist. The fire illuminated the Alfather's silver curls and his dark blue robes.

On all the ships the warriors began to sing the fallen into the next life. Hundreds of warriors.

The sun began to rise with their retreat. It was the end of the first Winter Night. Many had passed on, but all in high honour. The Alfather and his valkyries were guiding them all to Valhalla.

Longingly, Hilda watched them choose one corpse after another. Even as they floated further and further away, Hilda could pick out the Alfather and the silhouettes of his valkyries on the burning ship, and when they were too far away, Hilda turned her gaze to Magadoborg's gates. Her eyes searched for Einer's bear, but the town was too far away.

A white bear will lie in a lake of blood.

'Every living thing dies,' Hilda told the Runes to dismiss their warnings of doom. 'Kinsmen die, cattle die. We must die likewise.'

A white bear will lie in a lake of blood, they repeated, as though intent on scaring her.

'Fylgjur don't stay with corpses,' Hilda realised. At Midsummer, she had seen her father's raven fly off when he had died. Before his funeral. Right when he had died. And the *Northern Wrath* carried fresh corpses, but none of the warriors' fylgjur.

'Someday Einer too will die, but it won't be on this Winter Night,' Hilda said, certain of herself. That was what the Runes had wanted to tell her. 'He won't die in Magadoborg.' Einer was stronger than anyone else she knew, and he had his bear to protect him, and his berserker rage.

SIGISMUND

Chapter Sixty-Seven

THE WIND WAS so perfect that Sigismund was certain the gods were watching and blessing their journey home. Their stand against the southerners had been acknowledged and approved in the high halls of Asgard, and in reward of their sacrifice, they were gifted strong and steady winds to aid their retreat.

A warrior approached Sigismund and his two helmsmen. 'The snow fox wouldn't get off the ship,' he timidly said, urging them to do something about it.

'It knows we're going home,' Sigismund said. 'It dragged the corpses down to the ships with us.' That alone meant that they ought to respect it. It was no ordinary snow fox, perhaps it was a guide sent by the gods, or a god in disguise.

'The fox will bring us good fortune,' he added, but the unease among his warriors did not settle. They had lost much in the battle and their loss made them worry more than usual.

His crew were still visibly shocked by the sudden end to the battle, when Einer had raged through their ranks and thrown himself at the southerners. The sound of Einer's bear growl and the sight of him throwing away his shield and drawing his father's Ulfberht sword to fight with two blades. That was a sight Sigismund might never forget; none of them would.

Without Hilda, there was no one to stop Einer. No hope of calming his berserker rage and bringing him home. In a way, Sigismund was glad that it had been impossible to wrench Einer free from the battle. After Hilda's fall, he imagined that all Einer had wanted was to fall at her side. Now, at the very least, they would go to Valhalla together, like they had planned.

'But we can't keep a wild animal onboard,' the young sailor insisted.

Sigismund sighed. His breath froze into a white cloud. The sweat on his forehead from the fight hadn't cooled yet. The true damages and consequences of the battle had yet to be assessed, and already his crew had come up with a problem he needed to solve for them. 'Where is it?' he asked.

'Knut's place,' answered the young man. Then he shifted around to give a hopeful smile and nod to the warriors at the aft who waited to hear how his conversation with Sigismund had gone.

With another sigh, Sigismund left his steersman in charge and moved along the ship. The river-traps they had constructed in Hammaborg were lain out both at the fore and aft of the ship, in good positions to be thrown overboard further down the river.

No southern ships would follow them today, if at all.

With the cool morning wind, the season's first snow fell, whitening the *Storm*'s frost-ridden deck.

Careful not to get caught on the river traps, or slip on the frosted deck, Sigismund legged around the spear ends. As he cornered the river traps, Sigismund saw the snow fox. The warriors had left a large circle around it, and they all kept a watchful eye.

The white-coated fox sat on Old Knut's rowing position. After Knut had passed on, Hilda had sat on that rowing bench when she wasn't on duty, and the sight of the snow fox unexpectedly made Sigismund tear up. He had so many mixed thoughts about this revenge raid, and he had not had a chance to think about any of it.

The snow fox watched Sigismund approach and as he looked into its blue eyes, all he could see was Hilda. The fox gazed down the length of the ship and out to the horizon to the east where the sun was rising.

Sigismund swiped the newly fallen snow off the rowing bench next to the fox and sat down. The fox did not scare or startle at his movements.

Together they watched the sun rise through the increasingly snowy landscape.

Sigismund wondered how a snow fox of the far north had arrived so far south. At the same time, he knew that the manner in which it had arrived was irrelevant. The gods had sent it after they had taken Hilda back. After they had retrieved their runemistress. She had said the gods had plans for her.

The battle had not made Sigismund part with many of his own warriors, but he had parted with some good ones, and their loss was felt in the silence of the crew. Even in the aft, where the only warrior who had fallen in battle was Hilda.

Ten of Sigismund's sailors had passed on, one fifth of his crew. Others had it worse. He did not know the exact number of warriors who had passed on in the fight, but some of the crews were so bare that it was a wonder they could sail at all. Thora's crew sailed without a commander. Sigismund had ordered some of his own warriors to sail with them.

Thora would likely die, and their child with her. She had been breathing when he had pulled her free, but she had a dozen puncture wounds from arrows and spears. He supposed she would die before a healer could treat her, but he hoped that she would survive. He had gotten her down to the ships as quickly as he could after finding her. Perhaps the berserker caps would give her the strength to survive. She had already survived longer than most. He supposed that hundreds must have passed already. The corpses had filled the hull of the *Northern Wrath*.

Many had died on both sides of the fight, but perhaps because of this, many more would live.

The southerners were scared. The little girl Sigismund had left alive in the last house he had raided had been so terrified that she had fainted. She had watched her parents and brothers die at Sigismund's hand. It had not been a raid, it had not been fun, but Sigismund hoped that it had enough impact to keep the southerners away for many summers and winters.

The snow fox wailed; a high-pitched cry that brought Sigismund out of his thoughts.

Snow had settled on the fox's scarred eyebrows and covered its winter coat, so the few strands of fur that still had not turned white were hidden beneath the falling snow.

It looked so sad.

Sigismund held his hand out to the snow fox for it to sniff and get familiar with his scent. It pushed its wet snout against his hand, urging him to pet it, and he complied. The scars up its legs reminded him of the scars up Hilda's arms, and the blood that had flowed from her eyes like a permanent wound.

'Hilda,' he mumbled.

The snow fox snapped its attention up to him at the mention of her name. Its ears darted forward, and Sigismund felt compelled to say something more. 'Whatever glory you were looking for in Magadoborg,' he said. 'I hope you found it.'

HUGIN & MUNIN

Chapter Sixty-Eight

THROUGH THE COOL air, we glide.

I cock my head and spread my black wings. My vision is shielded by clouds and smoke. I croak for my brother to turn, and together we dash away.

My brother carries our memories, but I, Hugin, carry our thoughts, and it is I who thinks for the both of us. My brother remembers every battle fought, but only I understand the lessons, and why some day Valhalla will be emptied when the giants and gods go to war.

Together we emerge through the mist, and shake the snow of Midgard off our dark wings. Glad to be home in Asgard, my brother and I fly over the broad-leaved forests and out over Frey's farmyard. The clouds announce that soon rain will fall. Frey waves to me, and returns to his work. A true god of fertility, who knows the value of hard toil.

Munin does not notice how Frey hurries to bale his hay. My brother is too focused on his memories of what we've seen.

'Rain, rain,' I call to him.

Munin responds with a quiet look, and together we dart towards Valhalla's gold-red oak. We settle on the gold oak shields and search for Odin inside the hall.

'He's not there,' Munin caws. His black eyes, like mine, search through Odin's warriors, but the Alfather is not among them. I cock my head up and look around. He must be somewhere here, for I can feel his presence in my feathered chest.

At the edge of a field of anemones, more than a hundred short-lived corpses arrive in Asgard. From the skies Munin and I watched the battle from which they passed on.

I nudge Munin and together we take flight. We skip straight down to Valhalla's nearest gate, and settle on top.

The Alfather arrives to greet the newly dead. Like us he has been to Midgard, and has seen the battlefield. Out from the anemone-covered field march his guards, the valkyries, and from somewhere out there, comes the distant echo of song. Voices from another world sing the hundreds of corpses into the next world. Munin and I rock along to the echo of the short-lived voices.

Heavy rain begins to pour as the dead short-lived arrive in front of Odin's hall. The Alfather accompanies them with welcoming words. Finally, he looks up at us. He brushes his long silver hair, off his shoulder and Munin darts down to him.

I push away from the gate, and spread my wings. I make a sudden turn, and wrap my sharp claws around the shoulder of my god.

I strut my wet feathers on the shoulder of Asgard's commander, as the warriors of Valhalla welcome home their god. Thousands of warriors stand for him. Satisfied, the Alfather walks down the hall and gains a modest seat on a mail-covered bench. Proud, I sit on his shoulder and lean in to whisper what I have seen.

Every day my brother and I carry out the Alfather's commands. We visit short-lived mothers, fathers, sons and daughters. We, Hugin and Munin, witness everything; from their first walk to their last fall.

*   *   *

You HAVE HEARD what my brother Hugin has to say. Now it is time for you to see the nine worlds my way. My brother can only give Odin a vague account. It is I, Munin, who possesses the memories that can explain the latest bloody battlefield.

Before Magadoborg, there was Ash-hill's fight. The southerners came and burned every house. With a single cut, the nornir severed every destiny string. Together, Hugin and I watched hundreds of bodies decay.

"All shall be chosen as Valhalla's guardians," Odin ruled, as he stood in Ash-hill's cinders. Farmers and children, old folk and weavers, all were rewarded for their strength that night.

All of Jutland burned and bled, but few were those who honoured their sacred promises. Few stood up to protect their homes, but through ashes and flames, the villagers of Ash-hill fought for their place. Farmers with chopping axes as weapons, and honour as their armour.

Odin was far from glad about the attack on Jutland's towns. "None of us will survive," he muttered in this hall, and in a firm grip, crumbled the elderberries in his fist. Out over his hands dripped the berries' dark juice.

I shake the memories away. They won't explain Odin's current frown. Unlike my brother, Hugin, I'm not clever enough to understand what the Alfather has planned.

In Asgard's greatest hall, I have settled in the corner, quiet like a thrall. I groom a drenched feather. All around me, warriors curse the beginning rain outside. They will have to fight in the storm.

I cock my head and stare out through the open door. Outside, thunder strikes.

I hop around myself and turn my attention to the long hall's oak tree; where the darkest shadows fall. My brother sits and whispers into Odin's right ear. They sit at the far end of a long-table so the warriors can't hear.

Memories have no power without meaning, Odin once said. So, I never argue and let my brother have the first and last word. I've never mentioned that I too can form thoughts, because even I know that Hugin is a better thinker than me.

'Munin,' the Alfather mutters and calls me to him. I leap from the floor, and spread my limbs. The warriors are loud below me. I fly over them and land on the long-table in front of my brother and Odin. I settle my black eyes on my god, ready to meet his demands.

'Tell me about the half-jotun.' The Alfather leans in over the table and urges me to begin. His single eye shines with hunger for knowledge.

I hop a little closer so I don't have to caw as loud. 'He fights still. A berserker in Magadoborg. Southern arrows hit, but don't kill. Many summers will pass before he will join your ranks.'

The Alfather and my brother exchange a mysterious grin. 'The veulve has declared that Glumbruck's son shall sit in my hall before the end of winter,' the Alfather confides in me.

He sets down his cup.

'It is good that so many fought and died. I need all of my warriors to pass on and fill my hall.'

I stare at my brother to make certain that I understand what worries Odin. He nods to me. They were talking of last battle of gods and giants before I joined them.

'The last battle shall not be fought in Midgard, but right here,' Odin confirms. 'Outside this very hall. The last winter draws close.' Blankly, he stares at me. 'My bones ache with the knowledge. Soon we shall all fight and die.'

ACKNOWLEDGEMENTS

I USED TO think that being a Viking was all about war and fights, but being a sailor on a Viking ship taught me that it is so much more. Thank you to the crew of the *Sea Stallion* for accepting me and proving that being a Viking is cuddling up at night to shield yourself from the cold northern wind. It's making unexpected friends across generations and professions, all through a common sense of adventure. As Vikings we aim, not to speculate about what lies beyond the horizon, but to sail out there, and find out.

A novel like this would be impossible to write without a diverse cultural background. So, a big thank you to my parents for gifting me just that; the most precious thing you ever could. Thank you for telling me when I'm wrong, and for reminding me of what's important. Not only are you my first readers, you are my sparring partners, my eternal support and, as Siv does for Tyra, you have helped me carve my own way through the nine worlds.

May the little goddess Sif, who has already proven herself to be a true Viking, be gifted with much love in her long life, and explore the world, as a goddess would.

Thank you to Celia Brayfield, who helped shape me into a writer. I knew nothing when I first arrived in your classes, and unlike my peers, I had not been writing for long. Your honest critique and feedback over the years helped to shape my writing. I learnt a lot from you.

Only a standing ovation seems appropriate for my agent, Jamie Cowen, for believing in this book, its characters and knowing how to transform it. Together we have achieved what we set out to do during that very first meeting of burger eating. With your help and guidance, a half decent manuscript called 'Runes' bloomed into the brilliant novel *Northern Wrath* and found a home.

To David and the wonderful team at Solaris and Rebellion, I am glad I found a place for my series to flourish in a world of like-minded people. I lift my proud horn of meeting mead to you! Skál!

This novel started on my MA, but the journey my dear teachers and friends took me on from the beginning of my BA to my MA has shaped it like no other. Thank you to coffee friends on Fridays, bus rides home, and talks at Corsham Court with the backdrop of screeching peacocks.

Thank you also to my friends for providing writerly distraction and in-depth conversation in long-winded messages. Every writer needs some fun and distraction between work sessions, and you provided.

This novel was composed listening to the music of Wardruna and Agnes Obel, while Epik High and Bangtan provided the energetic symphony fit for editing.

ABOUT THE AUTHOR

Thilde Kold Holdt is a Viking, traveller and a polygot fluent in Danish, French, English and Korean. As a writer, she is an avid researcher. This is how she first came to row for hours upon hours on a Viking warship. She loved the experience so much that she has sailed with the Viking ship the *Sea Stallion* ever since. Another research trip brought her to all corners of South Korea where she also learnt the art of traditional Korean archery. Born in Denmark, Thilde has lived in many places and countries, taking a bit of each culture with her. This is why she regards herself as simply being from planet Earth, as she has yet to set foot on Mars...

Thilde is currently based in Southern France where she writes full-time.

FIND US ONLINE!

www.rebellionpublishing.com

/rebellionpub   /rebellionpublishing   /rebellionpublishing

SIGN UP TO OUR NEWSLETTER!

rebellionpublishing.com/newsletter

YOUR REVIEWS MATTER!

Enjoy this book? Got something to say?

Leave a review on Amazon, GoodReads or with your
favourite bookseller and let the world know!

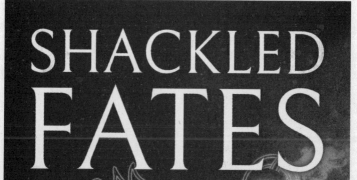